HARRY TURTLEDOVE

Settling Accounts: The Grapple

HODDER

Frist published in Great Britain in 2006 by Hodder & Stoughton
A division of Hodder Headline

A Hodder paperback

1

A CIP catalogue record for this title is available from the British Library

ISBN 978 0 340 82690 4
ISBN 0 340 82690 8

Typeset in Plantin Light by Palimpsest Book Production Ltd,
Grangemouth, Stirlingshire

Printed and bound by
Mackays of Chatham Ltd, Chatham, Kent

Hodder Headline's policy is to use papers that are natural, renewable and
recyclable products and made from wood grown in sustainable forests.
The logging and manufacturing processes are expected to conform to
the environmental regulations of the country of origin.

Hodder & Stoughton Ltd
A division of Hodder Headline
338 Euston Road
London NW1 3BH

Settling Accounts:
The Grapple

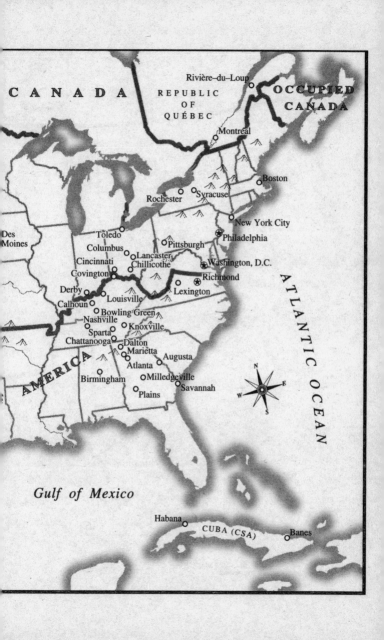

I

Funereal music poured out of the wireless set on Brigadier General Clarence Potter's desk. For three days, Confederate stations had played nothing but somber tunes and even more somber commentaries praising the courage of the army whose survivors had just surrendered in Pittsburgh.

Potter's mouth twisted. Behind steel-rimmed spectacles, his cold gray eyes flashed. That army should have taken Pittsburgh away from the damnyankees. With their great industrial center gone, the USA should have had to make peace. From everything the Intelligence officer knew, Pittsburgh was a wreck. That would hurt the United States. But the army that should have conquered it was gone, every man a casualty or a prisoner. That would hurt the Confederate States even more.

The latest dirge-tempo march ended. An announcer came on the air. 'Courage, self-denial, modesty, and the willingness to make every sacrifice are the highest virtues of the Confederate soldier,' he said. 'It was not the lust for conquest which caused the Confederacy to take up arms. This war was forced upon us by the destructive aims of our enemies.'

Well, what else could the man say? If he came right out and announced that Jake Featherston wanted to go to war long before he became President of the CSA, it wouldn't look good. Potter knew perfectly well that it was true. He also knew that what was true and what made good propaganda often had not even a nodding acquaintance with each other.

'Our soldiers are completely imbued with the importance and the value of the ideas now championed by the Freedom Party,' the announcer said. For better and for worse, Potter knew how true that was. The announcer went on, 'The Confederate soldier is convinced of them to the very depths of his innermost being, and that is why the Confederate armed forces form an invincible bloc having as its spiritual foundation the sublime ethics of a soldierly tradition. It is, moreover, inspired by belief in its high mission of protecting the Confederate States against the longtime enemy to the north, the enemy who would gladly deny our great nation its very right to exist.'

Again, he wasn't wrong. This was the fourth war between the USA and the CSA in the past eighty years. But if the Confederates were so bloody invincible, what went wrong in Pennsylvania? Potter, a confirmed cynic, would think of something like that. Would the average Confederate who was listening? Maybe not.

'We see the most magnificent example of this in the sacrifice of the troops fighting at Pittsburgh,' the announcer went on. 'That let our armies farther west build up new dams to hold back the raging Yankee torrent and continue to preserve the Confederacy from the annihilating rule of the USA. Cut off from all possibility of receiving reinforcements, surrounded by implacable foes, they fought on with bayonets and entrenching tools after their ammunition was exhausted. Truly their courage and devotion will live forever.'

The music swelled once more: yet another sorrowful tune. Potter sighed. Putting a good face on disaster was always hard. He wondered why he kept listening. Knowing what the rest of the country was going through was useful. That had something to do with it. The rest was akin to picking at a scab. The pain held a perverse attraction.

He started a little when the telephone rang. Turning down the music, he picked up the handset. 'Potter here.' If anybody needed to know what he did, that person had got hold of him by mistake.

'Hello, Potter there.' The voice on the other end of the line was a harsh rasp every Confederate citizen recognized at once. 'I need you to be Potter *here*, soon as you can get on over.'

'Yes, Mr. President. On my way.' Potter hung up. He turned off the wireless. When Jake Featherston said he wanted to see you as soon as you could come, you needed to get to the Gray House in a hurry.

Potter went upstairs. The door by which he came out on the ground floor had something innocuous painted on the frosted-glass window. You would never open it unless you already knew where it led.

Workmen labored to repair bomb damage. The damnyankees hit the War Department as often as they could. More and more of the business here went on underground – how far underground, even Potter wasn't sure any more. The men who bossed the work parties were whites too old or too crippled to help the war effort. Some of the men in the crews were colored, though a lot of Negroes had already been removed from Richmond. More workmen were Mexicans, up from Francisco José's ramshackle empire to find better-paying work in the CSA.

Some offices on the ground floor were still usable. The officers and clerks who worked in them took a sour pride in staying at those battered desks as long as they could. Several men waved to Potter as he walked past. He nodded in return.

All the motorcars outside the War Department were ordinary civilian models. Every so often, U.S. fighters streaked low over Richmond in broad daylight, shooting up whatever they could. No point giving them any special targets. As if at a cab stand, Potter got into the forward-most auto. 'The Gray House,' he told the driver.

'Yes, sir.' The soldier started the engine and put the Birmingham in gear.

More work crews repaired streets and gas lines and water mains and electric lines and telephone wires and . . . anything else that could be damaged when bombs fell on it or near it. Hardly any glass windows faced the world these days. Plywood and cardboard covered even the ones the damnyankees hadn't blown to smithereens.

Again, Mexicans did a lot of the work Negroes would have handled before. The Confederate States would be a different country when the war was through. Whites had anxiously watched blacks for much too long. Well, soon there'd be far fewer blacks to need watching. Potter had long opposed the Freedom Party, but he didn't mind its taking a shot at the Negro problem. He didn't know any white man who did.

As he'd expected, the driver had to detour several times before he got to the presidential mansion. Craters made some streets impassable. One block had sawhorses and warning signs all around. DANGER! UNEXPLODED BOMB! the signs shouted in big red letters. Maybe the bomb was a dud. Maybe a time fuse ticked inside it. Either way, Potter didn't envy the men who worked to get the ordnance out of there. They were skilled technicians. No matter how skilled they were, their average life expectancy was measured in weeks.

The snouts of sandbagged antiaircraft guns poked up from the Gray House grounds. Not much of the building was left above ground. The damnyankees kept doing their best to level it. They wanted Jake Featherston dead, not only because losing him would take the wind out of the Confederacy's sails, but also because Confederate bombs had killed U.S. President Al Smith.

'Here you are, sir.' The driver pulled to a stop in front of the rubble pile.

'Thanks.' Clarence Potter got out of the Birmingham. With a clash of gears, it rolled away.

Guards waited in among the wreckage. 'Let's see your papers, sir,' one of them said.

No one got anywhere in the CSA without proper papers these days. Potter displayed his. Once the guards were satisfied about who he was, one of them used a telephone. That done, he nodded to his pal. Together, they opened a heavy steel trap door.

Potter went down the stairs. They bent several times to foil blast that might penetrate the door above. In due course, he got to another door, this one even thicker. He pressed the button next to it. It swung open from the inside. More guards nodded to him. 'Come with us, sir,' one of them said.

'I know the drill,' Potter said.

They ignored him. He'd figured they would. All of what went on at the Gray House went on underground these days. People who spent a lot of time down there were as pale and pasty as . . . people who spent a lot of time underground at the War Department. Potter looked at the backs of his own hands, and at the veins clearly visible there. He wasn't a vampire, to whom the sun was death, but he often behaved as if he were.

Lulu, Jake Featherston's longtime secretary, nodded to him. 'He'll be with you in a moment, General,' he said.

'Thank you, ma'am,' Potter answered. You treated Lulu

with respect or you were sorry. No one ever talked about the authority secretaries and other such people had, which didn't make it any less real.

The moment stretched to about five minutes. Featherston wasn't in the habit of making people cool their heels just to be sitting. Something had to be going on. And something was. Nathan Bedford Forrest III, the head of the Confederate General Staff, came out of the President's office. He didn't look happy.

He looked even less happy when he saw Potter in the waiting room. Potter wasn't happy to see him, either. They weren't quite conspirators. If it looked as if Jake Featherston was dragging the CSA down to ruin, someone would have to try to dispose of him. If that worked, someone would have to try to run the country afterwards. As far as Potter could see, Nathan Bedford Forrest III made far and away the best candidate.

Forrest wanted the job as much as he wanted another head. That didn't mean he wouldn't try to do it – he had a strong sense of duty. It meant he hoped everything would turn out all right, even though he was the one who'd first wondered whether Jake Featherston was going round the bend.

Did Featherston know about those wary discussions? If he did, would Nathan Bedford Forrest III still be free? Potter didn't think so.

'You can go in now, General,' Lulu said.

'Thank you very much,' Potter said. From most Confederates, that would have been, *Thank you kindly*. He'd never lost the more than half-Yankee way of speaking he picked up to fit in while he was at Yale.

'Hello, Potter,' Jake Featherston said. The President of the CSA was in his early fifties, tall and rawboned, his close-cropped brown hair going gray. His eyes had dark pouches under them that hadn't been there a few years before. They still blazed, though. If ruthless determination could pull the CSA through, Featherston was the man to give it.

'What's up, sir?' Potter asked, hoping it had nothing to do with Nathan Bedford Forrest III.

'I need you to light a fire under Professor FitzBelmont. I don't care if you promise him prime pussy or promise you'll shoot his kids if he doesn't get his ass in gear, but get him moving. We really need that uranium bomb,' Featherston said.

The Confederate uranium program had got off to a slow start because the President didn't believe in it at first. Potter couldn't blame him for that; who in his right mind would have believed it? But when the Confederates learned the United States were going after uranium explosives as hard as they could, they'd had to follow suit.

'If lighting a fire will do anything, I'll do it.' Potter wasn't sure it would. Separating U-235 from U-238 was proving fiendishly hard and fiendishly expensive. 'They could use more money and more men, too.'

'Whatever they need, we'll give it to them,' Featherston vowed. 'If the damnyankees are ahead of us on this one, we're screwed. If we beat 'em to the punch, we win. Even Pittsburgh won't matter at all. It's about that simple. Or will you tell me I'm wrong?' He glared a challenge at Potter.

'No, sir.' Potter meant it. He might despise Jake Featherston the man, but Jake Featherston the leader was dead right here.

Major Jonathan Moss became a flier at the start of the Great War because he thought it would prove a cleaner, more chivalrous way of fighting than the mess on the ground. And he was right – for a while.

After a career as a lawyer in occupied Canada, he came back to flying not long before the new – the greater? – war broke out. With his wife and daughter killed by a Canuck bomber, he threw himself into aviation as much to stay sane as for any other reason. And he got shot down over Virginia and spent a while languishing in the Confederates' Andersonville POW camp. If not for a tornado that flung barbed wire in all directions, he would have been there yet.

Now he was a foot soldier, not because he wanted to be one but because he had no choice. The Negro guerrillas who found him would have killed him if he didn't join their band.

Chickens and chunks of pork roasted over campfires in the pine woods of southwestern Georgia. The white man from whose farm they'd been taken didn't need to worry about his livestock any more. Neither did his family. The USA and the CSA followed the Geneva Convention when they fought each other. The USA and the Mormon rebels in Utah played by the rules, too; the Mormons were, if anything, more scrupulous than their U.S. foes about keeping them. Between black guerrillas and Confederates, rules went out the window. It was war to the knife.

'Smells goddamn good,' Captain Nick Cantarella said. The infantry officer, much younger than Moss, had escaped from Andersonville with him. With his knowledge of how to fight on the ground, Cantarella had to be more valuable to the Negroes than Moss was.

'Be ready soon.' The black who led the guerrillas called himself Spartacus. He wasn't far from Moss' age. He'd fought for the CSA in the Great War, and reminded Moss of a career noncom in the U.S. Army. Jake Featherston didn't want any Negroes fighting on his side. Spartacus used everything he'd learned fighting for the Confederacy to fight against it now.

After Moss got outside of some hot, greasy pork and a tin cup of chicory-laced coffee, he asked, 'What do you aim to do next?' He had no trouble treating Spartacus as his CO, and it wasn't just because the black man could kill him with a word. Like most whites in the USA, Moss hadn't had much to do with Negroes. There weren't many in the United States, and most whites were happy to keep it that way. He'd always thought of Negroes as inferior; he hadn't had much reason to think otherwise. But Spartacus would have commanded respect as a man if he were green with blue polka dots.

He tossed a chicken bone back into the fire. 'Well, I was thinkin' o' comin' down on Plains again.' His voice was a smooth, rich baritone.

Moss stared. The band had raided the small town the autumn before. 'You don't think they'll be laying for us?'

'Reckon not.' When Spartacus grinned, his teeth gleamed white in his dark face. 'Reckon the ofays don't think even a nigger'd be dumb enough to come back so soon.'

Nick Cantarella laughed out loud. 'I like it. Fuck me if I don't.' He'd grown up in New York City, and sounded like it. Sometimes he and Spartacus had trouble understanding each other. For that matter, sometimes Moss, who was from Chicago, had trouble understanding Cantarella. He rarely did with Spartacus. The Negro might drawl and slur, but at least he spoke slowly. Cantarella's harsh consonants and clotted vowels came at machine-gun speed.

'Got me a couple people lookin' the place over,' Spartacus said. 'Don't seem like nobody doin' nothin' special there. They reckon they done got hit once, so they's immune now.' He grinned again. 'It don't work dat way.'

'All right by me,' Moss said.

But the raid didn't come off. Spartacus didn't want to move till he had everything just the way he wanted it. From a Regular Army commander, Moss might have thought that too cautious. But Regular Army commanders had men to spare, and regularly proved it. Spartacus didn't. He needed to be careful not to walk into a trap.

While he was waiting and getting ready, the situation changed. Two companies of soldiers who wore yellowish khaki uniforms and helmets of unfamiliar shape came into the area. 'Mexicans!' Nick Cantarella said in disgust. 'Goddamn bean-eating greasers! Wonder how the hell Featherston pried 'em outa Francisco José.'

'Screw that.' Spartacus didn't let the Mexican soldiers faze him. 'What I wonder is, can them fuckers fight?'

'When the U.S. Army broke through in Pennsylvania last fall, it broke through against the Mexicans,' Cantarella said.

'Uh-huh, but y'all got barrels an' airplanes an' all that good shit.' Spartacus was nobody's fool. 'All we got is us, an' we ain't got so many of us.' He frowned in concentration. 'Make them come at us, mebbe, an' see how good they is.'

'Always better to meet them where you want to, not where they want to,' Moss said.

'Make sense,' Spartacus agreed. 'Now we got to cipher out how them greasers can reckon they is doin' what they wants when they is really doin' jus' what we aims to have 'em do.'

Arranging to have a letter intercepted in Plains turned out to be the easiest thing in the world. Moss' only worry was that the Mexicans would decide it was too obviously a fraud. It told a fictitious comrade in the town where Spartacus' band would be and what they planned to do for the next four days. One of the blacks sneaked into

Plains at night and dropped the envelope that held the letter not far from the little hotel where Francisco José's soldiers were garrisoned. Another black, one who lived in town, brought word the envelope had been found.

As Spartacus hoped, the Mexicans moved down the road from Plains toward Preston, the next town farther west. They marched in good order, with scouts well forward and with men out to either side to make sure they didn't get hit from the flank. But the scouts saw nothing the guerrillas didn't want them to, and the flank guards weren't out far enough.

Spartacus approached field fortifications with the eye of a man who'd seen plenty of trench warfare. He had eight or ten riflemen dug in at the top of a tiny swell of ground. Jonathan Moss was one of them. He clutched his Tredegar with sweaty palms and hoped none of the blacks in the trench with him noticed how nervous he was.

The one thing he felt he could tell them was 'Don't open up too soon. We want to make the Mexicans bunch up in front of us, remember.' The Negroes nodded. Some of them still automatically acted deferential toward whites when they weren't trying to kill them. That was a funny business.

Moss had only a few minutes to wonder about it before the Mexicans' scouts came into sight. Their pale khaki might make good camouflage in northern Mexico, but it didn't do so well against the green woods and red dirt of Georgia. The guerrillas waited till the scouts got close, then shot all three of them down. Moss thought he hit one of them, and also thought they went down before they were sure where the killing fire came from.

Those gunshots brought the rest of the Mexicans at a trot. They came in loose order, so nobody in front of them could pick off too many men at once. They would soon have overwhelmed the Negroes in that trench – if those were the only men Spartacus had. But their commanding officer did what the guerrilla leader hoped he would: in concentrating on what lay ahead, he forgot all about what might might be waiting off to the flank.

And he paid for it. What waited off to the flank was an artfully concealed machine gun. The Negroes didn't take it with them everywhere they went; it was heavy and clumsy to move. But when they could set it up ahead of time . . .

When they could set it up ahead of time, it was the concentrated essence of infantry. The Mexicans hurried forward to deal with the roadblock in front of them. The machine-gun crew couldn't have had a better target for enfilading fire if they'd set up the enemy themselves.

When the machine gun started stuttering, the Mexicans toppled like tenpins. They were close enough to let Moss hear their cries of fear and dismay and agony. Some of them tried to charge the machine-gun position. That was brave, but it didn't work. The gun itself might have held them at bay. In case it didn't, other blacks with rifles were there to help protect it.

Realizing they'd run into a trap helped break the Mexicans. When they took heavy casualties without taking the machine gun, they fled east, back toward Plains. Some of them threw away their weapons to run faster. The guerrillas galled them with gunfire till they got out of range.

After the Negroes emerged from cover, they methodically finished off the wounded Mexicans. Some of the guerrillas carried shotguns or small-caliber hunting rifles. They replaced them with bolt-action Tredegars taken from Francisco José's men. A handful of the Mexicans carried submachine guns. Those also went into the blacks' arsenal. None of the dead men had the automatic rifles that gave

Confederate soldiers so much firepower. Moss wasn't much surprised; the Confederates didn't have enough of those potent weapons for all their own front-line troops.

Nick Cantarella went up to Spartacus, who was pulling clips of ammunition from the equipment pouches on a dead man's belt. 'We better haul ass outa here, and I mean now,' the U.S. officer said. 'Those greasers'll be back, either by themselves or with the local Freedom Party stalwarts. Ain't gonna make the same trick work twice, not here.'

'You don't reckon so?' The guerrilla leader didn't sound convinced. 'Them Mexicans ain't smart, an' the ofays who yell, "Freedom!" all the goddamn time, they's dumber.'

'Quickest way to end up dead is to think the guy you're fighting is a damn fool,' Cantarella said. 'Second quickest way is to get greedy. You try both at once, you're askin' for it, you hear what I'm sayin'?'

Spartacus looked at him. Jonathan Moss thought another quick way to end up dead was by pushing the Negro too far. Spartacus didn't take kindly to listening to whites. But Cantarella had the certainty that went with knowing what he was doing. He wasn't trying to show Spartacus up, just to give good advice. And he wasn't much inclined to back down himself.

Muttering to himself, Spartacus looked along the road toward Plains. 'Reckon mebbe you's right,' he said unwillingly. 'We done stuck 'em pretty good, an' that'll have to do.' He raised his voice to a shout: 'Let's git! Time to move out!'

The Negroes and their white advisers streamed away from the ambush. Moss didn't see how Spartacus could have wanted much more. He wondered if the Mexicans would push hard after the guerrillas again, or if one introduction like this would show them that wasn't a good idea.

When he asked Nick Cantarella, the infantry officer only shrugged. 'Have to find out,' he said. 'Pretty plain they never saw combat before. Whether they can't stand up to it or whether they figure they've got something to prove now – well, we'll see before long, I figure.'

'Guerrillas did well,' Moss remarked.

'Yeah.' Cantarella looked around, then spoke in a low voice: 'Wouldn't've thought the spooks had it in 'em. But if your ass is on the line, I guess you do what you gotta do, no matter who you are.'

'We just did,' Moss said. Nick Cantarella blinked, then nodded.

Scipio was almost too far gone to notice when the train stopped. The Negro and his wife and daughter were scooped up in Augusta, Georgia, a week earlier – he thought it was a week, but he could have been off by a day or two either way.

Along with so many others from the Terry – Augusta's colored district – they were herded into a boxcar and the door locked from the outside. It was too crowded in there to sit down, let alone to lie down. Scipio wasn't off his feet for a minute in all that time, however long it was. He couldn't make it to the honey buckets that were the only sanitary facilities, so he fouled himself when he couldn't hold it any more. He wasn't the only one – far from it.

He got a couple of sips from a dipper of water that went through the miserable throng, but nothing more. If the boxcar held any food, he never saw it. By the time the train finally got wherever it was going, his nose told him the car held dead bodies.

Had they made this journey in high summer, everyone would have died. He was as sure of that as he was of his own name – surer, since he'd gone by Xerxes for many years. Scipio was still a wanted man in South Carolina for his role in the Red Negro uprisings during the Great War.

But it was February, so heat and humidity didn't add themselves to starvation and overcrowding. *What a mercy,* Scipio thought.

'Bathsheba?' he croaked through a dust-dry throat. 'Antoinette?'

He heard no answer from either of them. Maybe they were dead. Maybe they were just too dry to talk. Maybe they couldn't hear his husk-filled voice. Or maybe the noise other people were making covered their replies. His ears weren't what they had been once upon a time. He was getting close to seventy. He'd been born a slave, back in the days before the Confederate States reluctantly manumitted their Negroes.

There was a bitter joke! Technically free, blacks didn't have a prayer of equality with whites even in the best of times. Here in the worst of times . . . Scipio wasn't worried about seeing another birthday now. He wondered if he would see another day, period.

Then what seemed like a miracle happened. The door to the boxcar opened. A cold, biting wind blew in. Fresh air hit Scipio almost as hard as a slug of whiskey would have. His eyes opened very wide. He thought his heart beat a little faster.

'Out!' White men's voices, harsh as ravens' croaks, roared out the word. 'Come on out o' there, you goddamn shitty niggers! Form two lines! Men on the left, women and pickaninnies on the right! Move! Move! Move!'

A few people stumbled out of the boxcar. A few corpses fell out. That eased the pressure that had held Scipio upright for so long. He started to sag to the planking of the floor. If he did, though, he didn't think he'd be able to get up again. And the way these ofays – guards; he could see they were guards – were screaming at people to come out, he could guess what would happen to a man who couldn't rise.

He wanted to live. He wondered why. After what he'd gone through, dying might have come as a relief. But he stumbled forward and awkwardly got down from the boxcar.

'Men on the left! Women and pickaninnies on the right!' the guards yelled again. Then one of them smacked a black man with a club he pulled from his belt. 'You dumb fucking coon, don't you know which one's your right and which one's your left? Get your lazy ass over where you belong!' Blood pouring down his face, the Negro staggered into the proper line.

Somebody touched Scipio's hand. There stood Bathsheba, with Antoinette beside her. They looked like hell, or maybe a little worse. Scipio tried not to think about what he looked like himself. It didn't matter. Nothing mattered except that they were all alive.

'We gots to get in our line,' Bathsheba said in a voice like ashes. 'The good Lord keep you safe, darlin'. We see you when we can.'

His wife had always been a churchgoing woman. She'd got Scipio to go with her a good many times. They were captured in church, in fact. Education and Marxism had corroded Scipio's faith. If they hadn't . . . Well, the trip he'd just finished would have turned St. Thomas Aquinas into an atheist. Somehow, though, it hadn't shaken Bathsheba, not that way.

'You move, old man.' The Mexican-looking guard who gave the order had three stripes on the left sleeve of his gray uniform tunic. 'You move, or you be sorry.' He didn't sound particularly mean. He just sounded like a man doing his job – and a man who would do it, whatever that took.

Was it better that he didn't seem to enjoy tormenting his captives? Or did that make it worse?

The guard sergeant (no, in a gray uniform he'd have some kind of silly Freedom Party rank) waited to see if Scipio would obey, or maybe if he could obey. His wife and daughter had already gone off to their line. Nothing held him here except exhaustion, thirst, and starvation.

'I goin',' he said, and discovered his feet still worked after all. The Mexican guard nodded and went to prod another sufferer into moving.

Standing in line wasn't easy. Several men begged for water. The guards ignored them. One of the Negroes fell over. A man in a gray uniform kicked him. When the Negro didn't respond, the guard peeled back his eyelid, then felt for a pulse. The white straightened, wiping his hand on his thigh. 'Son of a bitch is dead as belt leather,' he said. 'Gotta haul his worthless carcass outa here.'

A skinny black man in ragged shirt and dungarees out at the knee dragged the corpse away by the feet. A crew of similar wraiths were pulling bodies out of the train cars. Once, one of them called, 'This here fella ain't dead.'

A guard stood over the live Negro and fired a burst from his submachine gun. 'Sandbagging fucker is now,' he said. The man who'd announced the survival hauled away the body as if such things happened whenever a train came in. They probably did.

'Jesus God, you are the smelliest, most disgusting bunch of niggers I ever seen!' a guard officer shouted. *What else could we be?* Scipio thought. He knew how filthy he was. He knew he didn't have any choice about it, either. None of the lurching unfortunates in the line had any choice. The officer went on, 'Strip naked and we'll hose you down, get the worst shit off you.'

'What about our clothes?' somebody asked.

'Clean clothes inside,' the officer said. 'Get out of them duds! Move it!'

Despite the cold wind, Scipio was glad to shed the suit in which he'd gone to church. High-pressure hoses played over the black men. He feebly tried to wash and drink at the same time. He got a couple of swallows of water, and he got rid of some of his own filth. When he stood there naked and dripping, the north wind really did cut like a knife.

The blacks who'd hauled away corpses took charge of the discarded clothes, too. Some of the men whose clothes they were pulled long faces. Maybe they'd managed to hang on to money or valuables. Since Scipio hadn't, he was just as well pleased to be rid of his.

Bins of shirts and trousers and drawers and shoes and socks waited for the black men. As Scipio found clothes that more or less fit, he wondered who'd worn them before and what had happened to him. This time, his shiver had nothing to do with that biting wind. Better not to know, maybe.

Losing his clothes also lost Scipio his passbook. In a way, that was a relief. Without it, he could claim to be anyone under the sun. In another way, though, it was as ominous as those bins of clothing. A Negro couldn't exist in the CSA without a passbook. If the inmates of this camp didn't need passbooks . . . If they didn't, wasn't that an argument they didn't exist any more?

'Line up in rows of ten!' a guard shouted. 'Rows of ten, y'all hear? We got to get you coons counted. Soon as we do that, we can get your asses into barracks.'

'Food, suh? Water?' Several men called the desperate question at the same time.

'Y'all can get water once you're counted,' the guard answered. 'Food comes at regular time tonight. Now line up, goddammit. Can't do anything till we count you.'

Another man fell over dead waiting to be counted. More ragged, skinny Negroes seemed to materialize out of thin air to drag off the body. Would the clothes he had on go back into the bin? Scipio would have bet on it.

He got assigned to Barracks 27, which differed from the halls on either side only by its number. The wind blew right through the thin wallboard. Pails and cups told where the roof leaked when it rained. Bunks went up five and six high. Healthier, younger, stronger prisoners claimed the ones closest to the pot-bellied stove in the middle of the room. Scipio got a miserable bunk in the outer darkness near the wall. The only good thing about it was that it was on the second level, so he didn't have to climb very high. A burlap bag did duty for a blanket. Another, smaller, one stuffed with sawdust made a pillow of sorts. That was the extent of the bedclothes.

He staggered out and went looking for water. He found lines snaking up to three faucets. The lines were long. He wondered if he'd live till he got to the front of his. He did, and then drank and drank and drank. That brought some small fragment of life back to him. It also made him realize how hungry he was. But he wouldn't starve to death right away, while thirst had almost killed him.

He went back to his bunk. Lying down seemed a luxury after his time on the train. He fell asleep, or passed out – which hardly mattered. He would have slept through supper – he would have slept the clock around – if somebody didn't shake him back to consciousness. He wasn't sure the man did him a kindness. He was almost as weary as he was hungry.

Standing in line in someone else's clothes, in shoes that didn't quite fit, was a displeasure all its own. What he got when they fed him was another displeasure: grits and beans and greens. All in all, it wasn't enough to keep a four-year-old alive. His pants felt a little tight. He didn't think he'd need to worry about that for long.

After supper came the evening roll call. 'Line up in rows of ten!' a guard yelled. Scipio wondered how often he would hear that command in the days to come. More often than he wanted to; he was sure of that.

The count went wrong. For one thing, there'd been the influx of new prisoners. For another . . . The scrawny Negro standing next to Scipio muttered, 'These ofays so fuckin' dumb, they can't count to twenty-one without playin' with themselves.'

In spite of everything, Scipio snorted. 'Thank you,' he whispered – he'd already seen making noise during roll call could win you a beating.

'Fo' what?' the other black man said. 'Ain't nothin' to thank nobody for, not here. I's Vitellius. Who you be?'

The real Vitellius, if Scipio remembered straight, had been a fat man. This fellow didn't live up to the name. 'I's Xerxes,' Scipio replied. That was funny, too, in the wrong kind of way. He'd used Xerxes for years, fearing his own handle might get him sent to a camp. Well, here he was. What more could they do to him? One way or another, he'd find out.

Major General Abner Dowling's guns pounded Lubbock, Texas. Confederate artillery in and behind the city sent high-explosive death northwest toward Dowling's Eleventh Army. Back East, the Eleventh Army wouldn't even have made a decent corps; it had about a division and a half's worth of men. But the war out here in the wide open spaces ran on a shoestring, as the last one had. Dowling's men outnumbered the Confederates defending Lubbock.

Jake Featherston's soldiers were fighting with everything

they had, though. He couldn't push them out of Lubbock, and he couldn't flank them out, either. Up till recently, it hadn't mattered. As long as he kept them too busy to send reinforcements east to help rescue their army in Pittsburgh, he was doing his job.

But now Pittsburgh wouldn't fall to the CSA. Now Lubbock became valuable for its own sake, or as valuable as a city of 20,000 in the middle of nowhere could be. Dowling's headquarters lay in Littlefield, the last town northwest of Lubbock. He studied the map. He'd tried outflanking the Confederates to the south. Maybe if he swung around to the north this time . . .

His adjutant stuck his head into the map room. 'I've got some new aerial recon photos, sir,' Major Angelo Toricelli said. Toricelli was young and handsome and spry. Dowling was in his sixties, built like a breakfront, and wore a large, unstylish gray mustache. Even when he was young, he hadn't been spry. He'd played in the line at West Point just before the turn of the century. No, he hadn't been spry, but he'd been tough.

Several chins wobbled as he nodded to Toricelli. 'Let's see 'em,' he said. Both sides here were short on airplanes, too. Both sides here were short on everything under the sun, as a matter of fact.

'These are the deep-penetration photos, sir,' Toricelli said as he spread out the prints on top of the map. 'They go all the way down to Snyder, and to that . . . thing outside it.'

Snyder lay southeast of Lubbock. It was a bigger town than Littlefield, but not a whole lot bigger. Normally, Dowling wouldn't have worried about it, not where he was now. It was too small, and too far away.

Snyder was too small, yes. The . . . thing was another story altogether. It was called Camp Determination – so

Intelligence said, anyhow. And it was not small at all. 'How many niggers have they got crammed in there?' Dowling asked.

'Many, many thousands. That's the best Intelligence is willing to do, sir,' Toricelli said. Dowling thought he put it an interesting way, but didn't push him. The younger officer went on, 'There's a lot of incoming train traffic, too.'

'If there is, then this place must get fuller all the time, right?' Dowling said. Toricelli shook his head. Dowling raised an eyebrow. 'Not right?'

'No, sir.' His adjutant pointed to another photo. 'Looks like the overflow goes here.'

Dowling studied the picture. Trucks – they looked like ordinary C.S. Army trucks – stood next to a long, wide trench. The scale they provided gave him some notion of just how long and wide the trench was. It seemed to be full of bodies. Dowling couldn't gauge its depth, but would have bet it wasn't shallow.

The photo also showed several similar trenches covered over with dirt. The trenches went out of the picture on either side. Dowling couldn't tell how many filled-in trenches it wasn't showing, either.

'They go there, huh?' His stomach did a slow lurch. How many corpses lay in those trenches? How many more went into them every day? 'Any idea how they get from the camp to the graveyard?'

'How they get killed, you mean?' Toricelli asked.

'Yes, dammit.' Dowling usually despised the language of euphemism that filled military and bureaucratic life. Here, though, the enormity of what he saw made him unwilling to come out and say what he meant.

'Intelligence isn't quite sure of that,' his adjutant said. 'It doesn't really matter, does it?'

'It does to them.' Dowling jerked a thumb at that photo

with the trenches. 'Lord knows I'm no nigger-lover, Major. But there's a difference between not loving somebody and setting up a factory to turn out deaths like shells for a 105.'

'Well, yes, sir,' Major Toricelli said. 'What can we do about it, though? We aren't even in Lubbock, and this Snyder place is another eighty miles. Even if Lubbock falls, we'll be a long time getting there. Same with our artillery. And what good would bombers do? We'll just be killing spooks ourselves if we use 'em.'

'I know what I'm going to do,' Dowling said. 'I'm going to send these photos back to Philadelphia, and I'm going to ask for reinforcements. Now that Pittsburgh's ours again, we ought to have some men to spare. We *need* to advance on this front, Major. We need it a lot more than we do some other places.'

'Yes, sir. I think you're right,' Toricelli said. 'But will they listen to you back East? They see things funny on the other side of the Mississippi. We found out about that when we were trying to hold the lid down on the Mormons.'

'Didn't we just?' Dowling said. 'Tell you what – let's light a fire under the War Department's tail. Can you get another set of those prints made?'

'I'm sure I can, sir.'

'Bully!' Every once in a while, Dowling still came out with slang whose best days lay back before the Great War. Toricelli loyally pretended not to notice. Dowling went on, 'Send the second set of prints to Congresswoman Blackford. She's been up in arms about how the Confederates are treating their niggers ever since Jake Featherston took over. If she starts squawking, we're likelier to get those troops.'

'That's . . . downright byzantine, sir.' Major Toricelli's voice held nothing but admiration.

Dowling resolved to look up the word to see whether it carried praise or blame. He nodded to his adjutant. 'Get me those extra prints. I'll draft the letter to the General Staff. We'll want to encrypt that before we send it.'

'Oh, yes,' Toricelli said. When you were fighting a war with somebody who spoke the same language you did, you had to be extra careful about what you said openly. The only good news there was that the enemy had to be as careful as you were. Sometimes he slipped, and you could make him pay. Sometimes he pretended to slip, and you could outsmart yourself in a hurry if you weren't careful.

'Do that yourself, if you'd be so kind, Major,' Dowling said.

'Yes, sir. I'll take care of it.' Dowling's adjutant didn't even blink. This was a hell of a war all kinds of ways. When you couldn't be a hundred percent sure of the men in the cryptography section – you did without them whenever you could, or whenever you had something really important.

Rolling a sheet of paper into his Underwood upright, Dowling banged away at it, machine-gun style, with his forefingers. The machine was at least twenty years old, and had an action stiff as a spavined mule's. Fancy typists used all ten fingers. Dowling knew that – knew and didn't care. Being able to type at all put him ahead of most U.S. generals.

He tried to imagine George Custer pounding on a typewriter. The man under whom he'd served as adjutant during the Great War and for some years afterwards would have counted himself progressive for using a steel pen instead of a quill. Dowling wondered how many letters he'd typed up for Custer over the years. A whole great pile of them, anyhow. The old Tartar had had a legible hand. Dowling, who could fault him for plenty of other things, couldn't deny that.

Of course, Custer had spent more than sixty years in

the Army. He was one of the longest-serving soldiers, if not *the* longest-serving, in the history of the United States. Back when his career started, you had to be able to write with tolerable neatness. If you couldn't, no one would be able to make out what you were saying.

Dowling read through his draft, pen-corrected a typo that had escaped him while the paper was on the platen, and took it to Major Toricelli. 'Get this off to Philadelphia as fast as you can,' he said.

'I'll tend to it right away.' Toricelli had already taken the code book out of the small safe that accompanied Eleventh Army as it advanced – and, at need, as it fell back, too.

'Good. Thanks. Now I need to get a letter ready for those photos that'll go to Flora Blackford.' Dowling had met her before, in that she'd questioned him when he testified before the Joint Committee on the Conduct of the War. He hadn't appreciated her prodding then. If he could get her to prod in a way that did him some good, though, that was a different story. He wagged a finger at Toricelli. 'Make sure we get that other set of prints pronto, too.'

'Yes, sir.' Now his adjutant sounded resigned. Dowling knew he was guilty of nagging. How often had he sounded like that when Custer gave him the same order for the fourth time? At least he – sometimes – noticed when he repeated himself. He wrote the letter, signed it, and gave it to Major Toricelli. The younger officer, who was deep in five-letter code groups, nodded abstractedly.

When Dowling walked out of the house he'd commandeered for a headquarters, the sentries in front of the porch stiffened to attention. 'As you were,' Dowling said. The sentries had foxholes into which they could dive in case C.S. artillery reached Littlefield or enemy bombers came overhead.

A thick barbed-wire perimeter isolated headquarters

from the rest of the small west Texas town. The wire was far enough from the house to keep an auto bomb from doing too much damage if one blew up outside it. Soldiers and matrons frisked people entering the perimeter to make sure none of them carried explosives. Dowling didn't think he was important enough to make much of a target for a people bomb, but he didn't take chances, either.

Headquarters occupied one of the few undamaged houses in Littlefield. The Confederates had made a stand here. They fought wherever they could find an advantageous position. They didn't like retreating. But this country was so wide, they didn't have enough men to hold on to all of it. He'd flanked them out here. He wasn't having so much luck with that around Lubbock.

The Stars and Stripes floated above the house. Littlefield had been in the U.S. state of Houston till the Confederacy won the plebiscite here a little more than two years earlier. Now it was back in U.S. hands, and the locals liked that no better than they had before.

Dowling cordially despised the locals, too. He wished he could put up photographs of the murder camp and the mass graves outside Snyder – put 'em up all over town. He wished he could parade everybody *in* Littlefield past those graves, let people see what thousands of bodies looked like, let them find out what thousands of bodies smelled like. *You sons of bitches, this is what you bought when you went around yelling, 'Freedom!' all the goddamn time. How do you like it now?*

What really scared him was, they were liable to like it just fine. He could easily imagine them looking down at all those contorted corpses and saying, *Well, so what, you lousy damnyankee? They're only niggers, for cryin' out loud.*

He scowled out at Littlefield, wishing his imagination didn't work quite so well. All at once, he wanted nothing more than to wipe the town and everybody in it off the face of the earth.

Major Jerry Dover knew how to give men orders. He'd commanded at about the platoon level during the years between the wars. Bossing the cooks and waiters and bus-boys at the Huntsman's Lodge in Augusta, Georgia, gave him most of the experience he needed to put on the uniform and tell people in the Confederate Quartermaster Corps what to do.

Being white and the boss had given him authority over the staff at the restaurant. Military law made a good enough substitute in the field. Dover hadn't been out there long before one of his subordinates exclaimed, 'Jesus, sir, you work us just like a bunch of niggers!'

'Good,' Dover answered, which made the grumbling corporal goggle and gape. 'Good, goddammit,' Dover repeated. He was a foxy-featured man, wiry and stronger than he looked, with graying sandy hair and mustache. 'We've all got to work like niggers if we're going to whip those bastards on the other side.'

He drove himself at least as hard as he drove anybody under him. He left a trail of chain-smoked Raleigh butts and empty coffee cups behind him. He tried to be every-where at once, making sure all sorts of supplies got to the men at the front when they were supposed to. The men who worked under him didn't need long to figure that out. They swore at him as they shivered in the snow in southern Ohio, but his kitchen staff had sworn at him the same way while they sweltered over their stoves. The soldiers might not love him, but they respected him.

His superiors didn't know what to make of him. Most of them were Regulars, men who'd stayed in butternut all through the lean times before Jake Featherston started building up the C.S. Army again. A colonel named Travis W.W. Oliphant – he got very offended if you left the *W.W.* out of any correspondence addressed to him, no matter how trivial – said, 'You know, Major, you'll just kill yourself if you try to run through every brick wall you see instead of going around some of them.'

'Yes, sir.' Dover ground a cigarette out under the heel of his left boot (Boot, Marching, Officer's Field, size 9½C). He lit another one and sucked in smoke. Without a cloud of smoke around him, he hardly felt real. 'If you'll excuse me, sir, those damned idiots south of the Ohio finally got us about half as many of the 105 shells we've been screaming for as we really need. Gotta move 'em up to the people who shoot 'em out the guns.'

Travis W.W. Oliphant scratched his head. He looked like a British cavalry colonel, or what Jerry Dover imagined a British cavalry colonel would look like. 'See here, Dover, are you trying to mock me?' he said.

'Mock you? No, sir.' Dover scratched his head, too. 'Why would you say that? I'm just trying to do my job.'

'You're not a Regular,' the senior officer said.

'No, sir,' Dover agreed. 'So what? I can still see what needs doing. I can still get people to do it, or else do it myself.'

'There are people in this unit who think you're trying to show them up,' Colonel Oliphant said.

Dover scratched his head again. He blew out another stream of smoke. 'Sir, don't the Yankees give us enough trouble so we haven't got time to play stupid games with ourselves? I work hard. I want everybody else to work hard, too.'

'We won't get the job done if we wonder about each other – that's for sure,' Oliphant said. 'We've all got to pull together.'

'What am I supposed to do when I see some people who won't pull?' Dover asked. 'You know some won't as well as I do, sir. Plenty of men in the Quartermaster Corps who like it here because they're in the Army, so nobody can complain about that, but they aren't what you'd call likely to see a damnyankee with a piece in his hand and blood in his eye.'

'You're in the Quartermaster Corps,' Colonel Oliphant pointed out.

'So are you, sir.' Dover stamped out the latest cigarette and lit a replacement. 'You want to send me up to a line battalion, go right ahead. I happen to think I help the country more where I'm at, on account of I really know what the fuck I'm doing here. But if you want to ship me out, go on and do it. I was in the line last time around. Reckon I can do it again. Where were you . . . sir?'

Travis W.W. Oliphant didn't answer right away. He turned red, which told Dover everything he needed to know. Had Oliphant ever fired a rifle, or even an officer's pistol, in anger? Dover didn't believe it, not even for a minute.

'You are insubordinate, Major,' Oliphant said at last.

'About time somebody around here was, wouldn't you say?' Dover saluted and walked away. If the high and mighty colonel wanted to do something about it, he was welcome to try. Jerry Dover laughed. What was the worst Oliphant could do? Get him court-martialed? Maybe they'd drum him out of the Army, in which case he'd go back to the restaurant business in Augusta. Maybe they'd throw him in a military prison, where he'd be housed and fed and out of the war. About the worst thing the god-damn stuffed shirt could do was leave him right where he was.

Did Oliphant have the brains to understand that? Did the colonel know his ass from his end zone? Dover only shrugged. He didn't really care. Oliphant would do whatever he did. In the meantime, Dover would do what he had to do.

As soon as he stepped out of the butternut tent, a cold breeze from the northwest started trying to freeze his pointed nose off his face. 'Fuck,' he muttered. He hadn't been up in Ohio long, but the weather was really and truly appalling. Augusta got a cold snap like this maybe once in five years. Ohio could get them any time from November to March, by what he'd seen. He wondered why the hell the CSA wanted to overrun country like this in the first place.

Not all the trucks into which cursing Confederates were loading crates of shells had started life down in Birmingham. Some were captured U.S. machines, with slightly blunter lines, slightly stronger engines, and suspensions that would shake a man's kidneys right out of him on a rough road. They had butternut paint slapped on over the original green-gray. They had butternut paint slapped on their canvas canopies, too. Rough use and rough weather were making it peel off. Dover hoped that wouldn't get some luckless driver shot by somebody on his own side.

The drivers were safe if those trucks didn't get moving. Dover rounded on a quartermaster sergeant. 'What's the slowdown about?' he demanded.

'Sir, we were suppose to get a couple dozen military prisoners to help us load, and they ain't showed up,' the sergeant said stolidly. 'We're doin' what we can with what we got. Ain't like the last war – no nigger labor gangs up here.'

Jerry Dover muttered discontentedly. He'd never been a big Freedom Party man; he thought Jake Featherston was more a blowhard than anything else. Without Negroes, the Huntsman's Lodge either couldn't have operated at all or would have had to charge three times as much. Negroes had done a lot for the Army in the Great War. Not this time around. Featherston didn't trust them – and he'd given them abundant good reason not to trust him.

Before saying anything, Dover eyed the quartermaster sergeant's hands. They were muddy and battered, with a couple of torn fingernails. He'd been humping crates just like everybody else. Nobody could complain about effort. 'All right, Sergeant. Do the best you can. I'll track those damn convicts for you.'

'Thank you, sir,' the noncom said.

The convicts wouldn't work the way Negroes would have in the last war. They'd know they were doing nigger work, and they'd do it badly just to remind people they weren't niggers and the work was beneath their dignity. That they might get their countrymen killed because they worked badly wouldn't bother them. That they might get themselves killed wouldn't bother them, either. Showing they were good and proper white men counted for more.

Were Dover a convict, he knew he would act the same way. No less than the men who'd fallen foul of military justice, he was a Confederate white man. He'd probably had more experience with Negroes than any white since the days of overseers. That had nothing to do with the price of beer. There were some things a Confederate white man wasn't supposed to do.

Of course, one of the things Confederate white men weren't supposed to do was lose a war to the USA. If not losing meant they had to do some other things they wouldn't normally, then it did, that was all. So Dover thought, anyhow. Some of his countrymen seemed to prefer death to dirtying their hands.

Shells burst a few hundred yards away. Dover didn't flinch, didn't duck, didn't dive for cover. They'd have to come a lot closer than that before he started flabbling. Back in the last war, he'd learned to gauge how dangerous incoming artillery was. The knack came back in a hurry this time around.

Most of the older men working with these crates had it. Some of the younger ones didn't. What did worry Dover was that the damnyankees' guns were close enough to strike what should have been the Confederates' safe rear in Ohio. That showed how badly things had gone wrong. With so many men dead or captured in and around Pittsburgh, the defenses farther west were crumbling. One U.S. thrust was coming west from Pennsylvania and eastern Ohio, the other southeast from northern Indiana and northwestern Ohio. If they met, they would enfold even more irreplaceable Confederate troops in a pocket.

Dover went over to the field telephone station. The state of the art there had improved a lot since the Great War. Then people used Morse more often than they shouted into field telephones, just to make sure their message got through. Now you knew the guy on the other end of the line would hear you.

Whether he felt like listening to you might be a different story. For years, Dover had battled people who tried to palm off lower-quality meat and seafood and vegetables on him and to give him what he needed later than he needed it. Now he turned all his suavity and charm on the Confederate military policemen who hadn't delivered the promised convicts on time.

'This here's Major Dover in the Quartermaster Corps south of Columbus,' he rasped. 'Where the hell are they? You lazy sons of bitches, y'all tryin' to lose the war for us? How're we supposed to get the shit to the front if you hold out on us? . . . What do you mean, I can't talk to you that way? I'm doin' it, ain't I? An' if those convicts don't show up in the next hour, I'll sic my colonel on you, and we'll see how you like that!' He slammed down the phone without giving the MP he was talking to the chance to answer back – always a favorite ploy.

He knew Travis W.W. Oliphant was useless in these turf battles. He knew it, but the MP didn't. And the unhappy fellow evidently didn't care to take chances with an angry senior officer. The convicts arrived less than half an hour later.

'About fucking time,' Dover snarled at the driver who brought them. 'You should have got 'em here when you said you would, and saved everybody the aggravation.'

'Sir, I don't have nothin' to do with that,' the driver said. 'They load the truck, they tell me where to go an' how to git there, an' I do it.'

Dover wanted to tell him where to go and how to get there, too. He feared he'd be wasting his breath. Instead, he glowered at the convicts. 'You are going to work like mad sons of bitches, or else.'

'Or else what?' one of them said scornfully.

'Or else I will personally shoot your worthless ass off, and I'll laugh while I do it, too,' Dover replied. 'You reckon I'm funnin' with you, you go ahead and try me.' He waited. The convicts worked. He'd expected nothing else.

Sergeant Michael Pound had been in the U.S. Army a long time. He'd spent a lot of that time getting barrels to do what he needed them to do. He wasn't just one of the better gunners who wore green-gray coveralls, though he was that. He was also a damn good jackleg mechanic. A lot of barrel men were. The more repairs you could make yourself, the less time you had to spend in the motor pool. The less time you were out of action, the more trouble you could give the Confederates.

'Distributor cap, I bet,' he said when the mechanical monster wouldn't start up one rainy morning east of Columbus, Ohio. 'Damn thing gets wet inside too easy. It's a design flaw – it really is.'

'Can you fix it?' asked Second Lieutenant Don Griffiths, the barrel commander. He was perhaps half Pound's age: a puppy, like most second lieutenants. Unlike a lot of shavetails, he had a fair notion of what he was doing. He also didn't seem to think asking questions threatened his manhood.

'Yes, sir.' Along with a .45, Pound carried a formidable set of tools on his belt and in his pockets. He had the engine louvers off in nothing flat, and got the distributor cap off the engine almost as fast. One glance inside made him nod. 'Condensation, sure as hell.' The loader, Cecil Bergman, held a shelter half over his hands while he worked. The rain would only make things worse.

'What can you do about it?' Griffiths asked. 'A dry rag?'

'Even better than that, sir,' Pound said. He was stocky and wide-shouldered – built like a brick, really. His brown hair had begun to go gray and to retreat at the temples. His eyes were pale in a broad face more Scots than English: marksman's eyes. He pulled out a small bottle half full of clear liquid. 'Absolute alcohol,' he explained. 'I'll rub a little where it'll do the most good. It evaporates like anything, and it'll take the moisture with it.' He suited action to words.

The distributor cap went back on. So did the louvers that protected the engine from small-arms fire while letting its heat escape. Pound scrambled down from the engine compartment. 'Fire it up!' Bergman yelled to the driver.

There was a cough, a bang, and then the flatulent roar of a barrel engine coming to life. 'Nicely done, Sergeant!' Griffiths said.

'Thank you, sir.' Pound clambered up to the turret and opened his hatch. He paused before climbing in and sitting down behind the gun. 'Shall we get on with it?'

'I hope so, anyway,' Griffiths answered. 'If this rain starts thawing out the ground, though, we're liable to bog down.'

Pound didn't think that likely. It was a little above freezing, but only a little. He guessed the rain would turn to sleet or snow before long. But he didn't want to argue with Griffiths – which, considering how firmly armored in his own competence he was, was no small compliment to the young officer.

They rattled west in company with six or eight more barrels and several squads of foot soldiers. Only two of the barrels were the old models, with an inch-and-a-half gun. The improved machines, of which Pound's was one, featured an upgunned, uparmored turret and a more powerful engine to handle the extra weight. Their 2.4-inch cannon still weren't a match for the three-inchers new Confederate barrels carried, but they were the biggest guns the turret ring in the chassis would allow. And they were good enough to give the U.S. machines a fighting chance against the best the enemy could throw at them.

'After Pittsburgh, moving so fast seems strange,' Griffiths said.

'Yes, sir.' Pound nodded. In Pittsburgh, they'd measured progress in blocks per day, sometimes houses per day, not miles per hour. That was a fight of stalks and ambushes and strongpoints beaten down one by one. Now they were out in the open again, rolling forward. 'Only a crust here,' Pound said. 'Once we break it, they haven't got so much behind it.'

As if to give him the lie, a Confederate machine gun opened up ahead of them. Even through the turret, Pound had no trouble telling it from a U.S. weapon. It fired much faster, with a noise like ripping canvas. The Confederates, with fewer men than the USA, threw bullets around with reckless abandon.

'Can you see where that's coming from, sir?' he asked Lieutenant Griffiths.

Griffiths peered through the periscopes built into the commander's cupola. He shook his head. 'Afraid not, Sergeant,' he answered. 'Want me to stick my head out and have a look?'

He didn't lack for nerve. The barrel was buttoned up tight now. You could see more by opening the hatch and looking around, but you also ran a formidable risk of getting shot – especially anywhere in the neighborhood of one of those formidable machine guns.

'I don't think you need to do that, sir,' Pound said. Now that he'd found a junior officer he could stand, he didn't want the youngster putting his life on the line for no good reason. Sometimes you had to; Pound understood as much. Was this one of those times? He didn't think so.

But Griffiths said, 'Maybe I'd better. That gun'll chew hell out of our infantry.' He flipped up the hatch and stood up so he could look around, head and shoulders out of the cupola. Along with a flood of cold air, his voice floated down to Pound: 'I don't like staying behind armor when the foot soldiers are out there naked.'

Michael Pound made an exasperated noise down deep in his throat. Yes, a crewman in a barrel had face-hardened steel between himself and the enemy's attentions. An infantryman had nothing but his helmet, which wouldn't even keep out small-arms fire. On the other hand, nobody used antibarrel cannon or antibarrel mines or Featherston Fizzes to try to knock out individual foot soldiers. Lieutenant Griffiths wasn't thinking about that.

'There it is – about one o'clock,' Griffiths said. 'Do you see it now, Sergeant?'

As Pound traversed the turret, he looked through the gunsight. Sure enough, there was the malignantly flashing machine-gun muzzle. 'Yes, sir,' he said, and then, to the loader, 'HE!'

'HE!' Bergman loaded a white-tipped high-explosive round into the breech.

The gun roared. The noise was tolerable inside the turret. To Lieutenant Griffiths, out there in the open, it must have been cataclysmic. Soldiers joked about artilleryman's ear, but they were kidding on the square.

When the machine gun kept firing, Pound swore. A 2.4-inch HE shell just didn't carry a big enough bursting charge to be very effective. He'd seen that in Pittsburgh, and he was seeing it again in among the trees here. 'Give me another round,' he told Cecil Bergman.

'You got it, Sarge.' The loader slammed the shell home.

An instant before Pound fired, Don Griffiths groaned. Pound didn't let himself pay attention till the second HE round was on the way. He saw the Confederate machine gun fly one way and a gunner, or some of a gunner, fly another. But he had no time to exult; Griffiths was slumping down into the turret.

'How bad is it, sir?' Pound asked, swearing at himself – if he'd knocked out the gun first try, the lieutenant might not have got hit.

'Arm,' Griffiths answered through clenched teeth. He had to be biting down hard on a scream. Sure as hell, his left sleeve was bloody, and blood dripped from his hand down onto the shell casings on the fighting compartment floor.

'Can you wiggle your fingers?' Pound asked. Griffiths tried, but gasped and swore and shook his head. He'd had a bone shattered in there, then – maybe more than one. Pound took a morphine syrette from the wound pouch on his belt, stuck it into Griffiths' thigh, and pushed home the plunger. Then he said, 'Let's bandage you up.'

He had to cut away the sleeve to get at the wound. He dusted it with sulfa powder and packed it with gauze. As soon as he could, he'd get Griffiths out of the barrel and send him to the rear with some corpsmen.

'You've got yourself command here whether you want it or not.' The lieutenant sounded eerily calm, which meant the morphine was taking hold.

'Even if I did want it, sir, I wouldn't want it like this,' Pound said, which was true. 'You'll be back soon.' He hoped that was true.

He stuck his own head out of the cupola. With the machine gun gone, all he had to worry about were ordinary Confederate infantrymen and maybe snipers in the trees. He looked around. Sometimes luck was with you, though he wished it would have shown up a little sooner. But he did see a couple of corpsmen with Red Crosses on smocks and armbands and helmets. He waved to them.

'What's up?' one of them yelled.

Before Pound could answer, a bullet cracked past. He ducked. He knew it was a useless reflex, which didn't mean he could help himself. He hoped it was a random round. If it wasn't, the medics would have two casualties to deal with. *Unless, of course, I get killed outright,* he thought cheerily.

'Got a wounded officer. Forearm – broken bones,' he called after he straightened up.

'All right – we'll take care of him,' the corpsman said. 'Can you swing sideways so the barrel covers him while you get him out of the hatch?'

Pound liked that idea about as much as he liked a root

canal. Expose the barrel's thin side armor to whatever guns the goons in butternut had up ahead? But the medics weren't armored at all. Neither was Lieutenant Griffiths, and he'd gone and proved it.

Sometimes you needed a root canal. It was no fun, but you had to go through with it. This wouldn't be any fun, either. If they hustled, though, they ought to get away with it. 'Will do,' Pound called to the medics. He ducked down into the turret and told the driver to make a hard right and stop.

'Jesus! You sure?' The protest came back through the speaking tube.

'Damn straight. I wouldn't ask you if I wasn't,' Pound answered. 'Come on. Step on it. The lieutenant's bleeding all over everything back here.'

'It's not so bad now.' Griffiths sounded as if he hadn't a care in the world. The morphine must have hit him hard. Well, good.

Snorting, the barrel turned. The movement wasn't so sharp as it might have been. Try too tight a turn and you might throw a track, in which case you wouldn't go anywhere for a while. When Pound was satisfied, he yelled, 'Stop!' and the barrel did. He undogged the side hatch and sketched a salute to Don Griffiths. 'Out you go, sir. You did good. Hope I see you again one day.' He meant it. He wasn't the sort to waste compliments on people who didn't deserve them.

'Thank you, Sergeant.' Awkwardly, Griffiths scrambled out of the barrel. Pound helped him leave. The corpsmen took charge of him once he got through the hatch. They eased him down to the ground and got him moving away from the front. They were probably relieved to help somebody able to move on his own: they didn't have to lug him in a stretcher.

After waiting till they'd gone some distance from the barrel, Pound clanged the hatch shut and dogged it. He yelled into the speaking tube: 'All right, Miranda – square us up again.'

'You bet, Sarge!' The barrel jumped as the driver put the thicker steel of the glacis plate and the turret between the crew and the enemy.

Peering through the periscopes in the commander's cupola, Pound saw the heaviest action off to his left. He ordered the barrel over that way. For now, it was his.

II

Clouds and rain and sleet shrouded the North Atlantic. A few hundred miles to the west of the *Josephus Daniels* lay Newfoundland. To the east of the destroyer escort, probably, lay trouble. The British never stopped sending arms and men to Newfoundland and to Canada to give the rebellion against the USA a helping hand. Lieutenant Sam Carsten and the skippers of his fellow picket ships did everything they could to keep the limeys from getting through.

He halfheartedly swore at the weather. It made enemy ships all that much harder to find. The rain and sleet even interfered with the Y-ranging gear. The wireless waves bounced back from raindrops, too. A good operator could peer through the interference, but it sure didn't make life any easier. And the old-fashioned Mark One eyeball had a very short range here.

He swore only halfheartedly because the weather suited his own needs very well. He was a short step away from being an albino. His skin was pink, his eyes pale blue, and his hair white gold. It was even whiter these days than it had been when he was younger – he'd spent almost thirty-five years in the Navy now. Summer in the tropics was a never-ending misery for him. Summer in Seattle was a misery for him, and that took doing.

His executive officer was a young, auburn-haired lieutenant named Pat Cooley. If not for Sam, the exec might have been the the fairest man on the ship. Cooley had gone through Annapolis, while Sam was a mustang who hadn't made ensign till some years after the Great War.

Cooley was a comer, a hotshot. He'd have a ship of his own before long. Sam didn't want the exec promoted out from under him, but he knew things worked that way. As for himself, when he walked into the recruiting office all those years ago he never dreamt he would wear two stripes on his sleeve. He'd just been looking for a way to escape walking behind the north end of a southbound mule for the rest of his life.

The *Josephus Daniels* pitched down into the trough between two waves. Seas on the North Atlantic weren't quite so fierce and mountainous as they had been earlier in the winter, but they weren't any fun, either. 'You all right, Mr. Cooley?' Sam asked when the exec grabbed for something to steady himself.

'Yes, sir. Just clumsy.' Cooley's eyes were green as a cat's. Just now, he looked like a cat that had rolled off a bed and was trying to pretend it hadn't.

'Insides not turning inside out?' Sam had rounded the Horn more than once. Those were the only seas he knew that put the North Atlantic to shame. He hadn't been seasick. He might sunburn in anything this side of a cloudburst, but he had no trouble keeping his grub down.

Pat Cooley was a good sailor. The North Atlantic seemed intent on showing good sailors they weren't as good as they thought. Here, though, the exec shook his head. 'Not giving me any trouble right this minute,' he said: a precise man's cautious answer.

'Skipper?' That was a very young, very junior lieutenant, junior grade, named Thad Walters: the officer responsible for the care and feeding of the Y-ranging gear. He looked up from the green blips on his oscillo-scope screens. 'I've got something showing.'

'A ship?' Sam asked. Even troubled by the weather, the Y-ranging set was more likely to pick up limeys trying to run the U.S. gauntlet than lookouts were.

But the j.g. shook his head. 'No, sir. It's an airplane. Have we got a carrier in the neighborhood?'

'If we do, nobody told me, that's for damn sure,' Sam answered. Nobody'd warned him a British carrier was oper-ating in the neighborhood, either. That could be very bad news. A beat slower than he might have, he heard exactly what Walters said. 'Wait a second. *An* airplane?'

'Yes, sir. Y-ranging gear sees one. Speed two hundred. Bearing 085. Range . . . Range is twenty-five miles and closing – he's heading our way.'

'Just one, though?' Sam persisted. 'Not a bunch of them?'

Walters shook his head. 'Sure doesn't look like it. The set could pick them out at that range.'

'All right.' Carsten turned to the exec. 'Call the men to general quarters, Mr. Cooley. If he finds us in this slop, we'll have to try to shoot him down.' He'd been attacked from the air before, even back in the Great War. He didn't enjoy it, not even a little bit.

'General quarters. Aye aye, sir,' Cooley said. Klaxons hooted. Sailors started running like men possessed. They dashed into the turrets that held the *Josephus Daniels'* two 4.5-inch guns. And they manned all her twin 40mm anti-aircraft guns and the .50-caliber machine guns that sup-plemented them. The unknown airplane would get a warm reception, anyhow.

As soon as Sam heard the snarl of an airplane engine off in the distance, he said, 'Evasive action, Mr. Cooley.'

'Evasive action – aye aye, sir.' Cooley was a better

shiphandler than Sam was. Sam had never had his hands on a wheel till he took over the *Josephus Daniels*. He was a lot better now than he had been then, but the exec was better still. 'All ahead full!' Cooley called down to the engine room, and the throb of the destroyer escort's own engines picked up.

Cooley started zigzagging the ship across the ocean, lurching now to port, now to starboard, at random times and angles. But the *Josephus Daniels* was only a destroyer escort, not a full-fledged destroyer. She had a smaller crew, a smaller hull, and a smaller powerplant than a destroyer proper. She couldn't come within several knots of a real destroyer's speed. One of these days, that would hurt her. Sam felt it in his bones. He hoped today wasn't the day.

The airplane with the blue-white-red British roundel broke through the clouds. 'All guns open fire!' Sam shouted. They did. The racket was impressive. Even the popguns that were the *Josephus Daniels'* main armament could fire antiaircraft shells. Black puffs of smoke appeared around the British aircraft.

Sam nodded to himself in more than a little satisfaction. He was still no great shakes as a shiphandler, no. But gunnery aboard the *Josephus Daniels* was far better than it had been when he took over the ship. He'd been part of a five-inch gun crew before becoming an officer; he knew what was what there.

That airplane jinked and dodged like the destroyer escort, though much faster. It had a bomb slung under its belly. It also had floats under the belly and each wing. Despite its maneuvers, it bored in on the *Josephus Daniels*. The bomb fell free. The airplane raced away. Cursing, Pat Cooley swung the ship hard to starboard.

With a roar and a great gout of water hurled into the sky, the bomb burst about a hundred yards to port. The airplane vanished into the clouds. For all the shells the gunners threw at it, Sam didn't think they'd hit it. He hoped no splinters from the bomb casing had sliced into his crew.

'Nice job, Pat,' he said.

'Thank you, sir,' the exec answered. 'Every so often, this looks like work, doesn't it?'

'Maybe a little,' Carsten answered. They smiled at each other, both glad to be alive. Sam went on, 'Well, we don't have to worry about a limey carrier, anyway.'

'Sir?' Cooley said.

'Oh. I guess you were kind of occupied.' Sam chuckled under his breath. 'Son of a bitch was a floatplane. A freighter could catapult-launch it, let it scout around, and then haul it out of the drink with a crane.'

'Damn. My hat's off to the pilot,' Cooley said. 'I sure as hell wouldn't want to try putting a plane down on the water in seas like this.'

'Good point.' Sam hadn't thought of that, but he nodded. 'When I was on the *Remembrance,* we wouldn't launch or land aircraft from the flight deck in this, let alone try to get down on the sea. But that's not my worry. . . . Mr. Walters!'

'Sir?' the Y-range operator said.

'You still have that airplane on your screen? What's his course?'

'Flying out at 085, sir – going out on the reciprocal of the vector he came at us on.'

'All right.' Sam turned back to the exec. 'Mr. Cooley, bring our course to 080. Let's see if we can follow him back more or less down his trail and find the ship that sent him out.'

'Changing course to 080, sir.' Cooley's smile was predatory. 'You'd make a good duck hunter.'

'Thanks. You've got to lead them a little,' Sam said. 'The

limey'll still be heading west. If we get close, the Y-ranger will spot him.'

'Here's hoping, anyway,' Walters said.

'You've done it before,' Sam said. 'If we do find the ship, let's just hope she's not loaded for bear like the last one we met.'

'We'll be ready this time, anyhow,' Pat Cooley said. Sam nodded. The British had taken to mounting guns on some of their freighters. The *Josephus Daniels* got a nasty surprise the first time she ran into one of those. She'd outfought the *Karlskrona,* but Sam still shuddered thinking about what might have happened if one of those big shells had hit his ship.

He wondered how far that floatplane had come from. If it was a hundred miles, the destroyer escort would never find the ship that had launched it. He wouldn't have wanted to try to find the ship after flying a hundred miles each way through this kind of weather. He'd seen the limey pilot had guts. But wasn't there a difference between having guts and being out of your skull?

He'd sailed east and a little north for about an hour when Lieutenant Walters stirred at his set. 'Something?' Sam asked hopefully. The *Josephus Daniels* was up at the crest of a swell, which let the Y-ranging gear see a little farther.

'I – think so, sir,' the j.g. answered, and then grimaced. 'Gone now.' They'd slid into the trough. He waited till the ocean carried the ship higher again, then nodded. 'Yes, sir. Range, eight miles. Bearing 075.'

'Nice navigating, sir,' Cooley said.

'Thanks. Change course to 075,' Sam answered. In good weather, he would have seen the stranger's smoke before he got within eight miles. But the weather wasn't good, and wouldn't be for weeks.

He drew within a mile of the freighter before he spotted

her. The message he blinkered over was hard and uncompromising: HEAVE TO. SURRENDER. ANY FALSE MOVES AND WE FIRE WITHOUT WARNING. *Once bitten, twice shy,* he thought. Through binoculars, he could see the airplane that tried to bomb the *Josephus Daniels* stowed aft of the bridge.

The rustbucket ran up a white flag even as he ordered a shot across her bow. He wasn't the only man scanning her for anything the least bit wrong. If canvas was thrown aside to clear hidden guns . . . But it wasn't, not this time.

Feeling piratical, he sent across a boarding party armed with rifles and pistols and submachine guns. The British sailors offered no resistance. ' 'Ow the bleedin' 'ell did you find us?' their skipper asked when the Americans brought him back to the *Josephus Daniels*.

Sam almost told him. Why not? The limey wasn't going anywhere. But the urge to take no chances prevailed. 'Just luck,' he answered, and smiled to himself. 'Yeah, just luck.'

Twice built, twice destroyed. Sergeant Armstrong Grimes strode through the wreckage of Temple Square in Salt Lake City. The Mormons had risen during the Great War, and been brutally smashed. They waited for years. They finally got their civil rights back from President Al Smith. And then, no doubt with Confederate encouragement, they rose against the USA again. And now the Temple and the Mormon Tabernacle were rubble again, perhaps more finely pulverized rubble than they had been a generation earlier.

Armstrong's eyes flicked now this way, now that. Since Lieutenant Streczyk got wounded, he'd commanded a platoon. One of these days, a new junior officer might take charge of it. Armstrong wasn't holding his breath. The war in Utah got what the war against the CSA didn't need. Since the war against the CSA needed everything, the war in Utah got . . . hind tit.

Corporal Yossel Reisen walked through the wreckage, too. Like Armstrong, the Jew from New York City held his Springfield at the ready. Reisen took a drag at the cigarette that hung from the corner of his mouth. 'Well, here we are. We've liberated Temple Square,' he said.

'Yeah.' Armstrong looked around. He didn't see a piece of rock bigger than about two by two. The United States had expended a *lot* of bombs and shells on this place. 'We've liberated the living shit out of it, haven't we?'

Here and there, Mormon civilians who'd lived through the fighting were starting to come out of their holes. They said they were civilians, anyway. Orders were to treat them as civilians unless they showed signs of being dangerous. Armstrong didn't know why the U.S. government was trying to win the locals' hearts and minds. That had been a losing game for more than sixty years now. But he didn't shoot at people he would have tried to kill not long before.

That didn't mean he wanted the Mormons coming anywhere near him. One of the ways they could show signs of being dangerous was by blowing themselves up, along with whatever U.S. soldiers happened to be within range of the blast. Mormons had invented people bombs, and still used them to deadly effect.

And they weren't the only ones who did. Plainly, they'd hit upon an idea whose time had come. Blacks in the CSA used people bombs to strike at the Freedom Party. Half a dozen Balkans groups were using them against Austria-Hungary. Armenians blew themselves up to hit back at the Ottoman Turks. In Russia, the Reds had lost a long, brutal civil war to the Tsar. Now their remnants had a new weapon, too.

Other soldiers in green-gray kept chivvying the emerging Mormons away from them. Most of the civilians were women. That cut no ice with Armstrong Grimes. The first person he'd seen using a people bomb was a woman. And plenty of Mormon women picked up rifles and grenades and fought alongside their husbands and brothers and sons.

'You ever . . . pay a Mormon gal back?' he asked Yossel Reisen.

Reisen was watching the women, too. He shook his head. 'Not like that. You?'

'No,' Armstrong said. Not many Mormon women let themselves be captured. They had reasons for fighting to the death, too. The revenge U.S. soldiers took was basic in the extreme. Gang-raping captured Mormon women was against orders, which didn't mean it didn't happen.

Off to the north, artillery boomed. U.S. airplanes buzzed overhead, some spotting for the guns, others dropping bombs on Mormon positions. The Confederates would have hacked the lumbering, obsolescent bombers out of the sky with ease. Against enemies who didn't have fighters and didn't have much in the way of antiaircraft guns, they were good enough.

'Blow all the bastards to hell and gone.' Armstrong picked up a chip of granite that might have come from the Temple. 'Then we can get on with the real war.' He flung the stone chip away. It bounced off a bigger rock and disappeared in the rubble.

Yossel's expression changed. He bent and picked up a bit of stone, too. Tossing it up and down, he murmured, 'I wonder what Jerusalem is like these days.'

'Huh?' Armstrong knew what Jerusalem was like: a sleepy Ottoman town full of Arabs and Jews where nothing much had happened for centuries.

But his buddy said, 'We had our Temple destroyed twice, too.'

He didn't usually make a big deal out of being a Jew,

any more than he made a big deal out of being a Congresswoman's nephew – and not just any Congresswoman, but one who'd also been First Lady. 'You guys are real Americans,' Armstrong said. 'Hell, you're a gentile here – just ask a Mormon.'

'I know. I think it's a scream,' Yossel Reisen said. 'Yeah, we're real Americans – or we try to be, anyhow. But we sure didn't make real Romans a couple of thousand years ago. That's why the Second Temple got it.'

'I guess.' Except for what little Armstrong remembered from a high-school history class and from *Julius Caesar* in English Lit, ancient Rome was a closed book to him.

'We think the Mormons are nuts, and we treat 'em that way, and what happens?' Yossel said. 'Bang! They rise up. We treat Jews all right, and they're happy and quiet. The Romans thought my ancestors were nuts, and they treated 'em that way, and what happened? Bang! The Jews rose up.'

'Bunch of bullshit, if you want to know what I think,' Armstrong said. 'We were nice to the Mormons right before the war, and what did we get for it? They kicked us anyway, soon as we got busy with Featherston's fuckers.' He might not know ancient history, but he remembered the end of the occupation of Utah. Fat lot of good ending it did anybody.

'Yeah, there is that,' Yossel allowed. 'Maybe you just can't make some people happy.'

'Better believe you can't,' Armstrong said. 'These bastards have spent the last God knows how long proving it, too.' He was some small part of what the U.S. government had done to Utah, but that never entered his mind. Neither side, by then, worried much about who'd started what and why. They both knew they had a long history of hating, mistrusting, and striking at each other. Past that, they didn't much care.

Yossel Reisen pointed to another corporal trudging through the wreckage of Temple Square. He nudged Armstrong. 'You recognize that guy?'

Armstrong eyed the two-striper. He looked like anybody else: not too young, not too old, not too big, not too small. But he didn't look like anybody Armstrong knew, or even knew of. Maybe that didn't mean anything. Now that Temple Square had finally fallen, it drew its share of gawkers.

But maybe it did mean something. The USA had trouble fighting the Mormons just because they looked so ordinary. They had no trouble getting U.S. uniforms, either. Down in the CSA, the Freedom Party knew who was a Negro and who wasn't. Here . . . Armstrong unslung his Springfield. 'Let's go check him out.'

The corporal wasn't doing anything to draw notice; he ambled around with his hands in his pockets. Once he bent down and picked up a bit of rock and stowed it away. To Mormons, pieces of the Temple were sacred relics. But to U.S. soldiers who'd gone through hell to get here, they made good souvenirs. Carrying one didn't say a thing about what you were.

'Hey!' Armstrong said, quietly slipping off the Springfield's safety.

'You want something, Sarge?' The corporal sounded like anybody else, too. Mormons did.

'Yeah. Let's see your papers.'

'Sure.' The noncom started to take something out of his pocket.

'Hold it right there!' Yossel Reisen snapped. Armstrong didn't like the way the stranger's hand bunched, either. He sure looked as if he was grabbing something bigger than a set of identity documents. 'Take both hands out, nice and slow,' Yossel told him. 'If they aren't empty when you do, you're dead. Got it?'

'Who are you clowns?' the corporal demanded. 'You Mormons trying to hijack me? You won't get away with it!'

If he was trying to put the shoe on the other foot, he had balls. Armstrong gestured with his Springfield. 'Do like my buddy says.' His own balls tried to crawl up into his belly. If this guy was a Mormon and what he had in there was a detonator . . . But his hands came out empty.

Yossel reached into that pocket and pulled out a pistol: not an Army .45, but a smaller revolver, a civilian piece. Armstrong's suspicions flared. Then Yossel found the other corporal's papers. He looked from the photo to the man and back again. He shook his head.

'Let's see,' Armstrong said. His pal showed him the picture. It was of a guy noticeably darker and noticeably skinnier than the fellow in the uniform. Armstrong gestured with the rifle again. 'Come on. Get moving. You got a bunch of questions to answer.'

'I haven't done anything!' the corporal said. One thing he hadn't done was swear, not even once. Most U.S. soldiers would have. Mormons watched their mouths better.

'Well, you'll get the chance to prove it,' Armstrong said. 'Yossel, grab his rifle.'

Carefully, Yossel Reisen unslung the other corporal's Springfield. 'Move,' he told the man.

Still squawking – but still not cursing – the soldier who might not be a soldier moved. They led him back over the ground for which the Mormons had fought so long and so hard, the ground that was cratered and crumpled and crushed, the ground over which the stench of death still hung. That would only get worse when the weather warmed up. Armstrong wondered if it would ever leave the land, or if the foul, clinging odor would linger forever, an unseen but unmistakable monument to what Salt Lake City had gone through.

Sentries outside of regimental headquarters popped up out of the foxholes where they spent most of their time – not every sniper had been hunted down and killed. 'What the fuck's going on here?' one of them demanded. He talked the way most U.S. soldiers did.

'We caught this guy up by the Temple,' Armstrong answered. 'Yossel here spotted him.' It didn't occur to him till later that he might have taken the credit himself. He didn't want to screw his buddy. 'We figure maybe he's a Mormon. His papers don't match his face, and he was carrying this little chickenshit pistol – show 'em, Yossel.' Reisen displayed the revolver.

The sentry eyed the corporal who didn't seem to be a corporal. 'Waddayou got to say for yourself, Mac?' he asked, his voice colder than the weather.

'They're full of baloney,' the – maybe – two-striper said. Not *shit – baloney.* He added, 'I don't like a .45 – kicks too hard.'

'Huh,' the sentry said, no doubt noticing, as Armstrong did, that that – maybe – Mormon didn't say anything about his papers. The sentry nodded to Armstrong and Yossel. 'Bring him on in. They'll find out what's going on with him. And if it is what you think it is . . .' He didn't go on, or need to. If it was what they thought it was, the fellow they'd captured was a dead man. He wouldn't die quickly or cleanly, either. *Oh, what a shame,* Armstrong thought, and led him on.

Cincinnatus Driver hadn't been under fire for more than twenty-five years. He'd forgotten how much fun it wasn't. If he hadn't forgotten, he never would have volunteered to drive a truck in a combat zone again. He would have stayed back in Des Moines and found work in a war plant or tried to bring his dead moving and hauling business back to life.

But he'd been flat on his back in Covington, Kentucky, when the state passed from the USA back to the CSA. He supposed he was lucky: the car that hit him didn't kill him. It didn't seem like luck while he was recovering from a broken leg and a fractured skull and a smashed shoulder. Even now, almost two and a half years later, he walked with a limp and a cane and sometimes got headaches that laughed at aspirin.

He was finally exchanged for a Confederate the USA was holding – U.S. citizenship meant something, even for a Negro. It didn't mean everything; Negroes in the United States couldn't join the Army, couldn't pick up rifles and go after the enemies who were tormenting their brethren south of the Mason-Dixon Line. With his age and his injuries, Cincinnatus wouldn't have been able to join the Army if he were white.

This was the next best thing. He'd driven trucks for more than thirty years. He'd driven for the USA during the Great War. Here he was, doing it again, part of a long column of green-gray machines hauling ammunition and rations to the U.S. troops trying to drive the Confederates out of western Ohio.

The state of the art had improved over the past quarter-century. The Chevy truck he drove now had a much more powerful, much more reliable engine than the White he'd used then. It had a fully enclosed cabin, too, and a heater. It boasted a self-starter; he didn't have to crank it to life. Its headlights were electric, not acetylene lamps. With all-wheel drive, it could get through terrain that would have shaken the White to pieces.

But the driving wasn't much different. Neither was the fear when shells started bursting in the field to either side of the road. Cincinnatus' mouth went dry. His sphincters tightened. He wanted to stop and turn around and get the hell out of there.

A .45 lay on the seat beside him. He couldn't afford to let the Confederates capture him. It wasn't just that he was colored, though no black man in the USA wanted to think about falling into Confederate hands. But he was also on the CSA's list of dangerous characters. When they removed him from Covington, they made it very plain they didn't want to have anything to do with him ever again. They might regret it if they did, but he would never get over it.

Next to those bursting shells, the .45 seemed like small potatoes. Next to the dreadful immensity of the war, Cincinnatus himself seemed like small potatoes: just one man, and an ordinary man at that. But all you could do was all you could do. Everybody was just one person, doing what he or she could do. Added together, all those people made up the USA and the CSA – made up the war. If, added together, all the people of the USA could do more . . .

'They better,' Cincinnatus said, there alone in the cab of the Chevrolet truck. Imagining a North America dominated by the Confederacy and the Freedom Party . . . He didn't want to do it. He'd seen what Covington was like after the Stars and Bars replaced the Stars and Stripes. Thinking of that happening everywhere made him a little sick, or more than a little.

One of the incoming shells hit a truck a couple of hundred yards ahead of him. The truck, loaded with the same sort of cargo as his, went up in a fireball. Luckily, it careened off the road instead of blocking it. All the same, Cincinnatus hit the brakes. He didn't want to get any closer than he had to till that ammo finished cooking off.

Could have been me, he thought, and shuddered. It would have been him if one of the Confederate artillery men had paused to scratch an itch or stick a fresh chaw in his mouth before pulling the lanyard. About fifteen seconds later, his truck would have been where that shell landed.

He sped up when he went past the shattered deuce-and-a-half. Not a chance in hell the driver got out. He hoped the man died fast, anyhow. Given the size of that explosion, the odds seemed good.

Another shell left a crater in the road, forcing Cincinnatus over onto the soft shoulder to get around it. With power to all six wheels, he managed to get by without bogging down. He hoped the trucks that came after his would be able to do the same. Each one chewed up the ground more and more.

The truck column rolled into Findlay about five minutes later. Here and there around the town, tall columns of black, greasy smoke rose into the air: oil wells torched by the retreating Confederates. A team of U.S. engineers was trying to put one out as Cincinnatus came into town. He wondered if retreating U.S. soldiers had fired the wells a year and a half earlier, leaving the Confederates to get them working again. He wouldn't have been surprised.

He didn't get long to worry about it. 'Come on! Come on! Over here!' a sergeant bellowed, waving like a man possessed. Cincinnatus did his best to follow the noncom's instructions. At last, the sergeant threw up both hands, as if he'd just scored a touchdown. He stopped.

A swarm of soldiers descended on the truck, transferring the munitions and rations to several smaller trucks for the trip to the front. It wasn't far away; Findlay itself had fallen only a few days before. Shells still came down on the town, as they'd landed on the road to the northwest. The faster the explosives left Cincinnatus' truck, the happier he would be.

Of course, as soon as the deuce-and-a-half was empty, he had to drive back to the big depot in Defiance to load up again for another trip to Findlay. The CSA had heavily bombed Defiance earlier in the war. Not many enemy airplanes came over these days. U.S. fighters and bombers took off from airstrips on the outskirts of town. Antiaircraft guns by the score poked their long snouts up toward the sky. Camouflage netting masked some of them. Others stood out in the open, as if warning the Confederates they were there.

Cincinnatus gulped a sandwich and drank coffee while they filled his truck again. There was one other Negro driver in his transport unit. Douglass Butler came from Denver, of all places. He talked like a white man. Cincinnatus' son and daughter had grown up in Des Moines, and lost a lot of their Confederate Negro accent. Cincinnatus had lost some of it himself; he'd noticed that when he got stuck in Covington. But Douglass Butler didn't have any, and apparently never had had any. He puffed on a cigar, waiting for his truck to get reloaded.

'My dad went out to Colorado to see if he could get rich mining,' he said, every vowel sharp, every consonant distinct. 'He didn't – only a few people did – and he ended up running a grocery store. I started driving a truck for him, but I found I liked driving more than I liked the grocery business.'

'Folks out there give you a lot of trouble on account o' – ?' Cincinnatus brushed two fingers of his right hand across the back of his left to remind the other Negro what color they were.

'Well, I know what *nigger* means, that's for damn sure.' Butler shrugged. 'But Jews are kikes and Chinamen are Chinks and Irishmen are micks and Mexicans are greasers and Italians are wops and even Poles are lousy Polacks, for God's sake. I don't get too excited about it. Hell, my brother's married to a white woman.'

That made Cincinnatus blink. 'Work out all right?' he asked.

'They've been married almost twenty years. People are used to them,' the other driver said. 'Every once in a while, John'll hear something stupid if he's standing in line for a film with Helen or out at a diner or something like that, but it's not too bad.' He chuckled. 'Of course, he's my *big* brother – he goes about six-three, maybe two-fifty. I don't care if you're green – you want to be careful what you say around him.' He was of ordinary size himself.

'Does make a difference,' Cincinnatus agreed. He wondered if John Butler was named for John Brown; with two s's in his first name, Douglass Butler was bound to be named for Frederick Douglass.

Before he could ask, somebody shouted that their trucks were ready to roll. 'Got to get moving,' Butler said. 'I want to parade through Nashville or Birmingham or one of those places. And if I hear some Confederate asshole yell, "Freedom!" – well, I want to pull out my .45 and blow his fucking head off.'

He sounded altogether matter-of-fact about it, the way a U.S. white man would have. But for the color of his skin, he might as well have been a U.S. white man. He seemed as sure of his place in the world and as comfortable with it as any white man, whether from the USA or the CSA. Cincinnatus, whom life had left forever betwixt and between, envied him for that.

He climbed into the cab of his truck, slammed the door, turned the key in the ignition, and put the beast in gear. South and east he rolled, back toward Findlay. No shellfire fell on the road this time. U.S. guns, or maybe dive bombers, had silenced the Confederate batteries that were shelling it. Cincinnatus approved. Unlike Douglass Butler, he didn't want to use his .45 for anything. He had it. He could use it if he had to. But he didn't want to.

What if Jake Featherston was right in front of you? He glanced over to the pistol. Well, you could make exceptions for everything. Dream as he would, though, he didn't expect to be sharing a diner with the President of the CSA any time soon.

When he rolled into Findlay, he got waved through the town. 'What's goin' on?' he called to a soldier with wigwag flags.

'We broke through again, that's what,' the white man answered. 'They need their shit farther forward.'

'I like that,' Cincinnatus said, and drove on.

Shells were falling not far from the new unloading area, but they'd been falling in Findlay and beyond it only a couple of hours before. The men who hauled crates out of the back of his truck had an air of barely suppressed excitement. They didn't seem to think the Confederates would be able to slow this latest push.

Do Jesus, let 'em be right, Cincinnatus thought. That Ohio should be liberated didn't matter so much in and of itself – not to him, anyway. But he could see that U.S. soldiers would have to clear the Confederates out of their own country before they started doing what really did matter – to him, anyway. If the United States were going to lick Jake Featherston, they would have to do it on Featherston's turf.

Cincinnatus thought about the last time he'd driven trucks full of munitions through Kentucky and Tennessee. He thought about the Confederate diehards who'd shot up his column more than once. Then he thought about U.S. artillery and bombers blowing all those people to kingdom come.

War was a filthy business for everybody, no doubt about it. Cincinnatus wanted a little more filth to come

down on the other side. He didn't think that was too much
to ask.

Brigadier General Irving Morrell was a man in a hurry.
He always had been, ever since his days as a company commander at the start of the Great War. He took the first
position he ever attacked – and he got shot charging with
the bayonet when he ran out of ammunition. That taught
him an important lesson: like anything else, being in a hurry
had its disadvantages.

It also had its advantages, though. Massing barrels and
smashing Confederate lines made the CSA say uncle in
1917. At the Barrel Works at Fort Leavenworth after the
Great War, Morrell designed a machine with all the features a modern barrel needed: a reduced crew, a powerful
engine, a big gun in a turret that turned through 360
degrees, and a wireless set.

He designed it – and he found nobody in the USA
much wanted it. The Great War was over, wasn't it? There'd
never be another one, would there? Being a man in a hurry
sometimes put you too far ahead not only of the enemy
but also of your own side.

By the time it became clear the Great War wouldn't be
the last one after all, the state of the art all over the world
had caught up with Morrell's vision. Germany and Austria-
Hungary built barrels incorporating all the features he'd
envisioned more than fifteen years earlier. So did France
and England and Russia. And so did the Confederate States.

So did the United States, but belatedly and halfheart-
edly. When the fighting started, Morrell had to try to defend
Ohio without enough machines – and without good enough
machines. He failed. Even in failure, he alarmed the
Confederates. A sniper gave him an oak-leaf cluster for his
Purple Heart and put him on the shelf for weeks.

Returning to duty, he didn't have much luck in Virginia, a narrow land bristling with fortifications. But he was the architect of the U.S. thrust that cut off, surrounded, and destroyed the Confederate army that fought its way into Pittsburgh. Now the armored force he led was driving west through Ohio. He knew exactly what he wanted to do. If, somewhere south of Columbus, his force could meet up with the one pushing southeast from northwestern Ohio and Indiana, they would trap all the Confederates to the north of them in another pocket.

He didn't think Jake Featherston could afford to lose one army. He knew damn well the President of the CSA couldn't afford to lose two. What could be better, then, than giving Jake exactly what he didn't want?

Right this minute, Morrell was bivouacked with his lead barrels atop Mount Pleasant, in Lancaster, Ohio. The 250-foot sandstone rise looked down on the whole town. It had not lived up to its name. Not being fools, the Confederates put an observation post and several artillery batteries atop the rise, and protected them with pillboxes and machine-gun nests.

Clearing them out was a slow, bloody, expensive job. Morrell believed in bypassing enemy strongpoints wherever he could, letting slower-moving infantry clean up in the armor's wake. Some strongpoints, though, were too strong to bypass. This, unfortunately, was one of them.

Dive bombers helped pound it into submission. Several 105s sprawled in the snow, knocked ass over teakettle by 500-pound bombs. Dead soldiers in butternut lay there, too. Some of them wore white camouflage smocks over their uniforms, which struck Morrell as a good idea. Good idea or not, it didn't save them. Along with soot, their blood streaked the snow.

Crows and a couple of turkey vultures were feeding on

the bodies. Standing up in his barrel's cupola, Morrell waved his arms and yelled, 'Yaaah!' A few of the birds flew away. Most of them ignored him.

The gunner tapped him on the leg. 'What the hell, sir?' Corporal Al Bergeron said plaintively. 'You scared the crap out of me there.'

'Sorry, Frenchy,' Morrell answered. Bergeron was a good man and a good gunner – maybe not quite so good as Michael Pound, who was one of a kind in several different ways, but damn good just the same. Morrell explained why he made his horrible noise.

'Oh.' Bergeron thought about that for a little while. Then he said, 'Yeah, those damn things are filthy, all right. Tell you one thing, though: I'm glad they're chowing down on Featherston's fuckers and not on us.'

'Me, too,' Morrell said, though he knew the carrion birds didn't care whether their suppers came wrapped in butternut or green-gray. For that matter, the crows and vultures feasted on dead civilians, too.

'What's it look like off to the west?' Bergeron asked.

Before answering, Morrell scanned the way ahead with binoculars. Visibility wasn't everything he wished it were, but he could see enough to get some idea of what was going on. 'Sure looks like they're pulling back,' he said.

Corporal Bergeron summed up his reaction to that in two words: 'Well, shit.'

'You said a mouthful, Frenchy.' Morrell really had hoped he could cut off as many Confederates with this thrust as he had in and around Pittsburgh. Then, Jake Featherston forbade his men to withdraw. Morrell had hoped he would do it again. But evidently he was able to learn from experience. *Too bad,* Morrell thought. The Confederates were heading south in anything that would roll: truck convoys, barrels, commandeered civilian motorcars. Bombers and

artillery and saboteurs did everything they could to knock
the railroads out of action, but Ohio had such a dense net
of tracks that it wasn't easy. Every soldier, every barrel,
every gun, every truck that got out now was a soldier, a
barrel, a gun, a truck the USA would have to put out of
action later on.

Morrell scanned the horizon again. He knew he was
being foolish, but he did it anyhow. If he could have seen
the U.S. forces coming down from the northwest, the
Confederates would have been in even worse trouble than
they really were. When he sighed, the vapor threatened to
cloud the field glasses' lenses. That western column wasn't
so strong or so swift as this one. Even so . . .

'We get the country put back together again,' Frenchy
Bergeron said.

You didn't need to be a general to see that; a noncom
would do just fine. The Confederates' armored thrust had
carried them all the way from the Ohio River up to
Sandusky. They cut the United States in half. For more
than a year and a half, goods and men moved from east
to west or west to east by air (risky), on the waters of the
Great Lakes (also risky, with C.S. airplanes always on the
prowl), and over the Canadian roads and railroads north
of the lakes (of limited capacity, and vulnerable to sabotage even before the Canucks rebelled).

'It'll be better,' Morrell agreed. It probably wouldn't be
a whole lot better any time soon. The Confederates were
professionally competent. They would have done their best
to wreck the east-west highways and railroad lines they
were now sullenly abandoning. Putting the roads and rail-
ways back into action wouldn't happen overnight, especially since C.S. bombers would go right on visiting
northern Ohio.

But now the Confederates were reacting to what Morrell

and his countrymen did. For the first year of the war and more, the enemy had the United States back on their heels. The CSA called the tune. No more.

As Morrell watched, artillery rounds began falling near the Confederate convoy. The first few shells missed the road, bursting in front of or behind it. The trucks sped up. If they could get out of trouble . . . But they couldn't, not fast enough. A round hit the road. The convoy had to slow down to go onto the shoulder. And then a truck got hit, and began to burn.

That was all Morrell needed to see. He was commanding a large, complex operation. But he was also a fighting man himself. When he saw trucks in trouble, he wanted to give them more.

His barrel carried a large, complicated wireless set. He could talk with his fellow armored units, with artillery, with infantry, or with bombers and fighters. He didn't want to, not here. He used the company circuit any barrel commander might have clicked to: 'We've got a Confederate convoy stalled on the road a few miles west. Let's go get 'em!'

Along with the others nearby, his own machine rumbled down off Mount Pleasant. Even after giving up the high ground, they had no trouble tracking their quarry: the pyre from that one burning truck – and maybe from more by now – guided them straight to it.

They met a warm reception when they got there. The Confederates had to know trouble was on the way. They didn't stay in the trucks waiting around to get shot up. Some of them made their way south on foot. And others had manhandled an antibarrel gun into position, and opened up on the U.S. machines as soon as they came into range.

The Confederates hit one, too, fortunately with a round

that glanced off instead of penetrating. 'Front!' Morrell said.

'Identified!' Frenchy Bergeron answered. 'HE!' the gunner called to the loader. The barrel stopped. He fired a couple of high-explosive shells at the gun. He wasn't the only barrel gunner shooting, either. The Confederates serving the cannon had only a small splinter shield to protect them. They soon went down.

Brave bastards, Morrell thought, watching with his head and shoulders out of the cupola. Small-arms fire came his way, but not a lot of it. He ignored it with the stoicism of a man who'd known worse. One bullet was all he needed to make this as bad as it could be, but he didn't think about that.

Then something different happened. A projectile trailing smoke and flame seemed to come out of nowhere. It slammed into a U.S. barrel and set it afire. Morrell couldn't see if any of the men got out. He didn't think so.

'What the fuck was that?' Bergeron must have seen it through the gunsight.

'I'll be goddamned if I know,' Morrell answered.

He didn't have to wait long. A couple of minutes later, another one of those darts of fire lanced out to incinerate a U.S. barrel. 'It's some kind of rocket, like on the Fourth of July,' Frenchy Bergeron said. 'How the hell did they come up with that?'

'How? I don't know, but they sure did.' Morrell ducked down into the turret. 'Did you see where they're shooting it from?'

'Yes, sir,' the gunner answered. 'Behind that stone fence there near the road.'

'All right. If they pop up again, try and shoot them before they can let go with it. I've got to get on the horn to my people.' He flipped to the circuit that would connect him to senior armor officers. 'The Confederates have a portable antibarrel device, something an infantryman can use to knock out a machine at a couple of hundred yards. I say again, a foot soldier can use this thing to knock out a barrel at a couple of hundred yards.'

Life suddenly got more complicated. If foot soldiers really could fight back against armor without the suicidal impulse required to fling a Featherston Fizz . . . *We need something like that ourselves,* Morrell thought.

The coaxial machine gun chattered. '*Got* the son of a bitch!' Bergeron said.

Plainly, the C.S. rocket was new. Plainly, the Confederates here didn't have many rounds. Just as plainly, the damn thing worked. And how many factories would start turning it out as fast as they could? Morrell swore. Yes, life was a lot more complicated all at once.

When Jake Featherston wanted to fly into Nashville, his bodyguards didn't just have kittens. They had puppies and lambs and probably baby elephants, too. Their chief was a group leader – the Freedom Party guards' equivalent of a major general – named Hiram McCullough. 'Mr. President,' he said, 'your airplane could crash.'

Featherston scowled at him. 'My train could derail, too, if I go that way,' he growled.

'Yes, sir,' Group Leader McCullough agreed stolidly. That gave Featherston's ever-ready anger no good place to light. McCullough went on, 'The other thing that could happen is, the damnyankees could shoot you down. The country needs you too much to let you take the chance.'

Without false modesty, Jake knew the country needed him, too. He couldn't think of anyone else with the driving will to hold the CSA together if anything did happen to him. That was only the second half of what McCullough said, though. As for the first . . . 'How could the damnyan-kees shoot me down? They won't know I'm in the air till I've landed.'

'Sir, you don't know that for sure. Neither do I.' McCullough had a round, red face pitted with acne scars. He was good at looking worried, as a bodyguard should be. He looked very worried now. 'We don't know for a fact how many of our codes the Yankees can read. We don't know for a fact that they don't have spies who'd pass on where you're going and when. If you give the orders, I'll follow 'em. But do you want to take a chance you don't have to?'

Damn you, Jake thought. Since turning fifty – and since surviving two assassination tries, one by his own guards – he was more careful about his own safety. No one could question his courage, not after the record he'd racked up in the Great War. However much he wanted to, he couldn't deny that Group Leader McCullough had a point.

'All right, Hiram,' he said. 'I'll take the goddamn train.'

'Thank you, Mr. President!' McCullough said in glad surprise. Those doleful features hardly seemed able to contain the smile that lit them now.

Featherston held up a bony hand. 'Don't thank me yet. We'll keep the train real quiet – I mean *real* quiet. What you put out through the regular secure channels is that I am going to fly. Send my regular pilot, send my regular airplane, give it the regular fighter escort. Put somebody who looks like me on it. If the Yankees jump it, you win. If they don't, I'll damn well fly when I feel like it. You got that?'

'Yes, sir,' McCullough said. 'I'll take care of it, just like you want me to.' Just about everyone said that to the President of the CSA. It was what he liked to hear most. McCullough got to his feet. 'Freedom!'

'Freedom!' Jake echoed.

Two days later, an armored limousine took someone who looked like him from the ruins of the Gray House to the airport outside Richmond. Escorted by Hound Dogs, his personal transport took off for Nashville. With no ceremony at all, Jake went to the train station and headed west in a Pullman car.

He got to the capital of Tennessee six hours later than he expected to; U.S. bombs had knocked out a bridge. He was glad he wasn't scheduled to speak till that evening. Delaying his talk because of what the enemy did would be embarrassing.

Hiram McCullough went to Nashville a day ahead of him to make sure security was tight. The group leader met Jake at the train station. As soon as he could, he took Featherston aside. In a low voice, he said, 'Mr. President, two squadrons of Yankee fighters jumped your airplane before it got out of Virginia. They shot it down, and they shot down three of the Hound Dogs with it, too.'

'Jesus Christ!' Jake exploded.

'Yes, sir,' McCullough said. 'I'm mighty glad you stayed on the ground, Mr. President.' That was *I told you so*, but Jake didn't care. He was glad, too.

He said so. He didn't see how he could avoid it. Then he asked, 'How the hell are those bastards picking up our codes?'

'Don't know, sir,' McCullough answered. 'I'm going to be looking at that, though – you better believe I will. And I'll tell you something else, too: I won't be the only one, either.'

'Better not be,' Featherston said. 'Dammit, I'm gonna have to do more talking with Clarence Potter.' Potter was smart – sometimes too damn smart for his own good, but smart. And a breach like this would make him focus all of his formidable brainpower on it.

Unless he's the one who fed the damnyankees the codes in the first place. In Jake Featherston's shoes, you worried about everybody all the time, and for every possible reason. But Featherston couldn't make himself believe Clarence Potter would sell the CSA down the river. Potter didn't love him; he'd known that for many years. But the Intelligence officer was a Confederate patriot. If you didn't understand that, you didn't understand anything about him.

'I brought an armored car to the station, sir, to take you to the hotel,' McCullough said. 'Just in case.'

'Thanks.' Featherston couldn't deny that that made sense. If the Yankees knew he was on the way to Nashville, they might have people here who would try to strike at him. Of course, they might also be thinking they'd just killed him – in which case they were all probably out getting drunk and trying to lay their secretaries. He let out a nasty chuckle. Before long, they'd know he was still alive and kicking, all right.

The armored car looked impressive as hell. It had six big tires with cleated treads. Its angles were harsh and military. It sported a barrel-like turret with a cannon and a coaxial machine gun. But factories weren't making very many of them these days, and most of the ones that did get made were used against rebellious Negroes, not against the damnyankees. Armored cars made tolerable scout vehicles. Their steel sides kept out small-arms fire. But they were horribly vulnerable to any kind of cannon, and even with six wheels and all-wheel drive they weren't as good away from roads as tracked machines were.

This one, though, was fine to get him to the Hermitage Hotel. He peered out at Nashville through firing slits and periscopes. The city hadn't been bombed nearly so hard as Richmond had. It was farther from U.S. airstrips than the capital, and not so vital a target. But it had suffered, too.

So much to rebuild when this is over, Jake thought. A scowl made his rawboned features even harsher than they were already. As long as the United States needed to put more back together, it didn't matter.

Everybody at the Hermitage Hotel was nervous, though Featherston had stayed there on earlier visits to Nashville. The manager said, 'I hope the suite will be satisfactory,' about three times in the space of two minutes.

'Don't worry about it. It'll be fine,' Jake told him. The manager had to be scared he'd get skinned alive if the rooms weren't fancy enough. That only proved he didn't know the President of the CSA. Jake liked Habana cigars and good whiskey, but that was as far as he went along those lines. He hadn't got into politics hoping for riches and luxury. Power drove him, nothing else.

He didn't stay at the Hermitage very long: just long enough to freshen up after the train trip. Then he went across the street to the Nashville Memorial Auditorium, a ponderous concrete building that went up after the Great War.

He didn't have a full house in the auditorium, but he didn't care. This speech was for the wireless and the newsreels, not for the people actually in the hall. When it was filmed, the place would look full whether it was or not. Saul Goldman didn't hire cameramen who didn't know what they were doing.

'I'm Jake Featherston, and I'm here to tell you the truth.' He'd been opening with that line ever since he discovered the wireless. That was twenty years ago now. He found it hard to believe, but it was true. When he said it, he believed it. His speeches wouldn't have worked half as well if he didn't.

'The truth is, we are going to win this war!' When he said that, the Party stalwarts and fat cats in the Memorial

Auditorium started yelling as if it were going out of style. Maybe he inspired them. Maybe they were scared shitless and needed a pat on the fanny to make 'em feel better. If they did, he would give them one.

'We *are* going to win,' he repeated. 'They can't beat us, because we damn well won't quit! We'll never quit, not while we've got one free white man who can stand on his own two feet and aim a rifle at the enemy.' More applause came echoing back from the ceiling. The noise made Jake's heart beat faster. Talking in a wireless studio was one thing. Talking in front of a living, breathing, sweating crowd was something else, something better, something hotter.

'Truth is, the Freedom Party's had the right idea for twenty-five years now,' Jake went on. 'And if an idea's right to begin with, it will take up arms and struggle in this world. And once it does, nobody can beat it. Nobody, you hear? Every time someone persecutes it, that only makes it stronger!'

'Freedom!' somebody in the audience yelled. An instant later, everyone took up the cry. It washed over Jake Featherston. He scowled toward the north. If the damnyankees thought the Confederate States would fold up and die because things hadn't gone perfectly in Pennsylvania and Ohio, they could damn well think again.

'We're in this for the long haul!' he shouted. 'This isn't any ordinary war, and everybody needs to remember it. This is the kind of fight that will shape the new millennium. A war like this doesn't come along every day. It shakes the world once in a thousand years. We're on a crusade here, a crusade for—'

'*Freedom!*' The roar was louder this time.

Featherston nodded. 'That's right, friends. We can't quit now. We *won't* quit now, either. If the Confederate people give up, they won't deserve anything better than what they get. If they give up, I won't be sorry for them if God lets them down.' He paused to let that sink in, then softly asked, 'But we won't give up, will we? We'll never give up, will we?'

'*No!*' No hesitation, no backsliding. If they were there, he would hear them. As always, the Confederate States were going where he took them. And he knew where that was.

'We'll buckle down, then,' he said. 'We'll work hard at home. We'll whip the damnyankees yet. For every ton of bombs they drop on us, we'll drop ten tons on their heads, same as we've been doing all along. And we'll never get stabbed in the back again, on account of we're putting our own house in order, by God!'

That drew more frantic applause. Most of Nashville's Negroes were already in camps. Lots of Negroes went into camps in Alabama and Mississippi and Louisiana and Texas. They went in, but they didn't come out. That suited most of the whites in the CSA just fine. And if the Confederate States of America weren't a white man's country, then there was no such thing, not anywhere in the world.

Since the war started, wireless broadcasting was a tricky business. The USA and the CSA jammed each other's stations as hard as they could. As often as not, snarls of static strangled and distorted music and comedies as well as news.

But that wasn't the only reason the tune coming out of the wireless set in Flora Blackford's office sounded strange to her. Satchmo and the Rhythm Aces weren't an ordinary U.S. combo. They were colored men who'd escaped to the USA after being sent north into Ohio to entertain Confederate troops. Nobody in the United States played music like 'New Orleans Jump.' If the Negroes weren't minor heroes because of their daring getaway, they never would have got airtime for anything with such peculiar syncopations. As things were, they had a minor hit on their hands.

Congresswoman Blackford was happy for them. She'd met Satchmo and his less memorable bandmates. They were talented men. To her, they were a symbol of everything the Confederate States were wasting with their constant war against the Negro.

She clucked unhappily. To her countrymen, Satchmo and the Rhythm Aces were a curiosity, nothing more. Most people in the USA didn't want to hear about Negroes, didn't want anything to do with them, and didn't want to be told what the Confederates were doing to them. She'd tried her best to make her countrymen pay attention. Her best wasn't good enough.

'New Orleans Jump' struck her as fitting background music for what she was reading: the transcript of Jake Featherston's recent speech in Nashville. She'd got it from the War Department. The captain who gave it to her seemed angry that he had to.

Flora wondered what that was all about. She didn't think the young officer had any reason to be angry at her personally. She'd never set eyes on him before. She wasn't trying to cut off funding – who would, these days? You gave the Army and the Navy what they said they needed, and you hoped they found ways to shoot all the money at the enemy.

So why was the captain steaming, then? She picked up the telephone and called the Assistant Secretary of War, who was somewhere between a conspirator and a friend. 'Hello, Flora,' Franklin Roosevelt said genially. 'What can I do for you today?'

'A captain just brought me a copy of Featherston's latest speech,' Flora said.

'Jake's a son of a bitch, isn't he?' Roosevelt said. 'Pardon my French.'

'There's certainly no give in him – as if we didn't know that,' Flora said. 'But that isn't why I'm calling, or not exactly, anyhow. This captain seemed to be doing a slow burn, and I wondered why. It's not like I ever met him before.'

'Oh. I think I can tell you that on the telephone,' Roosevelt said. 'It's not as if the Confederates don't already know it. Dear Jake gave that speech in Nashville, right?'

'Yes.' Flora found herself nodding, though of course Franklin Roosevelt couldn't see her. He had a gift for inspiring intimacy. If infantile paralysis hadn't left him in a wheelchair, he might have tried to follow his cousin Theodore into the White House. And he was a solid Socialist, too, unlike Theodore the Democrat. 'What about it?' Flora went on.

'This about it: we knew Featherston was going to Nashville. We hoped we'd arranged things so he wouldn't get there.' Roosevelt sighed. 'Obviously, we didn't. He's a suspicious so-and-so, and he dodged the bullet. I wouldn't be surprised if that's why your captain was steaming. I'm steaming, too, to tell you the truth.'

'Oh.' Flora nodded again. 'Well, now that I know, so am I. If we could bump him off . . .'

'Wouldn't it be lovely?' Franklin Roosevelt said.

'It sure would.' Flora was sure she and the Assistant Secretary of War shared the same beatific vision: the Confederate States of America thrashing around like a headless snake if Jake Featherston got it in the neck. She had no idea who would or could replace Featherston if he got it in the neck. She doubted the Confederates had any more idea than she did. Jake Featherston made the CSA tick. If he wasn't there, wouldn't the country stop ticking?

'The other bad thing about it is, now they know we've broken some of their codes,' Roosevelt said. 'They'll change them, and that will complicate our lives for a while.'

Till we break them again, he had to mean. 'Too bad,' Flora said. 'Too bad all the way around, in fact. Thanks for letting me know. That does make me pretty sure the captain wasn't mad at me personally, anyhow.'

'Always a relief,' Roosevelt agreed. 'The last thing anybody wants or needs is a secret unadmirer.'

'Er – yes.' Flora tasted the phrase. 'But it's a shame Featherston's unadmirers here didn't stay secret enough.'

'Well, so it is,' the Assistant Secretary of War said. 'The Confederates didn't break off the flight because they're reading *our* codes. I think they put a decoy on it because one of their security people got jumpy. The good ones do, from everything I've heard, and Lord knows Featherston needs good ones.'

'Plenty of people on both sides of the border who want to kill him, all right,' Flora said. 'Did you notice inflation is coming back to the Confederate States?'

'No.' Roosevelt was suddenly and sharply interested. After the Great War, the Confederate dollar collapsed; when things were at their worst, enjoying a beer took billions. 'What do you mean? It would be wonderful if their economy went down the drain again.'

But Flora didn't mean that, however much she wished she did. 'Not what I was thinking,' she said sadly. 'When the war was new, though, Featherston promised to drop three tons of bombs on our heads for every ton we landed on the CSA. Now he's up to ten tons.'

'Oh.' Franklin Roosevelt laughed. 'I'd call that deflation

myself – as his spirits go down, his threats go up. He was lying then, and he's still lying now. The Confederates weren't that far ahead at the start of things, and they're behind us now. We're landing more on them than they are on us – quite a bit more, as a matter of fact.'

'Good,' Flora said, wondering how he knew. If she asked him, he'd probably tell her it was a very precise statistic he'd just made up. Odds were neither side knew exactly how much it was getting and receiving. She asked a different question instead: 'How are things out West?'

'They're doing quite well.' Roosevelt sounded enthusiastic, as he often did. 'It really does look like General Dowling *will* take Lubbock away from the Confederates. If he does, we may proclaim the state of Houston again. That will give the people in west Texas something to flabble about – something to fight among themselves about.'

'No one – except maybe them – would be sorry about that,' Flora said. 'It would also give him a base to go after Camp Determination.' The camps where the Confederates systematically got rid of their Negroes sickened her as nothing else ever did.

'Well, maybe.' Franklin Roosevelt didn't sound so enthusiastic about that. He spelled out his reasons: 'It's farther from Lubbock to the camp than it is from the border to Lubbock, quite a bit farther. Those are the wide open spaces out there. And detaching men from more urgent things farther east may not be easy, either.'

Flora could have argued that nothing was more urgent than saving the lives of untold thousands of innocent human beings. She could have, but she knew the Assistant Secretary of War wouldn't pay any attention if she did. He would say that wouldn't win the war, and winning the war was the most urgent item on the agenda. She would have a devil of a time showing he was wrong, too. So, again, she took a different tack: 'How are things farther west than that?'

Had Roosevelt started giving her chapter and verse about the skirmishes on the border between New Mexico and Sonora – and there'd never been more than skirmishes on that border, even though the war was heading towards its second birthday – she would have got angry. But he didn't. 'That seems to be going as well as expected, too,' he said.

'I'm glad to hear it.' Flora didn't expect to hear anything more, not over the telephone. The project centered on Hanford, Washington, sounded like something from the pages of a pulp magazine with bug-eyed monsters and scantily clad girls on the cover. In fact, though, someone had told her that those magazines had a lot of subscribers in Hanford – they were much more popular with scientists and engineers than with the general public. She hoped the Confederacy's spymasters didn't know that.

'I do think we're making progress. I really do,' Roosevelt said.

'Here's hoping.' Flora didn't think she'd ever heard of uranium till after the war began. Now she knew there was more than one kind. If the 235 could be separated from the 238, or if the 238 could somehow make some new element altogether – it all sounded more like medieval alchemy than science – the bombs that resulted might blow whole cities off the map. With luck, those would be Confederate cities. Without luck . . . 'Any word on how they're doing with this on the other side of the line?'

'Well, they do seem to be trying.' The Assistant Secretary of War sounded less jaunty than was his wont.

Fear clogged Flora's throat. If the cities blown off the map belonged to the USA, Jake Featherston would win his war in spite of the disasters the Confederates had suffered in Pennsylvania and Ohio. 'What can we do about that?' she asked. 'Can we do anything?'

'We won't let them get away with it if we can possibly stop them, I promise you that,' Roosevelt said.

'Good,' Flora said, before she asked herself how good it really was. What had Roosevelt promised? To stop the CSA from building a uranium bomb? No. He'd promised to try to stop the Confederates from building one. Of course the United States would do that. Flora found one more question: 'What can they do to stop us?'

'They haven't tried anything yet,' Roosevelt said – another answer that wasn't an answer. He went on, 'They may have done some reconnaissance – we're not sure about that. If they did, they won't be able to do it again. We've tightened up since the last time we think they came around.'

'Why weren't things tight right from the beginning?' Flora admired her own restraint. She didn't raise her voice at all, no matter how much she felt like yelling her head off.

'Because we were asleep at the switch.' Roosevelt could be disarmingly frank. 'We aren't any more. We won't be, either. That's about the best I can tell you, Flora.'

'All right,' she said, and hoped it was. 'I'm sure we'll do everything we can.' She said her good-byes then. She hoped the USA bombed the Confederates' uranium-producing plants to hell and gone. She hoped the CSA didn't do the same to the one the United States had. Was such hope enough? The only answer that occurred to her was painfully clichéd, which made it no less true. She'd have to wait and see.

III

'Mail call!' That shout always made the guards at Camp Determination hurry up to see what they had. Troop Leader Hipolito Rodriguez wasn't as good at hurrying as some of his younger, sprier comrades. He was still on the sunny side of fifty, but moved like an older man. He'd almost got electrocuted a year and a half earlier, and he'd never been the same since. He belonged to the Confederate Veterans' Brigades: men who couldn't hope to fight at the front, but who could still serve the CSA behind the lines.

All the men at Camp Determination, whether from the Veterans' Brigades or not, were Freedom Party guards, with the funny ranks that accompanied Party positions. Rodriguez had three stripes on the left sleeve of his gray uniform. He thought of himself as a sergeant. He did a sergeant's job and got a sergeant's pay. If they wanted to call him something silly, who was he to tell them they couldn't?

Because he had three stripes on his sleeve, Rodriguez didn't need to hurry as much as ordinary guards did. They got out of the way for him. They never would have if he hadn't been promoted. To most Confederates, greasers from Chihuahua and Sonora were only a short step up from niggers. Rank carried more weight than race, though.

And a short step could be the longest step in the world. Hipolito Rodriguez – Hip to men who grew up speaking

English – wasn't the only guard with Mexican blood. On the other side of the barbed wire were untold thousands of *mallates*. And the camp outside of Snyder, Texas, existed for one reason and one reason only: to kill them off as fast as possible.

The two-stripe assistant troop leader with the sack of mail started pulling out letters and stacks of letters held together by rubber bands and calling off names. As each guard admitted he was there, the corporal tossed him whatever he had.

'Rodriguez!' The noncom, a white man, made a mess of the name. Confederates born anywhere east of Texas usually did.

'Here!' Rodriguez knew the ways they usually butchered it. He raised his hand. The corporal gave him three letters.

He fanned them out like cards. They were all from Magdalena, his wife. He opened the one with the oldest postmark first. She wrote in the English-flavored Spanish middle-aged people in Sonora and Chihuahua commonly used. His children's generation, further removed from the Empire of Mexico, spoke and wrote a Spanish-flavored English. Another couple of generations might see the older language disappear altogether.

But that thought flickered through Rodriguez's mind and was lost. He needed the news from Baroyeca. He hadn't been back since he joined the Confederate Veterans' Brigades, and he might not get home till the war was over.

Magdalena had heard from the Confederate Red Cross: Pedro was a POW in the United States. Hipolito Rodriguez let out a sigh of relief. His youngest son was alive. He would come home one of these days. He'd done everything he could against the USA, and he was safe. No one could ask for more, especially since the news out of Ohio, where he'd fought, was so bad.

From what Rodriguez's wife wrote, his two older sons, Miguel and Jorge, were also well. By an irony of fate, Pedro had gone into the Army ahead of them. He was in the first class after the CSA reintroduced conscription, where his older brothers missed out till it was extended to them. Miguel was in Virginia now, while Jorge fought in the sputtering war on Sonora's northern border, trying to reclaim what the damnyankees annexed after the Great War.

Compared to that news, nothing else mattered much. Magdalena also talked about the farm. The farm was doing all right – not spectacularly, because it wasn't spectacular land and she had trouble keeping things going by herself, but all right. The family had no money problems. With her getting allotments from her husband and three sons, they probably had more in the way of cash than they'd ever had before.

Robert Quinn was wearing the uniform. That rocked Rodriguez back on his heels. Quinn had run the Freedom Party in Baroyeca since not long after the Great War. He'd put down as many roots as anyone who wasn't born in the village could hope to do. And now he was gone? The war was longer and harder than anyone imagined it could be.

Carlos Ruiz's son was wounded. The doctors said he would get better. That he would was good news. That he'd been hurt in the first place wasn't. Rodriguez and Ruiz had been friends . . . forever. They grew up side by side, in each other's pockets. *I have to write him,* Rodriguez thought.

And a couple of women were sleeping with men who weren't their husbands since the men who were their husbands went to the front. Rodriguez sighed. That kind of gossip was as old as time, however much you wished it weren't. Back in the Great War, Jefferson Pinkard, the man who was *comandante* at Camp Determination, had had the same kind of woman trouble.

Other guards read their letters from home as avidly as Rodriguez tore through his. Letters reminded you what was real, what was important. They reminded you why you put on the uniform in the first place. Helping the country was too big and too abstract for most people most of the time. Helping your home town and your family . . . Anybody could understand that.

Not all the news was good. One guard crumpled a letter and stormed away, his face working, his hands clenched into fists. A couple of his friends hurried after him. 'Can we help, Josh?' one of them said.

'That goddamn, no good, two-timing bitch!' Josh said, which told the world exactly what his trouble was. Rodriguez wondered if the letter was from his wife telling him she'd found someone new, or from a friend – or an enemy? – telling him she was running around. What difference did it make? Something he'd thought fireproof was going up in flames.

Rodriguez crossed himself, hoping he never got a letter like that. He didn't think he would; what he and Magdalena had built over the years seemed solid. But Josh didn't expect anything like this, either. The trouble you didn't see coming was always the worst kind.

He thought about that when he patrolled the women's side of the camp north of the railroad spur that came out from Snyder. He and the two guards with him all carried submachine guns with big drum magazines. If they got in trouble, they could spray a lot of lead around in a hurry.

But life-and-death trouble mostly wasn't the kind guards had to worry about here. In the men's side, south of the train tracks, you were liable to get knocked over the head if you were stupid or careless. Here, your biggest worries were probably syphilis and the clap. Like anybody else, the Negro women used whatever they had to keep themselves and their children alive. What they had was mostly themselves, and a lot of them were diseased before they came here.

'Mistuh Sergeant, suh?' a pretty colored woman in her twenties purred at Rodriguez. Like most people, she knew what three stripes were supposed to mean and didn't give a damn about Freedom Party guard ranks. 'Mistuh Sergeant, you git me some extra rations, I do anything you want – an' I mean anything.' If he had any doubts about what she meant, a twitch of the hips – damn near a burlesque-quality bump and grind – would have erased them.

He didn't even change expression. He just kept walking. When he did, she called him something that reflected badly on his manhood. 'I wouldn't mind me a piece of that, not even slightly,' said one of the younger men with him.

'You want her, you take her,' Rodriguez answered with a shrug. 'You think you pass shortarm inspection afterwards?' They had those now. Jefferson Pinkard pitched a fit when four men came down with the clap inside of three days. Rodriguez had a hard time blaming him.

The guard looked back at the woman. 'I don't reckon she's got anything wrong with her,' he said. Rodriguez didn't try to argue with him. She had a large, firm bosom and round hips, and that was all the younger man cared about. To Rodriguez, one of the things her looks meant was that she hadn't been here very long. Eat prisoner rations for a bit and the flesh melted off of you.

Another black woman nodded to him. 'Hello, Sergeant,' she said. She wasn't trying to seduce him. Her gray hair said she was older than he was. But she greeted him every time she saw him. Some people were just nice. Some people

were nice enough to stay nice even in a place like this –
not many, but some. She was one of them.

'Hello, Bathsheba.' He had trouble pronouncing her
name, which had two sounds right in the middle of it that
Mexican Spanish didn't use. Her smile said he'd done pretty
well today.

Her daughter came up beside her. Even though the girl
was darker than her mulatto mother, he found her very
pretty. But she wasn't one of those who tried to screw their
way to safety. Maybe she realized there was no safety to
be had. Or maybe she kept her morals. Some women did.

She nodded, too. 'Sergeant,' she said politely.

'*Señorita* Antoinette.' Rodriguez nodded back.

'Can you take a message to the men's side?' her mother
asked. Some women would do anything to get word to husbands or lovers.

'Is against regulations,' Rodriguez said.

'It's not anything bad, not anything dangerous,'
Bathsheba said. 'Just tell Xerxes we love him an' we's
thinkin' about him.' Antoinette nodded.

Rodriguez didn't. 'Even if I find him' – he didn't say,
Even if he's still alive – 'maybe it's code. I don't take no
chances.'

'Please, Mistuh Guard, suh,' Antoinette said. 'Ain't no
code – swear to Jesus. Ain't nothin' but a Christian thing
to do. Please, suh.' Unlike her mother, she was young and
pretty. Even so, she didn't promise to open her legs or go
down on her knees if Rodriguez did what she wanted.
Oddly, her not promising made him take her more seriously, not less. He lost track of how many times he heard
promises like that. More than he wanted to collect. More
than he *could* collect, too.

He sighed. 'I see this Xerxes' – he stumbled over the
peculiar name – 'maybe I tell him this. Maybe.' He wouldn't

make any promises of his own, not where the guards with him could hear.

The older woman and the younger both beamed at him as if he'd promised to set them free. 'God bless you!' they said together.

He nodded gruffly, then scowled at the other two guards in gray. 'Come on. Get moving,' he said, as if they'd stopped for their business, not his.

All they said was, 'Yes, Troop Leader.' That was what he said when someone with a higher rank came down on him. Now he had . . . some rank of his own, anyway. He enjoyed using it.

Would he pass on the message if he found that man on the other side? He didn't really believe it was code. He also didn't really believe it mattered one way or the other. Before long, that Xerxes was a dead man, and Bathsheba and Antoinette were dead women, too.

One of the Confederates up ahead of First Sergeant Chester Martin squeezed off a short burst from his automatic rifle. Martin had been about to jump out of his foxhole and move forward maybe twenty feet, maybe even fifty. Instead, he decided to stay right where he was for the next little while. He'd been wounded once in the Great War and once in this one. As far as he was concerned, that was enough and then some.

Didn't the Confederates know they were supposed to be on the run in this part of Ohio? Didn't they know they'd already pulled out of Columbus and they were hightailing it down toward the Ohio River? Didn't they know they would have to fall back across the Scioto River into Chillicothe on the west side? Didn't they know they couldn't hold Chillicothe, either?

By the way they were fighting, they didn't know any of

that. They were bastards, yeah, no doubt about it, but they were tough bastards.

More automatic-weapons fire came from the west. Somebody not nearly far enough from Chester Martin let out a screech and then hollered for a corpsman. That was a wound, but it didn't sound like too bad a wound. Martin knew what badly wounded men sounded like. He'd hear those shrieks in his nightmares till the day he died – which, given the way things worked, might be any day now.

From a hole in the ground not far from Chester's, Second Lieutenant Delbert Wheat called, 'Mortars! Put some bombs down on those gunners!'

Mortar rounds started dropping on the Confederate line. Mortars were handy things to have. They gave infantry platoons instant artillery support, without even adding boiling water. Lieutenant Wheat made a pretty fair platoon leader, too. Before him, Martin had served with a couple of much less satisfactory officers. One of the things a first sergeant was supposed to do was keep the shavetail set over him from making too big a jackass of himself. Most second lieutenants never understood that. They labored under the delusion that they were in charge of their platoon.

A lot of them got killed laboring under that delusion. A first sergeant was also supposed to keep them from killing too many other people on their own side. The second lieutenants who survived went on to bigger and better things. First sergeants who survived got brand-new second lieutenants to break in.

Martin saw only one thing wrong with Lieutenant Wheat's order. Just about every Confederate soldier carried either an automatic rifle or a submachine gun. The Confederates understood right from the start that they'd be outnumbered. They used firepower to make up for it.

These days, more than a few U.S. soldiers used captured C.S. automatic rifles. The biggest problem with them was that they needed captured ammunition to stay usable. Back when the Confederates were always pushing forward, captured ammo was hard to come by. Now Martin's countrymen often overran C.S. positions. Both rifles and cartridges were in pretty fair supply.

Lieutenant Wheat stuck his head up like a groundhog looking around to see if it cast a shadow. Another burst of Confederate fire made him duck in a hurry. He popped up again a couple of minutes later, which was asking to get his head blown off.

'You want to be careful there, sir,' Martin said. 'You show yourself twice running, the bastards in butternut are liable to have time to draw a bead on you.'

He didn't want this particular platoon commander to stop a slug with his face. Wheat had a pretty good idea of what he was doing; odds were anyone who replaced him would be worse. Or maybe nobody would replace him for a while. Officers weren't thick on the ground, and the brass might figure a first sergeant could handle a platoon for a while.

Martin figured he could, too. He led a company for a while during the Great War, when everybody above him got killed or wounded. They lost officers even faster in that war than they were losing them in this one. But, having proved he could command a company, Martin didn't want to take over the platoon now. They'd never make *him* an officer – who ever heard of a fifty-year-old second lieutenant? He had plenty to do the way things were.

'Thanks for the tip, Sergeant,' Wheat said, as calmly as if Chester advised him to lead the fourth highest from his longest and strongest suit. 'I'm trying to see how we can cross the Scioto.'

'*We* as in the division or *we* as in this platoon?' Chester asked, more than a little apprehensively. Before long, U.S. forces were bound to get over the Scioto somewhere. The luckless bastards who crossed the river first would pay the price in blood, though. They always did.

'This platoon, if we can,' Wheat answered, and damned if he didn't stand up and look around one more time. 'We're only about a mile from the river, and the Confederates are pulling back across it. They may not even notice we've got the bridgehead on the other side till we're too strong to throw back.'

What have you been smoking? Martin wanted to yell. The soldiers in butternut were alert. Just because they were the enemy, that didn't mean they were morons. Most of this war was fought on U.S. soil. That at least argued the dummies were the ones in green-gray.

Another sputter of bullets made Wheat duck down again before Chester could say anything at all. And then the Confederates threw something new at them. That screaming in the sky wasn't any ordinary artillery Martin had ever heard. And ordinary rounds didn't come in trailing tails of fire. You mostly couldn't see ordinary rounds at all till they burst.

Rockets, Chester thought. Featherston's men were firing them at barrels. These were different – much bigger and nastier. They slammed down and went off with roars like the end of the world. He didn't know how many burst all at once. A dozen? Two dozen? Something like that. However many it was, he felt as if God stamped on the platoon with both feet.

He wasn't ashamed to scream. Hell, he was too scared not to. Nobody heard him, not through that roar. Even if somebody did hear him, so what? He wouldn't be the only man yelling his head off. He was sure of that.

And he didn't even get hurt, except for being bruised and battered and half stunned by blast. He was one of the lucky ones. As his stunned ears came back to life, he heard soldiers screaming to the right and left and behind him. He scrambled over to the closest wounded man. Shrapnel had gouged a chunk out of the soldier's leg. As Chester dusted sulfa powder onto the wound and slapped a dressing over it, the soldier said, 'What the fuck was that, Sarge?'

'Beats me, Johnny,' Martin answered. 'I just hope to Christ we never see it again.' He injected the soldier with a morphine syrette, knowing all too well the Confederates would play with their new toy over and over again. Why would they do anything else? Wherever that salvo of rockets came from, it did a better job of plastering a wide area with explosives than any other weapon he'd ever seen.

'Fuck,' Johnny said again, biting his lip against the pain. 'When do we get something like it?'

That was another good question. 'Soon, I hope,' Martin said, which was nothing but the truth. Now that his side knew the other side had something new and nasty, how long would they need to copy it or come up with something on the same order? *Months*, he thought glumly. *Gotta be months*. That meant U.S. soldiers would be on the receiving end for months, too, which was anything but a cheery idea.

Chester yelled for the medics. So did Johnny. They didn't come right away. He wasn't surprised. They had to be dealing with a lot of casualties. If another salvo came in . . .

And then one did. The incoming rockets' shrieks put him in mind of damned souls. He did some more shrieking himself when they crashed down. Blast picked him up and smashed him into the dirt. 'Oof!' he said, struggling to breathe. He tasted blood in his mouth. If the Confederates threw in a counterattack just then, they could push as far as they wanted. The platoon – hell, probably the whole damn regiment – was in no shape to stop them.

'Boy,' Johnny said, 'it's a good thing they didn't have those a little while ago, or they'd still be in Pittsburgh.' He sounded detached, almost indifferent. The morphine was working its magic.

Chester wished he could be indifferent to the chaos and carnage around him. 'You ain't kidding,' he said. These rockets were very bad news. Somebody over in Richmond was probably kicking somebody else's ass around the block for not thinking of them sooner or for not getting them into production fast enough.

Motion behind him made him whirl, ready to plug whoever made it. 'Easy, buddy,' the soldier there said. The man wore the same uniform he did. Even that didn't have to mean anything. The Confederates sometimes put their guys in green-gray to raise hell behind U.S. lines. But this fellow had a Red Cross on his helmet, Red Cross armbands, and a white smock with big Red Crosses front and back. 'You got a wounded guy here?'

'That's me.' Johnny sounded halfway proud of himself. Part of that was the morphine talking. And part of it was knowing he had a hometowner. His wound wasn't enough to ruin him for life, but it was plenty to keep him away from the front for a while. Chester's wound in the Great War was one like that. He actually did go back to Toledo for a while to recuperate. Maybe Johnny would get to see his family and friends.

'We'll haul him out of here.' The corpsman yelled for buddies. They manhandled Johnny onto a stretcher and lugged him back toward the closest aid station. Chester hoped the rockets didn't knock it flat. They sure did a hell of a job up here.

Even if he got himself a hometowner this time around, they wouldn't ship him over to Los Angeles. He was as sure of that as he was of his last name. Yes, the CSA's retreat from northern Ohio meant the United States were no longer cut in half, but it would be quite a while before anything but the most urgent supplies and people crossed the gap. A general with a hometowner might fall into that category. A sergeant damn well didn't.

A bullet cracking past made him flatten out on the ground like a run-over toad. He didn't want to get shot again, not even with a hometowner. And life didn't come with a guarantee. You might not pick up a hometowner. You might turn into Graves Registration's business, not some corpsman's. Rita would never forgive him if he got himself killed, not that he'd be able to appreciate her anger.

Half an hour later, a thunderous U.S. artillery barrage came down on the heads of the Confederates withdrawing across the Scioto. Every gun the USA had handy opened up on the men in butternut. Some of them would be screaming for medics, no doubt about it.

But would all those guns match the horror the Confederates inflicted with a couple of salvoes of rockets? Chester Martin wasn't sure. Maybe the rockets seemed worse because he'd been shelled too many times before. And maybe they seemed worse because they *were* worse. He feared he would see them again often enough to make up his mind.

In a way, Dr. Leonard O'Doull wasn't sorry to get back under canvas again. It meant the front was moving forward. He'd spent longer than he wanted to working out of the University of Pittsburgh's medical center as the battle for the city swayed back and forth. He didn't want to think about how much work he did there.

Operating in a tent a few hundred yards back of the

line also had its drawbacks. What he'd done at the medical center reminded him of that. He'd worked in fully equipped operating rooms, with nurses at his beck and call and with X-ray equipment right down the corridor. He had it easy, in other words.

Now he was on his own again, doing the emergency work that patched people up well enough to get them farther back so other doctors could do a more thorough job if they had to. It was, or could be, satisfying work – he saved a lot of lives, and he knew it. But he also knew he might save more still if he had everything here that he had back at the hospital.

He worked like a man possessed, trying to save a private who'd got caught in the open by one of the Confederates' newfangled rockets. 'Who would have thought we'd see a new kind of wound?' he said, tying off a bleeder and extracting a chunk of casing with a forceps. 'Half blast, half shrapnel.'

'Best of both worlds. Happy day,' Granville McDougald said. 'Aren't we clever?'

Because O'Doull had an M.D., he held officer's rank – they made him a major when they talked him out of the Republic of Quebec and back into U.S. uniform for the first time in a quarter of a century. That didn't mean he would ever have to command a battalion. *A good thing for the battalion, too,* he thought. It did let him give orders to the men he worked with.

Granny McDougald was a sergeant. He'd been a medic as long as O'Doull had been a doctor – he didn't leave the Army after the Great War, the way O'Doull did. His knowledge was much narrower than the physician's. But, within its limits, it was just as deep. He was all too intimately familiar with the multifarious ways in which human bodies could get mangled.

He knew how to fix them, too. Even without formal training, he made a damn good surgeon. He was a more than capable anesthetist, too. O'Doull knew McDougald could do most of his work if anything happened to him.

The medic said, 'I wonder when they'll figure out how to pack gas into those rockets.' Above his mask, his gray eyes were grim.

'Bite your tongue, Granny!' O'Doull exclaimed. But what a U.S. medic could imagine, so, no doubt, could a C.S. engineer. Morosely, O'Doull said, 'Probably just a matter of time.'

'Uh-huh,' McDougald said. 'How's he doing there?'

'I *think* he'll make it,' O'Doull answered. 'I've got most of the wound cleaned up. The blast damage to his lungs, though . . . Damn rocket might as well have been a bomb.'

'Lucky they didn't point those things in our direction,' McDougald said. 'Doesn't look like they can aim 'em for hell.'

'*Tabernac!*' O'Doull muttered. He still swore in Quebecois French every once in a while; it was almost the only language he spoke for half his life. He never gave up reading English, because so much medical literature was written in it. But not much of his birthspeech came out of his mouth while he was living in Rivière-du-Loup. 'You get the nicest ideas, Granny.'

'Yeah, well, you go through a couple of wars and you figure anything that can come down can come down on your head.'

O'Doull had his own fair share of the cynicism so many medical men wear. When you spend your days looking at the way the human body can go wrong – or, in war, can be made to go wrong – you are unlikely to believe, as Candide did, that this is the best of all possible worlds. But Granny McDougald had his fair share and what seemed like two or three other people's besides.

'You know what we really need?' McDougald went on as O'Doull put in suture after suture.

'Tell me. I'm all ears,' O'Doull replied.

'Must make sewing up that poor bastard kind of clumsy, but all right,' the senior medic said. 'What we really need is a bomb so big and juicy, they won't waste it on the battlefield. They'll drop it on New York City or New Orleans, and *boom!* – it'll blow the whole place right off the map like *that.*' He snapped his fingers.

'*Calisse!*' O'Doull said, and then, 'Son of a bitch! Why would you want a bomb like that?'

'Because it's the only thing I can think of that's so awful that after you use it a few times and everybody sees how awful it is, it'll scare the shit out of people and they won't want to use it any more. If we had bombs like that and the CSA did and England and France and Germany and Austria-Hungary and Russia and the Japs, how the hell could you fight a war?'

'Carefully,' O'Doull answered. He set down his scalpel as Granville McDougald laughed. 'I've got this guy stabilized, or as stabilized as I can get him. If his lungs aren't wrecked and if the tissue the blast tore up doesn't go gangrenous on him, chances are he'll pull through.'

'Good job, Doc. I wouldn't have given more than about four bits for his chances when the corpsmen hauled him in,' McDougald said.

A couple of minutes later, at Leonard O'Doull's direction, the corpsmen sent the wounded man back to a real hospital several miles to the rear. He might finish his recovery there, or he might go farther back still. O'Doull would have bet on the latter – this guy would live, he thought, but wasn't likely to put on a helmet and pick up a Springfield again any time soon.

O'Doull shed his mask and tossed it in a trash can. He washed the soldier's blood off his hands and chucked his surgical instruments into a tub of alcohol. If he had time, he'd autoclave them before he used them again. If he didn't . . . Well, alcohol made a good disinfectant.

'I'm going outside for a smoke before they bring in the next poor miserable so-and-so,' he said. 'Come with me?'

'You bet,' McDougald said. 'Grab all the chances to loaf you can – they may not come your way again.'

With ether and alcohol and other inflammables inside the aid station, lighting up in there was severely discouraged – with a blunt instrument, if necessary. Once O'Doull had stepped away from the green-gray tent, he took out a pack of Niagara Falls.

'Oh, come on, Doc.' McDougald pulled a horrible face. 'Haven't you got anything better than those barge scrapings?'

' 'Fraid not,' O'Doull admitted. 'Smoked my last Confederate cigarette a couple of hours ago. U.S. tobacco won't kill me, and it's like coffee – bad is better than none at all.'

'Like booze, too,' the medic said, and the doctor didn't deny it. McDougald reached into his pocket and extracted a pack of Dukes. 'Here. Bad is better than none, but good is better than bad.'

'Thanks, Granny. I owe you,' O'Doull said. The noncom was a better scrounger than he was. Some headline that made. O'Doull took a cigarette and stuck it in his mouth. McDougald gave him a light. He inhaled, then smiled. 'My hat's off to the Dukes.'

'I ought to make you put up your dukes for one that bad.' Granville McDougald paused. 'Except mine was even worse, wasn't it?'

'Sure wasn't any better,' O'Doull allowed. 'But this tobacco is, and I thank you for it.'

'Any time,' McDougald said. 'Not like I haven't mooched butts from you a time or three.'

The roar of artillery from behind them drowned his last couple of words. The fire from the big and medium guns went on and on and on. Some of the shells flying west gurgled as they spun through the air. Leonard O'Doull winced at that sound: gas rounds. He tried to look on the bright side of things: 'Sounds like we're finally going over the river.'

'And through the woods, yeah, but where's Grandmother's house?' McDougald said. While O'Doull was still digesting that, the medic went on, 'About time we got across the damn Scioto, don't you think? Hanging on to Chillicothe like they have, the Confederates must have pulled God only knows how many men and how much matériel out of northern Ohio.'

'You sure you don't belong back at corps HQ or something?' O'Doull said. McDougald laughed at him.

They had time to finish their cigarettes, and that was about it. Then the familiar and hated shout of, 'Doc! Hey, Doc!' rang out again.

'I'm here!' O'Doull yelled. More quietly, he added, 'Well, let's see what we've got this time.'

They had a corporal with a bullet through his calf. He was cussing a blue streak. 'Hey, keep your shirt on, pal,' Granville McDougald said. 'If that's not a hometowner, there's no such animal.'

'Fuck hometowners,' the corporal snarled. 'And fuck you, too, Jack. For one thing, it hurts like shit. And besides, I don't want any goddamn hometowners. I want to blow the balls off some more of Featherston's fuckers.'

A man of strong opinions, O'Doull thought. His voice dry, he said, 'It's not usually smart to swear at the guy who's going to help fix you up. You might find out it hurts even more than you expected. And before you tell me where to head in, you need to know I'm a major.' Cussing out an officer was a good way for an enlisted man to run into more trouble than he ever wanted to find.

The noncom opened his mouth to draw in a breath. About then, though, the novocaine O'Doull injected by the wound took effect. What came out was, '*Oh,* yeah. That's not so fucking bad now. You can go ahead and sew me up.' He caught himself. 'You can go ahead and sew me up, *sir.*'

O'Doull decided he'd been given the glove. By Granny McDougald's barely smothered snort, he thought the same thing. But the corporal scrupulously stayed within regulations. O'Doull cleaned out the wound and sewed it up. 'Like it or not, pal, you've got a hometowner,' he said. 'I know you'd be happier if you didn't get shot, but you could have stopped it with your face or your chest, too.'

'Oh, yeah. I know. I've seen—' He broke off, then shook his head. 'I started to say, I've seen as much of that shit as you have, but I probably haven't.'

'Depends,' O'Doull answered. 'We see plenty of nasty wounds, but the poor guys who get killed on the spot don't make it back to us. Maybe it evens out.'

'Hot damn,' the corporal said. 'Tell you one thing, though – it's a bunch of fucked-up shit any which way.'

'Buddy, you are preaching to the choir,' Granville McDougald said solemnly. O'Doull decided he couldn't have put it better himself.

From the deck of the USS *Townsend,* George Enos watched two new escort carriers come into Pearl Harbor. Like the pair that had previously sailed from the West Coast down to the Sandwich Islands, the *Tripoli* and the *Yorktown* were as ugly as a mud fence. They were built on freighter hulls, with a flight deck and a little island slapped on topside. They had a freighter's machinery, too, and couldn't make better than eighteen knots unless they fell off a cliff.

But each one of them had thirty airplanes: fighters, dive bombers, and torpedo-carriers. They weren't fleet carriers; since the loss of the *Remembrance* more than a year earlier, the USA had no fleet carriers operating in the Pacific. Still, they were ever so much better than no carriers at all, which was what the United States had had in these waters for most of the time since the *Remembrance* went to the bottom.

'Well, doesn't look like the Japs are going to drive us back to San Francisco after all,' George remarked. He spoke with the flat vowels and swallowed r's of the Boston fisherman he was before he joined the Navy to make sure the Army didn't conscript him.

'Damn well better not,' said Fremont Blaine Dalby, the CPO who commanded the twin 40mm antiaircraft gun for which George jerked shells.

'Didn't look so good when they were bringing their carriers down from Midway and knocking the snot out of us here,' George said.

'They had their chance. Now it's our turn.' Chief Dalby was a man who knew what he knew. Even his name showed that: it showed he came from a rock-ribbed Republican family in a country where the Republicans, caught between the Socialists and the Democrats, hadn't amounted to a hill of beans since the 1880s.

'About time, too.' Fritz Gustafson, the gun crew's loader, talked as if the government charged him for every word he said.

'If we can get Midway back . . .' George said.

'That'd be pretty good,' Dalby agreed. *He* wasn't shy about talking – not even a little bit. 'Run the Japs out there, run 'em off Wake, too, so they don't come back to Midway, and then we can stop worrying about the real Sandwich Islands, the ones down here, for a while.'

'Gotta hang on to Hotel Street,' Gustafson said. George and Fremont Dalby both snorted. Hotel Street not only had more saloons and cathouses per square inch than any other street in Honolulu, it probably had more than any other street in the world. Sailors and soldiers and Marines might not give a damn about the Sandwich Islands as a whole, but they'd be bound to fight like men possessed to keep Hotel Street in American hands.

'Think four of these baby flattops are enough to take Midway?' George asked.

'Dunno. I ain't no admiral,' Dalby said. As a CPO, he had a much smaller sphere of authority than a man with a broad gold stripe on his sleeve. But within that sphere, his authority was hardly less absolute. 'Tell you what, though – I hope like hell there's a couple more of those babies somewhere halfway between here and the coast.'

'Yeah.' George nodded. There was a gap in the middle of the eastern Pacific that neither aircraft from Oahu nor those from the West Coast could cover very well. Japan had done her best to get astride the supply line between the mainland and the Sandwich Islands and starve the islands into submission. It didn't quite work, but it came too close for comfort, both metaphorically and literally.

Thinking of U.S. warplanes looking for enemy aircraft and ships made George notice the combat air patrol above Pearl Harbor. Fighters always buzzed overhead these days. Y-ranging gear should be able to give U.S. forces enough warning to scramble airplanes, but nobody seemed inclined to take chances.

'Wonder how come Jap engines sound screechier than ours,' George said. Japanese carrier-based fighters had strafed the *Townsend* more than once. He knew the sound of those engines better than he wanted to.

'They take 'em out of the washing machines they used to buy from us,' Dalby suggested. George laughed. Any joke a CPO made was funny because a CPO made it.

The *Townsend* sailed a couple of days later, escorting the *Tripoli* and the *Yorktown* north and west toward Midway. They wouldn't get there in a hurry, not at the escort carriers' lackadaisical cruising speed. George wasn't enthusiastic about getting there at all. He'd gone north and west from Oahu too many times, and sailed into danger each and every one of them.

You always ran to your battle station like a madman when general quarters sounded. When you didn't know if it was a drill or the real McCoy, you ran even harder.

Run as he would, George couldn't get to the twin 40mm mount ahead of Fremont Dalby. The gun chief seemed drawn there by magnetism instead of his legs, which were shorter than George's.

'What can I tell you?' he said when George asked him about it. 'I know I've got to be here, so I damn well am.' In a way, that didn't make any sense at all. In another way, it did.

Up above the bridge, the Y-ranging antenna spun round and round, round and round. It would pick up incoming Japanese aircraft long before the naked eye could. How much good picking them up ahead of time would do was an open question. They weren't any easier for guns on the destroyer to shoot down. With luck, though, fighters from the carriers could drive them off before they got within gunnery range.

Few of the islands north and west of Kauai were inhabited; if not for its position, Midway wouldn't have been, either. Albatrosses and other sea birds nested on the rocks and reefs rising above the Pacific. Some of the enormous birds glided past the *Townsend* and the other ships in the flotilla.

Pointing to a long-winged albatross, George said, 'I'm surprised Y-ranging doesn't pick up those things. They're damn near as big as a fighter.' He exaggerated, but not too much.

'I hear from the guys on the hydrophones that they've got to be careful, or else they really can mistake a whale for a sub – and the other way round,' Fremont Dalby said.

'That wouldn't be good,' George said.

'No shit!' No, Fritz Gustafson didn't talk a lot, but he got plenty of mileage out of what he did say.

As they got closer to Midway, tension built. George didn't want to do anything but stick close to his gun. The *Townsend* had come through a couple of ferocious attacks. Blazing away with everything you had gave you a chance to come through, but the pilots in the enemy airplanes were the guys in the driver's seat these days.

Dive bombers and escorting fighters roared off the escort carriers and flew up toward Midway. 'Still not obvious the Japs have Y-ranging,' Dalby said. 'If they don't, we can plaster their aircraft on Midway before they even know we're on the way.'

'Wouldn't break my heart,' George said. 'Bastards tried to do it to us at Pearl Harbor. Not like we don't owe 'em.'

'If they'd done it, I bet they would have followed up with a landing,' the gun chief said. 'Maybe we'll be able to do the same up here before long.'

'That wouldn't break my heart, either,' George said.

The more time went by without a warning over the PA that the Y-ranging gear was picking up enemy airplanes, the happier he got. Maybe the American bombers really were knocking the daylights out of whatever the Japs still had on Midway.

Then the speakers crackled to life. George groaned, and he wasn't the only one. 'May I have your attention?' the exec said, as if he didn't know he would. 'Our aircraft report the Japanese appear to have abandoned Midway . . . May I have your attention? Our aircraft report the Japanese appear to have abandoned Midway.'

'Fuck me,' Fremont Dalby said reverently.

'Wow,' George agreed.

'Little yellow bastards know how to cut their losses,' Dalby said. 'If they can't take the Sandwich Islands, what's Midway worth to 'em? It's out at the ass end of nowhere, and it's got to be even more expensive for the Japs to supply than it is for us.'

'What do you want to bet they've bailed out of Wake, too?' George said.

'I wouldn't mind,' the gun chief told him.

'Beats working,' Fritz Gustafson said.

'Oh, hell, yes,' Dalby said. 'If they're gone from Midway and Wake, what are we gonna do? Go after 'em? Charge through all their little islands and head for the Philippines? We need the Philippines like we need a hole in the head.'

'Amen,' George said. 'If they want to call this mess a draw, I don't mind. I don't mind a bit.' The rest of the gun crew nodded. They'd all developed a thoroughgoing respect for Japanese skill and courage. The Japs had already come too close to killing them more than once. George knew he wouldn't be sorry never to see any more maneuverable fighters with meatballs on their wings.

But that raised another question. George asked it: 'If the Japs are pulling back here, where are they going to use their ships and airplanes?' He assumed Japan would use them somewhere. In a war, that was what you did.

Fremont Dalby suddenly started to laugh. 'Malaya.

Singapore. What do you want to bet? Malaya's got tin and rubber, and Singapore's the best goddamn harbor in that whole part of the world.'

'But they belong to England,' George objected. 'England and Japan are on the same side.'

'Were,' Fritz Gustafson said.

Dalby nodded. 'I think you nailed that one, Fritz. England's busy in Europe. England's busy in the Atlantic against us. What can the fuckin' limeys do if Japan decides to go in there? Jack shit, far as I can see. When Churchill hears about this, I bet he craps his pants.'

'So let's see,' George said. 'Japan's at war with us, and England's at war with us, but away from all that they're at war with each other? You ask me, they're trying to set a world record.'

'Better them than us,' Dalby said. 'Only way England's stayed in the Far East as long as she has is that Japan's let her. If Japan doesn't want her around any more . . . Well, she may hang on to India—'

'Her goose is really cooked if she doesn't,' George said.

'Yeah. That's why she's got to try, I expect,' the gun chief said. 'But Japan's already in Indochina. She's already in the East Indies. Siam's on her side, not England's. What with all that, no way in hell the limeys keep her out of Malaya.'

'Japan has all that stuff, she'll be really nasty twenty, thirty years down the line,' Fritz Gustafson said.

'Let's worry about winning this one first,' George said, and neither of the other men chose to disagree with him.

Even though Jefferson Pinkard had run Camp Determination since the day it started going up on the west Texas prairie, he got his news on the wireless just like everybody else in the CSA. 'In heavy defensive fighting just southeast of Lubbock, Confederate troops inflicted heavy losses on the Yankee invaders,' the announcer said.

That same bulletin probably went out all over the Confederate States. If you didn't have a map handy and you didn't bother working out what lay behind what actually got said, it sounded pretty good. Like a lot of people, though, Jeff knew what lay behind it, and he didn't need a map to know where Lubbock was. *Defensive fighting* meant the Confederates were retreating. *Just southeast of Lubbock* meant the town had fallen. *Heavy losses on the Yankee invaders* meant . . . nothing, probably. And Lubbock was just up the road from Snyder – and from the camp.

Just up the road, in Texas, meant about eighty miles. Soldiers in green-gray wouldn't be here day after tomorrow. Jefferson Pinkard and Camp Determination were ready if the damnyankees did come close. The trucks that asphyxiated Negroes would drive away. The bathhouses that gassed them would go up in explosions that ought to leave no sign of what the buildings were for. The paperwork that touched on killings would burn. Nothing would be left except an enormous concentration camp. . . .

And mass graves. Jeff didn't know what to do about those. He didn't think he could do much of anything. Oh, bulldozers could cover over all of the trenches, but nothing could dispose of all the bodies and bones.

He got to his feet and stared out at the camp from the window in his office. He looked like what he was: a middle-aged man who'd been a steelworker when he was younger. Yes, his belly hung over his trousers and he had a double chin. But he also had broad shoulders and a hard core of muscle under the weight he'd put on as the years went by.

And he had the straightforward stubbornness of a man who'd worked with his hands and expected problems to go away if you put some extra muscle into them. Not all of a camp administrator's problems disappeared so conveniently. He knew that; he'd gained guile as well as weight over the years. Still, his first impulse was to try to smash whatever got in his way.

He couldn't smash the damnyankees single-handed. He'd fought in west Texas during the Great War as a private soldier. Even now, he had no particular clout with local Army officers. His Freedom Party rank – group leader – was the equivalent of major general, but he had no authority over Army troops.

No direct authority, anyhow. He did have friends, or at least associates, in high places. When he got on the phone to Richmond, he didn't call the War Department. He called the Attorney General's office. He didn't love Ferdinand Koenig, who kept piling responsibility onto his back as if he were a mule. Here, though, the two of them were traveling the same road. Pinkard hoped they were, anyhow.

'What can I do for you today?' Koenig asked when the connection went through. He assumed Pinkard wanted him to do something. And he was right.

'Any chance you can get more soldiers on this front, sir?' Pinkard asked. 'If Lubbock's gone, we got us some real trouble.'

'Well, now, you know that isn't my proper place,' Koenig said cautiously. 'I can't come out and tell the Army what to do.'

'Yes, sir. I know that. I damn well ought to. Damn soldiers won't listen to me, neither.' Jeff spoke with the resentment of a man who'd tried to get them to move but couldn't. 'But does the President want the damnyankees to take Camp Determination away from us?'

'You know he doesn't.' Now Koenig spoke without hesitation.

'Well, I sure *hope* he doesn't, anyway. But if he doesn't,

we better have the men out here to keep the USA from doing it,' Jeff said.

'We've got trouble other places, too,' the Attorney General reminded him.

'Oh, yes, sir. You don't need to tell me that,' Jeff said. 'But we got trouble here, too, and we're out in the back of fucking beyond – pardon my French – so who ever hears about it? Yankee general hasn't got much more than a scratch force himself. Some more men, some more airplanes, some more barrels, we can run him right back over the border.'

'I can't promise you anything,' Ferdinand Koenig said. 'I'll talk to the President, and that's as much as I can tell you.'

'Thank you kindly, sir. That's all I wanted,' Jeff lied. He wanted a couple of divisions rolling through Snyder on their way to driving the damnyankees back from Lubbock. He thought Camp Determination deserved to be protected. 'Wouldn't want the United States going on about this place if they grabbed it.'

'No, we don't want that,' Koenig agreed. 'I'll see what I can do, and that's all I can say.'

'All right.' Jeff knew he wouldn't get anything more. He tried to make sure he did get something: 'Doesn't even have to be regular Confederate soldiers. Most of what we need out here is bodies, so the damnyankees can't just go around us. Mexicans would do the trick, or Freedom Party guards.'

'Won't be Mexicans,' Koenig said. 'The Emperor doesn't want 'em going into combat against the USA, not any more. Only way the President talked him into giving us more was by swearing on a stack of Bibles he wouldn't use 'em for anything but internal security. Freedom Party guards, though . . .' He paused thoughtfully.

Pinkard was a fisherman from way back when. He knew he had a nibble. Trying to set the hook, he said, 'This might be a good place to let the guards show what they can do. If they fight harder than soldiers . . .' He paused, too. The Freedom Party guards were Ferd Koenig's own personal, private bailiwick. If they fought better than soldiers, or at least as well, then Koenig had his own personal, private army. He might not mind that. No, he might not mind that at all.

He was nobody's fool, either. If Jefferson Pinkard could see the possibilities, he would also be able to. But all he said was, 'Well, I'll see what the President wants to do.' He was a cool customer. He didn't get all excited – or he didn't show it if he did. And the odds were that somebody was tapping his telephone, too. Sure, he went back forever with Jake Featherston. All the more reason for Featherston to make sure he didn't get out of line, wasn't it?

Pinkard got off the phone. When you were talking with the higher-ups, you didn't want to waste their time. He'd done everything he reasonably could. Now he had to wait and see if the Attorney General could run with the ball.

And he had to make sure the camp went on running smoothly, regardless of where the Yankees were. Ever since he first started taking care of prisoners during the Mexican civil war in the 1920s, he'd been convinced the only way you could keep your finger on the pulse of what was going on was by seeing for yourself. A lot of ways, his office looked like any other Confederate bureaucrat's. Most bureaucrats, though, didn't have a submachine gun hanging on the wall by their desk. Pinkard grabbed the weapon, attached a big snail-drum magazine, and went out to take a look around.

A couple of junior guards fell in behind him when he did. That was all right; nobody armed had any business going into the camp alone except in an emergency. The puppies wouldn't cramp Pinkard's style. They wouldn't know where he was going and what he was doing because he wouldn't know himself till he started doing it. That often made his subordinates despair, but more than once it let him nip what could be trouble before it got too big to be easily nippable.

The guards at the barbed-wire-strung gates between the administrative compound and the camp proper saluted him. 'Group Leader!' they chorused.

'At ease, at ease,' he said, returning the salute. Part of him liked being treated like the equivalent of a major general. Another part, the part that was a private during the Great War, thought it all a bunch of damn foolishness. Right now, that part had the upper hand.

After the guards let him and his watchdogs through the inner gate, they closed it behind him. Then they opened the outer gate. He and the younger men walked into the camp.

Even the stink seemed stronger on this side of the barbed wire. Maybe that was Jeff's imagination. He couldn't prove it wasn't. But his nose wrinkled at the odors of unwashed skin and sewage. Skinny Negroes stared at him as if he'd fallen from another world. By the difference between his life and theirs, he might as well have.

The wreathed stars on either side of his collar drew the black men as honey drew flies. 'You gots to let me out, suh!' one man said. 'You gots to! I's an innocent man!'

'Kin we have us mo' food?' another Negro asked.

'My fambly!' said another. 'Is my fambly all right?'

'Everybody's in here for a reason.' Jeff spoke with complete certainty. He knew what the reason was, too. *You're a bunch of niggers*. Oh, the Freedom Party still ran camps for white unreliables, too. The whole camp system cut its teeth on them. But not many white unreliables were left any more. The Party also had better ways to get rid of them these days. Slap a uniform on an unreliable, stick a rifle in his hands, put him in a punishment battalion, and throw him at the damnyankees. Most of those people loved the United States, anyway. Only fair they should die at U.S. hands. And if they took out a few soldiers in green-gray before they got theirs, so much the better.

'Food!' that second Negro said. 'We's powerful hungry, suh.'

'I'm spreading out the ration best way I know how,' Pinkard said, which was true – all the inmates starved at the same rate. 'If I had more, I'd share it out, too.' That was also true; he was cruel because he found himself in a cruel situation, not because he enjoyed cruelty for its own sake. He understood the difference. Whether a scrawny black prisoner did . . . mattered very little to him.

When the scrawny black looked at him, it wasn't at his fleshy face but at his even fleshier belly. *You ain't missed no meals.* The thought hung in the air, but the Negro knew better than to say it. He turned away instead, hands curling into useless fists.

As for the man with the family, he was already gone. He must have realized he wouldn't get any help from Jeff Pinkard. And he was right. He wouldn't. Other blacks came up with their futile requests. Jeff listened to them, not that it did the blacks much good.

Every once in a while, though, somebody betrayed an uprising or an escape plot. All by itself, that made these prowl-throughs worth doing. The ones who did squeal got their reward, too: a big supper where the other inmates could watch them eat, and a ride out of Camp Determination . . . in one of the sealed trucks that asphyxiated their passengers.

That was a shame, but what could you do? The CSA had no room for Negroes any more, not even for Negroes who played along.

Guards kept a long file of men moving toward the bathhouse. 'Come on!' one of them called. '*Come* on, goddammit! You don't want to be a bunch of lousy, stinking niggers when we ship your asses out of here, do you?'

Jeff Pinkard smiled to himself. By the time the Negroes got out of the bathhouse, they wouldn't care one way or the other – or about anything else, ever again. But as long as they didn't know that beforehand, everything was fine.

'You, there! *Sí*, you. *Mallate!*'

Scipio stared in alarm. Were he white, he would have turned whiter. The guard with the sergeant's stripes was pointing at him. He hadn't been in Camp Determination long before he realized you didn't want guards singling you out for anything at all. And *mallate* from a Sonoran or Chihuahuan, as this fellow plainly was, meant the same thing as *nigger* from an ordinary white Confederate.

He had to answer. The only thing worse than getting singled out by a guard was pissing one off. 'Yes, suh? What you need, suh?'

'You named, uh, Xerxes?' asked the swarthy, black-haired sergeant.

'Yes, suh. That's my name.' At least the man wasn't asking for him as Scipio. Even though he used it here himself, hearing it in a guard's mouth might mean his revolutionary past in South Carolina had popped up again. If it had, he was a dead man . . . a little sooner than he would be anyway. Once you landed in here, your chances weren't good any which way.

The guard gestured with his submachine gun. 'You come here.' Did some special school teach guards that move?

They all seemed to know it. It was amazingly persuasive, too.

'I's comin',' Scipio said. If you told a guard no, that was commonly the last thing you ever told anybody.

Legs light with fear, Scipio stepped away from Barracks 27. Even *I's comin'* might be the last thing he ever told anyone. That sergeant and his two white flunkies looked ready to chalk him up to 'shot while attempting to escape.'

'You know two women named Bathsheba and Antoinette?' the guard demanded. In his mouth, Scipio's wife's name came out as *Bat'cheba;* Scipio almost didn't recognize it.

But he nodded. 'Yes, suh, I knows dey,' he said. Fear and hope warred, leaving his voice husky. 'Is dey – Is dey all right?' He had to fight to get the words out.

'They all right, *sí.*' The guard nodded, too. 'They say, they hope you all right, too.'

'Do Jesus!' Relief flooded through Scipio. 'Thank you, suh. Thank from from de bottom o' my heart. You see dey again, you tell dey I's doin' fine.' No black in Camp Determination was doing fine. His wife and daughter were bound to know that as well as he did. They didn't want him to worry, though, and he didn't want them to, either.

'I tell 'em.' The guard sergeant from Sonora or Chihuahua gave him one more brusque nod, then strode away, the two bigger men still at his heels.

Bathsheba and Antoinette were still alive. There was still hope. And Lubbock belonged to the Yankees. Like a lot of Negroes in the CSA, Scipio would have been a patriot if only the whites around him let him. The Confederate States were the only country he had. But if his own homeland set out to do horrible things to him and the people he loved, then its enemies became his friends.

He laughed, not that it was funny. From everything he'd

heard, the Mormons up in Utah were as firm in denying Negroes equality as white Confederates were, even if they had different reasons. He sympathized with them now, no matter what they believed. What the United States were doing to them wasn't that different from what the Confederate States were doing to blacks.

And yet you never could tell. Even in this hellhole, that guard went out of his way to deliver the message from Bathsheba and Antoinette. He didn't have to do that. He could have refused them straight out. He could have promised to pass along their words and then gone on about his business. He hadn't. Decency cropped up in the strangest places.

Scipio looked north. He could see the women's barracks, there on the other side of the railroad line that brought his family here. Not one but two barbed-wire perimeters separated him from his loved ones. He drew himself up a little straighter. The train ride from Augusta didn't kill him. If it didn't, could anything? He didn't believe it. He wouldn't believe it.

His gaze swung from the north, the unattainable, toward the northwest. The Yankees might well come down to Camp Determination. If Lubbock was gone, other west Texas towns could fall. He just had to stay alive till U.S. troops arrived.

Just. That made it sound easier than it was.

He still didn't know how many people died in that cattle car. He didn't know why he still lived, either. Plenty of men and women younger and stronger than he was were dead. If he could make the Yankees listen to his story, maybe his survival would mean something. Bathsheba would say so. She believed things happened for reasons. She believed God watched over people.

Scipio wished he could do the same. He also wished

God did a better job of watching over the Negroes in the CSA. He wished God did any kind of job of watching over them. As far as he could see, God was out to a film, leaving them to fend for themselves. The only trouble with that was, the Freedom Party had a lot more fending power than the Negroes did.

'Labor gang!' a guard shouted. 'Need fifty volunteers for a labor gang!'

Labor gangs left the camp with men chained to one another like criminals. They worked killing hours on little food. When they came back, the men in them were worn to nubs.

The guard could have got five hundred volunteers, or five thousand. Work on a labor gang was real work, and you did come back when you went out. Nobody knew what happened when you got shipped to another camp. A lot of people muttered about that. If you muttered too loud, you had a way of getting shipped out yourself. Then other people muttered about what happened to you.

Except for the labor gangs, there was nothing to do inside the camp but stew and starve. If the Confederate authorities were smart, they could have set up factories where the Negroes they'd dragged from the cities and countryside could make things for them. The authorities didn't bother. They just didn't care.

The only sport in camp was watching new fish come in. Scipio had been a new fish himself, not so long before. Now he watched other dazed, thirsty, half-starved – or sometimes more than that – men stagger into Camp Determination. Their astonishment was funny, as his must have been to those who arrived before him.

'What you lookin' at?' a black man would yell at the newcomers. 'Y'all reckon you's in New Yawk City?'

Scipio didn't understand why, but talking about New

York City never failed to send the prisoners into gales of laughter. For as long as he could remember, the biggest town in the USA had been the symbol of degeneracy and depravity to white Confederates. In films made in the CSA, New York City seemed entirely populated by villains and lounge lizards and slutty women. Maybe that was part of it.

But New York City was also full of riches and luxury. No matter how white Confederates despised the place, they couldn't deny or ignore it. That probably made the camp jokes funnier. And sometimes things didn't have to make any sense at all to be funny. Sometimes not making sense was the point of the joke.

'You park your Cadillac car outside befo' you come in?' the wit would call to the new fish. It was always a Cadillac car, never just a Cadillac. Scipio didn't know why that was so, but it was. It was one more thing that made the jokes funnier.

Sometimes a new fish would have spirit enough to say something like, 'You niggers crazy.'

That would send the camp veterans into capers as wild as they had the energy to perform. 'We sure is crazy,' someone would say. 'If you ain't crazy in dis here place, you gots to be nuts.'

At one level, that made no sense at all. At another level, it held a profound truth. Scipio was used to thinking in terms like that. Anne Colleton made sure he was thoroughly educated, not for his sake but so he made a better butler, a better ornament, for the Marshlands plantation. Marshlands was a ruin today. Anne Colleton was dead, killed in the early days of the war when U.S. carrier-based bombers hit Charleston.

And here I am, in Camp Determination. Much good my education did me, Scipio thought. The one thing that mattered in the CSA was his color. How smart he was? That he could quote Shakespeare from memory? Nobody white cared a bit.

The Negro who'd made the crack about craziness was just making a joke. Scipio was sure he didn't see that he was kidding on the square. He talked like a field hand. He certainly wasn't educated. He probably wasn't very smart. What difference did it make? Here he was, and here Scipio was. They had equality of a sort – equality of misery.

This batch of new fish had no trouble finding bunks – a large number of men were transferred to other camps just a couple of days before they got here. People came into Camp Determination. They went out. Nobody seemed to stay very long. That could have been why all the rumors swirled around the trucks and the bathhouses. Scipio hoped that was the reason.

And then he got the chance to find out for himself. When his barracks lined up for roll call one morning, a guard shouted, 'We're gonna ship your asses to Abilene. Head on over to the bathhouse. Don't want you bringin' lice an' fleas an' shit like that with you, so we're gonna wash you off and delouse you.'

'Befo' breakfast?' somebody said in dismay.

'You'll get breakfast on the trucks that take you east,' the guard said. 'They got bread an' all kinds of good stuff. From what I hear, they feed you better in Abilene than we do here.' That sent a buzz through the assembled Negroes. Whatever the food in Abilene was like, it couldn't very well be worse than it was here.

Nobody raised any particular fuss as the guards marched the Negroes to the bathhouse. Anyone who did raise a fuss would have been sorry; the guards carried automatic rifles as well as submachine guns, and looked very ready to use them. Among the guards was the Mexican-looking sergeant who'd delivered the message from Bathsheba and Antoinette. Seeing him made Scipio feel better. He didn't think the man would let anything bad happen to him.

Inside the bathhouse, the guards ordered the Negroes to take off their rags and store them in cubbies. One of the gray-uniformed men who watched them do it said, 'Remember where your shit's at. Anybody tries stealing somebody else's duds, he's gonna wish he was never born.'

A sign pointed the way to the delousing station. The naked black men walked along the corridor in that direction. It was a big chamber, but they filled it up. Scipio noticed the door was steel, with rubber gasketing around the edges. His unease began there. But for a few metal columns with grillwork at the bottom, the chamber was bare. A sign over a door in the far wall said, TO THE BATHS.

He'd heard veterans, both white and black, go on about Great War delousing stations. Either they'd changed the way things worked since or . . .

Some kind of gas started pouring out of the grillwork. Even a tiny whiff of it set Scipio's lungs on fire. He ran toward that door in the far wall. Other blacks got there ahead of him. They screamed in despair – the door didn't open. *They fooled us,* Scipio thought. *They fooled us good, damn them.* Half crushed in the panic, half poisoned by the gas, he crumpled. Blackness enfolded him.

IV

Up until a few years earlier, sharecroppers lived in this sorry little collection of shacks. Now the buildings stood sad and vacant under Georgia's mild spring sun. 'Where did everybody go?' Jonathan Moss asked. 'Did the Freedom Party catch the people who were here and send them to a camp?'

To his surprise, Spartacus shook his head. 'Don't reckon so,' the black guerrilla leader answered. 'Reckon they went to town, to look for work there. Weren't no' mo' work here, that's fo' damn sure.'

'Why the hell not?' Nick Cantarella asked. 'You got nothin' but miles and miles of cotton farms and tobacco farms and shit like that.'

Spartacus surprised Moss again, this time by chuckling in grim amusement. 'You is a city fella,' Spartacus said, not unkindly. 'You is a city fella, an' you don't see how the country work. Used to be plenty jobs fo' nigger field hands, yeah. Then the Freedom Party make all these tractors an' harvesters an' shit, throw Lawd only know how many niggers outa work. Goddamn bastards.'

'That's not all it did,' Cantarella said. 'Factories they built to turn out those tractors and harvesters, they're making barrels and armored cars nowadays. You can bet your ass on that.'

'Sly,' Moss said. 'Sly twice, because it let them drive the Negroes off the fields and let them gear up for turning out war machines without making the USA flabble about it.'

'Fuck me,' Spartacus said, looking from one of them to the other. 'I seen the first part o' dat, on account of it happen to me an' mine. But the other half . . . Didn't worry 'bout dat none.'

'Yeah, well, those Freedom Party fuckers wouldn't be half so dangerous if the guys running the show for 'em were dumb,' Cantarella said. 'Featherston's a maniac, but he's a goddamn smart maniac, you know what I mean?'

Jonathan Moss did, and wished he didn't. Fighting the war against the Confederates hadn't proved anything to him one way or the other. Soldiers were soldiers, and sometimes where they came from hardly mattered. Military life had rhythms of its own. But his time since escaping from Andersonville told a different story.

He'd wondered how the Confederates could hold down the countryside with so many whites of military age off fighting the USA. Now he knew. If Negroes in the countryside lost their jobs, a lot of them had to go to the CSA's cities and towns, where they were easier to keep track of and get hold of. No, the people at the top of the Freedom Party weren't dumb at all. Too damn bad.

Meanwhile, some of the blacks still in the countryside did their best to make the Confederates unhappy. Spartacus said, 'Reckon we kin spend the night heah. Ain't nobody round seen us go in. Better'n sleepin' on bare ground.'

Moss didn't argue with that. His middle-aged bones thought anything was better than sleeping on bare ground. War was a young man's game. As a fighter pilot, he'd made up in experience what he lacked in exuberance. Even so, he'd needed more rest and more regular rest than his young comrades, and he wasn't able to fly as many missions.

Here, on the ground in Georgia, his years shoved themselves in his face in all kinds of ways. He got tired. He got hungry. When the shooting started, he got scared. Spartacus' black guerrillas were mostly young and entirely fearless. When they attacked whites, they did it with a fierce joy, almost an exaltation, that left him admiring and astonished. He didn't think he'd ever felt that ferocious in an airplane over Canada in the last war.

Of course, he hadn't had such good reasons for ferocity, either.

He went into one of the cabins. It smelled all musty; it had been deserted for some time, and water and mold had their way inside. But even brand-new, it would have indicted the system that produced it. No running water. No plumbing. No electricity. No gas. Not even a wood-burning stove – all the cooking was done over a fireplace.

'I've seen horses with better stalls than this,' he said.

'Yeah.' Nick Cantarella nodded. 'Tell you something else, too – horses deserve better than this. So do people.'

Not much was left inside the cabin to show how the people who used it had lived. A cheap pine stool lay tumbled in a corner. A few dishes, just as cheap, some of them broken, sat on a counter. When Moss put the stool back on its legs, he found a rag doll, face leprous with mildew, forgotten behind it. Did some little colored girl cry and cry because that doll was lost? He'd never know now, any more than he'd know whether that little girl was still alive.

'Can't even light a fire,' Cantarella grumbled. 'Anybody white sees smoke coming out of the chimney, he'll sic the Mexicans on us.'

'Yeah, well, it could be worse,' Moss said. 'They could have guys after us who really want to fight.'

Nick Cantarella laughed, though he wasn't kidding. Francisco José's soldiers rapidly discovered the black guerrillas were desperately in earnest. Spartacus' men didn't need long to figure out that the soldiers from the Empire

of Mexico weren't, at least if not under direct attack. The
Mexicans didn't want to be in Georgia. They resented C.S.
whites almost as much for making them come up here as
they resented C.S. blacks for having the gall to shoot back.
It wasn't quite *a plague on both your houses,* but it came
close.

'What do we have for food?' Cantarella asked.

'I've got some ham and cornbread. How about you?'

'Cornbread, too, and I've still got a couple of ration cans
from that dead Mexican we found.' Cantarella grimaced.
'Damned if I know how the Confederates go on eating that
slop. I mean, the stuff we have is lousy, but this is a hell
of a lot worse.'

'It's pretty bad,' Moss agreed. Pilots ate better than soldiers in the field – most of the time, anyway. He went on,
'It's better than what we got in Andersonville, though,
except when the Red Cross packages came through.'
Rations for POWs were supposed to be the same as what
the captor's soldiers got. Theory was wonderful – either
that or the Confederate States were in more trouble than
anybody north of the Mason-Dixon Line suspected.

They shared what they had. It filled their bellies,
although a chef at the Waldorf-Astoria – or even a mess
sergeant – would have turned up his nose, or more likely
his toes. Despite lacking a fire, Moss appreciated being able
to sleep with a wall, no matter how drafty, between him
and the outside world. What Georgia called winter had
been mild by the standards of Ontario or Chicago, but it
still got chilly. Spring days were warmer. Spring nights
didn't seem to be.

Then again, Moss suspected he could sleep through an
artillery duel in the middle of a blizzard. Any chance for
sleep he got, he grabbed with both hands. He knew his age
was showing, knew and didn't care.

Captain Cantarella shook him awake much too early the next morning. Any time before the next afternoon would have been too early, but the sun was barely over the horizon. Moss' yawn almost made the top of his head fall off. 'Already?' he croaked.

' 'Fraid so,' Cantarella answered. 'They've got coffee going out there, if that makes you feel any better.'

'Not much,' Moss said, but he sat up. 'What they call coffee'll be nothing but that goddamn chicory, anyhow.'

'Maybe a little bit of the real bean,' Cantarella said. 'And chicory'll open your eyes, too.'

'Yeah, but it tastes like you're drinking burnt roots,' Moss said.

'That's 'cause you are,' Cantarella said cheerfully. 'If you don't get your ass in gear, though, you *won't* get to drink any burnt roots, on account of everybody else will have drunk 'em all up.' There was a threat to conjure with. Moss got to his feet. He creaked and crunched, but he made himself move.

After a tin cup full of essence of burnt roots – and maybe a little bit of the real bean – life looked better, or at least less blurry. Moss munched on a chunk of cornbread. Spartacus squatted beside him. 'Nigger come out from Americus in the night,' the guerrilla leader remarked. 'He say there's a train comin' we gots to blow. Gots to sabotage.' He spoke the last word with sardonic relish.

And Jonathan Moss liked the idea of striking a train better than he liked going into these half-assed Georgia towns and shooting them up. Shooting up a town annoyed the Confederates and made them flabble. Wrecking a train, though, meant the men and munitions aboard either wouldn't get into the fight against the USA or would get there late. 'Sounds good,' he said. 'What's on this one? Do you know?'

'Oh, I know, all right.' Spartacus sounded thoroughly grim. 'Niggers is on it.'

'Huh?' Even after the mostly ersatz coffee, Moss wasn't at his best.

'Niggers,' Spartacus repeated. 'From No'th Carolina, I reckon. They's headin' for them camps. They git there, they don't come out no mo'. So we gots to make sure they ain't gonna git there.'

Rescuing a trainload of blacks wouldn't do the USA much good, but Moss didn't even dream of trying to talk the guerrilla chieftain out of it. Spartacus had his own worries, his own agenda. When those took him on a track that also helped the United States, he didn't mind. When they didn't, he didn't care.

One of his men knew more about dynamiting train tracks than Nick Cantarella did, and Cantarella was no blushing innocent. The U.S. officer did suggest a diversionary raid a few miles away to give the explosives man – his name, also likely a *nom de guerre,* was Samson – a chance to work undisturbed. Spartacus liked that. 'Sneaky fucker, you,' he said, nothing but admiration in his voice.

He sent off a few of his men to shoot at trucks on the highway. That would be plenty to draw the Confederates' attention – and that of their Mexican stooges, too. The rest of the band lurked close by where Samson did his job.

The train pushed a heavily laden flat car ahead of the locomotive. That kept Samson's bomb from wrecking the engine itself. Against some kinds of sabotage, it might have mattered. But the bomb still made the train stop. Then the guerrillas sprayed the engine and the men inside with gunfire. Steam plumed from the punctured boiler.

Some of Spartacus' men ran forward to open the passenger cars and freight cars in the train. Others stayed back to cover them. Jonathan Moss was one of those who hung back – he doubted the Negroes in there would welcome any white face just then.

Blacks began spilling out, more and more and more of them. 'Sweet Jesus!' Cantarella said. 'How many smokes did those Freedom Party bastards cram in there?'

'Too many,' Moss said, and then, 'Now I believe every atrocity story I ever heard. You don't pack people in like that if you don't mean to dispose of them.'

He watched in horrified fascination as the Negroes scattered over the countryside. They didn't know where they were going, where they would sleep, or what – if anything – they would eat. But they were sure of one thing, and so was he: whatever happened to them here, they would be better off than if this train got to where it was going.

Most of the time, Irving Morrell didn't like getting called back to Philadelphia for consultation. Some things, though, were too big to plan on the back on an envelope. What to do once the USA drove the CSA out of Ohio seemed to fall into that category.

Brigadier General John Abell met him at the Broad Street Station. The tall, thin, pale General Staff officer was as much a product of the War Department as Morrell was of the field. Morrell was sure Abell distrusted him as much as he distrusted the other man, and for reasons probably mirroring his own.

'Good to see you under these circumstances,' Abell said, shaking his hand.

'Good to be here under these circumstances,' Morrell answered. Better by far to come to Philadelphia to plan the next attack than to figure out how to defend the city. More than eighty years had passed since a Confederate army reached Philadelphia. Morrell devoutly hoped the city never saw another one.

As they walked from the station to the auto Abell had waiting, the General Staff officer said, 'When we beat the Confederates this time, we're going to beat them so flat, they'll never give us trouble again. We'll beat them so flat, they won't even *think* about raising a hand against us from now on.'

'I like that,' Morrell said. The enlisted man driving the government-issue Chevrolet sprang out to open the back door for his exalted passengers. After Morrell slid into the green-gray auto, he went on, 'Can we bring it off?'

'Militarily? I think we can. It won't be easy or cheap, but we can do it.' Abell sounded coldly confident. 'We can, and we need to, and so we will.' As if to underscore his determination, the Chevy rolled by a downed Confederate bomber. Behind a barricade of boards on sawhorses, technicians swarmed over the airplane, partly to see if the enemy had come up with anything new and partly to salvage whatever they could.

'Oh, yeah – I think we can whip 'em, too,' Morrell said. 'But we have to occupy them once we do. Otherwise, they'll just start rearming on the sly the way they did after the Great War.'

John Abell nodded. 'You and I are on the same page, all right.' He let out a small chuckle; they'd known each other for close to thirty years, and that wasn't the kind of thing either one of them said every day. Then he went on, 'Plans for doing that are already being prepared.'

'Good. Are the planners working out how much it'll cost us?' Morrell asked. Abell made a questioning noise. Morrell explained: 'They hate us down there. They hate us bad. Maybe they hate their own Negroes worse, but maybe they don't, too. And it's awful easy to make a guerrilla war hurt occupiers these days. Auto bombs. People bombs. Land mines. Time bombs. These goddamn newfangled rockets.

It was bad when we tried to hold down Houston and Kentucky. It'll be worse now. "Freedom!" ' He added the last word with sour emphasis.

General Abell looked pained – not so much for the wit, Morrell judged, as for what lay behind it. 'Maybe it's a good thing you're here for more than one reason,' Abell said. 'You ought to write an appreciation with all that in mind.'

'No one will appreciate it if I do,' Morrell said.

That made Abell look more pained still. But he said, 'You might also be surprised. We're looking at this. We're looking at it very seriously, because we think we need to. If you point out some pitfalls, that will be to everyone's advantage – except the Confederates', of course.'

He was serious. The War Department was serious, then: whatever else you could say about John Abell, he made a good weather vane. 'If we occupy the CSA, we won't even pretend to be nice people any more,' Morrell warned. 'It'll be like Utah, only more so. We'll have to kill anybody who gives us a hard time, and maybe kill the guy's brother-in-law to make sure he *doesn't* give us a hard time afterwards.'

'That is the working assumption, yes,' Abell agreed matter-of-factly.

Morrell let out a soft whistle. 'Lord!' he said. 'If the Confederates are killing off their own Negroes the way we say they are—'

'They are.' Abell's voice went hard and flat. 'That's not just propaganda, General. They really are doing it.'

However many times Morrell had heard about that, he didn't want to believe it. Because the Confederates fought clean on the battlefield, he wished they played fair with their own people, too. But Abell's certainty was hard not to credit. Sighing, Morrell went on, 'Well, if they're doing that, and if we kill off any whites who get out of line, people are liable to get thin on the ground down there.'

'Yes, that's true.' Spring was here, but Abell remained blizzard-cold. 'And so?'

He envisioned massacre as calmly as Jake Featherston did. The only difference was, he might let whites in the CSA live if they stayed quiet. Featherston killed off Negroes whether they caused trouble or not – his assumption was that Negroes *were* trouble, period. The distinction didn't seem enormous. Morrell clung to it nonetheless.

'Either this town was already as beat-up as it could be or it hasn't taken a whole lot of new damage since the last time I was here,' he remarked.

'The Confederates still come over,' Abell said. 'Maybe not so much – and we can hurt them more when they do.'

'That sounds good,' Morrell said.

But when he got to the War Department, he went underground – far underground. Brigadier General Abell had to vouch for him before he even got into the battered building. The stars on his shoulders meant nothing to the guards at the entrance. That was how it should be, as far as Morrell was concerned. 'No one has been able to blow himself up inside yet,' Abell said with what sounded like pride.

They went down endless flights of stairs. Morrell revised his notions about whether people around here ever got exercise. Climbing those stairs on the way back up would be no joke. 'How close have they come?' he asked.

'Somebody dressed like a major took out a guard crew at the eastern entrance a couple of weeks ago,' Abell answered. 'One of the men there must have seen something he didn't like, and so. . . .'

'Yeah. And so,' Morrell said. 'I wonder how long it'll be before they start using two-man suicide crews. The first fellow blows himself up, then the next one waits till the place is crowded before he uses his bomb – either that or he uses the confusion to sneak into wherever he really wants to go. It works with auto bombs; I know the Negroes in the CSA have done it. It might work with people bombs, too.'

'You're just full of happy thoughts this morning, aren't you?' John Abell said. 'Well, put that in your appreciation, too. If you can think of it, we have to believe those Mormon bastards can, too.' He made a sour face. 'Probably not going to be many people left alive in Utah by the time that's all done, either.'

'No,' Morrell agreed. His own name for planning had suffered when a Great War attack against the rebels there didn't go as well as it might have. He was banished from the General Staff back to the field then – a fate that dismayed him much less than his banishers thought it would. He said, 'One thing – if we need to sow the place with salt, we won't have to go very far to get it.'

'Er – no.' Abell didn't know what to make of foolishness. He never had. To Morrell's relief, he left the stairwell before they got all the way to China. 'The map room is this way,' he said, reviving a little. Separate a General Staff officer from his maps and he was only half a man.

Officers ranging in rank from captain to major general pored over maps on tables and walls. Those maps covered the U.S.-C.S. frontier from Sonora all the way to the Atlantic. Some of the men in green-gray used their pointers decorously, like schoolteachers. Others plied them with brio, like orchestra conductors. Still others might have been knights swinging swords: they slashed and hacked at the territory they wanted to conquer.

Morrell was a slasher himself. He grabbed a pointer from a bin that looked like an archer's quiver and advanced on a map showing the border between the Appalachians and the Mississippi. 'This is what I want to do,' he said, and executed a stroke that would have disemboweled the Confederacy if it went across the real landscape instead of a map.

John Abell's pale eyebrows rose. 'You don't think small, do you?'

'I've been accused of a lot of things, but rarely that,' Morrell said. 'We can do it, you know. We should have started building up a little sooner, but I really think we can do it.'

Abell studied the map. He borrowed the pointer from Morrell and walked over to another map. His slash was as surgical as Morrell's, if less melodramatic. 'This would be your follow-up?' he inquired.

'Absolutely.' Morrell set a hand on the other man's shoulder. 'If we're thinking along the same lines, chances are this will really work, because we never do that. Or we never did — now it's twice in just a little while.'

'More likely we're both deluded,' the General Staff officer replied. Morrell laughed, hoping Abell was joking. Abell studied the map himself. 'This may be a two-year campaign, you know, not just one.'

'That's . . . possible,' Morrell said reluctantly. 'But I don't think the Confederates will have a whole lot more than wind and air once we breach their front. They shot their bolt, and they hurt us, but they didn't quite kill us. Now it's our turn, and let's see how they like playing defense.'

'Defense is cheaper than offense,' Abell warned. 'And they have some new toys of their own. These multiple rocket launchers are very unpleasant.' He hadn't come within a hundred miles of those rocket launchers — he was that kind of soldier — but he spoke with authority even so.

'Where are our new toys?' Morrell asked.

'I thought you might be wondering about that.' With the air of a stage magician plucking a rabbit from a hat, John

Abell took a folded sheet of paper out of his breast pocket. 'Tell me what you think about this.'

Morrell paused to put on reading glasses, a concession to age he hated but couldn't do without. He unfolded the paper and skimmed through it. The more he read, the wider his smile got. 'Well, well,' he said. 'This is more like it! But there isn't anything about when they'll be ready. Are we talking about soon, or is this in the great by-and-by?'

'Soon,' Abell said. 'Immediately, as a matter of fact. They're coming off the lines in Pontiac – and in Denver – even as we speak. Whatever you do this summer, you'll be able to use them.'

'That's the best news I've had in quite a while,' Morrell said. '*Quite* a while. We've always had to play catch-up to Confederate armor. If we've got better barrels for a change, that just makes it more likely we can give them a good sickle slice and cut 'em off at the roots.'

'Depending on what they're doing themselves along these lines,' Abell said. 'Our intelligence isn't perfect.'

'Really? I never would have guessed,' Morrell said. Abell gave him a sour stare. But with that piece of paper in his hand, with the idea for that campaign in his head, Irving Morrell wasn't inclined to pick a fight with his own side. 'Perfect or not, General,' he went on, 'we'll manage. I really think we will.'

Confederate shells crashed down outside of Lubbock. Inside the Texas town, Major General Abner Dowling was not a happy man. After Lubbock fell to his Eleventh Army, he'd hoped he could go on biting chunks out of west Texas, but it didn't work out like that. The Confederates, to his surprise – to everybody's surprise – threw fresh troops into the fight, and those men didn't seem to care whether they lived or died. They weren't here in more than brigade strength, but that was plenty to stabilize the line and even to push U.S. forces back toward Lubbock.

Major Angelo Toricelli stuck his head into Dowling's office. It did belong to a bank manager, but he took a powder before U.S. troops occupied Lubbock. 'Sir, you said you wanted to question one of those Confederate fanatics,' Toricelli said. 'We've got one for you.'

'Do you?' Dowling brightened fractionally. 'Well, bring him in. Maybe we'll have a better notion of what we're up against.'

His adjutant saluted. 'Yes, sir.'

In came a large, burly Confederate soldier, escorted by three large, burly U.S. soldiers with submachine guns. The Confederate had two stripes on his tunic sleeve. Tunic and trousers weren't the usual C.S. butternut, but a splotchy fabric in shades of tan and brown ranging from sand to mud. 'Who are you?' Dowling asked.

'Sir, I am Assistant Troop Leader Lee Rodgers, Freedom Party Guards,' the prisoner said proudly. He recited his pay number.

'Assistant Troop Leader?' Dowling pointed to Rodgers' chevrons. 'You look like a corporal to me.'

'Sir, they are equivalent ranks,' Rodgers said. 'The Freedom Party Guards have their own rank structure. This is to show that they are an elite.' He still sounded proud. He also sounded as if he was rattling off something he'd had to learn by rote.

Dowling had heard that before, though he didn't know the guards actually went into combat. He thought they were just prison warders and secret policemen and Freedom Party muscle. But they fought, all right, and they fought well. Their tactics left something to be desired, but not their pluck.

'What's your unit?' Dowling asked.

'Sir, I am Assistant Troop Leader Lee Rodgers, Freedom

Party Guards.' Rodgers gave Dowling his pay number again. 'Under the Geneva Convention, I don't have to tell you anything else.'

He was right, of course. Sometimes that mattered more than it did other times. Had Dowling thought Rodgers held vital information, he might have squeezed him. There were ways to do it that technically didn't violate the Convention. As things were, though, Dowling only asked, 'Do you tell the Negroes in that prison camp down the road about their rights under the Geneva Convention?'

'No, sir,' Rodgers answered without hesitation. 'They aren't foreign prisoners. They're internal enemies of the state. We have the right to do whatever we need to do with them.' He eyed Dowling. 'They might as well be Mormons.'

He was sharper than the average corporal. If the Freedom Party Guards really were an elite, Dowling supposed that made sense. 'We follow the Geneva Convention with the Mormons we capture,' Dowling said, which was – mostly – true. Then again, the Mormons had more than a few female fighters. They generally fought to the death. When they didn't, U.S. soldiers often avenged themselves in a way they wouldn't with Mormon men. That was against regulations and officially discouraged, which didn't mean it didn't happen.

Assistant Troop Leader Lee Rodgers only snorted. 'If you do, it just means you're weak and degenerate. Enemies of the state deserve whatever happens to them.' That sounded like another lesson learned by heart.

'How many Freedom Party Guards units are in combat?' Dowling asked.

'More every day,' Rodgers said, which gave the U.S. general something to worry about without giving him any real information. The prisoner folded his right hand into a fist and set it on his heart. 'Freedom!' he shouted.

The U.S. soldiers guarding him growled and hefted their weapons. Rodgers seemed unafraid, or else more trusting than most new POWs. Dowling scowled. 'Take him away,' he said.

'Yes, sir,' one of the men in green-gray said. 'Shall we teach him not to mouth off, too?'

'Never mind,' Dowling said. 'We'll see how mouthy he is when we start advancing again.' That seemed to satisfy the soldiers. They weren't more than ordinarily rough with the Freedom Party Guard, at least where Dowling could see them. The general commanding Eleventh Army sighed. 'He's a charmer, isn't he?'

'Yes, sir,' Major Toricelli said. 'That's why you wanted to see him, isn't it?'

'I wonder if they're all like that. All the Party Guards, I mean,' Dowling said.

'Well, they sure fight like it's going out of style,' his adjutant answered. 'Those people are fanatics, and the Freedom Party is taking advantage of it.'

'Huzzah,' Dowling said sourly. 'Do you suppose we have to worry about them turning into people bombs? That's what fanatics do these days, it seems like.'

Toricelli looked startled. 'Hadn't thought of that, sir. They haven't done it yet, if they're going to.'

'Well, that's good. I suppose it is, anyhow,' Dowling said. 'Of course, maybe they just haven't thought of it yet. Or maybe they're going to put on civilian clothes instead of those silly-looking camouflage outfits and start looking for the biggest crowds of our soldiers they can find.'

'Or maybe they'll start looking for you, sir,' Toricelli said. 'The Confederates like to assassinate our commanders.'

'I know I'm not irreplaceable.' Dowling's voice was dry. 'I suspect the Confederates can figure it out, too. Besides, how would they get me? I'm not about to go strolling the streets of Lubbock.' He yawned. 'I'd bore myself to death if I did.'

Lubbock held many more people than the other west Texas towns Dowling's troops held for the USA. It wasn't much more exciting. And the people here were as stubbornly pro-Confederate as in those small towns. When this part of Texas was the U.S. state of Houston, there were collaborators hereabouts. But they'd had the sense to get out when Jake Featherston conned Al Smith into a plebescite that returned Houston to Texas and the CSA. The ones who didn't have that kind of sense ended up in camps themselves.

Under both the Stars and Stripes and the Stars and Bars (whose display now violated martial law), Lubbock had been a dry town. Dowling tried to win some popularity among local drinkers by declaring it wet. A couple of saloons opened up – and a minister promptly petitioned him to close them down.

The Reverend Humphrey Selfe looked as if he'd never had a happy thought in his life. He was long and lean, all vertical lines. He wore stark white and funereal black. His voice sounded like that of a bullfrog that had just lost its mother. 'Wine is a mocker,' he told Dowling, aiming a long, skinny forefinger at him like the barrel of an automatic rifle. 'Strong drink is raging.'

'Judge not, lest ye be judged,' Dowling answered – he'd loaded up with his own set of quotations ahead of time.

Reverend Selfe glowered. He was good at glowering. His physiognomy gave him a head start, but he had talent, too. 'Do you make sport of me?' he demanded, as if he'd take Dowling out behind the woodshed if the answer was yes.

Dowling, however, declined to be intimidated by a west Texas preacher skinny enough to dive down a soda straw. 'Not at all,' he lied. 'But you need something more than fire and brimstone to tell me why a man shouldn't be able to buy a shot or a bottle of beer if he feels like it.'

'Because God says drinking is a sin,' Selfe said. 'I was trying to illustrate that for you.'

'But He also says things like, "And the roof of thy mouth like the best wine for my beloved, that goeth down sweetly," ' Dowling said – sweetly. 'How do you pick and choose? Remember, "Drink no longer water, but use a little wine for thy stomach's sake." '

Humphrey Selfe looked like a man who needed wine for his stomach's sake. He certainly looked like a man whose stomach pained him. 'You are a sinner!' he thundered.

'I shouldn't wonder if you're right,' Dowling answered, fondly recalling a certain sporting house in Salt Lake City. 'But then, who isn't? I have at least as many quotations that say it's all right to drink as you do to say it's wrong. Shall we go on, sir? I'll show you.'

'Sinner!' Selfe said again. 'Even the Devil can quote Scripture for his purposes.'

'No doubt,' Dowling said. 'Which of us do you suppose he's speaking through? And how do you aim to prove it one way or the other?'

'You do mock me!' the pastor said.

Dowling shook his head. He was enjoying himself, even if the Reverend Selfe wasn't. 'No, you said wine was a mocker,' he said. 'I haven't had any wine for weeks.' He didn't mention strong drink, lest Selfe start raging. 'Shall we go on with our discussion? It was getting interesting, don't you think?'

Humphrey Selfe wasn't interested in discussing. Like a lot of people, he wanted to lay down what he saw as the law. 'I shall denounce you from the pulpit!' he said furiously.

'Remember the line about rendering unto Caesar, too, your Reverence,' Dowling said. 'Lubbock is under martial law. If you try to incite riot, rebellion, or uprising, I promise you'll be sorry.'

'I shall preach on the subject of saloons,' Selfe said.

'You do that,' Dowling told him. 'I'm sure they can use the advertising. It will be fascinating to see how many of your congregants – is that the word? – decide to wet their whistles once you let them know where they can.'

The Reverend Selfe left most abruptly. The way he slammed the door, a large shell might have gone off. Major Toricelli opened the door again – to Dowling's surprise, it was still on its hinges – and asked, 'What did you do to him?'

'Talked about the Scriptures,' Dowling answered. 'Really, there's no making some people happy.'

'Uh-*huh*,' Angelo Toricelli said. 'Why do I think you made a nuisance of yourself . . . sir?'

'Because you know me?' Dowling suggested. Then he added, 'Sunday, we'll need people listening to the quarrelsome fool's sermon. If he goes overboard, we'll make sure he pays for it.'

'That will be a pleasure,' Toricelli said.

After his adjutant withdrew once more, Dowling cursed. He'd wanted to ask the Reverend Humphrey Selfe what he thought of that camp for Negroes down by Snyder. Then he shrugged. Odds were the preacher would have said he'd never heard of the place. Odds were that would be a big, juicy lie, but Dowling wouldn't be able to prove it.

More C.S. artillery came in. Some of those rounds sounded as if they were hitting in town, not just on the southern outskirts. *Maybe,* Dowling thought hopefully, *they'll knock Reverend Selfe's church flat.* He laughed. Who said he wasn't an optimist?

★

Another downstate Ohio town. Having grown up in Toledo, First Sergeant Chester Martin looked on the southern part of his own state with almost as much scorn as a Chicagoan viewed downstate Illinois. Maybe people down here didn't marry their cousins, but they were liable to fool around with them – so he uncharitably thought, anyhow.

Hillsboro had a couple of foundries and a couple of dairy plants. It sat on a plateau in the middle of Highland County. Because it lay on high ground, the Confederates were hanging on to it as an artillery base to shell the U.S. forces advancing from the north and east.

Martin was frustrated at the way the war in southern Ohio was going. 'We should have trapped all the Confederates in the state,' he grumbled as he waited for water to boil for his instant coffee. 'We should have given them the same business we gave the butternut bastards in Pittsburgh.'

'Isn't there a difference, Sarge?' asked one of the privates huddled around the little campfire.

'Like what?' Chester said. What was the younger generation coming to? When he was a buck private, he wouldn't have dared talk back to a first sergeant.

'When they were in Pittsburgh, they had orders not to pull back till after it was too late and they couldn't,' the kid answered. 'Here, they are falling back – looks like they'll try and make the fight on their side of the Ohio.'

'Everybody thinks he belongs on the damn General Staff,' Chester said. But that wouldn't quite do. 'Well, Rohe, when you're right, you're right. I forgot they had those orders, and it does make a difference.'

Somewhere off to the left and ahead, a Confederate fired a short burst from one of their submachine guns. A U.S. machine gun answered. So did a couple of shots from the guys with the Springfields who helped protect the machine-gun crew. Another Confederate fired, this one with an automatic rifle. The machine gun answered again. Silence fell.

By then, Chester and the rest of the soldiers around the fire had their weapons in their hands, ready to hurry to help the machine-gun position if they had to. The Confederates in front of Hillsboro defended aggressively, probing as if they intended to go over to the attack any minute now. Martin didn't think they would, but you never could tell.

'Gotta hand it to those bastards,' said one of the privates by the fire. 'They still have their peckers up.' That wasn't far from what Chester was thinking.

But brash Private Rohe said, 'Yeah, well, I wish I did.'

That got a laugh. One of the other men said, 'Hey, you can't get laid around here, you ain't tryin'. These Ohio broads are mighty glad – I mean *mighty* glad – we ran off those butternut bastards.'

Several men nodded. From what Chester had seen, the private wasn't wrong. Some of the local women seemed convinced they had a patriotic duty to celebrate the return of the Stars and Stripes. 'Do your prophylaxis, just like they're whores,' he said: a sergeantly growl.

'They aren't, though, Sarge. That's what makes 'em so much fun – they're nice gals,' Rohe said. More nods.

'You think you can't come down venereal from laying a nice gal, you better think twice,' Chester said. 'Remember, some of those "nice" gals were probably screwing Featherston's boys while they were here. They're laying you to take the whammy off.'

'They wouldn't do that!' Two young men spoke in identical dismay.

Chester laughed. 'Hell they wouldn't. There are collaborators on both sides. Always have been. Always will be.' He looked at his men. 'You may be handsomer than the bastards in butternut – but if you are, the Confederacy's got more trouble than it knows what to do with.'

The infantrymen jeered at him. He sassed them back. If they were laughing and loose, they'd fight better. They didn't worry about anything like that, but he did. That was why he had those stripes, and the rockers under them.

Airplanes droned by overhead. Chester and the rest of the men looked for the nearest hole, in case those airplanes carried the Confederate battle flag. But they unloaded their ordnance on Hillsboro. Great clouds of smoke and dust rose above the town.

'Hope our people got out of there,' Rohe said, eyeing the devastation a couple of miles away.

Some of the locals probably – no, certainly – hadn't. War worked that way. U.S. soldiers and armored vehicles started moving toward Hillsboro. Chester Martin sighed. He knew what would happen next. And it did. Lieutenant Wheat called, 'Come on, men! Now that we've got the Confederates softened up, it's time to drive them out of there once and for all!'

Chester heaved himself to his feet. 'You heard the man,' he said. 'Let's get moving. Stay on your toes as we move forward. The Confederates may not be as beat up as we hope they are.'

He feared they wouldn't be. He'd seen too many massive bombardments in the Great War yield little or nothing. He wouldn't be surprised to see the same thing all over again here.

Rohe took point as the platoon moved up. He was small and skinny and sly, a good man to spot trouble before he tripped over it. The guys Chester had lugging the platoon's machine guns were the ones who would have played the line in a football game. He would have been the sort to lug one himself in the last war.

He also had four or five men carrying captured C.S. automatic rifles. He blessed the extra firepower they gave. The whole platoon kept its eyes open for dead Confederates. Scrounging ammo never ceased – they didn't want to run dry just when they needed it most.

They'd got about halfway to Hillsboro when mortar rounds started falling out of the sky. 'Down!' Chester yelled. 'Dig in!' There were plenty of shell holes that needed only minimal improvement to become foxholes. Some of them were already pretty good. Chester dove into one of those. Dirt flew as if he were part mole. Pretty good wasn't good enough. He wanted outstanding.

The veterans in the platoon all dug in as fast as he did. New replacements stood around gaping and wondering what the hell was going on. Nobody'd had time to show them the ropes, and they didn't own enough combat experience to do what needed doing without having to think about it. The extra few seconds they stayed upright cost them.

One was gruesomely killed. Two more went down wounded, both screaming their heads off. 'Corpsman!' other soldiers shouted. 'Over here, corpsman!' A veteran scrambled out of his hole to help a wounded rookie, and another fragment bit him. He howled in pain and howled curses at the same time.

In due course, U.S. artillery thundered. The mortars fell silent. *Biding their time,* Martin thought gloomily. But he was one of the first ones out of those newly enlarged and improved holes. 'Come on!' he called to the rest of the men. 'We've got a job to do.'

It was a nasty, unpleasant job. The ground over which they advanced offered little cover. To the Confederates in Hillsboro, they had to look like bugs walking across a plate. Smoke rounds helped, but only so much. If Featherston's boys had one of those rocket launchers up there, they could put a hell of a crimp in anybody's morning.

U.S. barrels rattled forward. Chester always liked to see them. They could do things infantry simply couldn't. And they always drew enemy fire away from foot soldiers. He wasn't the only one who knew they were dangerous – the Confederates did, too.

One of the things the barrels could do was lay down more smoke. That helped shield the advancing men in green-gray from the Confederates on the high ground. The Confederates kept shooting, but now they had trouble finding good targets. Chester trotted on, ducking and throwing himself into shell holes whenever he thought he had to.

Out of the smoke loomed a man in the wrong uniform: dirty butternut instead of dirty green-gray, a helmet of not quite the right shape. Chester's Springfield swung toward the Confederate's chest. The enemy soldier dropped – in fact, violently cast away – his submachine gun and threw up his hands. 'Don't shoot, Yankee!' he moaned. 'You got me!'

'What do we do with him, Sarge?' one of Martin's men asked.

Chester thought, but not for long. They didn't really have time to deal with POWs. . . . 'Take him on up the road,' he said.

'Right,' the U.S. soldier said. He gestured with his Springfield. 'Come on, you.' Pathetically eager, the prisoner came. Martin went on advancing. A shot rang out behind him, and then another one. He swore softly. It was too bad, but they just didn't have the time. If he'd told his men to take the Confederate to the rear, that would have removed at least one of them from the fight. And so he used the other phrase, and the man was dead. At least he

wouldn't have known he was about to die till it[...]
That was something, though not much.

Martin was sure the Confederates played the g[...]
same way. It was too bad, but what could you do? I[...]king
a prisoner didn't inconvenience or endanger you, you'd do
it. Why not? But if it did . . . It was a tough war, and it
didn't get any easier.

*Shame he didn't have one of their automatic rifles – sub-
machine-gun cartridges don't matter so much,* Martin thought.
*Well, the guy who plugged him will get his cigarettes and what-
ever else he has that's worth taking.* And that was what a
man's life boiled down to: cartridges and cigarettes. Yeah,
it sure was a tough war.

Artillery and the barrels pounded the Confederates
ahead. The gun bunnies were in good form; hardly any
rounds fell short. More soldiers in butternut came out of
their holes with hands high. Chester did let them surrender.
When men gave up in a group, it was too easy to have
something go wrong if you tried to get rid of all of them
at once.

Hillsboro fell that afternoon. The enemy pulled back
when U.S. barrels threatened to cut off his line of retreat
to the Ohio. He did a professional job of it, moving his
guns out hitched to trucks and commandeered motorcars.
He even paused to fire a few Parthian shots as he went
south.

'We licked him here,' Private Rohe said, inspecting what
was left of Hillsboro. 'We licked him, yeah, but he ain't
licked yet.'

Chester was thinking about the same thing. 'As long as
we keep licking him, the rest doesn't matter. Sooner or
later, he'll be licked whether he likes it or not.'

'Yeah?' Rohe weighed that, then nodded. 'Yeah. Sounds
right, Sarge. So when do we go over the Ohio?'

'Beats me,' Chester said. 'Let's bundle the other guys across first. Then we can worry about us, right?' Rohe nodded again.

Major Jerry Dover watched from the south bank of the Ohio as trucks and infantrymen crossed the bridge back into Kentucky. The span was laid about a foot below the surface of the river. The damnyankees still hadn't figured out that trick. When no one was on the bridge, it was invisible from the air. U.S. bombers didn't keep coming over and trying to blow it to hell and gone.

The foot soldiers on the bridge looked like men walking on water. Dover turned to Colonel Travis W.W. Oliphant and said, 'If we keep it up, sir, we can start our own religion.'

'What's that?' Colonel Oliphant didn't get it. *I might have known,* Dover thought with a mental sigh. Then the light dawned on his superior. Oliphant scowled. 'I don't find that amusing, Major. I don't find that amusing at all,' he said. 'I find it the next thing to blasphemous, as a matter of fact.'

'Sorry, sir,' Dover lied. *Damned stuffed shirt.* It wasn't as if he didn't know as much. He did. Any man who got huffy over not one initial but two couldn't be anything but a stuffed shirt.

Colonel Oliphant went on trumpeting and wiggling his ears and pawing the ground. After a little while, Dover stopped listening to him. He was watching the stream of men and machines to make sure all the field kitchens safely returned to the CSA. Oliphant was supposed to be doing the same thing. He was too busy ranting.

'If we make God turn His face away from us in disgust, how can we prevail?' he demanded.

Dover thought about Negroes disappearing in Atlanta.

He thought about the people he lost from the Huntsman's Lodge in cleanouts. He wondered what was going on since he put on the uniform and went away. Was Xerxes still there? He could hope, but that was all he could do. 'Sir, do you know about the camps?' he asked Colonel Oliphant in a low voice.

'What?' The other officer stared at him as if he were suddenly spouting Choctaw. 'What are you talking about?'

'The camps,' Dover repeated patiently. 'The camps where niggers go in but they don't come out.'

He wondered if Travis W.W. Oliphant would deny that any such things existed. A little to his surprise, Oliphant didn't. 'Yes, I know about them. So what?' he said.

'Well, sir, if God will put up with those, I don't think He'll get too disgusted about a bad joke of mine,' Dover said.

Oliphant turned red. 'The one has nothing to do with the other, Major,' he said stiffly. 'The Negroes deserve everything that we're giving them. Your so-called joke, on the other hand, was completely gratuitous.'

'God told you the Negroes have it coming, did He?' Jerry Dover asked.

'See here, Dover, you don't have the right attitude,' Colonel Oliphant said. 'Whose side are you on, anyway?'

'I'm on the Confederacy's side . . . sir,' Dover answered. 'If you think a stupid joke will put us in bad with God, I'm not so sure you are, though.' He'd managed the Huntsman's Lodge too damn long. He wasn't inclined to take guff from anybody, even if the guff-slinger wore three stars on either side of his collar while Dover had only one.

'I will write you up for this insubordination, Major,' Oliphant said in a low, furious voice. 'You'll get a court-martial, by God – yes, by God!'

He failed to impress Dover, who said, 'Go ahead. One

of three things will happen. They'll throw my ass in the stockade, and I'll be safer than you are. Or they'll take the uniform off my back and ship me home, and I'll be a lot safer than you are. Or – and here's my bet – they'll tear you a new asshole for wasting their time with this picayune shit, and they'll leave me the hell alone. So sure, court-martial me, Colonel. Be my guest. I'll thank you for it.'

Travis W.W. Oliphant's mouth opened and closed several times. He might have been a freshly hooked perch. Subordinates were supposed to react to the threat of a court-martial with terror, not gloating anticipation. After his wordless tries, he finally managed to choke out, 'You're not a proper soldier at all, Dover.'

'That depends, sir. If you want me to keep people fed, I'll do it like nobody's business,' Dover said. 'If you feed me bullshit and tell me it's breakfast, I'm gonna puke it all over your shoes.'

Colonel Oliphant retreated in disorder, shaking his head. No summons to a court-martial ever came. Dover hadn't expected one.

Since he wasn't going to the stockade, he had plenty to do. The Confederate units that got out of Ohio were in a horrible tangle. They had to try to improvise a defense where they'd thought they wouldn't need to. The CSA hadn't had much time to fortify Kentucky before the war broke out, and neglected it afterwards. Confederate thinking was surely that Ohio was more important.

But now Ohio was back in the damnyankees' hands. Whatever happened next would happen because the United States wanted it to, not because the Confederate States did. How good was the Confederacy at playing defense? Nobody knew, probably including Jake Featherston.

When supplies didn't come up from farther south fast enough to suit him, Dover acquired an evil reputation with farmers all over northern Kentucky. He requisitioned what he needed, paying in Confederate scrip.

Some of the farmers' screams reached Richmond. They got Dover a letter of commendation in his promotion jacket. Colonel Oliphant ignored it. Colonel Oliphant ignored Jerry Dover as much as he could from then on out, too.

That suited Dover down to the ground. He got more work done without Colonel Oliphant than he would have with him. He moved depots closer to the river than Oliphant liked, too. He didn't think Oliphant was a coward – he'd seen the man blazing away at strafing U.S. fighters with a submachine gun, cool as you please. But the colonel's ideas about logistics formed during the Great War, and didn't move forward with the easy availability of telephones and wireless sets and trucks.

Front-line soldiers appreciated what Dover did, regardless of whether Travis W.W. Oliphant understood it. Dover got to the front himself whenever he could. The best way to make sure things worked as you wanted them to was to check them with your own eyes. He knew that from the restaurant business.

And he promptly caught one potbellied supply sergeant diverting rations to the local civilians – for a nice little rakeoff, of course. Of course. He landed on the enterprising noncom like a thousand-pound bomb. After the sergeant went off in irons – nobody wasted time being nice to mere noncoms – things elsewhere along the line of the Ohio tightened up remarkably.

Because of all his time at the Huntsman's Lodge, Dover knew better than to believe he'd worked miracles. He didn't labor under the delusion that he'd changed human nature. Thieves and grifters were going to keep right on being thieves and grifters. But he forced them to be careful for a while, which was better than a poke in the eye with a carrot.

'Way to go, Major,' a first lieutenant running a company right on the southern bank of the river told him. 'We've got more grub here than I reckoned we'd ever see.'

'Good,' Dover said. 'Good you've got it now, I mean. Not so good you gave up thinking you ever would.'

'Yeah, well, what can you do? Shit happens,' the lieutenant answered. 'We were up on the other side of the border for a long time. We could swap smokes with the damnyankees for some of their rations, and we could requisition on the farms when we ran low. But that don't go over so good when you're requisitioning from your own people. So we were making do and getting by down here, but it's a damn sight better now.'

'Dammit, this country grows enough food. This country cans enough food,' Dover said – and requisitioning from his own side bothered him not a bit. 'We ought to be able to get that stuff to the people who need it the most.'

'We ought to be able to do all kinds of shit,' the lieutenant said, and paused to light a cigarette. 'We ought to still be up at Lake Erie. We ought to still be in Pittsburgh. Fuck, we ought to be in Philadelphia.' He looked at Dover. He did everything but blow smoke in Dover's face. 'And if you want to report me for defeatism, go right ahead . . . sir. It's not like I give a good goddamn.'

'I'm not going to report you. I think you're right.' Only later did Dover wonder if the other officer was trying to entrap him. No hard-faced men in gray trenchcoats swooped down on the tent where he slept during the wee small hours. No one hauled him away for bright lights and hard knocks and endless rounds of questions.

That didn't keep him from almost getting killed. Just as the Confederates were trying to strengthen their defenses on the southern bank of the Ohio, so the damnyankees were building up north of the river. The first two summers of the war, the Confederates struck when and where they chose. This time, the United States enjoyed the initiative. What they would do with it remained to be seen.

One of the things they did with it was strike at the C.S. positions south of the Ohio from the air. Bombs blasted field fortifications. Fighters streaked low to shoot up anything that moved. Confederate airplanes were bound to be doing the same thing on the other side of the river, but that didn't help Dover when a Yankee fighter strafed his Birmingham.

'Oh, shit!' the driver said when he saw the airplane in the rearview mirror. He jammed the gas pedal to the floor, which shoved Dover back in his seat. Then he did something his passenger thought smarter than hell, even if it almost put Dover through the windshield: he screeched the brakes, hoping to make the fighter overshoot.

It almost worked, too. Most of the U.S. fighter's machine-gun bullets chewed up the asphalt in front of the Birmingham. Most – but not all. A .50-caliber slug almost blew off the driver's head. Bone and blood and brains showered Jerry Dover. Two more bullets, or maybe three, slammed into the engine block. Flames and smoke spurted up from under the hood.

If the driver weren't already stopping, the auto would have gone off the road at high speed, and probably rolled over and exploded. As things were, it limped onto the soft shoulder. Dover yanked open the door, jumped out, and ran like hell. He managed to get clear before the fire reached the gas tank. A soft *whoomp!* and the Birmingham was an inferno.

'Jesus!' Dover looked down at himself. He was as spattered with gore as if he were wounded himself. He could *smell* it. His stomach heaved, but he kept breakfast down.

Looking back at the pyre that marked his driver's last resting place, he felt guilty about not getting the man out. The rational part of his mind said that was ridiculous – you couldn't possibly live with nothing left of your head from the ears north. He felt guilty even so, maybe for living where the other man died.

Another Birmingham painted butternut stopped. The officer inside stared from the burning motorcar to Jerry Dover. 'You hurt, pal? You need a lift?' he asked.

'I'm all right. I do need a lift,' Dover answered automatically. Then he said, 'Christ, what I really need is a drink.' The officer held up a silvered flask. Dover ran for the other Birmingham.

Cincinnatus Driver rolled into Cincinnati, Ohio. His name didn't have anything much to do with the town, even if he was born in Covington, Kentucky, right across the Ohio River. Negroes in the CSA had long been in the habit of giving their babies fancy names, either from the days of ancient Greece and Rome or, less often, from the Bible. When you didn't have much but your name to call your own, you got as much out of it as you could.

Cincinnati looked like hell. The Confederates made a stand here before pulling back across the Ohio into Covington. As the USA taught the CSA in Pittsburgh, attacking a built-up area could be hellishly expensive. The bastards in butternut did their damnedest to make it so here.

Great flocks of metallically twittering starlings darkened the sky as they rose when Cincinnatus' truck convoy rolled by. The war didn't bother them much, except for the ones unlucky enough to stop bullets or bomb or shell fragments. Those made only a tiny, tiny fraction of the total.

Back when Cincinnatus' father was a little boy, there were flocks of passenger pigeons instead. Cincinnatus had seen only a handful of those; they were in a steep decline when he was a boy around the turn of the century. They were all gone now, every one of them. Confederate artillery fire killed the last surviving specimen, a female in the Cincinnati zoo, early in the Great War.

By the same token, he remembered starlings arriving in the area not long after the war ended. Some crazy Englishman brought them to the USA in the 1890s, and they'd moved west ever since. He wondered if they filled up some of the hole in the scheme of things that was left when passenger pigeons disappeared.

And then he had more urgent things to wonder about, like whether he'd live long enough to deliver the shells he was carrying in the back of his truck. The Confederates on the far side of the river went right on lobbing their own shells into the ruins of Cincinnati, trying to make them even more ruinous.

Fountains of upflung dirt and smoke rose from not nearly far enough away. Cincinnatus kept on driving. Why not? He was just as likely to stop a fragment standing still as he was moving forward.

The trucks in the convoy stayed well separated from one another. If a shell blew one of them to hell and gone, even one carrying munitions, the blast wouldn't take out the trucks in front of and behind it. Everybody hoped it wouldn't, anyhow.

He pulled to a stop in front of the city jail. A lot more than one shell had fallen on that squat, ugly building. The Confederates must have made a stand there. That made sense – a place designed to keep unfriendly people in would also be pretty good at keeping unfriendly people out.

When Cincinnatus got down from the cab of his truck,

he was laughing to beat the band. 'What's so funny?' asked one of the other drivers, a white man named Waldo something. 'Way you're going on, anybody would think you did a couple months in there.' He jerked a thumb toward the wreckage of the jail. A big grin took the sting from his words.

'You ain't so far wrong,' Cincinnatus answered. 'Damn Confederates jugged me across the river, over in Covington. But when they went an' exchanged me, they stopped here an' got some other guys out, too. So I ain't sorry to see this place catch hell, not even a little bit.'

'Suits me,' Waldo said. 'The more jails they blow up, the happier I am. I've done stretches in too goddamn many of 'em. Never any big shit, but I like to drink, and when I drink I like to fight, and so. . . .' His face showed that he'd caught a few lefts and rights, or maybe more than a few, as well as dishing them out. He sounded proud of his escapades. A moment later, in fact, he went on, 'I wonder if they got any saloons open in what's left of this town.'

'You sure you want to find out?' Cincinnatus asked. 'You got the government tellin' you what to do, they can give you a lot more grief if you get in trouble than some city *po*lice can.'

Waldo thought it over. He nodded. 'Makes sense. Thanks.' If he'd left it there, everything would have been fine. But then he added, 'You're pretty goddamn smart for a nigger, you know?'

The worst part was, he meant it for a compliment. 'Thanks a bunch,' Cincinnatus said sourly.

A few more 105s came whistling in, but none of them burst close to where swarms of young soldiers unloaded the trucks. Watching them, Cincinnatus remembered how he'd done the same thing during the Great War. A lot of years had landed on his shoulders since, a lot of years and that encounter with the motorcar he didn't see before it almost killed him. He still didn't remember getting hit. He didn't suppose he ever would.

A second lieutenant who looked even younger than the soldiers doing pack-mule duty wandered through the unloading zone with a clipboard in his hands. It made him seem official, so official that Cincinnatus got suspicious. The Confederates would have no trouble putting one of their people in a U.S. uniform and sending him up here to see what he could see. They were supposed to do stuff like that all the time. Cincinnatus hoped the USA did it, too.

Then the young lieutenant talked to an officer who came down with the truck convoy. That made Cincinnatus feel better. A spy wouldn't talk to anybody if he didn't have to – or so it seemed to Cincinnatus, anyway. The older officer nodded. He said something; Cincinnatus was too far away to make out what.

'Driver!' the second lieutenant yelled, plainly reading the name from his clipboard. 'Cincinnatus Driver!'

Alarm sleeted through Cincinnatus. What the devil did they want with him? And who were they, anyhow? 'I'm here,' he said, and picked his way through the rubble over to the shavetail. 'What's up?'

'My superiors need to talk with you,' the baby-faced officer said. He wore green-and-white arm of service colors on his collar, a combination Cincinnatus hadn't seen before. A badge – a wreath with the letters INT inside – gave him a pretty good idea of what those colors meant. Intelligence.

That made him feel better, not worse. He'd got out of Covington – and got out of its colored district – only a little while before. If the U.S. Army was looking for ways to use Covington's Negroes, he had some ideas. He also had the names of people they could get in touch with – and names of people to stay away from at all costs.

Sentries in green-gray uniforms stood in front of what used to be an office building. The young lieutenant needed to exchange password and countersign with them before they let him in. Nobody trusted anybody these days. Cincinnatus hoped that was just as true on the side of the line where the men wore butternut.

A white-haired fellow in civilian clothes was talking with a lieutenant colonel and a major when Cincinnatus followed the lieutenant into the room where they sat. The man's eyes were the light, almost golden brown of a hunting dog's – a most unusual shade for a man. Cincinnatus stiffened. He knew those eyes anywhere, and the clever, engagingly homely face that housed them. Luther Bliss was trouble with a capital T.

When Kentucky belonged to the USA between the wars, Luther Bliss headed the Kentucky State Police, an outfit that hunted Confederate diehards and black radicals with equal enthusiasm. Cincinnatus spent almost two years in a Kentucky State Police jail. Bliss was a law unto himself, and paid attention to other law only when he felt like it.

He nodded to Cincinnatus now. 'As long as you're against the Freedom Party, we're on the same side,' he said. To the officers, he added, 'We've had our run-ins, Cincinnatus and me, but he's all right. I'm glad his card came up.'

Cincinnatus wasn't sure he was glad his card – what card? – turned up. Forced to choose between Luther Bliss and Jake Featherston, he would choose Bliss. No black man could possibly disagree there. Forced to choose between Bliss and anyone else – anyone else at all . . . But that wasn't the choice he had.

Bliss went on, 'I was hooked in with Lucullus Wood and the other colored activists, but only from the outside.' He brushed one hand across the back of the other, noting his own white skin. 'Cincinnatus here, though, he knows all that stuff from the inside out.'

'Well, that's what we're looking for,' the major said. 'We want to try to stir things up in Covington so the Confederates will be busy when we go over the river.'

'You gonna stir things up with the whites, too, or just with the blacks?' Cincinnatus asked.

'What business of yours is that?' the lieutenant colonel demanded in a voice like winter.

Cincinnatus scowled at him. When the Negro eyed Luther Bliss, he saw that the secret policeman understood what he was talking about. 'Just the niggers rise up,' he told the light colonel, 'you let the Freedom Party bastards put 'em down, an' *then* you move. I know how you work. You get the CSA to solve your nigger problem for you, and your own hands stay nice an' clean.'

The officer with the silver oak leaves on his shoulder straps gaped like a boated bream. Luther Bliss laughed. 'You see, Ray?' he said. 'He's nobody's fool. He didn't come to town on a load of turnips.'

Cincinnatus had come to town on, or at least with, a load of 105mm shells. 'You ain't got no white folks to rise up, I ain't talkin' 'bout no niggers.' His own accent came out more strongly with every sentence. 'They got enough troubles – they got too goddamn many troubles – without me givin' 'em mo'.'

'You are insubordinate,' the major growled.

'Bet your ass,' Cincinnatus said proudly.

'Tell him what's going on,' Luther Bliss advised. 'He won't blab. He never said anything to me that he shouldn't have, and I squeezed him, too.'

'Most irregular,' the lieutenant colonel – Ray – muttered. Reluctantly, he said, 'The unrest will involve members of both principal racial groupings in Covington.'

'He means whites and Negroes,' Luther Bliss put in.

'Why don't he say so, then?' Cincinnatus asked. Bliss laughed. The lieutenant colonel looked irate and indignant. Cincinnatus didn't care. If the man meant whites and Negroes, why did he have to hide it behind a bunch of fancy talk?

'You going to give us a hand?' Luther Bliss asked. 'This'll happen with you or without you. It may work a little better, kill more of the right people and not so many of the wrong ones, if you give us a hand. How does that sound?'

'Sounds like the best deal I'm gonna get,' Cincinnatus said. He talked about the Red network centered on Lucullus Wood's barbecue shack. Bliss already knew a lot about that; he'd dealt with Lucullus himself. Cincinnatus also talked about the probable Confederate informers at the Brass Monkey, a saloon not far from his father's house. He told the Intelligence officers everything he knew, and he hoped to heaven that it did some good.

V

With a theatrical flourish, Brigadier General John Wade pinned a Silver Star on Michael Pound's chest. Then he pinned a small gold bar onto each shoulder strap on Pound's new shirt. The division commander stuck out his hand. 'Congratulations, Lieutenant Pound!' he said warmly. A flashbulb flared as a photographer immortalized the moment.

'Thank you, sir.' Pound feared he sounded as enthusiastic as he felt. He didn't want to be an officer. He'd also done things a lot more dangerous than the ones that got him this medal. Nobody'd paid any attention to them, though. This time, the wounded Lieutenant Griffiths went on and on in writing about what a wonderful fellow he was. And so . . . He had the decoration, which he didn't mind, and the promotion, which he did.

'You'll have a platoon of barrels,' General Wade said. 'I'm sure you'll fight them as bravely and effectively as you fought your own machine after the commander got hurt.'

'I'll do my best, sir.' Pound liked giving orders only a little better than he liked taking them. The other four barrel commanders in the platoon would be sergeants who didn't want to hear from a lousy second lieutenant, even if Pound wasn't your everyday shavetail. Getting them to pay attention to him would be a pain in the neck, or probably points south of the neck.

But then Wade said, 'Because of your excellent service

and your long experience, Lieutenant, we'll give you a platoon of the Mark III machines. These are some of the first ones we have, just down from the factories in Michigan.'

Suddenly, Michael Pound didn't mind the promotion. He didn't mind the prospect of giving orders to sergeants who didn't want to take them. He didn't mind a thing. He tore off a salute that would have turned a drill sergeant green with envy. 'Thank you very much, sir!' he exclaimed. 'Are they here? Can I see them?' He'd heard about the new machines, but he had yet to set eyes on them.

Brigadier General Wade smiled. He was somewhere close to Pound's age, with a chestful of medals and service ribbons – and with a scar on his face and a finger missing from his left hand that said he'd really and truly earned his decorations. 'I know enthusiasm when I hear it, Lieutenant,' he said. 'Why don't you come with me?'

'Sir, I'd follow you anywhere,' Pound said, and John Wade laughed.

Hamilton, Ohio, was an industrial town of about 50,000 people, maybe a third of the way from Cincinnati up to Dayton. It sat in a bowl of hills on both sides of the Great Miami River. The west side of town was the nice side, or had been before the Confederates made a stand there. Wade had formally commissioned Pound in the Soldiers, Sailors, and Pioneers Memorial Building, a two-story structure of limestone blocks that housed a museum dedicated to U.S. wars. Two cannon from old Fort Hamilton stood in front of the building; the names of the men from Hamilton who'd served in the Mexican War, the War of Secession, the Second Mexican War, and the Great War were carved into the walls.

Now some new military hardware had joined those late-eighteenth-century guns. Michael Pound eyed the sleek lines of the new barrels with as much admiration as he would have given those of Daisy June Lee, even if of a slightly different sort. The armor on the green-gray machines – splotched here and there with darker green to help break up their outlines – was as well sloped as anything the Confederates had ever built. And that long 3½-inch gun would make any C.S. barrel, including the enemy's latest and greatest, say uncle.

Brigadier General Wade looked as proud of the new barrels as if he'd designed them himself. 'Well, Lieutenant,' he said genially, 'what do you think?'

Pound knew what he was supposed to say. He was supposed to burble on about how wonderful the new barrels were and what a howling wilderness they would make of the Confederate States. If John Wade expected him to say things like that, it only went to show the general didn't know his newest and most junior officer very well.

'Sir, they're fine machines,' Pound said, and General Wade beamed – his new lieutenant was on the right track. Pound promptly proceeded to drive off it: 'I'd like them a lot better if we had them at the beginning of the war. And we could have, you know.'

General Wade's smile faded. 'That wouldn't have been easy,' he said, the geniality leaking out of his voice word by word. 'In fact, I doubt it would have been possible.'

'Oh, yes, it would, sir.' Pound didn't mind correcting an officer with a star on each shoulder strap – Wade was wrong, and anybody who was wrong needed correcting. (No wonder he went gray before making officer's rank himself.) He went on, 'We had everything we needed in place to build machines like this twenty years ago – and then we turned our backs on barrels, because they were too expensive and we probably wouldn't need them any more. If we'd just followed up, this is where we would have been going into the war, this or better.'

'And what makes you so sure of that, Lieutenant?' Brigadier General Wade asked unwisely.

'Sir, I was General Morrell's gunner at the Barrel Works in Fort Leavenworth – he was only a bird colonel back then, of course,' Pound answered. 'I remember the prototype he designed. It was just a one-off, in mild steel, but it pointed straight ahead to those machines. About the only thing missing was the sloped armor, and that would have come. Or if it didn't, we would have built thicker instead and used a stronger engine to haul around the extra weight.'

'I . . . see,' Wade said in slightly strangled tones. Officers often used those tones when talking to or about Michael Pound. Wade aimed a forefinger at him. 'If you were there then, Lieutenant, why in God's name aren't you a major or a colonel by now?'

'I liked being a noncom.' Pound spread his hands, as if to say, *There! Isn't that simple?* 'I've turned down more promotions than you can shake a stick at. If you gave me any chance to do it, I would have turned this one down, too.'

'My God,' John Wade muttered. He'd never even dreamt of turning down a promotion. No one who aspired to high rank ever did. 'Didn't you ever want to use your expertise on a wider scale?'

'My expertise is barrel gunnery, sir – and everything that has to do with keeping a barrel running, too, but anybody who's been in barrels a while gets good at that,' Pound said. 'But I can only shoot one cannon at a time, and the gun doesn't care whether I'm a sergeant or an officer. Besides, now that I'm going to be commanding a platoon, I won't get the chance to do my own shooting any more.'

'My God,' Wade said again. 'You're an unusual man, Lieutenant. Don't let anyone tell you any different.'

'I'll shoot the next so-and-so who tries,' Pound agreed, which only seemed to fluster the division commander more.

He went on, 'When do we go into Kentucky and start chewing up the Confederates? Soon, I hope, so they don't have much time to strengthen their defenses. We push southeast, maybe we can cut *them* in half.'

If General Wade gaped before, he downright goggled now. Pound had seen that expression on officers' faces before. They often didn't believe men in the ranks – or, in his case, just up from the ranks – could think on their own. Wade managed a ragged laugh. 'I put bars on your shoulders, and you think you're ready for the General Staff.'

'Oh, no, sir.' That might have sounded suitably modest had Pound left it there. But he didn't: 'I was wondering about this when I was still a sergeant. As long as we've got the initiative, we need to use it. Jake Featherston is the world's biggest son of a bitch, but he understands that. Do we?'

John Wade gave him a wry grin. 'If I tell you that, I tell you things I haven't told some members of my own staff. You tend to your knitting there, and I'll tend to mine. I don't think you'll end up disappointed.'

Michael Pound ended up disappointed with most of what his superiors did. Even he could see that saying so wouldn't win him any points. And he did have new knitting to tend to. He saluted and said, 'Yes, sir.' This time, Wade's smile wasn't wry. Pound smiled, too, if only to himself. Yes, they always liked that.

But the general wasn't wrong. Without waiting for permission, Pound started crawling all over the new barrel. He eyed the driver's seat and the bow gunner's spot next to it. Then he went into the turret. He sat in the gunner's seat, then got up from it with a sigh of real regret. Up till now, U.S. barrels were always outgunned. A U.S. machine's main armament could defeat a C.S. barrel most of the time (though taking on a new-model C.S. barrel's frontal armor with the 1½-inch gun on the oldest U.S. barrels was an invitation to suicide – you had to hit them from the flank to have any kind of chance). Now, though, he would have the advantage. *This* gun would penetrate enemy armor at ranges from which the Confederates couldn't hope to reply.

He shook his head. *He* wouldn't have the advantage. His gunner would. *He'd* be stuck telling other people what to do.

With another sigh, he sat down in the commander's seat. He stood up so he could look out of the cupola. Seeing what was going on mattered more than maybe anything else on the battlefield. Sometimes, though, you would get killed if you tried to look out. He closed the cupola's lid and peered through the built-in periscopes. The view wasn't nearly so good, but it wasn't hopeless, either.

This barrel happened to have a platoon commander's wireless set like the one he'd be using. He studied that with extra care. He would have to keep track of four machines besides his own. They would have to become extensions of his will, all working together to give the bastards in butternut a good kick in the teeth.

He frowned thoughtfully. He'd never tried anything like this before. Maybe officers earned their money after all.

He climbed out of the turret with a certain sense of relief. Brigadier General Wade eyed him with amusement. 'You're thorough,' Wade said.

'Sir, it's my neck,' Pound answered. Again, were he speaking to a less exalted personage, some other part of his anatomy would have occurred to him.

Yes, escaping the turret did bring relief with it. He felt as if he were leaving a platoon commander's responsibilities behind. Logically, that was nonsense, but logic and feelings had little to do with each other. He peered down through the engine louvers at the powerplant. 'Anything special I should know about the motor, sir?' he asked. 'Have they found any gremlins?'

'Some growing pains with the fuel pump, I've heard,' Wade answered. 'Engine seems fairly well behaved, though – it's a scaled-up model of the one we've been using in the older barrels.'

'I thought so from the look of it,' Pound said. 'Well, we'll see how it goes. How soon will we see how it goes?' One more probe couldn't hurt.

It also didn't help much. Chuckling, General Wade said, 'It won't be too long,' and Pound had to make what he could of that.

Armstrong Grimes still had his platoon. No eager young second lieutenant had come out of the repple-depple to take his place. He would have bet the replacement depot had no eager young second lieutenants. He was still very young himself, but not very eager. Nobody who'd been in Utah for a while was eager any more except the Mormons. They were getting pounded to bits a block at a time, but they had no give in them.

A commendation letter sat in Armstrong's file for capturing the corporal who turned out not to be a corporal. They'd promoted Yossel Reisen to sergeant for his part in that. Armstrong didn't flabble about not getting bumped up to staff sergeant. For one thing, he cared more about coming out in one piece than he did about rank. And, for another, getting promoted up to sergeant was pretty easy. Adding a rocker to your stripes wasn't.

His whole regiment was out of line for R and R, or what passed for R and R in Utah: real beds, food that didn't come out of cans, hot showers, and a perimeter far enough out to make it hard for the Mormons to snipe at you or drop mortar bombs on your head. No women, but there was an NCOs' club where Armstrong could buy beer. Rank did have its privileges. He enjoyed them while he could.

Now he couldn't any more. In a clean uniform, he trudged back up toward the fighting. The dirty, ragged, unshaven men coming south for R and R of their own eyed him and his comrades with the scorn veterans gave to anybody who looked new and raw. 'Does your mama know you're here?' one of them jeered – the oldest gibe in the world.

'Ah, fuck you,' answered one of the privates in Armstrong's platoon. It wasn't even a challenge – more an assertion that the man who'd spoken wasn't worth challenging.

The vet coming back understood that tone. 'Sorry, buddy,' he said. 'You didn't look like you'd been through it before.'

'Yeah, well, fuck you anyway,' the private said. This time, he did smile when he said it.

'Come on, keep moving,' Armstrong said. 'We've got so much to look forward to.'

'Funny,' Yossel said.

'Tell me about it,' Armstrong said. 'I'm gonna grow a long blue beard and join the Engels Brothers.' That made his buddy shut up. Armstrong could see the wheels going round in Yossel's head. He would be thinking that Armstrong had to know the Engels Brothers dyed their beards all the colors of the rainbow . . . didn't he? He would also be wondering how Armstrong intended to grow a blue beard. Since Armstrong was wondering the same thing himself, he let it go there.

As soon as they got into the outskirts of Salt Lake City, the sniping started. Armstrong swore as he hit the dirt. This was supposed to be territory the USA controlled. Civilians here were supposed to be disarmed. With Utah under martial law, the penalty for keeping firearms was death. So was the penalty for harboring Mormon fighters. No one seemed to worry about that.

After a few minutes and a burst of machine-gun fire, the sniping stopped. The soldiers got to their feet again and tramped on. 'Nice to be back at the same old stand, isn't it?' Armstrong said.

'Lovely.' Yossel Reisen modified the word with a participle that brought a sour smile to Armstrong's face.

The Mormons still held the military compound northeast of downtown Salt Lake City that the United States, with the tact that made the central government so beloved in Utah, called Fort Custer. Before becoming a national hero in the Second Mexican War, George Armstrong Custer hanged John Taylor – Brigham Young's successor – and several other prominent Mormons on the grounds of that fort. Afterwards, Custer said his biggest regret was not hanging Abe Lincoln, too.

U.S. artillery and aircraft pounded the Mormon garrison up there. The Mormons replied with mortars and screaming meemies and whatever else they could get their hands on.

A lieutenant led the platoon Armstrong and his men were replacing. The officer showed no particular surprise at briefing a noncom. 'A sergeant's got the other platoon in this company, too,' he said. 'Just dumb luck I haven't stopped anything myself.' A cigarette hung from the corner of his mouth. He looked beat to hell. But for the gold bars on his shoulders, he might have been a noncom, too.

Because he'd been through the mill, Armstrong gave him more respect than he would have otherwise. 'Hope you stay safe, sir,' he said. 'They got anything special up ahead of us I ought to know about? Places where they like to put mortars? Sniper spots? Infiltration routes?'

'Ha! You're no virgin, sure as hell,' the lieutenant said.

'Bet your ass,' Armstrong told him, and then, 'Uh, yes, sir.'

' "Bet your ass" will do fine.' The lieutenant laughed. 'Don't slip and say it back of the line, that's all, or it'll be *your* ass.' He pointed out the trouble spots on the other side of the line, and the places where U.S. soldiers had to keep their heads down if they didn't want to turn into sniper bait. And he added, 'Brigham's bastards have some kind of headquarters about half a mile ahead of us. That's what I figure, anyhow. More foot traffic up there' – he pointed – carefully – to show where – 'than anything else is likely to account for.'

'You put snipers on 'em?' Armstrong asked.

'Oh, hell, yes,' the lieutenant said. 'They're sneaky as snakes about it now, but the traffic won't go away.'

'Maybe some mortars'll shift 'em,' Armstrong said. 'Maybe they'll go away and be somebody else's headache. Hell, that'd do.' The lieutenant laughed again, for all the world as if he were kidding.

After the other platoon pulled back, Armstrong put his own snipers into some likely looking spots. He told them to pick off the first few Mormons they spotted. One of the snipers said, 'I got it, Sarge. You don't want those shitheels figuring we're a bunch of damn greenhorns.'

'Right the first time, Urban,' Armstrong answered. 'As soon as they know we know what the hell we're doing, they'll find somebody easier to pick on. Hell, I would.'

One of the Mormons took a shot at him as he left that nest. The bullet cracked past his head. He flattened out and crawled for a while after that. Yes, the guys on the other side were seeing what they were up against.

They tried a trench raid that night. Having acquired a nastily suspicious mind in the course of almost two years of fighting, Armstrong was waiting for it. He sited a couple of machine guns to cover the route he thought the enemy most likely to take, and he guessed right. The Mormons retreated as fast as they could – from the cries that rose, some of them were wounded. His platoon didn't lose a man.

They left him and his men severely alone for the next two days. That suited him fine, even if it did make him wonder what they were up to. He assumed they were up to something. They usually were.

On the third morning, a Mormon approached under flag of truce. Armstrong shouted for his men to stop shooting. One thing the Mormons didn't do was violate a cease-fire. They were scrupulous about that kind of thing. They always played fair, even if they played hard.

Armstrong stared at the Mormon. 'You!' he said.

'You!' the Mormon – a major – echoed. They'd met before. Armstrong had made him strip to his drawers to prove he wasn't a people bomb. The Mormons did their best to pay him back by turning him into a casualty. They didn't quite manage, but not for lack of effort. The officer went on, 'You'd better let me through this time.'

'Oh, yeah?' That automatically made Armstrong suspicious. 'How come?'

'Because—' The Mormon choked on his answer and had to try again: 'Because I'm coming to try to work out a surrender, that's why.' He looked like a man who badly, desperately, wanted to scream, *God damn it!* He didn't, though. In all too many ways, the Mormons were made of stern stuff.

'Oh, yeah?' In spite of himself, Armstrong didn't sound so hostile this time. The Mormon major's fury and frustration embittered his face as well as his voice.

'Yeah.' Again, the Mormon's fastidiousness seemed to

handicap him. 'If we don't, you people will murder all of us, the same as the Confederates are murdering their colored people.'

'Why should you piss and moan about Featherston's fuckers?' Armstrong said. 'You're in bed with 'em, for Christ's sake!'

He got a look full of hatred from the Mormon major. ' "The enemy of my enemy is my friend," ' the Mormon quoted. 'You ever hear that one? You people send guns to the Negroes. The Confederates give us a hand when they can. It evens out.'

'Oh, boy. It evens out,' Armstrong said in a hollow voice. 'How do we know you guys won't keep using people bombs even after you say you've given up?'

'Because we'll be hostages, that's how.' The Mormon major looked and sounded like death warmed over. 'How many of us will you murder every time anything like that happens? You'll set the number high – and you know it.'

'Like you won't deserve it,' Armstrong said.

'I don't have to dicker with you, and I thank God for that,' the Mormon said. 'Will you please pass me through to your officers? They're the ones who can say whether they'll let any of us live.'

Armstrong thought about making him strip again. He didn't do it this time. He wanted nothing more than getting out of Utah in one piece. A truce or a surrender or whatever you called it made that more likely. He did say, 'Come forward so I can pat you down. You still may be a people bomb.'

'Do whatever you think you need to,' the Mormon said. By itself, that went a long way toward convincing Armstrong he wasn't loaded with explosives. The man came up to him, lowered the white flag, and raised his hands. Armstrong frisked him and found the nothing he expected.

'Yeah, you're clean,' Armstrong said when he was satisfied. 'Come on with me. I'll take you back.'

'You're not gloating as much as I thought you would,' the Mormon major remarked.

'Sorry,' Armstrong said. 'I just want to get this over with so we can go on with the real war, you know what I mean?'

'Oh, sure,' the enemy officer said bitterly. 'We're just the sideshow, along with the trained ponies and the flea circus and the freaks.'

'You said it, pal – I didn't,' Armstrong replied. The Mormon gave him another dirty look. He ignored it.

He passed the Mormon major on to behind-the-line troops, then went back to his platoon. 'You think anything will come of it?' Yossel asked him.

'Beats me,' Armstrong said. 'Even if it does, are we ever gonna let up on these snakes again? Every time we try it, they give us one right in the nuts.'

'Be nice to get the hell out of Utah,' Yossel said wistfully.

'Yeah, and if they let us leave, you know where they'll ship our asses next?' Armstrong waited for Yossel to shake his head, then went on, 'Up to fucking Canada, that's where. We're good at putting down rebellions, so they'll give us another one.' Yossel, a look of horror on his face, flipped him the bird. Armstrong gave it right back. He knew how the War Department's mind worked – if you called that working.

Flora Blackford and Robert Taft glared at each other in the small conference room. The Congresswoman from New York and the Senator from Ohio were friends on a personal level. Though she was a Socialist and he a conservative Democrat, their views on prosecuting the war hadn't been very different. They hadn't been, but they were now.

'We have Jake Featherston to deal with,' Flora said. 'He's more important. We can worry about the Mormons later.'

'We've got them on the ropes now. We ought to finish them off,' Taft said. 'Then we won't have to worry about them later.'

'How do you aim to finish them?' Flora inquired. 'If you don't make peace when they ask for it, don't you have to kill them all?'

Taft gestured toward the front of Congressional Hall. Along with Confederate bombs from the air, it was also scarred by Mormon auto bombs and people bombs. 'Aren't they doing their best to kill us all, or as many of us as they can?' he said.

'But they can't, and we can,' she said. 'They're only trouble to us. We can destroy them. Isn't that reason enough not to?'

'How many bites do they get?' Robert Taft returned. 'Whenever we get in trouble with the Confederate States, the Mormons try to take advantage of it. They did it in the Second Mexican War. They did it in the Great War. If they just stayed quiet in Utah this time around and enjoyed being citizens again, nobody would have bothered them at all.'

' "Enjoyed being citizens again," ' Flora echoed. 'Do you think they might resent us a little for occupying them for twenty years?'

'Maybe,' Taft answered calmly. 'Do you think we might resent them a little bit for making us conquer the whole state of Utah house by house in the Great War? How many casualties did they cause? How many divisions did they tie down? And now they're doing it again. Do you think they can just walk away and say, "All right, we've had enough," and get off easy? Your nephew's there, isn't he? What does he say about that?'

'Yossel says he'd sooner fight the Confederates. That's the war that really counts,' Flora answered. He also said he worried about getting sent to Canada instead. She understood that. If a division showed it could put down one rebellion, wouldn't the War Department figure it was good at the job and ship it off to help put down another one?

'Even if the Mormons do surrender, or claim they're surrendering, how many troops will we have to leave behind in Utah to disarm them all and make sure they don't start fighting again as soon as our backs are turned?' Robert Taft asked. 'Just licking them isn't the only problem. We have to remind them that they're licked, and that they'll catch it even worse if they give us any more trouble. Even now, they're probably stashing guns and explosives as fast as they can.'

They probably were, too. She couldn't tell him he was wrong. But she said, 'If we say, "No, you can't surrender," what will they do? Fight till they're all dead. Send people bombs all over the country, and auto bombs, and poison gas if they can arrange that. They'll play Samson in the temple, except they won't be playing.'

Now Taft gave her an unhappy look, because that also seemed only too probable. 'You're saying we don't win even if we win, and they don't lose even if they lose.'

'Oh, they lose, all right,' Flora said. 'But so do we.'

'Maybe we ought to kill them all in that case,' Taft said.

Now Flora violently shook her head. 'No, Robert. I'm going to quote the New Testament at you, even if I am Jewish: "For what is a man profited, if he shall gain the whole world, and lose his soul?" You've seen the photos of those Confederate camp guards grinning while they hold their rifles and stand there on trenches full of dead Negroes. Do you want pictures like that with our soldiers in them?'

She waited. If Taft said yes, their cautious friendship was just one more war casualty. But he shook his head, too. 'No. Those photographs sicken me – almost as much for what massacres like that do to the guards as for what they do to the poor colored people. I don't want to murder the Mormons like that. But if they die in battle I won't shed many tears.'

'The question is, can we make real U.S. citizens out of the Mormons?' Flora said.

'We've been trying since before the War of Secession, and we haven't had much luck,' Taft said.

Almost two thousand years earlier, hadn't Roman senators and imperial officials in Palestine asked the same kind of questions about the Jews there? They didn't come up with any good answers. Discrimination and maltreatment sparked one Jewish revolt after another. The revolts sparked mass slaughter, plus more discrimination and maltreatment. Finally, the Romans ended up throwing most of the surviving Jews out of Palestine altogether.

Flora's head came up. 'I wonder if that would work here,' she murmured.

'If what would work here?' Robert Taft asked.

'Expelling the Mormons from Utah after they surrender,' Flora answered.

'Where would you put them if you did that?'

'Some place where they wouldn't make so much trouble.' Flora explained what she'd been thinking about her own people's past.

'Are they tied to Salt Lake City the way the Jews were to Jerusalem in days gone by?' Taft asked. 'I have to tell you, I don't know the answer to that. Does anyone? Somebody would probably be able to tell us. But where *would* you put them? In Houston, now that we have some of it back? Wouldn't they join the Confederates against us?

Would you send them up to Canada? Wouldn't they just stir up the Canucks? Aren't the Canucks stirred up enough already? Newfoundland? Wouldn't they start waving across the Atlantic to the British?'

Those were all good questions. Disagree with him or not, you judged Robert Taft a fool at your peril. Flora said, 'Maybe we could ship them to the Sandwich Islands. It looks like we'll be able to hold on to those now.'

'Wouldn't the Mormons yell for the Japanese?' Taft snorted laughter. 'And wouldn't they deserve each other?'

'Maybe we could keep them off the island with Honolulu and Pearl Harbor on it,' Flora said. 'The others don't matter so much to the military. What I'm thinking is that, if we get them out of Utah, we can search what they take with them. They wouldn't have years and years' worth of guns and ammunition and explosives squirreled away and hidden so well we couldn't find them.'

'They wouldn't when they left, no,' Taft agreed. 'How long would they need to start getting hold of them, though?'

'Twenty minutes – maybe half an hour if we take them all the way out to the Sandwich Islands,' Flora said. 'I know that, Robert. But we have to do *something* with those people, and I don't want to kill them all. I don't want to leave them in place, either. That's just asking for the whole thing to start all over again in another generation.'

'It won't if we keep an eye on them.' Robert Taft sighed and ran a hand over the bald crown of his head. He was a much slimmer man than his father, but William Howard Taft had kept his hair till his dying day. With another sigh, the Senator from Ohio went on, 'I don't suppose it's in the range of human nature to hold somebody down for much longer than a generation, is it? We couldn't even do it to the Confederates after the Great War.'

'Will we after this one?' Flora asked. 'If we don't, what

will they eventually do to us because we didn't?'

'Whatever they can, probably. We put off the evil day as long as we're able to, that's all,' Taft said.

'I suppose so.' Flora also supposed she sounded uneasy. If Taft knew about the U.S. project out in western Washington, he'd never given any sign of it. Flora didn't want to talk about the possibility of splitting atoms, or about the possibility of one bomb's being able to destroy a whole city. The Confederate States weren't so big a country as the United States. But they were plenty big enough to conceal a project like that.

If the Confederacy lost the war, that kind of project would also fall to pieces . . . wouldn't it? It would take lots of money and lots of equipment a beaten CSA wouldn't be able to afford or to hide. But the fastest way to go from a beaten country to one ready to stand on its own two feet again was to make a bomb like that.

'The Mormons.' She got back to the issue at hand. 'If we're not going to slaughter them all, we've got to accept their surrender. I don't see any other choice. Do you, really?'

'No-o-o.' Taft sounded most reluctant to accept his own conclusion, for which Flora could hardly blame him. 'But what *can* we do with them once we do?'

'Sit on them in Utah or sit on them somewhere else,' Flora said. 'Those are the only two things we can do. Which would you rather?'

'If we drive them out, we bring gentiles into Utah to take their place,' Taft said. 'That won't be easy or cheap, either.'

'Robert, from now on nothing this government does will be easy or cheap,' Flora said. Taft pursed his lips as if biting down on an unripe persimmon. Democrats hated letting the government spend money, except on guns. But he didn't contradict her. She went on, 'We have to worry about whether we do the right thing. Finding it won't always be easy, but we have to try.'

'Right now, nothing comes ahead of beating Jake Featherston,' Taft said. 'Nothing.'

'Well, I don't think you'll find many people in the USA to tell you you're wrong,' Flora said. 'I sure won't. He's a danger to us and he's a danger to his own country.' *And if he gets one of those uranium bombs, he's a danger to the whole world.* Again, she swallowed that worry. 'I don't like to speak ill of the dead, but you were right and Al Smith was wrong in 1940. We never should have allowed the plebiscites that gave Kentucky and Houston back to the CSA. Featherston uses the empty space in west Texas as a shield against us, and he used Kentucky as a springboard to attack us.'

'He said he was going to,' Taft said. 'He told us what he had in mind, and we didn't listen to him. It almost makes you think we deserve what's happened since. Aren't we paying for our own stupidity?'

'We're paying for our own decency,' Flora answered. 'It's not quite the same thing, or I hope it's not. And that brings us back to the Mormons, I'm afraid. Can we be right and decent at the same time?'

'If we don't wipe them off the face of the earth, if we do accept their surrender, how do we make sure we don't give them a chance to pay us back for letting them live?' Taft asked. 'That's what it comes down to.'

'Occupy the land they still hold. Disarm them as thoroughly as we can. Maybe ship them out of Utah; I don't know. Hostages for good behavior, I suppose.' Flora grimaced. She didn't like that. But she could see that it had a better chance of controlling the Mormons than a lot of other things did. Taft nodded at each suggestion. Then she said, 'Freedom of worship as long as they render unto

Caesar.' She laughed; she'd quoted the New Testament twice in the space of a few minutes.

'They'll use it as an excuse to take lots of wives. They'll use it as an excuse to get together and plot against us, too,' Taft said.

'We have to give them a carrot along with the stick,' Flora said. 'Otherwise, they'll just keep fighting. Wouldn't you, if you didn't get anything by quitting? And do you know what else? As long as all their marriages after the first one are unofficial, I'm sick of flabbling about them. Life is too short.'

Taft grumbled discontentedly. He was a straitlaced man. But when they discussed the surrender offer in the Joint Committee on the Conduct of the War, he didn't oppose her when she made the same proposal. She hoped that was a good sign.

From Pittsburgh to Cincinnati. In one way, Dr. Leonard O'Doull thought that was progress. When he'd labored in the hospital on the University of Pittsburgh campus, the Confederates still had a chance to break through, to run wild in the second year of the war as they did in the first.

That didn't – quite – happen. Now, after a hard winter and a rugged spring, the enemy was gone from U.S. soil east of the Mississippi. This summer, the United States would have the chance to show what they could do.

Granville McDougald summed up O'Doull's worries in one pithy sentence: 'How are we going to fuck it up this time?'

Even more than *To be or not to be?*, that was the question. The U.S. push toward Richmond had shown a lot of the ways not to fight a war. Daniel MacArthur seemed to do his best to acquaint the War Department with every single one of them. He hadn't come west to lead whatever the United States would do out here. That struck O'Doull as at least mildly encouraging.

But when he looked around at what was left of Cincinnati, when he thought about all the devastation between Pittsburgh and here, he came close to despairing. His church taught that despair was the one unforgivable sin, and he understood why, but it was hard to avoid anyway. 'Have we got enough left to do what we need to do?' he asked.

'Have the Confederates got enough left to stop us?' McDougald returned.

That was the other side of the coin, all right. Plainly, the Confederates had put everything they had into the invasion of Ohio and Pennsylvania. 'They aren't running up the white flag,' O'Doull said. The ruins of Cincinnati proved that, too. After sullenly pulling back across the Ohio – and after rescuing most of the force they had north of the river – Featherston's men started methodically shelling the Ohio city from emplacements in Kentucky. Their attitude seemed to be that if the United States wanted to use Cincinnati as a base from which to invade C.S. territory, they were welcome to try.

Most of the casualties U.S. doctors were treating came from artillery rounds. Bombs caused the rest; Confederate airplanes didn't come over every night, but they came whenever they could. U.S. bombers also did their best to smash up targets on the far side of the river.

'When do you think the balloon will go up?' McDougald asked. The hospital where they worked was painted white and had big Red Crosses on the walls and roof. O'Doull didn't think the Confederates shelled and bombed it on purpose. That didn't mean it didn't get hit every now and again. C.S. bombs and shells didn't have eyes; they couldn't see exactly where they were going.

O'Doull remembered other offensives in days and years gone by. 'When we've gathered everything together so there's no possible doubt about where we're going or what we're doing,' he answered. 'When we've given the Confederates all the time they need to get ready to knock us for a loop.'

McDougald raised an eyebrow toward the bald crown of his head. 'You're in a cheerful mood today, aren't you, Doc?'

'Well, hell, Granny, you asked,' O'Doull said. 'Tell me that's not how we usually do things.'

'Can't,' Granville McDougald admitted. 'Wish to God I could, but I damn well can't. Besides, it looks like we're filling Cincinnati up with everything under the sun so we can pop the Confederates in the nose.'

'Doesn't it just?' O'Doull said. 'And don't you suppose they've got a suspicion that we might want to cross the river here? Wouldn't you?'

'Not me. I've given up having suspicions. They end up getting confirmed, and then I'm unhappy,' the medic said. 'I don't like being unhappy. It makes me sad when I am.'

'Er – right,' O'Doull said. McDougald smiled back, calm as a cynical Buddha.

Before either one of them could go any further with it, they got called into an operating room. They had no room for a difference of opinion there. What needed doing was only too obvious: nothing any surgeon in the world could do would save an arm mangled like that one.

'Want to do the honors, Granny?' O'Doull said. 'I'll pass gas for you if you care to.'

'Sure, if you don't mind,' McDougald answered. 'A straight amputation I can manage, and he'll get the same result from me as he would from you. It's the complicated stuff where you've got an edge on me.'

To some degree, that was true. The degree was less than McDougald made it out to be. Scrupulously polite, the medic didn't pretend to have an M.D.'s skills. But he did have close to thirty years of experience at repairing wounded men. Plenty of doctors knew less than he did, and were more arrogant about what they did know.

O'Doull knew he was an amateur anesthetist himself. He'd knocked out patients back in Quebec before operating on them. He'd done it in the field, too, but he wasn't all that confident in his own skills.

Here, though, everything was straightforward. As soon as the man went out, McDougald got to work with scalpel and bone saw, taking the mangled arm off above the elbow. He tied off bleeders one after another, closed the dreadful wound, and sighed. 'Whatever that poor guy was, he won't be when he wakes up.'

'Maybe he was left-handed,' O'Doull said.

'Mm – maybe.' McDougald was a lefty himself. 'Odds are long, though. And even if a one-armed man has his good arm, he's still got a hard road in front of him.'

'Better than dying,' O'Doull said.

'I suppose you're right. I never once heard a dead man say he'd rather be the way he was than short an arm,' McDougald said.

'You never . . .' O'Doull's voice trailed away as he worked through the possibilities in that. 'How many dead people do you usually talk with?'

'Oh, not that many,' Granville McDougald said. 'Harder than anything getting a straight answer out of 'em.'

'I believe you,' O'Doull said. 'Have you noticed it's pretty damn hard getting a straight answer out of you, too?'

'Out of me? Nah.' McDougald shook his head. 'I'm as transparent as glass. The only problem with that is, too many of our people are as breakable as glass, which isn't so good.'

He could spin out nonsense, or sometimes stuff that seemed like nonsense but wasn't, faster than O'Doull could pin him down on it. O'Doull mostly didn't try; only the sheer outrageousness of the medic's latest effort pulled a protest out of him.

Before he could do any more squawking, an officer who pretty plainly wasn't a doctor came into the O.R. 'Major O'Doull?' the stranger asked. When O'Doull admitted he was himself, the newcomer said, 'I'm Vic Hodding. I'm a captain in Intelligence.'

Granny McDougald let out a soft snort. Above Hodding's surgical mask, his cat-green eyes swung toward the medic. McDougald blandly stared back. Nobody could prove a thing, even if the editorial message came through loud and clear. 'Well, Captain, what can I do for you?' O'Doull asked, wondering if he really wanted to know.

'We've got a wounded man we brought back from the other side of the Ohio,' Hodding replied. 'He knows some things we really need to find out. What are the drugs that would help pull them out of him?'

'Rack and thumbscrews often work wonders,' McDougald said, hardly bothering to hide his scorn.

Hodding glanced toward him again. 'Who is this man?' he inquired of O'Doull with a certain dangerous formality.

'Never mind,' O'Doull answered. 'If you need help from me, you don't need to know. And if you don't need help from me, I'll be damned if I tell you. And I'll do everything I know how to do to stop you from making trouble for him.'

Captain Hodding took that more calmly than O'Doull expected – more calmly than he would have himself, he thought. 'He must be good at what he does,' the

Intelligence officer remarked. O'Doull said nothing. Hodding went on, 'Anyway, we need answers from this guy. Strongarm stuff may just get us lies – and besides, we don't like to do it, no matter what Mr. High And Mighty there says. What goes around comes around, and the Confederates are too likely to pay us back if we get rough.'

O'Doull could see what Granny McDougald was thinking. *So then they pay us back with needles instead. Oh, boy.* But needles were less likely to wreck a man for life than some of the other things interrogators did.

'What do you think this guy knows?' O'Doull asked. Vic Hodding stood mute. O'Doull made an impatient noise. 'Look, I'm going to be there while you're questioning him, right? So what the hell are you flabbling about? You don't want me there, go find some other guy to do this for you.'

After some thought and an apparent wrestle with himself, Hodding nodded. 'Yeah, you're right, Doc. You have need-to-know.' The way he brought out the phrase would have told O'Doull he was in Intelligence even without any other evidence. He continued, 'We infiltrated some people down south of the river and extracted this guy. What he doesn't know about their trains and trucks in Kentucky and Tennessee isn't worth knowing. We should have got him out clean, but he put up more of a fight than we figured.' He shrugged. 'These things happen.'

'In films, the guy always has the secret for the new poison gas,' O'Doull said.

'Yeah, and the blonde with the big boobs teases it out of him, and he loves every minute of it,' Hodding said. 'Doctors in films never treat ringworm, either. But if the Confederates have trouble moving supplies, that makes our life a hell of a lot easier.'

He wasn't wrong. Granville McDougald murmured, 'Pentothal?'

O'Doull nodded. 'Best chance I've got.' He turned to the Intelligence officer. 'Sodium pentothal may make him not care so much about what he says. Or it may not. Drugging a guy and making him spill his guts is another one of those things that work better in films.'

'All right. Do what you can,' Hodding said. 'He's likelier to blab with the stuff in him than without it, right?' O'Doull nodded again – that was true, and didn't commit him to anything. Captain Hodding gestured toward the door. 'Come on, then.'

The Confederate officer was wounded in the leg and shoulder. He glared at O'Doull. 'I am Travis W.W. Oliphant, colonel, C.S. Army.' He gave his pay number.

'Pleased to meet you, Colonel. I'm Major O'Doull. I'm a doctor, and I'm going to give you something to make you feel a little better,' O'Doull said. Colonel Oliphant looked suspicious, but he didn't try to fight as O'Doull injected him.

After a little while, the Confederate said, 'I *do* feel easier.' Pentothal sneaked up on you. It didn't make your troubles go away, but it did mean you weren't likely to remember them once you came out from under it.

Captain Hodding started questioning Oliphant. The logistics specialist didn't seem to worry about what he said. A lot that came out was drivel, but enough wasn't to keep Hodding scribbling notes. O'Doull gave the colonel more pentothal. Too much and he'd stop making sense altogether. Not enough and he'd clam up. O'Doull found what seemed the right dosage by experiment.

'Thanks, Major,' Hodding said when Colonel Oliphant ran dry. 'I think you helped.'

'Well, good,' O'Doull answered, and wondered if it was.

Would he want to look in a mirror the next time he passed one?

Instead of going off to the peaceful, even bucolic campus of Washington University, Clarence Potter summoned Professor Henderson V. FitzBelmont to Richmond. Potter wanted the nuclear physicist to see what the war was doing to the capital of the CSA. Maybe then FitzBelmont wouldn't think of his experiments as abstractions that could move along at their own pace. Maybe.

If some Florida cinema studio needed a professor out of central casting, it could do much worse than Henderson FitzBelmont. He was tweedy. He was bespectacled. Clarence Potter wore eyeglasses, too, and had since he was a young man. But he didn't look perpetually surprised at the world around him the way Professor FitzBelmont did.

He met the physicist in Capitol Square, across Ninth Street from the War Department. The bench on which he waited was the one where he and Nathan Bedford Forrest III hadn't quite plotted against Jake Featherston. It gave a fine view of the bombed-out ruins of the Capitol, of the craters whose dirt sported new grass and even flowers as spring advanced, and of the sandbagged statues of George Washington and Albert Sidney Johnston. If you looked around, you could see more of what almost two years of Yankee air raids had done to Richmond.

Professor FitzBelmont came into Capitol Square at two o'clock, just when Potter asked him to. Potter stood up and waved. He kept waving till FitzBelmont spotted him. A look of relief on his face, the professor waved back and picked his way over the battered ground to the bench.

'Hello, uh, General,' FitzBelmont said, sticking out a hand.

'Professor.' Potter shook hands. Henderson FitzBelmont did have a respectable grip. Potter gestured to the bench. 'Have a seat. We've got some things to talk about.'

'All right.' Professor FitzBelmont looked around. 'I must say I've seen views that inspired me more.'

'You surprise me,' Potter said.

'I do? Why?' the physicist said. 'It's dreary, it's battered, it's sad – I can't think of one good thing to say about it.'

'That's *why* it ought to inspire you,' Potter said. Behind the lenses of his spectacles, Henderson V. FitzBelmont blinked. Potter went on, 'It shows you that your country's in trouble. If any one man can get us out of trouble, you're him. If we have uranium bombs, we win. It's that simple.'

'Mr. Potter—' FitzBelmont began.

'General Potter, please,' Potter broke in. He saw the faint scorn the other man didn't have the sense to hide. Nettled, he did his best to explain: 'It means as much to me as *Professor* does to you, and I had to go through a lot to earn it – not the same kinds of things you did, but a lot.'

Henderson FitzBelmont weighed that. He evidently didn't find it wanting, for he nodded. 'I'm sorry, *General* Potter. I'll remember from now on. You must understand, we are doing everything we know how to do to make a uranium bomb. One of the things we're finding out, unfortunately, is how much we don't know how to do. When you go through unexplored territory, that happens. I wish it didn't, but it does.'

He was calm, sensible, rational. Clarence Potter had no doubt that made him a splendid scientist. It didn't help a country at war, a country fighting for its life, a country whose fight for its life wasn't going any too well. 'How do we go faster?' Potter asked. 'Whatever you need, you'll get. President Featherston has made that very clear.'

'Yes, I certainly can't complain about the support I'm

getting, especially after the . . . sad events in Pittsburgh,'
FitzBelmont said – maybe he did own something resem-
bling discretion after all. But then he went on, 'What this
project needs most of all is *time*. If you can give me back
all the months when the President believed it a foolish waste
of money and effort, we will be better off; I guarantee you
that.'

So there, Potter thought. 'You're the physicist,' he said.
'If you can undo that . . . Hell, if you can do that, forget
about the uranium bomb.'

'Time travel is for the pulp magazines, I'm afraid,'
FitzBelmont said. 'No evidence that it's possible, and plenty
that it isn't. The bomb, on the other hand, is definitely possible – and definitely difficult, too.'

'I remember your saying before that working with uranium hexafluoride was giving you fits,' Potter said. 'Are you
doing better with that now?'

'Somewhat,' FitzBelmont answered. The physicist didn't
blink when Potter got *hexafluoride* out without stumbling.
He chose to take that as a mild compliment. Henderson
FitzBelmont continued, 'We've come up with some new
chemicals – fluorocarbons, we're calling them – that the
uranium hexafluoride doesn't attack. Nothing else seems
to, either. They'll have all kinds of peacetime uses – I'm
sure of it. For now, though, they give us much better control over the UF_6.'

UF_6? Potter wondered. Then he realized it was another
way to say *uranium hexafluoride*. If he weren't used to
hearing CO_2 for *carbon dioxide*, he would have been baf-
fled. 'All right,' he said after a pause he hoped FitzBelmont
didn't notice. 'So you've got better control over it. What
does that mean?'

'It puts fewer people in the hospital. It doesn't eat
through so much lab apparatus. Those are good starting

points,' FitzBelmont said, and Potter could hardly tell him he was wrong. 'Now we actually have a chance to separate the UF_6 with the U-235 from the UF_6 with the U-238.'

'You haven't done that yet?' Potter said in dismay.

'It's not easy. The two isotopes are chemically identical,' FitzBelmont reminded him. 'We can't add, say, bicarbonate of soda and have it do something with one and not with the other. It won't work. The difference in weight between the two molecules is just under one percent. That's what we've got to take advantage of – if we can.'

'And?' Potter said.

'So far, we seem to be having the most luck with centrifuges,' Henderson FitzBelmont said. 'The degree of enrichment each treatment gives is small, but it's real. And the centrifuges we're using now are a lot stronger than the ones we had when we started. They need to be – the old ones aren't worth much, not for this kind of research.'

'And when you treat the slightly enriched, uh, UF_6, you get slightly more enriched UF_6? Is that right?' Potter asked.

'It's exactly right!' By the way FitzBelmont beamed, he'd just got an A on his midterm. 'After enough steps, we do expect to achieve some very significant enrichment.'

'How far away from a bomb are you?' Potter asked bluntly.

'Well, I won't *know* till we get closer,' Professor FitzBelmont said. Potter made an impatient noise. Hastily, the physicist continued, 'If I had to guess, I'd say we're two years away, assuming everything goes perfectly. Since it won't – it never does – two and a half years, maybe three, seems a better guess.'

'So we wouldn't have this till . . . late 1945, maybe 1946?' Potter shook his head. 'We need it sooner than that, Professor. We need it a hell of a lot sooner than that.' All those months Jake Featherston wasted were coming back to haunt the CSA. The damnyankees sure didn't waste any time when they realized a uranium bomb was possible. Which raised another question . . . 'How soon will the United States get one of these things?'

'You'd do better asking someone in Philadelphia,' FitzBelmont said. Clarence Potter made another wordless noise, this one full of frustration. He was doing his best to spy on the U.S. uranium-bomb project, without much luck. Yankee authorities were holding their cards so close to their chest, they were almost inside their ribs. FitzBelmont added, 'You can do something about when the United States get theirs, you know.'

'How's that again?' Full of his own gloom, Potter listened to FitzBelmont with half an ear. Jake Featherston was going to come down on him like a thousand-pound bomb. Featherston wouldn't blame himself for stalling the Confederate project. He never blamed himself for anything. But the Confederacy couldn't afford the late start. The United States had more scientists and more resources. They had enough left over that they could afford mistakes. Everything had to go right to give the CSA a decent chance to win. For a while, it had. For a while . . .

'You can delay the U.S. bomb, General,' Henderson V. FitzBelmont said. 'If you damage or destroy the facility where the Yankees are working on it, you'll make them deal with what you've done instead of going forward on their own work.'

He wasn't wrong. He wasn't even slightly wrong. 'Son of a bitch,' Potter muttered. The U.S. project was hard for the CSA to reach – way the hell out there in Washington State. *Where there's a will, there's a lawyer,* he thought bemusedly. The Confederates could figure out how to attack it if they needed to badly enough. The way things looked now, they did.

Potter shook his head. He'd seen the race to the uranium

bomb as just that: a race. If the United States started out ahead and ran faster anyhow, what would happen? They'd get to the finish line first. And when they did, Richmond would go up in heat like the center of the sun, and that would be the end of that.

But it wasn't just a race. It was a war. In a race, you'd get disqualified if you tripped the other guy and threw sand in his eyes. In a war, you might buy yourself the time you needed to catch up and go ahead.

This time, Clarence Potter grabbed FitzBelmont's hand and pumped it up and down. 'Professor, I'm damn glad I called you into Richmond,' he said. '*Damn* glad!'

'Good,' the physicist said. 'As for me, I look forward to returning to my work. As long as I'm here, can I ask you send me, oh, five skilled workers? We're desperately short of them, and it seems next to impossible to pry the kind of people we need out of war plants.'

'You'll have 'em, by God,' Potter promised. 'Can you tell me who told you no? Whoever it is, he'll be sorry he was ever born.' Grim anticipation filled his voice.

FitzBelmont reached into the inside pocket of his herringbone jacket. 'I have a list right here. . . . No, this is a list of some of the things my wife wants me to shop for while I'm in Richmond.' He frowned, then reached into the other inside pocket. 'Ah, here we are.' He handed Potter the list he needed.

'I'll take care of these folks, Professor. They'll find out what *priority* means. You can count on that.' Potter carefully put the list in his wallet. He even more carefully refrained from mentioning, or so much as thinking about, how well FitzBelmont played the role of an absent-minded professor.

'Thank you, General. Are we finished?' FitzBelmont asked. When Potter nodded, the physicist got to his feet.

He looked around at Capitol Square, sighed, and shook his head. He started off, then stopped and looked back. 'Uh, freedom!'

'Freedom!' Potter hated the slogan, but that didn't matter. In Jake Featherston's CSA, not responding was inconceivable.

Henderson V. FitzBelmont walked north, toward Ford's Hotel. Under one name or another, the hotel had stood across the street from Capitol Square since before the War of Secession. Watching the physicist go, Clarence Potter sighed. Anne Colleton always stayed at Ford's when she came up to Richmond. Potter had stayed there himself, too, but his thoughts were on the South Carolina woman he'd . . . loved?

He nodded. No other word for it, even if it was a cross-grained, jagged kind of love, and one much marred by politics. She'd backed Jake Featherston when the Freedom Party was only a little cloud on the horizon. Potter laughed. He'd never leaned that way himself. He still didn't, come to that.

But now Anne was dead, killed in a Yankee air raid on Charleston. One of her brothers got gassed by the Yankees in the Great War, and was murdered at the start of the Red Negro uprising. The other went into Pittsburgh. Tom Colleton wasn't listed as a POW, so he was probably dead. A whole family destroyed by the USA.

'We need that bomb,' Potter murmured. 'Jesus, do we ever.'

'Wow!' George Enos said as the *Townsend* approached San Diego harbor. 'The mainland! I wondered if I'd ever see it again.'

'I'll kiss the pier when we get off the ship,' Fremont Dalby said. The gun chief added, 'Too goddamn many times when I didn't just wonder if I'd see it again – I was fucking sure I wouldn't.'

He'd been in the Navy since . . . Well, not quite since steam replaced sail, but one hell of a long time. He could say something like that without worrying that people might think he was yellow. George couldn't, which didn't mean the same thought hadn't gone through his mind.

Dalby nudged him. 'You can hop a train, go on back to Boston, see the wife and kiddies. All you need is a couple-three weeks of liberty, right?' He laughed and laughed.

'Funny,' George said. 'Funny like a broken leg.' Nobody was going to get liberty like that. The brass might dole out twenty-four- and forty-eight-hour passes, enough to let sailors from the destroyer sample San Diego's bars and brothels and tattoo parlors and other dockside attractions. George had never been here in his life, but he was sure they'd be the same as the dives in Boston and Honolulu. Sailors were the same here, weren't they? As long as they were, the attractions would be, too.

'Hey, nobody's shooting at us for a little bit,' Fritz Gustafson said. 'I'll take that.' From the loader, it was quite a speech.

'For a while, yeah,' Dalby agreed. 'Wonder where we'll go after they fuel us and get us more ammo and all that good shit? Probably down south against the Mexicans and the Confederates, I guess.'

That sounded like nasty, unpleasant, dangerous work to George. He'd seen enough nasty, unpleasant, dangerous work already. 'Maybe they'll send us up off the Canadian coast, so we can keep the Japs from running guns to the Canucks.'

'Dream on,' Dalby said. 'Fuck, if they send us up there, they'll probably send us to whatever the hell the name of that other place is – you know, with the Russians.'

'Alaska,' Gustafson said.

The CPO nodded. 'There you go. That's it. Nothing but emperors for us. We've been messing with the Mikado's boys for too long. Now we can tangle with the Tsar. And the seas up there are worse than the North Atlantic.'

George started to say that was impossible. He knew the North Atlantic well, and knew how bad it could get. But he'd also rounded Cape Horn. That was worse. Maybe the Pacific was godawful up in the polar-bear country, too.

'Russians hardly give a damn about Alaska anyway,' Fritz Gustafson said.

'Well, Jesus, would you?' Dalby said. 'It's more Siberia. They've got enough Siberia already. If somebody ever found gold in it or something, you'd have to remember it was there. Till then? Shit, who cares?'

San Diego wasn't Honolulu. The weather wasn't quite perfect. It got cooler at night than it did in the Sandwich Islands. It was just very good. To somebody who'd grown up in Boston, that would do fine.

George sent a telegram to Connie, letting her and the boys know he was all right. The clerk at the Western Union office said, 'It may take a while to get there, sir. We still don't have as many lines as we'd like to carry east-west traffic.' The man, who was more than old enough to be George's father, held up a hand when he saw him start to get mad. 'Don't blame me, sir. I don't have anything to do with it. I'm just telling you how things are. You got to blame somebody, go and blame Jake Featherston.'

Everybody in the USA had good cause to blame Jake Featherston for something or other. A telegram delayed was small change. Ohio's being torn to pieces badly enough to delay the telegram was rather larger. George didn't dwell on Ohio. The telegram ticked him off. Like politics, grievances were personal.

Sure enough, he got a twenty-four-hour liberty. He wished it were forty-eight, but anything was better than nothing. With the rest of the 40mm gun crew, he drank and roistered and got his ashes hauled. He felt bad about that afterwards – what was he doing going to bed with a whore with saggy tits right after sending his wife a wire? He felt bad afterwards, but it felt great while it was happening . . . and that was what he was doing lying down with the chippy.

He also got a tattoo on his left biceps – a big anchor. That didn't feel good while it was happening, even though he was drunk. But Fritz Gustafson was getting a naked woman on his right biceps, so George sat still for it. He wasn't about to flinch in front of his buddy. Only later did he wonder if Fritz took the pricking in silence because *he* was there getting tattooed, too.

His arm felt worse the next morning. He wasn't drunk then; he was hungover. All of him felt worse, but his arm especially. 'It'll get easier in a day or two,' Fremont Dalby said. That was rough sympathy, not hardheartedness: Dalby had ornaments on both arms and a small tiger on his right buttock.

He turned out to know what he was talking about. By the time the *Townsend* sailed a week later, George almost forgot about the tattoo except when he looked down and saw the blue marks under his skin. He also liked Gustafson's ornament, but Connie would clout him if he came home with a floozy on his arm. Fritz was a bachelor, and could get away with stuff like that.

The *Townsend* sailed south, toward the not very distant border with the Empire of Mexico. She was part of a flotilla that included three more destroyers, two light cruisers, a heavy cruiser, and two escort carriers. The baby flattops were just like the ones that helped make sure the Japs wouldn't take the Sandwich Islands away from the USA. They were built on freighter hulls, and had a freighter's engines inside. Going flat out, they could make eighteen knots. But each one carried thirty airplanes. That gave them ten or twenty times the reach of even the heavy cruiser's guns.

Although the flotilla stood well out to sea, it wasn't very long before Y-ranging gear picked up a couple of airplanes outbound from Baja California to look things over. 'Goddamn Mexicans,' Dalby said as George ran up to the antiaircraft gun.

'What did you expect, a big kiss?' George asked.

Dalby told him what Francisco José could kiss, and why. The CPO might have embroidered on that theme for quite a while, but Fritz Gustafson said, 'Next to what the Japs threw at us, this is all chickenshit. Take an even strain.'

Fighters roared east off the flight decks of the *Monitor* and the *Bonhomme Richard*. They came back in less than half an hour. A couple of them waggled their wings as they flew over the carriers' escorts. No Mexican airplanes appeared over the flotilla.

'Score one – I mean two – for the good guys,' George said.

'Yeah.' Fremont Dalby nodded. 'But now the greasers will start screaming to the Confederates. Gotta figure we're in business to yank Jake Featherston's tail feathers, anyway. So pretty soon we'll be playing against the first team.'

'Confederates don't have any carriers in Guaymas,' George said.

'No, but they've got land-based air, and they've got subs, and who knows what all shit they *do* have in the Gulf of California?' Dalby said. 'I guess that's what we're doing – finding out what kind of shit they've got there.'

'Such a thing as finding out the hard way,' George said.

When the flotilla got near the southern end of Baja California, bombers and fighter escorts left the escort carriers' decks to pummel the Mexican installations at Cabo San Lucas. Scuttlebutt said the installations weren't just Mexican but also Confederate. George wouldn't have been surprised. Cabo San Lucas warded the Gulf of California, which led to Confederate Sonora. And the place was isolated enough – which was putting it mildly – to keep word of Confederate soldiers doing Mexicans' jobs from spreading too far or too fast.

Cabo San Lucas lay at about the same latitude as Honolulu. Even lying well offshore, the *Townsend* got much hotter weather than she did in the Sandwich Islands. George wondered why. Maybe the North American continent screwed up the winds or something. That was all he could think of.

Then he stopped worrying about the weather. 'Now hear this! Now hear this!' the loudspeakers blared. 'We have two damaged aircraft returning from the raid on the Mexicans. They will come as far as they can before ditching, and we are going to go out after them. We don't want to strand anybody if we can help it.'

'Roger that!' George exclaimed. He imagined floating in a life raft, or maybe just in a life jacket, praying somebody would pluck him out of the Pacific before the sharks or the glaring sun did him in. He shuddered. It was worse than going into the drink after your ship sank, because you'd be all alone out there.

The *Townsend,* two other destroyers, and a light cruiser peeled off and raced toward the Mexican coast. Up there in the sky, the pilots would be nursing everything they could from their shot-up airplanes. Every mile west they made bumped up their chances of getting rescued.

A swarm of intact aircraft flew over the ships. They were

heading home to the carriers. Their pilots had to be thanking God they could get home. Then George spotted a dive bomber low in the sky and trailing smoke. Even as he watched, the airplane went into the Pacific. The pilot put it down as well as anybody could hope to. It skidded across the surface – it didn't nose in.

Did he ditch well enough? Only one way to find out. The *Townsend* was closer to the downed airplane than any of the other ships. She sped toward where it went down. By the time she got there, the dive bomber had already sunk. But George joined in the cheers on deck: an inflatable life raft bobbed in the blue, blue water. Two men crouched inside. A third, in a life jacket, floated nearby. They all waved frantically. One of them fired a flare pistol, though daylight overwhelmed the red glow.

Lines with life rings attached flew over the ship's side. The downed fliers put them on. Eager sailors hauled the men up on deck. 'God bless you guys,' said the one whom George helped rescue. 'You're prettier than my wife right now.'

He had a nasty cut over one eye and burns on his face and hands. All things considered, he was lucky. The fellow who wore the life jacket couldn't stand. 'Broken leg,' somebody by him said. 'Get him down to sick bay.'

'I don't mind,' the injured man said as they laid him on a stretcher. 'I figured I'd be holding a lily. But Jack there, he did a fuck of a job.'

'I hear somebody else was in trouble, too,' said the flier with the cuts and burns – Jack? 'I hope some of you sailor fellows find him, too.'

'We'll look for him, pal. That's what we're here for,' a sailor said. 'Ought to get you down to sick bay, too. I bet you need stitches.'

'For what?' Jack didn't even seem to know he was hurt. They took him below anyway.

A fighter was flying slow circles over where the other airplane went down, about forty miles east of the *Townsend*'s rescue. But all the destroyers and cruiser found when they got there was an oil slick and a little floating wreckage – no sign of the crew.

'Too bad,' George said.

'Can't win 'em all,' Fremont Dalby said. 'We broke even. Way things usually work out, that puts us ahead of the game.'

'I guess,' George said. The rescued men were here, yes. But the poor bastards who didn't make it out of their airplane . . . They didn't break even. They lost. Breaking even only mattered if you were on the outside.

VI

Jefferson Pinkard watched Confederate soldiers set up antiaircraft guns around Camp Determination. He went over to the major in charge of the job, an officer named Webb Wyatt. 'How much good d'you reckon this'll do?' he asked.

Wyatt shifted a chaw from one cheek to the other and spat a stream of tobacco juice much too close to Pinkard's highly polished boots. 'Well, I'll tell you,' he drawled. 'It's a hell of a lot better'n not doing anything.'

'Than not doing anything, *sir*,' Pinkard snapped.

The major in butternut looked him up and down. He was suddenly and painfully conscious that he wore Freedom Party gray himself. 'Well, I'll tell you,' Wyatt said again. 'I say *sir* to people who I reckon deserve it. What did you ever do to make me reckon that?'

Rage ripped through Jeff. It thickened his voice as he ground out, 'I'll tell you what I did, you little chickenshit asshole. I fought in the trenches when you were still in short pants. I joined the Party before you had hair on your nuts. I've been runnin' camps since Jake Featherston got to be President of the CSA. My rank's the same as major general. You want me to call up Ferd Koenig and ask him if *he* reckons you ought to call me sir? You cocksucking whistleass, how soon you reckon you'll see the inside of one of these here camps for your very own self? Well, motherfucker? Answer me, God damn you!'

Major Wyatt went very red. Then, as he realized how much more than he could chew he'd bitten off, he went white instead. Pinkard knew damn well he could send Wyatt to a camp. And he knew damn well he would, too, and enjoy every minute of it. Seeing that anticipation of pleasure yet to come helped break the Army officer.

'Please excuse me, sir,' Wyatt mumbled, and saluted as if on the drill grounds at VMI. 'I beg your humble pardon, sir.'

'You fuckin' well *better* beg,' Jeff said. 'Who ever told you you could talk to a superior officer that way?'

Wyatt bit his lip and stood mute. Pinkard knew what he wasn't saying: that he didn't think a camp guard really was his superior, regardless of what rank badges might show. Too bad for him. He'd picked the wrong man to rile.

'Let's try it again,' Pinkard told him. 'How much will these guns help?'

'Sir, if the damnyankees send a whole big swarm of bombers over, you're screwed.' Did Wyatt sound as if he hoped the USA did just that? If he did, he wasn't blatant enough to let Jeff call him on it. He went on, 'For small raids, or for driving off reconnaissance airplanes, they'll do a lot.'

'There. You see? You really can answer when you set your mind to it,' Jeff said. 'Now – how come we don't have more fighters to drive off those Yankee fuckers before they get here?'

'On account of all that stuff is back East, sir,' Major Wyatt answered. 'Far as Richmond is concerned, west Texas is strictly nowhere. Only good thing about that is, it's strictly nowhere for the damnyankees, too.'

He had a point, but less of one than he thought. Snyder, Texas, and even Lubbock, Texas, were indeed strictly nowhere to both CSA and USA. But Camp Determination

damn well wasn't. It was the biggest of the camps the
Freedom Party was using to solve the Confederacy's Negro
problem. That made it vital to the country and the Party.
And the Yankees used it for propaganda against the CSA.

'Can you use those guns against ground targets, too?'
Jeff asked.

'Reckon we can if we have to, sir,' Major Wyatt said.
'Antiaircraft guns make pretty fair antibarrel guns, no doubt
about it. But I think you're flabbling over nothing if you
figure we'll need to. USA won't get this far.'

'Well, if the damnyankees *don't* get this far, you know
how come that'll be?' Pinkard demanded, his temper rising
again. 'On account of Freedom Party Guards stopped 'em
– more than the Army could do by its lonesome. And you
know who asked 'em to send in the guards? Me, that's
who.' He jabbed a thumb at his own chest.

'Uh, yes, sir.' Wyatt was wising up.

He wasn't wising up fast enough to suit Jeff. 'You think
maybe people in uniforms that aren't the same as yours
deserve a salute every now and then, Major? How about
that, huh? What *do* you think?'

'Yes, sir, I think they do. I was wrong before.' As if to
prove the point, Major Wyatt saluted.

Pinkard returned the salute. He wasn't about to let the
Army man accuse him of not following etiquette. But as
far as he was concerned, Wyatt didn't prove a damn thing
except that he had maybe enough sense to try to save his
own neck.

With a small sigh, Jeff decided that would have to do.
He couldn't make the man in the butternut uniform love
him. All he could do was make Wyatt treat him with military courtesy. *I damn well did that,* he thought.

'Anything else, Major?' Pinkard asked.

'No, sir.' Wyatt saluted again. Jeff returned it again. The

major said, 'Permission to leave, sir?' He wasn't taking any chances now.

'Granted,' Jeff said, and Wyatt got out of there as if the seat of his pants were on fire. He probably thought his drawers *were* smoking.

Watching the Army man's ignominious retreat, Jeff smiled a slow, sated smile: almost the smile he might wear after going to bed with Edith. This was a different kind of satisfaction, but no less real. He was *somebody*, by God. He could throw his weight around. One hand rested on his belly. He had plenty of weight to throw, too. Not bad for somebody who'd figured on spending the rest of his life making steel at the Sloss Works in Birmingham. No, not bad at all.

Another sign he'd arrived was the driver who took him back into Snyder when his shift at Camp Determination was up. Some evenings he spent on a cot in the administrative compound. Not tonight, though. He smiled again as the camp receded behind him. Thinking about the kind of smile he'd have after going to bed with Edith made him want to put on that kind of smile.

Back in the days before the war, he might have had a colored chauffeur. He didn't suppose anybody had a colored chauffeur any more. Times were changing in the CSA. An ordinary camp guard had to do. That was all right. The guard was the Party equivalent of a private, and privates got stuck with nigger work. That was true in King David's day, and Julius Caesar's, and William the Conqueror's, and it was still true now.

The brakes squeaked when the driver parked the Birmingham in front of Jeff's house in Snyder. *Got to get that seen to,* Jeff thought. The driver jumped out and opened the door for him. 'Here you are, sir.'

'Thanks, Cletus.' Jeff made a point of learning the men's

names. It didn't cost him anything, and it made them feel good. 'See you in the morning – or sooner if anything goes wrong.' He never stopped worrying. That was probably why things went wrong so seldom.

'Yes, sir.' Cletus had no trouble remembering that he needed to salute. He jumped back into the auto and drove away.

When Pinkard walked into the house, his two stepsons were playing a game on the floor of the front room. It seemed to involve wringing each other's necks. They broke off as soon as he came in. 'Papa Jeff!' they both squealed in the shrill small-boy register just below what only dogs can hear. 'Hi, Papa Jeff!' They tried to tackle him. They weren't big enough, even together. But they were a lot bigger than when he married their mother the year before. One of these days . . .

He didn't want to think about that. And he didn't have to, not when Edith came out of the kitchen and gave him a kiss. 'Hello, Jeff,' she said. 'Wasn't sure if you'd be back tonight.'

'Wouldn't miss it,' he said, and gave her an extra squeeze to show what he had in mind. 'What smells good?' he added; an alluring odor followed her.

'I've got a nice beef tongue cooking – with cloves and everything, the way you like it.' She paused to eye her sons. 'Why don't you boys go out and play? I've got something to tell Papa Jeff.'

'Why can't we hear?' asked Frank, the older.

'Because I want to tell Papa Jeff, not you – that's why,' his mother answered. 'Now beat it, before I send you to your room instead.' He disappeared even faster than Major Wyatt had. So did his brother Willie.

'What's up?' Pinkard asked.

'I'm going to have a baby.'

Jeff had gone so long without getting a woman pregnant, he wondered if he was shooting blanks. 'Well, I'll be,' he said. Then he realized Edith had to be looking for something better than that. 'Wonderful!' He hugged her and kissed her and, with the boys out of the house, set a possessive hand on her backside.

She smiled. 'That's how this started.'

'I didn't reckon it was any other way,' Jeff answered. 'Jesus, yeah. Not us.'

'Don't you start.' Edith was a churchgoing woman. She took her faith much more seriously than Jeff took his. He believed in Jake Featherston the way she believed in Jesus. From everything he could see, Jesus didn't deliver.

Lately, though, Jake Featherston wasn't delivering, either. The Confederate States were gone from just about all the U.S. territory they took when the war was new. Not even the professional optimists on the wireless were predicting when the CSA would reinvade the USA. All the talk these days was of defense and of outlasting the enemy.

The Freedom Party Guards Ferdinand Koenig threw into the fight had stopped the damnyankees not far beyond Lubbock. They couldn't retake the town, though, and they couldn't push U.S. forces back very far. A good-sized chunk of west Texas remained under the Yankee boot heel.

'All right,' Jeff said to Edith, and then, in what had to seem like a change of subject to her but didn't to him, 'I hear the United States are going to start up that, uh, darn state of Houston again – give the collaborators something to do.'

'That's dreadful!' she exclaimed. 'They're so wicked. They've got no business doing anything like that.' She paused, then asked, 'How are things at the camp?'

'Going well enough.' He rarely gave her a detailed answer when she asked something like that. She wasn't really looking for one, either. She both knew and didn't know what went on inside the barbed wire. She didn't like to think about it. For that matter, neither did Pinkard. He said, 'What shall we name the baby?'

'If it's a girl, I'd like to call her Lucy, after my mother,' Edith said.

Jeff nodded. 'All right. It's a good name. And if it's a boy?'

'What do you think of Raymond?' she asked.

He hesitated. Her first husband was called Chick. What the devil was his real name? Jeff didn't want *his* son named after the camp guard who'd killed himself. Chick Blades' real name was . . . Leroy. Jeff almost snapped his fingers, he was so glad to remember. 'Raymond'll do fine,' he said. That was easy.

He ate more than his share at supper. So did his stepsons – they liked tongue. He smiled to see them stuff themselves. Maybe it would make them sleepy sooner than usual. And it did. He smiled again. Things were going his way.

Edith even let him leave the light on. She usually liked darkness better. 'You're beautiful,' he said. While he stroked her and kissed her, while she touched him, he believed it. And he made her believe he believed it, too.

'Oh, Jeff,' she said, and then, a little later, '*Oh*, Jeff.' Her nails dug into his back. He spent himself at the same time as she quivered beneath him. The damnyankees, even the camp, seemed a million miles away. They wouldn't in the morning, though, and that was a crying shame.

'Boston,' Lieutenant Sam Carsten said as a pilot guided the *Josephus Daniels* through the minefields that kept submersibles and surface raiders away from the harbor. 'Boston's a good town.'

'Oh, yes, sir,' Pat Cooley agreed. The exec went on,

'Good restaurants, theaters, all kinds of things you can do here.'

'Yeah.' Sam's voice was dry. When he was a rating, his liberties here revolved around saloons and whorehouses. Restaurants? Theaters? Those were for other people, people with time on their hands and without money burning a hole in their pocket.

The pilot swung the helm a little to port. 'How did you know to do that then?' Cooley asked.

'Simple, sir. Last time I didn't, I blew up,' the man answered, deadpan.

'That'll teach you, Pat,' Carsten said.

'Teach me what?' Cooley said in tones more plaintive than they had to be. The pilot chuckled and turned the ship again when he thought he needed to. The *Josephus Daniels* didn't explode. Sam was in favor of not exploding.

An hour later, the destroyer escort was tied up at a pier in the U.S. Navy Yard, across the river from Boston proper – and Boston improper – in Charlestown. The first liberty party went off to roister, just as Sam would have without gold stripes on his cuffs.

Since he had them, he went through the Navy Yard to report to his superiors. He gave a lot of salutes and returned just about as many. To his own amusement, he caused a lot of confusion. Here he was, a middle-aged man with several rows of fruit salad on his chest. Young lieutenant commanders and commanders – the up-and-comers in the Navy – would assume he had to be at least a captain, if not of flag rank. Their right arms would start to go up. Then they would see he was only a lieutenant and stop in the middle of their salute till Sam bailed them out with one of his own.

Sometimes they wouldn't notice they outranked him. When that happened, he gravely returned a salute with one of his own. He left a trail of bemused officers in his wake. He messed up their mental Y-ranging gear.

The men to whom he reported had no doubt about his grade. They were his age, and had the rank he could have aspired to if he weren't a mustang. 'Reporting as ordered, sir,' he said to the four-striper who headed things. He saluted first.

Returning the courtesy, Captain William McClintock said, 'Take a seat, Carsten.'

'Thank you, sir,' Sam said, though he wasn't sure he was grateful. He'd got used to being skipper of the *Josephus Daniels,* a potentate who gave orders and had to worry about receiving them only from a distance. Now, under the eyes of five senior officers, he felt more like a bug on a plate than a potentate.

'You've had a busy time in the North Atlantic,' McClintock observed. His craggy features and sun-baked skin said he'd spent a lot of time at sea.

'Yes, sir,' Sam answered. What McClintock said was true – and any which way, it was hard to go wrong saying *Yes, sir* to your superiors.

One of the other captains across the table looked down at some papers through bifocals, tilting his head back to read. Sam wore reading glasses, but still saw well enough at a distance. 'You've done pretty well for yourself, seems like,' said the captain – his name was Schuyler Moultrie.

'Thank you, sir,' Sam said – one more phrase where it was hard to go wrong.

'Have you had any . . . special disciplinary problems aboard the *Josephus Daniels,* Carsten?' Captain McClintock asked.

Sam knew what that meant. Any mustang would have. 'No, sir,' he answered. 'I try to keep a tight rein on my CPOs – not tight enough to choke 'em, you understand, because they have to do their jobs, but tight enough so they can't get away with murder.'

McClintock's mouth twitched in what looked like a swallowed smile. Sam knew what that meant, too – he'd said the right thing. A mustang who still behaved like a CPO himself was liable to let his chiefs run wild, and that wasn't good for the ship. One of the best pieces of advice he got after his promotion was to remember he was an officer. He always did his best to follow it.

'How badly are you hurting the British?' Captain Moultrie asked.

'Sir, you would know better than I do,' Sam said. Moultrie raised an eyebrow and waited. Sam went on, 'I know what we stop. I've got an idea of what the other ships in the squadron stop. But I don't think any of us knows how much gets through in spite of us.'

'Good answer,' said Ken Davenport, the captain at Sam's far left.

'Seems to be worthwhile, what we're doing,' McClintock said. He eyed Carsten from across the table. 'Anything special you'd like to tell us, Lieutenant? Anything you've found out that other skippers ought to know?'

'Not to trust the limeys as far as you can throw them,' Sam said at once. 'That freighter with the big guns, the catapult-launched fighter . . . They're sneaky bastards.'

McClintock's grin startled Sam. He hadn't thought the rugged badlands of that face could rearrange themselves so. 'Then what does that make you?' the senior officer asked. 'Whatever they threw at you, you beat.'

'I don't know that for a fact, sir,' Carsten answered. 'I wish I did, but I don't. If they were sneaky enough, they slid on by me, and I never knew the difference.'

'Not too likely, not with Y-ranging gear,' Captain Davenport said, which only proved he didn't know much about the North Atlantic in dirty weather. By the way Captain McClintock stirred, he was thinking the same thing. Before he could say anything, Davenport went on, 'I will say that recognizing the possibility does you credit.'

'Well, that's true enough,' McClintock said. 'We've got ourselves a raft of officers who think they're smarter than they really are. Finding one who thinks he's dumber than he really is makes for a refreshing change.' He eyed Sam. 'Well, Lieutenant, do you want to go back on patrol when your refit's finished?'

'Sir, I'll go wherever you send me,' Sam said. 'Real destroyers are probably better suited to that job than escorts like my ship, though. They've got more legs, so they can cover more ocean. Fewer things are likely to get past them.'

'He *is* a smart one,' Captain Moultrie remarked.

'So he is. Good for him,' McClintock said placidly. He turned back to Sam. 'You aren't wrong. The only trouble is, we haven't got enough real destroyers to go around. We're gaining on it, but we aren't there yet. And the ones we do have in the North Atlantic, we need farther east. Speed counts for even more there than it does on patrol duty.'

'All right, sir.' Where to send ships wasn't Sam's decision. 'If you want the *Josephus Daniels* back out there, that's where she'll go.'

'You're the fellow who landed those Marines on that Confederate coastal island, aren't you?' Moultrie asked.

'Yes, sir, I did that.' Sam wondered if he should have said he was panting to go back out on patrol. Coastal raiding made for exciting films, but if you were doing it for real you kept all your sphincters puckered tight till you got out of range of Confederate land-based air.

'We have anything like that in the hopper?' Davenport asked.

'Well, we *could*, if we had an experienced skipper to

handle it,' Moultrie answered. They talked as if Sam weren't there. He wished he weren't. He wasn't eager to volunteer for a dangerous mission, but he knew he wouldn't turn it down if they gave it to him. You didn't do that, not if you were an officer. You didn't if you were a rating, either.

'Gives us something else to think about.' Captain McClintock sounded pleased. Of course he did – he'd be giving somebody else the shitty end of the stick. But the ribbons on his chest said he'd done warm work himself. He nodded to Sam. 'We need to talk to some people ourselves, Lieutenant. If you stay in port an extra day or two, I'm sure it'll break your crew's hearts, won't it?'

'Sir, you'll probably hear them crying all the way over in Providence,' Sam said.

That made two or three of the captains snort. McClintock said, 'I'm sure I will. All right, Carsten – you'll hear from us one way or the other before long. You have anything to say before we let you go?'

'Whatever you give me, whatever you give my ship, we'll take a swing at it,' Sam said. 'I guess that's it. Oh – and my exec is ready for a command of his own. Past ready. I hate to say it because I hate to lose him, but it's true.'

'We know about Lieutenant Cooley – indeed we do,' the senior captain replied. The others nodded. Just how fast a track *was* Pat on? McClintock continued, 'As for the other – well, plenty of worse things you could tell us. All right – dismissed for now.'

When Sam got back to the *Josephus Daniels*, Lieutenant Cooley asked, 'What's up, Skipper?'

'Well, I don't exactly know,' Sam answered. He didn't say anything about the senior officers' regard for Cooley. That would come out in its own time, if it did. 'Maybe they'll send us out on patrol again, or maybe they'll give us something else to do.'

'Something hush-hush and sneaky?' Cooley said. 'Something where our ass is grass if the bad guys find out about it?'

'They didn't say that in so many words,' Sam said. 'It sounded that way to me, though. They remembered that time we carried the leathernecks.'

'They would,' the exec said darkly. 'They didn't tell you what, huh?'

'Nope.' Sam shook his head.

'Doesn't sound good.'

'Nope,' Sam repeated. 'Sure doesn't. Way I figure it, we'll sail up the James to Richmond, land our Marines to scoop up Jake Featherston, and shell the Tredegar Iron Works while we wait for them to bring the son of a bitch back.'

Cooley looked at him. 'I hope you didn't tell the brass anything like that. They'd take you up on it in a red-hot minute – and if they did, we wouldn't sail up the James. We'd go up that other creek instead – without a paddle, too.'

'Don't I know it!' Sam said. 'No, I didn't give them any fancy ideas. I may be dumb, but I'm not *that* dumb. Besides, they can come up with all kinds of fancy ideas all by themselves. They don't need any help from me.'

'Maybe they'll shift the whole crew to a river monitor so we can help when our guys go over the Ohio,' Cooley suggested.

'There's a cheery thought.' Carsten shivered. During the Great War, both sides put monitors on the Ohio and the Mississippi. Some of them carried guns worthy of a battleship. They gave heavy cannon mobility the big guns couldn't get any other way, but even then they were vulnerable to mines, which both sides sowed broadcast in the rivers. And monitors were even more vulnerable these days. They were slow and they had little room to maneuver,

which meant dive bombers cleaned up on them. Sam supposed he would rather command a river monitor than try
to defuse unexploded bombs, but neither job was his idea
of fun.

While waiting for orders, Sam did some discreet rois-
tering at places where officers could roister discreetly. He
enjoyed himself. He would have had more fun at the rau-
cous joints where he went before he became an officer, but
he kept that to himself. A mustang who still behaved like
a petty officer wasn't a good officer. Sam had seen enough
men who proved the point.

Pat Cooley plainly had a good time at those discreet
establishments. But then, he was an up-and-comer with an
Annapolis ring. He was supposed to know how to enjoy
himself like a gentleman.

They both happened to be aboard the *Josephus Daniels*
when the orders arrived, as if from On High. Sam read
them. Without a word, he passed them on to Cooley. 'Well,
well,' the exec said brightly when he finished going through
them. 'Doesn't this look like fun?'

'Now that you mention it,' Sam said, 'no.'

Troop Leader Hipolito Rodriguez was starting to dread
duty on the women's side of Camp Determination.
Whenever he went over there, Bathsheba and Antoinette
looked for him so they could give him messages to take to
Xerxes over on the men's side. And he had to make up
messages from Xerxes to give to them. Otherwise, they
would realize the truth.

This is what you get for being kind even once, Rodriguez
thought unhappily. He delivered one message. After that,
he took the old *mallate* to the bathhouse. Xerxes didn't care
about anything any more. And he wasn't about to send
messages back to the women's side on his own.

But how was Rodriguez supposed to tell the man's wife and daughter that he was dead? He saw no way, however much he wished he did. They would wail and scream and blame him. And he was to blame, too. Didn't he shepherd everybody in that barracks into the bathhouse? It needed doing; more Negroes filled the building now. Pretty soon, they would get what was coming to them, too.

When Rodriguez sent swarms of men and women he didn't know into the bathhouse or into the trucks that asphyxiated them, it was only a job, the way planting corn and beans on his farm outside of Baroyeca was only a job. He didn't think about it; he just did it. Didn't he back the Freedom Party because it promised to do something about the Negroes in the CSA, and because Jake Featherston kept his promises?

When it came to Bathsheba and Antoinette, though, they weren't just *mallates* any more. They were people. And thinking about killing people was much harder and much less pleasant than thinking about getting rid of abstractions, even abstractions with black skins.

Part of him hoped they would go in a population reduction while he was over on the men's side. Then they would be gone, and he wouldn't have to worry about it any more. But they kept hanging on. No matter what the guards' orders were, they didn't clean out the women's side as efficiently as the men's. Even those hard-bitten men found their hearts softening – some, at least.

Naturally, that meant the women's side got more crowded than the men's. Just as naturally, Jefferson Pinkard noticed. Rodriguez remembered when Jeff came back from what was plainly a disastrous leave during the Great War. Pinkard went hard and merciless himself after that. He hadn't changed since – if anything, he was more so now. What with the job he had to do, that wasn't surprising.

He lectured the guards about not softening up – once. When that didn't work, he found a new way to solve the problem. A work gang – male prisoners – ran up new barracks on the women's side of Camp Determination. Before long, new guards filled them. They wore the gray of Freedom Party Guards . . . but instead of gray tunics and trousers, they wore gray blouses and skirts. Jefferson Pinkard or somebody set above him decided that female guards would be as tough on women as male guards were on men.

And it worked. To Hipolito Rodriguez's way of thinking, it worked appallingly well. The new guards were all whites – no women from Sonora or Chihuahua. They were all tough-looking; Rodriguez would much rather have dallied with colored prisoners than with any of them. They carried the same submachine guns as their male counterparts, and they knew how to use them.

They wasted no time proving it to the Negro women, either. The first few days they started patrolling the north side of Camp Determination, they shot three women in separate incidents. It was as if they were warning, *Don't give us any guff. You'll pay for it if you try.*

And they didn't waste any time sending Negro women to the bathhouse on that side and for one-way rides in the asphyxiating trucks. They hardly bothered pretending the eliminations were anything but eliminations. The women's side began to bubble with terror.

With the female guards building up numbers over there, Rodriguez took a turn on that side less and less often. That wasn't bad; in a lot of ways, it was a relief. But he didn't like what he saw when he did a shift there, and he especially didn't like what he felt. The hair on his arms and at the back of his neck kept wanting to stand on end. That side was an explosion waiting to happen.

Because he was who he was, he had no trouble getting in to see Jeff Pinkard. Saluting his buddy from the trenches always felt funny, but he did it. 'What's on your mind, Hip?' Pinkard asked. 'You aren't one of those people who flabble for the fun of flabbling.'

'I hope not, *Señor* Jeff,' Rodriguez answered. 'But those guards on the women's side, those *lesbianos*' – he didn't know if they were or not, but if *some* of them weren't, he'd never seen any – 'they make trouble there.'

That got Pinkard's attention, all right. 'How do you mean?' he rapped out.

'They don't – how you say? – they don't keep the secret. You make the men do it. The lady guards, they should do the same thing,' Rodriguez said.

Pinkard drummed his fingers on the desk. 'That's not so good.' He got out of his chair, stuck his hat on his head, and grabbed his submachine gun. 'I'll have a look for myself.'

He said that whenever he found a problem. Rodriguez admired him for it. He didn't let things fester. If something was wrong, he went after it right away. He had no trouble making up his mind.

By that time the next day, three female officers and half a dozen noncoms in skirts were gone. Pinkard assembled the rest of the female Freedom Party guards and spoke to them for most of an hour while men patrolled the women's half of the camp. Rodriguez never found out exactly what the camp commandant said, but it seemed to do the trick. The female guards stopped being so blatant about what Camp Determination was for. Little by little, the women on that side relaxed – as much as they could relax while not so slowly starving to death.

Bathsheba and Antoinette still survived. The cleanouts missed them again and again. In a way, Rodriguez was glad. They *were* people to him now, and they hadn't done anything to deserve death except be born black. He liked the older woman. And the younger one would have been beautiful if she weren't so thin.

But they reminded him of exactly what he was doing here, and he didn't like that. Thanks to the hard-hearted female guards, they had a pretty good idea of what would happen to them. 'One o' these days, they gonna put an end to us. Ain't that right?' Bathsheba asked with no particular fear and no particular hatred.

'Ain't happened yet. Don't got to happen.' Rodriguez tried to dodge around the truth.

She wagged a finger at him. 'I ain't nothin' but a nigger cleanin' lady, but I ain't no blind nigger cleanin' lady. You wave somethin' in front o' my face, reckon I see it.'

'I don't wave nothin'.' He did his best to misunderstand.

She wouldn't let him. 'Don't reckon it's any different on the men's side, is it?'

'I don't know what you mean. You got women over here, men over there. Of course is different.'

Bathsheba sighed. 'I spell it out for you.' She laughed. 'I ain't hardly got my letters, but here I is spellin' fo' you. They killin' folks over yonder the same way they killin' folks here?'

He didn't answer. He couldn't answer. Saying yes would admit far too much. Saying no wouldn't just be a lie – that wouldn't bother him a bit – but an obvious lie. Obvious lies were no damn good, not when you were talking about life and death.

When you were talking about life and death, keeping quiet was no damn good, either. Bathsheba sighed again. 'Well, I do thank the good Lord fo' preservin' my sweet Xerxes along with me an' Antoinette,' she said. 'We is in a hard road, but we is in it together.'

Shame threatened to choke Rodriguez. Along with that shame, though, came an odd pride. Bathsheba and Antoinette still thought Xerxes was alive. That gave them pleasure and hope. And they thought so because of him.

'Ask you somethin' else?' Bathsheba said.

Rodriguez didn't sigh, though he felt like it. 'Go ahead,' he said, and wondered what sort of trouble her next question would land him in.

'Antoinette give herself to you, it keep her alive any longer?'

The question itself didn't surprise him. The brutal bluntness of it did. Again, he did his best to evade: 'I got a wife at home down in Sonora. I don't need nobody here.'

'Uh-*huh*.' Her agreement was more devastating than calling him a liar would have been. And he didn't tomcat around the women's side the way a lot of male guards did. Every now and then, yes, but only every now and then.

'Is true. I do,' he said. He usually felt bad after he took a woman here. But not while he did it – oh, no, not then.

'All right.' Bathsheba sounded as if that wasn't worth quarreling about. She got to the point: 'Antoinette give herself to some *other* guard, then, it keep her alive any longer?'

He couldn't very well get around that, however much he wanted to. He gave the best answer he could, saying, 'Maybe. Ain't no way to be sure.'

'Ain't no way to be sure about nothin', is there?' Somehow, Bathsheba still didn't sound bitter. 'Reckon some o' them ofays, they think it's funny to lie down with a girl one day an' reduce her population the nex'.'

She was righter than she knew, or maybe she knew the way guards' minds worked much too well. 'I never done nothin' like that,' Rodriguez said. That was true, but it didn't do him much good. And it didn't make him sound very good, even to himself.

'Didn't say you did,' Bathsheba answered. 'Wouldn't've

asked if I reckoned you was one o' them. I is pretty much used up. Don't want to go, mind, but if I gots to, I gots to. But Antoinette, she jus' startin' out. You do somethin' fo' her, you make an ol' nigger cleanin' lady happy.'

'I do what I can.' Rodriguez had no idea how much that would be. 'She don't got to do nothin' like that for me.'

Bathsheba started to cry. 'You is a good man,' she said, even if Rodriguez wasn't so sure of that himself right now. 'You is a *decent* man. I reckon you is a God-fearin' man.' She cocked her head to one side and eyed him, the streaks of tears on her cheeks shining in the sun. 'So what you doin' here, doin' what you doin'?'

He had an answer. He'd always hated *mallates,* ever since they did their level best to kill him after he put on the Confederate uniform. Like any Freedom Party man, he thought Negroes meant nothing but danger and misfortune for the Confederate States. The country would be better off without them.

But how did he explain that to a colored woman in rags, her hair going all gray, who'd just offered her only daughter to him not for her own sake but for the younger woman's? How did he explain that to a wife and daughter who loved an old man on the other side of the camp, an old man now dead, an old man whose death Rodriguez didn't have the heart to tell them about?

He couldn't explain it. Even trying was a losing fight. He just sighed and said, 'I got my job.'

'Don't seem like reason enough.' Had Bathsheba got mad and screamed at him, he could have lost his temper and stormed off. But she didn't. And that meant he couldn't. He had to listen to her instead. He had three stripes on his sleeve and a submachine gun in his hands. She had nothing, and chances were neither she nor her pretty daughter had long to live.

So why did he feel he was the one at a disadvantage? Why did he feel she could call the shots? Why did he wish he were still down on the farm outside of Baroyeca? He didn't know why. He didn't like wondering, not even a little bit.

Jake Featherston was not a happy man. Being unhappy was nothing new for him. He ran on discontent, his own and others', the way a motorcar ran on gasoline. He recalled only two times in his life when he *was* happy, and neither lasted long: when he took the oath of office as President of the CSA, and when his armies drove all before them pushing north from the Ohio to Lake Erie and cutting the United States in half.

Being President was still pretty good, but it was also a lot more work than he ever thought it would be. Hard work corroded happiness. And Al Smith, damn him, was supposed to lie down with his belly in the air after the Confederates went and licked him. When he didn't, he dragged Jake and the Confederacy into a long war, the last thing anybody on this side of the border wanted.

Now the CSA would have to take a Yankee punch, too. Jake muttered under his breath. Like any barroom brawler, he wanted to get in the first punch and clean up afterwards, especially when the other guy was bigger. He tried it, and he didn't knock out the USA. He didn't have enough to hit again. Standing on the defensive went against every ounce of instinct in him. Instinct or not, sometimes you had no choice.

His secretary looked into his office. 'The Attorney General is here to see you, sir.'

'Thank you kindly, Lulu. Bring him in,' Jake said.

Ferd Koenig seemed bigger and bulkier than ever. 'Hello, Jake,' he said – he was one of the handful of men these days who could call the President by his first name.

'Hello, Ferd,' Jake answered. 'Have a seat. Pour yourself some coffee if you want to.' A pot sat on a hot plate in the corner. Jake smacked a desk drawer. 'Or I've got a fifth in here if you'd rather have that.'

'Coffee'll do.' Koenig fixed himself a cup, then sat down. After a sip, he said, 'Want to thank you for letting that Freedom Party Guard unit go into action in west Texas. They've done a pretty good job.'

'Better than I expected, to tell you the truth,' Featherston said. 'You want to pick up recruiting for your combat wing, I won't tell you no.'

'Thanks, Mr. President. With your kind permission, I will do that,' Koenig said. 'We need a fire brigade when things get hot.'

'That's a fact. Other fact is, some of the generals are getting jumpy. I can feel it,' Jake said. 'A counterweight to the Army could come in goddamn handy one of these days. You never can tell.'

'Lord, isn't that the truth?' Koenig set the coffee cup on the desk. 'Pour me a shot in there after all, would you?'

'Help yourself.' Jake got out the bottle and slid it across the desk. 'Shame to do that to good sippin' whiskey, but suit yourself.'

'I want the jolt, but I run on coffee these days.' Koenig added a hefty slug of bourbon, then tasted. He nodded. 'Yeah, that'll do the trick.' He eyed Jake. 'You really mean that about the Guards units?'

'Hell, yes.' Jake poured himself a shot, too, only without the coffee. He raised the glass. 'Mud in your eye.' After a respectful drink – he couldn't just knock it back, not after he called it sipping whiskey – he went on, 'If Party guards aren't loyal, nobody will be. You raise those units, and by God I'll see they're equipped with the best we've got.'

'Army won't like it,' the Attorney General predicted.

'Fuck the Army,' Featherston said. 'That's the whole point. So what else have we got going on?'

'Did you forget?' Ferd Koenig asked. 'Day after tomorrow, we clean out Richmond. Isn't it about time the Confederate States had a nigger-free capital?'

'Oh, I remember, all right. You don't need to worry about that,' Jake said. 'All the cops and stalwarts and guards are geared up for it.' He chuckled. 'With the niggers gone, we won't need so many of those people around here. We can put some of 'em in the Army – and in your Party Guards outfits – and some in the factories, and we'll be better off both ways.'

'If we didn't have all those Mexicans coming in, we'd never be able to make enough to stay in the war,' Koenig said.

'Yeah, well, that's the carrot we give Francisco José,' Jake answered. 'He gives us soldiers to fight the niggers in the countryside, we keep the frontier open for his workers. That's his safety valve, like. They get jobs here instead of going hungry down in Mexico and stirring up trouble against him. He gives us a hard time, we close the border . . . and start shipping the rebels old bolt-action Tredegars we don't need any more. His old man made it through a civil war – we can see how he likes another one.' His laugh held all the cynicism in the world.

'Sounds like you've got that under control, all right.' Koenig's role was domestic. He didn't presume to mess around with foreign affairs. He had his place, he knew it, he was good at it, and he kept to it, all of which made him uniquely valuable to Jake Featherston. He added, 'The sooner we clean out all the niggers, the sooner we can throw everything we've got at the USA.'

'That's the idea, all right,' Jake agreed. Koenig didn't know anything about the uranium bomb. Featherston didn't tell him anything, either. That secret couldn't be too tightly held. He did say, 'Starting day after tomorrow, Richmond'll be a better place. You go in right at sunup like usual?'

'That's what I've got in mind. We'll have all day to move 'em out then. Yankee bombers aren't likely to complicate things by daylight, either,' Koenig answered, and Jake nodded. As far as he was concerned, the difference between day and night was largely arbitrary. He'd always been a night owl, and spending so much time underground only encouraged him to catnap around the clock.

He was asleep at sunrise the day the cleanout started, but he got a wakeup call: literally, for the telephone by his cot jangled. That telephone didn't ring unless something big was going on. He grabbed it in the middle of the second ring. 'Featherston,' he said hoarsely, and then, 'What the fuck have the damnyankees done to us now?'

'Not the damnyankees, Mr. President.' Ferd Koenig's voice was on the other end of the line. 'It's the goddamn niggers. We've got . . .' He paused, maybe looking for a way to sugarcoat what came next, but he almost always did speak his mind, and this morning proved no exception: 'We've got an uprising on our hands.'

Jake sat bolt upright. 'What's going on? Fill me in fast.'

'Damn smokes must've known we were coming for 'em,' the Attorney General answered. 'We've already had, I dunno, six or eight people bombs go off. They've got rifles and grenades and Featherston Fizzes and a couple of machine guns, anyway. They mined the streets into the colored quarter, the sneaky bastards, and they blew two armored cars to hell and gone. It's a *fight*, sir, nothing else but.'

'Son of a bitch. Son of a motherfucking bitch,' Jake Featherston said. 'All right, if they want a fight, they can damn well have one. Let me get hold of the War

Department. If we have to, we'll blow up the whole nigger part of town' – basically, southeast Richmond – 'and all the coons inside it. That'll do, by God.' He sounded as if he looked forward to it. The reason for that was simple: he did.

'All right, Mr. President. I wanted to let you know,' Koenig said.

'Well, now I know. Get off the line, and I'll get you what you need to finish the job.' Jake waited till the Attorney General hung up, then called Nathan Bedford Forrest III. He wasn't surprised to find the chief of the General Staff at his desk. 'Forrest, the niggers are raising a ruckus. What can we pull from north of here to squash those stinking, backstabbing shitheels flat?'

'Well, sir, there is a problem with that,' Forrest said slowly. 'If we pull too much or make it too obvious what we're doing, the damnyankees are liable to try and break through up there. They're liable to make it, too – we're already stretched pretty damn thin north of the city.'

'They won't do it.' Jake sounded very sure. He wondered why. Then he found an answer: 'They're building up out West, not right here. You know that as well as I do.' He even thought he was telling the truth. And he added, 'Besides, we can't let the niggers get away with this kind of crap, or we'll have trouble from here to fucking Guaymas. I want men. I want armor. I want artillery. And I want Asskickers. By the time they all get done, won't be a nigger left on his feet in there.'

He waited. If Nathan Bedford Forrest III did any more bitching, the C.S. General Staff would have a new chief in nothing flat. Forrest must have sensed as much, too, for he said, 'All right, Mr. President. They'll get here as fast as they can.'

'Faster than that,' Featherston said, but it was only reflex complaint; Forrest had satisfied him. He slammed down the telephone, quickly dressed, and did something he didn't do every day: he went up above ground.

Shockoe Hill gave him a good vantage point. When he looked southeast, he swore at the black smoke rising over the colored part of Richmond. He heard the rattle of small-arms fire and the occasional explosion, too. 'Christ!' he said. The police and stalwarts and Party Guards always came loaded for bear, just in case. Well, they found a bear and then some this time.

Nathan Bedford Forrest III proved good as his word. About half an hour later, the first Mule dive bombers screamed down out of the sky above the colored quarter. Whatever the blacks had in the way of small arms, they didn't have any antiaircraft guns. The flat, harsh *crump!* of bursting bombs echoed across Richmond.

But the Confederate Asskickers weren't the only air-planes in the sky. U.S. fighters, flying at not much above rooftop level, darted over southeastern Richmond to strafe the people cleaning out the Negroes. Then they zoomed away to the north again.

Jake Featherston did some more swearing at that, swearing sulfurous enough to make his guards and the crews of the antiaircraft guns on the cratered Gray House grounds stare at him in startled admiration. He didn't know whether the damnyankees had urged Richmond's Negroes to rise. He didn't know, and he hardly cared. He did know they had good spies inside the city, to hear about it and take advantage of it so fast.

He called for his driver and pointed toward the trouble. 'Take me down there, quick as you can.'

'Uh, yes, Mr. President.' The driver saluted. But then he went on, 'Sir, what good will you be able to do there? You don't want to give the coons a shot at you.'

'Don't tell me what I want to do,' Jake snapped. 'Just get moving, goddammit.'

The driver did. People were in the habit of doing what Jake Featherston said. *A good thing, too,* he thought. *A damn good thing.* Twenty minutes later, he was at what was for all practical purposes the fighting front. He found Ferd Koenig looking ridiculous with a helmet on his jowly head. A moment later, when a bullet cracked past, Featherston wished for a helmet of his own – not that any helmet ever made would stop a direct hit.

'It's a war, Mr. President,' Koenig said unhappily.

'I see that.' Featherston wasn't unhappy. He was furious. If the Negroes thought they could get away with this, they needed to think again. 'Send in everybody we've got,' he told Koenig. 'This has to be stamped out right now.'

'Shouldn't we wait till the soldiers get here?' the Attorney General asked, licking his lips. 'Been kind of hot for the manpower we have.'

'Send them in,' Featherston repeated. 'When we have the soldiers later, we'll use 'em. But if we can end it in a hurry, we'll do that. We've already got the Asskickers in action. What more do you want, egg in your beer?'

So the attack went in. And the Negro fighters, waiting in prepared positions, shredded it. Wounded whites staggered back out of the fighting. So did overage cops who looked as if they were on the point of having heart attacks. They killed some Negroes and brought out some others, but they didn't break the line. Jake Featherston swore yet again. Now he'd have to do it the hard way.

From the bridge, Sam Carsten looked at the *Josephus Daniels* with a kind of fond dismay. They'd done strange things to his ship. Her paint was the wrong shade of gray. Sheet metal changed the outline of the bridge and the gun turrets. Her sailors wore whites of the wrong cut. His own uniform was dark gray, not blue, and so were the rest of the officers'.

By the name painted on both sides of her bow, the *Josephus Daniels* was the CSS *Hot Springs,* a Confederate destroyer escort operating in the North Atlantic. The main danger coming south from Boston was that she would run into a U.S. patrol aircraft or submersible and get sunk by her own side. The Confederate naval ensign, a square version of the C.S. battle flag, completed the disguise.

'If they capture us, they'll shoot us for spies.' Lieutenant Pat Cooley didn't sound worried. He was almost childishly excited at playing dress-up. The possibility of getting shot hardly seemed real to him.

It didn't seem real to Sam, either, but for a different reason. 'Not a whole lot of POWs off Navy ships,' he said. 'If something goes wrong, they'll just damn well sink us.' That wasn't romantic. It had no cloak-and-dagger flavor to it. He didn't care. It was real.

By now, barring bad luck, they were too far south for U.S. airplanes to harry them. Subs were always a risk, but Sam didn't know what to do about it except monitor the hydrophones as closely as he could. The crew was doing that.

He had the best set of C.S. Navy recognition signals his U.S. Navy superiors could give him. He also had an ace in the hole, a deserter from the CSA named Antonio Jones. Normally, Sam would have been leery about a Confederate traitor. Anybody like that was too likely to be playing a double game. But he – and, again, his superiors – had a good reason for thinking Jones reliable.

The man was black as the ace of spades.

He came from Cuba, the only state in the CSA where Negroes had surnames. He pronounced his 'Hone-ace': he spoke English with an accent half Confederate drawl, half syrupy Cubano Spanish. He hated the homeland he'd left behind, and he burned to go back there. And so here he was, with a disguised destroyer escort for transport . . . among other things.

'Not the first time I've been in the gun-running business,' Carsten remarked.

'No?' the exec said, as he was supposed to.

'Nope. I took rifles into Ireland in the last go-round, just to help keep England busy,' Sam said. 'The Irish paid us off in whiskey. Don't expect that'll happen in Cuba.'

'No, suh,' Antonio Jones said. He wore a mess steward's uniform. High cheekbones and a strong nose argued for a little Indian blood in him. 'But maybe you get some rum.'

'Oh, *I* won't,' Sam said. 'That'll be for the fellows who do the real work. Long as they don't get drunk and disorderly, I'll look the other way.'

Pat Cooley raised an eyebrow, but lowered it again in a hurry. A lot of skippers would do the same thing, not just a man who was a mustang. The exec contented himself with saying, 'Let's hope they have the chance to drink it.'

'Not all these little tricks are easy,' Sam said. 'We just have to do what we can and hope for the best, same as always.'

They were off the coast of South Carolina when a seaplane of unfamiliar design buzzed out to look them over. The mock Confederate sailors ran to their guns. With luck, that wouldn't alarm the fliers in the seaplane, which also sported the Confederate battle flag on wings, fuselage, and tail.

After a couple of passes, the seaplane waggled its wings at the pseudo-*Hot Springs* and flew away. 'Let's just hope it didn't fly low enough to read our name,' Pat Cooley said.

'I don't *think* it did.' Sam hoped he wasn't whistling in the dark. The people the seaplane wirelessed probably wouldn't be surprised to find a C.S. destroyer escort in these waters. They probably *would* be surprised to find the *Hot Springs* around here. They also probably wouldn't be very happy. The *Josephus Daniels* wasn't fast enough to run away from everything they'd throw at her. She wasn't armed well enough to fight it off, either. All she could do was go down swinging.

'Y'all are *bueno*?' Antonio Jones asked.

'Well, I'll tell you – if we're not, we'll know pretty damn quick.' Sam went from the bridge to the wireless shack. 'Any Confederate traffic for us or about us?' he asked the men with earphones.

'Nothing for us, sir,' one of the yeomen answered. 'If there's anything about us, it's not in clear.'

'If it's in code, chances are we're shafted,' Sam said. 'All right – thanks.' He returned to his station, at least somewhat reassured.

Another seaplane examined them when they neared the southern tip of Florida. They must have passed that inspection, too. If they hadn't, cruisers and land-based dive bombers would have called on them. As far as Sam knew – as far as anybody in the U.S. Navy knew – the Confederates had no airplane carriers. It made sense that they wouldn't; they didn't need that kind of navy. Land-based air and coast-defense ships could keep the United States from mounting major operations against them, and submarines let them strike at the USA from far away.

'You know what our best chance is?' Sam said as the *Josephus Daniels* neared the northeastern coast of Cuba.

'Sure,' his exec answered. 'Our best chance is that the Confederates won't figure we're crazy enough to try anything like this in the first place.'

'Just what I was thinking – maybe we ought to get married,' Sam said.

'Sorry, sir. No offense, but you're not my type,' Cooley answered. They both laughed.

Antonio Jones looked from one of them to the other. 'This ain't funny, *amigos*,' he said. 'What that Featherston bastard is doing to colored people in my *estado*, it's a shame and a disgrace. We got to go to the mountains and fight back.'

'Sorry, Mr. Jones.' Sam didn't think he'd ever called a Negro *mister* before, but orders were to treat him like a big shot. 'We know your people are in trouble. We're not laughing about that. But my crew is in trouble, too, and it will be till we get back into U.S. waters.' *And even after that*, he added, but only to himself. 'We *can* laugh about that. We'd go nuts if we didn't, chances are.'

'Ah. Now I understand.' Jones sketched a salute. 'All right, *Señor Capitán*. We do this, too, against our worries.'

The sun sank into the sea with tropical abruptness. No long, lazy twilights in these latitudes; darkness came on in a hurry. Pat Cooley had the conn as the *Josephus Daniels* approached the Cuban coast. Sam didn't want to risk the ship in any way he didn't have to. What they were doing was already risky enough by the nature of things.

'One patrol boat where it's not supposed to be could ruin our whole day,' Cooley remarked.

'All the guns are manned, and Y-ranging should let us see him before he sees us,' Sam said. 'With luck, we'll sink him before he gets word off about us.'

Cooley nodded. Sam wondered how much luck they'd already used up when those C.S. seaplanes believed they were what they pretended to be. Did they have enough left? He'd find out before long.

Y-ranging gear also let them spot the Cuban coast. Although it was blacked out, the darkness wasn't so thorough as it would have been farther north. U.S. bombers weren't likely to visit here. Eyeing what had to be two fair-sized towns, Sam said, 'That's Guardalavaca to starboard, and that has to be Banes to starboard. We are where we're supposed to be. Nice navigating, Mr. Cooley.'

'Thank you very much, sir,' the exec said.

Sailors were hauling crates of rifles and submachine guns and machine guns and cartridges up on deck. Soon they'd be lowered into the *Josephus Daniels'* boats and brought ashore . . . if the destroyer escort got the recognition signal she was supposed to.

That thought had hardly crossed Carsten's mind before three automobiles on a beach aimed their headlights across the water in the warship's general direction. Antonio Jones breathed a sigh of relief. Sam breathed another one. Anxiety tempered his – were they sailing into a trap? He had to find out.

'Thank you, sir,' the black Cuban answered. 'God willing' – he crossed himself – 'the *Partido de Libertad* here will have some new worries.' They went out on deck together. Sailors in ersatz Confederate uniforms swung crate after crate down into the waiting boats. Jones continued, 'It is not as much white man against black man here as it is on the mainland of the CSA. There are many of mixed blood on this island, and even some whites help us as much as they can.'

'Good. That's good, Mr. Jones.' Sam did his best to pronounce it the way the Negro did. He was uneasily aware that his own country wasn't doing everything it could to help the Negroes in the Confederate States. Well, the United States were doing *something*. The proof of that was right here. Sailors scrambled down nets to board the boats and take the guns and ammo ashore.

Antonio Jones went to the port rail to go down himself. 'I hope you stay safe, *Capitán* Carsten,' he said.

'I hope you do, too,' Sam said. 'Maybe after the war's done, we'll get together and talk about it over a beer.'

'I hope so, yes.' Jones sketched a salute and swung himself over the rail. He descended as nimbly as any sailor. Motors chugging, the boats pulled away from the *Josephus Daniels* and went in toward the beach.

Nothing to do but wait, Sam thought. He would rather be doing. He'd smuggled arms into Ireland himself. He knew the ploy worked right away. If firing broke out on the beach now . . . *Well, in that case I'm screwed, too.*

The boats came back after what felt like years. His watch insisted it was more like forty-five minutes. Sailors hoisted the boats up one after another. 'Smooth as rum, sir,' said one of the men back from the beach. The simile made Sam suspicious, or more than suspicious. Remembering the good Irish whiskey he'd downed in the last war, he said not a word.

'Goddamnedest thing you ever saw, too,' a grizzled CPO added. 'They had this kid running things on the beach. If he was a day over sixteen, I'm a nigger. But he knew what was what, Fidel did. He gave orders in that half-Spanish, half-English they talk here, and people jumped like you wouldn't believe. He was a white kid, too, not a smoke like Mr. Antonio Jones.'

'Jones said whites and blacks were in it together down here,' Sam said. 'Do we have all the boats aboard? If we do, we better get out of here.'

They did. The *Josephus Daniels* made for the open ocean. Aboard her, sailors put on their own uniforms for the first time since setting out from Boston. They started dismantling the sheet-metal camouflage that turned her into a Confederate ship. When morning came, they would give her a proper paint job, too. They couldn't bring her back into U.S. waters looking the way she did, not unless they wanted her sent to the bottom in short order.

'We got away with it,' Sam said to Pat Cooley.

'Did you think we wouldn't, sir?' Cooley asked.

'Well, I'm damn glad we did,' Sam said, and let it go at that.

Clarence Potter fitted a new clip to his Tredegar automatic rifle. He worked the bolt to chamber the first round. That done, he was ready to empty the twenty-five-round clip into anything that looked even a little bit like trouble.

The Negro uprising in Richmond was having unexpected effects. One of them was reminding even officers who normally spent their time deep in the bowels of the War Department that war meant fighting, and fighting meant killing. Nathan Bedford Forrest III's great-grandfather first said that, and the cavalry general from the War of Secession knew what he was talking about.

Small bands of blacks had managed to get out through the barbed-wire perimeter that was supposed to seal the colored quarter off from the outside world. Bombed-out buildings gave them hiding places uncountable during the day. When night fell, they came out and shot whoever they could find. Rumor said a Negro'd come close to killing Jake Featherston. Potter didn't know if he believed rumor. He didn't know how he felt about it even if it was true, either. He didn't love the President of the CSA, but he knew the country needed him.

His own foxhole was just inside the colored district. 'Come on!' he shouted to the Confederate soldiers entering the perimeter. 'They're shooting back from over there, and from over there, too.' The Virginia Confederate Seminary ordained black preachers; it was as close to an institution of higher learning as Negroes could have in the CSA. For now, its large, solid buildings made a splendid strongpoint for Negroes armed with old-fashioned bolt-action

Tredegars, sporting rifles, shotguns, pistols, and whatever else they could get their hands on.

They even had a few mortars, perhaps captured, perhaps homemade, perhaps sneaked in by the damnyankees. But what they had was no match for the artillery, barrels, and air power the Confederacy used against them, to say nothing of the ground troops clearing them out one block, one building, at a time.

More Confederates, some in gray, some in butternut, led a long column of black captives out of the colored district. Any time a Negro hesitated, a soldier or Freedom Party guard shot him – or her. If Asskickers bombed apartment blocks into rubble, who could say how many people died in the explosions or in the fires that followed? And who cared, except the Negroes themselves? Anybody blown to bits now didn't need shipping to a camp later. Population reduction came in all different flavors.

Antiaircraft guns started going off. Clarence Potter swore and dove into a foxhole. The Yankees sent fighters into Richmond whenever they could. Helping the black uprising was good for them, just as helping the Mormons helped the CSA. But the U.S. border was much closer to Richmond than the Confederates were to Salt Lake City. *Too bad,* Potter thought.

The U.S. fighters came in low, the way they always did. They blasted whatever they could, then roared off. A few bullets slammed into the sandbags that helped strengthen Potter's foxhole. Dirt leaked out of them and onto him.

Leaking dirt he didn't mind. Leaking blood was a different story. Potter straightened up again when he was reasonably sure the enemy airplanes were gone. A latecomer shot past then, but didn't open up on him. He let out a sigh of relief. That could have been . . . unpleasant.

'Potter!' someone yelled. 'Potter!'

'I'm here!' Clarence Potter shouted back. By Jake Featherston's orders, no one named anyone else's rank inside the perimeter. Shouting out for a general only made the man a tempting target for snipers. Quite a few officers and even noncoms didn't wear their rank badges for the same reason. Potter did, but more from a sense of fussy precision than out of vanity.

He kept calling till the runner found his foxhole. 'Here you are, sir,' the man said, and handed him a sealed envelope.

'Thanks,' Potter said. Things did happen outside this colored district, though proving as much wasn't easy, not when the capital was on fire. He broke the seal, took out the papers inside it, read through them, and nodded to himself. 'So that's ready to get going, is it?'

'I don't know what you mean, sir,' the runner said. 'Do I need to take an answer back to anybody?'

'No, that's all right. This just lets me know something's going to happen. You can leave,' Potter answered. The young Confederate soldier didn't seem sorry to disappear. No doubt he would have been happier running messages through the War Department's miles of underground corridors. Potter couldn't blame him. Rifle and machine-gun bullets hardly ever flew down those corridors. Here, now . . .

Well, he'd got this message where it needed to go. Potter lit a match and burned it. Confederate bombers flying out of extreme northwestern Sonora were going to try to hit the U.S. uranium works in western Washington. It was a gamble in all kinds of ways. Other C.S. bombers taking off at the same time would head toward Los Angeles, Las Vegas, and Denver. With luck, the damnyankees' fancy electronics – better than anything the CSA had – would make them concentrate on those other bombers, not on the ones that really counted.

With a little more luck, the bombers would do some real damage when they got over the target. They had to fly a long way to get there: something on the order of 1,200 miles. The Confederacy didn't have long-range heavy bombers that could carry a big bomb load that far and then turn around and fly home. If the war broke out in 1945, say, instead of 1941, the Confederacy probably would have such airplanes. But the country needed to use what it could get its hands on now.

Even starting out with a light bomb load, those bombers wouldn't be coming home again. They would land at a strip on Vancouver Island, a strip of whose existence the United States were – Potter fervently hoped – ignorant. Assuming everything went the way it was supposed to, pilots and air-crews would eventually get smuggled back to the Confederacy. Canadian rebels would wreck the aircraft so the USA couldn't learn much from them. (So the Canucks claimed, anyhow. If they found people to fly those birds against the damnyankees, Potter suspected they would. He didn't mind. He wished them luck.)

Assuming everything went the way it was supposed to . . . Clarence Potter laughed, not that it was funny. Things had a habit of going wrong. Any soldier, and especially any soldier in the intelligence business, could testify to that.

He laughed again. Assuming everything went the way it was supposed to, Richmond's Negroes would all be in camps by now. Assuming everything went the way it was supposed to, Potter himself would be back under the War Department figuring out sneaky ways to make life miserable for the damnyankees and to keep them from making it miserable for his own country. That knowledge didn't give him any great faith things would go the way they were supposed to.

But the Confederate States had to try. The United States

started the race towards uranium sooner, and they were running faster. They had more trained people to attack the problem, and they had more industrial capacity to spare from straight-out, short-term war production.

'Thank you, Professor FitzBelmont,' Potter muttered, there in his foxhole. Who would have thought an unworldly physicist would see something a spymaster missed? Physics was FitzBelmont's business, but all the same. . . .

Even if everything did go the way it was supposed to, how long would this raid stall the United States? Days? Weeks? Months? Potter laughed at himself. He couldn't know ahead of time. Neither could anybody else.

'The longer, the better,' Potter said. And that was the Lord's truth. One raid on that facility might get through. A follow-up seemed unlikely to.

More Negroes came back past his foxhole. They were skinny and dirty. Despair etched their faces. They'd done everything they could to hold off the Confederate authorities. They'd done everything they could, and it wasn't enough. Plenty of their friends and loved ones lay dead in the rubble from which they were pulled, and now they were going off to the camps in spite of everything.

Potter felt like waving good-bye to them. He didn't – that was asking for a bullet. But the temptation lingered. Too bad, fools!

Of course, if the damnyankees won this war as they'd won the last one, they would jeer the Confederates the same way. And they would have won the right. Potter tried to imagine what the Confederate States would be like with U.S. soldiers occupying them. He grimaced. It wouldn't be pretty. The Yankees got soft after the Great War. They paid for it, too. They weren't as dumb as most Confederates thought they were. They weren't dumb enough to make the same mistake twice in a row. If they came down on the CSA this time around, they'd come down with both feet.

Of itself, Potter's gaze swung to the west, toward Washington University. How were Professor FitzBelmont and his crew of scientists doing? How much time did they need? How far ahead of them were their U.S. opposite numbers? How long would the C.S. bombers set the damnyankees back?

There. He was back where he started from. He had lots of good questions, and no good answers.

Rattling and clanking, a couple of Confederate barrels ground forward against the rebellious Negroes. They were obsolescent machines left over from the early days of the war: only two-inch guns, poorly sloped armor. Having to use them – and their highly trained crews – for internal-security work was galling just the same.

A machine gun in the ruins of a grocery opened up on the barrels. That wasn't a C.S. weapon; it came from the USA. Its slower rate of fire made it immediately recognizable. Potter cursed under his breath. Yes, the damnyankees helped the Negro revolt in the CSA, the same as the Confederates helped the Mormons. But the Mormon uprising was fizzling out, while Negroes went right on causing trouble.

Bullets ricocheted off the forward barrel's turret and glacis plate, some of them striking sparks from the armor. Even experienced soldiers tried to knock out barrels with machine guns, and it couldn't be done. A Confederate infantryman fired an antibarrel rocket into the battered store. The machine gun suddenly fell silent. Antibarrel rockets were made for piercing armor plate. Confederate soldiers had quickly discovered they also made excellent housebreakers.

The barrels clattered on. When somebody with a rifle

fired at them, the lead barrel sprayed the house from which he was shooting with machine-gun fire. But that rifleman was only a distraction. A skinny Negro kid – he couldn't have been more than fourteen – leaped up onto the second barrel, yanked open the hatch over the cupola, and threw in a Featherston Fizz.

A C.S. foot soldier with a submachine gun cut him down a moment later – a moment too late. Flames and black, greasy smoke burst from all the turret hatches. The gunner got out, but he was on fire. He took only a few steps before crumpling to the ground, and writhed like a moth that flew into a gas flame.

Then the barrel brewed up as its ammunition cooked off. Fire burst from it. Potter knew the commander and loader were stuck in there. He didn't think the driver or bow gunner got out, either.

Five good men gone. Five men who wouldn't fight the USA again. Five men the CSA couldn't afford to lose – but they were lost. Clarence Potter swore one more time. To his way of thinking, this proved the Confederacy had to get rid of its Negroes. What did they do but cause trouble and grief?

What the Confederacy might be if it treated Negroes like men and women rather than beasts . . . never even crossed his mind.

VII

Flora Blackford was listening to a Navy captain testifying about support for black rebels in the Confederate state of Cuba when a page approached her and whispered, 'Excuse me, Congresswoman, but you have an urgent telephone call outside.'

'Who is it?' she whispered back. This wasn't the most exciting testimony the Joint Committee on the Conduct of the War had ever heard, but it was important.

'Assistant Secretary Roosevelt,' the page answered.

'Oh.' Flora got to her feet. 'Please excuse me,' she told her colleagues. 'I'll be back as soon as I can.'

The page led her to one of the telephones outside the hearing room. 'He's on this line.'

'Thank you.' Flora picked up the handset and said, 'This is Congresswoman Blackford.'

'Hello, Flora,' Franklin Roosevelt said. 'Can you come by here?'

'Right this minute?' she asked.

'Well, you might want to,' Roosevelt answered. And what did that mean? Something like, *If you don't you'll be sorry*. Flora couldn't think of anything else it was likely to mean.

'On my way,' she said, and hung up. 'Please apologize to the rest of the committee for me,' she told the page. 'I'm afraid I need to confer with the Assistant Secretary of War.' The young man nodded and hurried away. Flora wondered what kind of connections he had, to be wearing a sharp blue suit instead of a green-gray uniform. She also wondered how long he would go on wearing his suit. Congressional pages did get conscripted. At least one had got killed.

And, as she hurried to the exit, she wondered what the other members of the Joint Committee on the Conduct of the War would think. People knew she often talked with Franklin Roosevelt. She hoped to heaven they didn't know why. If they didn't know why, what would they think? That she and Roosevelt were having an affair? He was married, but that mattered little in high government circles. Reporters knew better than to write such stories. People called it a gentleman's agreement, though Flora had never seen anything very gentlemanly about it.

She walked over to the War Department. Sentries there scrupulously compared the photo on her ID card to her face. They searched her handbag. A woman took her into a closed room and patted her down. And they called Roosevelt's office to make sure she was expected. Only when they were fully satisfied did a soldier escort her to that office far underground.

'Call when you need to come back up, ma'am,' the soldier said: a polite way of warning, *Don't go wandering around by yourself.*

'I will,' Flora promised.

Roosevelt's chief secretary or administrative assistant or whatever he was led her in to the Assistant Secretary of War. Then the man left, closing the door behind him. Did he knew about the work on uranium bombs? Flora wouldn't have cared to guess one way or the other.

'How are you, Franklin?' she asked.

'Oh, a little tired, but not too bad,' he answered. He looked worn and weary, as if he was running on too much coffee, too many cigarettes in that jaunty holder of his, and not enough sleep. Few people with important jobs were doing anything else. He nodded, perhaps trying to make himself believe it. 'No, I'm not too bad myself, but the news could be better.'

'What is the news?' Flora asked.

'The Confederates bombed our Hanford facility in the wee small hours this morning.'

'Gevalt!' She sank into a chair. Her knees didn't want to hold her up. 'How bad is it? Do I want to know?'

'Well, it's not good,' Roosevelt said. 'They know we're working on this, they knew where we're working on it, they know it's important, and they must be working on it, too, or they wouldn't try so hard to shut us down.'

Every word of that was true. But he hadn't told her what she most wanted to know. 'How much damage did they do?'

'Oh. That.' His resonant laugh filled the office. 'Now that the sun's up out there, we can see it's less than we feared at first. They don't have aircraft that can carry heavy loads a long way, and it's hard to bomb accurately at night anyway. They hit some of the works, but they didn't damage the plant where we're separating U-235 and U-238 or the pile – that's what they're calling the gadget that makes more energy than goes into it.'

'That would have been bad,' Flora said. 'Repairing those things would take a long time.' She didn't even mention money.

'Repair isn't the only worry. If the bombers hit those, we'd have to worry about radioactive contamination like you wouldn't believe,' Roosevelt said. Flora must have looked blank, for he went on, 'That kind of thing can cause cancer. It can poison you. If it's strong enough, it can come right out and kill you. And it's very hard to clean up.'

'But it didn't happen?' Flora said.

'It didn't happen. Hardly any contamination, in fact,' Roosevelt said.

'Good – I guess.' Flora hadn't even thought about – what did Roosevelt call it? – radioactive contamination. She hadn't known such a thing was possible, or that anybody needed to worry about it. She was just starting to realize how much she didn't know about this whole uranium business.

'It's very good, believe me,' Roosevelt said. 'They could have made things worse for us than they did. We're not badly delayed, anyhow.'

'That *is* good,' Flora said. 'What kind of program do the Confederate States have? How far along are they? How do we go about finding out?'

'I don't know, I don't know, and we'll have to find a way, respectively.' The Assistant Secretary of War sighed. 'That's all I can tell you right now. As I say, they're working on it, the same as we are. We're in a race, and we'd better win.'

Eight words. As far as Flora could see, they said everything that needed saying. 'If we knew where they're working, we could visit them the same way they just visited us,' she said.

'If we knew that, we would have done it a long time ago,' Roosevelt said. 'We've got to look harder, that's all.'

'It's a long way from Confederate territory to Washington State,' Flora said. 'That's one of the reasons you put the uranium works out there, I suppose. How did they manage to fly bombers all the way up there? And what happened to them afterwards?'

'They got cute,' Franklin Roosevelt said unhappily. 'I don't know what else to tell you. They flew a whole swarm of airplanes out of northwestern Sonora. Some of them headed for Los Angeles. Some attacked Las Vegas and Boulder Dam in Nevada. And some . . . some we just forgot about.' He looked angry and embarrassed at the same time. 'Airplanes flying over the middle of the country – too many people assumed they were ours and didn't worry about them. That won't happen again, either.'

'They didn't go back to the CSA, did they?' Flora asked.

He shook his strong-chinned head. 'No. We might have done something about that. I hope to heaven we would have done something about it, anyhow. But they flew on to Vancouver Island and landed at strips there. The crews were gone by the time we got people there, and they set fire to the airplanes – or maybe the Canadians who helped them get away did. I don't know about that. I do know it was a very smart operation, and we're lucky it didn't hurt us a lot worse than it did.'

'What can we do to make sure it doesn't happen again?' Flora asked.

'You do know the right questions to ask,' Roosevelt said. Flattery? Truth? Both at once? He went on, 'From now on, we'll have fighters overhead all the time. That's effective immediately. We'll beef up the antiaircraft guns as soon as we can, and we'll put a Y-ranging station close by so we can spot the enemy a long way off. And we'll hit Confederate airports in Sonora and Chihuahua and even Texas to make it harder for them to fly up north.'

'What do we do about auto bombs? What do we do about people bombs?' Flora asked.

'Well, the area is well fenced, and the fences are a long way out from the buildings – for one thing, we need room if experiments get out of hand,' Roosevelt answered. 'We have a garrison there.' He wrote himself a note. 'We'd better reinforce it, and we'd better add some armored vehicles, too. You *do* know the right questions.' Maybe he really meant it this time.

'Did we lose any important people?' Flora asked.

'No. Absolutely not. No. We don't have as many first-rate physicists as Germany does, but we've got plenty of good people to take us where we're going,' Roosevelt said. 'And the bombers didn't hit any of them last night, so *that's* all right. If we find the Confederates' project, striking them will hurt them more, or I hope so, anyway. They only have a third as many educated people as we do. They can't afford to lose anybody.'

'One more part of the price they pay for leaving their Negroes as nothing but field hands,' Flora said.

'I agree. But they aren't even field hands now. They're . . .' Roosevelt paused.

'Victims.' Flora supplied a word.

'Yes, that's what they are.' Roosevelt shook his head. 'Strange to use a word like that in this day and age. Strange to use it like that, anyhow. If people drown in a flood, they're victims. If a man runs a stop light and kills a grandmother, she's a victim. But those aren't accidents in the CSA. The Freedom Party is doing it on purpose.'

'Nobody up here wanted to believe that for the longest time,' Flora said.

'I still don't want to believe it,' Franklin Roosevelt said. 'But I have no choice. It's true, all right. You deserve a lot of credit for making people see that.'

'I don't want it. I wish I didn't have it,' Flora said. 'And speaking of such things, what are we doing to help the Negroes in Richmond?'

'What we can, which isn't much,' the Assistant Secretary of War answered. 'Our fighters strafe the Confederates. We bomb their positions as we can. Some of the weapons the Negroes are using, they got from us. Smuggling arms isn't easy, but we do what we can.'

'The Confederates did a pretty good job of helping the Mormons in Utah,' Flora said.

'More space and fewer people out there,' Roosevelt replied. 'Getting things into Richmond's never been easy. The Negroes are making the most of what we got them – and of what they got on their own. I will say that for them.'

'They really can fight, can't they?'

'It does seem that way.'

'Then why doesn't the U.S. Army let our Negroes put on the uniform and go after the Confederates?' Flora asked. 'God knows they have the incentive to do it.'

'I can't change that policy myself, you know,' Roosevelt said.

Flora nodded impatiently. 'Yes, of course. But you can recommend a course of action to the President. He could change it by executive order – I don't think he needs the consent of Congress to enlist Negro troops.'

'I'd say you're right about that,' Roosevelt replied. 'My one worry is, I don't know how our white soldiers would like Negroes fighting alongside of them.'

'Who'd have a better reason to fight hard than colored troops?' Flora said. 'If I were a black man in uniform, I wouldn't want to surrender to the Confederates. Would you?'

'When you put it that way, no,' Roosevelt admitted. 'I'll speak to President La Follette about this. You might do the same. The final decision will be up to him, though.'

'Yes,' Flora said. For the past year, Charlie La Follette wasn't just someone who could help make the upper Midwest vote Socialist. He was the man who decided things, and he seemed to be doing it well enough. 'I'll talk to him, and we'll see what happens after that.'

Brakes squealing, the train pulled into the station. 'Rivière-du-Loup!' the conductor called. 'All out for Rivière-du-Loup!' He spoke French, as most people did in the Republic of Quebec.

Dr. Leonard O'Doull hardly noticed. To him, French seemed at least as natural as English. *Home,* he thought, and got to his feet. After two years away, Rivière-du-Loup looked very good indeed. After almost two years of war, the Republic of Quebec – officially neutral in the war that convulsed the rest of North America – looked very good indeed, too.

People waiting on the platform waved as he and two other men and a woman got off the train. Nicole dashed up to him. He squeezed the air out of his wife, then did the same with his son. 'You should get married more often, Lucien,' he said. 'It lets me take leave.'

Lucien O'Doull sent him a severe look. 'You're as bad as Uncle Georges,' he said. 'I only intend to get married once, thank you very much.'

'As bad as me? Thank *you* very much, Lucien.' Georges Galtier, the younger of Nicole's two brothers, was the family wit, the family cynic, the family punster and practical joker. Most of the Galtiers were swarthy and slight. Georges was dark, but almost as tall as Leonard O'Doull, and half again as wide through the shoulders. His older brother, Charles, stopped picking on him in a hurry when he began to get his full growth. Charles was no coward, but also no fool. No Galtiers were fools.

Charles came up to O'Doull now. He looked achingly like his father. Lucien Galtier, after whom O'Doull's son was named, was several years dead. 'Good to see you again,' Charles said gravely. 'Good to see you safe.' He sounded like his father, too, though he didn't have much of the old man's whimsy. Georges had got all of that, and a little more besides. They both made successful farmers, though. Crops didn't care if you were funny or not.

Hand in hand with Lucien stood his fiancée. Paulette Archambault was a dentist's daughter; the match, if not made in heaven, was certainly one that had a lot of study behind it. Paulette had black hair and blue eyes and a nice figure. O'Doull had no trouble understanding what his son saw in her. 'Welcome to the family,' he said.

'Thank you very much,' Paulette said. 'There's . . . a lot of it, isn't there?'

As if to prove her point, Nicole's three sisters, Susanne, Denise, and Jeanne, greeted O'Doull, too, each with a husband at her side. Jeanne, the youngest, was pregnant again. O'Doull tried to remember if this would be her fifth or sixth. He couldn't. But all the Galtier children had big broods except for Nicole. Lucien O'Doull might be an only child, but he was an only with a raft of first cousins.

'You look tired,' Jeanne told Leonard O'Doull. She was a farm wife with a flock of children, and she was telling him *he* looked tired? If that wasn't madness, damned if he knew what would be.

O'Doull managed a – tired – shrug. 'I've been busier than I wish I were,' he said, and let it go there. Coming back to a country of peace, a country at peace, felt surreal. He'd got used to the tensions of emergency surgery, to the cries of wounded men, to the smells of ether and alcohol and pus and blood and shit, to washing gore from his hands more often than Lady Macbeth ever did. The only familiar odor on the platform was tobacco smoke. Perfume? For all he'd smelled it lately, perfume might be a Martian invention.

'You look like a man who needs a drink,' his wife said.

'Amen!' he exclaimed. Everybody laughed except Nicole, who understood he wasn't kidding. They'd known each other for more than a quarter of a century now. If one of them didn't understand the other, nobody ever would.

'Let's go back to the house,' Nicole said. With the six

Galtier children and their spouses and progeny leaving, the platform lost a big part of the crowd on it.

A house with a lawn in front of it. No broken windows. No bullet holes. No chunks bitten out by artillery or bombs. No craters in the front yard. No gunshots close by. No soldiers stumbling by with numb, stunned faces and thousand-yard stares. No, this wasn't Mars. It seemed more alien than that.

Instead of decay, O'Doull smelled cooking of a sort he'd almost forgotten. He knew Nicole would do herself proud when it came to food. But . . . 'Will we have enough to drink?' A lot of his nieces and nephews were getting old enough to hoist a glass. And Georges always seemed to have a hollow leg.

But Nicole said, 'Don't worry about it.' He *did* worry, till she went on, 'For one thing, I bought twice as much as I thought we'd need. And, for another, the farmer across the road from Charles makes the best applejack in Temiscouata County. He makes a lot of it, too.'

When Leonard O'Doull heard that, he stopped flabbling. A lot of people with apple orchards turned out homemade Calvados. Quality varied widely from one farm to another, often from one batch to another. None of it went through the tiresome formalities involving taxes. The Republic of Quebec loved distillers no more than the Dominion of Canada did before it, and had no better luck bringing them to heel.

O'Doull took packs of Raleighs and Dukes out of his suitcase and distributed them to his wife, his son, and his in-laws. They would have repaired his popularity had he lost it. Quebec got U.S. tobacco, and not enough of that. No one had tasted mild, flavorful cigarettes like these since the early days of the war.

'How did you get them through Customs?' Georges

asked. His face was wreathed in smiles, and in smoke.

'I'm in U.S. uniform.' O'Doull tapped the gold oak leaf on one shoulder strap. 'I speak pretty good French, too. And I let the inspectors have a couple of packs apiece, so they didn't bother me a bit.'

'Such things are wasted on those swine, but what is a man to do?' Georges said with a philosophical shrug.

If the man was Leonard O'Doull, he was to eat too much and to get drunk. He wasn't loud and boisterous, but he felt the applejack buzzing in him. He'd feel it in the morning, too, but he didn't worry about that. He ate, he drank, he talked – and he didn't tell war stories. His Quebecois extended family didn't know how lucky they were not to know much about what he did, and he didn't intend to enlighten them.

A lot of relatives stayed at the house. They slept in the front room, in the dining room, in the kitchen. O'Doull didn't mind. Even now, not everybody had a motorcar. For those who didn't, going back out to a farm and then coming into town again for the wedding the next day would be slow and inconvenient. All the same, he whispered to Nicole, 'You didn't ask one of your sisters to share the bedroom, did you?'

'Why would you want to know that?' his wife asked archly.

'Ha!' he said. 'You'll find out.'

'With so many people here?' Nicole said. 'It's upstairs, remember. If we're not careful, the bed will squeak, and they'll laugh at us.'

'We'll just have to be careful, then, won't we?' O'Doull said. Nicole was laughing at him, but she didn't say no.

She didn't say no later that night, either, though she did lock the door first and she did insist on turning off the light. After nearly two years away, O'Doull felt almost as if he were having his wedding night all over again, just ahead of his son's. He didn't have the stamina Lucien would doubtless display, but he had the sincerity.

'I've missed you more than I know how to tell you,' he said afterwards.

'Why did you go, then?' Nicole asked.

'It needs doing,' he answered. 'I'm a doctor. I'm good at putting people back together. A good many men are alive because I happened to be there.'

'So they can go back to the war and get killed somewhere else instead,' Nicole said tartly.

He shrugged. That made the bed squeak, where their side-by-side lovemaking hadn't, or not very much. It made Nicole squeak, too, in alarm. Laughing a little, O'Doull said, 'I can't do anything about that. God puts them where He wants them. I just patch them up when He looks the other way for a second.'

After the things he'd seen, he wondered how he still believed at all. Granny McDougald didn't, not so far as he could tell. But his own faith survived . . . as long as he didn't lean on it too hard. And he was strong-willed enough to make his own choices. As he usually did, he wore a rubber tonight. Nicole wasn't likely to catch; she was close to fifty. But why take chances? And if that made the Pope unhappy – O'Doull didn't lose much sleep about it.

He didn't lose much sleep about anything. He couldn't begin to guess how far behind he was. Nicole had to shake him awake the next morning. When he did come back to consciousness, the smells of coffee and of frying bacon helped reconcile him to the world. He found fried eggs and fried potatoes to go with the bacon. Susanne and Denise had been busy in the kitchen.

'Thank you, my dears,' he said after he finished breakfast. 'You're just about as wonderful as your sister.' They laughed. Susanne made as if to throw a spatula at him. He made as if to duck. Everybody laughed then. After flying shell fragments and machine-gun bullets, a spatula didn't seem very dangerous.

He thought about wearing uniform to the wedding. He might have, if it were in the USA. In Rivière-du-Loup, he didn't want to remind people he was a foreigner. He didn't want to remind himself, either. His tailcoat smelled of moth-balls, but he put it on anyway. It didn't match Lucien's hired suit, but that was all right: the groom was supposed to be noticed, while his father was perhaps the most easily disposable person in the wedding party. He wasn't even footing the bill – Alphonse Archambault was.

Doctor and dentist greeted each other at the Église St.-Patrice with a handshake and identical words: 'Hello, quack.' They laughed and clapped each other on the back.

Bishop Guillaume celebrated the mass. He wasn't a patch on the former Bishop Pascal, who'd returned to sec-ular life, but his lady friend hadn't had twins, either, which was why the former Bishop Pascal had returned to secular life.

Lucien lifted Paulette's veil and kissed her. The O'Doulls and the Archambaults stood in a receiving line and shook enough hands to make politicians jealous. Then everyone repaired to the Archambaults' house – only a few blocks from the O'Doulls' – and ate and drank with as much abandon as people had the day before. Archambault had either talked with Charles or knew somebody else who made damn good applejack.

Rivière-du-Loup didn't have a hotel. O'Doull and Nicole went down to old Lucien's farm – run by Charles these days – to give Lucien and Paulette the privacy they needed for their first night. In the morning, the newlyweds would catch a train to honeymoon at Niagara Falls – on the

American side, not the Canadian. The Canadian side was under martial law.

Nicole squeezed O'Doull's hand when they rolled past the hospital built on what was once Galtier land. 'If the occupiers hadn't wanted to punish your father by putting the hospital there, we probably wouldn't have met,' O'Doull said.

'See how many things we can blame on them?' Charles said from behind the wheel, his voice as dry as if he were Georges.

'Since Father did eventually get paid, I suppose we can forgive them now,' Nicole said.

'You don't have any other reasons?' O'Doull asked, and she poked him in the ribs.

The farmhouse hadn't changed much with Charles living there. Even most of the furniture was the same as it had been. 'So many memories,' Nicole murmured.

O'Doull nodded. He had a lot of memories of this place, too, though not so many as she did. But he also had other memories, more recent ones, darker ones. All too soon, he would have to get back on a train for himself, not for a honeymoon but to return to nightmare. *What was I doing? What was I thinking?* he wondered. Even though he saved lives, even though he wanted to save lives, he also wanted to stay here. He knew he couldn't, and got drunk again so he didn't have to remember.

Spring in Georgia. What could be finer? Mild air, occasional showers, everything green and growing, the countryside full of birdsong, hummingbirds flitting like bad-tempered jewels from flower to flower. Everything was lovely.

Cassius noticed none of it. He cared about none of it. All he wanted to do was stay alive one more minute, one more hour, one more day.

Had he gone to church with his family in Augusta that Sunday morning, he wouldn't be wandering the Georgia countryside now. When his father and mother and sister didn't come back, he went looking for them – and almost ran right into the cops and Freedom Party stalwarts who'd rounded them up. The ofays were still laughing and joking about their haul, and didn't notice him in the shadows. Every once in a while, a dark skin came in handy.

Of course, if he were born with a white skin, he wouldn't have ended up shut in behind barbed wire in the Terry like a zoo animal. He would have been on the other side of the wire – probably with a submachine gun in his hand and a Freedom Party pin on his lapel.

He didn't dwell on that. He did realize he had to get out of the Terry, and right away. If he didn't, the whites would nab him in a cleanout before long. Off he'd go to a camp. People didn't come out of those places.

He waited till after midnight that night. He had two weapons when he headed for the wire – a pair of tin snips and the biggest, stoutest knife from his mother's kitchen. If anyone spotted him, he aimed to fight. If he could kill somebody with a gun, then he'd have one. He didn't think about dying himself. He was too young to take the idea seriously.

All the heroics he imagined ahead of time evaporated. The tin snips cut through the wire well enough. Come morning, people would have no trouble figuring out where he'd got away, but he didn't care. He'd be long gone by then.

And he was, heading west. He couldn't very well stay inside Augusta. It wouldn't be thirty seconds till he heard, *Let's see your papers, boy!* Nothing in his passbook said he had any business being out and about. Again, they'd ship him off to a camp – or maybe they'd just kill him on the spot.

Out in the country . . . There'd be more Negroes there. Maybe he'd fit in better. And then he could start paying the Freedom Party goons back for everything they were doing.

He'd had connections with the resistance in the city – had them and lost them as people kept dying or getting seized. Now he had to rely on his wits and on the kindness of strangers: black strangers, of course. He'd long since given up on expecting anything from whites. His father always said he got on well with Jerry Dover. He even said Dover had kept their whole family safe more than once. Maybe so – but Dover was in the Army now, and the rest of Cassius' family was in a camp.

When the sun came up, Cassius was walking along a road heading west. He didn't know where he was going. All he knew was that he'd made it out of Augusta alive, and that he was getting hungry and getting thirsty. All the money that had been in the apartment was in his pocket. How long could he make $27.59 (he'd counted it to the last penny – counted it twice, in fact, hoping it would be more the second time around and absurdly disappointed when it wasn't) last? Well, he'd find out.

Maybe he'd find out. On the other hand, maybe he'd get killed before he came close to going through his meager funds. Every time he saw a motorcar, he ran for the pine woods through which the road ran most of the time. Nobody stopped to go after him. None of the vehicles that went by was an armored car, so nobody sprayed the woods with machine-gun fire.

That was good luck, as good luck for Negroes in the CSA ran these days.

Cassius didn't see it so. Aside from being hungry and thirsty, he had sore feet. He couldn't remember when he'd done so much walking. He didn't think he ever had. He wondered if he ought to throw his shoes away. For a while, he didn't. He didn't want to look like a shiftless country nigger. He might have argued with his father, but his attitudes faithfully respected the way he was raised.

He did a little thinking. *Why* didn't he want to look like a shiftless country nigger? Wasn't that his best bet for survival? Away went the shoes, and his socks, too.

Don't go barefoot. You get chiggers, an' hookworm, too. His old man's voice still rang in his ears, or rather, between them. Ignoring it wasn't easy, but Cassius managed. The blisters on his heels sighed with relief. Before long, though, his soles started to complain.

And his luck ran out with the pine woods. For miles ahead, the road ran through fields: cotton, peanuts, tobacco, even rice. He couldn't stay where he was. Living on what he could grub out of the ground – mushrooms and maybe berries – and on the squirrels and rabbits he killed with rocks wasn't living. It was just starving a little more slowly. For better or for worse, he'd grown up in the city. No doubt there were tricks to living out here. Only one trouble: he didn't know them.

He took a deep breath and set out down the road through the fields. A few years earlier, they would have been full of colored sharecroppers. Tractors and harvesters and combines drove Negroes off the land in swarms, though. Like so many towns in the CSA, Augusta had filled with farm workers who couldn't find work. Having them in the cities made it easier for the Freedom Party to scoop them up, too.

Here came a motorcar. It was fairly new and in good repair – not noisy, not belching smoke. That made it a good bet to belong to a white man. Cassius straightened up, squared his shoulders, and kept walking along as if he had every right to be there. Every Negro learned that trick: if you pretended you belonged somewhere, the ofays would believe you really did.

And it worked, damned if it didn't. The driver here wasn't a white man but a white woman, her blond hair blowing in the breeze that came in through the open windows. Her head didn't even turn toward Cassius. As far as she was concerned, he was part of the scenery, like a cow or a dog or a turkey vulture sitting on a telegraph pole.

In a way, that was good. She didn't notice him, and he couldn't afford to be noticed. In another way ... He thought he deserved to be more important than a cow or a dog or a turkey vulture. Whites in the CSA didn't see things like that. They never had. Odds were they never would.

We have to make 'em see, Cassius thought fiercely.

Then a white *did* notice him, and it made his heart leap into his throat. He was walking past a farmhouse when somebody shouted, 'Hey, you! Yeah, you, boy!' The farmer wore bib overalls and a big straw hat. He carried a shotgun, at the moment pointed down at the ground.

'What you want, uh, suh?' Cassius tried not to show how scared he was.

'You chop wood? Got me a pile of wood needs chopping,' the farmer said. 'Pay you a dollar for it when you get done.'

Part of Cassius wanted to leap at that. The rest ... The rest was naturally leery of trusting any white man. 'Half a dollar now, half when I get through,' he said.

'Reckon I'd stiff you?' the farmer said. Cassius just spread his hands, as if to say you never could tell. The farmer shrugged. 'All right. But if you take off halfway through, I'll send the sheriff after you, hell with me if I don't.'

'That's fair,' Cassius allowed. 'Reckon I could get me a ham sandwich an' maybe a Dr. Hopper at noontime 'long with my other four bits?' If he was going to bargain, he'd go all out.

The farmer took the request in stride. 'Don't see why not. Good Book says something about not binding up the mouths of the kine that tread the grain. Reckon that goes for people, too.'

How could he quote the Bible and go along with what was happening to Negroes in the CSA? Maybe he didn't go along, or not all the way, anyhow. He didn't ask to see Cassius' passbook, and he didn't ask any inconvenient questions about what a young black man in city clothes was doing here.

As soon as Cassius saw the mountain of wood he was supposed to chop, he understood at once why the man didn't ask questions. If he chopped all that, he'd earn his dollar three or four times over. He was tempted to light out with the farmer's two quarters in his pocket. One thing held him back: fear. County sheriffs were supposed to use bloodhounds to track people, just the way their grandfathers did back in slavery days. If this one caught him . . . He didn't want to think about that.

With a sigh, he set to work. Before long, sweat ran down his face even though the weather wasn't too warm. He got blisters on his palms bigger than the ones on his heels. The farmer came to check on him, took a look at those, and gave him strips of cloth to wrap around his hands. They helped.

At least an hour before noon, the man brought him an enormous sandwich, a big slice of sweet-potato pie, and a cool Dr. Hopper. The bottle was dripping; maybe it had been in the well. 'Much obliged, suh,' Cassius said.

'You're doing an honest job,' the farmer said. 'Looks like you could use a meal.'

'Maybe some.' Cassius wolfed down the food. He

savored the Dr. Hopper, and smiled when bubbles went up his nose. 'Can I pour a bucket o' water over my head? Feel mighty good if I do.'

'Go right ahead,' the farmer answered.

Cassius walked over to the well and did. He finished somewhere between three and four in the afternoon. The farmer didn't make any fuss about giving him the second installment of his pay, and even brought him another sandwich without being asked. 'Thank you kindly,' Cassius said with his mouth full.

'Want to stick around for a spell?' the white man asked him. 'I could use a hand, and you pull your weight. Say . . . four dollars a week and board?'

The money was chicken feed, though a place to sleep and three – or at least two – meals a day made up for some of that. But Cassius shook his head. 'I better keep movin' on,' he said.

'You won't find many better deals,' the farmer warned.

Not from ofays, Cassius thought. With Negroes, though, he had a chance for something this fellow couldn't hope to give him: vengeance. That still burned in him. 'Obliged,' he said again, 'but I got places to go.'

'And I know where you'll end up: in trouble,' the farmer said. 'You come sneakin' round here after dark raisin' Cain, I'll give you a bellyful of double-aught buckshot. Wouldn't be the first time.'

That meant guerrillas were active in these parts: for Cassius, good news. Still, he said, 'I wouldn't do nothin' like that with you, suh. You treated me fair. You treated me better'n fair, an' I know it.'

'How long will you remember, though?' The white man shrugged. 'Reckon we're quits. I don't have anything against you – you did a job of work there. Ain't seen anybody go at it like that for a long time.'

'I was hungry,' Cassius said with a shrug.

'Makes a difference,' the farmer agreed.

'You know what they're doin' in the city, suh?' Cassius asked. 'You know they got all the niggers shut up inside barbed wire? You know they're takin' 'em to camps an' killin' 'em? They took my ma and my pa and my sister yesterday.'

'No. I didn't know any of that. They don't talk about it much,' the farmer said.

Only after Cassius was a couple of miles down the road, still another sandwich tied up in a rag, did he realize the man had to be lying. Who were *they*? What *did* they say? He wondered why the man bothered to waste time lying to a black. Why not just tell the truth and gloat? One answer occurred to him after another half a mile or so. He'd been closer to the axe than the farmer was, and he'd shown he knew how to use it.

Armstrong Grimes was fit to be tied, and he didn't care who knew it. What was his reward, what was his regiment's reward, what was his division's reward for making the Mormons realize they couldn't throw enough bodies on the fire to put it out? Why, to go to Canada, to go up against a bigger rebellion. He'd called the shot too well.

'How many people in Utah?' he demanded of Yossel Reisen.

'I don't know,' his fellow sergeant answered as the train rattled along through the upper Midwest – or maybe it was in Canada. One stretch of plain looked just as dreary as another. Yossel went on, 'Half a million, maybe?'

'Yeah, and not all of 'em were Mormons, either,' Armstrong said. 'All right – how many people in Canada?'

'Millions,' Reisen said. 'Got to be millions.'

'Fuckin'-A it does. That's what I figure, too,' Armstrong

said. 'So what do we have to do? Kill every goddamn one of them?'

'Hey, don't get sore at me,' Yossel told him. 'I didn't give the orders. I've got to take 'em, same as you do.'

'I'll tell you what's sore. My ass is sore,' Armstrong grumbled. The car he was in had hard benches packed too close together to squeeze in as many soldiers as possible. The smell and a dense cloud of cigarette smoke thickened the air. The Army cared nothing for comfort. It valued efficiency much more. Armstrong shifted from one weary cheek to the other. He nudged his buddy. 'You oughta write your Congresswoman.'

'Armstrong, the first time you said that, it was funny,' Yossel Reisen said. 'The fifth time you said it, I could put up with it. By now, though, by now it gives *me* a fucking pain in the ass, you know?'

'All right, already. Got a butt?' Armstrong asked.

'Sure.' Yossel passed him a pack. He lit up. It helped pass the time. When Armstrong returned the pack, Reisen stuck one in his mouth. Armstrong leaned close to give him a light. After Yossel's first drag, he said, 'We've got to lick the damn Confederates. If we don't, we'll be stuck with our own shitty tobacco forever.'

'There you go.' Armstrong blew out a cloud of smoke. 'One more reason to hate Jake Featherston. I thought I already knew 'em all. We've got to kick his scrawny butt, all right. I wish *we* could do it, too, instead of fucking around with the goddamn stinking worthless Canucks.'

Yossel chuckled. 'I don't quite follow you. Tell us how you really feel.'

Before Armstrong could answer, he discovered they were already in Canada: somebody shot out a window in his railroad car. The bullet missed everybody, but glass sprayed soldiers. Everybody jumped and yelled and swore.

Machine gunners on the roofs of two or three cars opened up on the sniper. Armstrong had no idea if they hit him, but he did hope they made the bastard keep his head down. Then he said, 'My guys – you all right?' He still had his platoon. No eager young second looey had come out to take his place.

'I got somethin' in my eye, Sarge,' somebody right behind him said. 'Is it glass?'

'Lemme see.' Awkwardly, Armstrong turned around. 'Don't blink, Boone, for Christ's sake.' He yanked at the private's eyelid. Damned if he didn't see a chunk of glass not much bigger than a grain of salt. 'Don't flinch, either, dammit.'

'I'll try,' Boone said. Not flinching when somebody's hand came at your eye was probably harder than holding steady in combat. The soldier managed . . . pretty well.

'Hang on.' Armstrong peered down at his thumb. Sure as hell, he'd got the glass out. He flicked it away. 'Blink. How's your eye?'

'Better, Sarge,' Boone said in glad surprise. 'Thanks a million.' He blinked again. 'Yeah, it's all right now.'

'Bully.' Armstrong didn't know why he said that. He couldn't remember the last time he'd used it. He couldn't remember if he'd ever used it. Even his old man hardly ever said it. But getting something out of somebody's eye made you feel fatherly, and fathers talked in old-fashioned ways.

Yossel Reisen gave him a quizzical look. 'Bully?'

'Well, what about it?' Armstrong snapped. He was embarrassed he'd come out with it, too.

'Nothing,' Yossel said. But it wasn't nothing, because he added, 'You sounded like George Custer, that's all.'

'Thanks a lot, Yossel.' Armstrong had often wondered why his father gave him Custer's middle name and not his first one. George Grimes would have been a perfectly ordinary handle. Armstrong . . . wasn't. He shrugged. Yossel had a funnier name yet, although maybe not if you were a Jew.

A few minutes later, the train screeched and squealed to a stop. They weren't anywhere that Armstrong could see – just out in the middle of the damn prairie. Before long, though, officers started yelling, 'Out! Out!'

'What the fuck?' Boone said. Armstrong only shrugged. He didn't know what was going on, either.

He was standing out on the prairie with his men, waiting for somebody to tell him what to do next. Either nobody was in a hurry to do that or nobody knew. He looked around. In Utah, he'd got used to always having mountains on the horizon. No mountains here. This was the flattest country he'd ever seen; it made Ohio look like the Himalayas. The train tracks stretched out toward infinity. As far as he could tell, the two rails met there.

'Next town ahead is Rosenfeld!' yelled somebody with a loud, authoritative voice. 'Canucks ran the Frenchies out of there, and they hold the train station. We're going to take it back from them. Rosenfeld sits at a railway junction, so we need the place if we're going to be able to use both lines. You got that?'

'Goddamn Frenchies,' Armstrong muttered. The soldiers from the Republic of Quebec showed no enthusiasm for fighting their former countrymen. He'd heard Mexican troops in the CSA didn't jump up and down at the idea of shooting at – and getting shot by – the spooks down there. Both sets of soldiers from small countries probably figured they didn't really want to do big countries' dirty work for them. *Well, the hell with 'em,* he thought. *I don't want to get my ass shot off, either.*

Yossel Reisen, on the other hand, summed things up in

half a dozen words: 'This is where we came in.' Armstrong grunted and nodded. They'd got off the train and fought their way forward in Utah, too.

He hoped the Canadians wouldn't be as fanatical as the Mormons. He had trouble imagining how they could be, but a soldier's life was full of nasty surprises. The men in green-gray shook themselves out into skirmish lines and moved forward. A woman with hair once red but now mostly gray stood outside her farmhouse staring at them as they tramped past.

'She saw Americans come this way in 1914, too,' Yossel murmured.

'Yeah, and her husband probably made bombs or some-thing,' Armstrong said. Yossel trudged on for another couple of paces, then nodded.

One good thing, as far as Armstrong was concerned: this flat, flat ground offered far fewer ambush points than Utah's rougher terrain. The first gunfire came from a farmhouse and its outbuildings. The American soldiers went after the strongpoints with practiced ease. Machine guns made the Canadians stay down. Mortar teams dropped bombs on the buildings and set some afire. Only then did foot soldiers approach. A few Canucks opened up on them. More mortar and machine-gun fire silenced the position.

Then something new was added to the mix. A beat-up old pickup truck bounced across the fields. It turned broad-side to the American soldiers. 'Get down!' Armstrong yelled to his men. Whatever the bastard driving that truck was doing, it didn't look friendly.

And it wasn't. Two Canucks in the pickup's staked bed served a machine gun on a tall mount. The gun chattered. Bullets sprayed toward the Americans. Wounded soldiers shouted and screamed. A few men in green-gray had the presence of mind to shoot back, but only a few. Leaving a trail of dust in the distance, the truck bucketed away.

'Jesus!' Armstrong said, and then, 'Well, I will be damned.'

'How come?' Yossel Reisen asked.

'Because here's a way to make our lives miserable the fucking Mormons never thought of,' Armstrong answered. He pointed toward the pickup, which was long out of range. 'It's not as good as a barrel, but they can sure as shit chew us up from long range if they've got more than one or two of those stinking things. And they will. Bet your ass they will.' He spoke with a veteran's ingrained pessimism.

Yossel didn't tell him he was wrong. The other sergeant did say, 'A couple-three rounds through the engine block and those trucks won't go anywhere fast.'

'Sure – if we can do it,' Armstrong said. 'What about this guy, though? We never laid a glove on the mother.'

'He surprised us,' Yossel said.

'Sure as shit surprised me,' Armstrong agreed. 'Damn near punctured me besides.' He'd lasted two years with nothing worse than cuts and bruises and scrapes. He wanted to go on lasting, too. He'd seen too many horrible things happen to other people. He knew much too well that they could also happen to him.

'Now we know they've got 'em,' Yossel said. 'We'll spread our machine guns out more or whatever the hell. No soft-skinned trucks are going to make monkeys out of us.'

'Ook,' Armstrong said, and scratched under his armpits. Yossel gave him the finger, but he didn't care. As far as he was concerned, he was dead right. That damn machine gun must have wounded eight or ten men. The Americans were flabbling as if it was going out of style, but they weren't doing anything except flabbling. One lousy pickup truck knocked them back on their heels.

They needed most of an hour to start moving forward again. Half a mile closer to Rosenfeld, another defended farmhouse held them up. As soon as they went to the ground, two pickup trucks showed up. They stayed at extreme range and blazed away. Most of their bullets were bound to go wild. A few, though – a few would wound or kill.

Somebody with an antibarrel cannon made either a lucky shot or a great one and set a pickup on fire. The other truck zoomed up alongside, picked up the men who got out, and roared off. Despite all the U.S. bullets and shells that flew toward it, it got away.

'How many little trucks do you suppose the Canucks have?' Yossel asked.

Armstrong gave that the only possible answer: 'Too goddamn many.' His buddy nodded.

They fought their way into Rosenfeld a couple of hours later. The Canadian fighters didn't try to hold the little prairie town with the fanatical determination the Mormons showed over every inch of ground in Utah. But Canada had a hell of a lot more inches than Utah did. The defenders headed north, toward Winnipeg. They would make another stand somewhere else. Only at the train station and a diner called Pomeroy's did they put up much of a fight.

The Canucks wrecked the tracks in the station, blew up the building, and escaped. Pomeroy's was a different story. The rebels who holed up there didn't run and didn't give up. The only person who got out of the burning, battered building was a little boy about six years old. He'd lost the last joint of his left little finger. Otherwise, he didn't seem badly hurt.

'What's your name, kid?' Armstrong asked as he bandaged the boy's hand.

'I'm Alec.' The boy looked at him. 'You must be a god-damn Yank.'

'Yeah, well, I love you, too.' Armstrong pulled a squashed chocolate bar out of his pocket. 'Here. Want it?'

'Thank you,' Alec said gravely. 'But you're still a god-damn Yank.'

'You better believe it, you little bastard,' Armstrong told him, not without pride.

Vienna, Georgia, was as far as east as Spartacus' guerrilla band had gone since Jonathan Moss and Nick Cantarella joined them. Spartacus insisted on pronouncing the name of the place as *Vie*-enna. So did everybody else who talked about it. From everything Moss heard, it probably didn't hold two thousand people. But its name was proudly distinct from that of the capital of Austria-Hungary.

Mexican soldiers and overage white men patrolled the roads. The Negroes moved cross-country, past the ghosts of what had been their lives till the Freedom Party turned on them. The countryside was achingly empty: so many people either gone to towns to look for work or just gone, period.

Nick Cantarella was chortling over an article in a three-day-old copy of the *Albany Gazette* somebody had brought into camp. 'Listen to this,' he said, nudging Moss with his elbow. ' "Brave Canadian patriots with machine guns mounted on the back of pickup trucks have inflicted heavy casualties on the brutal U.S. occupiers in a series of lightning-like hit-and-run raids." Isn't that terrific?'

Moss gave the U.S. infantry captain a quizzical glance. 'Well, I guess it depends on whose side you're on.'

'Oh.' Cantarella laughed some more. 'Yeah, sure. But it's a terrific idea. We could do that right here. We *should* do it. And I was just laughing on account of Jake Featherston's propaganda asswipe told me about it.'

'All right. Now I get it. Color me dumb,' Moss said. 'Yeah, we could build a machine-gun mount if we had ourselves a truck.'

'Bet your ass we could,' Cantarella said. 'Couple-three of these smokes are better mechanics than half the guys you'd find in a motor pool. They're used to working with scrap metal and junk, 'cause they couldn't get anything else.'

'Let's talk to Spartacus,' Moss said.

They put their case to the guerrilla leader. 'Ain't hard gettin' us a truck, or as many as we need,' he said. 'All we gots to do is steal 'em.' He took the prospect for granted. 'Wish we had us mo' machine guns. We could fit 'em out like they was tanks, damn near.' That was the old-fashioned British word for barrels.

Cantarella shook his head. 'Well, no, not quite. The thing about barrels is, they're armored. Somebody shoots up one of these trucks, it's gonna be shot up, all right. Can't get too gay with 'em, or you'll be sorry quick. You hear what I'm sayin'?'

'I hear you,' Spartacus answered. 'Makes sense. Still and all . . . Reckon we can git some o' the ofays round these parts to shit their pants?' He grinned.

'Oh, I think we might. I think we just might,' Cantarella answered. 'We ought to make the mount so we can take it off a truck in a hurry. Sometimes a truck *will* get shot up. Sometimes we'll have to leave it behind 'cause we can't hide it. Shame to have to build a whole new mount again if something like that happens, you know?'

'That makes sense, too,' Spartacus allowed. His grin got wider. 'We's gonna put trouble on wheels.'

'Hell, yes,' Cantarella said.

Three pickups walked with Jesus in Vienna that very night. The guerrilla band's blacksmiths got to work on one the next morning. Spartacus stashed the other two in an abandoned Negro village a few miles outside of town. Jonathan Moss found places like that heartbreaking. How many of them were there, from one end of the CSA to the other? And what happened to the people who used to live in them? Nothing good – that was only too plain.

The colored blacksmiths got the idea about fitting a machine gun on a truck as soon as Cantarella started explaining. One of them – a man named Caligula – said, 'Don't need to give us no sermon on the mount, suh.' He sent the white man a sly smile.

Cantarella winced. Moss groaned. The Negroes broke up. Moss looked at them with new eyes from then on. Anyone who made puns that bad was – damn near had to be – a real live human being, and deserved to be slapped down just like anybody else.

And the mount the blacksmiths came up with was beautifully simple. They fastened a short length of upright iron pipe to the truck bed. If they lost the truck, they would lose it, too. Into it they stuck a longer pipe whose outer diameter matched the inner diameter of the bottom part of the mount. And on top of that they fixed the machine gun.

Jonathan Moss admired the result. 'If you were going to make these as a regular thing, you couldn't do any better,' he said. 'Where did the pipe come from?'

'Reckon some plumber wonder where the pipe go, suh,' Caligula answered with another sidelong grin.

All the Negroes were eager to take their new toy out on the road, so eager that they almost came to blows. They all knew how to serve the machine gun. Only a handful of them, though, could drive. That was funny, in a frightening way. Spartacus sidled up to Moss and asked, 'How you like to be our driver?'

How would *I like that?* Moss wondered. He was less useful to the guerrillas than Nick Cantarella, simply because he knew less about the infantryman's trade. But he damn well could drive a truck. 'Sure,' he said after no more than a second's hesitation. 'Put somebody who knows where he's going in the cab with me, though. I didn't grow up around here, so I don't know all the little back roads that'll get me out of trouble.'

'I go with you my ownself,' Spartacus said. 'Reckon I knows this country tolerable good.' He let out a nasty chuckle. 'Reckon we gonna give the ofays a little bit of a surprise, too. Yeah, jus' a li'l bit.'

What will the Confederates do to me if they recapture me fighting alongside the black guerrillas? Moss decided he didn't want to know, not in any detail. He also decided he couldn't afford to be taken, not any more. 'Let me have a pistol,' he said, and mimed shooting himself in the head.

'Oh, yes. We takes care o' dat,' Spartacus promised, and he did. The .45 he handed Moss the next morning was an officer's sidearm. It would do the job, all right.

Strategy was simplicity itself. About an hour after sunup, they set off up the road from Vienna, heading north toward the even smaller town of Pinehurst about ten miles away. Anything they passed, they shot up. The first auto they came up to was driven by a fat, gray-haired white man. He started to give Moss a friendly smile as the pickup truck passed his beat-up gray Birmingham. The smile changed to a look of horror when he saw Spartacus on the seat beside Moss. A moment later, a burst of machine-gun fire finished him and set his motorcar on fire.

Spartacus and the blacks in the back all whooped. 'Do Jesus!' the guerrilla leader yelled. 'This here gonna be fun!'

That white man wouldn't think so. But then, if he was one of the yahoos who went around yelling, 'Freedom!' he was helping the Confederate States' government visit wholesale slaughter on their blacks. If he happened to get in the way of a little retail slaughter coming the other way – well, too damn bad.

A tractor sat in a cotton field not far from the side of the road. 'Stop the truck!' Spartacus told Moss. He followed the black man's order. Spartacus pointed out the window. 'Put some holes in that fucker!' he yelled. The gun crew obeyed. The tractor sent a plume of black, greasy smoke up into the sky.

They wrecked two more tractors and a combine. Jonathan Moss nodded to himself. Those were the tools that let white farmers get along without black sharecroppers. They were handy, yes, but they were also expensive. How would those whites like watching them go up in flames?

The gunners sprayed an oncoming automobile with bullets. It went off the road, flipped over, and burned like a torch. 'This *is* fun!' Spartacus shouted. Moss nodded. Destruction for the sake of destruction brought a nasty thrill with it, almost as if he were a staid married man visiting a whorehouse.

There was a checkpoint outside of Pinehurst: a sleepy one, manned by three or four Great War veterans too old or too infirm to do anything more strenuous. They were just going through the motions. They didn't expect any trouble as the pickup truck drew near. Spartacus ducked down so they couldn't see him next to Moss.

When the machine gunners in the back of the pickup opened fire, the guards toppled like tenpins. 'Git!' Spartacus told Moss. 'Go left, then left again soon as you can.'

The road up to Pinehurst was paved; the one onto which

Spartacus put Moss was nothing but a dirt track. Red dust rose in choking clouds, for it hadn't rained lately. 'The dust will let them track us,' Moss said.

'So what?' Spartacus answered. 'We be long gone by the time they catch up to us – an' if we ain't, they be sorry.' He probably wasn't wrong about that. Pursuers – even riflemen – coming up against a machine gun would get a lethal surprise.

He sent Moss and the pickup bouncing along back roads and tracks nobody who hadn't known these parts for years would have been able to follow. Moss' teeth clicked together more than once. They weren't necessarily *good* tracks. One of them had a hog wallow right in the middle. Spartacus pointed straight ahead. Moss gunned the engine and leaned on the horn. The machine gunners solved the problem a different way. As hogs scrambled out of the muck, the gunners shot them.

The truck sprayed stinking mud as it went through. 'Stop!' Spartacus yelled when it got to the other side. Moss hit the brakes. The machine-gun crew hopped out and threw three carcasses into the back of the pickup. 'We don't just shoot up the ofays,' Spartacus said happily. 'We eats good today, too.'

A white man with a shotgun charged out of a farmhouse a couple of hundred yards away. He didn't want to yield his porkers without a fight. The machine gunners sprayed a burst in his general direction. He ran away even faster than he'd come out.

'We don't take shit from nobody!' Spartacus roared as Moss put the pickup in gear again. Riding around with a machine gun in the back of your truck worked wonders for your confidence.

Those side roads brought the pickup almost back to where its rampages had begun. The machine gun and the top part of the mount came off neat as you please. One of the gunners carried the weapon. The other shouldered the long pipe. More guerrillas emerged from the undergrowth to take charge of the dead pigs.

Roast pork and a ten-mile stretch of road shot to hell and gone made for a celebration that evening. So did a couple of jugs of raw corn whiskey. The stuff tasted like paint thinner and burned its way down like a lighted kerosene lamp. After a few swallows, Moss started forgetting things. A few more, he knew, and he'd have trouble remembering his name.

But he needed to remember something. 'You've got to tell people,' he said to Spartacus, the homemade hooch adding urgency to his voice.

'Tell which people?' the guerrilla leader asked. 'Tell 'em what?' He was drinking harder than Moss.

'Got to tell the other colored fighters.' Moss was proud of himself. He did remember! 'Got to tell them what these pickup trucks can do.'

'Don't you worry none about dat,' Spartacus said. 'Be all over Georgia day after tomorrow. Be all the way to Louisiana this time nex' week. Yes, suh. You best believe it will. We done hit the ofays hard. Folks is gonna hear about it. You best believe folks is gonna hear about it.'

Moss turned to Nick Cantarella. 'You're a hero.'

'My ass,' Cantarella said. 'I didn't even get to drive the truck.' But he hadn't drunk himself fighting mad, for he went on, 'What I really like about this is that their own damn propaganda upped and bit 'em. I never woulda thought of mounting a machine gun on a pickup and raising hell. But since those stupid pricks went and told me how—'

'Here's to propaganda,' Moss said. They both drank.

*

Colonel Terry DeFrancis was one of the youngest officers of his rank Major General Abner Dowling had ever seen. Remembering how long he'd taken to get to bird colonel himself, Dowling eyed the boy wonder with suspicion.

'My orders from the War Department are to subordinate myself to you and to smash C.S. air power in west Texas,' DeFrancis said. 'I think my wing has brought enough fighters and bombers out here to do the job, too.'

'I wouldn't begin to argue with you there, Colonel,' Dowling said. In one fell swoop, the air power at his command had tripled. 'But why does Philadelphia care now when it didn't before?'

'Sir, I can answer that in three little words,' DeFrancis told him.

'If you're going to say, *I love you,* Colonel, I'll throw you out on your ear,' Dowling warned, straight-faced.

Terry DeFrancis stared at him, then laughed like a loon. 'You're not what I expected, sir, not even slightly,' he said. 'No, what I was going to say is, *I don't know.* Have Featherston's boys been pulling off air raids that hurt?'

'If they have, nobody told me about it,' Dowling answered. 'They haven't had enough airplanes out here to hurt us very badly. We haven't had enough to do much to them, either. Sounds like things are going to change, though.'

'That's what I'm here for,' Colonel DeFrancis agreed. 'That's what my boys are here for. We're going to make them sorry if we can.'

'Good,' Dowling said. It was good in all kinds of ways. If the War Department had aircraft to spare for an out-of-the-way outfit like his Eleventh Army, it was bound to have even more farther east, where the real decision would lie. And . . . 'Tell me something, Colonel: when they sent you out here, did they say anything about Camp Determination?'

'No, sir,' the younger man answered. 'Is that ours or theirs? Sounds like something the Freedom Party would name.'

'There's a reason for that – it *is* something the Freedom Party named. Here. Take a look at these.' Dowling's desk had a locked drawer. He unlocked it and took out the aerial reconnaissance photos of the camp near Snyder . . . and of the mass graves not far away.

DeFrancis studied them with meticulous care. He was frowning as he looked up at Dowling. 'Interpreting stuff like this isn't always easy, especially when you're seeing it for the first time. What exactly am I looking at here?' Dowling told him exactly what he was looking at there. DeFrancis' jaw dropped. 'You're making that up . . . uh, sir.'

'Colonel, I wish to Christ I were,' Dowling answered, and the disgust and horror in his voice had to carry conviction. 'It's the truth, though. If anything, it's an understatement. They really are killing off their Negroes, and they really are doing it by carload lots. Literally by carload lots – that's a railroad spur between the two halves of the camp.'

'Yes, sir. I saw that it was.' Colonel DeFrancis stared down at the pictures again. When he looked up this time, he wasn't just frowning. He was slightly green, or more than slightly. 'You know, I thought all those stories were bullshit. Propaganda. Stuff we pumped out to keep the civilians all hot and bothered about the war effort. Back in the last war, the British said the Germans boiled babies' bodies to make soap. That kind of thing.'

'I felt the same way till I got out here,' Dowling said grimly. 'Who wouldn't? If you're halfway decent yourself, you figure the guy on the other side is, too. Well, the guy on the other side here is Jake Featherston, and Jake

Featherston really is just as big a son of a bitch as everybody always thought he was.'

DeFrancis eyed the photographs once more. Dowling understood that. They had an evil fascination to them. In their own way, they were just as much filthy pictures as the ones you could buy in any town where soldiers or sailors got leave. 'What can we do about this, sir?' DeFrancis asked. 'We can't just let it go on. I mean, I haven't got any great use for niggers, but. . . .'

'Yeah. But.' Dowling reached into another desk drawer. He pulled out a half-pint of whiskey and slid it across the desk to the younger man. 'Here. Wash the taste out of your mouth.'

'Thank you, sir.' DeFrancis took a healthy swig, then set the flat bottle down. 'What *can* we do? We've got to do something.'

'I think so, too, though you'd be amazed at how many people on our side of the border don't give a rat's ass,' Dowling said. 'I've had the time to think about it now. Way it looks to me is, we can't just bomb hell out of the camp. If we do that, we go into the nigger-killing business ourselves. Like you said, I don't have much use for them, but I don't want to do that.'

'I agree,' DeFrancis said. 'Like I told you, sir, my first priority is blasting enemy airstrips and aircraft, but now I see what I do next.'

Dowling scratched his head. The War Department suddenly seemed to have a wild hair about C.S. airstrips here in the West. Had the latest raids on Los Angeles and Las Vegas and Denver rattled people back East so much? If they had, why? Dowling shrugged. That wasn't his worry – and, as often as not, the ways of the gods back in Philadelphia were unfathomable to mere mortals in the field.

'I haven't operated out here before,' Colonel DeFrancis said. 'What's the fuel situation like?'

'We don't have a problem there,' Dowling said. 'The refineries in Southern California are working with local crude, so they're at full capacity. We get what we need. A lot of the airplane plants are out there, too, so you should be able to get your hands on spare parts.'

'Assuming they don't decide to send all of them – and all the avgas – to Ohio and Virginia,' DeFrancis said.

'Yes, assuming,' Dowling agreed. 'We can't do much about that, so there isn't much point to worrying about it, is there?'

'No, sir.' The young officer eyed him. 'I think we're going to get on pretty well, sir.' He might have been announcing a miracle.

'Well, here's hoping,' Dowling said. 'I put up with General Custer for a lot of years. My thought is, if I managed that, most people ought to be able to stand me for a while.'

'Er – yes, sir.' Colonel DeFrancis gave him an odd look now. To DeFrancis, as to most people, George Armstrong Custer was a hero up on a marble column. He wasn't a whiskey-drinking, cigar-smoking, skirt-chasing (whenever his wife wasn't too close), evil-tempered, mule-stubborn old man. Reminding people that a hero had feet of clay (and sometimes a head of iron) seldom won you friends.

No matter what DeFrancis thought about General Custer, he knew what to do with airplanes. He built his strips close to the front, relying on the Eleventh Army not to lose ground and leave them vulnerable to artillery fire. Dowling thought he could oblige the flier there. But he was gloomily certain the Confederates would find out where the new fields were as soon as the bulldozers and steamrollers started leveling ground. No matter whether you called this part of the world west Texas or part of a revived U.S. state of Houston, the people here remained passionately pro-Confederate. And the land was so wide and troops scattered so thinly, those people had no trouble slipping across the front to tell the enemy what they knew.

Or rather, what they thought they knew. Terry DeFrancis proved devious to a downright byzantine degree. Earth-moving equipment laid out and flattened several dummy fields along with the ones his airplanes would actually use. Confederate bombers called on more of the dummies than the real airstrips, wasting their high-explosive sweetness on the desert ground.

And then DeFrancis' medium and heavy bombers roared off to respond. Dowling drove back to one of the strips – irreverently named Fry Featherston Field – to watch them go. They and their escort fighters kicked up ungodly clouds of dust. Coughing, Dowling said, 'We've got our own smoke screen.'

'Yes, sir,' DeFrancis shouted over the engines' thunder. 'We could use one, too. I'm not used to operating in broad daylight. It's a different war out here. New rules.'

'No, Colonel.' Dowling shook his head. 'Only one rule, the same one you find anywhere. We've got to beat those bastards.'

DeFrancis pondered that, but not for long. 'We'll do it, sir. We'll beat 'em like a drum.'

He kept fighters in the air when the bombers came back for fuel and ordnance. A few bombers – and a few fighters – didn't come back. The Confederates had fighters of their own, and antiaircraft around their airfields. You couldn't fight a war without taking losses. Colonel DeFrancis looked grim. The men who went down weren't just fliers to him. They were friends, almost family.

Wireless technicians monitored signals from the U.S. airplanes, and also from the Confederates. They marked maps and brought them to DeFrancis and Dowling. 'Looks like we're doing pretty good, sir,' one of them said.

'We're plastering the fields we know about, all right,' DeFrancis said.

'How many fields have they got that we don't know about?' Dowling asked.

'That's always the question,' DeFrancis said. 'We'll find out how hard they hit back, and from where. Then we'll go blast hell out of those places, too. Sooner or later, they won't be able to stand the gaff any more.'

He sounded confident. Dowling looked inside himself – and found he was confident, too. Enemy bombers returned, but at night: the Confederates had paid too high a price to go on with day bombing. That was a sign they were hurting, or Dowling hoped it was. Night bombing spared their airplanes, but wasn't very accurate.

The Confederates managed to sneak auto bombs onto a couple of fields. They blew up one bomber in its revetment and cratered another runway. The runway was easy enough to repair; the bomber was a write-off. Terry DeFrancis cashiered the officers in charge of security at those strips.

When Dowling heard about the auto bombs, he telephoned and asked what the wing commander had done about them. When he found out, he grunted in sour satisfaction. 'If you didn't give 'em the boot, I would have,' he said.

'Figured as much, sir,' DeFrancis said. 'But I can shoot my own dog, by God. And I shot both those sons of bitches. They had no business falling asleep at the switch. This isn't Nebraska, for God's sake. Enemy action shouldn't catch them playing with themselves.'

'In two words, Colonel, you're right.' Dowling hung up feeling better about the world than he had in quite a while. DeFrancis was an officer after his own heart.

On the ground, the Eleventh Army wasn't making much progress. Dowling used what he had as aggressively as he could. He'd already made the Confederates send that elite unit to stall his advance. The Party Guards did it, too. He was disappointed about that, but not crushed. Whatever the Freedom Party Guards did here, they weren't doing in Ohio or Kentucky or Virginia, places that really mattered.

He wondered if the Confederates would send more bombers west to contest the skies with Terry DeFrancis' airplanes. They didn't. Their counterattacks dwindled. Before long, they were reduced to harassment raids from biplanes that sounded like flying sewing machines – Boll Weevils, the Confederates called them. They came straight out of the Great War: their pilots heaved five- and ten-pound bombs from the cockpit by hand.

That sounded laughable, till the first time one of those little bombs blew up an officers' club. The Boll Weevils flew at what would have been treetop height if there were any trees close by. Y-ranging had a devil of a time spotting them, and nothing else could, not till they got right on top of whatever they intended to hit.

They would never win the war for the CSA. Even so, they kept Dowling and DeFrancis back on their heels. U.S. air power had won part of the fight here in west Texas, but not all of it. Abner Dowling fumed in Lubbock. Nothing ever went quite the way you wished it would.

VIII

George Enos had never crossed the country on a train before. That he could now said the war had come a long way in the past few months. The *Townsend* sat in dry-dock in San Diego, getting a refit and repairs. They'd given him enough liberty to go to Boston, stay a few days, and then hop another train heading back to the West Coast.

The one he was on now would have gone faster if it could have made anything better than a crawl at night. But blackouts were strictly enforced. The cars had black curtains. Along with conductors, they had hard-faced blackout monitors who carried .45s and made sure nobody showed a light at night.

Those monitors had good reason to look tough. The farther east the train traveled, the more often George saw wrecks shoved off to one side of the railroad. The government no doubt figured they were part of the cost of making war. The government had a point. George doubted the people in those ravaged trains would have appreciated it.

He came through Ohio during the day, so he could see what the war had done. He stared in astonishment. It looked more like the mountains of the moon than any human landscape. How many years would this part of the country take to recover from the devastation? Would it ever? How could it?

He didn't go through Pittsburgh. From everything he'd

heard, that was even worse. That he could get through at all was plenty. *This time last year, things were even worse,* he thought. He shook his head. It seemed impossible.

Even Boston had taken bomb damage. He'd heard that, too. Seeing it as the train slowed and then stopped was something else again. *Those bastards hit my home town.* The fury that stirred up amazed him.

He wasn't overjoyed about coming into town three and a half hours behind schedule, either. He wasn't surprised, but he wasn't overjoyed. He hoped Connie and his sons weren't waiting for him on the platform. The boys would be bouncing off the walls if they'd had to sit around all that time.

When the train stopped, he jumped up, grabbed his duffel, and slung it over his shoulder. He almost clobbered another sailor. 'Sorry, buddy,' he said. Then a sergeant almost clobbered him. He laughed. What went around came around, but not usually so soon.

There was a traffic jam at the door to the car. Everybody wanted to get out first. Eventually, the door opened and people squeezed out. Most of the passengers were soldiers and sailors coming home on leave. Screaming, weeping women rushed toward them.

'George!' That was redheaded Connie – she was there after all. She almost knocked him off his feet when she threw her arms around him.

'Hi, babe,' he said. Then he kissed her, and that took a lot of careful attention. He felt as if he stayed submerged longer than any submersible in the U.S. Navy. At last he came up for air, his heart pounding. He noticed his wife was there by herself. 'Where are the kids?' he asked.

'My mother's got 'em,' Connie answered. 'I figured the train would be late, and I was right. . . . What's so funny?'

'You talk like Boston,' George said. 'So do I, but I'm

about the only guy on my ship who does. I'm not used to hearing it any more.'

'Well, you better get used to it pretty darn quick, on account of it's how people talk around here,' Connie said. 'What do you think of that?'

He hadn't let go of her. 'Your ma's got the boys?' he said. His wife nodded. 'At her place?' Connie nodded again. George squeezed. 'In that case, I know exactly what I think.' He squeezed her again, tighter.

'Oh, you do, do you? And what's that?' Connie pretended not to know.

'Let's go back to the apartment. You'll find out,' he said.

'Sailors.' She laughed. 'Sure, let's go. You won't be fit to live with till we do.' Her mock-tough tone softened. 'And I've missed you.'

'Missed you, too, babe,' George said, and it was true. He did his best to forget his occasional visits to whores. He told himself they didn't really count. He didn't do anything like that when he was at home. And his visits to pro stations must have worked; he'd passed every shortarm inspection. He wouldn't be bringing Connie any unexpected presents. *That* was a relief.

When they got to the subway station, the ticket-seller wouldn't take his nickel. 'Free to men in uniform, sir,' she said. Before the war, everybody who worked in the subway system had been male. One more thing the pressure of fighting had changed.

'I hate these cars. They're so crowded,' Connie said as the train rattled along. George nodded purely for politeness' sake. It didn't seem that bad to him. He'd got used to being packed tight with other people on fishing boats. The Navy pushed men together closer still. No subway car could faze him.

He dropped the duffel inside the front door to the apartment and looked around in amazement. The living room was so big! And the kitchen and the bedrooms lay beyond! And a bathroom just for the family, with a door that closed! 'I swear to God, hon, the skipper on the *Townsend* doesn't live half this good!' George said.

'I should hope not,' Connie said, and pulled her dress off over her head.

That wasn't what George meant, but it wasn't bad, either. He would have dragged her down on the floor and done the deed right there. Why not? With a carpet down, it was softer than the decks he'd been walking since going to sea. But, giggling, she twisted away and hurried back into the bedroom. He followed, standing at attention even while he walked.

A bed was better than even a carpeted floor. Afterwards, sated for the moment, George was willing to admit it. 'Wow,' he said, lighting a cigarette and then running a hand along Connie's sweet curves. 'Why'd I go and join the Navy?'

'I asked you that when you went and did it,' Connie said. 'See what you've been missing?'

'It's good to be home, all right,' he said. 'But the Army would've got me if I didn't put on a sailor suit. If I could've gone on doing my job, that would've been different. But conscription would've nailed me. I'd rather be a sailor than a soldier any day of the week, and twice on Sundays.'

He wondered why. Putting to sea wasn't safer than staying on dry land. He'd seen as much in the endless clashes with the Japanese over the Sandwich Islands. But he'd been going out to sea since he was in high school. He'd never gone through the middle of the USA till this train trip from the West Coast. He was doing what he was used to.

Connie poked him in the ribs. He jerked. 'What was that for?' he asked.

'What do you do when you come into port when you're halfway around the world from me?' his wife said. 'Do you go looking for floozies, the way sailors do when they get into Boston?'

'Not me,' he lied solemnly. If he hadn't expected that question, he couldn't have handled it so well. 'I'm a married guy, I am. I like being a married guy.' To show how much he liked it, he leaned over and started caressing her in earnest. He wasn't ready for a second round as fast as he would have been a few years earlier, but he'd gone without for a long time. He didn't have much trouble.

Smiling in the afterglow, Connie said, 'I like the way you argue.'

'Me, too,' George said, and they both laughed. She wouldn't have liked it so much – which was putting things mildly, with her redhead's temper – if he'd told her the truth. He never felt like straying if she was anywhere close by. If they were thousands of miles apart, though, if he wasn't going to see her for months . . . As long as he didn't come down with the clap and pass it along, what she didn't know wouldn't hurt her. And then he poked her the same way she'd poked him. She squeaked. 'What about you?' he asked. 'You looking at the handsome delivery guys and truck drivers while I'm gone?'

'That's a laugh,' she answered. 'These days, the delivery guys and truck drivers have white mustaches or hooks or wooden legs – either that or their voices aren't done changing yet. Besides, if I was stupid enough to do something like that, you'd find out about it. Somebody would blab. Somebody always does. But you're off in those places where nobody ever heard of you, so who knows what you could get away with if you wanted to?'

She was right. She was righter than she knew – and righter than he ever intended to let her find out. And she was right that word about straying wives did get back to husbands. A couple of men on the *Townsend* had got that kind of bad news from people in their home towns: either from relatives or from 'friends' who couldn't stand keeping their big mouths shut.

Connie teased him about going off the reservation, but she didn't really push him, which could only mean she didn't really think he was doing it. That left him relieved and embarrassed at the same time. She said, 'Now that you've acted like a sailor who just got home, do you want to see your children?'

'Sure,' George. 'Let's see if they remember me.'

Patrick and Margaret McGillicuddy had a house not far from the Enos' apartment. Connie's father was a fisherman, too, and out to sea right now. He was well past fifty; they weren't going to conscript him no matter what. Connie's mother was a lot like her, even if she'd put on a little weight and her hair wasn't so bright as it used to be. Margaret McGillicuddy didn't take guff from anyone, even her grandsons. To George's way of thinking, that made her a better grandma, not a worse one.

He missed his own mother – a sudden stab of longing he could never do anything about now. If only she'd never taken up with that worthless, drunken bum of a writer. He'd shot himself, too, not that that did George any good.

When George walked into the McGillicuddys' place, Leo and Stan were playing with tin soldiers, some painted green-gray, others butternut. Stan, who was younger, had the Confederates. He was losing, and not happy about it. Being a little brother meant getting the dirty end of the stick. George was the older of two children, and he had a sister. He hoped Mary Jane was doing well. He'd find out . . . soon.

For now, the boys looked up from their game, yelled,

'Daddy!' and knocked everything over. They charged him. He picked them both up. That was harder than it had been before he joined the Navy – they'd grown a hell of a lot since.

'Hey, guys!' he said, and kissed each of them in turn. 'Are you glad to see me?'

'Yeah!' they screamed, one into one ear, one into the other. The roar from the *Townsend*'s main battery might have been louder, but not a lot. Leo added, 'We don't ever want you to go away!'

'Neither do I,' Connie said softly.

'I don't want to, either,' George said. 'Sometimes you've got to do what you've got to do, though, not what you want to do.'

'That's so,' Mrs. McGillicuddy said. She turned to Connie and went on, 'Do you think I want your father to put to sea and stay away for weeks? But that's how he keeps us fed, and that's what he's got to do.'

Connie couldn't even say being in the Navy was dangerous and being a fisherman wasn't. Storms out in the Atlantic claimed too many boats for that to be true. 'I know,' she did say. 'But I still don't like it.'

'Well, I don't like it, either,' George said. He put down his sons. 'They're heavy. I think you must be feeding 'em rocks.' That made Leo and Stan giggle. Connie rolled her eyes. George aimed to enjoy his leave as much as he could. And when it was up . . . when it was up, he would go back, and that was all there was to it.

With the front stabilized not far southeast of Lubbock, Jefferson Pinkard stopped worrying about the damnyankees. He had more urgent things to worry about instead – making sure Negroes went through Camp Determination in a hurry chief among them. He didn't have numbers to let him know how the other camps in the CSA were doing, but if his wasn't the biggest he would have been mightily surprised. One thing seemed clear: they were reducing population faster than blacks could possibly breed. Every day they did that was a victory.

And then the United States started making his life difficult. U.S. bombers and fighters came overhead with little opposition from Confederate Hound Dogs. The antiaircraft guns around the camp boomed and bellowed, but didn't shoot down many enemy airplanes. Jeff telephoned the local C.S. field commander to ask for more help. 'If I could give it to you, I would,' Brigadier General Whitlow Ling said. 'I don't have the aircraft myself, though.'

'Where'd they go?' Jeff asked. He didn't quite add, *Did they fly up your ass?* He wanted the Army man to give him the facts, and pissing Ling off wouldn't help.

'Damnyankees pounded the crap out of 'em, that's where,' Ling said glumly. 'They got a whole new air wing sent in, and it gives 'em a big edge, dammit.'

'Why can't we get more, then?' Pinkard demanded.

'I'm trying.' Ling sounded harassed. 'So far, no luck. Everything we make, they're keeping east of the Mississippi.'

'But the *Yankees* can afford to send airplanes out here,' Jeff said.

'That's about the size of it.'

'And we can't?'

'Right now, that's about the size of it, too.'

'Shit,' Jeff said, and hung up. If the USA could do some things the CSA couldn't match, the Confederacy was in trouble. You didn't need to belong to the General Staff to figure that out. Only a matter of time before the damnyankees used their air superiority to . . . do whatever they damn well pleased.

And before long, what they pleased became pretty

obvious. They started bombing the railroad lines that led
into Snyder. You needed a lot of bombs to tear up train
tracks, because the chances of a direct hit weren't good.
The USA *had* plenty of bombs. And U.S. fighters strafed
repair crews whenever they could.

U.S. airplanes started pounding Snyder, too. That ter-
rified Jefferson Pinkard, not for the camp's sake but for his
own. If anything happened to his pregnant wife and his
stepsons, he had no idea what he'd do. *Go nuts* was all he
could think of.

The house where Edith and Frank and Willie were
staying – the house where Pinkard stayed when he didn't
sleep at Camp Determination – wasn't that close to the
tracks. But when the damnyankees hit Snyder, they didn't
seem to care. They did their best to knock the whole town
flat. Maybe they figured that would interfere with the way
Camp Determination ran. And maybe they were right, too.

Pinkard got a call from Ferdinand Koenig. 'What's this
I hear about niggers piling up on sidings halfway across
Texas?' the Attorney General barked. 'Doesn't sound like
your camp is doing its job.'

The injustice of that made Pinkard want to reach down
the telephone line and punch Koenig in the nose. 'Mr.
Attorney General, sir, you repair the railroads for me,' he
growled, clamping down on rage with both hands. 'You get
the fighters out here to shoot down the Yankee airplanes
that are chewing up the line. You do that stuff, and then if
I fall down on the job you can tell me I'm slacking off. Till
you do it, though, you just back the hell off.'

'Maybe you want to watch your mouth,' Ferd Koenig
said. How often did people talk back to him? Not very –
Jeff was sure of that. The Attorney General went on, 'I can
have your job like *that*.' He snapped his fingers.

'If you're gonna blame me for shit that's not my fault,

you're damn well welcome to it,' Jeff said. 'If I screw up, that's fine. Rake me over the coals on account of it. But if you want me to take the heat because some asshole on the General Staff won't send airplanes way the hell out here, I'm damned if I'll sit still for it. Go and find some other whipping boy. Then see how long *he* lasts. Me, I'll get the fuck outa here and go someplace safer.'

A long, long silence followed. At last, Koenig said, 'Maybe I was hasty.'

'Maybe you were . . . sir,' Jeff said. 'I've got my family. Maybe you ought to can me. Then I can send them back to Louisiana, and I won't have to worry about getting 'em blown to smithereens.'

'I'll get back to you.' The Attorney General hung up.

He didn't call back. Pinkard hadn't really thought he would. Nobody wanted to admit he'd got his ears pinned back. But no more C.S. fighters appeared in the skies above west Texas. Maybe the CSA truly couldn't spare them, no matter how much this front needed them. If the Confederacy couldn't . . .

One more thing Jeff didn't want to think about.

He was in Snyder for the worst air raid he'd ever gone through. His driver had just delivered him to his house and sped away when the sirens began to howl. Bombs started falling a few seconds later. Snyder boasted no fancy electronic detection gear – or if it did, Pinkard didn't know about it. Somebody had to eyeball those airplanes before the sirens could cut loose.

He almost knocked down the front door flinging it open. 'Get in the cellar!' he roared.

Edith was already herding her boys into it. 'Come on, Jeff – you, too,' she said.

'I'm coming.' He tried not to show how scared he was. A storm cellar gave almost perfect protection against a

tornado, as long as you got there in time. Against bombs
. . . There was no guarantee. Nothing this side of reinforced concrete gave you a good chance against a direct
hit. A wooden trapdoor wasn't the same.

But going into a cellar was a lot better than staying out
in the open. Fragments couldn't get you. Blast probably
wouldn't, not unless the bomb came down right on top of
the house.

'Make it stop, Papa Jeff!' Frank wailed as explosions
shook the earth.

'I can't. I wish I could,' Pinkard said.

His stepson stared up at him in the dim yellow light of
a kerosene lantern. 'But you can do anything, Papa Jeff.'

That was touching. If only it were true. 'Only God can
do everything,' Pinkard said. And the way things were going
for the CSA, even God looked to be falling down on the
job.

'God and Hyperman,' Willie said. The younger boy
sounded utterly confident. There was another comic with
a similar name in the USA, but that one was banned down
here. Its hero frequently clobbered Confederate spies and
saboteurs. But it was so vivid and exciting, banning it wasn't
good enough. People smuggled it over the border till the
powers that be in Richmond had to come up with an equivalent. Even now, from what Jeff heard, the Yankee comic
circulated underground in the CSA. But Hyperman, who'd
wrecked New York City at least three times and Philadelphia
twice, made a good enough substitute.

Edith might have explained that God was real and
Hyperman only make-believe. She might have, but bombs
started falling closer just then. The thunder and boom, the
earth rocking under your feet, made you forget about fun-
nybooks. This was real, and all you could do was hope you
came out the other side.

One hit so close that the lantern shuddered off the tabletop and started to fall. Jeff caught it before it hit the ground – miraculously, by the handle. He put it back where it belonged. 'Wow!' Frank said, and then, 'See? I told you you could do anything.'

Catching a lantern was one thing, and – Jeff knew, even if Frank didn't – he was lucky to do even that. Making the damnyankees stop dropping their bombs was a whole different kettle of fish. Jeff had no idea how to say that so it made sense to a little boy, and so he didn't try.

All he could do, all anybody in Snyder could do, was sit tight and hope a bomb didn't come down right on his head. Pinkard also hoped the Yankees weren't bombing the camp. They hadn't yet. What did that say? That they valued niggers' lives more highly than those of decent white folks? Jeff couldn't think of anything else – and if that was true, then what choice did the Confederacy have but to fight those people to the last cartridge and the last man?

After the longest forty minutes in the history of the world, the bombs stopped falling. 'Do you reckon we can go up now?' Edith asked.

'I guess so,' Pinkard answered, though he wasn't sure, either. His wife seemed to think he'd been through things like this before, and knew what to do about them. He wished it were true, but sitting in a cellar getting bombed was new for him, too. Back in the Great War, airplanes couldn't deliver punishment like this.

When they opened the door and went up, the house was still standing and still had all the roof. But window glass crunched and clinked under their feet. If they'd stayed up there, it would have sliced them into sausage meat. Edith softly started to cry. The boys thought it was fun – till they cut themselves on some razor-edged fragments. Then they cried, too.

Jeff went outside. 'Jesus,' he muttered. The house across the street had taken a direct hit. It had fallen in on itself and was burning fiercely. People stood around staring helplessly. Whoever was in there didn't have a chance of getting out. One of the houses next door to the wrecked one had half collapsed, too.

A little farther down, a bomb had gone off in the middle of the street. Water welled up onto the asphalt from a shattered main. That would make fighting fires harder, if not impossible. Telephone and power lines were down. He hadn't noticed that the electricity was out when he came up from the cellar, but he'd had other things on his mind.

And he smelled gas. 'Jesus!' he said again. He'd been about to light a cigarette, but he thought better of that. Then he changed his mind and lit up anyhow. If that blaze across the street didn't set off the gas, his Raleigh wouldn't.

Plumes and clouds of smoke rose all over Snyder. It was just a little Texas town, lucky to have one fire engine. The siren wailed like a lost soul as the firemen did whatever they could wherever they could.

Edith came out, too, and looked around in disbelief. 'This was a nice place,' she said. 'It really was. Look what those goddamn sons of bitches went and did to it.'

Pinkard's jaw dropped. She never talked like that. But she was right, no matter how she put it. Nodding, Jeff said, 'Do you want to take the boys back to Alexandria, then? Y'all'd be safer there.'

'No,' she said, which surprised him again. 'I want to stay right here with you. And I want us to lick the devil out of the USA.'

Looking around at the wreckage, Jeff knew the Yankees had just licked the hell out of Snyder. And . . . 'They're liable to come back, you know. I don't think they'll just hit us once and go away.' If they wanted to foul up Camp Determination, wrecking the way in would help.

'I'm not afraid,' Edith said. 'God will watch over all of us. I know He's on our side.' Everybody in every war since the world began was convinced God was on his side. Half the people in every war since the world began ended up being wrong. Jeff didn't know how to say that, either. He did know Edith wouldn't listen if he tried, and so he let it go.

Major Jerry Dover didn't know what the hell had happened to Colonel Travis W.W. Oliphant. Dead? Captured? Deserted? He couldn't say, and he didn't much care. With Oliphant out of the picture, keeping central Kentucky supplied landed on his shoulders. He could do it. Without false modesty, he knew he could do it better than his thick-headed superior did.

Oliphant, of course, was a Regular. He went to VMI or one of the other Confederate finishing schools for officers. No doubt he was a good enough subaltern during the Great War. But it wasn't the Great War any more, and Oliphant had had trouble figuring that out.

'Trucks!' Dover shouted into the telephone. 'We need more trucks up here, dammit!' He might have been back at the Huntsman's Lodge, screaming at a butcher who'd shorted him on prime rib.

'We're sending up as many as we've got,' said the officer on the other end of the line, an officer much more safely ensconced down in Tennessee. 'Damnyankees are giving us a lot of trouble, you know.'

That did it. Dover blew up, the same way he would have at a cheating butcher. 'Give me your name, damn you! Give me your superior's name, too, on account of I'm going to tell him just what kind of a clueless git he's got working for him. You want to know what trouble is, come up where you can hear the guns. Don't sit in a cushy office miles and miles away from anywhere and tell me how rough you've got it. Now give me your name.'

Instead of doing that, the other officer hung up on him. Jerry Dover said several things that made the other logistics officers in the tent outside of Covington, Kentucky, look up in amazement. Then he called back. Someone else down in Tennessee picked up the telephone.

'Who was the last son of a bitch on the line?' Dover demanded.

'Brigadier General Tyler just stepped out,' the other man replied. 'Who are you, and who do you think you are?'

'Somebody who's looking for Tyler's superior,' said Dover, who didn't back away from anybody. He had a short-timer's courage: he was a man with no military career to wreck. They wouldn't shoot him – the damnyankees were much more likely to do that. They wouldn't jail him for long. The worst they were likely to do was cashier him, in which case he'd go home and be better off than he was now. 'I'm going to get what I need up here in Kentucky, or I'll know the reason why.'

'I'm Major General Barton Kinder,' the officer said. 'Now, one more time – who the dickens are you?'

'I'm Major Jerry Dover, and I want Brigadier General Tyler to pull his trucks out of his asshole and get 'em on the road up here,' Dover said.

A considerable silence followed. Then Kinder said, 'A major does not speak that way to a general officer.'

'So sue me,' Dover said. 'All I know is, the damnyankees are building up like you wouldn't believe on the other side of the Ohio. We're lagging, on account of we can't get what we need where we need it. And one of the reasons we can't is that you guys won't turn loose of your trucks.

If we get swamped, you reckon anybody in Richmond's going to give a rat's ass that you've got all your fucking trucks?'

The silence lasted even longer this time. 'I could have your head, Major,' General Kinder said at last. 'Can you give me one good reason why I shouldn't?'

'I can give you two, sir,' Dover said. 'You give me the boot, you'll get somebody up here who doesn't know what the hell he's doing, and that'll screw up the war effort. There's one. And two is, ten minutes after that new sucker gets here, he's gonna be on the horn screaming his head off to you, wondering how come you're not shipping him the shit he needs.'

'You can't possibly be a Regular,' Major General Kinder said after yet another pause.

'Not me,' Jerry Dover agreed cheerfully. 'I come out of the restaurant business. But I'm mighty goddamn good at what I do. Which counts for more . . . sir?'

'The restaurant business, eh? No wonder you're such a foul-mouthed son of a bitch,' Kinder said, proving he'd had at least one other restaurant manager serve under him. 'All right, Major. We'll see what we can do.'

'Thank you very much, sir.' Dover's respect for military courtesy rose in direct proportion to how much his superiors were inclined to do what he wanted.

'You almost pushed it too far, Major,' Barton Kinder said. 'I wouldn't try that again if I were you.' He hung up before Dover could answer, which might have been lucky for all concerned.

One of the other logistics officers, who couldn't possibly have heard what Major General Kinder said, told Dover, 'Boy, you like to walk close to the edge, don't you?'

'The damnyankees can blow me up. The damnyankees *will* blow me up if we give 'em half a chance – maybe even if we don't,' Dover answered. 'If a brass hat on my own side wants to throw me in the stockade or take the uniform off my back, what the hell do I care? The worst thing my own people can do to me is leave me right where I'm at.'

'I wish I could look at it that way.' The other man had a VMI class ring on the third finger of his right hand, so he was a career officer. That meant he was missing . . .

'Freedom!' Dover said. He was no Party stalwart, but the slogan rang true here. 'Isn't that what this damn war's all about? If we aren't free to do what we want and tell everybody else to piss up a rope, what's the point?'

Before the VMI graduate could answer, the world blew up. Alarms started howling and screeching. Bombs started dropping. Shells started bursting. Men started screaming, 'Gas! Gas!'

'Fuck!' Jerry Dover said, with much more passion than he'd used to say, *Freedom!* He had to rummage in his desk for a gas mask. As he fumbled it on, he knew what this was. He knew what it had to be. The Yankees had been building up for a long time. They weren't building any more. They were coming.

Invasion! No word could rouse greater dread in the CSA. For the first two summers of the war, the Confederates had had everything their own way. The United States had a lot of debts to pay. Now it looked as if they were laying their money on the table.

'Out!' somebody shouted. 'Out and into the trenches!'

That struck Jerry Dover as some of the best advice he'd ever heard. He flew out through the tent flap – not that he was the first man gone, or even the second. The trenches weren't far away, but one of the men who got out ahead of him stopped a shell and exploded into red mist. Dover tasted blood on his lips as he ran by. He spat and spat, feeling like a cannibal.

He jumped into the trench feetfirst, as if going into a swimming hole when he was a kid. Then he looked around for something to dig with. Being merely a logistics officer, he had no entrenching tool on his belt. A board was better than nothing. He started scraping his own dugout from the side of the trench.

Shell fragments screeched past above his head. A wounded man shrieked. Not everybody made it to the trench on time. Some Confederate guns started firing back. The noise of shells going out was different from the one they made coming in.

Bombs whistled down out of the sky. They were what really scared Dover. If one of them burst in this stretch of trench, that was it. He was safe enough from artillery here, but not from bombs.

Somebody punctuated a momentary lull by screaming, 'This is it!'

'Make it stop!' someone else added a moment later, his voice high and desperate and shrill.

Jerry Dover wished it would stop, too, but it didn't. It went on and on, till it reminded him of one of the unending bombardments from the Great War. He was convinced whoever'd let out that first cry was dead right – or, with better luck, still alive and right. This had to be it. If the damnyankees weren't coming over the Ohio right here, this was the biggest bluff in the history of the world.

More Confederate guns boomed, but the noise they made seemed almost lost in the thunder of the Yankee barrage. Officers and sergeants shouted for men to move now here, now there. Dover wouldn't have left his hole for all the money in the world, or for all the love in it. Moving about up there was asking to be obliterated.

Overhead, U.S. airplanes droned south. Dover swore as he listened to them. The Yankees weren't just going after front-line C.S. troops. They were trying to tear up roads and railroads, too. The better the job they did, the more trouble the Confederacy would have bringing up men and matériel to beat them back.

And the better the job they did, the more trouble Jerry Dover would be in, not only from the U.S. soldiers but also from his own superiors. They wouldn't believe any disaster that befell the CSA was their fault. God forbid! Easier to blame the major who used to manage a restaurant.

A four-engine bomber fell out of the sky, its right wing a sheet of flame. It smashed down less than a quarter of a mile from where Dover huddled. Its whole bomb load went off at once. The ground shook under him. Blast slammed him into the side of the trench. He tasted blood again. It was his own this time.

'Corpsman!' 'Medic!' the shouts rose again and again, from all directions. *God help these poor bastards,* Dover thought. Riflemen and machine gunners – mostly – turned their weapons away from the soldiers who wore Red Crosses. Shells and bombs didn't give a damn.

After four and a half hours that seemed like four and a half years (Dover kept checking his watch every three months and being amazed only fifteen minutes had gone by), the gunfire let up. He waited for shouts of, *Here they come!* He was surprised he hadn't already heard those shouts. The damnyankees could have carved out a formidable bridgehead under cover of that barrage.

Then, just when he started to wonder if it was a bluff after all, more shells came in, these close by the river. 'Smoke!' Again, the shout came from everywhere at once. U.S. light airplanes buzzed along the southern bank of the Ohio, spraying more smoke behind them. They got away with it, too. They made perfect targets, but the Confederates near Covington were simply too battered and rattled to shoot back.

Slowly, slowly, the smoke screen cleared. Jerry Dover started to look up, but the rattle of machine-gun fire made him duck back into the trench again. Those small airplanes came back and sprayed more smoke. The sound of machine guns and rifles roared from it.

'Reinforcements!' someone bawled. 'We got to get us reinforcements, before they break out and go hog wild!'

'Fuck me!' That shout of despair came from close by Dover. 'They've got barrels over the river!'

Dover looked up. Sure as hell, through the smoke that now thinned again he spied several squat, monstrous shapes. The growl of their engines added more noise to the racketing gunfire.

A Confederate shell burst in front of a barrel – and it ceased to be. It didn't brew up; it didn't catch fire. It . . . vanished. 'It's a goddamn balloon!' Dover exclaimed.

There were no real barrels close by – only more balloons. The noise of engines and gunfire came from phonograph records and loudspeakers. Whoever'd planted them had disappeared. *The biggest bluff in the history of the world,* Jerry Dover thought again. And it had worked. It froze the Confederates by Covington. Now . . . Where was the real blow landing?

Irving Morrell was wary of repeating himself. Irving Morrell was wary of repeating himself. The armor commander shook his head, wondering if he was going out of his tree. He wanted to drive Jake Featherston out of *his* instead. Crossing a river the size of the Ohio wasn't easy. When George Custer did it in the Great War, he paid a heavy price – and he went on paying a heavy price while his troops ground their way southward a few hundred yards at a time.

Back in 1917, Morrell got men over the Cumberland

east of Nashville much more quickly, much more neatly. But he had to figure the Confederates now knew all about what he did then and how he did it. They were bastards, but they weren't dopes. If he tried the same thing twice, they would hand him his head. And he would deserve it.

And so, in football terms, he was doing his best to fake them out of their jocks. He laid on ferocious barrages in front of Covington and Louisville, and one on an open stretch of river between the two Kentucky towns. He used all the sneaky ingenuity the Army could come up with – and some straight out of Hollywood, too. Inflatable rubber barrels and sound-effects records kept the Confederates guessing a crucial extra little while. So did shells that gurgled as they flew through the air but didn't hold any gas. A sensible man would figure no one wasted gas shells on a bluff. And a sensible man would be right. Morrell saved the real ones for the genuine assault.

The state of the art of crossing rivers in the face of enemy fire had improved since 1917. You didn't have to throw pontoon bridges across or send men over in wallowing barges. Armored landing craft delivered soldiers, barrels, and artillery in a hurry. Only a direct hit from a 105 or a bigger cannon yet could make them say uncle. Once the soldiers carved out a lodgement, then bridges could span the river.

No, the tricky part wasn't the crossing itself. The tricky part was moving men and matériel into southern Indiana without letting the bastards in butternut know what was going on. Lots of trucks made lots of trips carrying nothing to fool Featherston's fuckers into thinking the real blow would fall farther east. Lots of others carried men who promptly reboarded them under cover of darkness. More inflatable barrels and wooden artillery pieces left the impression of buildups where there were none.

So did acres of tents just out of range of C.S. artillery.

Now Morrell had to hope all his deceptions were deceptive enough, his security tight enough. That the Confederates had spies on the northern bank of the Ohio went without saying. That U.S. Intelligence hadn't rooted out all of them was also a given. How much they reported, how much they were believed . . . Those were the questions only battle would answer.

So far, everything looked good. The U.S. concentration lay between two tiny Indiana riverside towns with odd names: Magnet and Derby. Magnet hadn't attracted any particular Confederate attention. That made Morrell want to tip his derby to the men under him who'd made the crossing work.

He wanted to, but he didn't – he wasn't wearing a derby. He was wearing a helmet with two stars painted on the front. On a parade helmet, the stars would have been gold so they stood out. Morrell didn't want them to stand out. One sniper had already hit him. He wasn't anxious to make himself a target for another one. His rank emblems were dull brown, and invisible from more than a few feet away.

His own headquarters were in Derby, the more southerly of the two towns. People there talked with a twang that reminded him of the wrong side of the border. Intelligence assured him they were no more disloyal than anybody else. He hoped Intelligence knew what it was talking about. But his hackles rose whenever he listened to any of the locals.

Through field glasses, he watched artillery and dive bombers pound northern Kentucky. The Confederates were trying to hit back, but they seemed a little punch-drunk, a little slow. The corners of Morrell's mouth turned down. Two years earlier, he and Abner Dowling were a beat late when they tried to meet the C.S. thrust into Ohio. About time the other side found out what that felt like.

A soldier from the wireless shack came up to him and saluted. 'We've reached Objective A, sir,' he reported.

Morrell looked at his watch. Two in the afternoon, a few minutes past. 'Almost an hour ahead of schedule,' he said. They'd driven the Confederates out of rifle and machine-gun range of the Ohio: pushed them back more than a mile. Jake Featherston's men wouldn't have an easy time driving the invaders into the river now. And Morrell had another reason to beam. 'With Objective A taken, I can cross myself.'

'Yes, sir,' the noncom said. Morrell had strict orders from Philadelphia to stay north of the Ohio till the Confederates were cleared from the riverside. He obeyed orders like that only when he felt like it. Here, reluctantly, he saw they made good sense.

'General Parsons!' he shouted now.

His second-in-command came running. 'Yes, sir?' Brigadier General Harlan Parsons was short and square and tough. He didn't have much imagination, but he didn't have much give, either.

'As of now, you're in command,' Morrell said. 'Keep 'em crossing the river, keep 'em moving forward. When I get south of the Ohio, I'll take over again. My barrel's got enough wireless circuits to do the broadcasting for New York City.' He exaggerated, but not by much.

Parsons saluted again. 'I'll handle it, sir,' he said, and Morrell had no doubt he would. 'I'll see you when we get to Objective B.'

'Right,' Morrell said. They would have to drive the Confederates out of artillery range of the Ohio – say, ten or twelve miles back – to meet their second objective. If everything went according to plan, that would take another two days. But who could say what the plan had to do with reality? You went out there and you saw what happened.

Morrell hurried toward his fancy barrel with the eager-ness of a lover going to his beloved. The rest of the crew stood around the machine, waiting. As soon as the four enlisted men saw him, they scrambled into the machine. The engine roared to life even as he was slipping down through the hatch atop the cupola and into the turret.

'Take us onto the landing craft,' he called to the driver as soon as his mouth reached the intercom mike.

'Yes, sir!' The barrel rumbled forward, first on the soft riverside earth and then on the steel ramp that led up into the ungainly, slab-sided, river-crossing contraption.

Sailors – they wore Navy blue, not Army green-gray – raised the ramp. It clanged into place, hard enough to make the barrel shake for a moment. A series of clangs meant the ramp was stowed and now had become the boat's stern or rear end or whatever the hell you called it. The boat's engine started up. The vibration made Morrell's back teeth ache. Well, a dentist could wait.

The landing craft was as graceful as a fat man waddling along with an anvil. But a fat man lugging an anvil would sink like a stone if he went into the water. The landing craft didn't. God and the engineers who designed it no doubt knew why it didn't. Irving Morrell had no idea. He took the notion on faith. Somehow, believing in the landing craft was easier than his Sunday-school lessons had been.

Crossing the Ohio took about fifteen minutes. A few Confederate shells splashed into the river not far away. Fragments clanged off the landing craft's sides. Nothing got through. Up front, the barrel driver said, 'Thank you, Jesus!' He still believed in what he'd learned in Sunday school.

Then, with a jolt that clicked Morrell's teeth together, the barrel wallowed up onto dry land again. The ramp thudded down. Morrell hadn't felt the boat turn in the water, but it faced away from the Ohio. The barrel went into reverse and left its steel nest. Morrell felt like cheering when the tracks bit into soft ground. Here he was, on Confederate soil at last after spending most of the two years trying to defend his own country.

'Forward!' he told the driver. 'Toward the fighting!' Then he played with the dials on the big, bulky wireless set that cramped the turret. 'Nest, this is Robin,' he said, wondering who'd picked such idiotic code names. 'Nest, this is Robin. Do you read?'

'Read you five by five, Robin.' The answer resounded in his earphones. He was back in touch, back in command. After fifteen or twenty minutes of glory – and responsibility – Harlan Parsons could go back to being number two.

'What is the situation?' Morrell asked. 'Any changes?'

'Negative, sir,' the wireless man replied. 'Everything's on schedule, or maybe a little ahead of schedule.'

'Sounds good to me,' Morrell said. Before the Nest could answer, a noise like a giant frying bacon filled his earphones. Swearing, he yanked them off his head. The Confederates were starting to jam signals. That was a sign they were getting their wits about them and seriously starting to fight back. Morrell swore some more. He would have liked the enemy to stay stunned a while longer. You didn't always get everything you wanted. As long as the USA had enough . . .

The barrel jounced past the burning ruin of a C.S. machine. Four soldiers in blood-soaked butternut coveralls – the barrel crew – sprawled close by in death. Maybe the fifth man got away. Or maybe he never got out, and was nothing but charred meat inside the barrel.

Morrell rode toward the front standing up in the turret, head and shoulders out of the cupola. He wanted to see what was going on. Enemy fire was light. Machine guns and other small arms farther forward chattered. Every Confederate foot soldier carried either an automatic rifle or a submachine gun. The bastards in butternut had plenty of firepower. Did they have enough big guns, enough barrels, enough airplanes, enough *men*? Morrell and the United States were betting they didn't.

A salvo of those newfangled rockets screamed in from the south. Morrell just had time to duck down into the turret and slam the cupola hatch shut before the rockets burst. Blast rocked the barrel. It could flip even one of these heavy machines right over. It could, but it didn't this time. Fragments clanged off armor.

'Son of a bitch!' Frenchy Bergeron said. 'Those fuckers are no fun at all.'

'Right the first time,' Morrell told the gunner. Yes, the Confederates were fighting back. No reason to expect they wouldn't, no matter how much Morrell would have liked it if they rolled over onto their backs like whipped dogs.

Another salvo of rockets came down, this one a little farther away. 'God help the poor infantry,' Bergeron remarked. Morrell nodded. For plastering a wide area with firepower, those rockets were world-beaters. Bergeron went on, 'How many of them have they got, anyway?'

'Good question,' Morrell said. 'Best answer I've got is, not enough to stop us.' He hoped he was telling the truth. Somewhere in Alabama or Texas or Georgia, the CSA had factories working overtime to turn out the rockets and their launchers, though the latter were simplicity itself: just iron tubing and sheet metal. But the more rockets the Confederates made, the less of something else they turned out. Bullets? Automatic rifles? Barrel tracks? Canned corn? Something – that was for sure. Keep the pressure on them and they couldn't make enough of everything they needed and keep an army in the field at the same time, not when they were fighting a country more than twice their size.

Things had worked that way in the Great War, anyhow. The United States ought to have a bigger edge this time, because the Confederates were persecuting their Negroes instead of using them. But industrialized agriculture and factory efficiency were both a lot further along than they were a generation earlier. Farms and factories kept fewer men away from the field than they had.

The bow machine gun on Morrell's barrel fired a quick burst. 'Scratch one!' the gunner said. A Confederate who did make it to the battlefield wouldn't go home again. Morrell nodded to himself. Now – how many more would it take before Jake Featherston said uncle?

Cincinnatus Driver sat in a tent north of Cincinnati, hoping the other shoe would drop here. U.S. forces were already over the river farther west, driving from Indiana into western Kentucky. Meanwhile, Cincinnatus shoved money into the pot. 'See you an' raise you a dollar,' he said. He was holding three jacks, so he thought his chances were pretty good.

One of the other truck drivers still in the hand dropped out. The last driver raised a dollar himself. Cincinnatus eyed him. He'd drawn two. If he'd filled a straight or a flush, he'd done it by accident. Odds against that were pretty steep. Cincinnatus bumped it up another dollar.

Now the other man – a white – eyed him. He tossed in one more dollar of his own. 'Call,' he said.

'Three jacks.' Cincinnatus showed them. The other driver swore – he had three eights. Cincinnatus scooped up the pot. The other driver, still muttering darkly, grabbed the cards and shuffled them for the next hand.

He'd just started to deal when artillery, a lot of artillery, roared not far away. All the men in the card game cocked their heads to one side, listening. 'Ours,' one of them said. The rest nodded, Cincinnatus included.

'Don't sound like they're dicking around,' said the fellow who'd held three eights. He was a wiry little guy named Izzy Saperstein. He had a beard so thick he shaved twice a day and the most hair in his nose and ears Cincinnatus had ever seen.

'Put on a bigger barrage earlier,' another driver said. 'Made the bastards in butternut keep their heads down and made sure they wouldn't move soldiers west. Chances are this is more of the same.'

'Maybe.' Saperstein scratched his ear. With that tuft sprouting from it, he likely itched all the time. Cincinnatus wondered if he couldn't cut the hair or pluck it or something. It was just this side of disgusting.

They played for another couple of hours, while the guns boomed and bellowed. None of them got excited about that. They'd all heard plenty of gunfire before. As long as nothing was coming down on their heads, they didn't flabble. Cincinnatus won a little, lost a little, won a little more.

He was up about fifteen bucks when a U.S. captain stuck his head into the tent. 'Go to your trucks now, men,' he said. 'Head for the depot and load up. We've crossed the Ohio, and our boys'll need everything we can bring 'em.'

'Crossed the Ohio? Here?' Izzy Saperstein sounded amazed.

Cincinnatus was surprised, too. He hadn't really believed the USA would try to force a crossing here. He didn't know many people who had, either. If folks on this side were caught by surprise, maybe the Confederates would be, too. 'We fighting in Covington, sir?' he asked. 'I was born there. I know my way around good. I can lead and show folks the way.'

'Thanks, Driver, but no,' the captain answered. 'We're going to skirt the town, pen up the enemy garrison inside, and clean it out at our leisure. Now get moving.'

Only one possible answer to that. Cincinnatus gave it: 'Yes, sir.' Along with the other men, he headed for his truck as fast as he could go.

A self-starter was so handy. A touch of a button and the motor came to life. He remembered cranking trucks in the Great War. That was even more fun in the rain – and if your hand slipped, the crank would spin backwards and maybe break your arm. He didn't have to worry about that now. No – all he needed to worry about was getting shot or incinerated or blown sky-high. *Happy day,* he thought.

Soldiers with dollies filled the back of the truck with crates of God knew what. Ammunition, he guessed by the way the truck settled on its springs. 'Go get 'em, Pop!' one of the young white men yelled to him. Cincinnatus grinned and waved. He was plenty old enough to be that kid's father. And *Pop* didn't burn his ears the way *Uncle* would have. The soldier would have said the same thing to a white man Cincinnatus' age. In the CSA, *Uncle* was what whites called a Negro too old to get stuck with *boy*.

The truck convoy rumbled south, toward the river. With so much weight in the rear, Cincinnatus' deuce-and-a-half rode a lot smoother than it did empty. He drove past gun pits where gun bunnies stripped to the waist worked like men possessed to throw more shells at the Confederates. Some of the U.S. soldiers were already lobster-red from too much sun. Cincinnatus glanced at his own brown arm. There weren't many things white men had to worry about that he didn't, but sunburn was one of them.

Every so often, incoming shells burst. Think what you would about the men who followed Jake Featherston, but they had no quit in them. Wherever they could hit back, they did.

'This way! This way!' A sergeant with wigwag flags directed the trucks toward slab-sided boats plainly made to cross rivers no matter what the unpleasant people on the other bank had to say about it. Cincinnatus rolled into one.

'All the way forward!' a sailor told him. 'We hold two trucks, by God.' Cincinnatus rolled up till his front bumper kissed the landing craft's rear wall. The sailor rewarded him with a circle from his thumb and forefinger. Cincinnatus waved and nodded, as he had with the young soldier who loaded the truck. He knew how the man in blue meant the gesture. Whether the sailor did or not, though, Cincinnatus also happened to know that to Germans (many of whom had crossed from Cincinnati to Covington in the easygoing days before the Great War) a very similar hand sign meant you were an asshole.

Another truck followed his into the ungainly boat. It didn't quite have to bump his machine to let the boat's crew raise the ramp and dog it shut. 'Do I leave my motor on?' Cincinnatus called to the closest sailor.

'Bet your butt, buddy,' the man answered. 'You're gonna wanna hit the ground running, right?'

Cincinnatus didn't say no. He wished he were someplace where the Confederates couldn't shoot at him or shell him or drop bombs on his head. *Why didn't you stay in Des Moines, then?* he asked himself. A little – no, much – too late to worry about that now. And he knew why he didn't stay there: he owed the CSA too much. But understanding that and liking it when he headed into danger were two different things.

On land, the landing craft ran well enough to get down into the river. On the Ohio, it ran well enough to cross.

On the other side, it got up onto the bank. It didn't do any of those things very well. That it could do all of them, even if badly, made it a valuable machine. The wall against which Cincinnatus' truck nestled also proved to be a ramp. It thudded down. He put the truck in gear and rolled off. The other truck in the landing craft followed him.

A corporal pointed at him, and then at some other trucks. 'Follow them!' the man yelled. Cincinnatus nodded to show he understood. He wasn't sure those other trucks came from his unit. That wasn't his worry, not right now. Somebody'd told him what to do. He just had to do it.

He began to wonder if they'd caught the Confederates flatfooted. There wasn't a lot of incoming enemy fire. He didn't miss it, and he hoped that what there was kept missing him. Whenever he could, he glanced east, toward Covington. He could see . . . exactly nothing. He hoped the police and Freedom Party stalwarts and guards hadn't shipped all the Negroes in town off to camps farther south. He hoped Lucullus Wood and the other black Reds were finding ways to give the Confederates a hard time, even from behind barbed wire. All he could do was hope. He couldn't know.

The convoy stopped by a battery of 105s. Soldiers swarmed aboard his truck and unloaded it with locustlike intensity. He waited to see if they would start swearing, the way they might if, say, he carried crates full of machine-gun belts. When they didn't, he decided the corporal had sent him to the right place after all.

'Where do I go now?' he asked when the truck was empty. 'Back across the river to load up again?'

'No, by God.' A U.S. soldier pointed south and west. 'We just took a Confederate supply depot. I mean to tell you, the guy who was running it must've been a fucking genius. Everything from pencils to pecans to power tools. Ammunition out the ass, too.'

'That don't do us much good,' Cincinnatus said. 'They don't use the same calibers as we do.'

'Yeah, but we got a lotta guys carrying their automatic rifles. Damn things are great, long as you can keep 'em in bullets,' the soldier said. 'We got enough of their ammo at this here dump to keep a lot of our guys going for a long time.'

Cincinnatus liked the way that sounded. When he got to the depot, he decided the soldier who'd sent him there was right: the quartermaster who'd set it up was a genius. If he was still alive, he was bound to be gnashing his teeth that everything he'd labored to gather now lay in U.S. hands. The Confederates hadn't even got the chance to blow up the ammunition.

This time, Cincinnatus could see what went into the back of his truck. RATIONS, CANNED, the crates said. No doubt U.S. authorities would use them to feed soldiers in green-gray. And no doubt the soldiers in green-gray would grumble when they got them. U.S. canned goods were better than their C.S. equivalents. But Confederate rations were ever so much better than no rations at all.

Confederate prisoners marched glumly up the road toward the Ohio. The U.S. troops in green-gray who herded them along got them off the highway and onto the shoulder to keep them from slowing down the southbound trucks. Some of the men in butternut stared at Cincinnatus' dark face in the cab of his truck. He sent them a cheery wave and went on driving. So they didn't think Negroes were good for anything, did they? Well, he hoped he gave them a surprise.

The U.S. soldiers who unloaded the truck didn't seem so happy. 'We've got our own canned goods, dammit,' one of them said. 'We don't want this Confederate shit.' His pals nodded.

'Don't blame me, friends,' Cincinnatus said. 'I just brung what they told me to bring.'

'Why didn't they tell you to bring us a shitload of Confederate cigarettes?' the soldier said. 'That woulda been worth somethin'.'

'Fuck it,' said another young man in green-gray. 'We're heading down into tobacco country. We'll get our own smokes before long.'

'Yeah!' Two or three U.S. soldiers liked the sound of that. So did Cincinnatus, for different reasons. They weren't more than ten or twelve miles south of Covington, but they thought they could go a lot farther. He'd seen that arrogance in Confederate soldiers before, but rarely in their U.S. counterparts. If they thought going into a fight that they could lick the enemy, that made them more likely to be right.

'General Morrell, he knows what the hell he's doing,' the first soldier said. Again, he got nothing but agreement from his buddies. Again, Cincinnatus wondered if he was hearing straight. U.S. soldiers usually thought of their generals as bungling idiots – and usually had good, solid reasons for thinking of them that way.

Up ahead, Confederate guns boomed. A few shells came down not too far away. The soldiers laughed. 'If that's the best those bastards can do, they won't even slow us down,' one of them said.

'They pulled this shit on us two years ago,' another one added. 'Hell, I was in Ohio then. They caught me, but I slipped off before they took me very far. We didn't know how to stop 'em. And you know what? I bet they don't know how to stop us, either.'

No sooner had he spoken than several rocket salvos screamed down out of the sky. They didn't land on the trucks, but half a mile or so to the east. Where the artillery hadn't, they sobered the U.S. soldiers. 'Well, maybe it won't be quite so easy,' the first one said. 'But I bet we can do it.'

Lieutenant Michael Pound thought he was getting the hang of commanding four other barrels instead of doing the gunning for one. He hoped he was, anyhow. None of the other barrel commanders in the platoon was complaining. They'd plunged deep into Kentucky, and all five machines were still intact.

He studied the map. The next town ahead, on the north bank of the Green River, was called Calhoun. The hamlet on the south side of the river, Rumsey, was even smaller. They probably didn't have a thousand people put together.

John Calhoun, Pound remembered, was a Southern politician before the War of Secession – and, therefore, a son of a bitch by definition. A town named after him deserved whatever happened to it. Pound didn't know who Rumsey was. Nobody good, probably.

Calhoun and Rumsey together wouldn't have mattered if not for the bridge between them. The James Bethel Gresham Memorial Bridge, the map called it, and noted that it was named for a Kentuckian who was one of the first Confederate soldiers to die in the Great War. *He had it coming,* Pound thought unkindly.

He eyed the bridge from the edge of the woods that encroached on Calhoun from the north. Binoculars made it seem to leap almost to within arm's length. Some Confederate soldiers milled around in Calhoun, but not many, and they didn't seem very well organized.

As usual, Pound didn't need long to make up his mind. He got on the all-platoon circuit of his wireless: 'Men, we are going to take that bridge away from the enemy.'

'How, sir?' That was Sergeant Frank Blakey, the next

most senior barrel commander. 'Won't they just blow it when they see us coming?'

'Sure – if they recognize us,' Pound answered. 'But if they don't . . .' He explained what he had in mind.

When he finished, Sergeant Blakey whistled. 'You've got the balls of a burglar, sir. If we try it, though, we just have to hope you don't get 'em draped over a doorknob.'

'If you think it won't work, sing out,' Pound said. 'I spent years telling officers they were a bunch of damn fools – and they mostly were, too. My ears won't fall off if you tell me the same thing.'

Despite reassurances, none of the noncoms under him spoke up right away. At last, Blakey said, 'I think we've got a chance, sir. Like you say, they sure as hell won't be expecting it.' He laughed. 'I wouldn't – you better believe that.'

'Let's go, then.' When an idea struck Pound, it struck hard. This one was no exception. He threw open the cupola lid and climbed out of the barrel. 'Come on,' he called to his gunner and loader. 'Time's a-wasting.'

They descended from the machine, too. They both looked faintly dubious, or more than faintly, but they went along. Crewmen also got out of the other four barrels. Like Michael Pound and his men, they started cutting down bushes and leafy branches and tying them to the decking and turrets of their machines, breaking up their silhouettes and hiding a lot of the green-gray paint that covered them.

An infantry lieutenant came up to Pound. 'What the hell are you guys doing?' he asked. 'Playing Queen of the May?'

'I hope not.' Pound pointed to the span between Calhoun and Rumsey. 'I aim to take that bridge. I'll probably need your help to do it.' He told the other officer – who was at least twenty years younger than he was – his plan.

'You got your nerve, don't you?' The infantry lieutenant echoed Sergeant Blakey. But he nodded. 'Yeah, we can do that. Keep quiet till you make it onto the bridge or you get in trouble, then open up with everything we got.' He had a tough-guy, big-city accent – Pound guessed he was from Chicago. He added, 'You know that's liable to be kinda too late, don't you?'

'Chance you take.' Pound's broad shoulders went up and down in a shrug. 'If we go down, we'll go down swinging.'

'Hope you don't. We'll back your play.' The other lieutenant stuck out his hand. 'Luck.' He didn't say, *You'll need it*, but it was written all over his face.

Pound shook hands with him anyway. 'Thanks. If this does work, come on down once we're where we need to be and help us take charge of things.'

'Right,' the infantry lieutenant said. *Fat chance*, his face declared.

When the barrels were camouflaged to Pound's satisfaction, he led the parade down into Calhoun. The other four machines stayed buttoned up. He couldn't stand that. He wanted to see everything that was going on – and he thought he might need to talk his way past some of the men in butternut.

Along State Highway 81 they rumbled, past Seventh, Sixth, Fifth, Fourth. Calhoun didn't seem to have any street with a number bigger than Seventh. They got down to Mayberry, four blocks past the county seat and only a block away from the river, before anybody thought to challenge them. A Confederate sergeant stepped out into the narrow road and called, 'What do y'all reckon you're doin'?'

'Securing the bridge, of course.' As usual, Michael Pound acted as if he had not a doubt in the world.

Frowning, the sergeant hefted his automatic rifle. The

barrel's bow machine gun could cut him in half before he started shooting . . . Pound hoped. 'You talk funny,' the noncom said. 'Where you from?'

'New Orleans,' Pound answered. The Crescent City's half-Southern, half-Brooklyn speech pattern was different from anything else in the CSA. His own accent was much closer to Canadian than anything else; he'd grown up not far from the border. It didn't sound much like that of a native Louisianan, but if this Confederate wasn't expecting anybody from the USA. . . .

And he wasn't. He stepped aside, saying, 'Wish to God somebody woulda told us we were getting barrels sent in.'

Life is full of surprises, Pound thought, but he didn't say anything out loud – the less he opened his mouth where Confederates could hear, the better. The barrel turned right on First and rumbled west toward the bridge to Rumsey. The bridge was about a quarter of a mile away. Pound's machine had covered a little more than half the distance when somebody shouted, 'Holy Jesus! They're Yankees!'

'Shit!' Pound said, without originality but with great sincerity. A burst of submachine-gun fire clanged off the side of the barrel. He dove down into the turret. 'Gun it for the bridge!' he yelled to the driver. To the bow gunner, he added, 'Shoot anybody who gets in our way or tries to blow the bridge!'

'Yes, sir,' both men answered. The barrel's engine went from rumble to roar. The ponderous machine couldn't leap, but it could scoot pretty fast. It could – and it did.

'What if they can blow the damn thing from the Rumsey side, sir?' the gunner asked.

'There's a technical term for that, Sergeant,' Pound answered. 'In that case, we're screwed.' He startled a laugh out of Mel Scullard. A moment later, he added, 'Once we're *on* the bridge, I want you to make sure nothing alive has the chance to come up from Rumsey and blow it. Can you do that for me?'

'Yes, sir,' Scullard said, which was the right answer. He gave the loader a one-word order: 'Canister!'

'Canister,' Private Joe Mouradian echoed. The shell went into the breech. Barrels carried only three or four rounds of canister in their racks because they needed it so seldom. When they did need it, though, they were liable to need it bad. It turned the main armament into an enormous shotgun. Anybody who came within a hundred yards or so was asking to get blown to bits.

The driver turned left onto the bridge so sharply, Pound thanked the God in Whom he only sporadically believed for not letting the barrel throw a track. One of the machines behind him fired a round from its main armament. He couldn't see what it was shooting at – he had his eyes on the forward-facing periscopes that showed the far end of the bridge and the village of Rumsey beyond.

'Stop just at the end of the bridge,' he told the driver.

'At the end of the bridge – yes, sir.' No sooner had the driver stopped than soldiers in butternut started running toward the barrel. The bow machine gun chattered. The Confederate soldiers went down, some dead or wounded, others diving for cover. Civilians appeared in the streets, too, but they were running for cover.

After the first impromptu charge from Rumsey failed, the Confederates paused to put together a proper attack. Whoever led it was plenty smart. He had plenty of people with automatic rifles and submachine guns going forward in front of the men with Featherston Fizzes and the Confederates' newfangled antibarrel rockets. If the troops making the racket with the small arms could distract the barrel crew . . .

But the Confederate commander reckoned without can-

ister. Pound waited till the closest enemy soldiers were very
close indeed before he shouted, 'Fire!'

Even he was awed by the carnage a 3½-inch canister
shell could cause. Men and pieces of men lay and writhed,
broken, in front of the barrel. Several dropped Featherston
Fizzes added flames to the horror. 'Shall I give 'em another
round, sir?' Scullard asked.

'By all means,' Pound answered.

The second round of canister, when added to the steady
rattle of death from the bow machine gun, convinced the
handful of Confederates still on their feet to get away if
they could. 'Give me one more round,' the gunner told the
loader.

'Hold up on that.' Pound overrode him. 'Use HE instead,
and start knocking down the houses closest to us. I don't
want one of those bastards with a rocket to be able to get
off an easy shot at us.'

'I'll do it, sir,' Scullard said, and he did, with the peculiar gusto a man has when destroying property that belongs
to the other side. A secondary explosion from inside one
of those houses in Rumsey made Pound think he'd barely
beaten the Confederates to the punch: if that wasn't a
rocket blowing up, what was it?

Sergeant Blakey's barrel came up alongside Pound's. The
other three in the platoon held the north end of the bridge
against the Confederates in Calhoun. Their cannon and
machine guns thundered and barked. Pound hoped the
U.S. foot soldiers in the woods north of Calhoun were
pressing down into the town. Squeezed between them and
the barrels on the bridge, what could Featherston's men
do but get out?

The Confederates inside Rumsey had an antibarrel
cannon: an inch-and-a-halfer from the days when the war
first started. It had two virtues – it was easy to haul around,

and it fired rapidly. Against one of the new U.S. barrels, though, it was hardly more than a doorknocker. Its shells had no hope of penetrating that thick, well-sloped armor.

'There it is, sir!' Scullard said. 'In the bushes by that big house.'

'You're right,' Pound said. 'Do the honors, then.'

'Yes, sir,' the gunner said, and then, to the loader, 'HE!' Two shells sufficed to upend the gun and send a couple of the men who served it flying. Pound nodded to himself in somber satisfaction. If the other side wanted to play the game but didn't have good cards . . . well, too bad for them.

He looked through the periscopes facing back toward Calhoun. Alarm tingled through him. Soldiers were on the bridge. Could he traverse the turret fast enough to fire at them before they reached the barrel? But then he relaxed – they wore green-gray, not butternut.

'We have Calhoun,' he said happily. 'And we have the bridge – intact, by God. We can keep rolling right on through Kentucky. Let's see Featherston stop us. Let's see anybody stop us.'

IX

In the reinforced-concrete shelter under the ruins of the Gray House, Jake Featherston fumed. He had the feeling of being a bug pinned down on a collector's board. Wiggle as he would, the pin held him helplessly in place.

He'd had that feeling in the last war, when U.S. artillery and barrels inexorably pushed the Army of Northern Virginia back from Pennsylvania through Maryland and into the state for which it was named. He'd sworn he would never feel that way again. He'd sworn the Confederate States would never let anybody on earth do that to them again. For two years, near enough, his barrels and dive bombers made good on the boast. Now . . .

Now the damnyankees had barrels and dive bombers, too. Their machines were just as good as the CSA's. From the dismayed reports from the field, their latest barrels were better than anything the Confederates had. And the United States had swarms of barrels and cannon and airplanes and men, while the Confederates had . . . what was left from the adventures of the past two years.

Lulu stuck her head into the office. 'Mr. President, General Forrest is here to see you.'

'Thanks,' Featherston said. 'Please send him in.' He could order Negroes sent to camps by the tens of thousands, by the hundreds of thousands, without batting an eye, but he was always polite to his secretary.

Nathan Bedford Forrest III came in and gave him a perfunctory salute. 'Mr. President,' he said, and then, plainly with an effort, 'Freedom!'

'Freedom!' Jake echoed; the Party slogan never felt stale to him. He waved the head of the General Staff to a chair. Seeing how haggard Forrest looked, he took out the bottle of whiskey that lived in his desk drawer. 'Need a snort?'

'Don't mind if I do, sir.' Forrest poured himself a healthy shot. 'Mud in your eye.' He knocked it back. Jake Featherston also drank. Forrest eyed him. 'That was good, but I don't reckon I can drink enough to make me forget how much trouble we're in.'

'You're the fellow who's supposed to get us out of trouble like that,' Jake said.

'With what . . . sir?' Forrest asked. 'Talk about making bricks without straw – I feel like I'm trying to make bricks without mud out there. How can I stop the damnyankees when they're throwing everything but the kitchen sink at me and I don't even have the goddamn sink?'

'It can't be that bad,' Featherston said.

'No, sir. It's worse,' Nathan Bedford Forrest III said. 'We . . . lost a lot of men and we lost a lot of matériel in Pittsburgh and falling back afterwards.'

'The Yankees must have lost a lot, too.' Featherston eyed the whiskey bottle. He still drank, but he couldn't remember the last time he really *drank*. Getting plowed, forgetting all this crap, was an enormous temptation. But the crap wouldn't go away, and it would get worse while he wasn't looking at it. And so, regretfully, he looked but he didn't grab the bottle again.

'They did, sir. No doubt about it,' the chief of the General Staff said earnestly. *He's getting ready to call me a damn fool,* Featherston thought. *He'll be polite about it, but he'll do it just the same.* And sure as hell, Forrest went on, 'But they've got more men and more factories than we do.

They can build up faster than we can, and they can go on building up to a level . . . we have trouble matching.'

A level we can't match – that's what he almost said. 'They've got more men. We can't do much about that,' Jake said. 'But we've got better men, by God, and we've got better weapons. The automatic rifles, and now the rockets . . .'

'All that's true, sir, and it's why things aren't worse,' Forrest said. 'But our artillery's no better than theirs, and they've got more. Our airplanes aren't better, and they've got more. That's really starting to hurt. And when it comes to barrels – sir, when it comes to barrels, they've got a step up on us. That's starting to hurt bad, too.'

'Goddammit, why can't we keep up?' Jake Featherston snarled. 'We were ahead when the war started.'

'We don't have enough engineers, sir. We don't have enough factory hands,' Forrest said. 'Damn near every healthy white man in the country from eighteen to fifty's in uniform.'

'Women are taking up some of the slack in the factories – more every day, in fact.' Forrest was angry he'd taken too long to see how important that was. He didn't like giving women such jobs. In the long run, it would twist the CSA out of the shape he wanted the country to have. But if you got smashed in the short run, the long run didn't matter. So women went to work in war plants, and he'd worry about what it all meant later – if there was a later.

'We still need more bodies in there, sir.' Forrest took a deep breath. 'If there was any way we could get more use out of our niggers—'

'No,' Featherston said in a low, deadly voice. 'The niggers are Party business. They're *my* business. Don't you go sticking your nose in where it doesn't belong. We are gonna come out of this war nigger-free. Nigger-free, you hear me?'

'Mr. President, how much do we have to pay to make that happen?' Forrest asked. 'We needed most of a division to clean Richmond out – a division we couldn't use against the damnyankees. If that happens too many more times, it'll put us in a world of trouble. I'm sorry I have to tell you such things, sir, but somebody needs to.'

He had nerve. Not many people who came before Jake Featherston told him anything but what they thought he wanted to hear. Clarence Potter did, but Potter had almost official gadfly status. Even Ferd Koenig hesitated. Forrest might be hesitant, but he was saying what he thought.

'The worst is over,' Jake said. 'Most towns are cleaned out.' That still left the black belt from rural South Carolina through Louisiana largely unaffected, but he wasn't about to split hairs with Nathan Bedford Forrest III. Besides, he had Mexican soldiers dealing with the coons there. He didn't need to pull so many of his own men away from more urgent – not more important, but more urgent – things.

'I hope you're right, sir,' the chief of the General Staff said. 'I hope so, but. . . .'

I haven't convinced that man, Jake thought. He changed the subject from his own shortcomings to those of the Army: 'We've got to stop the Yankees. They're carving their way through Kentucky like we did through Ohio.'

'That's what I'm trying to tell you, Mr. President,' Forrest said. 'We're using every man and every piece of machinery we can get our hands on. We can't get our hands on enough men or machines.'

'If you stop retreating, if you start hitting back—'

'Sir, that's not fair to the men fighting and dying in Kentucky. You can hang me out to dry if you want – I'll be your scapegoat. But they're doing everything flesh and blood can do. They're making stands every chance they get, and they're counterattacking every chance they get, too. We'd be in worse shape if they weren't, and you can take that to the bank.'

His passion startled Featherston. The President of the CSA would have thrown him to the wolves without a qualm – if he'd had someone in mind to replace him. But the only officer who came to mind for the job was George Patton, and Patton was too valuable in the field to bring him back to Richmond.

So instead of canning Nathan Bedford Forrest III, Featherston said, 'Let's take a look at the map.'

'Of course, sir.' Did Forrest sound relieved? If he didn't, he damn well should have.

But the map mattered. Jake Featherston slashed a line across it with his forefinger – almost exactly the line Irving Morrell had slashed across a map of the CSA in Philadelphia some months earlier. Whatever Featherston's flaws, he had a gift for seeing the big picture. 'This is what the sons of bitches aim to do to us.'

Nathan Bedford Forrest III blinked. He worried about trees; he hadn't looked at the forest as a whole for a while. 'You don't think small, sir,' he said after a moment's pause for thought.

'Neither do the damnyankees,' Jake answered without the least hesitation. The truth burned hot and clear in his mind. (Lies burned just as hot and clear, which helped make him as effective as he was. But this was no lie; he wasn't trying to fool either himself or the chief of the General Staff.) 'The damnyankees hurt us bad the last go-round, but that was all they did – they hurt us. With barrels that really haul ass, with airplanes that really bomb, they'll fucking kill us this time. And that's how they'll do it – Chattanooga, Atlanta, the ocean.'

Forrest eyed the map as if a rattlesnake had crawled out

from behind it. He licked his lips. 'They can't do that!' he blurted.

'They can unless we stop 'em,' Jake answered. 'How do you aim to? Losing Atlanta'd be bad enough. All the oil from Louisiana and Texas comes east through there. Atlanta goes down the toilet, everything north and east of it stops running. We are screwed, blued, and tattooed.'

'They can't possibly do all that this year,' Forrest said.

Jake would have liked the assessment much better without the qualifier – and if it didn't so closely match his own. He asked, 'How much more can we pull out of Virginia to send west?'

'If we pull more out, the United States will just waltz into Richmond, you know,' Forrest said. 'I'm not sure we can stop them if they push hard now.'

'If we have to, we can keep fighting without this town, right?' Jake knew losing the capital of the CSA would hurt. It would be a psychological blow that would start people plotting against him – if they weren't already plotting against him, which they probably were. And Richmond wasn't just the capital. It was one of the most important industrial towns in the CSA, right up there with Birmingham and Atlanta and Dallas. But . . . 'If it comes down to choosing between Richmond and Atlanta, we have to hold on to Atlanta, because so many other things depend on it. If the damnyankees take this place away from us, they can't go much farther. Is that right, or do you see it different?' He meant the question. Forrest was welcome to make him change his mind – if he could.

But the chief of the General Staff kept eyeing the map, and the slash Jake had cut across it. 'I'm afraid it is right.' Forrest sounded unhappy about it, which convinced Jake he was telling the truth.

And if he was, and if Jake had things straight, the answer

seemed plain: 'We have to stop the USA as far this side of Atlanta as we can. Stop the damnyankees, then drive 'em back. They did it to us. Let's see how they like getting hoist with their own waddayacallit.'

'Petard,' Forrest said automatically. 'I hope we *can* do it, sir. The one big difference between us and the United States is that they have more margin for error than we do. They fell all over themselves in the Ohio campaign, but we did everything we could do to get as far as we did. If things don't go just right for us . . .'

'Yes, yes.' Jake Featherston had heard that too many times. One reason he'd heard it so often was that it was true. He didn't want to think about that, and no one in the CSA could tell him he had to. He said, 'We'll just have to make things go worse for the damnyankees, that's all. Stir up the Canucks wherever we can, try and talk Quebec into pulling its soldiers out of the rest of Canada so the United States have to send more men in, see if we can fire up the Mormons one more time . . .'

'Will it be enough?' Forrest asked.

'Of course it will,' Jake said. 'It's got to be.' He also didn't want to think about what would happen if it wasn't, and no one in the CSA could tell him he had to do that, either.

For a long time, Camp Determination had bustled. Load after load of Negroes came into the place. Load after load of corpses went out. It was, in a way, a factory, with death as its chief product. And it ran very efficiently.

Troop Leader Hipolito Rodriguez longed for the old days. So did all the other guards, up to Jeff Pinkard himself. The only people who liked the way things were now were the Negroes still inside the camp, and their opinions didn't count.

Fewer and fewer Negroes were left. Thanks to the damnyankees' air raids, trains had a hard time getting to Snyder, Texas, and the camp just beyond it. The bathhouses that weren't bathhouses and the asphyxiating trucks went right on working, emptying barracks one by one. Blacks went to their deaths without too much fuss; the story now was that they were being moved for their own protection. They knew how many bombs fell on Snyder. They didn't know bombs wouldn't fall on them. And so they walked into the bathhouses and climbed onto the trucks – and they never worried about anything else after that.

All of a sudden, Camp Determination had more guards than it needed. Rodriguez and the other men from the Confederate Veterans' Brigades didn't worry about going anywhere else; they were useless at the front. The tough females who did most of the guarding on the women's side didn't need to fear trading their gray uniforms for butternut, either. But the young men, the Freedom Party Guards . . .

'Shows what kind of people the damnyankees are,' one of them said at supper after another day when no trains came in. 'They'd sooner help niggers and blow decent white folks to hell and gone.'

Rodriguez gnawed on a barbecued pork rib. As far as he was concerned, Texans only thought they knew how to barbecue. Down in Sonora, now, they did things right. He found himself nodding to the young guard, though he was neither black nor white himself.

Another youngster said, 'How long till there aren't any niggers left here at all?'

'They aren't shipping so many spooks out this way, I hear,' said the guard who'd spoken first. 'More and more are going to camps farther east, where the U.S. bombers can't hit the train tracks so hard.'

'That's not good,' the second guard said. 'Camp Determination was made to be the biggest and the best. Country can't do a proper job of reducing population if this here camp isn't doing its bit.'

'They didn't think about no Yankees when they made it,' Rodriguez put in.

'You're right, Troop Leader,' the first young guard said. Without three stripes on his sleeve, Rodriguez would have been just another damn greaser to him. With them, the Sonoran was a superior. Party discipline ran deep.

'We've got to do something,' the second guard added. 'We've got to push the United States back into New Mexico.'

Go ahead – volunteer, Rodriguez thought. Guards outfits were fighting alongside C.S. Army troops northwest of the camp. Even if he were hale, he wouldn't have volunteered himself. He'd seen too much infantry combat in west Texas in the last war. He didn't want or need any more.

'Maybe if we sneak in the spooks at night . . .' another guard said.

'Got to have lights to move 'em from the railhead into the camp,' Troop Leader Tom Porter said. The veteran was an outstanding noncom; Rodriguez tried to model himself after him. Porter went on, 'Can you imagine what would happen if we lit this place up like a Christmas tree? Damnyankees'd be on it like ants on potato salad at a picnic.'

'They'll blow up the niggers if they do that,' one of the young guards said. 'They could hit this place any time they please. They don't do it, on account of they love coons so goddamn much.'

Porter frowned. 'Maybe you're right. Maybe. But if they figure out they can take out a whole bunch of guards all at once, they might reckon it's worthwhile. I mean, it's not like we won't reduce the niggers' population anyway.'

The young guard grunted. So did Rodriguez. That sounded as if it made good military sense. 'Why don't they just bomb the camp anyhow, then, though?' the youngster said. 'They'd just be blowing up the smokes a little bit before we take care of them.'

'Well, you're right,' Porter said bleakly, which wasn't what the young guard expected to hear. 'That's why we've got shelters in this place now. If they want to blast the living shit out of us, they can – no two ways about it.'

'What about the antiaircraft guns around the camp?' Two or three guards asked the question in almost identical words.

'What about 'em?' Porter said. 'Antiaircraft guns don't mean you can't bomb a place if you want to bad enough. They just mean it costs more. If you're willing to pay, you can do it. You bet your ass you can. You reckon they don't have antiaircraft guns all over Richmond and Philadelphia? You reckon those places don't get bombed? Ha!'

Nobody said anything for a while after that. Hipolito Rodriguez found himself looking at the ceiling, as if to see bombers overhead. He would have been embarrassed if he were the only one doing it. But he wasn't – nowhere close.

He almost panicked when droning airplane engines woke him later that night. He was ready to run for the shelter, not that his middle-aged, almost-electrocuted body could run very fast. But the enemy airplanes went on to the east. Whatever they were after, it wasn't Camp Determination or Snyder.

Two days later, Jefferson Pinkard sent another contingent of female guards packing. The men who had to go over to the women's side to take their shift didn't know exactly why the guards left. All their guesses were lewd, though. It wasn't as if Pinkard minded brutality, as long as it stopped short of the point where prisoners rebelled.

Rodriguez wondered if he would find Bathsheba and Antoinette alive. To his surprise, he did. They'd lasted longer than most camp inmates. Both of them were dreadfully thin now; the older woman coughed all the time. But they greeted him with smiles. 'It's the nice sergeant,' Bathsheba said. 'How is that Xerxes? How is our man?'

Dead. Rotting in a trench a bulldozer scraped in the ground, piled in with God knows how many other bodies. He couldn't tell them that. He didn't have the heart. He'd led so many men to their death – what was telling the truth about one of them next to that? Nothing, logically, but logical didn't seem to have much to do with it.

And so he lied: 'He is good. He is about like you. He says hello. He says he loves you both. He says he misses your son.' He remembered Bathsheba had one, and that the boy or young man didn't come to the camp.

'I misses Cassius, too,' the older woman said, and Antoinette nodded. Bathsheba went on, 'I hope he's all right.'

Wherever he was, if he wasn't in a camp he was better off than the rest of the family. Rodriguez didn't say that – why belabor the obvious? He did say, 'You got messages for – for your man?' He couldn't pronounce *Xerxes* to save his own life, and nothing would save Xerxes' now.

They poured out their hearts to him. That only made him feel worse about lying to them. But they would hate him all the more for deceiving them if they found out the truth now. And so he listened to words of love for a dead man and promised to bring back answers from beyond the grave.

None of the other guards knew what he was doing. Had they known, they would have laughed at him or said he was doing it to get Antoinette to lie down with him. If he wanted her, he thought he could have her. But what was the point? She and her mother couldn't last much longer, not the way things were. And when she was dead, he'd be sad she was gone. He'd be sad when she was gone even if she didn't sleep with him; he liked her.

He didn't miss the black women he did lay. They were just . . . bodies. Now they were dead bodies, and so what?

'If they was to drop bombs all over this place,' Bathsheba said, 'you reckon a couple o' skinny colored ladies could run off without nobody noticing?'

'You don't ask me that!' Rodriguez exclaimed. 'I got to keep people inside here, not tell nobody how to get away.'

'You keepin' people in here?' Bathsheba shook her head. 'Don't reckon so. Ain't nobody in the whole wide world could keep *people* in a place like this. What you're doin' is, you're keepin' niggers here. Niggers ain't people, not to the folks who go 'round yellin', "Freedom!" all the damn time.'

'Mama . . .' Antoinette said.

Bathsheba laughed. 'It's the truth, ain't it? 'Course it is. You afraid I git in trouble on account of tellin' the truth? Girl, how kin I git in trouble that's any worse'n what I'm in already? You answer me that.' She turned to Rodriguez. 'You answer me that, too, Mistuh Sergeant, suh.'

Rodriguez had no answers, and he knew it. He was a twenty-year Freedom Party man. He'd shouted, 'Freedom!' and '*¡Libertad!*' plenty of times, more times than he could count. He had no use for blacks; if anything, *mallate* was even more insulting, even more demeaning, than *nigger*. He still believed Negroes caused most of the Confederacy's troubles. And without blacks, whites would come down on Mexicans instead.

But this skinny old woman did something no one else had ever been able to do: she made him ashamed of the uniform he wore, of the stripes on his sleeve, of the Party badge on his chest. Bathsheba did indeed tell the truth, and Hipolito Rodriguez wasn't too far gone to know it.

'Where you goin'?' she called after him. He didn't answer. He just went away, anywhere away from the terrible truth, as fast as his legs would take him.

'Now look what you went and done, Mama,' Antoinette said reproachfully, as if, despite everything that had happened to them, this could still be her mother's fault.

'Me? I didn't do nothin',' Bathsheba answered, and then, more quietly but not too quietly for Rodriguez to hear, 'He done it to hisself.'

And there was another piercingly painful truth. Rodriguez had done it to himself. He looked beneath the face of population reduction and saw murder. He looked at niggers, at *mallates*, and saw people. He looked at what he'd been doing and saw. . . .

'*Madre de Dios*,' he whispered, and crossed himself. '*¡Ai, madre de Dios!*' But could even the Virgin forgive him for such a mountain of sins? He had trouble believing it. No – he couldn't believe it. That made a difference. That made all the difference in the world.

He crossed himself again. The gesture seemed extraordinarily pointless, extraordinarily futile. He was damned. He felt the certainty of his damnation like that mountain of sin falling on him.

He'd known for a long time that Edith Pinkard's first husband was a camp guard who killed himself. He'd heard of other men who did the same thing. Up till now, he'd thought they were crazy. All at once, he didn't. How could you live with yourself when you understood what you were doing, what you were helping your country do?

He looked down at his hands. How much blood was on them? A river? A lake? An ocean? He looked at the submachine gun in those bloodstained hands. It was made for one thing: killing people. It was perfectly designed for the job, too. He clicked off the safety, flicked the change lever to full automatic fire. Then, like a man in a trance, he put the muzzle of the conveniently short weapon in his mouth. It smelled and tasted of metal and gun oil.

'Look out!' a woman cried. 'He gonna—'

And he did. He pulled the trigger, hard. And that was most definitely that.

Chester Martin had never gone south of the Ohio River. He'd spend the Great War in Virginia, on the Roanoke front in the west and then, after recovering from his first wound, in the northern part of the state, pushing down toward Richmond. He'd been not far from Fredericksburg when the fighting ended in 1917 – and not far from the same town when he got wounded twenty-five years later.

He liked Kentucky better. He especially liked how far the U.S. Army had driven into Kentucky, and how fast it was moving. They'd passed Madisonville and were heading south toward Earlington. Madisonville was a tobacco town. The crop was nowhere near ripe, which didn't stop several U.S. soldiers from plucking their own, drying or half cooking the leaves, and trying to smoke them afterwards. They proved one thing in a hurry: making cigarettes wasn't as easy as it looked.

Earlington, by contrast, made its living from coal. U.S. Army engineers dynamited the entrances to one mine after another. 'Is that smart, sir?' Martin asked his platoon commander. 'Shouldn't we be using those mines ourselves?' He knew how much coal the steel industry needed, and it wasn't the only one.

Lieutenant Wheat only shrugged. 'I guess the first thing is to deny this coal to the enemy,' he answered. 'We can worry about everything else later. It's not like we don't mine plenty of our own.'

'I suppose so, sir.' If Chester didn't sound convinced, it was because he wasn't. But he didn't decide such things, even if the news would have come as a surprise to the men in the platoon.

Somewhere not far away, a rifle went off. He and Lieutenant Wheat both reached for their weapons – that wasn't a Springfield. It also wasn't one of the Confederates' automatic rifles, or an older bolt-action Tredegar. Martin didn't know exactly what it was – some kind of squirrel gun, he supposed. He would have bet whoever squeezed the trigger wasn't aiming at a squirrel.

The same thought must have gone through Delbert Wheat's mind, for he said, 'They don't love us around here, do they?'

'Not hardly,' Chester said. The .22 or whatever it was barked again. 'I bet we're going to have to take more hostages.' Soldiers in butternut were trying to hold a line on the southern fringes of Earlington, and they would have to fall back from there in the next day or two. But Confederate civilians had rediscovered the thrills of guerrilla warfare. Kids and old men and even women turned into bushwhackers whenever they saw the chance.

The laws of war said people who weren't in uniform but took up arms anyway were fair game. Those laws didn't say taking hostages was all right, but every army on enemy territory did it. Sometimes it helped. Sometimes it just made more civilians want to pick up squirrel guns.

'We kill enough of these fuckers, sooner or later the rest will get the idea,' Wheat said. 'Or if they don't, we'll kill all of them.' He didn't sound worried – more as if he looked forward to it.

After a third shot rang out, Martin got to his feet.

'Somebody ought to do something about that damn sniper,' he said.

He hadn't gone more than a step or two before a U.S. machine gun stuttered out a short burst, and then another one. A triumphant shout went up: '*Got* the son of a bitch!'

'Talk about service,' Lieutenant Wheat said. Chester grinned and nodded and hunkered down again. He pulled out a pack of Raleighs – properly grown, properly cured tobacco – and lit up. After a deep drag, he nodded again. Yeah, this was what smokes were supposed to taste like.

A soldier trotted back to him and the lieutenant. 'There's a Confederate captain with a flag of truce, wants to talk to us about civilians,' he said.

'Bring him back here,' Wheat said. 'We can talk.'

'Blindfold him first,' Chester added. 'No point letting him see what we've got. That may be part of what he's after.' The platoon commander nodded. The soldier saluted Wheat and hurried away.

'Would you like to sit in on this?' the lieutenant asked politely.

'If you don't mind, sir,' Chester answered, as politely. The platoon leader didn't want to let the Confederates hornswoggle him. Chester was his ace in the hole, and appreciated being invited without having to invite himself.

When the C.S. captain took off his blindfold, he proved to be about thirty, with the ribbon for the Purple Heart – a decoration that went back to George Washington, and that both sides used – on his chest. He said his name was Wilbur Pease. He didn't seem surprised to find a first sergeant sitting in with a second lieutenant, which showed he knew how the world worked.

Wheat did the talking: 'Well, Captain, what's on your mind?'

'I've had reports of atrocities against civilian citizens,

Lieutenant, and I've come to investigate and to protest,' Pease answered.

'Considering what the Confederate States are doing to their Negroes, aren't you in a poor position to talk about atrocities?' Wheat asked.

Wilbur Pease didn't even blink. 'Civilian citizens, I said. Negroes are only residents, not citizens. They don't have the rights of citizens.' *We can do whatever we want to them,* Martin translated. Captain Pease went on, 'I'm talking about white people, people who matter.' His racism was so complete, so perfect, he didn't know he had it.

'We have a problem with – what's the fancy French for it, Sergeant?'

'*Francs-tireurs,* sir.' Chester pronounced it *franks-teeroors;* he knew no more French than Chinese.

It satisfied both Lieutenant Wheat and Captain Pease. The U.S. officer went on, 'If we catch people out of uniform shooting at us, we're going to kill them. It's as simple as that, Captain. We nailed one a few minutes ago. If we have to take hostages to make them think twice, we'll do that, too. And we'll shoot the hostages if it comes to that. I'm sorry, but these jerks with guns need to understand that we're serious.'

'The laws of war—' Pease began.

'You did the same damn thing on our soil,' Chester Martin said. 'Don't get all high and mighty about it.'

'And don't encourage the, uh, *francs-tireurs,* either,' Wheat added. 'That way, everybody will be better off.'

Captain Pease scowled. His troops wouldn't be better off. The more U.S. soldiers flabbled about civilians with rifles, the more distracted from fighting the regular Confederate army they were. 'I deny that we encourage civilians to take up arms against invaders,' he said.

'Of course you do, Captain,' Wheat said.

'And the stork brings babies and sticks 'em under cabbage leaves,' Chester added.

'All right,' Pease said angrily. 'I can see you don't take this seriously.'

'Oh, we do,' Wheat said. 'We take it so seriously, we'll do whatever we have to to stamp it out. And if that means you run short on civilians, we won't lose any sleep about it. Whatever people in these parts try to do to us, we'll do worse to them. I promise you that, Captain. It worked in Utah. It should work here.'

'If you want that kind of fight, I'm sure you can have it,' Wilbur Pease said. 'You'd better put my hoodwink back on – I'd like to return to my side of the line.'

'I'll do it, sir,' Chester said to Lieutenant Wheat. As he blindfolded Pease, he went on, 'We don't have anything in particular against the Confederate Army. You play fair when you fight us. Civilians playing soldier – that's a different story.'

'Yes, it is. You'll see.' Pease held out his hand. 'Someone take me back, please.'

A soldier led him through the U.S. positions. Chester's face was troubled as he watched the Confederate officer go. A different story . . . He wondered if his own words would come back to haunt him. Auto bombs, people bombs . . . The Kentuckians hadn't started making life as miserable for the U.S. Army as they could.

'How much trouble do you think civilians can make?' By the troubled note in Lieutenant Wheat's voice, he was worrying about the same thing.

'It can't be worse than Utah. That's all I know for sure.' Martin paused for a moment. 'Of course, Utah was pretty bad.'

A brief burst of gunfire came from the Confederates, formally marking the end of the truce. A U.S. machine gun fired back, and after that it was time for everyone to keep his head down again.

The Confederates launched a salvo of their rockets. Most of them came down on Earlington. Civilians hadn't evacuated the town, and bore the brunt of the hellish weapons' bursts. 'So much for taking care of their own,' Martin said into Delbert Wheat's ear; they both crouched in the same shell hole. If something came down on them, the platoon would need new leaders.

'They don't give a damn. They never have,' the young officer answered. 'All they care about is scoring points off us.'

Chester nodded. It looked like that to him, too. Chaos reigned in the town. Wounded U.S. soldiers screamed for medics. So did wounded civilians. The corpsmen dealt with soldiers first. That was likely to hurt their popularity with the locals. They didn't seem to care. Chester didn't, either.

U.S. warplanes streaked low overhead. They were fighters, but each one carried a bomb slung under its belly. They were bound to be slower and less maneuverable till they dropped those bombs. Explosions on the Confederate side of the line said they weren't wasting any time.

Barrels rumbled down toward the front, too. One platoon particularly caught Chester's eye. All five machines were the newest U.S. model, sleek and deadly as so many tigers. All five were unbuttoned, too, their commanders and drivers looking out to see where they were. When they got closer to the firing, the drivers would close their hatches. Some barrel commanders liked to stand up in the cupola as long as they could. They took chances doing that, but their machines fared better.

One of those commanders drew Chester's notice as he rolled down Highland Park and into the northern outskirts of Earlington. He spotted Chester, too, and no surprise, for they were about the same age: middle-aged survivors in a world of young men. Over the din of his engine, he called, 'You went through it before and you came back for another round?' His accent said he came from somewhere close to the Canadian border.

'Yeah, I'm a glutton for punishment – just like you,' Chester shouted back. They grinned and waved at each other. 'Stay safe,' Chester added.

'You, too.' The barrel commander laughed. So did Martin. If they wanted to stay safe, what were they doing here?

Lieutenant Wheat gave Chester a quizzical look. 'You know that guy?'

'No, sir,' Chester answered. 'But us old farts, we've got to stick together.'

His platoon went into the line not long after the barrels clattered past. With help from the armored behemoths, they shoved the Confederates all the way out of Earlington. More rockets came in from the south. Featherston's soldiers had lots of nasty weapons. Whether they had enough men to use them was a different question. For all their firepower, Confederate troops seemed thin on the ground.

That barrel commander fought his machine aggressively. His gunner hit a Confederate barrel at what had to be over a mile, and set it afire. Two other Confederate barrels decided they'd be better off somewhere else. They trundled away in a hurry. Chester approved – the less he had to worry about enemy armor, the happier he was. Before too long, he trudged past the burning enemy machine. The push south rolled on.

Cincinnatus Driver made sure the .45 on the seat of his truck was loaded and sat where he could grab it in a hurry – he never let it slide out of reach. The road between Paris and Winchester wasn't safe for U.S. convoys. The drive south had pushed the Confederate Army out of this part of Kentucky. But C.S. stragglers and bushwhackers who didn't wear uniforms still took potshots at U.S. vehicles from the trees that grew too damn close to the side of the road.

A bloated body hung from a telegraph pole. The placard tied around the man's neck said, FRANC-TIREUR. That was officer talk for *bushwhacker.* No doubt U.S. authorities hanged him there to warn his buddies. His wasn't the first corpse Cincinnatus had seen. They didn't seem to do much to intimidate the Confederates.

He sighed. Things hadn't been that much different in the Great War. You did what they told you to do, and you hoped you came out the other side in one piece. *You volunteered for this,* Cincinnatus reminded himself. *Were you born stupid, or did you have to study?* He concluded he was born stupid; he'd never been much for studying. But he'd had too recent a close-up look at the Confederacy. Any black man who did, naturally wanted to kill the country with an axe.

Since he didn't have an axe, truckload after truckload of supplies would have to do. In the Great War, the USA was content to make the CSA say uncle. This time, the United States seemed to want to kill the Confederate States with an axe. Cincinnatus understood why, too. The United States almost had the axe fall on them.

The lead truck in the convoy didn't run into an axe. It ran over a land mine, and started to burn. The lead truck never carried munitions, just because it was most likely to go boom. The driver probably didn't have a chance. A different truck, chosen by lot, led every convoy. *That could have been me,* Cincinnatus thought, gulping.

No matter what happened to the lead truck, the convoy

had to get through. The second truck drove off the road onto the soft shoulder on the right – and ran over another mine and blew up. 'Do Jesus!' Cincinnatus yelped. He hit the brakes. There was going to be a holdup here – he could see that. If the third truck went off the road to the left, would it go sky-high, too? The driver didn't want to find out. Cincinnatus wouldn't have, either. The Confederates who planned this one had outthought their U.S. opposite numbers.

Just how badly they'd outthought them became obvious a moment later. When the U.S. trucks in the convoy were all stopped and all bunched up behind the two that were in flames, a machine gun and assorted automatic rifles and submachine guns opened up on them from the woods to the left. As soon as Cincinnatus heard the gunfire and saw muzzle flashes winking over there, he bailed out. He paused only to grab the .45 as he slid across the seat. He was damned if he'd get out of the truck on the driver's side and make himself a perfect target for the C.S. holdouts or guerrillas or whoever the hell they were.

His bad leg and bad shoulder both howled protests at what he was making them do. He paid them no attention. Getting hit by an auto had been bad, very bad. Getting chewed up by machine-gun fire was one of the few things he could think of likely to be worse. He didn't want to find out the hard way.

No more than a second or two after he threw himself to the ground and crawled behind a tire, a burst of bullets chewed up the cab of the truck. Glass from the windshield and the driver's-side window blew out and then fell like rain.

Had the engine caught fire, he would have had to abandon the truck and make for the woods to the right. He would also have had to pray Confederates didn't infest them, too. For the moment, though, the truck wasn't burning.

A couple of wounded drivers cried out in pain. Other men, like Cincinnatus, crouched and sprawled in whatever cover they could find. One of them called, 'Be ready! Those fuckers are liable to rush us.'

Can they be that smart and that dumb at the same time? Cincinnatus wondered. If he were in the woods, he would have kept shooting at the trucks till they all caught fire or started exploding. The Confederates had put themselves in a position where they could do that. Why wouldn't they, then?

Confederate soldiers probably would have reasoned the same way he did. The men in the woods turned out not to be soldiers. They were amateurs, bushwhackers, guerrillas. They cared about the trucks, yes, but they wanted to kill people, too. Once they'd peppered the trucks with bullets, set some on fire, and flattened a lot of tires, they loped forward to deal with the drivers.

They must have thought they'd killed and wounded more men than they had. That was the only thing Cincinnatus could think of. With just a pistol, he had to let them come near before he opened up. He eyed the bushwhackers. They wore dirty dungarees and dirtier flannel shirts. They were poorly shaved. When they got a little closer, they would probably stink.

They never got that close. One of the drivers had a Springfield, not a .45. He fired from behind a tire, worked the bolt, and fired again. Two guerrillas fell. The others started spraying lead as if it were going out of style.

The drivers fired back. They didn't want the bushwhackers to concentrate on the man with the best weapon. Cincinnatus used the two-handed grip to steady the .45, but it still bucked like an unbroken stallion when he pulled the trigger. The man he aimed at ducked, the way almost everyone did when a bullet came too close.

Several bullets came too close to Cincinnatus. He was already down on his belly. He tried to flatten out like a squirrel after a deuce-and-a-half ran over it. Another guerrilla fell. The drivers' cheers were punctuated by a shriek as one of them got hit.

In the films about fighting Indians on the Great Plains, the cavalry always charged over the hill in the last reel. It wasn't the cavalry this time. It was an armored car and two command cars that carried .50-caliber machine guns. As soon as the U.S. soldiers in them got a look at what was going on, they hosed the irregulars down with gunfire. The men who fought for the Confederacy broke and flew toward the woods. Not many of them got there.

Even then, the bushwhackers didn't give up. The machine gun hidden among the trees started shooting at the oncoming vehicles. The armored car didn't need to worry about that, but the thin-skinned command cars did. The armored car had a small cannon, not just machine guns of its own. After it sent half a dozen rounds crashing into the woods, the enemy machine gun shut up in the middle of a burst.

Somebody in one of the command cars or the armored car must have used the wireless, because four or five fighter-bombers roared in and dropped their presents on the stand of trees. Cincinnatus hoped they blew the bushwhackers to hell and gone. No matter what he hoped, he knew some of them would get away. Maybe they would think twice about messing with the U.S. Army from now on. More likely, he feared, they wouldn't.

He didn't want to get out from behind his tire even after the armored car took up a position between the woods and the shattered convoy. Nobody could call him a cowardly coon, either, not when the white drivers also stayed right where they were.

A soldier got out of one of the command cars for a closer look at a dead irregular. A bullet from the woods made him throw himself flat. The armored car and the command car lashed the trees with machine-gun rounds. Another defiant bullet clanged off the armored car's turret.

Nobody went anywhere till more trucks brought soldiers forward, some to clear the woods and others, engineers, to get rid of the rest of the mines the bushwhackers had planted. After that, still more trucks had to come up to salvage what the Kentuckians hadn't destroyed – and to pick up the drivers.

'I'm getting too old for this shit,' one of them said wearily as he climbed into the back of a deuce-and-a-half.

'I was too old for this shit a long time ago,' Cincinnatus said. 'Remind me how come I signed up to do it again.'

'On account of you're a damn fool,' the other driver said. Before Cincinnatus could even start to get mad, the white man added, 'Just like me.' That took care of that.

The front lay just north of Winchester. Cincinnatus wished it were farther south still. He knew that was unfair. The U.S. Army had done in a couple of weeks what took months of slogging in the last war. And this wasn't even the main U.S. thrust. That was farther west, and was moving faster.

He got a new truck that afternoon, and a new assignment. The kid lieutenant in the motor pool gave him a dubious look. 'You sure you're up for this, Gramps?' he said.

'It's gonna help whip Jake Featherston, ain't it?' Cincinnatus said.

'That's the idea, yeah,' the lieutenant answered.

'Then I'm up for it,' Cincinnatus declared.

After another pause, the lieutenant – he was younger than Cincinnatus' son Achilles, which made him seem very young indeed – nodded. 'Well, when you put it that way—'

'I do,' Cincinnatus said.

'Fair enough. I can see why,' the lieutenant said. 'Good luck.'

Cincinnatus drove within artillery range of the front. Nothing came down too close, for which he thanked God. 'What the hell took youse guys so long?' said the quartermaster sergeant who took charge of the supplies the truck convoy delivered. 'We been waitin' for youse.' He was a hairy little Italian guy from New York City. His accent and Cincinnatus' were a long way from each other.

He was also a long way from any place where bullets flew. His uniform was clean. It was even pressed. 'Sorry to disoblige you, Sergeant,' Cincinnatus said, 'but before I got down here, bushwhackers hit the convoy I was in. We had trucks blown up an' men killed, so maybe you better do your grousin' somewheres else.'

'You gotta lotta noive, talkin' t'me that way,' the sergeant growled. 'Who do you think you are?'

'I'm an uppity nigger tryin' to kick Jake Featherston's raggedy ass,' Cincinnatus answered. 'We on the same side or not?'

The noncom's eyes almost bugged out of his head. 'You can't talk to me like that. You can't, you hear? Tell me your name. I'm gonna put you on report.'

'I'm Cincinnatus Driver. Do whatever you damn well please,' Cincinnatus said calmly. 'Whatever you do, it ain't gonna be worse'n what happened this morning.'

'You want to put him on report, put us all on report,' a white driver said. 'He just told you what everybody was thinking. I'm Hal Williamson. Write it down.'

'Bruce Donovan,' another driver said. Everybody in the convoy gave the quartermaster sergeant his name. Somebody in the back of the crowd added, 'You sad, sorry chickenshit asshole.'

'That does it! That fuckin' does it!' the sergeant shouted. 'Youse guys have had it.' He stormed off and returned a few minutes later with a captain in tow. 'Listen to these wiseguys, sir!'

Cincinnatus and the other truckers were happy to let the captain listen. 'We almost got killed today,' Cincinnatus said. 'I don't see him with no Purple Heart or Silver Star or nothin'.' Again, the rest of the drivers chimed in on his side.

After listening to them, the captain turned to his sergeant and said, 'Take an even strain, Cannizzaro. It's not like they were holding you up on purpose.'

'But, sir—' Sergeant Cannizzaro began.

'Take an even strain, I said,' the captain told him, more sharply this time. 'The stuff is here now. Let's get it out to the troops who need it.' He walked away, leaving the quartermaster sergeant staring after him. *An officer with sense,* Cincinnatus thought. He'd run into some before, but it didn't happen every day.

Jerry Dover had a promotion. He wanted a second star on either side of his collar about as much as he wanted a third leg, but he was now officially a lieutenant-colonel. He was doing everything Colonel Travis W.W. Oliphant did before he went missing and more besides, so the powers that be seemed to have decided he deserved at least some of the vanished Colonel Oliphant's rank.

Lieutenant-colonel wasn't enough. To get the boneheads down in Tennessee to pay attention to him, he would have needed to be at least a lieutenant general – not a rank the Confederate States dished out every day.

'Listen, dammit,' Dover snarled over a bad telephone connection, 'if you don't get more ammo and gasoline up here pretty damn quick, you won't need to worry about me pissing and moaning any more, that's for sure.'

'You don't know how bad things are down here,' said the colonel on the other end of the line. 'The Yankees are bombing the shit out of the dams President Featherston built. We've got floods like you wouldn't believe. Half the time we don't have power, on account of they made so much of it. Roads are out, railroads are out—'

'If you don't send us what we need to fight with, *we're* out,' Dover interrupted. 'You'll be arguing with some damnyankee quartermaster, not me.' Some damnyankee quartermaster was enjoying the depot he'd put together outside of Covington. Nobody but nobody had dreamt the USA could move so fast.

'We're trying,' the colonel said.

'You sure are,' Jerry Dover told him, but it went over his head. Dover would have bet on that. He went on, 'This is a war, in case you didn't notice . . . sir. If we don't do it, we're going to fucking lose.' He didn't care what he said when he talked to a supplier. That was just as true when he talked to C.S. Army quartermasters as it had been when he talked to rascally butchers in Augusta.

'I am certain you are doing everything you can, Colonel,' said the officer down in Tennessee. 'Why don't you give me and my men credit for doing the same?'

Because from up here it looks like you've got your head up your ass. But Dover didn't say that, though it was a damned near-run thing. What he did say was, 'Get as much forward as you can. They've promised me they'll hold on to Bowling Green no matter what.'

They'd also promised they would hold on to Covington no matter what. He'd believed them, which only proved anybody could be a fool now and then. He was more ready to evacuate and wreck this depot than he had been when the line lay farther north. Some Yankee writer once said, *Trust everybody – but cut the cards.* That struck Jerry Dover as good advice.

Even the colonel down in Tennessee, who had to worry about nothing worse than bombers and floods – mere details in Dover's harried existence – could see they might have promised more than they could deliver. 'Keep your options open,' he said, and hung up.

'Options. Right,' Dover said tightly. At the moment, he didn't know whether to shit or go blind, and that about summed up his options. The western U.S. column was already down about even with Bowling Green. The eastern one was still northeast of his current center. In a way, that was good news. It meant that, for the time being, he could resupply both crumbling Confederate fronts. But it also meant both fronts were liable to converge on him here, or even behind him. If that happened . . .

If that happens, I have to move like a son of a bitch to save anything, Dover thought glumly. *Take what I can, blow up what I can't.* He already knew what was what, what would go and what would go up in smoke.

If this turned into the front, he was liable to have to turn into a combat soldier to get free of it. He muttered to himself; like every other white man his age in the CSA, he'd done a spell in the trenches in the last war. He wasn't eager to repeat it. But if the damnyankees got in his way, he would try his best to run them over.

The telephone jangled. If it was that officious idiot in Tennessee, telling him something wouldn't show up because somebody'd lost the paperwork . . . 'Dover here,' he growled, a note of warning in his voice.

'This here is Major Kirby Bramlette by Elkton,' the

caller said. Dover had to look at a map to find Elkton south-east of Hopkinsville, which had fallen to the USA only the day before. It was also definitely south of Bowling Green, which wasn't good news. Bramlette sounded right on the edge of being frantic as he went on, 'You got any more o' them antibarrel rockets, the ones infantrymen can shoot off? Looks like every Yankee barrel in the world is heading right at me.'

'You'll have some in a couple of hours, if U.S. fighters don't shoot up my trucks on the way,' Dover answered.

'Sooner'd be better,' Bramlette said. 'Two hours from now, I'm liable to be dead.' He didn't say anything about pulling back. The Confederates did that only when they couldn't help it.

'Fast as we can get there.' Dover hung up and ran outside, yelling for drivers. When he'd assembled half a dozen, he said, 'Load up on antibarrel rockets and get 'em to Elkton on the double.'

'Where the fuck is Elkton?' one of them asked.

'Follow me. I'll get you there.' By his accent, the man who spoke was from around these parts. You'd have to be, to know where Elkton was.

'Take your trucks to gate number nine,' Dover said. 'Go in through there and make the first left you can.' He'd laid out the depot himself. He knew where everything was. If Major Bramlette needed cold-weather socks or prophylactics, he would have known where they were off the top of his head, too.

Confederate soldiers loaded the rockets and their stovepipe launchers onto the trucks. In the last war, Negroes would have done it. Not here, not now. The soldiers didn't even grumble about nigger work. They just fetched and carried without a second thought. If blacks were working now, most of the soldiers working the depot could have been at the front with automatic rifles in their hands. That seemed obvious to Jerry Dover. The trouble he would land in if he said so out loud seemed even more obvious, so he kept his mouth shut.

Inside of half an hour, the trucks were on the way. Dover went back to his office and telephoned Major Bramlette. 'Barring air strikes, they should get there in an hour or so. It's what, about forty miles from here to where you're at?' he said.

'Something like that, anyways,' Bramlette answered. 'Thank you kindly, Colonel. You've done what you could. Now we just have to see if we can hold on that long.' As if to punctuate the comment, explosions came over the telephone line. All of a sudden, he didn't have a connection. He swore, hoping the trouble was in the line and not because of a direct hit on Bramlette's headquarters.

He didn't find out till the trucks got back a little before sunset. 'We delivered the rockets, sir,' said the head driver, a master sergeant named Stonewall Sloane. (Dover had seen his papers – that was his real name. Why his parents couldn't have picked a different Confederate hero to name him after . . . Jerry Dover shrugged. How many babies born between 1934 and now were called Featherston? Too many – he was sure of that.)

'All right – you delivered them,' Dover said. Sloane nodded. He neither looked nor sounded happy. Dover asked the question he had to ask: 'What went wrong?'

'Damnyankees had already shoved our guys out of Elkton by the time we got there, sir.' Stonewall Sloane paused to light a cigar. Dover had a cigarette going – but then, he usually did. The sergeant went on, 'I *hope* the rockets can help us blow some of the Yankees to hell and gone. If they can't . . .' He sent up gloomy smoke signals.

'Shit,' Dover said. 'Whereabouts exactly did you make

your delivery? Was it south of Elkton or east of it?'

'East, sir,' Sloane answered: a world of bad news in two words.

'Shit,' Dover said again. 'They're heading this way, then.'

'Don't know if they want to take Bowling Green or get in behind it and cut it off,' Sergeant Sloane said. 'They've been doing a lot of that crap lately. We did it in Ohio, so I reckon the United States learned their lessons from us.'

'Did they have to learn them so goddamn well?' Dover stubbed out his cigarette and lit another one. Stonewall Sloane managed a thin smile. After a deep, savage drag, Dover asked, 'You think we'll have to get out of town? The more time we have, the more stuff we'll be able to save.'

'Sir, I honest to God don't know,' Sloane replied. 'If you told me a month ago the Yankees could come this far this fast, I would've told you you were out of your goddamn tree. Uh – meaning no disrespect.'

'Don't worry about it,' Dover said dryly.

Stonewall Sloane sent him an appraising glance. The cigar twitched. 'You're all right, aren't you?'

'Well, I try.'

'Yeah.' Sloane scratched his head. 'Where was I? Oh, yeah. They've already done more than I reckoned they could, so who knows what the fuck they're liable to do next? Do you want to take chances?'

Before Dover could answer, air-raid sirens wailed. 'We're going to take chances whether we want to or not,' he said, and grabbed his helmet and ran for the closest trench. Sergeant Sloane was right behind him.

Antiaircraft guns around the depot thundered. Dover was glad he had steel between his skull and the chunks of shrapnel that would start falling out of the sky any second now. You were just as dead if your own side killed you as you were any other way.

Fighter-bombers streaked by low overhead, the U.S. eagle in front of crossed swords plainly visible. One trailed fire and smoke. It slammed into the ground and blew up. 'That'll learn 'em!' Sloane yelled.

But other explosions came from the depot not far away. Some were single, others multiple: bombs touching off more explosions on the ground. What Jerry Dover had to say scuttled several commandments. He'd arranged ordnance in small lots with thick earthen dikes between them. That minimized the damage, but didn't, couldn't, stop it.

The surviving U.S. airplanes came back for another pass at the depot and the trucks, this time with their cannons and machine guns. Dover said something even worse. He yanked his .45 out of its holster and fired several shots at the U.S. warplanes. That did no good, of course. He'd known it wouldn't. 'Goddamn useless thing,' he growled in disgust.

'Antiaircraft guns aren't doing a hell of a lot better,' Stonewall Sloane said.

'Fuck them, too,' Dover said. The veteran noncom blinked, then laughed. Dover wasn't laughing. He was furious. 'We ought to have something that really will shoot airplanes down, dammit. All these things do is make noise.' The guns, at the moment, were making a godawful racket.

'Rockets, maybe?' Sergeant Sloane didn't sound as if he took that seriously, even if he was the one proposing it.

But Dover said, 'Why the hell not? They've got 'em for barrels. Why not airplanes? They're a lot easier to wreck.'

'Harder to hit, though,' Sloane said.

'That's for the guys with the high foreheads and the thick glasses,' Dover said. 'I bet we've got people working on it. I bet the damnyankees do, too. If they figure it out first, that's bad news.' He scrambled out of the trench and trotted toward the depot to do what he could to control the damage – and to see how much damage there was to control. Right now, he couldn't find much good news for the CSA.

Cassius skirted Milledgeville, Georgia, the way he skirted every town he approached. Milledgeville was a fair-sized place, with maybe 5,000 people in it. It was laid out with the idea that it would become the state capital – and it did, till brawling, bumptious Atlanta displaced it after the War of Secession. A sign on the outskirts bragged that Milledgeville was where Georgia legislators voted to leave the Union. Cassius didn't think that was anything to be proud of.

What would life be like in the United States? It probably wouldn't be good; he didn't suppose life for Negroes was good anywhere. But it couldn't be like *this*. He was skinny and dirty. He smelled bad – the only chances he got to wash were in streams he walked past. He was hungry most of the time.

And, at that, he didn't have it so bad. He wasn't in a camp. He didn't know what his family was going through, not exactly. Nobody knew exactly except the people who got carted away. The only thing people on the outside knew was that the ones who got carted away didn't come back.

Most Negroes in the cities had been rounded up and taken away. It was harder out in the countryside. They were more scattered, harder to get into one place with barbed wire all around it. Guerrillas scared some whites out in the country to death. Others, though, weren't so bad. Quite a few let you do odd jobs in exchange for food and a place to sleep and maybe a dollar or two.

Some of the farms had women running them, all the menfolk gone to war. Cassius learned it was harder to get a handout or even a hearing at those places than at the

ones with white men on them. Women on their own commonly carried shotguns or rifles, and didn't want to listen
to a hard-luck story. 'Get lost before I call the sheriff,' they
would say – either that or, 'Get lost before I shoot.'

But they didn't call the sheriff. In spite of an Augusta
passbook, Cassius hadn't had any trouble going where he
pleased. If he stole, that might have been a different story.
Except for trifles – a few eggs here, some matches there –
he didn't. His parents had raised him the right way. *He*
wouldn't have put it like that, not after the way he knocked
heads with his father, but that was what it amounted to.

He stayed in the pine woods after getting run off a farm
west of Milledgeville. With summer coming soon, nights
were mild. Mosquitoes tormented him, but they would have
done that anywhere except behind screens. He didn't worry
about animals; bears and cougars were hunted into rarity.
People, on the other hand . . .

He'd already seen Mexican soldiers on the march. He
made sure they didn't see him, ducking into a stand of
trees once and hiding behind a haystack another time.
Those yellowish khaki uniforms made him angry – what
were they doing in his country? He wouldn't have got nearly
so upset about butternut or gray.

That was his gut reaction, anyhow. When he thought
about it, he laughed at himself. As if the Confederate States
were his country, or any Negro's country! The idea was
ridiculous. And native whites would have been rougher on
him or anyone else his color than these foreigners were.

He chopped wood for a farmer later that day. The blisters he'd got the first time he did it were starting to turn
to calluses. The farmer gave him ham and grits and a big
mug of homebrew. Making your own beer was against the
law in Georgia, but plenty of people both white and black
turned criminal on that score.

'You work good,' the farmer said, spitting a stream of tobacco juice.

'Thank you, suh,' Cassius answered.

As others had before him, the white man asked, 'Want to stick around?' He gave Cassius a shrewd look. 'Sooner or later, you're gonna run into trouble wandering around the countryside – or else trouble's gonna run into *you*.'

Cassius only shrugged. Whatever happened to him out here couldn't be worse than what had happened to his father and mother and sister in Augusta. 'Sorry, suh, but I got to be movin' on,' he said.

'Whatever you want.' The farmer shrugged, too, but Cassius didn't like the glint in his eye. He left a little earlier than he would have otherwise, and headed south where he had been going west. As soon as he got out of sight of the farmhouse, he took the first westward track he found. Luck was with him, because he came up to another farm just as the sun was going down. He scouted the place from the edge of the woods, and didn't see or hear any dogs. When it got really dark, he sneaked into the haystack, which gave him a much better bed than bare ground would have.

He hadn't fallen asleep yet when gunfire split the night: several bursts from submachine guns, with single shots from a pistol in between them. He wondered what that was all about. No, actually he didn't wonder – he feared he knew. Had that farmer called the local sheriff or militia commander or whoever was in charge of the people with guns and said, 'There's an uppity nigger southbound from my place. Reckon you ought to take care of him'?

Deputies or Mexicans must have picked on the first Negro they saw heading south on that road. That black wasn't Cassius, but they didn't know or care – especially after he started shooting back at them. Cassius felt bad about snaring the other colored man in his troubles, and hoped the fellow got away.

If they were after me, they would've snagged me, he thought, shivering as he burrowed deeper into the sweet-smelling hay. *If I didn't notice that damn ofay looking all sly . . .*

He woke up before sunrise, and got out of there before the farmer could come outside and discover him. Once he was back in the woods, he took off his clothes and made sure he brushed all the hay off of them. He didn't want to look like somebody who had to sleep in a haystack, even if that was what he was – especially if that was what he was.

He heard gunfire again that afternoon: not just a little, the way he had the night before, but lots. Both sides had plenty of firepower and weren't shy about using it. *Now I know what war sounds like,* Cassius thought, which only proved he'd never come anywhere near a real battlefield.

But this would do. He walked toward it, thinking – foolishly thinking – he would watch what was going on from a safe distance, as he might have watched a football game back in Augusta. Even the first bullet that came close enough for him to hear the *crack!* as it zipped past wasn't enough to deter him. He got behind a pine tree and imagined he was safe.

Negro guerrillas held what had been a sharecropper village. Mexican soldiers were trying to push them out of it or kill them if they stayed inside. Hardly even noticing that he was doing it, Cassius leaned forward. This was more exciting than any football game he'd ever watched.

It stayed an exciting game till a Mexican took a bullet to the temple. The other side of his head exploded into red mush. His rifle fell from his hands as he crumpled to the ground. Even with that surely mortal wound, he didn't die right away. He jerked and flopped and twitched, like a chicken that had just met the chopper.

Cassius gulped. He almost wished someone would shoot the Mexican again to make him hold still. No, this wasn't a game, no matter what it looked like. People were really dying out there. When another bullet snapped past Cassius, he didn't just flinch. He felt as if somebody'd jabbed an icy dagger into each kidney. *This is what fear feels like,* he thought.

And fear had an odor, too. He could smell it coming off of himself. He could probably smell it drifting over from the Mexican soldiers and their Negro foes. And smelling it only made him more afraid, at some level far below conscious thought.

He heard footfalls coming through the woods toward him. They made him afraid, too. They were all too likely to come from Francisco José's men. And if the greasers spotted him, what would they do? They'd shoot him, that was what. He was a young Negro man. Of course they would think him an enemy.

And he was, even if he didn't carry a Tredegar. His heart was with the embattled blacks in the little hamlet. Not only his heart, either. Before he knew what he was doing, he ran for those shacks as fast as he could go.

Bullets chewed up the ground under his feet. They cracked and whirred past his head. He didn't know if the Mexicans or the Negroes were shooting at him. Both, probably. If the two sides weren't so busy blazing away at each other, they might have paid him even more attention than they did, not that it was attention he was likely to live through.

He dove behind a crate, hoping everybody would forget about him. 'Who the hell're you?' one of the Negroes shouted at him.

'Name's Cassius,' he answered, not that that told them much. 'There's soldiers in them trees I run out of.'

'Oh, yeah?' said the voice from behind him. 'We can shift them fuckers, I reckon.'

They did, too. They had a couple of machine guns, and they didn't seem short of ammunition for them. Shrieks from the woods said they'd scored at least a couple of hits. Nobody used the trees to outflank the hamlet, which the Mexicans had probably wanted to do.

Cassius lay very still behind the crate. The Mexicans seemed to forget he was there, which suited him fine. He didn't want to remind them. After another half hour or so, the firing on both sides tapered off. 'They's goin'!' someone behind him shouted.

'Reckon you can come out now, whatever the hell your name was,' someone else added.

Wearily, Cassius got to his feet. A couple of Negro men with rifles in their hands showed themselves. One of them gestured to him. 'Looks like you jus' joined us,' the man said. He was short and wiry, with a knife scar pulling the left side of his mouth up into a permanent sneer. 'Coulda had some trouble if them Mexicans got where they was goin'.'

'Looked that way to me,' Cassius said.

'You know anything about guns?' the scarfaced man asked.

'No, suh, but I reckon I can learn,' Cassius replied.

The older Negro nodded. 'That's a good answer. Now I got another question fo' you: you take orders? Folks call me Gracchus.' He jabbed a thumb at his own chest. 'I runs this outfit. You don't like that, you hit the road. No hard feelin's, but we don't want nobody who's out for hisself and not for all of us. The outfit gotta come first.'

'I'll take orders,' Cassius said. 'If you gave dumb ones, I reckon you'd be dead by now, not runnin' things here.'

'Expect you're right,' Gracchus said. 'Well, my first order

is, tell me about yourself. What's your name again? Where you from?'

'I'm Cassius. I got out of Augusta when the ofays nabbed my folks.'

'How come they didn't catch you, too?' Gracchus sounded coldly suspicious. Cassius wondered why. Then he realized the rebel leader might fear he was bait, and would betray the whole band when he saw the chance.

'They went to church,' he answered truthfully. 'Me, I stayed home.'

Gracchus nodded again. 'God didn't help 'em much, did He?'

'You reckon there's a God?' Cassius said. 'I got a hard time believin' any more. Either God likes ofays, or there ain't none. I got to choose between a God that loves Jake Featherston an' one that ain't there, I know which way I go.'

For the first time since he shouted out his warning, Gracchus eyed him with something approaching approval. 'Maybe you's all right after all,' he said.

'Give me a rifle. Teach me what to do with it,' Cassius said. 'Reckon I show you how all right I am.'

X

Irving Morrell rolled into Bowling Green with a smile on his face. The burnt-out Confederate barrels he rolled past were what made him happy. The Confederates had fought hard outside – they'd fought hard, and they'd got smashed. The one thing they managed to do was empty out most of their big supply dump and wreck what they couldn't take away. The U.S. Army wouldn't be able to salvage much. Given what the CSA had in Kentucky, logistics was one of the enemy's strengths. Some capable officer or another probably needed killing.

Almost without thinking about it, Morrell brought his left hand up to his right shoulder. It still twinged every now and again. Now both sides used snipers and bombs and any other way they could find to try to murder their foes' better leaders. It hardly seemed like war. Neither USA nor CSA seemed to care. Any weapon that came to hand, either side would use. When this war ended, one country or the other would lie flat on its back. The winner would have a booted foot on the loser's neck, and would try to keep it there as long as he could.

Somebody'd painted FREEDOM! on a wall. Somebody else – or maybe the same Confederate patriot – had added several blue X's: quick and easy shorthand for the C.S. battle flag. The Stars and Stripes might fly over Bowling Green, but the people still longed for the Stars and Bars.

Only a long lifetime ago, this town – this whole state –

belonged to the USA. They spent a generation back in the USA after the Great War. The Negroes in Kentucky had liked that fine. Most of the whites had hated it. They thought of themselves as Confederates, and didn't want to be U.S. citizens. The ones who did fled north when the CSA won the plebiscite in early 1941.

All of a sudden, Morrell stopped muttering and swore with savage fluency. 'What's wrong, sir?' Frenchy Bergeron asked.

'Nothing,' Morrell said. That was so patently untrue, he had to amend it: 'Nothing I can do anything about, anyway.' How many whites – and maybe even blacks – who fled Kentucky after the plebiscite were really Confederate spies? That hadn't occurred to him till now. He hoped it hadn't because he was innocent and naive. He intended to send a message to the War Department anyway, on the off chance that everybody else was just as naive.

'Thinking about the next big push, sir?' the gunner asked.

'I'm always thinking about that,' Morrell said, and Sergeant Bergeron chuckled. He was a good gunner, even a very good gunner. He wasn't quite in Michael Pound's league, but who was? Now that Pound was an officer at last, he was finding new ways to annoy the Confederates. Seizing the crossing over the Green River between Calhoun and Rumsey probably put the western prong of Morrell's offensive a couple of days ahead of where it would have been absent that.

A couple of artillery shells burst off to the south. The Confederates *were* fighting hard – if anything, harder than Irving Morrell had expected. No matter how hard they were fighting, they were still losing ground. They were losing it almost fast enough to suit Morrell's driving perfectionism – almost, but not quite. When he conceived his plan, he wanted the CSA wrecked in a single campaigning season. Unless the bastards in butternut flat-out collapsed, he didn't think he could bring that off. He would have to slice the Confederacy in half in two installments. John Abell was right about that.

'Ask you something, sir?' Frenchy Bergeron said.

'Sure,' Morrell answered. 'What's on your mind?'

'When do we go for Nashville?' Bergeron asked. Morrell started to laugh. The gunner coughed reproachfully. 'What's so damn funny, sir? Isn't that's what's coming next?'

'You bet it is,' Morrell said. 'And that's what's so damn funny. The War Department probably hasn't figured out where I go from here, but you damn well have. I want to get moving as fast as I can, too, before the Confederates think I'm ready.'

He never denied the military talent facing him. After what happened in Ohio, after what came much too close to happening in Pennsylvania, he would have been a fool to do that (which didn't always stop some of the more feverishly optimistic U.S. officers). What he wanted to do was make sure the Confederates' talent didn't matter much. If they lacked the men and barrels and airplanes to stop his thrusts, what was talent worth?

'Nashville . . . Nashville could be a real bitch,' Bergeron said. 'Uh, sir.'

Why do I always get gunners who think they belong on the General Staff? Morrell wondered wryly. It wasn't that Frenchy was wrong. The problem, in fact, was that he was right. Along with George Custer, Morrell had planned and executed the attack that crossed the Cumberland and took Nashville in 1917. That wasn't quite the blow that won the Great War, but it did knock the Confederates back on their heels, and they never got over it afterwards.

Meanwhile, Sergeant Bergeron was waiting for an answer. 'I expect we'll come up with something,' Morrell said.

'Oh, yes, sir,' Frenchy said. 'Don't want to try crossing the river where you did the last time, though. What do you want to bet Featherston's little chums'll be laying for us there?'

'Jesus!' Morrell exploded. 'You really do belong on the General Staff!'

'Not me, sir. I don't want to go back to Philly. The people back there, they just talk about what's supposed to happen. Me, I want to make that shit happen myself. They're smarter'n I am, but I have more fun.'

'I feel the same way,' Morrell said, which was only partly true. No way in hell did he think the high foreheads back in Philadelphia were smarter than he was. A lot of the time, he thought they thought they were smarter than they really were. Of course, Frenchy might have been sandbagging, too.

'You know what you're gonna do?' Bergeron persisted. 'Anything happens to you, I may be the guy who has to talk through the fancy wireless set for a little while.'

He was about as far removed from the chain of command as a soldier could be. That didn't necessarily mean he was wrong. If, say, Morrell got hit standing up in the cupola, which could happen easily enough, somebody who knew what things were like at the front might have to do some talking to keep an attack moving smoothly till Brigadier General Parsons could take over. It would be highly unofficial. Chances were it wouldn't show up in the after-action reports. It could be important, though.

'You're going to be an officer before this war is done,' Morrell said.

How many times had he tried to promote Michael

Pound? How many times had Pound said no? Now Pound was a lieutenant himself, and proving he deserved his rank. Morrell hadn't expected anything different. As for Frenchy Bergeron, he said, 'I hope so, sir.'

'I'll promote you right now if you want,' Morrell said. 'Only thing I don't like about the deal is that I'll have to break in a new gunner.'

'Thank you, sir!' Bergeron said. 'You want to wait till we get past Nashville, then? I figure there'll be a lot of fighting up to there, and you'll need me.'

'Deal,' Morrell said at once. 'And I think you're right. Getting over the Cumberland won't be fun. But if we made it across the Ohio, we can do that, too.'

The U.S. spearhead broke out of Bowling Green heading south three days later. Air strikes took out a battery of Confederate rockets before they could salvo. Hearing that cheered Morrell no end. Those damn things could hamstring an advance before it really got going.

As usual, Morrell's place was at the front. He wanted to see what happened, not hear about it later from somebody else. Officers who served on the General Staff didn't understand that. To them, war was arrows on a map. To Morrell, it was shells going off and machine guns hammering and barrels brewing up and sending pillars of noxious black smoke into the sky and prisoners staggering out of the fight with shell shock on their faces and with their hands in the air. It was exhaust fumes and cordite and the sharp stink of fear. To the men of the General Staff, it was chess. They didn't understand both sides were moving at once – and trying to steal pieces and knock over the board.

Morrell's barrels raced by – raced through – a column of refugees U.S. fighter-bombers had hit from above. In 1941, the Confederates gleefully strafed Ohioans who didn't care to live under the Stars and Bars. Refugees clogged roads. Refugees who'd just been hammered from the air clogged them even better. So the Confederates taught.

And now they were learning the same lesson for themselves. Kentuckians – or maybe they were Tennesseans by now – who didn't want to live under the Stars and Stripes fled south as people from Ohio had fled north and east two years earlier. When they got hit by machine guns and cannon fire and bombs from above, it was as horrible as it had been in the USA.

Dead and wounded children and women – and a few men, mostly old – lay in the roadway. Children with dead parents clutched corpses and screamed grief to the uncaring sky. People's most precious possessions were scattered everywhere. Automobiles burned.

A woman standing by the body of a little girl stared at Morrell with terrible eyes as his barrel rattled past. The shoulder was wide here – the oncoming barrels didn't need to plow straight through what was left of the refugee column. The woman picked up a rock and threw it at Morrell. It clanged off the barrel's side. 'What the hell?' Frenchy Bergeron said.

'It's all right.' Morrell ducked down into the turret. 'Just a dissatisfied customer. If that was me out there and all I had was a rock, I expect I'd throw it, too.'

He straightened up and looked out again. The Confederates didn't try to hold back the advancing U.S. troops till they got to a hamlet called Westmoreland. Morrell looked for it on his Kentucky maps, didn't find it, and checked the sheets for northern Tennessee. That was how he was sure he'd crossed the state line. A sign said, WEST-MORELAND – STRAWBERRY CAPITAL OF THE WORLD. Here as May passed into June, the crop was no doubt coming to full, sweet ripeness . . . or it would have been, anyhow.

The treads of Morrell's barrel and all the others speeding south with it churned the strawberries into jam.

Was that motion, there behind a farmhouse by Hawkins, the street leading into Westmoreland from the northwest? Morrell brought up his binoculars. 'Front!' he sang out. 'In back of that yellow clapboard house.'

'Identified!' Bergeron said, and then, 'Clapboard? That house go to a whorehouse?'

Morrell snorted and wheezed. He had to try twice before he could ask, 'What's the range?'

'Just over a mile, sir.'

'Can you hit it?'

'Bet your ass. I'll *kill* the fucker, and he won't dare open up on us till we get closer.'

'Do it, then.' Morrell ordered the barrel to a halt. The gunner traversed the turret till the long 3½-inch cannon bore on the C.S. barrel. The roar almost took Morrell's head off. He used the field glasses again. 'Hit!' he yelled. 'Way to go, Frenchy! Son of a bitch is burning!'

'Damn straight,' Bergeron said. 'They got any others hanging around, they'll know they better clear out.' Other U.S. barrels started finding targets and setting them afire at a range the Confederates couldn't hope to match. Sullenly, the surviving C.S. machines did pull back. They had to hope for wooded terrain where they had a better chance to strike from ambush. U.S. foot soldiers and barrels pushed into Westmoreland. The streets proved to be mined. That slowed them up, but not for long.

U.S. bombers left two major dams in northern Tennessee untouched – the one by Carthage and the one farther east near Celina. They didn't do it out of the goodness of their hearts: they didn't want the floods downstream to disrupt their own advance. The Confederates, desperate to slow

U.S. ground forces however they could, blew both dams as they fell back over the Cumberland.

Michael Pound was not pleased. The floodwaters washed over the banks of the river and flowed across what had been fertile farmland. They turned it into something that more closely resembled oatmeal.

The new U.S. barrels had wide tracks. That meant each part of the track carried less weight than was true in older machines. It also meant they could keep going where older barrels would bog down. It didn't mean they had an easy time.

Here and there, Confederate antibarrel guns and hold-outs with rocket launchers lingered north of the Cumberland. 'I hate those damn stovepipes,' Sergeant Mel Scullard said, using the name the men in green-gray had hung on the launchers. 'Doesn't seem fair, one miserable infantry son of a bitch able to take out a whole barrel all by his lonesome.'

'Especially when it's your barrel – and your neck,' Pound observed dryly.

'You bet,' the gunner said.

'They always could, with a Featherston Fizz,' Pound said.

'That's different,' Scullard insisted. 'You could see those assholes coming, and you had a chance to kill 'em before they got to you. These guys, they stay hidden, they fire the lousy thing, and then they run like hell.'

'I know,' Pound said. 'We've got to get something just like that so our guys can give the Confederates what-for.' Had he been as mouthy to his superiors when he was a noncom? He smiled reminiscently. He was sure he had.

That evening, he got summoned to an officers' con-clave. This was the sort of thing he'd always had to find out about from his own superiors till he finally couldn't evade promotion. It proved less impressive than he'd imagined it would. A dozen or so officers, ranging up from his lowly second lieutenanthood to a light colonel, gathered in a barn that smelled maddeningly delicious: the former owners had used it for curing tobacco.

The lieutenant colonel lit a U.S. cigarette, whose nasty smoke seemed all the viler by comparison with the aroma of choice burley. 'Intelligence says the Confederates have some Freedom Party Guards units in the neighborhood,' he announced. 'You want to watch out for those guys.'

'What's so special about 'em, sir?' a captain asked. 'If you shoot 'em, they go down, right? If you shoot 'em enough times, they stay down, right?' Michael Pound smiled. Meeting someone who thought the way you did was always nice.

After another drag on his cigarette, the senior officer (who was younger than Pound) looked at it in distaste. 'I think they made this thing out of camel shit,' he said. How he knew what camel shit tasted like when he smoked it was probably a question for another day. No matter how little he liked the Niagara, he kept on smoking it. 'What's so special?' he echoed. 'They're supposed to be Featherston's elite force. They've got the best men, and they've got the best equipment. Just about all of them carry those goddamn automatic rifles, they've got plenty of stovepipes' – he used the new handle, too – 'and their armor is the best the Confederates have.'

'Not good enough.' Pound and two other U.S. officers said the same thing at the same time.

The lieutenant colonel shook his head. 'Even up, out in the open, we've got the edge. If they shoot from ambush when we're out in the open . . .' He didn't go on, or need to. Pound nodded reluctantly, but he nodded. A hit from a three-inch gun could kill his barrel. It wasn't a sure thing, but it could.

'How do we know 'em when we see 'em?' somebody asked.

'They wear camouflage uniforms, not ordinary butternut,' the light colonel said. 'They've caused a lot of trouble in Texas. This is the first report of 'em east of the Mississippi.'

'Just our luck,' Pound said. A couple of the other men in the barn sent him curious looks. He was the junior officer present. He was also the oldest man there. The combination was odd and awkward – awkward for other people, anyhow. Michael Pound didn't much care. If they busted him back down to sergeant, he wouldn't say boo. He'd found he could do more as an officer than as a noncom. That was nice, and the Confederates had reason to regret it on the Green River. But he wouldn't mind looking through a gunsight again, either. That 3½-incher was a gunner's delight. High muzzle velocity, a flat trajectory, better sights than earlier barrels had, too . . .

'You need to be aware they're around,' the lieutenant colonel said. 'And be aware our engineers are in the neighborhood, too. They'll do their best to make ways for you to go forward where the flooding's worse than usual.'

Now Pound beamed. That was good news. Army engineers were on the ball. Fighting wasn't their job, but they did it when they had to. And they worked under fire without a peep. Solid men, sure as hell. He stuck up his hand. The lieutenant colonel nodded. 'Sir, will they have bridging equipment to get us over the Cumberland?' Pound asked. 'The sooner we can grab a bridgehead on the other side, the more the Confederates'll have to flabble about.'

'You don't think small, do you?' the light colonel said.

'No, sir.' Pound took the question literally and answered with a straight face.

He nonplused the colonel. The younger man rubbed his

chin. 'If we get that far, Lieutenant, I figure we'll find some way to get over, too. Does that satisfy you?'

'Oh, yes, sir,' Pound said. 'But as long as those bastards are down, I want to keep kicking them. I want to kick their teeth in.'

Again, he sounded perfectly earnest. Again, he made the lieutenant colonel pause. At last, the man made the best of it, saying, 'Your spirit does you credit. You can serve as an example for all of us. Any more questions?' He waited. Nobody said anything. He clapped his hands together once, softly. 'All right, then. Let's go get 'em.'

'What's the word, sir?' Sergeant Scullard asked when Pound came back from the meeting.

Pound hid a grin. How many times had he asked officers the same question when he was a sergeant himself? More than he could count, that was for sure. 'We drive for the Cumberland – and cross it if we can,' he answered, which overstated the case a bit. 'The engineers will give us a hand. We may have Freedom Party Guards units in front of us. They're supposed to be tough, and they've got A-number-one equipment, but we'll make 'em say uncle.'

'Sounds good to me.' The gunner was a man after his own heart.

The attack went in the next morning. Infantrymen in trucks and half-tracked armored personnel carriers kept up with the barrels, though the trucks had trouble with the mud and mostly stayed on the roads. Engineers rode in combat cars and in bulldozers with steel plating welded around the driver's position. Some of the dozers sported machine guns, too. Those were informal, nonregulation additions, but the engineers were in a position to do that if anybody was.

Resistance was light at first. Pound had just begun to doubt whether that lieutenant colonel knew what he was talking about when all hell broke loose. An enemy barrel nicely hidden behind an overturned truck blew up two personnel carriers in quick succession. The crew, no fools, started to fall back to another position. 'Front!' Pound sang out.

'Identified!' Scullard answered. What he identified, he could hit. He could – and he did. The C.S. barrel started to burn. Pound thought some of the men inside got away – it was long range for a machine gun. That was a shame; those soldiers plainly knew what they were doing. As soon as they got a new machine, they'd cause the USA more trouble.

But not now. When an antibarrel rocket took out a green-gray barrel, foot soldiers descended from their conveyances and started hunting the Confederates nearby. The enemy troops were plainly outnumbered, but nobody seemed to have told them anything about retreating. Holding their ground till they were overrun, they died in place, and took a lot of U.S. soldiers with them.

'Those the Freedom Party Guards, sir?' Scullard asked.

'I think so,' Pound said. 'Either they've all got a lot of mud on their butternut or they're wearing camouflage. And they fight hard – no two ways about that.'

'We smashed 'em for now, looks like,' the gunner said.

'Yup,' Pound agreed. 'And that means we ought to gun for the river fast as we can, before the Confederates bring more troops back to this side.'

He stood up in the cupola and looked around to see if he could spot any engineers. His wireless set couldn't communicate directly with theirs, which he considered an oversight not far from criminal. But he spotted an armored bulldozer only a couple of hundred yards away. He had his driver go closer so he could shout back and forth with the man inside. The dozer driver waved and nodded.

Then it was on toward the Cumberland for his platoon and the foot soldiers with them, and blast anything that got in the way. The Confederates really didn't have much left on this side of the river. Michael Pound cheerfully went about reducing what they did have. He wondered how they planned on fighting the war next year and the year after if they were wrecking some of their most productive land and the United States were wrecking some more.

After a bit, he decided the Confederates didn't care about next year and the year after. If they couldn't stop the United States *now,* they were much too likely to lose the war *this* year. He nodded. Yeah, that might be so. The more he thought about it, the better he liked it. The better he liked it, the harder he pushed his platoon. Other green-gray barrels stormed toward the Cumberland with them. And dozers and other engineering vehicles did their damnedest to keep up.

Even before he got to the river, he realized his chances of seizing a bridge intact, the way he had between Calhoun and Rumsey, were slim and none. The Confederates had blown the bridges over the Cumberland themselves, and were using it for a barrier. And if they hadn't, the flood they turned loose by blowing the dam upstream would have swept away any surviving spans.

He had hoped the engineers would be able to bridge the river in a hurry. But the Cumberland was too wide for anything engineering vehicles could carry on their backs. It would have to be pontoons, which took longer to rig and let the enemy concentrate his fire.

But Lieutenant Pound wasn't the only officer with a driving urge for speed. General Morrell had it, too, and had the authority to do something with it. The pontoon bridges started reaching across the river as soon as it got too dark for the Confederates on the southern bank to see what U.S. forces were up to. Morrell or someone else with a good head on his shoulders ordered an artillery barrage laid on several miles to the west. The Confederates naturally replied in kind, and fired star shells to light up the Cumberland there to discover what the men in green-gray were doing. The soldiers and engineers there weren't doing anything much but shelling. Lulled, Featherston's men fired back.

At a quarter to four, a captain of engineers asked Pound, 'You ready to go like hell, Lieutenant?'

'Yes, sir!' Pound answered around a yawn. He'd been up all night.

The captain nodded. 'Good. That's the right answer. Won't be long. Haul ass when you get the word.'

'I can do that, sir,' Pound said. And, ten minutes later, he and his platoon did. They weren't quite the first U.S. barrels over the Cumberland, but not many were in front of them. Infantry in half-tracks crossed right behind them. By the time the sun came up, they'd carved out a solid bridgehead on the south bank.

'Gas!' somebody shouted as U.S. shells rained down on the Confederate positions south of the Cumberland. Jorge Rodriguez already had his mask on – he'd heard the gurgle gas rounds made flying through the air. He huddled in a hastily dug foxhole and prayed nothing would come down on his head.

Too much had landed on him in the past few weeks, not literally but metaphorically. Virginia had been fairly quiet. Getting transferred to the Tennessee front was like getting a bucket of ice water in the face. But getting word that his father had died in Texas was like getting thrown into ice water with no way out. The telegram gave no details, which only made things worse. Jorge had written to his mother down in Sonora, but he was still waiting for an answer.

He had little time to brood on it. That was the one good thing about getting thrown into combat fierce enough to give him a brush with death almost every day. He'd asked his company commander for compassionate leave. Captain Nelson Cash had looked at the telegram and shaken his head. 'I'm mighty sorry, George,' he said, that being what most English-speakers called Jorge. 'I'm mighty sorry, but maybe you noticed there was a war on?'

'Yes, sir.' Jorge hadn't really expected anything different, but he had to try. He thought about going AWOL, thought about it and then thought again. He was a long way from Texas, an even longer way from Sonora. Someone at a train station was bound to check his papers. They were making examples of deserters these days.

Of course, what the Army and the Freedom Party were doing to deserters wasn't a patch on what U.S. bombs and bullets might do to him. He was in his late twenties, older than a lot of the conscripts who filled out his company, old enough to know God didn't have a carved stone somewhere that said he would live forever.

Even getting to the front hadn't been easy. He'd had to go all the way down to Atlanta and then north again, traveling mostly by night. The Yankees had torn up and bombed the railroad lines going west from Virginia into Kentucky, and also the ones going west from Asheville, North Carolina, to Knoxville, Tennessee. They wanted to keep the Confederates from hitting them in the flank while they pushed south. By all the signs, they knew how to get what they wanted, too.

All that meant the C.S. reinforcements from Virginia reached the front a couple of days later than they would have with everything going smoothly. It meant the front was farther south than it would have been had they got there in good time. And it meant that the mission they'd been given when they left Virginia – throwing the U.S. bridgehead south of the Cumberland back over the river – was nothing but a pipe dream by the time they got there.

Jorge knew about all that only because of occasional grumbles from his superiors. He'd never been in Tennessee before. He wasn't sure where the Cumberland was, let alone any of the towns south of it. The only thing he knew was that his outfit had to fight like hell whenever it got where it was going. In a way, such a state of almost blissful ignorance wasn't bad for an ordinary soldier.

He got off the train somewhere not far south of Murfreesboro, and climbed into a truck for the journey up to the front. Jorge was sorry to change vehicles; he'd won more than two hundred dollars in the poker game that started back in Virginia. He was a good-tempered, easy-going fellow. A measure of how popular he was with his buddies was that nobody called him a goddamn greaser no matter how much he won.

Murfreesboro had taken a pounding. A lot of the places where Jorge was stationed in Virginia had taken a pounding, too, but they'd been at or near the front since 1941. Some of them had taken a pounding in the Great War, too, and even in the War of Secession.

Murfreesboro . . . Hell had opened up on Murfreesboro in the past few days. The ruins still had sharp edges. Smoke still curled up from them. The women and kids and old men who grubbed through them still looked stunned, astonished that such things could happen to them. The smell of death was very sweet, very strong. Jorge's stomach turned over. He gulped, trying to keep his rations down.

The move east from Murfreesboro also came by night. The butternut trucks had most of their headlights covered over with masking tape. The slits that remained shed more light than cigarette coals, but not a whole lot more. The truck convoy had to go slow. Even so, Jorge rattled past one machine that had driven off the side of the road and into a shell hole.

'That driver, he's gonna catch hell,' he said. His English had an accent different from those of the white men in the truck with him. Every so often, he used a word that wasn't English anywhere except Sonora and Chihuahua. But the other soldiers understood him. His father spoke mostly Spanish when *he* went off to fight in 1916. His mother was still more at home in it than in English. But he and his brothers, like most of the younger generation, embraced the tongue the rest of the CSA used.

'Maybe he will,' someone else said, 'but the guys he was drivin', I bet they give him a medal for makin' 'em late.'

'Wish *our* driver'd go off the road,' another soldier said. He didn't sound like a man making a joke. On the contrary – he seemed painfully serious. His name was Gabriel Medwick. He was about six feet three, at least 200 pounds, blond, jut-jawed, and handsome. He could have posed for a Freedom Party recruiting poster, as a matter of fact. And he sounded like a man just this side of shitting himself with fear.

Jorge was afraid, too. Anybody who'd seen combat and wasn't afraid had some screws loose somewhere. He hadn't seen a whole lot, and what he had seen wasn't too intense. The company was probably heading into something worse. But knowing that the all-Confederate boy sitting in the truck with him was more afraid than he was – or less able to hide his fear, which amounted to the same thing – helped steady him.

'Aw, fuck,' Medwick muttered when the truck stopped. It was getting near dawn; gray light had started leaking in through the rear-facing opening in the canvas canopy over the cargo area. *That's what we are – cargo,* Rodriguez thought. *They use us up, like rations or bullets or barrels.* He wished that hadn't occurred to him.

'Come on. Get out. We got to head on up to the front.' Sergeant Hugo Blackledge would never show up on a recruiting poster. He had hairy ears and more hair sticking out of his nose and a black five o'clock shadow that came out at noon. His eyebrows grew together above that beaky nose. His chin was barely there at all. He was little and skinny and mean. If he was afraid, he never showed it. He ran his squad with no pretense of fairness or justice. But he never sent anyone anywhere he wouldn't go himself. And he could whip all of them, Gabriel Medwick included. He wouldn't fight fair to do it, which only made the men more willing to follow his lead. They'd seen enough to know that fighting fair was for civilians and other fools.

'Where the hell are we, anyways?' someone asked as they scrambled out of the truck.

'Where we're supposed to be,' Blackledge answered. 'That's all you assholes need to know.' He didn't expect to be loved. That wasn't his job.

Captain Cash, on the other hand, was friendly to his men. He could afford to be; he had bastards like Blackledge under him to handle the dirty work. 'That town up ahead is Sparta,' he told the soldiers piling out of several trucks. 'It's still ours. We've got to make sure it stays ours. Any questions?'

A bird piped in a tree. All the birds up here in the north sounded strange to Jorge. Even the jays were peculiar. They acted quite a bit like the black-throated magpie-jays he knew back home, but they were only about half the size they should have been. That meant they could only screech half as loud.

'What are the Yankees throwing at us?' somebody asked after a pause.

'Everything but the outhouse,' Sergeant Blackledge answered before the captain could say anything. 'If they figure out a way to dump that shit on us, they'll use it, too.'

After that, no one seemed to want to know anything else. 'Come on,' Captain Cash said into the uncomfortable silence. 'Let's go forward.'

When Jorge and his companions went into the line in Virginia, they'd replaced other soldiers who left the front for rest and refit and recuperation. Here, nobody was coming back as the replacements went forward. That couldn't mean all the Confederates up there were dead, or the damnyankees would storm through the breach. But it probably did mean the high command couldn't afford to take anybody out of the line, and that wasn't good news or anything close to it.

Confederate 105s banged away at the enemy. Jorge was glad to hear them. They meant things hadn't all gone to the devil, anyhow. The sun came up. It looked like a nice day.

Then U.S. guns started answering the 105s. Jorge knew enough to throw himself flat. He pulled his entrenching tool off his belt and started a foxhole. He'd long since learned how to dig without raising up more than a few inches off the ground. Pretty soon, he was in a hole, with the dirt heaped up in front of him to help block fragments.

Foxhole or not, though, he was still liable to get killed. The Yankees had more guns than his side did, and they weren't shy about using them. That was when the gas started coming in. He hadn't seen this kind of bombardment in Virginia. By the time he got there, the war had settled down to skirmishes, with neither side trying very hard to break through.

It wasn't like that here. He needed no more than a few minutes to see as much. The damnyankees had already broken through – if they hadn't driven all the way through Kentucky, they wouldn't have been over the Cumberland and deep inside Tennessee. The Confederates were doing what they could to counterattack and throw the enemy back.

So far, everything they could do wasn't nearly enough.

Even before the shelling stopped, fighter-bombers made it worse. Because they flew so low, they could put their bombs almost exactly where they wanted. They hit the C.S. artillery positions hard, and then came back to strafe whatever else looked interesting.

And then, from up ahead, Jorge heard a shout no foot soldier ever wanted to hear: 'Barrels!'

The big, snorting monsters advanced in wedges. Jorge needed a little while to realize they weren't all the same. The damnyankees put the largest and toughest ones in the lead. They blasted the way clear for the older barrels that came behind. *Where are* our *barrels?* he wondered. Wherever they were, they weren't close enough to do anything about these machines.

One of the U.S. machines hit a mine and threw a track. Its machine guns and cannon went on firing even so. Jorge picked off a barrel commander standing up in the cupola with a quick burst from his automatic rifle. That barrel kept on coming, though, and sprayed machine-gun bullets all around.

'Back!' Sergeant Blackledge screamed. 'We gotta get back, or we're all dead!'

'What's Captain Cash say?' Jorge asked.

'How can you say anything when you got your fucking head blown off?' the noncom said.

Jorge had no answer for that. The Confederates in and

around Sparta, Tennessee, had no answer for the oncoming Yankees. Jorge didn't want to get out of his foxhole, but he didn't want to get killed where he crouched, either. He ran for a shattered house and made it. Then he ran again. He was lucky. A lot of people weren't.

Brigadier General Clarence Potter had got used to long faces. Everybody in the War Department looked as if his favorite aunt had just walked in front of a bus. By the news leaking out of Kentucky and Tennessee, the whole Confederacy might have walked in front of a bus.

What goes around comes around, he thought unhappily. Up in Ohio, the CSA had taught the United States a lot of lessons about how to use armor and mechanized infantry and aircraft together. Who would have figured the damnyankees made such good students? Now they were giving lessons of their own.

And they had more in the way of blackboards and chalk and books than the Confederates ever did. Jake Featherston had counted on a quick, victorious war. When he didn't get one, when he got another grapple instead . . . A good big man didn't always lick a good little one, but that was sure as hell the way to bet.

If Potter wore a vinegar phiz, then, and if just about everybody he saw looked the same way – well, so what? People had earned the right to look gloomy. He took frowns as much for granted as he took the smell of smoke and corruption in the air and the sight of plywood or cardboard over almost every window. He hardly even noticed that the corners of everybody's mouth turned down.

He hardly noticed, that is, till a young lieutenant – who wore the same hangdog expression as everybody else – escorted Professor Henderson V. FitzBelmont into his office. No matter how tweedy FitzBelmont was, he looked as happy as if he'd just got engaged to an eighteen-year-old bathing beauty. Seeing his smile was like getting a surprise flashbulb in the kisser. Clarence Potter couldn't remember the last time he'd met such unalloyed joy.

'What's up?' he asked. 'Whatever you're drinking, I want a slug, too.'

Professor FitzBelmont had learned the ropes about security. He didn't let out a peep till the lieutenant saluted, left, and closed the door behind himself. Only after the latch clicked did he say, 'General, we are self-sustaining!'

'That's nice,' Potter answered, deadpan. 'So you're making enough money that you don't need a handout from the government, are you?'

'No, no, no!' FitzBelmont didn't quite say, *You damned fool*, but the thought plainly hovered in his mind. Then he sent Potter a suspicious stare over the tops of his spectacles. 'I believe you're having me on.'

'Who, me?' Potter sounded as innocent as a guilty man could. 'I don't know what you're talking about.' But he quickly grew serious. 'I'm not sure I do know what you're talking about, so suppose you spell it out for me.'

'We have a lattice of uranium – enriched uranium, with more U-235 than you'd find in nature – and graphite that is producing more neutrons in each generation than it needs to generate in order to produce the next generation.'

'I see . . . I think. Does that mean it'll go boom if you pull out all the stops or whatever you need to do?'

'Well – no,' FitzBelmont admitted. 'But it is an indispensable first step.'

'Have the United States already done it?' Potter asked.

'You would know for a fact better than I, General,' Professor FitzBelmont said. Potter wished that were true. He knew the damnyankees had that establishment out in Washington State, but that was all he knew. He hadn't been able to sneak any spies into the project – or, if he had, they hadn't managed to get any reports out, which amounted to the same thing. U.S. security there was tight, and all the tighter after the Confederates' bombing raid a few months before. FitzBelmont, meanwhile, went on, 'While I don't know for sure, I'd say it's highly likely.'

That matched Potter's opinion better than he wished it did. The United States wouldn't be committing the kind of resources they were if they didn't think they had a winner. Were they spending more than the Confederacy was? They hid the budget as best they could (so did his own government), but he thought they were. 'So they're still ahead of us?' he said.

'Again, I can't prove it. Again, if I were a gambling man, I'd bet that way,' FitzBelmont said.

'We're all gambling men right now, Professor,' Potter said. 'We're gambling that you and your people can get this done before the damnyankees do – and before they rip our guts out just in the ordinary way of making war.'

'Rip our . . . ?' Henderson FitzBelmont frowned. 'Do I take it that the true state of affairs in Kentucky and Tennessee is less salubrious than the press and the wire-less make it out to be?'

'Less . . . salubrious. That's one way to put it.' Abstractly, Potter admired the professor's choice of words. The damnyankees were tearing the Confederacy a new asshole out West, and nobody seemed able to slow them down much, let alone stop them. 'We are in trouble over there. They're aiming at Chattanooga right now. They haven't got there, but that's where they're heading.'

'Oh, my,' Professor FitzBelmont said. 'That's . . . a long way from the Ohio River.'

'Tell me about it,' Clarence Potter said. He'd almost got sent west a couple of times himself, not as an

Intelligence officer but as a combat soldier. The War Department was throwing every experienced officer into the fight. Only Jake Featherston's loud insistence that he needed a spymaster had kept Potter in Richmond this long. Even Featherston's insistence might not keep him here forever.

'Unfortunate,' FitzBelmont murmured. 'Um . . . You are aware that my team's experiments require large amounts of electricity?'

'Yes,' Potter said. 'And so?'

'The supply has been erratic lately, erratic enough to force delays,' FitzBelmont said. 'I have no idea who can do anything about that, but I'd appreciate it if someone would. If you are the person to ask, I hope you'll pass the word to the proper authorities.'

Clarence Potter didn't know whether to laugh or to cry. He ended up laughing, because he didn't want Henderson FitzBelmont to see him cry. 'Have you been paying attention to the war news, Professor? Any attention at all?'

'I know it's not good,' FitzBelmont said. 'We were just talking about that. But what does it have to do with the electricity supply?'

He was good at what he did. There wasn't a better nuclear physicist in the CSA. Potter knew that. He'd had every one of the small band of physicists investigated. But outside his specialized field, Henderson V. FitzBelmont lived up to almost every cliché about narrowly specialized professors. As gently as he could, Potter said, 'You know we've lost a lot of dams on the Cumberland and the Tennessee? The Yankees blew some, and we blew others to try to slow them down.' *And it didn't work well enough, dammit,* he added, but only to himself.

'Well, yes, certainly, but . . .' Much more slowly than it should have, a light went on in FitzBelmont's eyes. 'You're telling me those dams produced some of the electricity I use.'

'Not just what you use, Professor, and you aren't the only one feeling the pinch,' Potter said. 'Some of our factories have had to cut production, and we just can't afford that.'

'If we don't have adequate power, heaven only knows how we can go forward,' FitzBelmont said. 'This isn't something we can do with steam engines and kerosene lamps.'

'I understand that. But you need to understand you're not the only one with a problem,' Potter said.

How much did that matter? Would the Confederacy let factories work more slowly to make sure the uranium-bomb project stayed on track? Without the weapons the factories made, how were the Confederate States supposed to hold back the latest U.S. thrust? The other side of that coin was, could the Confederates hold back the latest U.S. thrust even with all those factories going flat-out?

If the answer to that was no . . . *If the answer to that is no, what the devil were we doing getting into this war in the first place?* Potter wondered. Jake Featherston had counted on his quick knockout. The difference between what you counted on and what you got explained why so many people had unhappy marriages.

But if the Confederate States had to count on the uranium bomb for any hope of victory, and if there was no guarantee they would ever get it built, and if there was a more than decent chance the United States would beat them to the punch . . . If all that was true, the Confederacy was in a hell of a lot of trouble.

'Do you want to see the President, Professor?' Potter asked. 'I'm sure he'd be glad to have this news straight from the horse's mouth.' *Well, straight from some part of the horse, anyhow.*

Henderson FitzBelmont shook his head. 'Thank you, but that's all right. You can deliver it. I don't mind. I don't mind at all. President Featherston, uh, intimidates me.'

'President Featherston intimidates a lot of people,' Potter said. That was true. Featherston intimidated *him*, and he was a lot harder to spook than any tweedy professor ever born. In fairness, though, he felt he had to go on, 'I don't think he would try to be intimidating after news like this. I think he'd be much more likely to pull out a bottle and get drunk with you.'

By the look FitzBelmont gave him, that was intimidating, too. How many years had it been since he went out and got drunk? Had he ever done anything like that? With most people, Potter would have taken the idea for granted. He didn't with the professor.

'Do I need to know anything else?' he asked. 'You've got a self-sustaining reaction, and you need all the electricity you can steal. Is that it?'

'That is the, ah, nucleus, yes.' Professor FitzBelmont smiled at his own joke.

So did Clarence Potter, in a dutiful way. As quickly as he could, he eased the professor out of his office. Then he called the President of the CSA – this couldn't wait. 'Featherston here.' That harsh, furious voice was familiar to everyone in the CSA, and doubly so to Potter, who'd heard it in person long before most Confederate citizens started hearing it on the wireless.

The line between his own office and the President's bunker was supposed to be secure. He picked his words with care all the same: 'I just had a visit from the fellow at the university.'

'Did you, now?' Jake Featherston said with sudden sharp interest. 'And what did he have to say?'

'He's jumped through one hoop,' Potter answered. 'I'll

send you the details as soon as I can. But we really are moving forward.'

'Hot damn,' Featherston said. 'The fucking Yankees are moving forward, too. I swear to God, Potter, sometimes I wonder if this country *deserves* to win the war. If we let those nigger-loving mongrels kick the crap out of us, we aren't the kind of people I reckoned we were.'

'I don't know anything about that, sir,' Potter said, in lieu of something like, *I see. It's not your fault we're losing the war. It's God's fault.* Potter didn't think that was true. But even if it were, it didn't help, because what could a mere mortal do about God? 'I do know our friend thinks he can get this done.'

'Does he think he can get it done in time?'

Hearing that question made Potter feel better. It showed the President still had a feel for the essential. 'I don't know. I don't think anyone knows. It depends on how far along the United States are with their own project.'

'Screw the United States,' the President said. 'Question is, can we keep our heads above water any which way till the professors come through?' That showed a feel for the essential, too. All things considered, Clarence Potter wished it didn't.

Dr. Leonard O'Doull had been with a retreating army. Now he served with an advancing one. From things he'd heard, most people's morale was sky high these days. His wasn't. At an aid station, you saw just as much misery going forward as you did going back. The only difference was, he didn't suppose the Confederates were so likely to overrun the tent while he was operating.

'It doesn't seem like enough,' he said, looking up from a resection of a kid's ripped-up lower intestine.

Granville McDougald looked at him over his surgical

mask. 'Yeah, well, you take what you can get, Doc,' the veteran noncom said. 'Only thing worse than fighting a war and winning is fighting a war and losing.'

'Is that really worse?' O'Doull put in another suture, and another, and another. Sometimes he felt more like a sewing machine than anything else. 'This poor bastard's going to be left with a semicolon instead of a colon any which way.'

'A semi – ?' McDougald sent him a reproachful stare. 'That's awful, Doc. Period.'

Did he really say *awful*? Or was it *offal*? He was right either way. But once you started making puns, you also started hearing them whether they were there or not. And wasn't that one short step from hearing the little voices that weren't there?

'*Is* it better to get shot in a war your side wins than in one where you lose?' O'Doull persisted.

'Better not to get shot at all,' McDougald said, a great and obvious truth to which too many people who went down in history as statesmen were blind. But he went on, 'If you have to get shot, better to do it so not so many people on your side will get shot after you. Do you really want to see Featherston's fuckers opening up with machine guns whenever they feel like target practice all over the USA?'

'Well, no,' O'Doull admitted. He dusted the wounded soldier's entrails with sulfa powder. Maybe the kid would escape the wound infection that surely would have killed him in any earlier war. Maybe. O'Doull started closing. If the soldier did live, he would have an amazing scar. 'Still and all, though, Granny, I wonder if I should have come back from Quebec.'

'So you were thinking about French leave, were you?' McDougald said, and O'Doull winced. Undeterred, McDougald went on, 'Can't say as I blame you.'

'I was tempted,' O'Doull admitted. 'I don't *think* Quebec would have let the USA extradite me. But I put the uniform on, and I can't very well take it off again till things are done.' Nicole had a different opinion, but he didn't mention that.

'Hey, Doc!' That shout from outside the aid tent warned another casualty was coming in. This time, though, Eddie added, 'Can you work on a civilian?'

The tent wasn't far south of Sparta, Tennessee. Not all the Confederate civilians had fled fast enough. O'Doull had already patched up several. Chances were they wouldn't be grateful, but he figured C.S. surgeons had done the same up in Ohio for equally ungrateful U.S. citizens. So he answered, 'Sure, Eddie, bring him in. I'll do what I can for the miserable bastard.' He paused and turned to McDougald. 'Or do you want me to pass gas while you do the honors?'

'Sure. Why not? Thanks, Doc,' McDougald answered.

But when Eddie and the other corpsmen brought in the casualty, it turned out not to be a him but a her. She was about thirty, groaning the way anyone else with a blood-soaked bandage on the belly would have. 'Aw, shit,' O'Doull said softly. Most of the time, he didn't get reminded that whole countries were at war, not just armies. When he did, it was like a slap in the face.

'You take the case, Doc,' Granny McDougald said. 'All I know about female plumbing stops about nine inches deep.'

'God, what a braggart you are,' O'Doull said. Eddie snorted. The wounded woman, fortunately, was too far gone to pay any attention to the byplay. 'Get her up on the table,' O'Doull told the corpsmen. 'I'll do what I can for her.'

She feebly tried to fight when McDougald put the ether cone over her mouth and nose. How many soldiers had done the same thing? More than O'Doull could count. He and Eddie held her hands till she went limp.

'Get a plasma line into her,' O'Doull said. 'She's lost a lot of blood.'

'Already doing it,' McDougald said, and he was. 'I'll put a cuff on her, too, so we can see what we've got.' With unhurried speed, he also did that. 'Pressure is . . . 100 over 70 – a little low, but not too bad. Pulse is . . . 85. A little thready, maybe, but I think she's got a chance.'

'Let's see what's in there.' O'Doull opened her up – actually, he extended the wound she already had. 'Shrapnel, sure as hell,' he said, and then, 'I'm going to have to do a hysterectomy.'

'Your case, all right,' McDougald said. 'I wouldn't even know where to start.'

'I haven't done all that many myself,' O'Doull said. He reached for a scalpel, and then, after he felt the womb, for forceps. 'Here's what did it, all right.' He held up a jagged piece of metal about the size of a half-dollar. 'Must have been nearly spent, or it would've torn her up worse than this.'

'Happy day. I'm sure she's real glad of that,' McDougald said.

'Yeah, I know,' O'Doull agreed. 'She's got a tear in her bladder, too, but I can fix it. Guts don't seem bad. With any luck at all, she'll make it.'

'That'd be good,' McDougald said. 'She's harmless now. She can't have any kids to shoot at U.S. soldiers when we try this again in 1971.'

'Christ!' O'Doull's hand almost jerked. 'There's a cheery thought.'

'It'll happen unless we really knock 'em flat and sit on 'em,' McDougald said. 'You hope we will, but what are the odds?'

'Beats me,' O'Doull said. 'But we'd have to be crazy to give them a third chance to cream our corn for us.'

'Yeah? And your point is . . . ?'

O'Doull winced again, but went on suturing. 'What are we supposed to do? We can't occupy the whole CSA. They'll shoot at us from behind trees and throw Featherston Fizzes at us forever if we try. But how do we hold 'em down without occupying them?'

'Kill 'em all,' McDougald said. 'Resettle the place from the USA.'

'Congratulations,' O'Doull told him. 'You get an A in Jake Featherston lessons.'

'Them's fightin' words,' McDougald said. 'Put up your dukes.'

'Later,' O'Doull said. 'Let me finish sewing this gal up first.'

'This is a funny business, isn't it?' McDougald said. 'She's not bad-looking, and there are you messing with her private parts, but she's not a broad or anything. She's just a patient.'

'Yeah, that crossed my mind, too.' O'Doull paused for a moment to make sure a suture was good and tight. 'Once upon a time, between the wars, I went to a medical conference in Montreal, and I got to talking with this hotshot gynecologist. I asked him if he ever got tired of looking at pussy all day. He kind of rolled his eyes and said, "Oh, Jesus, do I ever!" '

The medic laughed. 'Well, all right. I guess I believe that. Of course, a lot of what he's looking at belongs to little old ladies. The young, healthy, pretty gals mostly don't bother coming to him.'

'I wasn't finished yet.' O'Doull put in another stitch, then went on, 'A couple of years later, this guy's wife divorced him. Not easy to do in Quebec – it's a Catholic country. She had to prove infidelity, and she did – with three different patients of his. So not all the young, pretty ones stayed away.'

That made Granville McDougald laugh some more. 'See, I know what happened. You asked the wrong question. Maybe he got tired of looking, but do you ever get tired of touching?'

'Good point.' O'Doull looked down at the wounded woman. 'I do believe she'll pull through. Haven't had to try that particular surgery for quite a while.'

'You looked like you knew what you were doing, whether you really did or not,' McDougald said.

'Thanks a lot, Granny. You really know how to make a guy feel good about himself.' As O'Doull started closing the outer wound and the incision that had widened it, a new thought struck him. 'Where are we going to put her? Can't just dump her with the wounded POWs, you know.'

'No, that wouldn't work,' McDougald agreed. 'Where's the closest civilian hospital?'

'Beats me. Somewhere north of us – that's all I can tell you. Oh, there are bound to be some farther south, too, but passing her through the lines won't be easy. And if we keep moving forward, we're liable to blow wherever she's staying to hell and gone.'

'Be a shame to waste your hard work,' McDougald said. 'Tell you what we ought to do – we ought to just send her back to the division hospital and let them figure out what to do with her. They've got more room for her and more people to deal with her than we do, anyway.'

O'Doull had dealt with the military bureaucracy long enough to know a perfect solution when he heard one. 'We'll do that, all right,' he said. 'Fixing her up was my worry. Let the guys in back of the line figure out where she's supposed to go.'

She went off to the rear in an ambulance with the wounded soldier on whom O'Doull had operated not long before. 'They'll probably be pissed off,' McDougald remarked.

'Too damn bad,' O'Doull answered. They both stood outside the tent, watching the ambulance head off toward Sparta. 'What's the worst they can do? Write me a reprimand, right? Like I give a shit.'

'There you go, Doc,' McDougald said. 'That's one nice thing about coming in for the duration – you don't care what the brass hats who run things think of you. Must be nice.' He sighed wistfully.

'You're in about the same place, aren't you?' O'Doull pulled out a captured pack of Raleighs. 'They probably won't bump you up to lieutenant, and you'd really have to screw up big for them to take your stripes away. You're free.' He lit a cigarette and smiled as he inhaled.

'Let me have one of those, would you? . . . Thanks.' McDougald leaned close for a light, then took a deep drag of his own. 'You're right and you're wrong, Doc. Yeah, I can tell 'em where to head in, I guess. But I don't really want to most of the time, 'cause this is my outfit. I'll be here till they don't want me any more. You're freer than that.'

'I suppose.' One of O'Doull's hands touched the oak leaf on his other shoulder. He didn't feel very free. 'If it weren't for the honor of the thing, I'd rather walk. That's what the fellow said when they tarred and feathered him and rode him out of town on a rail, isn't it?'

'You know who told that joke the first time?' McDougald asked, and O'Doull had to shake his head. 'Abraham Lincoln, that's who.'

'Did he?' O'Doull decided he wouldn't tell it again. Eighty years ago, the things Lincoln did – and the things he didn't do – made sure the USA and the CSA would go at each other till the end of time. Few Presidents were better remembered: Washington and Jefferson, perhaps (their memories somewhat tarnished in the USA because they were Virginians), and undoubtedly Teddy Roosevelt. But only James G. Blaine came close to Lincoln as a failure, and Blaine wouldn't have had the chance to botch the Second Mexican War if Lincoln hadn't botched the War of Secession. Yes, that was one joke Leonard O'Doull would forget.

Jefferson Pinkard eyed the letter in front of him with several different kinds of pained incomprehension. He understood that it was from Magdalena Rodriguez down in Sonora. But he didn't understand much that was in it because, although she tried to write English, what they thought of as English in Sonora wasn't the same as it was in the rest of the CSA. Still, he knew what she had to be asking: why the devil did her husband go and shoot himself?

'I wish to Christ I knew,' Pinkard muttered. Every once in a while, a guard couldn't stand what he was doing, and he ate his gun or got rid of himself some other way. Pinkard knew that – nobody knew it better. If it weren't true, he wouldn't be married to Chick Blades' widow. But that Hip Rodriguez should blow off the top of his head . . . 'Goddammit, he fucking *hated* niggers!'

Still muttering, Jeff wondered if he ought to call in another guard from Sonora or Chihuahua to get an exact translation. After a few seconds, he shook his head. Whatever was in the letter would be all through the guard barracks in nothing flat if he did. He shook his head again. He didn't want that to happen. Hipolito Rodriguez was a good man. He didn't deserve to get his name dragged through the mud any more than it had to be. And that wasn't Jeff's only reason. . . .

'He was a *friend,* dammit,' Jeff said. And that scared him a couple of different ways. Anything that happened to Hip might happen to him, too. Ever since Rodriguez shot himself, the weight of the ceremonial .45 on Jeff's hip seemed larger and more ominous than it ever had before. And when he picked up a submachine gun to walk through Camp Determination, he often shivered. *What* was Hip thinking when he turned his the wrong way?

And Jeff hadn't realized how much having a real friend here mattered till he suddenly didn't any more. He could talk about stuff with Hip without fearing that Ferd Koenig or Jake Featherston would find out what he said. He could use his war buddy as a back channel to the guards – and they could use Rodriguez as a back channel to him, too. It worked well for everybody.

Except now it didn't. And under all that lay the hole one friend's death left in the life of another who survived. Hip and Jeff went through desperate and deadly times together. No one else remembered them – no one else Jeff knew, which was all that mattered. When he and Hip talked, they both understood the mud and the blood and the stinks and the fear and the occasional flashes of crazy fun that lit up the horror and the wild drunken furloughs they'd got to take too seldom. Now all that stuff was locked inside Jefferson Pinkard's head. He could explain it to other people, but that was the point. He never needed to explain it to Hip. Hip *knew.*

The telephone rang. Pinkard jerked in his swivel chair. 'Son of a bitch!' he burst out. His hand shook as he reached for the telephone. *I'm jumpy as a goddamn cat,* he thought. *Can't let anybody see that, or I'm in big trouble.* 'Pinkard here.' His voice came out as a satisfactory growl. 'What's up?'

'Sir, we've got a new shipment coming in.' The guard officer at the other end of the line sounded both pleased and more than a little astonished. 'Should be here in an hour or two.'

'Good God!' Pinkard said. 'Why the hell didn't somebody tell us sooner?'

'Only thing I can think of, sir, is that they didn't want the damnyankees listening in,' the officer replied.

Jeff grunted – that did make some sense. 'Could be,' he said. 'And maybe they'll let up on this place for a while anyway. They've had their damn propaganda offensive. It's not like they *really* give a rat's ass about niggers. I mean, who does, for Christ's sake?'

'Not me, sir,' the youngster on the other end of the line replied with great conviction.

'Didn't reckon you would,' Pinkard said. 'Let everybody know what's what. We want to give these coons a nice, juicy Camp Determination hello – and then a nice, juicy good-bye, too.'

If he had to, he aimed to raise hell to make sure the guards were ready. Because of the way U.S. airplanes had pummeled the railroads coming west to Snyder and the camp, things had been painfully slow lately. It would have been easy for the men in gray uniforms to slack off. But they didn't, which made Pinkard proud. He could tell when the call reached the barracks. Guards exploded out, almost as if they were in a comedy film.

But it wouldn't be funny when that train got here. Pinkard was at the railroad spur watching when it pulled into the camp. He didn't say anything. He would if he had to, but the men in charge of the welcoming committee – he chuckled when he thought of it that way – deserved the chance to handle things themselves till they showed they couldn't.

Engine puffing, brakes squealing, the train stopped right where it was supposed to. The engineer was on the ball, then. That was good, because he didn't fall under Jeff's command. Doors opened. The familiar rank stench that rolled out of the jam-packed cars was even richer and riper than usual: the weather was warming up.

'Out!' guards screamed, gesturing with their submachine guns. 'Move, you lousy, stinking coons! *Move!*'

'Men to the left!' officers added. 'Men to the left, women and brats to the right!' One of them kicked a dazed black man, who fell with a groan. 'Get up!' the officer roared. '*Get* up, you dumb fucking prick! You too goddamn stupid to know which is your left and which is your right?'

The Negro probably was. How many days had he been stuck in that jam-packed car, with nowhere to turn around, nowhere to sit down, nowhere to ease himself, nothing to eat, nothing to drink? How many bodies would the guards and the Negro trusties find when they went through the train? There were always a good many. Because summer was here, there would probably be more than there had been on runs earlier in the year.

A submachine gun stuttered out a quick burst. Jefferson Pinkard nodded to himself. Every trainload, a few Negroes thought they could beat the odds by playing possum. Every trainload, they found out they were wrong.

'No, you stupid fuck, you can't carry your suitcase into the camp!' Every time, some Negroes managed to bring things along. What was confiscated was supposed to go straight into the war effort. Some of it did. The guards took what they wanted first, though. That was one of the perquisites that went with this job.

Many of them barely able to stay on their feet, the black men shambled through the gate and into the southern half of the camp. The women and little children went into the northern half. Every time, men and women waved to one another and promised they would be together again soon. *Yeah, you will, all right – in hell,* Jeff thought.

He sighed. Sure as hell, the senior female guard officer would come around and complain that her girls didn't get a chance to help with the unloading. She'd done that at least half a dozen times. She wanted them to get what she thought was their fair share of the loot.

'Too damn bad,' Pinkard muttered. In case something out here went wrong, he didn't want a bunch of flabbling women trying to fix it, even (or maybe especially) if they carried submachine guns, too. They were all right with barbed wire to back them up. They even had advantages over men. Fewer of them had affairs with Negro women. But when they did, they really fell in love with their colored partners. That happened much less often with the men.

By now, the female guards knew how to get the colored women and children into the asphyxiating trucks and the bathhouse on that side of the camp without panicking them. The ones who couldn't manage that were gone. Jeff had had to be firm about that; the guards in skirts had powerful backers in Richmond. But nobody was more powerful than Ferd Koenig and Jake Featherston, and he'd got his way.

Camp Determination got another shipment of Negroes the next day, and two more the day after that. It seemed like old times again. Barracks started filling up as prisoners came in faster than the camp could process them. That was how Jeff thought of it, and that was how it went down on every report. It seemed so much more . . . sanitary than talking about killing.

There was some trouble with the prisoners from the last trainload on the second day. As they lined up to 'get deloused and bathed,' a man shouted, 'You ain't gwine give us no baths! You gwine kill us all!'

He wasn't wrong, either in general or in particular. Two guards emptied their submachine guns at him. By the time they got done, he had more holes than a colander. They hit other prisoners, too – only fool luck kept them from hitting other guards. Nobody could stay smooth and polite after that. The only way the guards got the Negroes into the bathhouse was by threatening to kill them all on the spot if they didn't get moving.

'An ugly business,' Jeff said when he got to the bottom of it. 'I hope that damn troublemaking nigger cooks in hell forever. All his fault.'

'Yes, sir,' agreed the guard officer in charge of those prisoners. 'We did everything we could.'

'We got the job done – that's what counts most,' Pinkard said. 'Maybe things'll slow down again so all the spooks who saw this get processed. Then they won't have the chance to say anything to anybody else. That's what really matters.'

'Yes, sir,' the guard said.

'We'll have endless trouble if we don't keep it smooth. I mean endless,' Jeff went on. 'Most of the guards I've got here, they didn't serve at a place like Camp Dependable. They don't know what it's like when you have to reduce populations by hand.' He meant marching Negroes out into the swamp and shooting them. Saying what he said was easier on the spirit. 'They don't know what it's like to have the niggers knowing their population's gonna get reduced, neither. It's like sitting on a bomb with the fuse primed, that's what. You hear me?'

'Uh, yes, sir,' the guard officer said once more. He was getting more than he bargained for, more than he wanted, but he couldn't do a thing about it.

And Jefferson Pinkard still wasn't through. 'If any little thing goes wrong then, the fuse catches and the bomb goes up. And then it blows your fuckin' ass off. You aim to let that happen? We gonna let that happen?'

'No, sir!' Now the guard got to say something else. It was the right answer, too.

'All right, then,' Jeff growled. 'Get the hell out of here, and we'll see if we can pick up the processing. More niggers we do handle before we get the next trainload in, easier things'll be from then on out.'

Instead of agreeing this time – or even disagreeing – the guard got the hell out of there, as Jeff had said. Pinkard nodded to himself. Telling other people what to do was an awful lot better than getting told. Where he was now, the only people who could tell him what to do were the Attorney General of the CSA and the President. *No wonder I don't like getting calls from Richmond,* he thought.

Then he laughed, because somebody else could tell him what to do: his wife. He laughed again. That was true of any ordinary family man, and what else was he? 'Got a new young one on the way,' he said wonderingly. He hadn't expected that, but he liked it pretty well, even if Edith did have morning sickness all day long. He looked out over the camp and nodded. 'I'm doing this for him, by God.'

XI

Major Angelo Toricelli stuck his head into Abner Dowling's office. 'I have the reply from the War Department decoded, sir.'

'Oh, good,' Dowling said, and then, after getting a look at his adjutant's face, 'No, I take it back. It isn't going to be what I wanted to hear, is it?'

'I'm afraid not, sir.' Toricelli walked in and set a sheet of paper on Dowling's desk.

'Thanks.' The commander of the U.S. Eleventh Army peered down through his reading glasses. When he looked over the tops of them, Toricelli was in perfect focus, but the typewritten text in front of him blurred into illegibility.

He would just as soon have had it stay unreadable. Philadelphia told him he not only couldn't have any more barrels – he couldn't have any new artillery, either. He got the impression he was lucky to be able to keep what he had, and that it had taken special intercession from the Pope, or possibly from the Secretary of War, to keep him supplied with ammunition.

'So much for that,' he muttered.

'Sir?' Toricelli said.

'Philadelphia got all hot and bothered about Camp Determination – for about a month,' Dowling said. 'Now they've got bigger fish to fry. Morrell's drive into Tennessee is going well. I'm not complaining, mind you – don't get me wrong. We need to give Featherston a couple of good ones right in the teeth. Lord knows he's given us too many. But that means they're forgetting everybody west of Morrell again.'

'Colonel DeFrancis—' his adjutant began.

Dowling shook his head. 'His aircraft have been hitting other targets lately, too. I don't blame him – we do need to knock out the enemy's factories. But nobody seems to be paying attention to the poor damned niggers.'

'I'm afraid you're right,' Major Toricelli said. 'Signs are that the Confederates are shipping more blacks to the camp and taking more bodies away from it. We've got aerial recon photos showing they've dug a new trench in that field where they get rid of the bodies.'

'Bastards,' Dowling said. The word didn't seem nearly strong enough. He doubted whether the language had words strong enough to say everything he thought about the Confederates who ran Camp Determination, the ones who fed Negroes into it, and the ones who, by backing the Freedom Party, proclaimed that it ought to exist.

Major Toricelli shrugged. 'What can we do, sir?' By his tone of voice, he didn't think the Eleventh Army could do anything.

Under normal circumstances, Dowling would have agreed with him. But circumstances here in west Texas weren't normal. He couldn't win the war here, no matter what he did. He couldn't lose it no matter what he did, either. When he got plucked from Virginia and sent to the wilds of Clovis, New Mexico, they told him he'd be doing his job as long as he didn't let the Confederates take Santa Fe and Albuquerque. Well, the Confederates damn well wouldn't. They had to be flabbling about what was going on in Kentucky and Tennessee even more than the United

States were. Their defensive force wouldn't get many new men. He was still surprised it had got that unit of Freedom Party Guards.

'I want you to draft some new orders, Major,' Dowling said. Toricelli raised a questioning eyebrow. Dowling explained: 'I want you to order this army to concentrate in and around Lubbock and to prepare for an advance as soon as possible. And get hold of Terry DeFrancis and tell him to get his fanny over here as fast as he can, because we'll need all the air support we can get.'

'Yes, sir.' Toricelli hesitated. He'd already given the only proper answer a subordinate should. Even so, he went on, 'What if the Confederates try getting around our flanks while we're concentrating?'

'Well, what if they do?' Dowling returned. Major Torricelli's eyebrow didn't just rise this time. It jumped. Dowling didn't care. 'They haven't got enough men or enough barrels around here to surround us and cut us off. This isn't Pittsburgh, and it damn well won't be. I aim to make enough of a commotion in these parts so that Philadelphia will *have* to notice me.'

'What happens if something goes wrong?' his adjutant asked.

'I go up before the Joint Committee on the Conduct of the War and they chop off my head,' Dowling said. That shut Major Toricelli up. Dowling was too old and too stubborn to worry much about what failure would do to his career. Toricelli doubtless worried about *his*, which was tied to his general's. 'Best way to keep everyone except the Confederates happy is to make sure things *don't* go wrong. Draft those orders, Major, and get DeFrancis here on the double.'

'Yes, sir.' Toricelli saluted with mechanical precision and left.

Dowling chuckled under his breath. He'd given General Custer plenty of those halfhearted salutes. *Somehow or other, the old boy made it work in the end,* he thought. *I will, too. See if I don't.*

Terry DeFrancis arrived within the hour. 'What's up, sir?' he asked. 'Your adjutant made it sound like you've got something interesting cooking, but he wouldn't go into any detail on the telephone.'

'Good for him,' Dowling said. When Confederate sympathizers weren't cutting the telephone lines, they were tapping them. Security in occupied west Texas was an unending nightmare. Dowling explained what he had in mind.

'I like it,' Colonel DeFrancis said with a grin when he finished. 'The more we do, the better we do, the more attention Philadelphia has to pay us. May I make one suggestion, though?'

'Go ahead,' Dowling told him.

'I think the axis of attack ought to be northeast, not southeast. For one thing, they'll be looking for a drive on the camp. For another, it's not much farther from here to Childress' – he used a map to show what he meant – 'than it is to Snyder. If we take Childress, we cut Amarillo off from the east by road and by rail.'

Dowling had to think about that. Cutting Amarillo off was a bigger military objective than threatening Camp Determination. But the camp was a bigger political plum. Not without regret, he shook his head. 'No, Colonel, we'll continue on our present line for now. If we get the reinforcements we're after, *then* we can worry about Amarillo. Prepare your mission plans accordingly.'

'Yes, sir,' DeFrancis said. Like Major Toricelli, he sounded dubious. Dowling didn't care. One way or another, he was going to ram this through. If George Armstrong

Custer's ghost was looking over his shoulder, the old bastard must have smiled.

Shifting soldiers from yon to hither occupied the next four days. Dowling left only tiny screening forces on his flanks, calculating that he wasn't likely to deceive the Confederates any which way – and also calculating that they didn't have the manpower or the driving will to hurt his army while it was on the move.

He proved right. On the fifth morning, U.S. guns in and around Lubbock thundered. Bombers overhead dropped tons of death on the enemy. Fighters streaked low over the Confederate lines to shoot up trucks and command cars and troop columns and anything else they caught out in the open.

Two hours after the bombardment started, Dowling ordered his infantry and the little armor he had forward. He went forward himself, in a command car bristling with almost as many wireless aerials as a porcupine had spines. Major Toricelli, who was in the car with him, was also bristling. Dowling didn't care about that, either. He wanted to see what happened at the front, not just hear about it from people who were really there.

The first thing he saw was a long file of prisoners in plain butternut and camouflage brown tramping back toward Lubbock, herded along by grinning U.S. soldiers in green-gray. Several of the U.S. soldiers carried captured C.S. automatic rifles – the perfect tools to use if prisoners got out of line. The glum Confederates seemed likely to behave themselves.

'Y'all don't fight fair!' a Confederate yelled at the command car. Dowling waved back as if acknowledging a compliment.

Naturally, the terrain right on the Confederate side of the line had taken the heaviest pounding from U.S. bombs and shells. Dowling saw scenes right out of the Great War: cratered trench lines, rusty barbed wire with stretches smashed down flat by barrels so foot soldiers could get through, wrecked field guns lying on their sides. The only thing missing was the all-pervasive stink of death a landscape got after it changed hands three or four times, with neither able to bury all the corpses. Then the rats smiled and grew fat and frolicked as they fed on noisome flesh.

Not all the Confederates had surrendered or died. A nest of them were holed up in a farmhouse and barn. Though cut off and surrounded by U.S. soldiers, they wouldn't quit. An officer in green-gray approached the barn with a white flag to see if he could talk them into coming out. They fired a burst over his head. They weren't trying to hit him, but they were letting him know they didn't intend to give up. He drew back in a hurry.

'Is that a bunch of Freedom Party Guards?' Dowling shouted to a sergeant serving a mortar.

'Those camouflage cocksuckers?' The noncom paused to drop a bomb down the tube. After a surprisingly small bang, it arced through the air to come down between the house and the barn. 'Yes, sir, that's them. They fight hard.'

'If we get rid of them, then, the Confederates will be in more trouble,' Dowling said.

As if the holed-up elite troops had heard him, they aimed one of their machine guns his way. He hadn't been under gunfire for a while: not since he and Daniel MacArthur were trying to hold this part of Texas in the USA before Al Smith's plebiscite. 'Get down, sir!' Major Toricelli yelled when bullets kicked up puffs of dust not far from the command car.

'Get down, hell!' Dowling swung the pintle-mounted machine gun toward the barn and let it rip. He had a .50-caliber weapon to play with, not the rifle-caliber gun that was shooting at him. His fired bullets almost as big as his thumb. The barn had to be more than a mile away – not much more than a dot on the horizon. Even so, he had confidence he was doing the enemy some harm.

And the jackhammer roar of the gun was as much fun as a roller-coaster ride. The stink of cordite and the clatter of brass as empty cartridges flew from the breech and fell to the floor of the command car only added to the kick. He went through a belt as happily as a twelve-year-old plinking at tin cans with a .22.

If he could have made the Confederates surrender all by himself, that would have been great. No such luck. A couple of truck-drawn 105s pulled up and flattened both buildings in which the Freedom Party Guards were holed up. The shells set the barn and the farmhouse on fire. Even so, when U.S. infantrymen cautiously advanced, the surviving Confederates opened up on them with automatic weapons.

All in all, the Freedom Party Guards fought a first-rate delaying action. They did what they set out to do: they tied up enough U.S. soldiers to let their buddies withdraw in better order than they could have otherwise.

But Abner Dowling, with the bit between his teeth, was determined not to let that matter much. He had more men than the Confederates, and more artillery, and more barrels, and many more airplanes. *As long as I don't do anything stupid,* he told himself, *I can drive them a long way.* Could he drive them all the way back to Camp Determination? He aimed to find out.

Flora Blackford had needed a while to get used to picking up the *Philadelphia Inquirer* and reading good news day after day. It seemed strange, unnatural, almost un-American. But instead of stories of disaster in Ohio and retreat in Pennsylvania, the paper was full of the U.S. drive through Kentucky and Tennessee, and of other progress elsewhere. By everything she could tell, U.S. bombers were hitting Richmond harder than the Confederates were hitting Philadelphia these days. New U.S. airstrips farther south meant Birmingham and Atlanta were starting to catch it, too.

Even the news west of the Mississippi seemed good, though it often got shoved back to page four or page six. Out in Texas, Abner Dowling was quoted as saying, 'With more men, I could move even faster.'

Flora wanted General Dowling's army to move faster. If U.S. soldiers could walk into Camp Determination, or could even take closeups of the vast boneyard where Jake Featherston's men disposed of dead Negroes, the world would have to sit up and take notice . . . wouldn't it?

She wished she hadn't had that last little afterthought. When the Tsar turned the Cossacks loose on the Jews in another pogrom, did the world sit up and take notice? When the Turks enjoyed their ancient sport of slaughtering Armenians, did the world try to stop them? When the Germans treated the blacks in the Congo even worse than the Belgians had, did anybody get up on his hind legs and complain?

No, and no, and no. So why would the world flabble unduly – or at all – about what the Confederates were doing to their own people?

'To hell with the world, then,' Flora said, there in the more-or-less privacy of her office. '*I* care, whether it does or not.'

Her secretary stuck her head into the office. 'Did you call me, Congresswoman?'

'No, Bertha. It's all right,' Flora said. The other woman retreated. Flora shook her head. It wasn't all right, or even close to all right. And if the world didn't care, wasn't that a sign something was wrong with the poor old globe?

She looked at the newspaper again. Why should Dowling complain that he didn't have enough men? He was doing something vitally important. Shouldn't he get all the soldiers he wanted, and more besides?

Her first impulse was to summon the Joint Committee on the Conduct of the War and hold the General Staff's toes to the fire. In 1941, she would have done it. She still might do it, but she'd learned other tricks since then. She called the Assistant Secretary of War instead.

'Hello, Flora!' Franklin Roosevelt boomed when she got through to him. 'Let me guess – you're going to want me to send about six divisions to west Texas, and to have them all there yesterday.'

'Well – yes.' Flora didn't like being so predictable. 'And now you're going to tell me why you claim you can't do it.'

'Simplest reason in the world: we need 'em more farther east,' Roosevelt said. 'If they go to Kentucky and Tennessee, they gut the Confederacy. Gut it, I say. If I send them out to Abner Dowling, they step on its toes. That will hurt, no doubt about it. But it won't kill, and we want the CSA dead.'

'Sending troops to Texas will stop Jake Featherston from murdering Negroes,' Flora said.

'Sending troops to Texas will stop Jake Featherston from murdering Negroes . . . at Camp Determination,' Roosevelt said. 'It won't do a damn thing – excuse me, but it won't – to stop him from murdering them in Louisiana or Mississippi or east Texas. The only thing that will keep him from murdering them there is knocking the Confederate States flat. Taking land away from the enemy, taking away his factories and his railroads and his highways – that will stop him.'

He made more sense than she wished he did. 'Is there any way we can compromise?' Flora asked. 'I can see why you don't want to send a lot of men and a lot of equipment to Texas. I don't like it, but I can see it. Can you send some, though? The Confederates are bound to be having a hard time out there, too. Even a small reinforcement could tip the balance our way.'

'You're very persuasive. You ought to be in Congress.' Roosevelt laughed merrily. 'Tell you what I'll do. Let me talk to the gentlemen with the stars on their shoulder straps. What they say we can afford, we'll send. If they say we can't afford anything—'

'They can come before the Joint Committee and explain why not.' Flora reminded him she had the stick as well as the carrot.

He only laughed again. 'You're *very* persuasive,' he said. 'I suspect you may squeeze a few soldiers out of them after all.'

Flora suspected she might squeeze out some soldiers, too. Generals were often happier facing amputation without anesthesia than they were about coming before the Joint Committee on the Conduct of the War. Amputation only cost you your leg, not your career, and the pain didn't last nearly so long.

'Anything else?' Franklin Roosevelt asked.

'How's the other business doing?' Flora wouldn't go into detail or name names over the telephone. Lines into and out of Congress and into and out of the War Department were supposed to be extra secure. Some things were too important to entrust to a line that was supposed to be secure, though. She still couldn't be sure who besides Roosevelt was listening.

He was equally careful, saying only, 'Everything seems to be coming along well enough right now.'

'That's good. They've made all the repairs they need?'

'I haven't heard anything different.'

'All right. Anything new from the foreign factories?' Flora hoped he would understand she was asking how the Confederacy and Germany and England and France – and Russia and Japan, too, come to that – were faring in their quest for a uranium bomb.

'I haven't heard anything new lately,' he replied. 'Of course, just because I haven't heard it, that doesn't mean it hasn't happened.'

'I know,' she said unhappily. That was true even of the Confederates' project, and they were right across the border and spoke the same language. How much *could* the USA find out about what the Germans, say, were doing? They were allies, but they were being tight-lipped about anything that had to do with uranium. The Russians and the Japanese were probably behind in the race – Flora hoped they were, anyway – but she didn't see how her country could learn anything about what they were doing unless they got amazingly careless with their codes.

'If I hear anything, you'll know about it,' Roosevelt promised, and then, 'Oh, that reminds me.'

Did he sound a little too casual? Flora thought he did. 'Reminds you of what?' she asked, trying not to show it.

'I'd like to send a team to your office and to your apartment, to sweep them for microphones,' he said. 'Don't want to take chances, you know.'

'No, I suppose not.' Flora sighed. 'All right – go ahead.' Of course, the Confederates – or any other spies – could plant mikes again right after the inspection team finished. A whore might be healthy when a government doctor looked her over, then catch something nasty from her next customer and spread it till she was inspected again. In both cases, though, you had to try.

'Thanks, Flora. The leader of the team is a master sergeant named Bernstein. If he's not there, go somewhere else and call the guards.'

'Will do,' Flora said. ' 'Bye.' She hung up.

The team showed up at her office the next morning. She exchanged Yiddish gibes with Sergeant Bernstein. If he was by any chance a Confederate spy, he was a brilliant one. Bertha squawked when he and his men ran their detectors over her desk. 'Sorry, lady. Gotta be done,' he said. 'Anything, Bob?' he asked the tall, blond soldier who was checking there.

'Looks like zip, Carl,' the private answered. He towered over his boss, who was little and dark and probably hadn't combed his hair in three or four days.

They also didn't find anything in Flora's office. 'Either you're clean or the Confederates are smarter than they look,' Sergeant Bernstein declared.

'Which is it likely to be?' Flora asked.

'Never can tell,' he said seriously. 'Most of their sh – uh, stuff – is just a little behind ours, but they're mighty good with it. And some of what they use *is* ours.' He made a sour face. 'You can walk into a wireless shop and buy it right on the street, and the bastards do.'

'Is that the price we pay for being a free country?' Flora asked.

'Don't ask me. I'm just a *shlemiel* with stripes,' Bernstein answered. 'But if we stop being free because those *mamzrim* can steal too easy, that ain't so good, neither.' He turned to the other soldiers. 'Come on, Bob, Dick. We got other places to check.'

Flora found one more question as the men in green-gray packed up to go: 'Secretary Roosevelt said you'd come to my apartment, too. When will that be?'

Sergeant Bernstein checked some papers in a clipboard.

'Day after tomorrow, probably in the morning. You be there?'

'If I won't, my son will,' Flora said. 'I'll tell him you're coming, and that he should let you in.'

'Oughta work.' Bernstein looked from one of his men to the other. 'You guys aren't ready yet? Watsamaddawidya?' To get that all out in one word, he had to hail from New York City.

'Well, let me say this—' Dick began.

Bernstein cut him off. 'No, don't say it. Just come on.' To Flora, he added, 'Get him started and he won't shut up.' Dick's blackly stubbled face burned with resentment, but the sergeant got him out of there before he could loose any of it.

When Flora got home, she was all set to tell Joshua about the soldiers who would stop by in a couple of days. But that never happened. Her son showed her an envelope. 'Look what came today!' He sounded excited about it.

That particular envelope, as Flora knew too well, hadn't changed much since the days of the Great War. The Old English typography on the cheap paper was almost the same, too:

𝔘.𝔖. 𝔄rmy 𝔇epartment of 𝔖election for 𝔖erbice.

Joshua might be excited. Flora knew nothing but horror. 'We can beat it,' she said automatically. 'We can quash it.'

'No,' Joshua said. 'This is my country. I'll fight for it, the same as anybody else would.'

'It's not a game, Joshua.' Flora knew she sounded desperate. She felt desperate. 'Uncle David walks on one leg. Cousin Yossel never knew his father. If anything happened to you, I don't think I could stand it.'

'Nothing will happen, Mother.' At eighteen, Joshua was

confident in his own immortality. An uncle? A cousin's father? So what? Joshua had never known the first Yossel Reisen, either. He went on, 'After the war, they'll ask me, "What did you do?" Shall I say I hid behind your skirts?'

Yes! Please God, yes! Flora wanted to scream it. Only the certain knowledge that it wouldn't help kept her quiet. She started to cry instead. That didn't help, either, but she couldn't help herself.

Somewhere out ahead in the Atlantic, the British and French fleets prowled. Sam Carsten kept glancing toward the *Josephus Daniels'* Y-ranging screens. Nothing showed up except the returns from the U.S. ships all around the destroyer escort. No enemy airplanes had smelled out where the U.S. fleet lay.

'This could be the big one,' Pat Cooley said.

'You're right – it could,' Sam agreed. 'I went through the Battle of the Three Navies, and I never thought there'd be a bigger fight than that. But maybe I was wrong.'

'This would be a different kind of fight,' the exec said.

'Oh, just a little,' Carsten said. Southwest of Oahu, U.S. warships had slugged it out with their British and Japanese counterparts with big guns. This time around . . . 'Chances are we'll never see the fleet that sends airplanes at us, and they won't see our ships, either.'

'We've got some battlewagons along just in case,' Cooley said, 'but I think you're right.'

'I know they're here. The *Dakota*'s one of 'em.' Sam shivered. 'I don't ever want to go on another wild ride – you can just bet your ass I don't.' A shell hit had jammed the battleship's steering, and she sped on a mad arc through the U.S. fleet, ending up much too close to the enemy. She took a lot of hits, but she kept shooting back, too. To this day, both sides claimed victory in that fight near the

Sandwich Islands. As far as Sam could tell, they'd both lost.

Lieutenant, j.g., Thad Walters stiffened in front of the Y-ranging set. 'Sir, I've got a bogey to the northeast,' the youngster said, his voice quivering with excitement.

'Give me range and bearing,' Sam snapped. As soon as he had them, he swung the destroyer escort's blinker light toward the closest cruiser to pass the word. The whole fleet, of course, sailed under wireless silence. Before he started flashing, the cruiser began sending him a signal. As he read it, he laughed.

So did Pat Cooley. 'Well, sir, at least their Y-ranging operator isn't asleep at the switch.'

'Swell,' Sam said. The exec smiled. So did Sam, wryly. He couldn't win, and he knew it. If he said something like *swell*, he marked himself as an old-timer trying to sound up to the minute. But if he said something like *bully*, he marked himself as an old-timer not bothering to stay up to date, which had to be even worse.

U.S. fighters from the combat air patrol streaked toward the foreign airplane. If they let it keep coming, it would find the fleet and pass the word on to the enemy ships somewhere off to the east. If they shot it down before it found the U.S. ships, that would also tell the limeys and frogs something, but not so much. And if they made it try to run before they shot it down, they might be able to use its flight path to get an idea of where the enemy lay.

Sam watched the fighters till they vanished from sight, then went over to the Y-ranging screens and watched them there. He could tell just when the enemy aircraft spotted them: it broke off its advance and turned away as fast as it could go.

'What's that bearing?' he asked Walters.

'Sir, the course is 105 – a little south of east,' the Y-ranging officer answered.

'So somewhere along that line from where it started, that's where the ship that sent it out is likely to be,' Carsten said.

'Well, we don't know that for a fact, sir – that airplane could be bluffing, trying to throw us off,' Walters said. 'But I think it's a pretty good bet.'

'Me, too,' Sam said, and then, 'Mr. Cooley, is the cruiser reporting that scout aircraft's course?'

'No, sir.'

'Then signal it over there, if you please. Chances are they're checking it themselves, but I don't want to take even the smallest chance with something this important.'

'Aye aye, sir.' Cooley was faster with Morse than Sam was himself.

'Sir, we've got a hydrophone contact!' That was Chief Bevacqua. The CPO was the best man on the ship at making sense of what came back from the pings the underwater equivalent of Y-ranging sent out. 'Bearing 165, range about half a mile. It's shallow, sir, and the contact feels like a god-damn submersible.'

'Jesus Christ!' Ice shot up Sam's back. A sub that close could sink the *Josephus Daniels* easy as you please. 'Change course to 165 – we'll give it the smallest target we can. Man the ashcan flinger! Pat! Signal the cruiser that we've got the worst kind of company!'

'Aye aye, sir!' Cooley said again, but before he could finish the signal the submarine announced its own presence. It cared little for anything as small as the destroyer escort. The light cruiser made a much more tempting target. Two torpedoes slammed into her. As soon as she was hit, the submersible dove.

By then, though, the *Josephus Daniels* hovered over the

sub. Depth charges splashed into the Atlantic. Down below, the submersible would be doing everything it could to get away, but its underwater electric motors were painfully slow. The skipper down there – British? French? Confederate? – would have heard the ashcans going into the water. Could he get away? Could he get deep enough to avoid and evade?

Even up on the surface, each burst from the spread felt like a kick in the teeth. Then Sam heard a noise like a slammed metal door – the pressure hull caving in from the explosions. 'We got him,' he said soberly.

'He got us, too,' Cooley said – the cruiser was listing badly.

'Do they want us to take men off, or does their skipper think she'll stay afloat?' Sam asked. Rage filled him, rage at himself. Destroyers and destroyer escorts sailed with the fleet to keep submarines away. He hadn't done his job. Any enemy country would gladly trade a sub for a cruiser.

'For now, they think she'll stay up,' Cooley answered. More flashing Morse came from the cruiser. 'We get an "attaboy" for sinking that submersible. They heard it cave in over there, too.'

'Hot damn,' Sam said bitterly. He spoke to the hydrophone operator: 'Keep your ears open, Bevacqua.'

'Will do, sir,' the petty officer replied. 'I feel like hell on account of that fucker suckered me. He must've snuck in under a warm layer or something. Even so—'

'Yeah. Even so,' Sam said. 'Well, do your damnedest.' He didn't look forward to the after-action report. He had to hope he lived to write one.

More airplanes came off the carriers' flight decks, and more, and still more. They formed up into attacking squadrons above the U.S. fleet, then zoomed off to the east. 'I think we've found the enemy fleet,' Cooley said.

'That's what we came for.' Sam paused. 'Of course, they came to find us. If they don't already know where we're at, seeing where our airplanes are coming from will kind of give them a hint.'

'I know the limeys have Y-ranging. From what I've heard, theirs may even be better than ours,' Cooley said. 'I'm not so sure about the French.'

'Well, once they see the limeys launching airplanes, they won't do a whole lot of waiting around after that,' Carsten said, and the exec nodded. Sailors wrestled more depth charges up on deck to replace the ones the *Josephus Daniels* used to sink the enemy submersible.

Half an hour went by. Then Thad Walters said, 'We've got aircraft coming in from the east, sir. They're not likely to be friendlies.'

'How far out are they?' Sam asked.

'Maybe fifteen or twenty minutes.'

'All right. Thanks.' It wasn't, and Sam had no reason to be grateful, but he said the polite words anyway. Then he got on the PA system: 'We're going to have company in a little while. Chances are they'll go after the airplane carriers and battleships ahead of us, but you never can tell. Any which way, our job is to get as many rounds in the air as we can. Some of them will do some good, I promise. We've put a lot of work in on our gunnery. This is where it pays off.'

'We're a lot better than we were when you took over this ship, sir,' Cooley said.

'Thanks, Pat.' This time, Sam did mean it. But he went on, '*Better* doesn't count. Are we *good enough*? Well, we'll find out pretty damn quick.'

Some of the ships farther east, at the very forefront of the U.S. fleet, started firing. Black puffs of smoke fouled the blue sky. Peering between the puffs with a pair of field glasses, Sam spotted wings and fuselages glinting in the sun. His belly tightened. His balls wanted to crawl up from his scrotum. He'd been on a ship attacked from the air as early as 1917. He'd been on the *Remembrance* when the Japanese sank her. Good men were going to die here in the middle of the Atlantic. So would good ships. With luck, more of them would die a couple of hundred miles to the east, out over the curve of the world. Neither side's ships would see the other's today.

With a thunderous roar, the *Josephus Daniels'* guns cut loose: .50-caliber machine guns, twin 40mm antiaircraft guns, and the 4.5-inch popguns that were her main armament. Those could reach higher and farther than the lighter weapons, but couldn't fire nearly so fast. 'Evasive action, Mr. Cooley,' Sam said. 'All ahead flank speed!'

'Aye aye, sir!' The exec relayed the command to the engine room. He started zigzagging as the ship's speed built up. It wouldn't build up enough. Sam wished for the extra six or seven knots a real destroyer could give him. But then, how much difference would they make against an airplane?

A burning fighter slammed into the Atlantic before Sam could see which side it belonged to. A great black cloud of smoke rose from a stricken ship. He swore. He'd known it would happen, but that didn't make it any easier to take.

'We've got to keep *some* carriers,' Sam said, more to himself than to anyone else. 'Otherwise, we won't be able to land our airplanes when they come home.'

A fighter with a blue-white-red British roundel dove on the destroyer escort, guns blazing. Bullets whined through the air and clanged off metal. Here and there, men sprawled in spreading pools of blood. Sailors got the wounded down to the sick bay. The ship had no doctor, only a couple of pharmacist's mates. They would have to do what they could.

When things calmed down, they could transfer the men hurt worst to a bigger ship with a real surgeon or even to a hospital ship.

Uncounted tracers pursued the enemy airplane, but it got away. Exultant shouts rang out a few minutes later, when a torpedo airplane splashed into the sea. Sailors at the forward 40mm guns jumped and swaggered and pounded their hairy chests like so many gorillas.

Too much was going on too fast in too many places for Sam to have more than a vague idea of how this end of the fight was going – and he had no way to know what was happening off to the east. If everything here and there went perfectly, the battleships could storm off and pound the enemy ships to pieces . . . but he didn't think things were going perfectly. Now several greasy black smoke plumes rose into the clean, salt-scented air.

'I hope we're hurting them worse than they're hurting us,' Pat Cooley said, exactly echoing his own thought.

After most of an hour, no more enemy aircraft remained overhead. They'd either gone down or flown off toward the east. They might clash with returning U.S. airplanes coming west. As Sam steered the *Josephus Daniels* toward a listing escort carrier, he realized he might have fought in two great naval battles now where nobody had the faintest idea who'd won.

'A great naval victory in the Atlantic!' blared the wireless set behind the bar in the sleazy seaside San Diego saloon. 'British and French claims of triumph are the spasmo bleating of frightened sheep!'

'Baaa!' George Enos said, looking up from his beer. 'What do you think, Chief?'

'Just have to wait and see,' Fremont Dalby answered. 'What happens next will tell the story. They said we were licking the Confederates in Ohio, too, when the bastards were really kicking our ass. Or does it look different to you?'

'Nah, that sounds about right,' George said.

'If we go on and blast the crap out of the convoys coming up from South America, then we honest to God did whip the limeys,' Dalby continued, for all the world as if he had an admiral's broad gold stripe on each sleeve. 'If they go on and link up with the Confederates and give us a hard time in our own waters, they walloped us instead.'

'I got you,' George said. 'And if neither one happens—'

'It's a push,' Fritz Gustafson put in.

'There you go.' Dalby nodded emphatically. The empty glass in front of him, and the ones that had preceded it, no doubt had something to do with that emphasis. He put money on the bar, and the man in a boiled shirt and bow tie behind it gave him a full glass and took away the empty one. After a sip, the gun chief went on, 'I mean, I think we really are no shit smacking the Confederates around, 'cause we wouldn't be down in fucking Tennessee if we weren't. Past that, though . . . Well, who knows how much to believe?'

'Who cares?' As usual, Gustafson got a lot of mileage out of a few words.

'That's it.' George drained his beer and nodded to the bartender. The man worked the tap but didn't hand over the beer till he got paid. George sipped, then sucked foam off his upper lip. 'We've got to keep doing our job no matter what the big picture looks like. We'll figure out what it all means later on.'

Down at the far end of the bar, two Marines started slugging at each other. Sometimes, as George knew too well, a brawl like that made the whole joint explode. This time, other young men in forest-green uniforms grabbed the brawlers and sat on them. 'Lots of leathernecks in town lately,' Dalby remarked.

'They train here,' George said.

Dalby shook his head. 'I mean even besides that,' he said. 'Something's up, I bet.'

'Could be,' George said. 'Maybe they're going to go down and take Baja California away from the Mexicans.'

'Possible,' Dalby said thoughtfully. 'We tried that in the last war, and it didn't work. Maybe we'd have more luck this time around.'

'We could blockade the Confederates at Guaymas.' George warmed to the idea – it was his, after all. 'If we did, they couldn't even get their subs out. That would make it like they didn't have any ports on the Pacific.'

'I've heard notions I liked less,' Fremont Dalby allowed.

'Me, too,' Gustafson said, which was a solid accolade.

'If they send the Marines south, I bet we go along, too,' George said. 'We could do shore bombardment and keep the submersibles away from the landing craft.'

Dalby laughed at him. 'You tell 'em, Admiral,' he said, reversing the thought George had had a moment before. But that held more admiration than derision, for he turned to Fritz Gustafson and said, 'He's not as dumb as he looks, is he?'

'Not always, anyhow,' Gustafson said – more praise, of sorts.

The next morning, George hardly remembered his prediction. You could get hung over on beer if you worked at it, and he'd been diligent the day before. Black coffee and aspirins took the edge off his pounding headache, but left his stomach feeling as if shipfitters were using blowtorches in there. His buddies seemed in no better shape. That was some consolation, but only some.

Two days later, the *Townsend* put to sea with several

other destroyers, the escort carriers that had raided Baja
California before, and a gaggle of slow, ugly landing craft.
Surveying them as they waddled along, Fremont Dalby
said, 'It's a good thing the Empire of Mexico has a horseshit Navy. A real fleet could sink those sorry wallowers
faster than you can say Jack Robinson.'

George would have argued, except he thought Dalby
was right. 'I'm glad *I'm* not on one of those scows,' he said.

'Amen, Brother Ben!' Dalby exclaimed. 'You'd be puking
your guts out every inch of the way. I know you've got a
good stomach – I've seen it. But you could put a statue
into one of those damn things and it'd barf brass by the
time we got down to Cabo San Lucas.'

They didn't get down to Cabo San Lucas. The Marines
went ashore about halfway down the Baja peninsula. That
had Dalby and the handful of other old-timers on the
destroyer muttering to themselves. The Army had landed
in almost the same spot during the Great War, and had
had to pull out not much later. George couldn't see that it
mattered one way or the other. Once you got south of
Tijuana, Baja California didn't have enough of anything
except rocks and scorpions – but it sure had plenty of
those.

The Mexican coastal garrison held its fire till the
landing craft got close, then opened up with several batteries of three-inch guns that were a generation out of
date on the big battlefields farther east but that still worked
just fine.

Keeping quiet let those guns escape the fury of the dive
bombers that flew off the escort carriers to soften up the
landing zone before the Marines went in. As soon as they
started firing, all the real warships with the flotilla blasted
away with their main armament from ranges at which the
smaller land-based guns couldn't reply. One by one, the

Mexican cannon fell silent. They weren't playing possum this time, either. George wouldn't have wanted to be on the receiving end of that shellacking.

But they'd done more damage than anyone on the U.S. side would have expected. A couple of landing craft were on fire, and a couple of more had simply gone down to the shallow bottom of the Pacific. Machine guns greeted the men in those dark green uniforms who splashed ashore.

The dive bombers returned and pounded the machine-gun nests. So did guns from the *Townsend* and her comrades. Fighters strafed the rocks just beyond the beach. Peering shoreward with binoculars, Fremont Dalby said, 'We're whaling the crap out of them. Only bad thing is, you can't hardly see them at all – their khaki matches the landscape real good. The leatherheads stick out like sore thumbs, poor bastards.'

'Somebody was asleep at the switch, not giving them the right kind of uniforms,' George said. 'The Confederates are starting to wear camouflage, for Christ's sake. Least we could do is have our guys not look like Christmas trees in the desert.'

'Probably figured we were only fighting Mexicans, so what difference did it make?' Dalby said. 'That's how they think back in Philadelphia. But anybody with a rock in front of him and a gun in his hands is trouble. What are we doing making things easier for him?'

'Acting dumb,' Fritz Gustafson said, which was all too likely to be true.

They had the time to gab, because the *Townsend* didn't come close enough to shore for them to open up with their 40mm guns. That would have let the Mexicans shoot back. No enemy airplanes appeared overhead. If they had, the fighters from the escort carriers would have dealt with them before the antiaircraft guns could – George hoped so, anyhow.

He watched the Marines hack out a toehold on the barren Mexican coast. 'Boy, if the Confederates weren't over on the far side of the Gulf of California, I'd say the Mexicans were fucking welcome to this Baja place,' he remarked.

'You notice the Confederate States didn't buy it when they picked up Sonora and Chihuahua,' Fremont Dalby said. 'You notice we didn't take it away after we won the Great War. Goddamn Mexicans *are* welcome to it.'

George looked at his wristwatch. 'Other crew's coming on pretty soon. They're welcome to it, too. I want some shuteye.' He yawned to show how much he wanted it. 'This watch-and-watch crap is for the birds.'

'What? You don't like four hours on, four hours off around the clock?' Dalby said in mock surprise. 'You want more than a couple-three hours of sleep at a time? Shit, Enos, what kind of American are you?'

'A tired one,' George answered. 'A hungry one, too. If I eat, I don't get enough sleep. If I don't eat, I still don't get enough sleep, but I come closer, and I get hungry like a son of a bitch. I can't win.'

Dalby scraped his index finger over his thumbnail. 'There's the world's smallest goddamn violin playing sad songs for you. That shows how sorry I am. You're not talking about anything I'm not doing.'

'I know, Chief,' George said quickly. One advantage of Gustafson's usual silence was that he couldn't get in trouble by opening his big mouth too wide and falling in.

When the other crew took over at the twin 40mm, George raced down to the galley and snagged a ham sandwich and a mug of coffee. He inhaled them, then climbed into his hammock. It was hot and stuffy belowdecks, but he didn't care. The destroyer's five-inch guns roared every so often, but he didn't care about that, either. He thought he could have slept on top of one of them.

He was punchy and groggy when he got shaken awake, and needed a minute or two to remember where he was, and why, and what he was supposed to be doing. 'Oh, God,' he groaned, 'is it that time already?'

'Bet your ass, Charlie,' his tormentor said cheerfully, and went on to rout other victims from sleep.

The sun had set. On the shore, tracers zipped back and forth. The U.S. Marines used yellow or red tracer rounds. Maybe the Mexicans had been buying theirs from the Empire of Japan, because they were ice blue. It made for a bright and cheerful scene – or a scene that would have been bright and cheerful if George hadn't known that those tracers, along with all the ordinary bullets he couldn't see, were fired with intent to kill.

'Looks like we're holding more ground than we were when I sacked out,' he said.

'Yeah, I think so,' Fremont Dalby agreed. 'Now that we're holding it, though, what are we going to do with it?'

'Beats me,' George said. 'But I'll tell you one thing – I'd sooner be fighting Francisco José's boys than Hirohito's any old day.'

'Well, if you think I'll argue with that, you're crazier than one man's got any business being,' the gun chief replied. 'The Japs are tough, and their gear is as good as ours. These guys . . . They're using stuff left over from the last war, and you have to figure most of 'em don't want to be here.'

'Would you?' George said. 'It's got to be hell on earth. Hot sun. Rocks. Rattlesnakes – gotta think so, anyway. Most of those guys probably just want to go back to their farms and make like none of this ever happened.'

'Sounds good to me,' Dalby said. 'If we go home and the Confederates go home, who's left to fight? See? Piece of cake. They'll be calling with the Nobel Peace Prize any goddamn day now. Want to split it?'

'Sure? Why not?' George said. On the barren, desolate coast of Baja California, something blew up with a rending crash. 'Hope that was on the Mexican side of the line,' George said. Fremont Dalby nodded.

A private came up to Chester Martin with a half-grim, half-sick expression on his face. Seeing that, Martin knew what he was going to say before he said it. But say it he did: 'Sarge, they found Don. Bushwhackers caught him. It ain't pretty.'

'Shit,' Chester said. 'This is worse than Kentucky, all right.' Kentucky had gone back and forth between the CSA and the USA. Most people there hated Yankees, but a fair-sized minority didn't. Even some of the ones who hated Yankees understood they didn't come equipped with horns and tails.

Here in central Tennessee, none of the locals seemed to have got the news. They reacted to soldiers in green-gray as if to demons from hell. Some of them ran, while the rest tried to fight back. Civilians weren't supposed to fight back. If anybody'd told that to the Confederates, it didn't sink in.

'What are we going to do, Sarge?' the private asked.

'I know what I want to do,' Chester answered. 'I want to take hostages. And if the bastard who did that to Don doesn't turn himself in, I want to shoot the son of a bitch.'

'Yeah!' the private said savagely.

'I can't do it on my own,' Chester said. 'My ass'd be in a sling if I tried it. But I bet Captain Rhodes can.'

Hubert Rhodes was newly in command of the company,

which had had two COs wounded on back-to-back days before he arrived. Unless he was unlucky, Martin didn't think he'd be easy to kill. He was tough and skinny, with a thin, dark mustache and gray eyes that seemed to see everywhere at once. He didn't mind having a noncom head up a platoon, which gave him another good mark in Chester's book.

When Chester found him, he was field-stripping and cleaning a captured Confederate automatic rifle. He carried it himself, in lieu of the usual officer's .45. He put himself where the enemy could shoot at him, and he wanted to be able to answer with as much firepower as he could.

He looked up before Chester got very close. You couldn't get close to him without his knowing it. 'What can I do for you, Sergeant?' he asked. By the way he talked, he came from somewhere in the Midwest.

'Damn Confederate bushwhackers just murdered one of my men, sir,' Martin replied. 'Murdered him and did nasty things to the body after he was dead. I hope after, anyway.'

Rhodes' mouth was never wide and giving. It tightened more than usual now. 'What do you want to do about it?' he asked. 'What do you want *me* to do about it?'

'Take hostages, sir,' Chester said. 'We may not make 'em stop this shit, but we can make it expensive for 'em.'

Without looking at the weapon he was working on, Rhodes reassembled it. His hands didn't need his eyes' help to know what they were doing. He got up and lit a cigarette: also Confederate plunder. 'Sounds good. Let's do it,' he said. 'You think ten's enough, or do you want twenty?'

'Twenty,' Martin said. 'This isn't the first man we lost like that. If Featherston's soldiers shoot us, it's one thing. We shoot them, too. But these cocksuckers . . . They think nobody can touch 'em because they're in civilian clothes.'

'We'll do it,' Captain Rhodes said. 'Your men up for firing-squad duty if it comes to that? Chances are it will, you know.'

'Yes, sir,' Chester said without the slightest hesitation. 'If it's a Confederate, they'll shoot it.'

'Old men? Boys too young to shave? Maybe even women?' Rhodes persisted. 'Won't be a lot of men of military age in this Woodbury place. The ones who did live there, the war's already sucked 'em into uniform.'

'Any Confederate hostages we take, they'll shoot,' Chester Martin said confidently. 'They know damn well the Confederates'd shoot them if they got the chance.'

'Then let's round up some soldiers, and let's round up some hostages,' Rhodes said.

Rounding up soldiers was the easiest thing in the world. By then, the whole company had heard about what happened to their comrade. Had Captain Rhodes given the order, they wouldn't just have taken hostages in Woodbury, Tennessee. They would have wiped the place off the face of the earth.

Woodbury might have held five hundred people before the war started – fewer now, of course. The stores in the center of town were old and weathered; the courthouse – it was a county seat – so shiny and new, it had probably gone up in Jake Featherston's administration. Slopes north of the courthouse square were given over to crops; those to the south held houses.

Soldiers formed a perimeter around the houses. Then they went through them and seized twenty men, all under eighteen or over fifty except for one who'd lost his right arm, probably in the last war. They also killed one old man who fired a shotgun at the U.S. soldiers heading up his walk. He must not have taken careful aim: he winged one man in green-gray, but most of the blast went over the soldiers' heads.

Once the hostages were taken, Captain Rhodes assembled the rest of the townsfolk in the square. They stared at him with sullen hatred only slightly tempered by the snouts of the machine guns staring at them from sandbagged revetments.

'We had a soldier murdered by bushwhackers,' Rhodes told the locals. 'That kind of cowardice runs dead against the laws of war, and we don't aim to put up with it. We've taken hostages. If the killer doesn't come forward inside of twenty-four hours, we will execute them.'

'I did it.' A man with a white mustache stepped forward. 'You can shoot me if you've got to shoot somebody.'

'What did you do to the body after it was dead?' Chester asked.

The man blinked. 'I smoked a cigarette over it, by God. Then I went home.'

'You're a liar. You're brave, but you're a liar,' Chester said. 'Get back where you belong.' Crestfallen, the man went back into the crowd.

'Anybody else?' Captain Rhodes asked. No one said a word. He looked at his watch. 'All right. The clock is ticking.'

One of the hostages started to blubber. 'You got no business doing this to me,' he said. 'No business, you hear? I never done nothin' to nobody.'

'Too goddamn bad,' said a man in Chester's platoon. 'You wasted a hell of a chance, then, didn't you?'

'This won't bring your soldier back,' another hostage said.

'That's true,' Chester said. 'But maybe it'll make somebody else with a squirrel gun and not a hell of a lot of sense think twice. And even if it doesn't, it pays you people back.'

'An eye for an eye and a tooth for a tooth,' Captain Rhodes agreed. 'Except we're taking a whole mouthful of teeth.'

Confederate artillery came in that evening. Maybe someone managed to slip out of Woodbury and let the enemy soldiers know what was going on. But the shells mostly fell short – the front kept moving south. Chester wasn't sorry not to be right up on the firing line for a while. He slept in his foxhole with his Springfield beside him. If anybody tried to give him trouble, he aimed to give it first.

But he slept till sunup, and woke with nothing worse than a stiff back. He didn't remember being so tight and sore the last time around. Of course, that was more than half a lifetime ago now. He'd been a young man then. He scratched his belly, which was larger these days. No, he wasn't a young man any more.

'Anybody come forward?' he asked, opening a ration can.

'Get serious, Sarge,' answered one of the soldiers who was already eating. 'Those fuckers are brave enough to shoot somebody who isn't looking, but they won't put their own necks on the line when it counts.'

'That one geezer who tried to volunteer had balls,' Chester said.

'Sure. But the point is, he didn't really do anything,' the soldier replied. 'The fellow who did sneak around, he's still sneaking.'

'He must be pretty sneaky, too,' Martin said. 'If the people with kin who got taken hostage knew who he was, you have to figure somebody'd rat on him to save a husband or a son or a brother.'

The soldier only shrugged. 'Hasn't happened – that's all I can tell you.'

'Well, they've got . . . what, another couple of hours?'

Chester said. The soldier nodded. Chester shrugged. 'We'll see what happens then, that's all.'

What happened then was what he'd expected: U.S. soldiers paraded the hostages out to the town square. Some soldiers had set a post in the ground in front of the courthouse. Captain Rhodes ordered the townsfolk of Woodbury out to watch the executions. 'This is what you get when civilians try to fight in a war,' he said. 'You'd better remember it.' He gestured to Chester Martin. 'Will you do the honors?'

'Yes, sir. Don was in my platoon.' Chester waited till the soldiers had tied the first hostage to the pole. Then he gestured to the men in the firing squad. 'Ready!' They brought up their Springfields. 'Aim!' The riflemen drew a bead on the white paper pinned over the hostage's heart. 'Fire!'

A dozen rifles barked as one. The hostage slumped against his bonds. Blood poured from his wounds. He writhed, but not for long. In the crowd, a couple of women screamed. Another one fainted. So did a man.

U.S. soldiers cut the dead hostage down and marched another one, a young one, over to take his place. The youth's shout of 'Freedom!' cut off abruptly when the men from the firing squad pulled their triggers. More screams rang from the crowd. A girl about his age tried to charge the soldiers. Not too roughly, they kept her from hurting them or herself, then shoved her back to her relatives. The locals held on to her to make sure she didn't try again.

Most of the hostages died as well as men could. Four or five wept and begged. It did them no good. Chester called, 'Ready! . . . Aim! . . . Fire!' over and over again. Finally, the men in green-gray cut down the last bloody body.

'Bury your dead,' Captain Rhodes told the townsfolk. 'And remember, chances are whoever made us do this is still right here with the rest of you. Some of you may even have a pretty good notion who he is. But he kept quiet, and you kept quiet, and this is what you get. You leave us alone, we won't harm you. If you break the laws of war, you'll pay. You have paid.'

The courthouse square stank of cordite and blood and shit. It stank of fear, too; Chester had smelled that smell too many times to have any doubts about what it was. For once, he didn't smell his own fear.

He made sure he patted each man from the firing squad on the back. 'You did good,' he told them. 'That wasn't easy, doing what you guys did. I'm proud of you.'

'Those fuckers had it coming,' said one of the men in green-gray. Several other soldiers nodded.

But another man said, 'You're right, Sarge – it wasn't easy. They were just . . . people. They didn't hurt anybody. I did this once, but I don't think I ever want to do it again.'

'All right, Lewis. You won't, then,' Martin promised. 'Go off and smoke a cigarette. If you've got any booze, take a knock. I'll look the other way. You earned it.'

'I don't, Sarge,' Lewis said mournfully.

'Don't worry about it, Frankie,' another soldier said. 'I got a pretty good idea where you can get your hands on some.'

Chester turned his back so they wouldn't see him smile. They were kids doing a man's job. *What about me?* he wondered. *I'm no kid any more.* He was trying to do a man's job, too, and it wasn't any easier for him than it was for them.

A rifle on his shoulder, Jonathan Moss trudged along through the muggy hell that was summertime in Georgia. He turned to Nick Cantarella and remarked, 'Up at 25,000 feet, where I'm supposed to be fighting, it's cold enough for me to need fur and leather. Even up above this, it's still that cold.'

'Yeah, well, that's how the ball crumbles,' the infantry officer answered. 'That's the way the cookie bounces.'

Spartacus looked from one escaped U.S. POW to the other. 'You damnyankee ofays, you fuckin' crazy, you know dat?' the guerrilla leader said.

'Thanks,' Moss said, which wasn't likely to convince Spartacus he was wrong. Cantarella chuckled. A couple of the blacks who were close enough to listen to the byplay tapped index fingers against their temples or spun them by their ears to show whom they agreed with.

The guerrillas held the countryside. It did them less good than Moss wished it would. With so many big farms growing one big crop – cotton or peanuts or tobacco – and with so many Negroes taken off the countryside after agriculture was forcibly mechanized, the rebels had a devil of a time feeding themselves. Some of their raids on towns came from no better reason than the need to steal enough food to keep from starving.

Towns were going hungry, too. Trains had cars that mounted machine guns and cannon. Trucks traveled in convoys with machine-gun-toting command cars. Guerrilla bands shot at them and planted explosives under roads and along railroad tracks anyway. Spartacus' machine-gun-carrying pickup had done some nasty work driving along-side roads and shooting up trucks that stuck to them.

'What are we going to do next?' Moss asked Spartacus. Back in the USA, he wouldn't have imagined ever taking orders from a black man. But Spartacus unquestionably led this band. A word from him to his followers and both Moss and Cantarella would die the next instant.

But all he said was, 'Don' know fo' sho'. Wish to Jesus I did. Best thing I kin think of is to keep on movin' east.

Foraging do seem better over dat way.' He had a Tredegar slung over one shoulder – and a ham slung over the other.

'Not so many Mexicans over that way, neither,' Nick Cantarella said. Moss could follow Cantarella when he spoke. He could follow Spartacus when he spoke, too. Trying to follow one of them on the heels of the other sometimes made him feel he was shifting mental gears too fast for comfort.

'Not yet,' Spartacus said. 'Dey hear we's operatin' in them parts, though, dey git over there pretty damn quick.'

'Maybe,' Moss said. 'But maybe not, too. They aren't what you'd call eager to mix it up with us.'

'Not their fight,' Cantarella said. 'I was them, *I* wouldn't want anything to do with a bunch of crazy-ass smokes.'

'Ofays hereabouts make them greasers fight,' Spartacus said. 'Make 'em pretend to fight, anyways. How good they aim, how hard they push when they comes after us . . . Mebbe a different story.'

'Has been so far,' Moss said. Francisco José's soldiers showed no more enthusiasm about being in Georgia than Moss would have shown in the Yucatan. And if peasants in the Yucatan tried to kill him when he came after them, he wouldn't go after them very hard.

'Big worry is, they're liable to find an officer with a wild hair up his ass,' Cantarella said. 'They get a guy who makes his troops more afraid of him than they are of us, they can give us trouble.'

Before Moss or Spartacus could answer, the guerrillas' point man waved. Everybody stopped. They were coming out of pine woods into more open, more cultivated country. Or maybe they weren't coming out. 'What's up?' Spartacus asked in a penetrating whisper.

'Somethin' don't look right up ahead,' answered the point man, a small, scrawny, very black fellow named Apuleius.

'Don't look right how?' Spartacus asked. 'What you mean?'

Apuleius shrugged. 'Dunno. Too quiet-like, maybe.'

'Reckon somebody's layin' for us out there?' Spartacus asked. The point man shrugged again. Spartacus frowned. 'Can't go back or stay here fo' good,' he said. Nobody argued with him; that was self-evidently true. His frown got deeper. 'We gonna have to smoke 'em out, then. I'll go out, see what they do.'

An Army officer would have sent a private, or several privates, into the open to do the same job. Spartacus led by force of personality, not force of military law. He had to show the men who followed him that he was worth following. That meant exposing himself to danger instead of them.

Out of the woods he sauntered. He left his Tredegar and the ham behind; he might have been a happy-go-lucky Negro without a care in the world. He might have been . . . if Jake Featherston and the Freedom Party hadn't made Negroes without a care in the world extinct.

Along with the rest of the band, Moss and Cantarella watched from the woods. Moss knew more than a little relief that Spartacus hadn't told the two white men to scout what was up ahead. If Mexican soldiers lurked in the fields, their color might have done the trick. But their accents would have betrayed them to Confederates as soon as they opened their mouths.

For a moment, Moss thought Apuleius was flabbling about nothing. Spartacus strolled along, and nobody bothered him. Then a shout rang out, seemingly from nowhere. Like a chipmunk popping out of its hole, a gray-haired Confederate in a gray uniform stood up in what looked like a plain old field of peanuts. He pointed a rifle at Spartacus.

Three other white men appeared and went over to the

Negro. One of them held out his hand. Spartacus produced papers. They were more or less genuine; the Negro whose picture was on them even looked something like the guerrilla leader. Spartacus pointed east down the road toward Perry, the closest town.

The whites put their heads together. After a minute or two, they waved for him to pass on. He sketched a salute and walked off in the direction toward which he'd pointed.

Back in the woods, the men he led scratched their heads. 'What you reckon we should oughta do now?' one of them asked Nick Cantarella. He wasn't Spartacus' second-in-command in any formal sense. But the Negroes recognized that he had a professional's sense of tactics.

'Now we know where they're at,' Cantarella said, and the black man nodded. The U.S. officer went on, 'We could set up the machine gun over there, say' – he pointed – 'and attack from a different angle while they're trying to take it out.'

'Could work,' the Negro agreed.

'Yeah.' Cantarella nodded. 'But it'd make a lot of noise, and probably draw everybody and his goddamn dog over this way. That ain't good news. Other thing that occurs to me is, we could just sit on our asses here till dark and try and get past this position then. Spartacus'll be waiting up the road for us somewhere – you can count on that.'

After talking it over in low voices, the guerrillas decided to wait it out. Moss thought that was a good idea. 'We can't send for reinforcements if things go sour,' he said. 'There's a saying – there are old pilots, and there are bold pilots, but there are no old, bold pilots.'

'Makes sense,' Apuleius said. As point man, he recognized the need for caution more than most of the others. If he got bold when he shouldn't, he'd end up killing himself, and probably a lot of his comrades, too.

They waited under the trees. Midges and the nasty little biting flies the Negroes called no-see-'ems buzzed around. Eventually, the sun sank. As darkness deepened, Cantarella peered east with a pair of field glasses some Mexican officer didn't need any more. 'Fuck me,' he said softly.

'Now what's wrong?' Jonathan Moss asked.

'They've got somebody cute in charge of them,' Cantarella answered. 'They aren't leaving. They're moving to new positions closer to the road so they can make sure nobody sneaks by. What I wouldn't give for a mortar right now.'

'Fight our way through?' Moss didn't like the idea, and he was sure his dislike showed in his voice.

'I don't want to,' Cantarella said. 'Even if we win, it'll cost us. And it'll draw more of these militia assholes and Mexican soldiers down on us just like shit draws flies.'

'You say the ofays is by the road?' Apuleius asked. Nick Cantarella nodded. 'Is all of 'em there?' the Negro persisted.

'I don't know for sure, 'cause I don't know how many of 'em were out there to begin with,' Cantarella said. 'But a good many of 'em moved. How come?'

'On account of mebbe I kin git us around 'em in the dark,' Apuleius replied. 'Wouldn't want to try in the daytime. They see us sure. But at night, without no moon . . . Got a fair chance, anyways.'

'Let's do it.' Cantarella wasn't a man to whom hesitation came naturally. 'We'll go in full combat array, ready to fight if we have to, but we'll sneak if we can.' Then he seemed to remember he wasn't a U.S. Army captain any more, and couldn't just give orders. He had much less authority here than Spartacus did. 'Is that all right with youse guys?' he asked the guerrillas.

Nobody said no. They got to their feet and shook themselves out into a line from which they could go into

action if they needed to. Everyone checked to make sure
he had a round chambered and his safety off. Then, as
quietly as they could, they left the corner of the pine
woods and sneaked left, following Apuleius one man at
a time.

The point man found or knew about a track through
the fields. A lot of the Negroes were barefoot. They moved
as silently as ghosts. Their dark skins also made them harder
to spot. Moss, shod and with what didn't feel like enough
dirt on his face and arms, felt conspicuous every time one
of his feet came down.

He waited for a shout from near the road, which didn't
seem far away at all. Worse, he waited for a volley from
the white men's rifles, thunder and the lightning of muzzle
flashes splitting the night. Those old-timers in gray couldn't
be so blind and deaf . . . could they?

Maybe they could. Moss spotted a couple of glowing
coals in the militiamen's positions. They were smoking, and
they weren't being careful about it. 'Jesus, if I was a fuckin'
sniper . . .' Cantarella whispered.

Moss didn't want to say a word, for fear his voice would
carry. But he nodded. The same thing had occurred to him.
The whites over there should know better. Careless
smoking in the trenches got plenty of soldiers killed in the
Great War.

No challenge rang out. Nobody fired. None of the guerrillas tripped over his own feet or dropped his weapon or
did any of the other simple, deadly things that were all too
easy to do. Apuleius led the line back toward the road. If
the militiamen had had a deep position . . . But there weren't
enough of them for that.

Just when Moss thought he was safe, when he could
breathe more than tiny sips of air, a human shape loomed
out of the darkness ahead. He almost fired from the hip.

Then he realized it was Spartacus. 'I was hopin' y'all didn't run off an' leave me,' the Negro said dryly.

'Not us. That other gal, she nothin' but a pretty face,' Apuleius answered. Laughing softly, the guerrillas tramped on through the night.

XII

Sergeant Armstrong Grimes looked at Winnipeg from the prairie due south of the city. As usual, smoke shrouded the view. Bombers the Confederates would have hacked out of the sky with ease were more than good enough to lower the boom on enemies who didn't have fighters or antiaircraft guns. That was as true in Canada as it had been in Utah.

How much good the endless bombing would do . . . 'It's gonna be craters like on the moon,' Armstrong said, pausing to light a cigarette.

Not far from him, Yossel Reisen was doing the same thing. He said something even worse: 'It's gonna be craters like Salt Lake City.'

'Fuck,' Armstrong muttered, not because Yossel was wrong but because he was right. Every pile of bricks in Salt Lake hid a rifleman or a machine gun. If it worked the same way here . . . If it worked the same way here, the regiment would take a hell of a lot of casualties.

A harsh chatter rang out in the distance. Armstrong and Yossel looked at each other in dismay. 'It's one of those goddamn machine-gun cunts,' Yossel said, and Armstrong nodded. They hadn't been in Canada long, but soldiers' language didn't need long to hit bottom. Machine-gun pickup went through machine-gun whore on the way down.

An antibarrel cannon boomed. The Canucks on the pickup truck went right on shooting back. Pickups were a lot faster than barrels. On flat ground, they were a lot more mobile, too. And they made much smaller targets. The antibarrel cannon fired again – and missed again.

'Put your spectacles on the next time, dears,' Armstrong said in a disgusted falsetto. Yossel snickered.

The antibarrel cannon boomed one more time. A couple of seconds later, there was a different boom, and a fireball to go with it. 'They listened to you!' Yossel exclaimed.

'Yeah, well, that makes once,' Armstrong said.

An officer blew a whistle. Soldiers trotted forward. Armstrong and Yossel veered apart from each other. They both dodged like broken-field runners, and bent as low as they could. They didn't want to make themselves easy to shoot.

Every time Armstrong saw a motorcar, he shied away from it. The Canadians used auto bombs, as the Mormons had. They'd added a new wrinkle, too: wireless-controlled auto bombs. They loaded a motorcar with explosives, put it where they pleased, and blew it up from a mile away – from farther than that, for all Armstrong knew – at the touch of a button when they saw enough U.S. soldiers near it to make the detonation worthwhile.

Sooner or later, explosives men – most of them borrowed from bomber squadrons – would go over the motorcars one by one to defang the machines that did carry explosives. That was dangerous, thankless work. The Canadians had booby-trapped some of their auto bombs to go off when somebody tried to pull their teeth.

'One thing,' Armstrong said when he and Yossel happened to dodge together again. The fire from up ahead wasn't bad – he'd known plenty worse. The Canucks didn't have many defenders in the outermost suburbs of Winnipeg, anyhow.

'What's that?' Yossel asked.

'If an auto bomb blows up while you're trying to defuse it, you'll never know what hit you,' Armstrong said.

A bullet kicked up dirt between the two men. They both flinched. 'Yeah, you got something there,' Yossel said. Each of them had seen – and listened to – men die knowing exactly what had hit them, and in torment till death released them. Armstrong had never killed a man to put him out of his misery, but he knew people who had. He knew he would, if he ever found himself in a spot like that. He hoped somebody would do it for him, if he ever found himself in a spot like *that*.

Which was not the sort of thing he wanted to be thinking when he got shot.

One second, he was loping along, happy as a clam (how happy were clams, anyway?). The next, his left leg went out from under him, and he fell on his face in the dirt. He stared in stupid wonder at the hole in his trouser leg, and at the spreading red stain around it.

'Oh, for Christ's sake,' he said, more in annoyance than anything else. *I stay lucky for two years, and then this shit happens,* he thought.

Then the pain reached his brain, and he howled like a wolf and clutched at himself. He knew what had hit him, all right, and wished to God he didn't. He scrabbled for the pouch that held his wound dressing, the sulfa powder he was supposed to dust on the wound before he used the bandage, and the morphine syrette that might build a wall between him and the fire in his leg.

'Sergeant's down!' somebody yelled.

'Corpsman!' Two or three soldiers shouted the same thing.

Armstrong detached the bayonet from the muzzle of his Springfield and used it to cut away his trouser leg so he could give himself first aid. He felt sick and woozy. He also bit his lip against the pain. The wound hadn't hurt for the first few seconds after he got it, but it sure as hell did now.

My old man got hit just about like this, he thought as he sprinkled sulfa powder into the hole in his calf. He'd never had a whole lot in common with his father. This wasn't the way he wanted to start. Merle Grimes still used a cane to take some of the weight off his bad leg. Armstrong hoped that wouldn't happen to him.

He slapped on the bandage. Then he yanked the top off the syrette, stuck himself, and pushed down on the plunger. He felt more squeamish about that than he had about the bandage, or even the wound. He was hurting himself on purpose. He knew he would feel better soon, but knowing didn't make a whole lot of difference.

Once he'd done what he could for himself, he looked around for cover. He didn't see anything close by. He pulled his entrenching tool off his belt and started digging. It wouldn't be much of a hole, no doubt, but anything was better than nothing. He piled the dirt from the scrape in front of him. Enough of it might stop a bullet, or at least slow one down.

He'd just got up a halfway decent dirt rampart when medics crouched beside him. 'Here you go, Sergeant,' one of them said. 'Can you slide onto the stretcher?'

'Sure.' Armstrong was amazed at how chipper he sounded. He didn't care about anything. The morphine had taken hold while he was digging. He didn't slide so much as roll onto the stretcher.

Another medic looked at his wound. The man with the Red Cross armbands and smock and helmet markings poked at it, too, which hurt in spite of the shot. 'He did a pretty good job patching himself up,' he reported. 'I don't think the bones are broken. Looks like a hometowner to me.' He gave Armstrong an injection, too, before the wounded man could tell him not to bother.

'Where you from, Sergeant?' asked one of the corpsmen at Armstrong's head.

'Uh, Washington. D.C., I mean,' Armstrong answered vaguely. That second shot was kicking like a mule. He felt as if he were floating away from himself.

The medic didn't seem to see anything out of the ordinary in the way he talked. The man laughed. 'If that's your home town, you're safer staying away. Damn Confederates have worked it over pretty good, I hear.'

'Folks are all right, as far as I know,' Armstrong said. Then the corpsmen picked up the stretcher and carried it away. Armstrong had felt as if he were floating before. Now he floated and bounced.

Red Cross flags flying around the aid station and Red Crosses painted on the tents themselves told the Canucks not to shoot this way – or gave them targets, depending. One of the medics let out a yell: 'Doc! Hey, Doc! We got a casualty!'

That's what I am, all right. With two shots of morphine in him, the idea didn't bother Armstrong a bit. 'Bring him in!' somebody yelled from the other side of the canvas. In Armstrong went. He smelled ether and other chemicals he couldn't name – and blood, enough blood for a butcher's shop. 'Where are you hit, soldier?' a bespectacled man asked from behind a surgical mask.

'Leg,' Armstrong answered.

The corpsmen slid him off the stretcher and onto the operating table. The doctor peeled off the bandage he'd put on and studied the wound. 'You're lucky,' he said after perhaps half a minute.

'My ass.' Even doped to the gills, Armstrong knew bull-shit when he heard it. 'If I was lucky, the fucker would've missed me.'

'He's got you there, Doc,' one of the medics said, laughing.

'Oh, shut up, Rocky,' the surgeon replied without rancor. He turned back to Armstrong. 'I'm going to give you a shot of novocaine to numb you up. Then I'll clean that out. It should heal fine. You may not be as lucky as you like, but you'll do all right.'

He wasn't especially gentle, and he didn't wait for the novocaine to take full effect before he started working with a probe and forceps and a scalpel. Armstrong yipped a couple of times. Then he did more than yip. 'Christ on a crutch, Doc, take it easy!' he said.

'Sorry about that.' The surgeon didn't sound very sorry. He didn't take it easy, but went on, 'No offense, but I want to get you taken care of in a hurry so I can deal with a bad wound if one comes in.'

'Thanks a lot,' Armstrong said. 'Easy for you to talk like that – it ain't your goddamn leg.'

'Well, no,' the medico said. 'But it's not an amputation, either, or a sucking chest, or a belly wound, or a bullet in the head. You'll be back on duty in six weeks or so. In the meantime, you get to take it easy while you heal. Could be worse.' As he spoke, he did some more snipping. Armstrong yelped again.

After what seemed like forever and was probably about ten minutes, the surgeon gave him a shot. 'What's that?' Armstrong asked suspiciously.

'Tetanus – lockjaw,' the man answered. He eyed Armstrong over his mask. 'Locking your jaws might be an improvement, all things considered.'

'Funny, Doc. Har-de-har-har. I'm laughing my ass off, you know what I mean?'

'Get him out of here,' the surgeon told the corpsmen. 'Some other poor bastard'll come along pretty damn quick.'

They carried Armstrong over to a tent next to the aid station and put him on a cot. 'Ambulance'll be along in a while,' one of them said.

'Happy day,' he answered. They were shaking their heads when they left the tent. He couldn't have cared less.

The tent held a dozen cots. Counting his, five of them were occupied. None of the other wounded men was in any shape to talk. One of them had bloody bandages around his head. One had lost an arm. Two had torso wounds. Three, including the man who'd been shot in the head, were deeply unconscious. The other one moaned from time to time, but didn't come out with any real words.

Looking at them, listening to them, Armstrong reluctantly decided the smartass surgeon had a point. If he had to get wounded, he could have done a lot worse than catching a hometowner. Despite the morphine and novocaine, his leg barked again. He muttered under his breath. Then he brightened – a little, anyhow. His old man had always thought he wasn't quite good enough, that he never did enough. If his father tried saying that now, Armstrong promised himself he'd knock his goddamn block off.

Lulu looked into Jake Featherston's office. 'General Forrest is here to see you, Mr. President,' she said.

'Send him in, then,' Jake growled. His secretary nodded and ducked out to bring back the chief of the Confederate General Staff.

Nathan Bedford Forrest III looked pale and pasty: the look of a man who spent most of his time underground and didn't see the sun very often. Featherston looked the same way, but he hardly noticed it – he saw himself all the time. Forrest nodded to him. 'Mr. President,' he said.

'Hello, General.' Jake leaned forward across the desk. 'Are we ready to hit back at those damnyankee sons of bitches?'

'General Patton thinks so, sir, and he's the man on the spot,' Forrest answered.

'He's the man on the spot, all right,' Jake Featherston said. His eyes went to the map on the wall of his office. The Confederates had been gathering men and matériel east of the Appalachians for weeks, aiming to strike at the U.S. flank. If everything went the way it was supposed to, they could cut off the Yankees in Tennessee and bundle the ones in Kentucky back to the Ohio. That would put the war on even terms again. But if things didn't go the way he wanted them to . . . 'We can't afford to fuck this up.'

'Yes, sir,' Nathan Bedford Forrest III said stolidly.

Jake swore under his breath. He'd never thought it would come to this when he ordered his armies into motion against the USA. The Yankees were the ones who were supposed to be fighting for their lives, not his side.

He swore again, on a different note, a moment later. He'd already survived two assassination tries. If the war kept going down the toilet, he knew damn well he'd have to worry about another one. Even a Vice President as pliable as Don Partridge might start getting ideas. So might Clarence Potter – as if he didn't have them already. But he might decide to do something about them, the cold-blooded son of a bitch. Nathan Bedford Forrest III might get some of his own, too.

'Is security tight?' Jake asked.

'Tight as we know how to make it,' Forrest answered.

'It better be. It better be tight as a fifty-dollar whore's twat,' Jake said, and the chief of the General Staff let out a startled laugh. Featherston went on, 'If the damnyankees figure out what we're up to before we get rolling, they can give us all kinds of grief, right?'

'You'd better believe it, sir. If they've got a gopher

planted somewhere between here and General Patton's headquarters, that's a problem,' Forrest replied. 'And if he can pass on whatever he knows, I mean.'

'Yeah, yeah,' Jake said impatiently. 'What are the odds?'

'Mr. President, I just don't know.' Nathan Bedford Forrest III spread his hands. 'We still have gophers in the USA and with U.S. forces. The Yankees are bound to be doing the same thing to us. Too goddamn hard for one side to root out all the spies from the other. We just sound too much alike. Whether they've got somebody in the right place, whether the son of a bitch can pass on what he picks up, if he picks up anything . . . We'll have to find out. I hope to God we don't find out the hard way, but I can't be sure.'

Most men in Forrest's place would have told Jake Featherston what they thought he wanted to hear: that everything was fine, that of course the United States had no chance of finding out what was going on. Reluctantly, Featherston respected the younger man's honesty. If you promised the moon and couldn't deliver, wasn't that worse than not promising in the first place?

'All right. We'll see what happens.' Jake tried telling himself what he wanted to hear: 'Maybe the Yankees won't believe we'd try coming through the mountains even if some stinking spy tells them we will.'

'Maybe.' But General Forrest sounded dubious. 'Remember, sir, that's General Morrell in charge of their spearhead. He won't be easy to fool. He's the kind who'd take armor through the mountains himself, so he's too likely to think we'd try it, too.'

'I suppose.' Featherston forced himself to nod. 'No, you're bound to be right, dammit. I sure wish we'd punched his ticket for good. Some lousy busybody of a sergeant threw him on his back and toted him out of the line of fire, I hear.'

Nathan Bedford Forrest III didn't say anything. The expression on his face was hard for Jake to fathom – and then, all of a sudden, it wasn't. Sure as hell, Forrest was thinking, *Takes one to know one.* And sure as hell, he was right. Jake damn well had been a lousy busybody of a sergeant. Clarence Potter remembered that, even if Forrest couldn't.

'Anything else?' Jake asked.

'No, Mr. President. That's what's going on now.'

'We'll go from there, then. Tell Patton to give 'em hell. Tell him I said so.'

'I will, sir – when I'm sure the damnyankees can't hear me do it.' Forrest got to his feet, saluted, and left the office.

Once Jake was sure the general was on his way back to the War Department, he stuck his head out and asked, 'Who's next, Lulu?'

'The Attorney General is waiting to see you, Mr. President.'

'Well, you know you can send him in,' Featherston said.

Ferdinand Koenig lumbered into the office a moment later. Unlike Forrest, he was older than Jake, and also much heavier than the President, who retained a whipcord leanness. 'Good morning,' Koenig rumbled.

'I hope so,' Jake said. 'You couldn't prove it by me, though.' He pointed at the map. The U.S. thrust aimed straight at Chattanooga. It was getting too close, too.

'I expect you'll do something about that before too long.' Ferd Koenig didn't know the details. He didn't need or want to know them, either.

'I expect I will, too.' Jake said no more than he had to. The less you told people, the less they could blab. Ferd wasn't the kind of guy who ran his mouth; Featherston wouldn't have put up with him for a second if he were. But even an inadvertent slip might hurt badly here, so why take chances? The President said, 'What's on your mind today?'

'About what you'd expect: the mess in Texas.'

Jake Featherston grunted. It *was* a mess, no two ways about it. 'When we built Camp Determination way the hell out there at the ass end of nowhere, we never reckoned the damnyankees would give us so much trouble about it.'

'*That's* the truth,' Koenig said unhappily.

'Only goes to show the bastards really are a bunch of nigger-lovers,' Jake said. 'How far from the camp are they?' He already knew, but didn't feel like admitting it.

'About forty miles now. They're throwing everything they've got out there into the attack,' the Attorney General said. 'They've got more out there than we do, too. We need reinforcements, Mr. President. We need 'em bad.'

'I can't give you more Army men, dammit.' Jake pointed again to the map showing the ominous Yankee bulge. 'Everything we can grab, we're using against that.' He sighed. Talking about Texas meant talking about Kentucky and Tennessee after all. He might have known it would. Things fit together; however much you wished you could, you couldn't look at any one part of the war in isolation.

'Can I have more Freedom Party Guards, then?' Koenig asked. 'I've got to do something, Jake, or the damnyan-kees'll take the camp away from us. We can't afford to let that happen – you know we can't. It screws up the whole population-reduction program, and it hands the USA a propaganda victory like you wouldn't believe.'

He wasn't wrong. Sometimes, though, propaganda defeats had to take a back seat when you were nose-to-nose with real military defeat. Jake didn't want anything to get in the way of cleansing the Confederacy of Negroes, but he didn't want to lose the war, either. He felt more harried than he'd ever dreamt he could. Never a man who compromised easily, he knew he had to now.

'Yeah, you can raise some more Guards units,' he said. 'We aren't short of weapons and we aren't short of uniforms, by God. But I'll tell you something else, too – we better set up a new camp some place where the damnyankees sure as hell can't get at it. When it's ready to roll, just move the guard staff and start shipping in niggers.'

'What about the ones who're already in Camp Determination?' Koenig asked.

'Well, what about 'em?' Jake said. Ferd was a sharp guy, but sometimes even sharp guys missed seeing the obvious.

'Oh.' The Attorney General turned a dull red. To hide his embarrassment, he made a small production of lighting up a Habana. After a couple of puffs, he went on, 'Yeah, that'll take care of itself, won't it? Jeff Pinkard won't be happy about moving, though. Camp Determination's his baby.'

'Tough titty,' Featherston said. 'Where it's at, his baby's getting to be more trouble than it's worth. If there's no camp in west Texas, the United States don't have any reason for pushing farther in. Except for Determination, what's there?'

'Lubbock,' Koenig said. 'Amarillo.'

'Big fucking deal.' Jake was massively unimpressed. 'The United States are welcome to both of 'em. They want to set up their phony state of Houston again, they're welcome to do that, too. Far as I can see, they got more grief from it last time around than anything else.'

'You've got a good way of looking at things,' Koenig said.

'Well, I hope so. Right now, what we've got to do is take care of the shit that won't wait.' Featherston aimed a forefinger at the map one more time. 'After we've dealt with that, then we go on with the rest of it.' He made everything sound simple and obvious and easy. He'd always had that knack.

Usually, making things sound easy was good enough. In a fight for your life, though . . . Ferd Koenig could see that, too. 'We need to hit the Yankees hard,' he said.

'Bet your sweet ass, Ferd.' Jake was thinking of Henderson V. FitzBelmont, about whom, he devoutly hoped, the Attorney General knew nothing or next to it. 'We will, too. You better believe it.'

'I've believed you for twenty-five years now,' Koenig said. 'I'm not about to quit.'

'Good.' Jake meant it from the bottom of his heart. 'You've believed in me longer than anybody these days.' That was true. Of people he still knew, Clarence Potter had met him before Ferd did. But Potter hadn't always followed him. He wasn't sure if Potter ever really followed him. Potter was loyal to the country, not to the Freedom Party or to Jake Featherston himself.

'We've come a long way, you and me,' Ferd said. 'We've brought the country a long way, too. We're not nigger-free, but we're getting there.'

'Damn straight,' Jake said. 'We'll get where we're going, by God. Even if the damnyankees come up Shockoe Hill and we have to fire at 'em over open sights, we won't ever quit. And as long as we don't quit, they can't lick us.'

'I sure hope not,' Koenig said.

'Don't you worry about a thing. You don't see any U.S. soldiers in Richmond, do you?' Featherston waited till his old warhorse shook his head, then went on, 'And you won't, either. Not ever. We're going to win this son of a bitch. Not just get a draw so we can start over twenty years from now. We're going to win.'

'Sounds good to me,' the Attorney General said.

It also sounded good to Jake Featherston. He hated relying on a goddamn professor, but knew too well he was.

Irving Morrell dismounted from his command barrel a few miles north of Delphi, Tennessee. His force wasn't within artillery range of Chattanooga, not yet, but U.S. guns weren't far from being able to reach the linchpin of the first part of the campaign. The United States had come farther and faster than he'd dreamt they could when the summer's fighting started. To his mind, that said only one thing: the Confederates had thrown everything they could into their opening offensives, and it hadn't been enough. They didn't have enough left to fight a long war.

Which didn't mean he wasn't worried about what they did have. The bright young captain whose command car rolled to a stop near Morrell's barrel wore a uniform with no arm-of-service colors or badges. If a cryptographer got captured, he didn't want the enemy knowing what he was.

He also didn't want to spread around what he knew. Morrell's barrel carried every kind of wireless set under the sun; that was what made it what it was. But if the United States were deciphering C.S. codes, you had to assume the Confederates were doing the same thing to U.S. messages. What the enemy didn't overhear, he couldn't very well use against you.

'Hello, Captain Shaynbloom,' Morrell said. 'What have you got for me today?'

Sol Shaynbloom was thin and pale, with a bent blade of a nose and thick glasses. He looked too much like someone who would go into cryptography to seem quite real, but he was. He handed Morrell a manila folder. 'Latest decrypts, sir,' he said, 'and some aerial photos to back them up.'

'Let's see what we've got.' Morrell studied the decoded messages and the pictures. 'Well, well,' he said at last. 'They are getting frisky over there, aren't they?'

'Yes, sir,' Captain Shaynbloom said. 'More of a buildup on our flank than in front of us, as a matter of fact.'

Morrell had a map case on his hip. He pulled out a map and unfolded it. 'So – here and here and here, eh?' He pointed. 'That's probably what I'd do in their shoes, too. They'll try to cut us off and roll us back to the Ohio.'

'Can they?' the codebreaker asked.

'I hope not,' Morrell said mildly. But that wasn't what the other man wanted to hear. Smiling a little, Morrell went on, 'I think we're ready for them. If we are, your section will have an awful lot to do with it.'

Shaynbloom smiled. 'That's what we're here for, sir.' Then his smile disappeared. 'If we do smash them as they try to break through, I hope they don't realize how well we're able to read their codes.'

'No, that wouldn't be good,' Morrell agreed. 'But sometimes the cards aren't worth anything unless you put them on the table. This feels like one of those times to me.'

'All right, sir. I guess you're right,' Captain Shaynbloom said.

I'd better be, Morrell thought. *Being right in spots like this is what they pay me for.* He wasn't in it for the money, but the extra salary he earned with stars on his shoulder straps acknowledged the extra responsibility he held. And if he was wrong a couple of times, they wouldn't take the rank or the pay away from him. They would just put him in charge of the beach in Kansas or the mountains in Nebraska and try to forget they'd ever had anything to do with him.

Another command car pulled up alongside the first. 'What's this?' Morrell said. 'I thought they only gave one to a customer.' He made it sound like a joke, but his hand dropped to the butt of the .45 on his belt even so. The Confederates had already tried to assassinate him once. They might well be up for another go at him.

But he recognized the officer who got out. First Lieutenant Malcolm Williamson bore almost a family resemblance to Sol Shaynbloom. Both were skinny and pale and fair, and both looked more like graduate students than soldiers. Williamson also wore an unadorned uniform. Saluting both Shaynbloom and Morrell, he handed the latter an envelope. 'We just got this, sir.'

'Let's have a look.' As Morrell opened the envelope, he asked, 'Do you know what's in it? Can I talk about it in front of you?'

'Yes, sir, and in front of the captain,' Williamson answered. 'It's not that kind of thing – you'll see in a second.'

'Fair enough.' Nodding, Morrell unfolded the paper in the envelope and read the message someone – maybe Williamson – had scrawled on it. 'Well, well,' he said. 'So General Patton will be in charge of the Confederate thrust. I'm honored . . . I suppose.'

'I wondered if he would be,' Shaynbloom said. 'He's sort of fallen off the map the past few weeks.'

'He's back on it now,' Morrell said. 'It's a compliment to me, I guess, but I could do without it.' He'd heard from someone or other that Patton developed his slashing style by studying his own campaigns during the Great War. Maybe that was true, maybe it wasn't. If it was, it made for another compliment Morrell didn't really want. Patton was too good at what he did.

'We'll lick him, sir.' As a lieutenant, Williamson wasn't prone to the doubts that could cloud a general's mind. 'Who gives a damn how tough he is? We've got the horses to ride roughshod over him.' He didn't even mix his metaphors, a common failing for everyone from the President on down.

'Do we know their precise start time?' Morrell asked. 'If we do, we can disrupt them with spoiling bombardments ahead of time. The more we can do to throw their plan and their timing out of whack, the better off we'll be.'

Williamson and Shaynbloom looked at each other. They even wore the same U.S.-issue steel-framed spectacles, though Shaynbloom's lenses were noticeably stronger. As one man, they shook their heads. 'Haven't got it yet, sir,' they chorused, Shaynbloom adding, 'But it can't be long.'

'You're right about that,' Morrell said. 'They'll know they can't hide a concentration very long. It'll have to be soon. If you find out exactly when *soon* is, let me know as fast as you can. We'll counterpunch if we have to, but getting in the first lick is even better.'

'Yes, sir.' Their voices didn't sound alike; Williamson's was an octave deeper. They tore off almost identical salutes, returned to their command cars, and roared off to wherever they worked their code-breaking magic. Morrell didn't know where that was; what he didn't know, he couldn't spill if captured.

As things worked out, the Confederates announced their own attack. They chose early afternoon to open their bombardment, hoping to catch U.S. soldiers off guard. By the rumble from U.S. batteries, they didn't.

U.S. airplanes roared into the sky. Morrell couldn't see where they were taking off from; the fields lay farther behind the lines. But he knew they were up there, which was what counted. The Confederates wouldn't catch them on the ground, the way they'd caught so many fighters and bombers in Ohio. U.S. Y-ranging gear was pointed east, ready to warn the pilots to get airborne before enemy air attackers arrived. And these days, unlike the way things were in 1941, everybody took Y-ranging – and the Confederates – very seriously indeed.

Those fighters and bombers with the eagle in front of crossed swords didn't get airborne just to escape C.S. attacks, either. They were loaded for bear. The Confederates had to deploy through several gaps in the mountains before they could debouche. The harder they got bombed and strafed while still in column, the slower and clumsier their deployment would be. *The less they can bring to the dance,* Morrell thought, remembering how he met Agnes not long after the Great War.

She and their daughter, Mildred, were all right. He'd had a letter not long before. The war hadn't really touched Fort Leavenworth. Out beyond the Mississippi, fighting came in harsh spatters: one that seemed unending over the oil fields in Sequoyah, which each side torched whenever the other seemed about to retake them, and another in west Texas that had heated up lately. Looked at logically, there was no reason on God's green earth to fight over west Texas. Dark mutters said logic had little to do with it, that the Confederates were up to something really horrible out there, something that needed suppressing regardless of logic.

Having fought without much luck to hold the state of Houston in the USA before Al Smith's plebiscite, Morrell was ready to believe the worst of west Texas. He was also ready to believe the worst of Jake Featherston and all his Freedom Party pals. The only question in his mind was how bad the worst was out there.

He didn't even have time to worry about that, except when he got out of the command barrel to stand behind a tree or smoke a cigarette. He spent almost all of the next forty-eight hours in the turret, as a less mobile commander might have spent them in a map room in a headquarters somewhere far behind the line. He was wryly amused to find it worked out about the same either way. Now much of the front – most of the places where the Confederates were trying to break through – lay behind him.

A map room proved better than the turret for at least one reason: it had the space to put up the maps. He was constantly unfolding and refolding them and using cellophane tape to stick them here and there for a little while. Frenchy Bergeron finally lost patience with him. 'What happens if the Confederates attack us here, sir?' the gunner asked pointedly. 'How am I supposed to fight those fuckers off if I can't even load my piece?'

'If the fate of this army depends on this barrel and some other one can't do the job, we're in a hell of a lot more trouble than I think we are,' Morrell said mildly.

'Well, all right, sir,' Bergeron said. 'I can see that. But my own neck might depend on shooting that gun, even if the army doesn't.'

'I think we're good even so,' Morrell told him. 'With everything the Confederates are throwing at our left, I don't see how they can have much to use against our front here.'

The gunner grunted. Like almost everyone else in the two opposing armies, Bergeron fancied himself a strategist. He came closer to being right than a lot of other people, some of whom held significantly higher rank than his. And he listened to what Morrell didn't say as well as to what he did. 'They're hitting us from the one side, sir? Not from both sides at once?'

'That's right.' Morrell nodded. 'They don't have the men for that. And even if they did, they could never get them into place west of us. The mountains help screen their positions in the east, and the travel's easier to get there, too. What they're doing is about as good a counterattack as they can hope to put together.'

'But not good enough, right?' Frenchy Bergeron said confidently.

Morrell yawned. He'd been in the saddle for a devil of a long time. 'Don't quite know yet,' he said. 'I hope not, but I can't be sure yet.'

'What happens if they do break through?' the gunner asked.

'Well, I can give you the simple answer or the technical one,' Morrell said. 'Which would you rather?'

'Give me the technical one, sir.' Sure enough, Bergeron figured he knew enough to make sense of it.

He was right, too. 'The technical answer is, if that happens, we're screwed,' Morrell replied.

Bergeron started to laugh, then broke off when he saw Morrell wasn't even smiling. 'You're not kidding, are you, sir?' he said.

'Not me,' Morrell said. 'Not even a little bit. So the thing we want to make sure of is, we want to make sure they don't break through.'

Brigadier General Clarence Potter thought of himself as a cosmopolitan man. He'd gone to college at Yale, up in the USA. He'd traveled up and down the east coast of the CSA, and west as far as New Orleans. He thought he knew his own country well.

But he'd never been to Knoxville, Tennessee, before. He'd never been anywhere like Knoxville before. The Confederacy's interior had been a closed book to him. The longer he stayed in and around the town, the more he wanted to get back to Richmond and the War Department. Knoxville made daily U.S. air raids seem good by comparison.

He'd spent most of his time in Charleston and Richmond. Those were sophisticated places. Back before the Freedom Party seized power, they'd had substantial opposition groups. Chances were they still did, though the opposition had to stay underground these days if it wanted to go on existing.

Knoxville . . . By all appearances, Knoxville had never heard of, never dreamt of, opposing Jake Featherston. People here were shabby and tired-looking, the way they were in Richmond. The men came in three categories: the very, very young; the ancient; and the mutilated. An awful lot of women wore widow's weeds. But people in Knoxville greeted one another with, 'Freedom!' Potter hadn't heard them say it without sounding as if they meant it. Jake Featherston's portraits and posters were everywhere. Even with U.S. soldiers in Tennessee on the other side of the mountains, the locals remained convinced the Confederate States would win the war.

Without sharing their confidence, Potter envied it. He wouldn't have come to Knoxville himself if the CSA weren't in trouble. If pulling someone out of Intelligence and expecting him to command a brigade wasn't a mark of desperation, what was it?

He needed a while to realize that question might not be rhetorical. Jake Featherston could have had reasons of his own in assenting to Potter's transfer. The first that sprang to mind was the one most likely true: the President of the CSA might not shed a tear if his obstreperous officer stopped a bullet.

Who will rid me of this turbulent priest? Henry II shouted, and in short order Thomas à Becket was a dead man. Featherston was more polite: instead of simply ordering his own men to do Potter in or even hinting that he wanted him dead, he sent the man he mistrusted off to where danger was apt to lie thicker on the ground than it did in Richmond.

Remembering some of the U.S. air raids he'd been through, Potter wondered if that was really so. But his was not to reason why. His was to do or, that failing, to die. He didn't want to die and he wasn't sure he could do, which left him in an unpleasant limbo.

He was in limbo another way, too: nobody'd ordered his brigade forward yet. If everything was going according to plan, it would have been committed two days earlier. He didn't think the officers set over him were keeping the outfit in reserve because it had a green CO. A lot of brigades did these days. No, he feared the outfit hadn't got the call because things up at the front were going to hell.

Even though he came out of Intelligence, he couldn't get a handle on what the war west of the mountains looked like. Nobody wanted to say anything. That in itself was a bad omen. When things were going well, people – and the Freedom Party propaganda mill – shouted it from the housetops. When they weren't . . .

Good news had a thousand fathers. Bad news was an orphan. The orphanage in Knoxville got more crowded by the day. Potter began to wonder if his brigade ever would get sent to the front. If it didn't, why the devil *had* they called him out of Richmond? Had optimism run that far ahead of common sense? Maybe it had.

He was just about convinced he would go back to the capital without ever seeing real action when he got the order to move forward. That amused him about as much as anything ever did, and in the usual sardonic way. He had trucks. He had fuel. He'd made damn sure he did. The outfit was rolling inside of an hour. He might have left a few men behind in Knoxville, men who'd got leave and whom the military police hadn't scraped out of the bars and whorehouses. He would worry about and, if need be, punish them later. Better to get where he needed to go when he needed to get there with not quite so many men than to wait around for the rest and show up late.

But he showed up late anyhow, though he didn't intend to. Everything went fine till the brigade rolled past Harriman, about thirty-five miles west of Knoxville. Up till then, Highway 70 had been in pretty good shape. Occasional craters were patched up; Confederate engineers had repaired bombed bridges or set up makeshift spans to do duty for the ones the damnyankees had blown to smithereens.

After Harriman, it was a different story. The Yankees had hit the road hard enough and often enough to get ahead of the repair crews. Potter hadn't seen such devastation since the Great War . . . except in Richmond, after a bad air raid. But those raids disrupted civilian life. These delayed soldiers on the way to the front, a much more serious business – especially if you were one of those soldiers.

Going off the roads and into the fields alongside them helped, but only so much. For one thing, the fields were cratered, too. Even trucks with four-wheel drive weren't barrels; they didn't laugh off big holes in the ground. And the lead trucks chewed up the ground and made it worse for the ones that came behind.

The worse the bottlenecks got, the more worried Potter grew. 'We have to get rolling,' he said to whoever would listen to him, and scanned the western skies like a farmer fearing rain at harvest time. He feared something worse than rain. 'If the damnyankees hit us while we're stuck here . . .'

'Bite your tongue, sir,' advised the corporal at the wheel of his command car. 'You say that kind of stuff, you're liable to make it come true.'

To Clarence Potter, that was superstitious nonsense. He

didn't say so, though – what was the point? Fifteen minutes later, with the brigade still snarled, what both he and the corporal dreaded came true: the howl of airplane engines, rising swiftly to a scream.

He'd done what he could to get ready for air attack. He'd deployed the antiaircraft guns attached to the brigade and the heavy machine guns. He and his men weren't caught flatfooted when the U.S. raiders struck them. Things could have been worse. As it worked out, they were only bad. Bad proved grim enough.

The damnyankees didn't use Asskickers or their equivalents. They just mounted bomb racks under fighters, which turned their explosives loose from not much above treetop height. They hit the trucks on the road and those to either side of it. Fireballs blossomed. Chunks of blazing metal hurtled through the air. So did chunks of blazing flesh.

Like most, Potter's command car carried a pintle-mounted machine gun. He banged away at the enemy airplanes. He'd gone through the whole Great War without firing a weapon at U.S. forces. Now he could hit back. The shattering noise and the stream of hot brass spitting from the breech filled him with fierce, primitive joy. Whether he hurt the damnyankees any was a different question. The unsleeping rational part of his brain knew that, even as the animal inside him whooped and squeezed the triggers and played the stream of tracers like a hose.

A fighter slammed into the ground not far away. That fireball dwarfed the ones the trucks sent up. Splashes of burning gasoline caught running soldiers. They dropped and writhed and rolled, screaming their torment all but unheard.

After the fighters unloaded their bombs, they came back to strafe the stalled column. The Confederates had invented the tactic two years earlier. Potter could have done without the flattery of U.S. imitation. He got more chances to use his machine gun. And the fighters, armed with four machine guns and two cannon each, got more chances to turn their weapons on *him*.

They badly outgunned him. They were making better than 300 miles an hour, while he was a sitting duck. The wonder wasn't that they kept missing him. The wonder was that all their weaponry didn't chew him to red rags.

Bullets cracked past his head. When bullets cracked, they came too damn close. Others kicked up puffs of dust from the dirt a few feet to the left of the command car, and then, a moment later, from the dirt a few feet to its right. He went on firing. Hardly even knowing he was doing it, he changed belts on the machine gun when the first one ran dry.

After what had to be the longest ten or fifteen minutes of his life, he ran out of targets. The U.S. fighters roared off toward the west. He looked around to see what they'd done – and discovered that what had been a brigade was no more than a shattered mess. Not all the trucks were on fire, but about one in three was. Some of the burning trucks carried ammunition, which started cooking off. Flying rounds would cause more casualties, and likely set more fires, too.

The stinks of cordite and burning fuel and burning rubber and burning meat filled the air. So did the cheerful *pop-pop-pop!* of exploding cartridges and the not so cheerful screams and moans of wounded men. Officers and noncoms shouted commands, trying to bring order out of chaos by sheer force of will. Order did not want to be born; chaos wasn't ready to die.

Potter's driver looked around and summed things up in a handful of words: 'Jesus, what a fucking mess!'

'Now that you mention it, yes.' Potter sounded dazed,

even to himself. He thought he'd earned the right. He'd had reports of what air strikes could do to troops. He'd read them carefully. He'd imagined he understood them. *So much for that,* went through his mind. The difference between reading about an air strike and going through one was about like the difference between reading about love and making love.

'You did good, sir,' his driver said. 'That took balls, standing up there and firing on those bastards. A lot of guys would've run for the trees fast as they could go.'

Not far from the command car lay the corpse of a soldier who'd been running for the trees when a cannon round caught him in the middle of the back. The corpse was in two pieces – top half and bottom half. They lay several feet apart. 'Running's not guaranteed to keep you safe,' Potter said. Standing your ground and shooting back at the enemy didn't guarantee it, either. A bomb had landed right by one of the brigade's antiaircraft guns. The blast blew the gun itself ass over teakettle. Not much was left of the men who'd served it.

'Can we still go forward?' the driver asked.

'We have to,' Potter said. The question and the automatic answer helped get his brain working again. He hopped down from the command car and started adding orders of his own to the ones that came from his subordinates. Fighting fires, getting the wounded and the dead off to one side, clearing wrecked vehicles from the roadway . . . It all took time, time the brigade should have used to travel. They were going to be late getting where they were supposed to go.

And they wouldn't get there at better than two-thirds strength. The Great War was a war of attrition, a war the CSA lost. Attrition had just fallen out of the sky and jumped on his brigade. A few minutes of air strikes, and it was barely combat-worthy. It wouldn't be able to do the things planners assumed a fresh brigade of reinforcements could do. It couldn't come close.

How many other Confederate units were in the same boat? And which boat was it, anyway? One that just stopped a torpedo? It sure looked that way to Clarence Potter.

He did the best he could, praying all the while that U.S. fighter-bombers wouldn't come back. He was agnostic leaning toward atheist, but he prayed anyhow. *It can't hurt,* he thought. And enemy aircraft did stay away. The brigade, or what was left of it, got moving again. The men could still do their best . . . however good that turned out to be.

Lieutenant Michael Pound was not a happy man. He'd been happy driving the Confederates from Pittsburgh back into Ohio and then down into Kentucky and Tennessee. Forcing the CSA to dance to the USA's tune made him happy.

Now, instead of pushing on toward Chattanooga, he and his armored platoon had to leave the front line and shift to the east. If they didn't, the Confederates were liable to drive in the U.S. flank. If that happened, very bad things would follow. Pound could see as much. He took it as a personal affront.

'We'll make them pay – you see if we don't,' he growled when his platoon stopped to rest and – at his orders – to maintain their barrels. 'If they think they can side-track us—'

'They're right, aren't they?' Sergeant Frank Blakey asked. The barrel commander had a large wrench in his hands. He was tightening the links in his barrel's left track.

Pound approved of a commander who could do his own maintenance. He also approved of a noncom who talked back to officers. He'd done plenty of that when he had stripes on his sleeve instead of these silly gold bars on even sillier shoulder straps. A lot of men who became officers late in their careers did their best to ape the style and ambitions of those who'd gained the privilege sooner. Not Michael Pound. He still thought like a top sergeant, and didn't labor under the delusion that those little gold bars turned him into a little tin god.

So he just laughed and nodded. 'Yeah, they are – right this minute, anyhow. But when we get through with them, they're going to be worse off than if they never tried this attack in the first place.'

'How do you figure, sir?' That was Mel Scullard, his own gunner. His crew had learned even faster than the others that he didn't get pissed off when people spoke their minds.

'We've got air superiority. We've got more barrels than they do, and better ones now. We've got more artillery than they do, too, in spite of their damn rockets,' Pound answered. 'If they come out and slug toe-to-toe with us, they just make themselves better targets. They're harder to get rid of when they hang back and make us come at them. It worked like that in the Great War, and it still does.'

Sergeant Scullard grunted. 'Well, that makes sense.' He gave Pound a crooked grin. 'How did you come up with it?'

'Accidents will happen,' Pound said dryly, and everyone laughed. Pound went on, 'What we have to do is, we have to clobber the Confederates for coming out in the open to bang with us, and then we have to get back down to the real front and push on to Chattanooga.' Everything always sounded easy when he started talking about it. It sometimes didn't turn out like that for real, but he was convinced that was never his fault.

'We'll put a lot of driving miles on our barrels,' Sergeant Blakey pointed out.

'Sure.' Pound nodded. Barrels were complex machines that performed right at their limits all the time. This war's models were less prone to breakdowns than the lumbering monsters of a generation earlier, but they still failed much more often than he wished they would. He said, 'The better we take care of them while we're on the road, the less trouble they'll give us.'

All the men he led nodded at that. A barrel crew that took care of its machine spent a lot more time in combat than one that let things slide. Barrels were the logical successors to horsed cavalry. Back in the old days, Pound had heard, a mounted trooper took care of his horse before he worried about himself. The same rule held good with armored units, though Pound would sooner have used a curry comb on his barrel than a screwdriver. He was old enough to remember the way horses responded when you groomed them. Barrels never would do anything like that.

But, in an age of mechanized warfare, horsed cavalry couldn't hope to survive. Soldiers in barrels stayed alive and hurt the enemy. That was what the game was all about.

'Are we ready to get rolling?' Pound asked. Nobody said no. The soldiers got back into their steel shells and rumbled northeast.

Before long, they passed a barrel whose men were busy replacing a track. 'We hit a mine,' one of the soldiers in coveralls said in response to Pound's shouted question. 'Lucky this is all that happened to us.'

'You'd better believe it,' Pound said. 'Well, hurry along – we'll need everybody we can get our hands on before long.' The other barrelman waved in agreement and returned to his backbreaking work.

The northeast road ran from Dalton toward Pikeville,

at the head of the Sequatchie Valley, where the Confederates were trying to break out. Pikeville was a county seat – a sign still standing near the edge of town so declared. All the same, the place couldn't have held much more than 500 people before the fighting started. Michael Pound doubted it had half that many now. The locals, like most people with half an ounce of sense, didn't want to stick around while bullets chewed up their houses and bombs and shells came down on their heads. They'd lit out for the tall timber, wherever the tall timber was – probably in the mountains to the east.

U.S. artillery was set up south and west of Pikeville, throwing shells at the Confederates as they tried to push forward. The gun bunnies, most of them naked to the waist, nodded to Pound as he and his barrels rattled past. U.S. fighter-bombers roared past overhead. Pound smiled to hear bombs going off not too far away. The harder the enemy got hit before he made it to Pikeville, the less trouble he'd be when he finally did.

Bomb craters said Confederate aircraft were hitting back as best they could. A burnt-out Hound Dog had crashed in a field just outside of town. The front half of the fighter was a crumpled wreck. The Confederate battle flag on the upthrust tail was as much of a grave marker as the pilot was likely to get.

Houses on the east side of Pikeville faced the mountains from which the enemy would come. Pound's barrel pushed its way into one of those houses – literally, knocking down the western wall and poking the gun out through a window on the east side. The other machines in his platoon deployed close by, behind fences and piles of wreckage. They weren't the only barrels taking up positions there. If the Confederates wanted Pikeville and what lay beyond, they would have to pay.

Pound peered out through the now glassless window, waiting. He would have been happier if the enemy never made it as far as Pikeville. If the artillery and fighter-bombers could stop Featherston's columns in their tracks, so much the better. It would let him turn around and head back toward important fighting – fighting that led to advances into the heart of the Confederacy.

But no such luck. Less than an hour after Pound got to Pikeville, U.S. infantrymen who'd been screening the way ahead fell back into the little town. 'Up to us now, I'd say,' Pound remarked. Without the foot soldiers and the artillery and the airplanes, the Confederates would have been in Pikeville ahead of him, and probably spilling out to the west. He didn't think about that, only about what needed doing next.

'Front!' he called as a Confederate barrel rolling through the cornfields made itself plain.

'Identified!' the gunner sang out. 'Range just over a mile, sir.'

'Can you hit the son of a bitch?' Pound asked.

'Hell, yes!' Scullard sounded confident as could be, the way a good gunner should.

'Then fire when ready.' Pound almost nagged Scullard about leading his target – at that range, the shell had a flight time of a second and a half, and the enemy barrel could move enough to make remembering it matter. But in the end he kept his mouth shut. The gunner knew what he was doing. He'd remember to lead the barrel . . . or if he didn't, Pound would come down on him after he screwed up.

The gun swung slightly. Then it roared. Michael Pound thought his head would come off. He was head and shoulders out of the turret but still in an enclosed space, and the noise was cataclysmic.

Was it a hit or . . . ? Smoke spurted from the enemy barrel. 'Got him!' Pound yelled. 'Good shot! You led him just right!' He laughed at himself. He was going to get the lesson in come hell or high water, wasn't he?

Other barrels opened up on the advancing Confederates. Several more enemy barrels brewed up. The longer U.S. barrelmen used the 3½-inch gun on the new models, the better they liked it. It fired a flat, fast round that could kill anything it could reach. And the improved gunsight made hits more likely. Pound wished he were shooting it himself.

Little by little, he'd decided he might be able to do more good as an officer than he had as a noncom. Coordinating five barrel crews wasn't the piece of cake he'd thought it was till he tried it himself. He kept shouting into the wireless, finding out what was going on with all the others and making sure they did what he wanted them to do. And he had to fight his own barrel, too. It was enough to give the one-armed paperhanger a galloping case of the hives.

And the Confederates wanted Pikeville. They *needed* Pikeville. And they were doing their damnedest to take it back from the U.S. soldiers inside it. Their barrels didn't swarm forward to be massacred in the open, the way Pound hoped they would. Instead, smoke rounds from C.S. artillery back in the mountains came down between the advancing Confederate forces and the defenders in the little town. Before long, the streamers came together in a ragged fogbank that hid most of what lay behind it.

Out of the fogbank came . . . trouble. Confederate foot soldiers armed with antibarrel rockets and launching tubes ran through the smoke, flopped down behind the closest cover, and started working their way forward. U.S. machine-gun fire picked off some of them, and more of the riflemen who protected them, but they kept coming in the little rushes experienced troops used.

Before long, rockets trailing tails of fire flew toward Pikeville. More than one U.S. barrel that had stayed too long in its original firing position got hit. Michael Pound's platoon came away unscathed; he'd ordered the machines back to secondary firing positions in the lull the smoke screen gave them.

A rocket slammed into the house where his barrel had been hiding. The house started to burn. Pound smiled to himself. The Confederates would think they'd killed the barrel. They might make some embarrassing mistakes if they thought their mischief-makers had done more than they really had.

And sure enough, a few minutes later a couple of platoons of C.S. barrels charged through the thinning smoke ready to break into Pikeville or die trying. Michael Pound earnestly preferred the second alternative. He was standing in the cupola of a machine that could make his preferences felt. The leading barrels were the latest Confederate model: excellent in their own right, but half a step behind his. They were out in the open. He had cover. It hardly seemed fair. But then, he didn't want a fair fight. He wanted a fight he'd win.

'Front!' he shouted.

'Identified!' Sergeant Scullard continued with the ritual.

Three shots from Pound's barrel killed two Confederate machines, and they were the leading two. One turned into a fireball. A couple of men got out of the other barrel. Machine-gun bullets reached for them, but they might have made cover. Part of Pound hoped they did. He'd bailed out of a stricken barrel himself. He knew what it was like. They were enemies, but they were also men doing the same job he was.

The Confederates kept coming. Another U.S. barrel set the last of theirs on fire less than a hundred yards outside of Pikeville. Several more green-gray barrels were also burning by then, some from enemy cannon fire, others from those damnable antibarrel rockets.

But the Confederates didn't get into the town. They didn't get around it, either. U.S. reinforcements poured in to make sure they couldn't. Pound was only half glad to see them. He wished they'd stayed farther south and stormed toward Chattanooga.

Lieutenant-Colonel Jerry Dover had the ribbon for the Purple Heart. He didn't much want it. Nobody on either side much *wanted* a Purple Heart, but Dover didn't think he'd earned his. A chunk of shrapnel had torn a bloody line across his forearm. As far as he was concerned, it wasn't worth fussing about. But the rule was that you got a medal if you bled. And so he had one.

Not a lot of officers in the Quartermaster Corps owned a decoration that said they'd been in combat. In a way, it was handy: it made line officers – and even line noncoms – take him seriously. But the wound was so trivial, the decoration embarrassed him.

It did when he had time to think about it, anyway. More often than not, he barely had time to breathe, let alone eat. He smoked like a chimney. As long as he kept breathing, he could do that. It didn't keep him from doing the usual seventeen other things at the same time.

He knew before almost anyone else that the Confederate thrust from the east wasn't going as well as the planners back in Richmond wished it were. As soon as the front just north of Chattanooga got its supply priority restored, he realized the Confederates either had an extravagant success and would soon swarm up from the south or had failed and would soon need to hold on for dear life here. The shipments of barbed wire and land mines said they wouldn't be advancing.

He sent out the supplies as front-line units shouted for them. In the meantime, he quietly swore under his breath. A generation earlier, he'd seen what a losing war looked like. Now he stared another one in the face. He hadn't thought Jake Featherston would land the Confederacy in a mess like this. Who had? Surely Featherston himself hadn't. *And a whole fat lot of good that does anybody,* Dover thought.

Confederate gunboats came up the Tennessee River as far as Chattanooga and fired big shells at U.S. forces to the north. Then they turned around again and scooted south as fast as they could go, for U.S. airplanes struck at them whenever they got the chance. Land-based guns couldn't be as big or move as fast as the ones the gunboats carried. But the boats had trouble moving fast enough to stay safe.

Dover could cheer for them without worrying that their performance reflected on him. The C.S. Navy was responsible for keeping them in fuel, hardtack, and munitions. Some Navy commander had to flabble about that. Dover just hoped their shells blew plenty of damnyankees to hell and gone.

His own worries were the usual sort: getting munitions and other supplies up from the rear and then making sure they reached the front. Keeping his dumps as close to the fighting as he could went a long way toward solving the second problem. The first was harder, especially since he had to deal with new sets of gatekeepers. The dumps in southern and western Tennessee that had nourished the Confederate armies were now withering themselves. Most of Dover's shipments came up from Atlanta, and the quartermasters there had carved out a tidy little empire for themselves, one they didn't care to disturb just because there was a war on.

'Your demands are excessive,' a colonel safely behind the lines told Jerry Dover. 'You can't possibly be expending so many antiaircraft shells.'

'No, huh?' Dover said. 'What do you think I'm doing with 'em, pounding 'em up my ass?' Had that colonel in Atlanta been handy, Dover might have done some pounding with him.

Even though he didn't say it, that message must have got across. In frigid tones, his superior said, 'You are insubordinate.'

'Yes, *sir*,' Dover said proudly. 'People keep telling me that. But the ones who do are always farther from the fighting than I am. The guys who really have to go out and shoot things at the Yankees, they like me fine. And you know what, sir? If I have to choose between them and you, I'll take them any old time.'

'Have a care how you speak to me.' The colonel in Atlanta sounded like a man on the verge of apoplexy. 'You'd better have a care, by God. I can have you court-martialed like that – like *that*, I tell you.' He snapped his fingers.

'Big fucking deal . . . sir.' Dover had heard such threats before. 'If you do, they'll kick my ass out of the Army. I'll go to prison, where it's safe, or I'll go home to Augusta, where it's safe. And I hope they ship you up here to take my place. It'd goddamn well serve you right. And if I don't get those shells, my next telegram goes to Richmond, not to you.'

'You can't do that!' the colonel gabbled. 'It violates the chain of command!'

No doubt that would have impressed an officer who'd had proper training. It didn't bother Jerry Dover one bit. 'You think Jake Featherston will give a damn about the chain of command when he hears somebody isn't doing his job and won't do it? *I* think he'll have you for breakfast . . . without salt.'

He was bluffing. He didn't think any telegram of his would reach the President of the CSA. No doubt the colonel down in Atlanta didn't, either. But there was always that chance. . . . And if Featherston did descend in wrath on an obstructive colonel, that man would end up nothing but a smear on the bottom of his shoe.

Dover got his antiaircraft shells. That meant the front got its antiaircraft shells. If he had enemies down in Atlanta, he didn't give a damn.

He camouflaged his supply dump as elaborately as he could. Netting and mottled tarps covered crates and boxes and stacks. Branches and uprooted saplings made the place next to invisible from the air. That wasn't just Jerry Dover's opinion. He sent up a Confederate artillery spotter in a light airplane to look the place over from above. The man said he had a devil of a time finding it. Dover felt proud.

Proud, however, had nothing to do with anything. Dover was also paranoid. Half a mile from the concealed dump, he ordered a dummy depot built right out in the open. He made some token efforts at camouflaging it: the kinds of things a busy, not very bright, not very diligent officer would do so his superiors couldn't come down on him for not doing anything, but nothing that would really keep enemy bombers from spotting the site.

His men grumbled at the extra work. That ticked him off. 'Look,' he said. 'The name of the game is being able to hang on to our shit till we have to move it up to the front. If the damnyankees drop bombs on the wrong place, we've got a better chance of doing that. Or do you want the bastards to plaster us here?'

Nobody said yes to that. He would have got rid of any man who did. A lot of officers would have given a man like that a rifle and sent him up to the forwardmost positions to see how he liked things there. As Dover had shown at the Huntsman's Lodge, though, he was more vindictive toward superiors than toward subordinates. He would have palmed reluctant enlisted men off on some other supply officer; sending them up to the front to get shot didn't cross his mind.

U.S. reconnaissance aircraft buzzed above Chattanooga almost every hour of the day. Antiaircraft fire didn't discourage them. There weren't enough Confederate fighters to drive them away. West of the Appalachians, the United States had air superiority. The Confederates could harry and harass, but they couldn't stop the Yankees from doing most of what they wanted to do.

Bombs rained down on the dummy depot, smashing it to hell and gone. 'You see?' Dover said to anybody who would listen. 'You see? We fooled the sons of bitches!' He got busy repairing the dump, just as if it were the real one. He was proud of his realism. He'd even had a few barrels of waste oil at the dummy site so they could send up convincing plumes of greasy smoke.

Enemy bombers hit the fake depot again two days later, even harder. Jerry Dover was so pleased with himself, he could hardly even breathe. He felt like dancing because he'd done such a good job of fooling the damnyankees. How many tons of bombs had they thrown away, smashing up worthless tents and empty crates? Enough to make some of their supply officers very unhappy if they found out about the waste – he was sure of that.

Again, he had his crew run around as if trying to set things to rights. After two wasted U.S. raids, they'd found some enthusiasm for trying to trick U.S. fliers. Antiaircraft guns sprouted like toadstools around the dummy depot. Only a handful of the guns were real. The rest were Quaker cannons: logs trimmed and painted to look like the real thing, on mounts made from whatever junk the soldiers could scrounge. Close up, they were jokes. From a couple of miles in the air, or from a fighter-bomber streaking by as fast as it could go, they seemed damned convincing.

When he heard the thrum of U.S. bomber engines overhead yet again, Jerry Dover smiled: a smug, complacent grin. The good humor behind that smile went up in smoke – literally – when the Yankees blasted the kapok out of his genuine dump. All the antiaircraft guns around the real installation were in good working order. They knocked down a few bombers, but not nearly enough. The USA clearly won the exchange.

'How?' he shouted, even as firemen poured streams of water on the smoking wreckage. 'How the fuck did they know where we were at?'

'I bet some goddamn nigger tipped 'em off that we were running a bluff,' a sergeant answered.

Dover started to say that was ridiculous, but he stopped with the words unspoken. It wasn't ridiculous, not one bit. Every black man – and woman – in the CSA had to hate the present government as much as the government hated blacks. Not many Negroes were left in these parts. Even one would have been plenty if he reached the damnyankees.

'I bet you're right,' was what came out of his mouth.

'Fucking black bastards,' the noncom said. 'Freedom Party should've done a better job of cleaning 'em out. What did we elect those assholes for, anyway?'

Politics didn't rear its head so often in this war as it had in the last. A lot of people in the CSA were afraid to talk politics these days. They worried – and with reason – that they could end up in camps if they said the wrong thing to the wrong person. Anything that criticized the government or the Freedom Party was too likely to be the wrong thing, although Jerry Dover hadn't expected anybody to come down on the Party for not doing enough to get rid of blacks.

'You want to kind of watch your mouth, Pete,' Dover told the sergeant. 'Some of these Party people, they don't take things the right way.'

'Yeah, well, I didn't figure you for a stalwart or anything like that,' Pete answered. 'You don't sound like you're ready to come when you go, "Freedom!" '

'No, huh?' Dover said dryly.

'Nope.' The sergeant shook his head. He stuck a chaw of Red Man in his mouth. His jaw worked; he might have been a cow chewing its cud. But a cow wouldn't have spat a stream of brown the way he did. He winked at Dover. 'Besides, sir, if you turn me in, you'll get stuck with some dumb shithead who doesn't know his ass from the end zone. You like people with a little something upstairs. Me, I like broads with a little something upstairs.' He held his hands in front of his chest.

Dover laughed. 'Go on, get out of here,' he said. 'You've got other things to do besides driving your CO crazy.'

With a sketched salute, Pete ambled off. Jerry Dover stared after him. No wonder people didn't talk politics any more. Whenever you did, you felt you were suddenly part of a plot. Say anything bad about the powers that be – even listen to someone else saying bad things about the powers without denouncing him on the instant – and you were complicit in indiscretion. You had a hold on the other guy, and he had a hold on you.

'Shit,' Dover muttered. 'It shouldn't be this way.' He felt that very strongly. Not being able to speak your mind had to hurt the war effort. Having people go after people who did speak their minds had to hurt the war effort, too. All the labor wasted in chasing down grumblers could have been turned against the damnyankees instead.

The effort used in chasing down Negroes? Dover wasn't like Pete; he didn't think the Freedom Party wasn't doing enough. But the question of whether the Party should be doing anything at all along those lines never crossed his mind. He might despise the numskulls set over him, but he was still a man of his country and his time and his color.

XIII

Dr. Leonard O'Doull finished the amputation. 'There we go,' he said. 'All things considered, the poor bastard's lucky.'

'Just losing a foot? I should say so.' Granville McDougald nodded. 'Sometimes you lose a leg when you step on a mine. Sometimes it just plain kills you. Or if you step on one of those new bouncing bastards the Confederates are using, it pops up in the air and blows your nuts off. Some fun.'

'Yeah.' O'Doull hated the bouncing mines with a fierce and terrible passion. They were designed to make the ghastliest wounds they could. Some C.S. engineer had probably won himself a bonus for coming up with the idea. He looked at the patient etherized upon the table. 'He should do pretty well, though. He just found an ordinary one.'

Pretty well. It was true. The man would live. He probably wouldn't get a wound infection. Once he healed enough to wear a prosthesis, he'd be able to get around without too much trouble. How much agony lay between the moment of stepping on the mine and that reasonably favorable prognosis, though? How much had he gone through before he was carried back to the aid station? No way in hell to measure such things, but he'd already tasted his share of hell, his share and then some.

'Let's get him off the table,' McDougald said. 'We're

bound to have more business before long. Ain't life grand?'

'*Mauvais tabernac,*' O'Doull said, and added, ' '*Osti!*' for good measure. Granny McDougald laughed, the way he always did when O'Doull swore in Quebecois French. Sometimes, though, the blasphemy of the French curses felt more powerful than the blunt Anglo-Saxon obscenities O'Doull had gone back to using more often than not.

They did get more business, too, but not the kind they expected. Mortar bombs started bursting not far away. 'Shit!' McDougald said, and Leonard O'Doull wasn't inclined to argue with him. They both grabbed the wounded man and lugged him along as they hurried out of the tent. They would have to rebandage him later, but that was the least of their worries. Leaving him there for shrapnel to slice up would have been worse.

'Careful with him, Granny,' O'Doull said as they slid him down into the trench near the tent, the trench they always hoped they wouldn't have to use.

'I'm trying,' McDougald said. Another mortar round burst nearby. Fragments screeched past O'Doull. McDougald gasped. Then he said, 'Shit,' again, this time in an eerily calm tone of voice.

'You hit?' O'Doull had heard that tone too many times to have much doubt.

'Afraid so,' McDougald answered. 'Two wars up at the front, and my very first Purple Heart. Lucky me.' Then he said, 'Shit,' again, most sincerely now. 'Son of a bitch is starting to hurt.'

'Get down in here,' O'Doull told him. 'I'll do what I can for you, and I'll get you on the table as soon as they stop landing things on us.'

'Right,' the medic said tightly. 'Well, nice to know I'm in good hands.' Like any other soldier, he carried a mor-phine syrette in the aid kit on his belt. As soon as he flopped down into the trench, he stuck himself. His left trouser leg was dark and soggy with blood.

Most soldiers would have used a belt knife or a bayonet to cut away the heavy fabric and get a look at the wound. O'Doull had a scalpel. It didn't do a better job than any other sharp blade would have, but it felt natural in his hand. He found a long, nasty tear in McDougald's thigh. 'Not too bad, Granny,' he said. 'We can patch it up – that's for damn sure.'

'You're the doctor,' McDougald said through clenched teeth. 'When is that morphine going to kick in? How long does it take, anyway?' He'd injected himself only a minute or so before. When he was caring for someone else, he could gauge exactly how long the painkiller needed. He wasn't objective about his own wound, his own torment. Who could be?

'Won't be long,' O'Doull promised, as soothingly as he could. 'I don't have my needles and suture material with me. I'm going to pinch off a couple of bleeders in there and safety-pin you together till I can get you under the gas for a proper job.'

'You're the doc,' McDougald said again. He braced himself as O'Doull got to work. On anyone else, he would have watched what his friend was doing. Why not? For a wound like this, he could have done just as well himself. When he was the wounded party, though, he looked anywhere and everywhere except at his injury. In a macabre way, it was funny. He even laughed when O'Doull remarked on it. But he swore savagely when O'Doull pinned the wound's lips together. Then he laughed again, shakily. 'Crazy how much that little crap hurts, isn't it?'

'Yeah. Crazy.' O'Doull started bandaging the gash. 'You're going to have yourself a hell of a scar, you know?'

'Oh, boy. Just what I always wanted.' But then

McDougald let out a sigh. 'Ah, there's the dope. Christ, that feels good. Almost worth getting hit for, you know? Somebody said it was like kissing God. Now I know what he meant.'

'Don't like it too much.' O'Doull had known a few doctors who did like morphine too well. Army medics weren't immune from using the stuff for their own pleasure, either. The powers that be landed on them like a rockslide when they got caught, but a lot of them were sly and careful. People who used drugs weren't always the crazed addicts in melodramas. A lot of them used just enough to stay happy, and lived more or less normal lives aside from their habit.

More shell fragments whistled and screeched overhead. Even staying in the trench didn't necessarily do O'Doull and McDougald and the anesthetized soldier with a missing foot any good. If a mortar bomb came down on top of them, that was it. End of story – or the start of a new and horrible one.

Far back of the line – well north of Delphi – U.S. artillery started thundering. The mortar fire stopped as suddenly as it had begun. Did that mean the C.S. mortar crews were casualties? O'Doull hoped so. He didn't like people shooting at him, not even a little bit.

Eddie the corpsman stared down into the trench. 'Jesus, Doc, what the hell happened here?' he asked.

'What do you think happened? I was elected Queen of the May, and I'm about to go into my dance,' Granville McDougald said before O'Doull could get a word out. Morphine might have dulled his pain, but not his sarcasm.

'Granny got his leg sliced when we were moving the wounded guy on account of the mortar fire,' O'Doull said. 'Can you help me get him up and out so I can work on him?'

'Let me round up a couple more guys. It'll go better if I do.' Eddie disappeared before O'Doull could say yes or no. *Nobody's paying any attention to me today,* O'Doull thought aggrievedly. He hoped the Confederates wouldn't get their mortars upright and shooting while Eddie was looking for help.

They didn't. Maybe the U.S. artillery really had knocked out the enemy crews. Three more corpsmen jumped into the trench with O'Doull. They got the man with an amputated foot up onto a stretcher and then, grunting, lifted him out of the trench. 'What's going on?' he said vaguely – he was starting to come out from under the anesthesia. He wouldn't feel pain for a while, though; O'Doull had shot him full of morphine while he was still out.

Once the corpsmen got him off the stretcher, it was Granville McDougald's turn. 'Take it easy, Granny,' Eddie said as they lifted him.

'Well, how else am I going to take it?' McDougald answered.

He rolled off the stretcher once they got it up to the level of the top of the trench. Morphine or not, that made him say several pungent things. They got out of the trench themselves, put him back on the stretcher, and carried him into the aid tent.

Sharp, jagged steel fragments had done a good job of ventilating the tent. A big one was stuck in one of the operating table's front legs. It was only about a foot from the cylinder of ether and oxygen up there. If it had punched into that . . . O'Doull was just as glad it hadn't. Maybe the tent would have gone up in flames, or maybe it would have just gone up – halfway to the moon.

'Well, Granny, I'm going to put you under so I can do a proper job on this,' O'Doull said, reaching for the mask connected to the cylinder.

'Sure, Doc. Do what you gotta do.' McDougald had anesthetized God only knew how many men himself. But when the mask came down over his nose and mouth, he tried to fight it, the way a lot of wounded soldiers did. It was reflex, nothing more; O'Doull knew as much. Eddie and another corpsman held McDougald's hands till he went to sleep.

O'Doull cleaned the wound, closed off some more bleeders, and then sutured things firmly and neatly. He nodded to himself. 'He'll be all right, won't he, Doc?' Eddie asked. 'He's a good guy.'

'You bet he is,' O'Doull answered. 'And yes, he ought to do fine. But he'll need at least a couple of months before he's back on the job.'

'We'll be getting a new number-one medic, then.' Above the mask he'd put on, Eddie blinked. 'That's gonna be weird.'

'Boy, no kidding.' O'Doull had come to take Granny McDougald's unflustered competence very much for granted. Now he'd have to break in somebody else, some-body who'd probably be half his age and who wasn't likely to know anywhere near as much as McDougald did. O'Doull muttered under his breath. He and McDougald had got on fine living in each other's pockets for most of two years. It wasn't a marriage, but it was intimate enough in its own way. Could he do the same with a new guy? He'd damn well have to.

They took McDougald away, still unconscious. O'Doull washed his hands and his instruments. He shook his head all the time he was doing it. He'd imagined himself get-ting hurt plenty of times. McDougald? He shook his head again. No, not a chance – he'd thought. The veteran noncom seemed enduring as the Rockies.

Which only went to show – you never could tell. O'Doull

was still fine, not a scratch on him, and McDougald was lucky he hadn't lost a leg. O'Doull thought about that, then shook his head. The medic was unlucky to have been wounded at all. But it could have been worse. With all O'Doull had seen himself, he knew how much worse it could have been.

U.S. fighter-bombers roared by overhead, flying south to pound the Confederate positions outside of Chattanooga. O'Doull didn't look forward to that fight. He couldn't imagine how taking the enemy bastion would be easy or cheap. *More work for me,* he thought. But he could do without more work. His ideal day was one where he sat outside the aid tent reading a book and smoking cigarettes. He hadn't had an ideal day since putting the uniform back on. He didn't expect to have one till the war finally ended. But every man, even a military doctor, deserved his dreams.

One way not to have to patch up wounded soldiers was to get hit himself. He looked down at his hands. He didn't have Granville McDougald's blood on them any more. He thought about the replacement medic or a surgeon farther behind the front trying to patch him up. He'd seen too many wounds. He didn't want one of his own.

What he wanted might not have anything to do with the price of beer. Only fool luck Granny stopped that fragment and he didn't. He wondered how – and whether – to tell Nicole that McDougald was injured. He talked about Granny in every letter he wrote. She would notice if he suddenly stopped. But she would flabble if he came right out and said his friend and colleague had got hurt. If it happened to Granville McDougald, she would say, it could happen to him, too.

And she would be right.

O'Doull knew he couldn't admit that to her. He didn't want to admit it to himself. The more you thought about

things like that, the less you slept, the more likely you were
to get an ulcer, the more likely your hand was to shake
when it shouldn't . . .

But how were you supposed to *not* think about something? If someone said, *Don't think about a blue rabbit,* of
course nothing else would fill your mind. 'You just have to
go on,' O'Doull murmured. 'You just have to go on.'

On the bridge of the *Josephus Daniels,* Sam Carsten said,
'I guess maybe we won that fight with the limeys and the
frogs after all.'

Pat Cooley nodded. 'Yes, sir. I guess maybe we did,' the
exec said. 'We wouldn't be trying to take Bermuda back if
we didn't, would we?' He didn't sound a hundred percent
convinced – more as if he was trying to convince himself,
and Sam, too.

'Well, I hope we wouldn't, anyway.' Carsten had been
aboard the *Remembrance* when a British attack on U.S.
fishing boats lured the carrier north – and left Bermuda
vulnerable to amphibious assault. Now the United States
were trying to return the favor, if that was the word.

U.S. surface ships and airplanes and submersibles kept
the British from reinforcing or resupplying the outpost in
the western Atlantic. But the British garrison wasn't ready
to throw in the sponge. Lots of Royal Marines and soldiers were on the ground. The British had plenty of artillery
– some of the heavy pieces big enough to damage a battleship or blow a destroyer escort like the *Josephus Daniels*
clean out of the water. And they had fighters and dive
bombers at least as good as the Americans could throw at
them, and enough fuel to keep their airplanes flying at least
for a while.

Along with carriers and battlewagons and smaller escort
vessels like the *Josephus Daniels,* troopships and landing

craft wallowed toward Bermuda. Sam watched them with a reminiscent smile on his face. 'It looked like this in 1914,' he said, 'when we landed on the Sandwich Islands.'

'You were there for that?' Cooley asked.

'You bet. I was still an able seaman in those days – hadn't even made petty officer,' Sam answered. 'I was on the *Dakota*. My battle station was at one of her five-inch guns.' He chuckled. 'Secondary armament, right? Sure. Bigger guns than we've got on this tin can.'

'We can do what we need to do.' The exec patted the destroyer escort's wheel, as if to say the ship shouldn't listen to her skipper's insults. But he couldn't help adding, 'You've seen a lot of action.'

'I've got a lot of miles on me, you mean,' Sam said with another laugh.

Airplanes roared off the carriers' decks and flew south and east toward the island. They hadn't had strike forces like that in the old days. The *Dakota* had carried a catapult-launched biplane scout that seemed to be made of sticks and baling wire. When it came back – if it came back – it landed on the sea, and the battleship fished it out with a crane. Nowadays, fleets didn't even see each other. Airplanes did the heavy lifting.

He hoped they would do the heavy lifting against Bermuda. If they plastered the runways on the island so the British fighters and bombers couldn't take off . . . If they did that, his own life expectancy would go up. He'd been lucky in war so far. He'd had a battleship hit and a carrier sunk under him, but he'd barely got scratched. He hoped that would go on – he liked his carcass the way it was.

Most of the time, Navy men were lucky compared to their Army counterparts. They slept in bunks, or at least in hammocks, not wrapped in a blanket in the mud. They ate pretty good chow, not the canned rations soldiers had to put up with. Most of the time, they were in transit from here to there; except for lurking submersibles, nothing put them in danger minute by minute for days or weeks at a stretch.

But . . . There was always a but. When things went wrong for sailors, they went wrong in a big way. If a ship went down to the bottom, she could take hundreds of men – even a couple of thousand on a carrier – down with her.

He wished he hadn't had that thought. He reached out and rapped his knuckles on the wheel. Pat Cooley sent him a quizzical look. 'What's up, sir?'

'Nothing, not really. Just snapping my fingers to keep the elephants away.'

The exec looked around. 'Nothing but the Atlantic for miles and miles,' he said. 'I didn't know the enemy was issuing heavy-duty water wings.'

'Gotta watch out for those water elephants,' Sam said gravely. 'Next time you see something sticking out of the Atlantic, it won't be a periscope – it'll be one of their trunks instead.'

'No doubt, sir,' Cooley answered. 'And the trunk'll probably be packed, too – with explosives or with bushwah, depending.'

'Bushwah – no doubt about it,' Sam said, his face still straight. 'An essential wartime ingredient.'

'Wouldn't surprise me a bit,' the exec said.

Carsten studied the charts of the waters around Bermuda. The one thing he was sure of was that he didn't want to get too close without a pilot aboard who knew them like the back of his hand. There were too many reefs marked, too many names like Cow Ground Flat and Brackish Pond Flats. There were also too many wrecks charted, some from the eighteenth century, some of blockade runners during the War of Secession, and ungodly numbers from the days of the Great War. He wondered how many wrecks *weren't* marked. He didn't want to add the *Josephus Daniels* to that number.

'Sir, we've got airplanes outbound from Bermuda,' the Y-ranging officer said. 'They don't intend to sit there and take it.'

'And we're still a hundred miles offshore,' Carsten said. 'Well, we already knew the limeys have their own Y-ranging gear.'

'Sure looks that way, sir,' Lieutenant Walters said. 'Seems like they're trying to keep us from doing too much to the island.'

'Can they?' Sam and his executive officer asked the same thing at the same time.

'No way to tell yet,' Walters answered. He watched the screens for another couple of minutes, then grunted. 'That's funny.'

'What's up?' Sam asked.

'I'm picking up incoming aircraft with a bearing of about 250 – a little south of west.' The Y-ranging officer laughed. 'Gadget must have the hiccups. It does that once in a while.'

Sam didn't think it was funny, not one little bit. He looked at Pat Cooley. The exec was looking back at him, similar consternation in his eyes. 'How far is it from Cape Hatteras to Bermuda, Pat?' Sam asked.

'About six hundred miles, sir,' Cooley answered.

'That's what I thought,' Sam said. 'If the Confederates wanted to try bombing us, they could, in other words.' He didn't wait for a reply this time. He just snapped out an order: 'Bring the ship to general quarters. Signal the rest of the fleet what we've spotted and what we think it means.' Other Y-ranging sets would pick up those airplanes, too, but would the men eyeing the screens know what they were seeing?

Klaxons hooted. Sailors dashed to their battle stations as if someone had tied torches to their tails. 'If the limeys can put up airplanes at the same time as the Confederates, things are liable to get interesting,' Lieutenant Cooley remarked, sounding calmer than he had any business being.

'Interesting. Yeah,' Sam said tightly. 'And I hear that the ocean is wet, and Jake Featherston doesn't always tell the truth, and you're liable to get hurt if a .50-caliber slug hits you.'

Cooley gave an uncertain chuckle, plainly having trouble making up his mind whether the skipper was being sardonic or had just flipped his lid. The blinker on the closest cruiser started sending Morse. Cooley and Carsten both turned field glasses toward the signal. CONFIRM C.S. AIRCRAFT, it said, one letter at a time. PREPARE TO DEFEND. AIR COVER LIMITED.

That was all, no matter how much Sam waited and longed for more. 'Happy day,' he said, and whistled something without much tune. He went to the speaking tube that connected the bridge to the engine room: 'Be ready to give me flank speed at my order. We're facing air attack any minute now.'

'Flank speed at your order. Aye aye, sir.' Nobody down in the black gang sounded ruffled. They never did down there. They did all they could do, and they didn't worry about anything beyond the noise and heat of their province. Sam envied them their simplicity. It was the one thing he missed from his days as a rating. Now he had to think about the whole ship and the tactical situation at the same time.

'One thing,' Cooley said. 'The Confederates probably won't throw Asskickers at us. They don't have the range to come out this far and make it back to the mainland. That means medium bombers hitting from high altitude, and they aren't nearly so accurate.'

'Can Asskickers dive-bomb us and then land on Bermuda?' Sam asked.

His exec looked quite humanly surprised for a moment. 'I hadn't thought of that.' Cooley sounded less self-assured than usual. He checked some reference books, and didn't look happy when he closed them. 'Probably, sir. They may not be able to carry a full bomb load, but I think they can get here.'

'One more piece of good news,' Sam said.

The cruiser that had signaled them opened fire with her five-inch guns. A moment later, the *Josephus Daniels'* pair of four-inchers opened up, too, and then the twin 40mm guns, and then the .50-caliber machine guns. The racket was terrific, astonishing, deafening. Sam knew he didn't hear as well as he would have liked. Artilleryman's ear, soldiers called it. This wouldn't help.

Sure as hell, a gull-winged Confederate Mule stooped on the cruiser. Sam saw the dive bomber release the bomb it carried under its belly a split second before a big shell connected with it. The airplane turned into a fireball. Fragments rained down into the Atlantic. But the bomb caught the cruiser just abaft the bridge. The big ship staggered in the water. A great plume of smoke rose from her.

'Pilot's a damn fool,' Cooley said. Sam made a questioning noise. The exec explained: 'They should be going after the troopships and the carriers. In a fight like this, escorts are chump change.'

He'd just called his own ship chump change, which didn't necessarily mean he was wrong. Another burning Asskicker plunged into the sea. The combat air patrol over the fleet was doing something, anyhow. And the guys at one of the forward 40mm mounts started whooping and dancing like men going out of their heads. They'd shot down an enemy airplane, or they sure as hell thought they had.

More Asskickers pulled out of their parabolic dives and fought for altitude. They were most vulnerable then, since they weren't moving very fast as they climbed. Several of them got hacked out of the sky. But other ominous smoke pillars rose from the fleet.

'It's a big game,' Sam said. 'I wish I knew what the score was.'

'If we get troops ashore on Bermuda, we're winning,' Pat Cooley said. 'If we don't . . . If we don't, the Navy Department had a lousy idea.'

No sooner had he said that than another destroyer signaled them – the damaged cruiser was no longer close. ADVANCE WITH US TO BOMBARD ISLAND, the other ship's signal lamp flashed.

'Acknowledge and tell 'em we're on the way,' Sam said to Cooley.

'Aye aye, sir.'

Bermuda was actually made up of several low-lying islands linked by bridges and causeways. The *Josephus Daniels'* fire went in against the airstrip in the northeast. The gunners worked their pieces with furious haste, knowing that the more damage they did, the less chance British and C.S. airplanes would have of getting off the ground and striking back.

Landing boats waddled forward from troopships that stayed out of the artillery range. Hidden gun emplacements opened up on them. Here and there, a boat was hit and went up in flames or simply sank. But most of the landing craft made it to the beach. U.S. bombers and fighters pounded all the enemy positions they could find. U.S. Army men and Marines swarmed forward. Sam hoped for the best.

Till Armstrong Grimes got wounded, he'd never been in upstate New York in his life. But a lot of U.S. military hos-

pitals were in that part of the country, because Confederate
bombers had to fly a long way to get there. The one where
he was recuperating lay somewhere between Syracuse and
Rochester. Since he wasn't sure which town was which, he
would have had trouble nailing it down any better than
that.

Lying around doing nothing with nobody to yell at him
for it felt strange, almost unnatural. Not worrying about
snipers or machine guns felt even stranger. He got plenty
of chow – not wonderful chow, but better than the canned
stuff he'd been eating most of the time. He got all the cigarettes he wanted, even if they were U.S. barge scrapings
instead of Confederate tobacco.

And the nurses were . . . nurses. Women. Some of them
were tough old battleaxes who'd been taking care of people
since the Great War. Others, though, were young and cute
and friendly. Armstrong hoped some of them would prove
more than friendly. Guys who'd been there a while told
stories about nurses who helped soldiers recuperate by hopping into bed with them. But soldiers always told stories
about women. Armstrong didn't see anything like that, no
matter how much he wished he would.

Even so, he couldn't remember the last time he'd been
around women who didn't want to blow his brains out. It
reminded him there was a bigger world out there than the
one that involved storming the next apartment building full
of Mormons or Canucks.

So did reading newspapers and listening to the wireless.
Oh, they were full of things like the reconquest of Bermuda
and the U.S. drive aimed at Chattanooga. But that wasn't
all. They didn't go on about the war twenty-four hours a
day. There were stories about crime and scandal and films
and a lady in Schenectady who'd had quadruplets.

That one impressed the nurses more than it did

Armstrong. 'Men!' one of them sniffed when she found out Armstrong didn't get it. 'Can you imagine trying to take care of four little tiny babies all at once? Can you imagine trying to take care of four two-year-olds all at once? My God!' She rolled her eyes.

Armstrong couldn't imagine anything like that. But, since Susan was young and cute instead of being a battleaxe, he did his best. 'Bad?' he asked.

'My God!' she repeated. 'My kids are almost two years apart, and they still drive me nuts. But four of them doing the same things, making the same messes, getting into the same trouble all at the same time? I hope she's got lots of people helping her, that's all I can tell you.'

She wore a wedding ring. Armstrong hadn't even noticed before. *Damn,* he thought. 'Where's your husband stationed?' he asked.

'He's in west Texas right now,' Susan answered. 'He's been lucky so far.' She reached out and knocked on the nightstand by his iron-framed cot. 'But when I see what can happen to you guys . . .' She grimaced.

'I'm getting better,' said Armstrong, not the least self-centered young man around. But then he realized that might need something more with it. He did his best: 'Most of us are getting better.'

He won a smile from the nurse. 'I know,' she said. 'But I still worry. How can I help it?'

'I guess you can't, but it doesn't do you any good,' Armstrong said. 'It doesn't do your husband any good, either. What's his name, anyway?' He didn't give a rat's ass what the guy's name was, but asking might make Susan like him better, and who could say where that would take him?

Her smile got bigger – she did appreciate the question. 'He's Jerry,' she said. 'He's so sweet . . .' Her face went all mushy. If she'd looked at Armstrong that way, he would have been in business. Since she was thinking about Jerry instead, he just lay there and smiled himself and nodded. He didn't hope the guy would stop an antibarrel round with his face, but he didn't exactly love him, either.

He watched Susan's perky behind as she went to check on the wounded man in the next bed. He wasn't the only recovering soldier watching her. The guys in this ward were wounded, yeah, but they were a long way from dead.

That afternoon, Susan bustled up to him with a different kind of smile on her face. She was pleased for him. 'You've got visitors,' she announced, then turned and said, 'You can come in now.'

In walked his father and mother. His mother gave him a big hug and a kiss. His father squeezed his hand hard and said, 'I'm proud of you, son.'

'What? For getting shot?' Armstrong said. 'I'm not proud of that. It was just bad luck.'

'No, not for getting shot.' Merle Grimes' left hand stayed on the head of his cane. 'For being brave enough to fight in the front line, and for doing it well.'

His old man had done his fighting a generation earlier, and he must have forgotten how things worked. You didn't go to the front line because you were brave. You went there because some slob with stars on his shoulder straps decided your regiment could do a particular job – or maybe because you drew the short straw. And if you didn't go forward when the other guys did, the Army made sure you caught hell. If you did go forward, you had a chance of coming through, anyway.

'You're going to be all right,' his mother said. 'The nurse told us so.'

'Yeah, Mom,' Armstrong said. 'I probably won't even have a limp.' They were talking about putting him back on duty once he healed up, so he figured the chances he'd be able to walk straight were pretty fair.

'That's good,' Edna Grimes said. 'Not that it would be the end of the world,' she added hastily, looking at her husband.

'I understood what you meant,' Merle Grimes said. 'I'm not ashamed of my limp or anything – I earned it honestly. But I wouldn't be sorry if I didn't have it.'

'Thanks for coming, both of you. You didn't have to do anything like this,' Armstrong said.

'Oh, yes, we did,' his mother and father said together.

'Who's taking care of Annie?' he asked. His little sister was getting big these days; she didn't need as much care as she would have a few years earlier.

'Your Aunt Clara has her,' his mother answered. 'She says she hopes you get better soon – Clara does, I mean. So does Annie, of course.'

'That's nice,' Armstrong said, as politely as he could. He didn't like his aunt, and it was mutual. Clara was his mom's half sister, and only a couple of years older than he was. They hadn't been able to stand each other ever since they were little kids. He was surprised Clara didn't hope he'd got his dick shot off.

His mother always tried to pretend things weren't as bad as they really were. His father, who didn't, chuckled. 'She doesn't want to see you dead, Armstrong,' he said. 'Not unless she does it herself, anyway.'

'Merle!' By her tone, Edna Grimes would make Dad pay for that, no matter how true it was.

'Oh, come on, Edna. I was joking,' he said. At the same time, though, he tipped Armstrong a wink. He wasn't joking a bit, but he didn't feel like fighting with his wife. He looked at the bandages on Armstrong's leg. 'How did it happen?'

'We were pushing north toward Winnipeg. The Canucks

had a strongpoint in a farmhouse,' Armstrong answered. 'I was one of the guys moving up, and the damn machine gun got me. Bad luck, that's all, like I said before.' He paused. 'How did you get wounded, Dad?' He'd never felt able to ask before. Now they both belonged to the same fraternity. He'd had himself a .30-caliber initiation.

'It was a trench raid,' Merle Grimes answered without the slightest hesitation. 'We used to pull them all the time, to grab a few prisoners and see what the guys on the other side were up to. The front didn't move then the way it does nowadays. We got in, we threw some grenades around, we caught some Confederates, and we were on our way back when some son of a bitch – excuse me, Edna – nailed me from behind. Stinky Morris and Herm Cassin got me back to our side of the line, and it was off to an aid station after that. It hurt like a . . . Well, it hurt like anything.'

'Yeah. I found out about that. For the first little bit, it was just like somebody knocked me down. But not for long.' Armstrong shook his head. 'No, not for long.' He didn't want to remember that, so he asked, 'How are things back in D.C.?'

'Well, we aren't occupied,' his mother said. 'It was bad when the Confederates took the town last time around, and it was really bad when the USA took it back. I wasn't much older than you are now when that happened. But in between there was a long stretch that was pretty quiet, when the front was too far north to let guns reach us. Bombers weren't so much back then.'

'They are now,' his father said. 'The Confederates still come over us two or three nights a week. We're not far from their fields, so they can really load up. We go to the cellars when the sirens start howling, and we hope for the best. You can't do much else. It's almost like being in the line, except you don't get to shoot back yourself.'

'I guess.' Armstrong had no idea what civilian life in wartime was like. He'd been a conscript when the shooting started. 'You have enough to eat and everything?'

'*That's* better than it was the last time around,' his mother said.

'I was in the service the last time around, so I can't compare,' his father said, 'but it's not too bad. Not much meat – there's this horrible chopped ham that comes in cans.' He and Armstrong's mother both made faces. He went on, 'What we get mostly isn't exciting, and a lot of the fruits and vegetables are canned, too. But nobody's going hungry. Your rations sound like they're better than what we ate in the trenches. Boy, I never wanted to see another bean after I got out.'

'We always bitch about what we get,' Armstrong said.

His father laughed. 'King David's soldiers probably did the same thing.'

'Yeah, probably,' Armstrong said. 'But the biggest thing I don't like is that you get bored. There aren't that many different kinds of rations, and some guys won't like some of them, so that cuts it down more. You're always happy when you can scrounge some chickens or a pig. Once in Utah, we ate a goat.'

His mother made a disgusted noise. His father just sounded interested as he asked, 'How was it?'

'Better than I expected,' Armstrong answered. 'Kinda tough and kinda gamy, but we had this Polack in the squad – Eyechart, we called him, 'cause his name looked really weird with all those s's and z's and w's – who stewed it and stewed it, and it ended up so it was better than rations, anyway.'

'Sounds like he had some practice in the old country,' his father said.

'Him or his folks – I think he was born here,' Armstrong

said. 'But the coffee's lousy and the cigarettes are worse. That's the, uh, dirty end of the stick.'

Merle Grimes chuckled at the just-in-time censorship. Then he said, 'Close your eyes.' Armstrong did. When his father said he could open them, he found himself looking at three packs of Raleighs. 'These are for you.'

'Wow, Dad! Thanks!' Armstrong knew he would have to share them with his wardmates. He didn't care. They were wonderful anyhow. 'Where'd you get 'em?'

'A friend of mine has a son who captured a Confederate truck crammed full of them,' his father answered.

'Wow,' Armstrong said again. Short of nabbing Jake Featherston, he couldn't think of anything better. 'That guy should've won the Medal of Honor.' He hadn't thought a visit from his parents could turn out so well. A truckload of Raleighs! That was almost better to think about than Susan.

Nothing official ever came of Cincinnatus Driver's run-in with Sergeant Cannizzaro. He hadn't thought it would. Technically, he was a civilian, so they couldn't even court-martial him. The most they could do was take away his gun and ship him home. That would have pissed him off, but it wouldn't have broken his heart. He knew he had a better chance of living to a ripe old age in Des Moines than he did hauling supplies through the CSA.

But there were more kinds of results than official ones. The way he handled himself when the Confederates hit the supply column and the way he stood up to the jerk of a U.S. quartermaster sergeant won him respect from his fellow drivers.

'You're all right, you know?' Hal Williamson sounded half surprised when he said it as they dug into ration cans somewhere in central Tennessee. 'Never had much to do with colored fellows before. Ain't a whole lot of 'em in Manchester, New Hampshire. You kinda believe what folks say. But like I said, you're all right. You're just – a guy.'

'What did you expect?' Cincinnatus paused to light a Raleigh. The Confederate from whom he'd taken the pack wouldn't be smoking again, unless he smoked down in hell. 'I ain't got horns. I ain't got a tail.' He was thinking about hell, all right.

'Not what I meant.' Williamson cast about for a way to say what he did mean. He was about Cincinnatus' age, with steel-rimmed bifocals and with three fingers gone from his left hand. He gestured with that mutilated hand to make his point. 'I didn't figure you people'd have the balls to do some of the things you done.'

'Niggers're like any other folks.' Cincinnatus used the word on purpose. He *could* use it, though he would have slugged Williamson had he heard it from the white man's lips. 'Some's smart, some's dumb. Some's brave, some's cowards. Some's good-lookin', some's mullions.' Hal Williamson blinked at that bit of black slang, but he followed it. Cincinnatus went on, 'Maybe I got balls, maybe I don't. But even if I do, that don't say nothin' about what niggers're like. It only goes to show what *I'm* like. You see what I mean?'

'Maybe.' Williamson lit a cigarette of his own. 'It's like sayin' all Jews are cheap or all Mexicans'll pull a knife on you if you look at 'em sideways.'

He probably knew even less about Mexicans than he did about Negroes. There might be a Negro or two in Manchester, but Cincinnatus would have bet there were no Mexicans. Still, he got the point. 'That's what I'm sayin',' Cincinnatus told him. 'Biggest difference between black folks and white folks is, you're white and we're black. Next biggest difference is, you been on top. If we was on top, you bet we'd treat you just as shitty as you treated us.'

Williamson blinked again behind those glasses. Cincinnatus chuckled silently; the idea that Negroes *could* be on top plainly had never occurred to the other driver. 'Son of a bitch,' Williamson said after a moment, and then, 'Well, I bet you would. It's . . . What do you call it? Human nature, that's what.'

'Reckon so,' Cincinnatus said. 'Tell you some more human nature: I ever get my hands on Jake Featherston . . . Do Jesus!'

'Yeah,' the white man said. 'But for me it's on account of he jumped my country. It's personal for you, ain't it?'

'You might say so.' Cincinnatus stubbed out his cigarette and twisted his hands as if he were wringing a chicken's neck – or a man's. 'Yeah, you just might say so.'

They got rolling again a few minutes later, carrying this, that, and the other thing down past Delphi to where the United States were building up for the attack on Chattanooga. Armored cars accompanied the column. So did a couple of half-tracks full of soldiers. The powers that be probably cared very little about the truck drivers' safety. What they were hauling? That was another story. Here in Tennessee, the column needed all the protection it could get. The only land the United States really held here was land their men were standing on. Everything else belonged to the Confederates.

Even shot-up autos by the side of the road could be deadly dangerous. One of them blew up with an enormous roar as an armored car went by. The vehicle got two flat tires and a dent, but otherwise withstood the blast. Whoever set off the auto bomb would have done better to wait for a soft-skinned truck.

U.S. machine guns sprayed the woods, but that was a forlorn hope. They also fired at other roadside wrecks, which turned out to be a good idea. One burnt-out command car exploded while the closest U.S. vehicle was still a quarter of a mile away. Cincinnatus whooped when it did. 'One of Featherston's fuckers cussin' his head off now!' he said jubilantly.

The jubilation didn't last. It never did. Infiltrators or holdouts started shooting at the trucks. A deuce-and-a-half lurched off the road with a driver wounded or dead. Another coughed to a stop when it took a bullet through the engine block. A couple had tires flattened and had to change them. An armored car stayed behind with them to obstruct the snipers and to shoot at them if they broke cover. Along with most of the other drivers, Cincinnatus went on.

Night was falling when they got to the supply dump. Soldiers holding dim red flashlights guided them to the unloading point. More men waited there with wheelbarrows and dollies. Off in the distance, artillery rumbled.

'Come on, youse guys! Move it!' a familiar voice shouted. Cincinnatus swore under his breath. If that wasn't Sergeant Cannizzaro, he was a blond. 'Took youse long enough to get here!' the quartermaster sergeant complained.

Telling him where to go and how to get there was bound to be more trouble than it was worth. Cincinnatus just sat in the cab of his truck and wished he could have a cigarette. Signs all over the dump screamed NO SMOKING! at the top of their printed lungs.

'Here you go, Jack.' Somebody handed him a sandwich through the open window.

'Why, thank you kindly,' Cincinnatus said in glad surprise. He was even more surprised – and even gladder – when he bit into it. That thick slab of ham had never lived in a U.S. Army ration can. He didn't know where the soldier came up with it, but it was mighty good.

He wished for a bottle of beer to go with it. No sooner had he wished than another soldier came along and gave him a bottle of . . . Dr. Hopper. Soda pop wasn't the same, but it wasn't bad, either. It had to be plunder, same as the ham. The taste reminded him he was back in the CSA. Dr. Hopper didn't come over the border – at least, he'd never seen it up in Des Moines. He hoped they dropped a bomb on the factory that made the stuff . . . maybe after he'd got hold of a couple of cases for himself for old time's sake.

Swearing soldiers unloaded his truck. He thought the cussing in this war was even worse than it had been the last time around. People then sometimes seemed faintly embarrassed at what came out of their mouths. Nowadays, men didn't even notice they were turning the air blue. They swore as automatically as they breathed – and profanity seemed as necessary as air.

'Hey, Sergeant!' somebody called. 'You got beds for us?'

'What? You ain't goin' back right away?' Cannizzaro sounded genuinely amazed.

A volley of curses – purposeful, not automatic – washed over him. Cincinnatus added his two cents' worth to the barrage. The idea of crawling along in the dark with useless taped-up headlights, waiting for raiders he couldn't see to open up, was less than appealing.

Sergeant Cannizzaro knew when he was outgunned. 'Awright, already!' he said. 'Stay here.' He might have been outgunned in the literal sense. Cincinnatus had traded in his .45 for a captured Confederate submachine gun. Other drivers carried Springfields or even C.S. automatic rifles – although U.S. infantrymen in the line grabbed most of those. 'Like I said, ain't got no beds,' Cannizzaro went on. 'Youse can spread out bedrolls on the ground, or youse can sleep in your trucks. Ain't nobody gonna give you no trouble till morning, honest to God.'

Cincinnatus slept under his truck. More men stayed in their cabs, but he couldn't stretch out at full length in there. With his battered carcass, sleeping all scrunched up mostly meant not sleeping. A crumpled-up jacket made a good enough pillow. Cincinnatus' battered bones creaked as he turned and twisted to get as comfortable as he could. All that wiggling might have kept him awake for – oh, an extra thirty seconds.

He came back to himself the next morning when somebody gave him a shake and said, 'You fuckin' die under there, Pop?'

'I was restin',' Cincinnatus said with as much dignity as he could manage around a yawn.

'Yeah, well, you'll be *ar*rested if you don't get your ass in gear,' the other soldier said, and he went off to torment somebody else.

Breakfast was scrambled eggs and more slices of that terrific ham. Wherever it came from, Cannizzaro and his merry men had a lot of it. 'You ever see anybody skinny in the Quartermaster Corps?' Bruce Donovan asked.

'Yeah, well, what the hell?' Most of the time, Cincinnatus would have been as eager as the other driver to slander Sergeant Cannizzaro and his ilk. Since the guys at the supply dump were sharing their bounty this morning, he was willing to let them off easy.

He wasn't jumping up and down at the idea of going back up north to get more supplies. Oh, the Army needed them – no doubt about it. But running the gauntlet again, even with armored escorts, didn't thrill him.

That hardly crossed his mind before Donovan said, 'To think I volunteered for this shit.' Cincinnatus couldn't have put it better himself. Since he couldn't, he finished his coffee and limped back to his truck.

The convoy hadn't gone far before it had to stop. The

Confederates must have sent bombers over in the night, and a couple of them had scored direct hits on the highway. The bombs must have been big ones, too – the craters were thirty or forty feet wide and at least half that deep. Nobody was going anywhere on that road, not for a while, especially since similar craters pocked the fields to either side.

Army engineers with bulldozers were busy repairing the damage. Soldiers in green-gray went through the bushes to clear out snipers so the engineers could work without harassing fire. That made Cincinnatus jealous, but the engineers weren't even moving targets. They were sitting ducks.

More engineers were stretching lengths of steel matting – the kind used to make emergency airstrips – across the field to serve as a makeshift road while the real one was getting fixed. After about half an hour, the job was done well enough to suit them. They waved the lead truck forward.

Cincinnatus was glad he wasn't driving lead. But where the deuce-and-a-half ahead of him went, he followed. The matting was a little higher than an ordinary curb would have been. His truck didn't like climbing up onto the stuff, but it could. He bumped along, then jounced down, then climbed up onto another strip of matting. Skirting the bomb craters went slowly, but it went. And those soldiers out there beating the bushes were keeping him safe along with the engineers. He tipped his cap to them, though they couldn't see him do it.

Everybody stepped on the gas once he got back onto the paved highway. Cincinnatus was happy to mash the pedal down to the floorboard. He knew he might be rushing toward danger, not away from it. All the same, he'd felt like a sitting duck himself back there. He was glad to get away.

Nobody got hurt on the run north from Delphi, which made it a good one. Only three or four shots were fired at the column. They sounded like .22 rounds to Cincinnatus. Those wouldn't come from Confederate soldiers, who had better weapons, but from some civilian with a squirrel gun and a grudge. U.S. authorities had confiscated all the firearms they could. The penalties for holding on to rifles and pistols were bloodthirsty. The Confederate citizenry didn't seem to care. Cincinnatus wished he were more surprised.

Halfway to Camp Determination. That was how Abner Dowling looked at it. He wished he'd come farther. He wished his men could have moved faster. But he'd been stalled in front of Lubbock too damn long. The Eleventh Army – such as it was – was moving again. How much anybody back East cared . . . might be a different story.

He hadn't got the reinforcements he hoped for. Everything the U.S. Army could lay its hands on was going into the drive toward Chattanooga. Dowling didn't much like that, but he understood it.

One reason he wasn't going as fast or as far as he wished he could was that the Confederates *were* bringing in reinforcements: Freedom Party Guard outfits that fought as if there were no tomorrow. They made Dowling scratch his head for all kinds of reasons.

'They've got fewer men in Tennessee and Kentucky than we do, right?' he asked his adjutant one hot, sticky summer morning.

'Certainly seems so,' Major Angelo Toricelli agreed.

'They're in trouble over there and we're not, right?' Dowling persisted.

'Unless our newspapers and wireless people are lying even harder than Featherston's, yes, sir,' Toricelli said. 'Possible, I suppose, but not likely.'

'Bet your ass it's not,' Dowling said, which made the

younger officer blink. 'All right, then. We keep saying we can't afford to send anything out here to the ass end of nowhere. But Featherston's sending people, sending equipment, out here like it's going out of style. I know he's a son of a bitch, but up till now I never thought he was a *dumb* son of a bitch, you know what I mean?'

'Yes, sir,' Toricelli said. 'I can only think of one thing.'

'Well, you're one up on me if you can. Spit it out.' Dowling had always enjoyed feeling smarter than George Custer. Now he watched his own adjutant feeling smarter than he was.

'To the Confederates, sir, this isn't the ass end of nowhere,' Toricelli said.

'Well, yes, but why not?' Dowling asked. 'You can't really mean they think killing off Negroes as fast as they can is more important than keeping us out of Chattanooga?'

The words hung in the air after he said them. The oppressive humidity might have borne them up. Major Toricelli nodded. 'That's it, sir. That *is* what I think. Nothing else makes sense to me.'

'Then Featherston really is off the deep end,' Dowling exclaimed.

'Could be, sir. I don't know anything about that. I'm no head-candler. But whether he's nuts or not, he's still running the CSA, and nobody's trying to stop him that I know of. When he yells, "Jump, frog!" they all ask, "How high?" on the way up.'

'Good God,' Dowling murmured. 'If you'll let your country go down the drain so you can do this instead . . . I'm not sure a head-candler can help you.'

'I hope nobody can help him,' Toricelli said. 'But he's been at war with Negroes about as long as he's been at war with the USA. Don't they say he had a chance to stop the uprisings in the last war, only his superior wouldn't let him take a servant in for questioning? Something like that, anyway.'

'I think you're right, or close enough,' Dowling said. 'But if he beats us, he can do what he wants with the Negroes later. If he goes on killing them and we lick him . . .'

'They're gone, and he dies happy,' Toricelli said.

'He sure as hell dies,' Dowling said. 'Send the War Department a report showing the reinforcements we've run up against. Send them a summary of what we've been talking about, too. They should know we think he thinks that way. Don't be shy about giving yourself credit, either. You were there ahead of me.'

'Thank you, sir.' Major Toricelli sounded as if he meant that. Dowling understood why. When he served under Custer, nothing was ever the great man's fault. Anything good accrued to the great man's credit. Here, Dowling consciously tried not to imitate his old boss.

He sent an armored probe forward – and got it bloodied. Yes, the Confederates finally were reinforced. They had new armor of their own, and that meant trouble. They'd go nipping in after his supply line next. He had the feeling he'd come about as far as he could, or maybe a little farther.

One thing the enemy didn't have was much air power. Dowling summoned Colonel DeFrancis. 'I want you to go after those barrels and self-propelled guns, Terry,' he said. 'Go after their fuel dumps, too. Let's see how much we can slow 'em down.'

'I'll do my goddamnedest, sir,' DeFrancis said. 'We've got some new inch-and-a-half guns mounted under dive bombers. Turns 'em into barrel busters. They dive, fire from close range, pull up and climb, then do it again. Engine decking hasn't got a prayer of standing up to an armor-piercing round like that.'

'Sounds good to me,' Dowling told him. 'Turn 'em loose. Let 'em hunt. Let's see what they can do. Let's see if they can keep those bastards off our necks.'

'Yes, sir!' Terry DeFrancis sounded enthusiastic. He often did, especially when Dowling was turning him loose on a new and exciting hunt. For most officers, as for most other people in executive positions, what they did was a job. Some of them were better at it than others, but for the able and not so able alike it was work. DeFrancis was different. He enjoyed what he did. He had a good time doing it. Maybe he got a hard-on watching things blow up. Dowling didn't know – he didn't ask. But the colonel's enjoyment made him a better combat officer. He constantly looked for new ways to put the enemy in trouble. Chances were he grinned when he found them, too.

West Texas made good barrel country. It was nice and flat – you could see for miles. There weren't a lot of forests for barrels to hide in, either. That made for a wide-open fight, and also for a fair fight. But if barrels had trouble hiding from one another, they also had trouble hiding from airplanes. The USA controlled the skies hereabouts. Abner Dowling aimed to make the most of it.

His headquarters wasn't close enough to the airstrip to let him hear DeFrancis' dive bombers and fighter-bombers take off. Why put all your eggs anywhere near the same basket when the prairie was so wide? He stayed where he was, strengthened his flanks in case the aircraft didn't do as much as he hoped they would, and waited to see what happened next.

Custer wouldn't wait, he thought. *Custer would charge ahead regardless.* And no doubt he was right, because Custer always aimed to get the bit between his teeth and charge ahead regardless. About four times out of five, he ended up wishing he hadn't. The fifth time . . . The fifth time left him with his reputation as a great general, because the fifth time he charged the other side shattered instead of his own.

Dowling knew he wouldn't go down in the history books as a great general. The two likeliest candidates this time around were Irving Morrell and George Patton. Patton got off to a fast start in Ohio, but Morrell was making up ground – literally as well as metaphorically – in Kentucky and Tennessee. Who held higher honors in the books would probably depend on who won the war.

Some men who realized they weren't going to be great generals turned into failures instead. They drank too much, or they became sour martinets, or they forgot about discipline for themselves and everybody under them. Dowling tried not to commit those particular sins. If he couldn't be a great general, he could be a pretty good one, and that was what he aimed at.

He awaited developments, then. A great general probably would have forced them. A pretty good general could decide he was in no position to force them, which seemed plain as a punch in the nose to Dowling. He consoled himself by deciding it would take a great general to beat him, and so far his Confederate counterpart had shown no signs of greatness. If anything, the fellow on the other side seemed to have more trouble making up his mind than Dowling did.

The awaited developments . . . didn't develop. No column full of Freedom Party Guards and enemy armor crashed into Dowling's flank from the wide open spaces to the north or south. Dowling briefly wondered whether his opposite number had had his imagination surgically removed when he was only a lad.

Then the aerial reconnaissance photos came in. Terry DeFrancis came in with them – and with a spring in his step and a cigar in his mouth. 'Will you look at these, sir?' he said. 'Will you just look at them?'

'If you quit waving them around, I will,' Dowling said.

'Sorry, sir.' DeFrancis set them on his desk.

Dowling spread them out so he could look at several at once. They all seemed to feature vehicles on fire and pillars of smoke mounting up to the sky. Some of the burning vehicles were trucks, but quite a few were barrels. 'You hit them hard,' Dowling said.

'Sir, we fucking pulverized them, pardon my French,' DeFrancis said. 'They were driving along without a care in the world, right out in the open, and we caught 'em naked with their legs spread. We screwed 'em, too. We screwed 'em to the wall.'

'With news like that, you can speak French to me any old day,' Dowling said.

'Thank you, sir.' Colonel DeFrancis grinned around the cigar. He grew a little more serious as he went on, 'Air power matters here. It *really* matters. We've got it, and the other guys don't. That gives them just as much trouble approaching us as a fleet of battleships has approaching an airplane carrier.'

'Don't get carried away,' Dowling warned. 'They can do things battleships can't. They can camouflage themselves. They can spread out, so you don't catch so many of them together. I suppose they can even use dummies and hit with their real force while you attack those.'

DeFrancis eyed him. 'Sir, I'm glad we're on the same side. You've got an evil, nasty, sneaky mind.'

'You say the sweetest things, Colonel.' Dowling batted his eyelashes at the younger man. Watching a portly, six-tyish general simper and flirt was almost enough to make DeFrancis swallow his stogie. As his air commander had before, Dowling quickly sobered. 'You're doing a terrific job, Terry. I just don't want you to get too confident.'

'Fair enough, sir,' DeFrancis said. Dowling hoped he meant it. When you were winning, when things were going your way, it was easy to think victory was meant to be. Custer always did. Hell, Custer thought victory was meant to be even when he'd just taken a shellacking. His confidence made his troops pay a fearful butcher's bill.

In the end, Custer made his vision of victory real. Dowling wanted DeFrancis to do that without causing his own side the misery Custer had. 'What's the next thing you can do that would hurt the enemy most?' Dowling asked.

'Catch another column flat-footed,' DeFrancis replied at once.

Dowling tried again: 'What's the next thing you can do that would hurt the enemy most, assuming he's not an idiot?'

Colonel DeFrancis took longer to answer this time. At last, he said, 'Well, the more we pound his supply lines, the more trouble he'll have hitting us.'

'Fine,' Dowling said. 'Do it. Even if the War Department won't send us more men, they don't seem constipated about shipping us ordnance. As long as we've got it, we might as well drop it on the Confederates' heads.'

'I like the way you think, sir,' DeFrancis said.

'I just hope the bastards in butternut don't,' Dowling answered. 'Keep hammering them. If we can soften 'em up enough, we *will* drive on Camp Determination.' He spoke with no small determination of his own.

'Hey, Sarge!' one of the soldiers in Chester Martin's platoon called to him.

'What's up, Frankie?' Martin asked.

'Found this out on patrol. Figured I better bring it in so you could see.' Frankie held out a piece of paper.

'Thanks – I think.' Chester took it. It was cheap pulp, not much better than newspaper grade. The printing was cheap, too: letters blurred, ink smeary. The message, though, was something else again. YANKEE MURDERERS! it began, and went downhill from there.

The gist was that U.S. soldiers who'd shot hostages couldn't expect to be treated as prisoners of war. *We shoot mad dogs,* it read, *and anyone who slaughters innocent Confederate civilians puts himself forever beyond the pale of civilized warfare.*

'What do you think, Sarge?' Frankie asked.

'Me? I think there's no such thing as an innocent Confederate civilian, except maybe in his left ear,' Chester answered. 'You tell anybody else about this little love letter?'

Frankie shook his head. 'No, Sarge. Not me.'

'Don't flabble about it if you did – bound to be lots more copies out there,' Martin said. 'But don't go yelling it from the housetops, either. You did good, bringing it to me. I'm going to let Captain Rhodes have a look at it.'

Rhodes studied the flyer, then looked up at Chester. 'Thanks for showing this to me, Sergeant. I'll kick it up to Intelligence, let the boys there check it out. I'd say we hit a nerve.'

'Sir?' Chester said. 'How do you mean?'

'Looks to me like the Confederates are saying they can't protect their own, and they're trying to scare us into being nice little boys and girls,' Rhodes answered. 'Or do you think I'm wrong? You've been around the block a few times – you know what's what.'

'I don't know my ass from a hole in the ground half the time.' Chester thought about it. 'You may be right. I don't know that you are, but you may be.'

'Fair enough,' Captain Rhodes said. 'We'll see what the Intelligence johnnies think. Hell, they won't pay any attention to me – I'm just a dumb line officer, so what the fuck can I know?'

'You're a damn good company commander, sir,' Martin said. 'I've been around *that* block – I ought to know.'

'Thanks. When you say something like that, I know you're not blowing smoke up my ass, 'cause you don't need to,' Rhodes said. 'I know damn well we've got more good company-level officers than first sergeants.'

He wasn't wrong. The worst thing he could do to Chester was take away his platoon. And if he did, if some baby-faced shavetail started commanding it instead, who would really be running things any which way? Chester and Hubert Rhodes both knew the answer to that one.

'Do we have any notion when we're going after Chattanooga, sir?' Chester asked.

'I'm sure *we* do, if we counts the big brains back in Philly,' Rhodes answered. 'If you mean, do *I* have any notion, well, no.'

'Can't be too much longer . . . can it?' Martin said.

'I wouldn't think so. Both sides are building up as fast as they can,' the company commander said. 'As long as we keep building faster than the Confederates, everything's fine. And I think we are. We've got air superiority here – we've got it just about everywhere except between Richmond and Philadelphia. We can smash them when they try to move men and supplies forward, and they can't do that to us.'

'We've got more men to start with, too,' Chester said. 'Their small arms make up for some of that, but not for all of it.'

'Now our barrels are better than theirs, too – till they run out their next model, anyway,' Rhodes said. 'We can lick 'em, Sergeant. We can, and I think we will.'

'Sounds good to me, sir,' Chester said.

If the Confederates thought their U.S. opponents could beat them, they did a hell of a job of hiding it. Chester had seen that in the last war. You could beat the bastards in butternut, but most of them kept their peckers up right till the end. They kept fighting with everything they had.

Maybe they didn't have as much as they would have if U.S. airplanes weren't bombing the crap out of their supply lines. Chester didn't know about that. They still seemed to have plenty of artillery ammunition. Their automatic rifles and submachine guns didn't run short of cartridges, either. They had enough fuel to send barrels and armored cars forward when they counterattacked – and they counterattacked whenever they thought they saw a chance to take back some ground.

The terrain south of Delphi didn't need long to turn into the sort of lunar landscape Chester had known and loathed during the Great War. The stench of death hung over it: something even uglier than the view, which wasn't easy. Soldiers sheltered in craters and foxholes. Trench lines and barbed wire were thinner on the ground than they had been a generation earlier, mostly because barrels could breach them.

Nobody liked this kind of fighting, going back and forth over the same few miles of ground. 'When do we break out, Sarge?' Frankie asked one day. He was scooping up pork and beans from a can. 'We go somewhere new, maybe it won't smell so bad.'

'Maybe.' Chester's ration can was full of what was alleged to be beef stew. The grayish meat inside might have been boiled tire tread. Chester had never found a piece with GOODYEAR stamped on it, but that didn't mean he wouldn't. And the Confederates thought Yankee chow was better than what their own quartermasters dished out! That was a scary thought. He went on, 'I asked Captain Rhodes the other day. He didn't know, either.'

'Well, if he don't, chances are nobody does. He's a hell of a smart man, the captain is,' Frankie said.

'That's a fact,' Chester said.

They were still eating when a Confederate junior officer came forward with a white flag. He asked for a two-hour truce for both sides to pick up their wounded. Martin greeted him with a glare. 'Yeah? Suppose you get some of our guys? You gonna shoot 'em once you take 'em back behind the lines?'

'Good God, no!' the C.S. lieutenant said. 'We don't do things like that!'

'Except maybe to niggers,' Chester said.

He watched the enemy soldier turn red. But the man didn't even waste his breath denying it. 'We don't do that to soldiers in a declared war,' was all he said.

'Sounds like bullshit to me, buddy,' Chester said. 'What about that goddamn leaflet you've been spreading all over creation?'

The C.S. lieutenant blushed again. 'That wasn't soldiers who did that. It was Freedom Party guys from the Director of Communications' office.'

'How the hell are we supposed to tell the difference? You've even got Freedom Party Guards coming into the line along with regular soldiers. What are we supposed to do? Kill all of you bastards and let God worry about it afterwards?'

'I don't have anything to do with ordering that stuff,' the Confederate said. 'If they come up here, they're soldiers. They perform like soldiers, don't they?' He waited. Martin couldn't very well deny that. Seeing that he couldn't, the officer went on, 'Honest to God, Sergeant, if we find your people, we'll take 'em prisoner. If we start doing things to 'em and you people find out, you've got our POWs to get even with.'

That made a certain brutal sense to Chester. He nodded. 'All right, Lieutenant. Two hours. Your medics and ours – and probably a little bit of trading back and forth. Got any coffee?' Not much came up into the USA. The Army got most of what there was and stretched it as far as it would go, which made it pretty awful.

'Swap you some for a couple cans of deviled ham. That's the best damn ration around,' the lieutenant said.

Before talking to him, Chester had made sure he had some. He would have bet the Confederate wanted it. The lieutenant gave him a cloth sack full of whole roasted beans. Just the smell, the wonderful smell, was enough to pry his eyelids farther apart. 'Yeah, that's the straight goods, sure as hell,' Chester said reverently.

'I got me some eggs,' the lieutenant said. 'Got me some butter, too. Gonna scramble 'em up with this ham . . .' For a moment, they both forgot about the war.

Then the Confederate officer turned and waved to his men. Chester also turned. 'Cease-fire!' he yelled. 'Two hours! Medics, forward!' He nodded to the lieutenant. 'You can head on back now.'

'Thanks.' The officer raised his hand in what wasn't quite a wave and wasn't quite a salute. Away he went.

From both sides of the line, men with Red Cross smocks and with the Red Cross painted on their helmets moved up to gather casualties – and to share cigarettes and food and coffee and maybe an unofficial nip or two from a canteen. Men on both sides stood up and stretched and walked around without fear of getting shot. If they were smart, they tried not to show exactly where their hiding places were. Snipers had a nasty habit of remembering stuff like that.

Corpsmen brought back a soldier with a wound dressing on his leg. 'How you doing, Miller?' Chester asked.

'I'm out of the fucking war for a while, anyway.' Miller didn't sound sorry he'd got hit. A lot of people who caught hometowners felt the same way.

Chester kept smelling that wonderful coffee. He wanted to smash up the beans with the hilt of his belt knife or find a hammer to do it and to make himself three or four cups' worth of joe right then. The enemy lieutenant had probably brought it forward the same way he'd carried the cans of deviled ham. The fellow had to know what a damnyankee would want.

Another wounded man came in, this one with a blood-soaked bandage on his head. The medics looked grim. 'Bad?' Chester said.

'About as bad as it gets,' one of the medics answered. 'Head wound, in one side and out the other. God knows how he's still breathing, with half his brains blown out. Take a miracle for him to get better.'

'Take a miracle for him to still be breathing this time tomorrow,' another medic said. The man who'd spoken first didn't tell him he was wrong. Shaking their heads, the stretcher team carried the wounded soldier back towards an aid station.

'Fuck,' Chester Martin said softly. Krikor Hartunian – hell of a name – didn't belong to his platoon. But he came from Captain Rhodes' company. He was a baby when his folks were lucky enough to escape from the Ottoman Empire. An awful lot of Armenians hadn't been so lucky. Some people said the massacres the Turks pulled off helped give Jake Featherston the idea for getting rid of the CSA's Negroes.

Chester had no idea if that was true. All he knew was that a Confederate bullet had slaughtered Krikor – usually called Greg. The kid's folks had a farm somewhere in central California nowadays. Pretty soon, a Western Union messenger would deliver a Deeply Regrets telegram from the War Department. People didn't want to see Western Union messengers these days. Chester remembered his folks talking about that during the last war. These days, they called the poor kids – who were only doing their job – angels of death. Wasn't that a hell of a thing?

Here in southern Tennessee, death came without angels. When the truce ran out, both sides fired a few warning shots. Anybody still up and around and out in the open ran for cover. Then they got back to the business of murder.

XIV

Gracchus' band of black guerrillas kept growing. At first, Cassius thought that was wonderful. Then he noticed how worried the rebel leader looked. 'What's the matter?' he asked.

Gracchus eyed him with something less than joy. 'How'm I gonna keep all you sons of bitches fed?' he burst out.

'Oh.' Cassius had no answer for that. He'd eaten well his whole life in Augusta. He'd gone on eating well, or as well as any Negro could, after the Freedom Party enclosed the Terry in barbed wire. Only after he escaped did he discover what living with his belly bumping his backbone was like. A full stomach was better. How his father, his old, fussy, precise father, would have laughed at him for that brilliant discovery! He hoped Scipio, wherever he was, still could laugh. What he hoped and what he feared were very different things.

'Oh,' Gracchus echoed sardonically. 'Yeah. You kin say, "Oh." But you only gots to say it. I gots to do somethin' about it.'

Cassius paused to fiddle with the sling to his Tredegar. When he first got the rifle, he messed with it all the time, trying to make the nine-pound weight comfortable. Now, as often as not, he forgot he was carrying it. If the sling hadn't found some way to twist, he wouldn't have noticed it.

'When I was in the city, I reckoned country niggers lived in these little villages,' he said. 'Y'all'd grow your own corn and raise chickens and pigs and like that. An' I reckoned there'd be plenty o' vittles.'

'Used to be like dat,' Gracchus said bitterly. 'I was a sharecropper. Had me a pot belly – best believe I did.' He was skinny as a snake now, and at least as mean. 'Freedom Party git in, they start makin' all kinds o' harvesters an' combines an' shit. Put all us niggers outa work, fucked them villages like you wouldn't believe.'

'Got the factories set up so they could make barrels, too,' Cassius said.

'That's a fact.' Gracchus eyed him. 'You ain't dumb, is you?'

'Me?' Cassius said in surprise. He always thought of himself as pretty dumb. He measured himself against his father – what young man doesn't? His father, as far as he could tell, knew everything there was to know. He could even talk white, and do it better than most whites could. He'd tried to teach Cassius some of what he knew. Cassius could read and write and cipher. Past that, he hadn't cared to learn. For the first time, he wondered if he'd made a mistake. It was too late, of course. Life didn't hand you many second chances. If you were black in the CSA, life didn't hand you many first chances.

'I ain't talkin' about Demosthenes over there,' Gracchus said. Demosthenes was larger than Cassius, stronger than Cassius, braver than Cassius. As far as Cassius could tell, Demosthenes feared nothing and nobody. He was hung like a horse, too. On the other hand, he was so dumb he had to remind himself out loud how to tie his shoes. Gracchus went on, 'We need folks who'll do whatever somebody tells 'em to do, an' do it *right now*. Gots to have folks like dat, no two ways about it. But we gots to have people who kin think some, too.'

'Me?' Cassius said again.

'Reckon so,' Gracchus answered. 'Next thing we gots to see is if folks jump when you tells 'em to. We fight the damn Mexicans again, you try it. See what happens. Things go good, got us a new officer.'

'Me?' Cassius knew he was starting to sound like a broken record. What he didn't know was whether he wanted to be an officer. He didn't like other people ordering him around. His father could speak volumes on that . . . if he was in a position to speak volumes on anything. Cassius didn't see why other people would want him ordering them around, either.

But Gracchus had no doubts. From everything Cassius had seen, Gracchus hardly ever had doubts. That was one of the things that made him a leader. 'You,' he said now, with a decisive nod. 'If you kin do the job, you better step up an' do it.'

That cut close to the bone. Francisco José's Mexicans had made most unwilling soldiers when they first came to the CSA. Now they seemed to realize they weren't going home any time soon, and that it was the black guerrillas' fault. Just as blacks wanted revenge on whites, so the Mexican soldiers wanted revenge on blacks.

And if they didn't, unconscripted Confederate whites did. The lame, the halt, the old, the very young . . . Some of them could take rifles out into the field and go after the rebels haunting Georgia. And even the ones who couldn't served as sentries and guards and did all they could to make life difficult for raiding bands of Negroes – and to fire up the Mexicans so they fought harder, too.

All of which made this march through the central part of the state grim and hungry. Gracchus had scouts out before and behind, to the left and to the right. He knew the guerrillas were hunted, all right. So far, though, they kept slipping through the net.

And how much good does it do? Cassius wondered. He wished he hadn't thought of the raiders as haunting the Georgia countryside. That made them too much like ghosts of what had been there before, what would never come back to life again. Whites in the towns were real. Everything out here . . . Well, so what? A lot of town dwellers had to see things that way, anyhow.

But without the countryside, where would the Confederates States get their cotton and peanuts and tobacco, their corn and rice and hogs? Thanks to the Freedom Party and the machinery, the countryside needed far fewer workers to produce its crops than it had ten years earlier. But it still needed some, and it still needed the machines. If farmers and farmworkers got shot, if combines got torched, how was the Confederacy supposed to bring in any kind of harvest at all?

Nobody challenged the guerrilla band as it tramped along a narrow blacktop road. Gracchus probably knew where the fighters were going, but Cassius had no idea. The countryside was a whole different world, and not one where he belonged. He knew every alleyway and corner of the Terry – and much good that ended up doing him. Now he had something new to learn. And he would . . . if he lived long enough.

Something buzzed overhead. For a second, Cassius thought it was a stupid country bug that didn't come into cities. Then he saw other guerrillas pointing and heard them swearing. His eyes followed their upraised fingers. The biplane circling up there had been obsolete as a fighting machine since the mid-1920s, if not longer. But it did just fine spotting people who couldn't shoot it down.

'Goddamn thing,' Gracchus snarled. 'Bet your ass some fucker with a wireless set bringin' sojers down on us.'

That struck Cassius as much too likely. But the biplane

pilot had other things in mind, too. He dove on the guerrillas. 'Scatter!' three blacks yelled at the same time.

The airplane mounted two machine guns set above the engine and firing through the prop. Cassius could see them winking on and off, on and off, as the pilot fired one short burst after another. Afterwards, he couldn't have said why he didn't run like most of the other men. It wasn't lack of fear. With bullets from the guns cracking past and with others pinging and shrieking as they ricocheted off the paving, he would have been an idiot not to be afraid. Hadn't Gracchus just called him a smart fellow?

Wounded men screamed to either side of the road. Cassius raised his rifle to his shoulder and fired two shots at the swooping biplane. He knew he wasn't the only guerrilla shooting at it. But he was sure one of his shots caught the pilot in the chest. He had a good bead on the man, and saw him throw up his arms when he was hit. The biplane never pulled out of the dive, but slammed into the ground less than a hundred yards away.

'Do Jesus!' Cassius exclaimed through the crunching thud of the impact and the roar of the fireball that went up an instant later. '*Do* Jesus!' Machine-gun rounds in the burning wreck started cooking off, *pop! pop! pop!*, like firecrackers on the Fourth of July. A bullet snapped past Cassius' head, as if the pilot were still fighting back from beyond the grave.

'You the one who nailed that ofay asshole?' Gracchus asked, coming out from between the rows of corn that grew to either side of the road.

'Reckon I am,' Cassius answered. Then he coughed. The breeze was blowing back from the downed airplane toward him. It was thick with the smells of burning fabric, burning fuel, hot metal – and charred flesh. He thought that odor would stay with him the rest of his life.

'How come you didn't run and hide?' the guerrilla leader asked.

'Beats me,' Cassius said honestly. 'Just didn't think to, I guess.'

'Didn't think to? Didn't fuckin' think to?' Gracchus came up and gave him an affectionate clout in the side of the head. 'Hope you do some more not thinkin' real soon now, you hear? You know what the ofays gonna do when they find out you shoot down their fancy airplane? They gonna shit, that's what.' He clouted Cassius again, which the younger man could have done without. Cassius knew better than to say so.

He looked down at the asphalt around his feet. Bullet scars pockmarked it. The white man in that airplane had done his level best to kill him. One of the bullet marks lay right *between* his feet. He started to realize just how lucky he was. It didn't make him feel proud or brave. No, it made him want to shiver instead.

Not everybody was so lucky. The guerrillas were doing what they could for their wounded. What they could do was pitifully little. They could bandage. They could suture – crudely. They could put alcohol or iodine on injuries. If they were desperate enough, they could put ether on a rag and go after a bullet with stolen forceps. Past that . . . no. Was there a black doctor, a black surgeon, anywhere in the CSA? Cassius didn't think so. Oh, maybe in New Orleans. People went on and on about what Negroes in New Orleans were supposed to be able to do.

Were there any Negroes, surgeons or otherwise, in New Orleans these days? Or had they all gone to the camps like the rest of Cassius' family? If they had, would any of them ever come out again?

Cassius feared he knew the answer. He knew it, but he didn't want to think about it. Thinking about it would have meant thinking about his mother and father and sister.

'We gots to get outa here,' Gracchus said. 'Even if that fucker wasn't on the wireless – an' he was bound to be, damn him – they gonna come see how come their airplane done crashed.'

'Ambush 'em?' Cassius asked.

Gracchus blinked. He thought. At last, reluctantly, he shook his head. 'Don't reckon we could pull free an' disappear fast enough afterwards,' he said. 'They be on our trail like bloodhounds.' Had he ever read *Uncle Tom's Cabin*? Cassius had, though the novel remained banned in the CSA sixty years after the slaves were – allegedly – manumitted. But he didn't think Gracchus could read at all.

He couldn't very well argue with the guerrilla leader about the risks. Since he couldn't, he made himself nod instead. 'Whatever you say.'

To a commander, that was always the right answer. Because it was, Gracchus condescended to explain: 'This ain't the Army. I lose my men, I can't pick up no telephone an' git mo'. I gots to find 'em, same way I found you. Sometimes I gots to learn 'em to fight, way I learned you. Don't want to lose 'em. Happens, but I don't want it to. Want the ofays an' the Mexicans to lose their bastards instead.'

He'd learned war in a sternly practical school. Cassius knew he himself remained a beginner, even if he was a beginner who'd just luckily aced an important test. He nodded and gave back the magic words once more: 'Whatever you say.'

'I say we gets outa here,' Gracchus declared. And they did. If Cassius wished for what might have been . . . this wasn't the first time, nor the most urgent. He hurried away with the rest.

*

Every time Jonathan Moss read in captured papers about U.S. advances deeper into Tennessee, he wanted to head north. When he and Nick Cantarella escaped from Andersonville, he never imagined men in green-gray could penetrate the Confederacy the way the USA's soldiers were. Jake Featherston's butternut-clad troops were pushing into western Pennsylvania then, and it hadn't been clear whether anything or anybody could stop them.

No matter what Moss wanted to do now, his desires ran up against reality in the shape of Spartacus. 'Tennessee line still a hell of a long ways from here,' the guerrilla leader said. 'Got to git around Atlanta some kinda way if we heads up there. That ain't country I know.'

'Could you pass us on to an outfit that operates north of you?' Moss asked. 'You know, like the Underground Railroad in the old days?'

Spartacus only shook his grizzled head. 'Yankee sojers come down here, fine. Till then, I needs you an' Nick too much to turn loose of you.'

And that was that. The two white men might slip away on their own, but what could they do next? They would be all alone in a country that hated them, all alone in a country where their accents gave them away whenever they opened their mouths. Could they get up to Chattanooga on their own? It seemed unlikely. The only hope for help they had came from other bands of black guerrillas. And would some other band's chieftain be any more willing to let them go than Spartacus was? One more unlikelihood.

And if Moss and Cantarella got caught trying to slip away, they would forfeit Spartacus' trust. That wouldn't be good. That would be about as bad as it could get, in fact. So they didn't go north. They went east with the guerrillas instead.

They moved mostly by night. More and more often,

Confederate authorities – or maybe it was just the locals on their own – put up a barnstormer's review of antique airplanes during the day to keep an eye out for guerrilla bands. Moss watched the two-deckers from the cover of pine woods with a fierce and terrible longing.

'You could fly one of those fuckers, couldn't you?' Nick Cantarella asked one day, first making sure no blacks were in earshot.

'In my sleep,' Moss answered at once. 'I flew worse junk than that in the Great War – not a lot worse, some of the time, but worse.'

Cantarella looked around again and dropped his voice even lower. 'You think we could steal one?'

'You're reading my mind – you know that?' Moss spoke hardly above a whisper. 'I only see one hitch.'

'Yeah? Walking up to the damn thing, hopping in, and flying off?'

Moss paused. 'Well, two hitches,' he said sheepishly.

'What's the other one?'

'From here, we need a full tank of gas to get up to the U.S. line. We run low, we can't stop at the local Esso station and tank up.'

'Not hardly.' The younger man laughed. Then he sobered again. 'So how do we know how much gas is in the son of a bitch we take?'

'I fire up the engine and look at what the fuel gauge says,' Moss answered. 'No matter what it says, though, I've got to take off after that. This isn't one of those deals where you can try again if you don't like what you see.'

'Suits me,' Cantarella said. 'Suits me fine. Far as I can tell, we've done our duty by these people and then some. Time to do our duty for the US of A, too. And you know what else?'

'Tell me,' Moss urged.

'We got one great big thing going for us when we waltz up to that airplane.' Cantarella waited till Moss made a questioning noise. Then he said, 'We're white. They won't be looking for ofays' – he grinned when he used the word – 'to up and steal a flying machine, not in a month of Sundays they won't.'

Moss didn't need to think about that very long before he nodded. 'Well, you're right. Too bad we won't be able to see the looks on their faces after we take off.'

It sounded so good, so easy, so inevitable, that they overlooked something: they weren't anywhere near an airstrip. They didn't come anywhere near one for quite a while, either. Their sole relationship with airplanes was hiding from them.

After a few days, Moss told Cantarella, 'You ought to suggest to Spartacus that we go hit an airport so they can't spy on us so well.'

'*I* ought to?' The Army officer pointed at him. 'What about you?'

'No.' Moss shook his head. 'If it comes from you, it's strategy. He's used to that. If it comes from me, it's *The pilot wants to get his hands on an airplane.* And he'd be right, 'cause I do. Better the other way.'

Whiskers rasped under Cantarella's fingers as he scratched his chin. 'Yeah, that makes sense. I'll do it,' he said at last. 'Don't know whether he'll listen to me, but it's a pretty good shot.'

'A lot depends on how well they guard their airstrips,' Moss said. 'If they're locked up tight, Spartacus won't want anything to do with them, and how do you blame him? But if he knows one where the locals are asleep at the switch . . .'

If there was an airstrip like that, Spartacus *would* know about it. The grapevine worked. Not all Negroes had disappeared from Confederate society – just most of them. There were still cooks and maids and janitors. They heard things. They knew things. And what they heard, what they knew, they managed to pass to guerrilla leaders like Spartacus.

Nick Cantarella planted the seed. He and Moss waited to see if it would bear fruit. While they waited, they tramped along. They couldn't stay anywhere for more than a couple of days; if they did, they started eating the countryside bare. It seemed bare enough to Moss as things were.

'Got a question,' Spartacus said as they marched through a weary night. 'You git your hands on an airplane with machine guns in it, could you shoot at the Confederates with it?'

'As long as I have fuel. As long as I have ammo. As long as the motor keeps working the way it's supposed to,' Moss said.

'You do it in the nighttime, or you have to wait fo' daylight?'

'Daylight would be better,' Moss answered. 'A lot better. I wouldn't want to try to land in the dark without good airport lights and without somebody on the wireless talking me down. Night flying's a whole different ballgame.'

'All right.' Spartacus nodded. 'Reckon that means we gots to hit at daybreak, so you kin git the airplane up an' shoot up the town before you lands it somewhere an' we gits you out.'

'What town?' Moss asked.

'Name o' the place is Pineview,' Spartacus said. 'We's about ten miles from there now. They got an airstrip outside – reckon we could swoop down on it.'

'Do you want to do that?'

The guerrilla chieftain nodded. 'Any way I kin hurt the ofays, I wants to do it. Strips won't be guarded much. I's sure of dat. Ofays don't know we got us a pilot. They reckon we ain't nothin' but a bunch o' dumb fuckin' niggers. We show 'em. We fuck 'em good – you'd best believe it.'

Later that day, Nick Cantarella tipped Moss a wink. If Moss hadn't been looking for it, he never would have noticed. He gave back a discreet thumbs-up.

Spartacus didn't charge ahead without checking. He sent scouts out under cover of darkness to give the airstrip a once-over. They reported a few strands of barbed wire and some sleepy guards ambling around the perimeter. 'We kin take 'em out, then?' Spartacus said.

'Oh, hell, yes, boss,' one of the scouts said. The other black man nodded.

Spartacus smacked his right fist into his cupped left palm. 'Let's go do it, then,' he declared. 'We gonna make the ofays shit.' All the colored guerrillas who heard that grinned and clapped and whooped. So did Jonathan Moss and Nick Cantarella. If they had reasons of their own that the Negroes knew nothing about . . . then they did, that was all.

Since the attack on the airstrip outside of Pineview wouldn't go in till morning twilight brightened the sky, the guerrillas had plenty of time to grab some sleep early in the evening and deploy as soon as the moon went down. Moss had trouble getting any rest. He was always nervous before missions. Cantarella snored like a buzz saw biting into a knot. If he worried ahead of time, he didn't show it that way.

Flopped down in the dirt, mud smeared on his face so it wouldn't show, Moss peered hungrily at the airstrip. There wasn't much to see: a couple of runways flattened with steamrollers, a couple of old-fashioned airplanes at the end of one of them, a sentry with a limp who patrolled this stretch of barbed wire. Moss knew what wire was supposed to be like. This barely counted for a token effort.

'Let's go,' Spartacus said. Three men with wire cutters slid forward. The strands of barbed wire parted with soft twangs. The men waved. The rest of the guerrillas loped toward the gaps. Someone shone a flashlight toward the rear. The prize pickup with the machine gun in the bed would be coming, too.

'Halt! Who goes there?' A white man spoke in peremptory tones. When he didn't get the answer he liked, his rifle barked. Moss saw the muzzle flash. Half a dozen answering shots rang out. The sentry screamed and toppled.

'Come on!' Spartacus shouted. 'Ain't got much time now.'

He was wrong. They had no time at all.

Electric lights blazed on, illuminating the advancing raiders much too well. 'Get down!' Nick Cantarella yelled. 'It's a – !' Before he could say *trap* or *ambush* or whatever he was going to say, three machine guns opened up and said it for him.

Spartacus' men were caught out in the open on flat ground at short range. The pickup went up in flames before it even got to the barbed-wire perimeter. Maybe some of the Negroes who'd fed Spartacus information did the same thing for their white bosses. Maybe the whites told them what to feed him. However that worked, the result was a massacre.

Moss hugged the dirt. Bullets cracked past hardly more than a foot over his head. The gunners were shooting low, trying to pick off anything that moved. He couldn't stay where he was, not if he wanted to stay alive. He crawled toward the pine woods from which the guerrillas had come.

Was somebody with binoculars watching them all the time while they advanced? Moss wouldn't have been surprised.

They'd trusted too much, and they'd walked right into the meat grinder. Somebody behind him screamed. Would anyone get away?

'Spartacus still alive?' Nick Cantarella asked.

'Beats me,' Moss answered. 'I'm amazed I'm alive myself.'

'Tell me about it,' Cantarella said. 'They fucked us good, the bastards. Talk about a sucker punch . . .'

'I know,' Moss said mournfully. 'I was just thinking that. Are we far enough away so we can get up and run?'

'Go ahead if you want to. Me, I'm staying flat a while longer.'

Moss stayed flat, too. Cantarella knew more about this business than he did. Of course, he'd thought Spartacus knew more about it than he did, too. And he'd been right. But Spartacus didn't know enough to keep from making a disastrous mistake. Even if the leader survived, his band was a shambles.

By the time Moss reached the woods, his knees and elbows were bloody. But he didn't get shot, so he was one of the lucky ones. Spartacus made it back, too. 'Do Jesus!' he said over and over again, his voice and his face stunned. 'Do Jesus! What do we do now?'

'Keep on fighting or try and disappear,' Cantarella said. 'Those are your only two choices.'

'How *can* I fight after this?' Spartacus said. 'How? Do Jesus!' Neither white man had any answer for him.

The first thing Flora Blackford did when she got up in the morning was turn on the wireless to find out how the war had gone while she slept. The wireless didn't always tell the truth; she knew that. In the black days of 1941 and 1942, news reports of Confederate advances often ran days behind what really happened. Losses to enemy bombs were minimized, as were U.S. casualties. The uprisings in Utah and Canada had got short shrift – the one in Canada still did.

But, if you knew how to listen, you could get a pretty good notion of what was going on. Today, for instance, the broadcaster declared, 'Confederate air raids over Bermuda are of nuisance value only. The enemy has suffered severe losses in terms of bombers and trained crewmen.'

That was true, but, like a lot of true things, didn't tell the whole story or even most of it. The Joint Committee on the Conduct of the War had had some pungent things to say to the generals and admirals in charge of the reconquest of Bermuda. It was back in U.S. hands, but the whole business had proved much more expensive than anyone expected.

Why hadn't the generals and admirals figured Confederate bombers would keep paying nighttime visits? It wasn't stupidity, not exactly. As far as Flora could see, it was more like the blind certainty everything would go fine, and an unwillingness to examine ways in which things might not go fine.

To the men on the low-lying ground who had to put up with bombs coming down on their heads, it probably looked a lot like stupidity even if it wasn't.

Flora made coffee and scrambled a couple of eggs. They were the only ones she would eat this week. She made a point of sticking to the limits rationing imposed on everybody else. Not all Representatives and Senators did, but she didn't see how government could force such things on the country without observing them itself. Tomorrow it would be corn flakes or toast and jam. She was low on butter, too, but she couldn't get more till after the first of the month.

'In Europe,' the newscaster went on, 'German wireless

reports that the Kaiser's armored units have driven British forces over the Dutch border. For the first time since the outbreak of war, Germany is free of invaders. British Prime Minister Churchill denies the German claim and insists that strong British counterattacks are imminent.'

How can he do both at once? Flora wondered. But Churchill was formidable, no doubt about it. He'd over-shadowed Mosley in the British government, and Britain was overshadowing France in the anti-German alliance, though *Action Française* had held power longer.

'Russia claims the German assault column aimed at Petrograd has been turned back with heavy losses,' the broadcaster continued. 'More weight would attach to this claim if the Tsar's government hadn't made it repeatedly over the past few weeks, each time without its being true. The situation in the Ukraine, however, remains as confused and chaotic as it has been since the beginning of the war.

'Serbian terrorists have taken credit for the people bomb that exploded in Budapest day before yesterday and killed several prominent Hungarian military officials. The Austro-Hungarian Empire has vowed reprisals.'

Flora sighed as she put salt on her eggs. The cycle of revenge and reprisal was lurching forward another couple of cogs. She saw no end to it. Serbs, Croats, Bosnians, Albanians, Macedonians, Bulgarians . . . Austria-Hungary had security worries that made the USA's seem simple by comparison.

'In sports . . .' Flora got up and poured herself another cup of mostly ersatz coffee. She didn't care about the foot-ball scores. Joshua would have, and no doubt still did. But he was off doing his basic training. The apartment seemed empty without him.

Somewhere out in Washington State, scientists were trying to build a bomb that might make soldiers obsolete.

With Joshua in uniform, Flora had one more reason to hope they succeeded soon.

And somewhere down in the CSA, other scientists were trying just as hard to build the same damn thing. Flora didn't think the Confederates could win the war as a slugging match, not any more. But if they got that bomb ahead of the USA . . . Roosevelt thought the enemy was running behind. Was he right?

The Joint Committee on the Conduct of the War couldn't hold hearings to find out. As far as Flora knew, she was the only committee member who'd ever heard of uranium bombs or understood the difference between U-235 and U-238. There, though, she didn't know how far she knew. Robert Taft might share the secret. So might any other member. The only way to find out was to ask, and asking meant breaching security. She kept quiet. So did any other members who knew. Maybe it would all come out after the war.

She went downstairs and flagged a cab. They were easy to get on this block, where so many Congressmen and Senators lived. 'Where to, ma'am?' the driver asked. In most of Philadelphia, Flora would have been *lady,* the same as in New York City. This fellow remembered where he was, and took no chances.

'Congressional Hall,' Flora said.

'Yes, ma'am.' He probably thought she was a secretary, but politeness could still be good for his tip.

He had to detour from the shortest route a couple of times. Sawhorses and ropes blocked the street. Signs said, BOMB DAMAGE. 'Do you know what's going on?' Flora asked. 'I didn't hear any bombers overhead last night.'

'Neither did I, ma'am,' the cabby agreed. 'But I heard one of 'em was an auto bomb and the other one was a people bomb.'

'*Oy!*' Flora said. 'Has anyone claimed responsibility? Confederates? Mormons who don't want to give up? Canadians?'

'God only knows,' he said. 'You can walk along minding your own . . . darn business, and out of the blue – *kaboom!*'

'Out of the blue makes it worse,' Flora said, and the driver nodded. When someone said he'd planted an auto bomb, when a group proclaimed that one of its members hated you enough to blow himself to red mist to hurt you, at least you knew why you'd been injured. When the question hung in the air . . . When the question hung in the air, what could you do but stay afraid all the time? Flora didn't *think* the cabby had several hundred pounds of TNT in the trunk of his beat-up Packard or under the floorboards, but she couldn't prove he didn't. And he couldn't know she hadn't strapped an explosive belt around her waist. Scary times, all the way around.

As if to prove as much, concrete barricades kept motorcars from getting too close to Congressional Hall. Flora paid the driver. The Packard wheezed away. She approached the building. Despite her status, despite her Congressional ID, security guards went through her handbag and attaché case. A hard-faced policewoman patted her down. She'd got complaints that some of the women who frisked other women enjoyed themselves as much as men would have. She didn't know what anyone could do about that. This one seemed all business. 'You can go on,' she said when she finished.

'Thank you so much,' Flora said. The sarcasm rolled off the policewoman like rain off a tin roof.

Her secretary was in the office before Flora got there. 'Good morning, Congresswoman,' she said. 'Coffee's just about ready.'

'Thanks, Bertha. It smells good,' Flora said. 'Isn't it terrible about the bombs this morning?'

'I should say so,' Bertha answered. 'I hear the people bomb was one of those horrible Mormons.'

'Was it? How do they know?' Flora asked.

'I don't know, but I'd believe anything about those people,' her secretary said. 'They caused us so much trouble, so much misery – why wouldn't they go on doing it even now?'

That wasn't evidence. It wasn't anything even close to evidence. Flora knew as much, even if Bertha didn't. The cease-fire in Utah was holding . . . mostly. But there were Mormons who weren't ready to give up the fight against the government that had spent a lifetime abusing them. Some didn't care if they lived or died. The United States were painfully learning that men or women who didn't value their own lives were the hardest kind of foes to stop.

'What are my appointments this morning?' Flora already knew most of them, but Bertha couldn't go on ranting about Mormons if she had to check.

'Senator Taft called a few minutes ago and said he'd like to come by,' she answered. 'I told him it was all right. I hope that wasn't wrong?' She didn't like making mistakes, which made her a good secretary. Flora had known some who just didn't give a damn one way or the other.

She nodded now. 'I'm always glad to see Senator Taft,' she said. They disagreed politically more often than not – they disagreed on almost everything, in fact, except that Jake Featherston needed suppressing. But they had an odd, acrid friendship, each knowing the other was sincere and honest. Flora went on, 'Did he say what it was about?'

'Not to me, he didn't.' Bertha sniffed. 'Like a secretary should know what was going on? Noooo.' She stretched the word out into a long sound of complaint.

'All right. I'll find out when he gets here.' Flora carefully didn't smile.

Robert Taft came in about twenty minutes later. 'Good morning, Flora,' he said. He was only half the man his father had been – literally. He was lean and spare, where William Howard Taft had been wide as a football field. William Howard Taft had been deceptively clever, a good mind darting out from that vast bulk. There was nothing deceptive about Robert Taft's cool, dry, piercing intelligence.

'Good morning.' Flora brought him a cup of coffee – he would have done the same for her in his office. 'What can I do for you today?' She was sure he wanted her to do something; he didn't waste time on social calls. His father, who'd lived up to the clichés about fat men, had been far more outgoing.

Sure enough, Robert Taft went straight to business: 'I want your support for the measure readmitting Kentucky and Tennessee to the United States.'

'Do you really think the time is ripe?' Flora asked. 'We don't hold all of either one – we don't hold most of Tennessee. I know some white people in Kentucky really are pro-USA. But in Tennessee, we'd only have Negroes to work with, and how many has Jake Featherston left alive?'

'Some Tennessee whites will work with us. You can always find front men,' Taft said, which was probably true. 'But the real reason for readmitting them is to show that we aim to end this war by ending the Confederate States, and that Featherston can't stop us. That was the rationale for reviving Houston, too. And the more states we take back, the more states that fall out of the Confederacy, the more political pressure we put on Richmond. How long will the Confederate people and the Confederate Army go on backing a loser?'

'These U.S. states would be shams – and they'd elect Democrats, not Socialists,' Flora said. 'Isn't that part of what you have in mind?'

'We can work out an arrangement like the one we used in Utah, if that's what's troubling you,' Taft said. 'As long as they stay under martial law, they don't vote in national elections. You won't see the House and Senate swamped with undesirables.' He smiled a wintry smile.

Flora considered. A deal like that only put off the evil day. But it was liable to put off the day for a long time, because no Confederate state would be reconciled to returning to the USA any time soon. Anyone who remembered the interwar histories of Kentucky and Houston knew that. She found herself nodding. 'I think we have a deal,' she said.

'Here you are, Mr. President.' Lulu set the latest pile of wireless intercepts and press clippings from the USA on Jake Featherston's desk.

'Thank you kindly,' he said, and put on his reading glasses to go through them. He never let himself be photographed wearing the damned things, but without them print was just a blur these days.

He waited till Lulu left his underground office before he started swearing. She didn't like it. He could cuss out his generals, but he wouldn't swear in front of his secretary. That was crazy, but it was how things worked. Of course, he couldn't stand most of his generals, and he liked Lulu. Keeping her happy mattered to him.

But he had plenty to cuss about. The damnyankees, now that they'd grabbed the ball, showed no signs of wanting to let go of it. Jake shook his head in furious wonder. That wasn't how things were supposed to work. The Confederate States were supposed to jump on the United States with both feet and never let them up again. Jake had intended to make the CSA the dominant country in North America. What he'd intended and what was going on . . . didn't turn out to be the same thing, dammit.

The damnyankees were methodically building up in Tennessee, the same way they'd built up north of the Ohio before slamming down into the Confederacy. The counterattack through the mountain gaps into their flank hadn't fazed them. Featherston muttered in profane discontent as he shook his head. The counterattack hadn't fazed them *much*. Without it, they might already be in Chattanooga. Even so, they were gloating about how far they had come.

They were gloating about how well things were going in what they called Houston, too. Part of that was thumbing their noses because they'd revived the state that everyone who lived in it hated. Part of it was a threat; a U.S. officer out there said, 'Before too long, we hope to shut down the Confederates' murder factory near Snyder.'

'Fuck you, asshole,' Featherston growled. That hit him where he lived. Getting rid of the CSA's Negroes was at least as important as putting the United States in their place, as far as he was concerned. If the Yankees thought they could stop him, they would have to think again.

He made a note to himself to talk to Ferdinand Koenig about that. Before he could do anything about the note, Lulu stuck her head in again and said, 'Major General Patton is here to see you, sir.'

'Send him in,' Jake said. Lulu nodded and withdrew.

Patton came in wearing what was practically dress uniform, with medals hanging on his chest in two rows. That wasn't the way to make Jake Featherston love him. Not that Jake had anything against courage, but he had everything in the world against show-off officers.

Patton's salute could have come straight out of VMI,

too. The holsters on his belt were empty, though; the President's guards had his pistols. 'Mr. President,' he said in his gravelly voice.

'Sit down, General.' Featherston waved Patton to a chair. When Patton had taken his seat, Jake fixed him with his stoniest glare. 'You didn't give me what I needed, General. You didn't give the country what it needed. What have you got to say for yourself, eh?'

'Two things, sir,' Patton replied. 'First is, if you're not satisfied with me, put in someone you like better and stick me in a penal battalion. I'll fight for the Confederate States any way you please. Second thing is, whoever you put in my place will have as much trouble succeeding as I did unless we can get some air cover. My men were naked under the sky, and they paid a dreadful price for it.'

Featherston stared at Patton again, this time sourly. The high and mighty general had just taken much of the wind out of his sails. Anyone who volunteered for a penal battalion . . . Those outfits were made up of officers and men who'd disgraced themselves one way or another. Commanders threw them in wherever the fighting was hottest. Soldiers who redeemed themselves could earn their old rank back. Most of the poor damned bastards ended up as casualties instead. They were there to end up as casualties, and with luck, to help the cause a little before they did.

'I goddamn well ought to throw you in a penal battalion,' Jake growled, but even he could hear his heart wasn't fully in it.

'Do whatever you need to do, Mr. President. I'll go.' Patton was nearly as stubborn as Jake was himself.

'I'll get more mileage out of you if I keep you in command.' Featherston didn't like that conclusion, but he'd had to deal with a lot of things he didn't like lately. 'Can you hold Chattanooga?'

'I can try,' Patton answered. 'If they mass enough force to outweigh us six to one or something like that, though, I don't know how I'll manage it. I'm a better than decent general, sir, but I don't work miracles.'

'Will you fight house by house and block by block, make those damnyankee sons of bitches pay the way we paid in Pittsburgh?'

'Yes, sir.' Patton didn't hesitate. In that, too, he was like the President of the CSA.

'All right, then. Go do it,' Featherston said. It wasn't all right, or anywhere close to all right, but Jake came from the school that didn't believe in showing where it hurt. Anything that gave anyone a grip on you was to be avoided.

Patton rose and saluted again. 'You won't be sorry, sir. Or if you are, I'll be too dead to know about it.' Without waiting for a reply, he did a smart about-turn and marched out of the office: a procession of one.

'I'm already sorry,' Jake muttered. He was sorry he had to use an attacking general to defend. He was sorry he had to defend so deep inside the Confederacy. He'd planned to fight this war almost entirely on U.S. soil. Well, what was life but the difference between what you planned and what you got?

He walked to the door and asked Lulu, 'Who's next?'

'General Potter, Mr. President.' She sniffed. She didn't like Clarence Potter – mostly because Jake Featherston didn't like him.

Jake hid a smile. That was about as funny as anything he had going on these days. But like Potter or not, the President knew he was useful. 'Send him in.'

'Yes, sir.' Lulu sighed.

Although Jake felt like sighing, too, he didn't, not around Potter. He didn't trust the Intelligence officer enough to show that he didn't enjoy his company. All he said after the usual formalities was, 'Being in the line isn't as easy as it looks, is it?'

'No, sir. It's like juggling knives when someone's shooting at your feet,' Potter answered. 'Maybe experience helps. I hope to God it does, anyway. I've got a little now – the hard way. They were grabbing for anybody they could find with wreaths on his collar, and they tapped me. I gave it my best shot. What else could I do?'

'Go out there and kick those Yankees' asses?' Featherston suggested, not at all sardonically.

'Sir, I would have loved to,' Potter said. 'But we hardly even got to the front, let alone fought there. U.S. air power chewed us to pieces coming through the gaps – slowed us down, gave us casualties, tore the crap out of our trucks and armor. We wouldn't have been in good shape even if we had done more fighting. We need more airplanes and more pilots.'

'We need more of everything, goddammit,' Jake said.

'Yes, sir. We do.' With four words, Potter skewered every Freedom Party policy – every policy of Jake Featherston's – at least as far back as the President's first inauguration. And Featherston couldn't do one damn thing about it, because all the cross-grained Intelligence officer had done was agree with him.

In lieu of snarling at him for agreeing, Jake asked, 'Were you able to keep putting Professor FitzBelmont's feet to the fire while you were in the field?'

'By messenger, yes, sir,' Potter answered. 'It meant letting one more man in on the secret, but Chuck doesn't blab. And I figured that was better than doing it by telephone or wire or letter. With a messenger in the know, I could really speak my mind.'

'Fair enough,' Jake said. 'FitzBelmont's got to know how bad we need that bomb, and how important it is for us to get it before the United States do.' If the Confederate States got uranium bombs ahead of the USA and kept on getting more of them, shortages of everything else – even airplanes, even manpower – would stop mattering. If the CSA had uranium bombs and the USA didn't, the Confederacy would damn well win.

'If he doesn't know, it's not because he hasn't been told,' Potter said. 'I believe he's doing everything he knows how to do. I believe he's the best man we've got for the slot, too. Whatever else he is, he's bright.'

'What about the men the damnyankees have?' Featherston asked. 'Have you worked out some kind of way to hit 'em up in Washington again?'

'If we can land a mortar team by submersible, it might be able to get close enough to shell their operation,' Potter said. 'I'm not sure how far out their ground perimeter extends. I don't think we can hit them from the air again. They're alert for that now. A lot of things you can do once, chances are you can't do 'em twice. The ground operation would be a suicide run, too, chances are.'

'Yeah, chances are,' Jake agreed. 'Either you get dedicated people who don't care or you don't tell 'em beforehand how dangerous the mission is. Both ways work.'

'If I can, I'll use people who know what they're doing and are willing to do it anyhow,' Potter said. 'I don't like sending people off to die when they don't know that's in the cards.'

'If you can, fine. But if you can't, do it the other way. Don't get thin-skinned on me, Potter,' Jake said. 'This country is in trouble. If blasting the crap out of the U.S. uranium factory helps get us out of trouble, we do it. Period. We do it. You got that?'

'Oh, yes, Mr. President. I've got it. You're always very plain about what you want.' Clarence Potter spoke respectfully. He spoke obediently. How, then, did he make Jake feel as if he'd just got slapped in the face? He had all kinds of unpleasant talents.

Jake held up a hand. 'One other thing I need to find out. Any sign the Yankees know where our uranium works is at?'

'Sir, the first sign of that you'd get would be every U.S. bomber ever built coming straight at Washington University with the heaviest load of bombs it could carry,' Potter answered.

He was bound to be right. And he was serious, too; when he talked about the Confederate uranium-bomb project, the subtle mockery disappeared from his voice. He was a Confederate patriot. Jake Featherston used that button to keep him loyal to the Freedom Party – and loyal to the President of the CSA, too. If Potter ever separated Jake Featherston's cause from the Confederacy's . . . *If that ever happens, I've got to get rid of him, because then he turns as dangerous as a rattler in my bed,* Jake thought. *I'd better keep a closer eye on him.*

None of his thoughts showed on his face. All he said was, 'You're doing a good job of keeping the secret, then. Thanks. That's one more thing the country needs.'

'Yes, sir.' Again, Potter sounded brisk and assured. But he couldn't resist one more gibe: 'We'd be further along now if FitzBelmont got funding sooner.'

'Oh, give me a break!' Jake exclaimed – that rubbed him the wrong way. 'He came to me with this blue-sky story an idiot dog wouldn't believe. So maybe it'll turn out to be true. I hear a dozen blue-sky stories every day, and damn near all of 'em are nothing but shit. Would *you* have believed this one way back then?'

Potter pursed his lips. 'Well, no,' he admitted – he was almost compulsively honest. 'But somebody made the

United States believe it. I wonder how that happened.'

'The United States follow the Germans wherever they go – maybe that's got something to do with it,' Jake said. 'I wonder how far along England and France are. Got any ideas?'

'No, Mr. President. They aren't talking to me.'

'To me, neither,' Jake snarled. 'They reckon I'm a poor relation. Well, when we get this here bomb, I'll show 'em who's a poor relation to who, by God. See if I don't. The whole damn *world*'ll see if I don't.'

Jefferson Pinkard heard the distant boom of artillery off to the northwest. He'd heard it before, but only as a rumble on the edge of audibility. Now it was louder and more distinct than he'd ever known it. That meant only one thing: the damnyankees were closer to Camp Determination than they'd ever got before.

When Pinkard called the local commander to complain, Brigadier General Whitlow Ling said, 'If you want to put your guards under my command and send 'em off to the front here, I'll listen to you. Otherwise, butt out of my business.'

'I can't do that,' Jeff said.

'Then butt out of my business,' the Army man said firmly.

'But Camp Determination is important to the whole country,' Jeff said.

'And I'm doing every damn thing I know how to do to keep the U.S. Eleventh Army away from it,' Ling said. 'If you think you're helping when you joggle my elbow, you'd better think twice, 'cause it ain't so.'

'We set up this camp way the hell out here so the Yankees couldn't get at it,' Pinkard said. 'We've got important business to take care of here.'

'I don't know anything about that,' Ling said. 'All I know is, General Dowling has more men than I do. He has a better logistics train than I do. He has a fuck of a lot more airplanes than I do. You want miracles, go talk to Moses.'

'So don't fight him straight up,' Jeff said. 'Go around him.'

'And how am I supposed to do that, when Richmond won't give me the barrels I need?' Brigadier General Ling seemed sure the camp commandant wouldn't have an answer for him.

But, thanks to the newspapers and magazine, Jeff did. 'Load machine guns and cannons onto a bunch of trucks and go raiding,' he said. 'The Canucks are doing it to the USA. Hell, the damn niggers in Georgia and Mississippi are doing it to us. Can we fight as smart as a bunch of coons? Hope to God we can.'

Had he laid that on too thick? Would Ling hang up on him instead of listening? If Ling thought he could get away with that, he had another think coming, because Jeff would get on the horn to Ferdinand Koenig. If the Attorney General couldn't make a mere soldier say uncle, Jeff was backing the wrong horse.

Ling didn't hang up. He said, 'You want us to turn guerrilla, then?'

'I don't care what you call it, General,' Pinkard answered. 'I want you to make the damnyankees stop. I want you to make 'em go backwards. I don't give a rat's ass how you do it. Here's something you haven't tried, that's all. It's worked good some other places. What have you got to lose?'

He waited. 'It wouldn't be that expensive,' Ling said in musing tones. 'Wouldn't cost that many men, wouldn't cost that much matériel. Might be worth a shot.'

'Anything's worth a shot right now, wouldn't you say?' Jeff answered.

Ling only grunted. That was probably as it should be. A soldier wouldn't admit his side was in trouble, even if it was – maybe especially if it was. If he hurt the troops' morale, what would that do? Cause his side more trouble still. 'We'll see what happens,' Ling said at last, and he did hang up.

'Hooked him, by God,' Jeff said happily as he set down his own telephone. 'I do believe I hooked him.' He hadn't been sure he could.

He looked out through his window at the men's half of Camp Determination. A long queue of Negroes waited to go into the bathhouse and delousing station. They would go in, all right, but they wouldn't come out again – not breathing, anyhow. Guards with submachine guns flanked them to either side, to make sure nobody did anything stupid or desperate. Right this minute, everything seemed calm.

The camp was busier than it had been for a while, too. U.S. bombers had eased up on the railroad line leading into Camp Determination. They still hit it every so often, but repairs stayed ahead of damage now. And they'd eased up on Snyder, too. Pinkard thanked God for that. He had his family to worry about, and it mattered more to him than anything else in the world.

As much as he hated to do it, he'd just about decided to send Edith and her boys back to Louisiana. Maybe he would have looked at things differently if she weren't expecting. But Alexandria was safe in a way Snyder wasn't. Even though it also had a camp nearby, the United States were in no position to bomb it. If they brought bombers south, they wouldn't bother with a half-assed target like Alexandria. They'd go and unload on New Orleans, which really mattered.

Jeff watched the queue snake forward. Everything went

smoothly. He'd set it up so everything would, but seeing that it did still made him feel good. It wasn't a guarantee these days. A year ago, all the Negroes who went through the camp believed the guards when they said the bath-houses and the trucks were just procedures to be put up with as they got transferred somewhere else. Not now. The blacks brought out of colored districts and the captured Red guerrillas had a pretty good idea of what went on here. Jeff blamed damnyankees propaganda for that. It made Camp Determination harder to run, because the inmates understood they had nothing to lose.

He breathed a silent sigh of relief when the last Negro moved through the barbed-wire gate and into the bath-house. That meant he could go back to his paperwork with a clear conscience. It never went away, and it was the part of the job he hated most. He hadn't signed up to be a bureaucrat. He'd signed up to *do* things, by God. But you couldn't just do things, not in the CSA you couldn't. You had to keep records to show you'd done them, too.

And you had to keep records about things that went wrong. He'd just sent away two more guards from the women's side for having lesbian affairs with the prisoners, and one male guard who'd got caught cornholing colored boys. Those involuntary separations required a mountain of forms. You couldn't just fire somebody for something like that. You almost had to catch people in the act, because those accusations could ruin somebody's life.

One of the women was raising a stink. She denied every-thing on a stack of Bibles. Jeff didn't care. He had wit-nesses to prove she'd been carpet-munching. That was dirty enough when a man did it to a woman (though Pinkard sure didn't complain when Edith went down on him – oh, no!). When another woman did it, it was about as disgusting as cornholing. This gal had to go, and she would.

She'll probably end up a girls' gym teacher, someplace where word of this hasn't spread, Jeff thought. Under the Freedom Party, records were a lot more thorough and complete than they had been back in the old days, but they weren't perfect, not by a long shot.

He'd just signed the last of the papers that would get rid of the dyke when air-raid sirens started wailing and airplane engines droned overhead. A minute or so later, the antiaircraft guns around Camp Determination thundered into action. In the camp compound, he watched guards hastily don helmets. Falling shrapnel could cave in a man's skull.

The colored prisoners, of course, had no helmets. Jeff only shrugged. That wasn't his worry. If one of the smokes got clobbered, well, so what? It only meant he was buying his plot a little sooner than he would have otherwise.

A thunderous explosion rattled the window in his office. It was safety glass reinforced with chicken wire, but it almost blew out anyhow. That wasn't a bomb going off. That was a bomber crashing, and its whole load blowing up at once. The gunners didn't nail very many, but every once in a while they came through.

Prisoners in the yard were pointing up in the sky at the bomber stream. They were cheering and dancing and urging the damnyankees on. Rage ripped through Pinkard. How *dared* they root for the other side? They deserved everything they were catching, all right. Whether they would have cheered for the United States if they weren't catching hell from the Confederate States never once crossed his mind.

Not surprising, not when he had other, more important, things to worry about. The bombers started unloading on Snyder again. More antiaircraft guns protected the towns, but flak alone couldn't keep bombers away. If the Confederacy had some fighters of its own in the air . . .

But the Confederacy damn well didn't. Basically, Snyder had to sit there and take it. *I will get Edith and the boys back to Alexandria, so help me God I will,* Jeff thought. If the damnyankees were going to bomb innocent civilians . . . Again, he didn't dwell on what the Confederates had done to innocent civilians on the other side of the border, let alone on what the men he commanded were doing to civilians right here in this camp.

He hated those strings of *boom! boom! boom!,* one right after another. Sure, Edith and Willie and Frank would be down in the storm cellar. Sure, it would take a direct hit to harm them. The odds against that were long. But it could happen, as he knew too well. And he couldn't do one damn thing about it. He hated that even more.

Here inside Camp Determination, he was safe as houses. The Yankees had never bombed the camp. They cared more about the worthless niggers inside it than they cared about the honest white people they were trying to murder.

Another bomber exploded. This one sounded as if it blew up in midair. The United States were paying for things today, anyhow. Sometimes the bombers got off scot-free. That was just plain embarrassing. At least the gunners weren't standing around with their thumbs up their asses.

Jeff knew losing a few bombers wouldn't keep the USA from coming back. He also knew how helpless he was to do anything about it. What choice did he have but wait here till the raid ended and then go back to Snyder and see if he still had any family left?

None. None at all.

Bombers stayed above Snyder for most of an hour. As soon as the bombs stopped falling, Jeff jumped into the Birmingham that was his to use. He didn't wait for a driver, but gunned the engine to life and roared off to find out if his family was all right.

He had to go off the road and onto the shoulder a couple of times to avoid craters. He was glad it hadn't rained any time lately, or his auto might have bogged down. But the fires rising from Snyder made him mutter and curse and pray, all in a confused jumble. *He* knew what he meant, but he doubted anybody else, even God, would have.

Once he got into Snyder, he had to make more detours, both because of holes in the streets and because of burning buildings. The bombs hadn't smashed the town's one fire engine. Its bell clanged like the shrieks of a lost soul as it raced from one disaster to the next. How much good could it do at each stop? Some, maybe.

Jeff's heart was in his throat when he turned onto his street. A house half a block in front of his had taken a direct hit. Part of a body lay on the front lawn. Pinkard gulped and looked away.

But there were Edith and Frank and Willie. His wife was bandaging a neighbor lady who looked to have been cut by flying glass. His stepsons watched with more interest than horror. They'd seen things like this before. Kids got used to war and other disasters faster than grownups did. For them, it soon became routine.

For Jeff . . . 'Thank God you're all right!' he called as he sprang from the motorcar and ran over to Edith.

'This was a bad one, but we made it into the cellar quick as we could. The windows are already cardboard and plywood, so we didn't lose any glass. I don't smell gas. The power's out, but it'll come back.' As Edith talked, she went on bandaging the neighbor lady's head. 'There you go, Vera. It's not too deep, and I don't think the scar will be bad.'

'Thank you, Edith.' With middle-class politeness, Vera

nodded to Jeff. 'Hello, Mr. Pinkard. Sorry we have to run into each other like this. It's a miserable war, isn't it?'

'It sure is, ma'am.' Jeff coughed on the smoke in the air. He shook his fist toward the west. 'It's a miserable war, but by God we'll win it.'

Cabo San Lucas wasn't quite the ass end of nowhere, but you could see it from there. George Enos knew damn well he wasn't any place he wanted to be. As usual, nobody in the Navy bothered asking his opinion. The Marines had taken the place away from the Empire of Mexico. U.S. Army troops were pushing down from San Diego to occupy the rest of Baja California. The godawful terrain and the heat and the lack of water were giving them more trouble than Francisco José's soldiers were.

Also annoying, or worse than annoying, to the men in green-gray and forest green were air raids across the Gulf of California from Confederate Sonora. C.S. bombers struck by night, when they were harder for U.S. fighters to find and shoot down. The Confederacy didn't keep a lot of airplanes in Sonora, but the ones they had did what any small force was supposed to do: they made the other side hate their guts.

And they were the reason the *Townsend* lingered by Cabo San Lucas. More and more escort carriers came down the coast of Baja California. Sooner or later, they'd try to force their way into the Gulf of California and put C.S. air power in Sonora out of business. When they did, they would need escorts to deal with Confederate and Mexican surface raiders and submersibles. That was what destroyers were for.

'This would go quicker if we got a couple of fleet carriers instead of all these chickenshit little baby flattops,' George grumbled. 'An escort carrier isn't big enough to hold many airplanes, and the damn things can't make twenty knots if you throw 'em off a cliff.'

Fremont Dalby gave him the horselaugh. 'Now tell me another one,' he said. 'Like they're gonna waste fleet carriers down here. Fast as we build more of 'em, they go into the Atlantic. It's just like last time: we cut off England's lifeline to Argentina and Brazil, we screw her to the wall.'

'Yeah,' George said. That was what the father he barely remembered was doing in 1917, and how the senior George Enos died after the CSA threw in the sponge.

Dalby didn't notice George was feeling subdued. 'Maybe – *maybe* – the Sandwich Islands get one,' he said. 'Depends on how serious we are about going after the Japs.'

'Makes sense, I guess,' George said. 'If it's up to me, though, we wait till we're done with the really important stuff, and *then* we kick their scrawny yellow asses.'

'That's how I'd do it, too,' Dalby agreed. ' 'Course, that doesn't mean it's how the admirals will want to handle it. Expecting the brass to do shit that makes sense is like expecting a broad to understand if you screw around on her. You can expect it, yeah, but that don't mean it's gonna happen. Like for instance, you know what I heard?'

'I'm all ears,' George said.

'You'd look even funnier than you do now if you were, and that's saying something,' Dalby told him, altogether without malice. George flipped the gun chief the bird. Since Dalby was ribbing him personally, he could get away with that. Had the conversation had anything to do with duty or the ship, he would have had to take whatever abuse the older man dished out. Dalby went on, 'Anyway, scuttlebutt is they're keeping a flotilla bigger'n this one off the northwest coast, near where the Columbia lets out into the Pacific. Carriers, escorts, subs, the whole nine yards.'

'That's pretty crazy,' George said. 'Why would they put so many ships up where they don't do any good?'

Fremont Dalby shrugged and lit a cigarette. He held out the pack to George, who took one, too. After a couple of puffs, Dalby said, 'It's almost like they're guarding that whole stretch of coast, like there's something up there they don't want the Japs to hit no matter what.'

'What could there be?' George asked. 'They think the Japs'll bomb the salmon-canning plants, or what?'

'Beats me,' Dalby said. 'Like I told you, this is all scuttlebutt. Maybe it's just a cloud of stack gas, but the guys I heard it from say it's the straight skinny.'

'Something's going on that we don't know about,' George said.

Dalby gave him exaggerated, silent applause. 'No kidding, Sherlock,' he said. George laughed. Maybe it would all make sense after the war was over. Maybe it would never make sense. Some of the dumb stunts the brass pulled were like that, too.

The *Townsend* was one of the lead escorts when a flotilla centered on three escort carriers steamed into the Gulf of California. The flotilla had minesweepers along, too, in case the Confederates and Mexicans had surprises waiting for any newcomers. George would have if he were waiting for trouble from the USA.

'Tell me about it,' Dalby said when he worried out loud. 'Mines are simple, mines are cheap, mines'll blow your sorry ass sky-high if you hit one. What more could anybody want from the fuckers?'

They didn't hit any mines the first day inside the gulf. On the second morning, klaxons hooted the men to general quarters. 'Now hear this! Now hear this! Aircraft approaching from the northeast! Aircraft approaching from the northeast!'

Fighters zoomed off the baby flattops' decks. From what George had heard, Confederate Asskicker dive bombers were great when they operated unopposed, but they were sitting ducks for fighters. He didn't know if what he'd heard was the gospel, but had the feeling he'd find out pretty damn quick.

Confederate fighters escorted the dive bombers. Up till recently, land-based aircraft were always hotter than their carrier counterparts, which needed heavier airframes to stand up to the stresses of catapult-aided takeoffs and landings cut short by tailhooks and arrester wires. But the latest U.S. carrier-based fighters were supposed to be as tough and fast as anything in the air.

An airplane tumbled down toward the sea. Fremont Dalby had a pair of binoculars. 'That's an Asskicker!' he said. 'Got the fixed landing gear and flies with its wings going up on either side like a goddamn turkey buzzard.'

Another airplane plummeted. 'Who's that?' Fritz Gustafson asked.

'Dunno,' Dalby answered. 'I *think* it was one of ours, though. They've got blunter noses than C.S. Hound Dogs do.'

Two more machines fell out of the sky, both burning. Keeping track of who was doing what to whom got harder and harder. The rolling, roiling fight drew ever closer to the flotilla.

'Here we go.' At Fremont Dalby's orders, the gun layers swung the twin 40mm mount toward the closest Confederate airplane. George Enos passed Fritz Gustafson two shells and got ready to give him more. Dalby put the guns exactly where he wanted them and opened fire.

Casings leaped from the breeches. George fed shells as fast as he could. Thanks to Gustafson's steady hands, the twin 40mms devoured them just as fast. Black puffs of smoke appeared all around the oncoming C.S. bombers and fighters. All the other guns on the *Townsend* were blasting away, too: not just the 40mm mounts but the dual-purpose five-inch main armament and the .50-caliber machine guns that were stationed wherever the deck offered a few feet of space. The noise was terrific, impossible, overwhelming.

'Got one!' Everybody at George's mount yelled the same thing at the same time. George couldn't be sure a shell from one of his guns hit the Hound Dog, but he thought so. The fighter pilot tried to crash his airplane into the destroyer, but fell short – he went into the drink about a quarter of a mile off the port bow.

George never saw the Asskicker that hit the *Townsend* till too late.

One second, he was passing shells as fast as he could. The next, altogether without knowing what had happened, he was flying through the air with the greatest of ease, like the daring young man on the flying trapeze. Unlike the daring young man, he didn't have a trapeze. He didn't have a net, either. The Gulf of California reached up and smacked him in the face and in the gut. If his wasn't the worst bellyflop of all time, he surely got no lower than the bronze medal.

At least the water was warm. He didn't swallow too much of it. His life vest kept him from sinking. He looked up just in time to watch a C.S. Mule zoom off not far above the waves. Dalby was right – with those uptilted wings, the damn thing was as ugly as a turkey vulture.

It made a much better killing machine, though.

He didn't realize what had happened to the *Townsend* till he looked back at his ship. Before that, he thought whatever happened to him was some sort of private accident – though how a private accident could have hurled him close to a hundred yards was anything but obvious. He slowly decided he wasn't thinking very well at all.

But he didn't need to be a genius to see the destroyer was history. Her back was broken. Smoke billowed from her. The Gulf of California all around her was full of sailors, some with their heads out of the water and paddling, others facedown and still and dead.

'Holy Jesus!' George blurted. 'We got nailed.' That was, if anything, an understatement. Even as he watched, the *Townsend* settled lower in the water. She wouldn't stay afloat much longer.

But George only thought he was afraid till he saw gray dorsal fins knifing through the water. He'd watched sharks from the destroyer's deck. That was fine. Watching them from the sea with a free-lunch course spread out all around . . . George crossed himself. The *Ave Maria* he blurted out might not help, but it sure couldn't hurt.

He looked around not just for sharks but also for his buddies. He didn't see Fremont Dalby anywhere. A big blond body floated not far away. Was that Fritz? George didn't paddle over to see. He didn't want to know that bad.

Fuel oil spread from the stricken destroyer. George swam away from it. That stuff would kill you if you swallowed it. He'd seen as much in the Sandwich Islands. His voice rose with others, calling for nearby ships to pick them up.

The minesweeper that had led the flotilla swung back toward the *Townsend,* whose deck was almost awash now. When the destroyer went down, her undertow dragged luckless sailors too close by under with her. George had got too far away for that to happen to him. But someone not nearly far enough from him screamed. Dorsal fins converged as red spread through the deep blue. George rattled off more Hail Marys, and an Our Father for good measure.

A life ring attached to a line splashed into the sea maybe fifty yards off. He swam over and put it on. Sailors aboard the minesweeper hauled him in like a big tuna. The ship had nets down. They helped him scramble up the side.

'Well, well – look what the cat drug in,' Fremont Dalby said. He was soaked, of course, but he already had a cigarette dangling from the corner of his mouth. Drop Dalby in horseshit and he'd come out with a pony. But his sardonic grin slipped as he asked, 'Spot any of the other guys?'

'Maybe Gustafson.' George pointed his thumb down at the deck.

'Fuck.' The gun chief looked at the oil slick and the bobbing men and debris that were the sole remains of the *Townsend*. 'That Asskicker sure kicked our ass, didn't he? Hit us right where it did him the most good, the son of a bitch.'

Airplanes were still mixing it up overhead. George Enos hardly noticed. He was luxuriating – rejoicing – in being alive. 'We just got ourselves some leave,' he said. 'And you know what? I wish to God we didn't.' Dalby nodded.

XV

Jorge Rodriguez and Gabriel Medwick made unlikely friends. Jorge was skinny and swarthy and spoke with a Spanish accent. Medwick was big and blond and hand-some in a jut-jawed way. If not for the war, they never would have met. But they'd shared in the grinding Confederate retreat through Tennessee. Now, just outside of Chattanooga, the powers that be were saying C.S. troops wouldn't fall back another yard. Jorge didn't know if they were right, but they were saying it.

A lot of men who'd come over from Virginia with Jorge and Gabriel were dead or wounded now. Jorge didn't think much of their replacements. Old-timers in the company doubtless hadn't thought much of him when he first joined it, either. Two company commanders had gone down since Captain Hirsch. They were both supposed to recover, but that didn't help much now. A first lieutenant named Jubal Frisch had the company at the moment, and didn't seem to know what to do with it.

Sergeant Hugo Blackledge hadn't got a scratch. He was another reason Jorge and Gabriel were friends – they both hated him. He had a platoon now, not just a squad. That let him spread his bad temper around more, but did nothing to make it good.

'Why don't they bring in a lieutenant to take over for him?' Medwick mourned.

'Even if they did, he'd still be running the platoon,' Jorge said. 'That's what sergeants do. The officer would just be – how do you say? – the guy in front.'

'The front man,' Medwick said.

'That's it. Thanks. The front man, yeah,' Jorge said. 'Blackledge, he can handle a platoon – no doubt about that.'

'Oh, I know. I know.' Gabriel Medwick looked around carefully and lowered his voice to a near-whisper. 'He can run it, sure. That ain't the problem. The problem is, he's a fuckin' asshole.'

'You got that right,' Jorge whispered. They both nodded, satisfied they'd figured out at least one small part of how the universe worked.

Blackledge couldn't have heard them. He would have come down on them harder than a six-inch shell. Somehow or other, though, they both ended up on sentry-go that night. The front wasn't quiet. Snipers and raiding parties slipped back and forth. That was the small change of war, and nobody worried much about it one way or the other except the people who got wounded or killed. But sentries were a trip wire, too. If a big push came, they were supposed to get word back to the main force.

Jorge peered out into the darkness, all eyeballs and nerves and apprehension. Every time an owl hooted, he thought it was a damnyankee signal. Every time a firefly blinked, he feared it was a muzzle flash. He clutched his automatic rifle and hoped nothing would happen till his relief took over.

Out of the darkness came a low-voiced call: 'Hey! You there! Yeah, you, Confederate!'

Jorge crouched in good cover. Even if a machine gun opened up, he was safe enough. So he cautiously called back: 'Yeah? What you want?'

'Got some smokes?' The other man had a funny accent

– a Yankee accent. 'Wanna swap 'em for rations? I can use coffee, too, if you got it.'

'I got cigarettes,' Jorge answered. 'Not much coffee. You got deviled ham?'

'Buddy, I got a dozen cans,' the U.S. soldier said proudly. 'I came prepared – bet your butt I did.'

'I got three-four packs I can trade you,' Jorge said. 'You see a stump by a rock up in front of you?'

A pause, presumably while the would-be merchant scanned the area. 'Yeah, I see it.'

'Bueno,' Jorge said. 'Put four cans on it, then go away. I put four packs on it, then I go away. You come back and get 'em.'

'And you shoot my sorry ass off,' the U.S. soldier said. 'I'll put two, you put two, then we do it again. Got to be some kind of way to keep both of us interested in the deal all the way through.'

'All right,' Jorge said, though he didn't much care whether it went through or not. The only thing that kept him going was the reasonable certainty that killing him would cause more trouble than it was worth. 'Go ahead. I don't shoot.'

'Fuckin' better not,' the U.S. soldier said, which was true enough under the circumstances.

He moved quietly. When he came, Jorge didn't know he was there till he got to within a few feet of the stump and boulder. He set down the cans, waved in Jorge's general direction, and disappeared again. But he had style; he made more noise retreating than he had advancing, so Jorge could be sure he really was leaving.

Even so, Jorge's heart pounded as he went up to the stump. If more Yankees waited nearby, they could jump out and capture him. He'd picked this spot himself, but. . . .

He grabbed the cans and almost forgot to set down the

cigarettes. After he did, he headed back to his foxhole. Up came the U.S. soldier. 'Yeah, you play fair,' he said as he snatched up the packs. 'Here's the rest.' He set down two more cans and withdrew again.

After Jorge took them and left the last two packs of Dukes, he was tempted to shoot the U.S. soldier when he came forward. But what was the point? It wouldn't win the war. It wouldn't move the war toward being won by even a hair's breadth. It would only start a firefight in which he was liable to get hurt himself. He would fight when he had to. When he didn't have to, he didn't want to.

Like a ghost, the U.S. soldier materialized. 'Thanks, buddy,' he said, collecting the last two packs of Dukes. 'Stay safe. I won't plug you unless I've got to. Try and do the same for me.' He vanished into the darkness again.

The deviled ham would be good. Jorge could always get more smokes. He wondered how long that would last, though. The United States had overrun a lot of tobacco country. How long could the Confederacy go on turning out cigarettes? There was a scary thought.

When his relief came up, he almost shot the other Confederate soldier. It wasn't even that his countryman messed up the password; he was just jumpy. He went back to the company's forward position, rolled himself in his blanket, and slept till sunup.

He got coffee and fried eggs from the company cook. When he spooned deviled ham into his mess kit to go with the eggs, his buddies gave him jealous looks. 'Where'd you get that?' Gabe Medwick asked.

'Found it on a tree stump,' Jorge answered, which was technically true but not what anybody would call responsive. Medwick rolled his eyes.

Sergeant Blackledge was blunter: 'You trading with the enemy?'

'Uh, yes, Sergeant.' Jorge didn't have the nerve to lie.

'Didn't pay more than one pack of smokes for a can, did you?' Blackledge demanded.

'Uh, no, Sergeant.'

'Goddamn well better not. You jack up the price for everybody else if you do.' The sergeant tramped off. Jorge let out a sigh of relief louder and more heartfelt than the one that had escaped him after he finished the deal with the damnyankee.

He was just finishing his coffee when somebody yelled, 'Mail call!' He hurried over to see if there was anything from his brothers (POWs were allowed occasional letters, so Pedro sometimes wrote) or from his family back in Sonora. The field-post corporal had a devil of a time pronouncing his last name, but a lot of ordinary Confederates did, so he took that in stride.

'Who's it from?' Gabe Medwick asked. He had a large family in Alabama, and got letters all the time.

'My mother,' Jorge answered. 'Got to remember how to read Spanish.' He said that only for effect. He wouldn't have any trouble, and he knew it.

When he opened the letter, what he got wasn't what he expected. *They say your father killed himself*, his mother wrote. *I don't believe them. I will never believe them, not just because killing yourself is a mortal sin but because your father would not do it. He would only do such a thing if he found out he had committed some great wrong and he had no other way to make up for it. And that is not so. He was doing something great, something wonderful, something important. He always said so when he wrote me. And so it must be a lie. Maybe they tell me these things because he died fighting and he promised me he would not go into any danger when he left to put on the uniform again. I cannot think of anything else that would make them say such things. And they are paying me a pension for him. Would they do that if he really killed himself? I don't believe it.*

Jorge stared at the scrawled words. He read them two or three times, and they made no more sense than they had at the beginning. He couldn't believe his father would kill himself, either. *Some great wrong,* his mother said. What could his father have done that was wrong? It wasn't in his father to do such a thing . . . was it? He didn't see how.

'You all right, buddy?' Gabriel Medwick asked. By the look on his face, Jorge got the idea he'd asked the same question before, maybe more than once, and hadn't got an answer for it. Gabe went on, 'You look like somebody just reduced your population, man. You got bad news from home?'

A white Confederate from Alabama could no more read Spanish than he could fly, Jorge reminded himself. He didn't want to lie, but he didn't want to tell the truth, either. 'It's not as good as it could be, anyhow,' he said.

'Not more trouble on top of your dad, I hope?' Medwick knew Hipolito Rodriguez was dead. He didn't know how – up till this moment, Jorge hadn't known how himself. *I still don't, dammit,* he thought fiercely.

'No, not on top of my father, *gracias a Dios,*' Jorge said, which was even true. 'Just . . . trouble winding up his affairs, I guess you would say.'

'That's no good,' Gabe said seriously. 'Stuff like that can get a whole family riled up, with lawyers or maybe guns, depending. Some neighbors of ours started feuding over a will, and now everybody hates everybody else. You don't want something like that to happen.'

'No, no,' Jorge said again. 'I don't think it will. But everything is more . . . more complicated than anyone thought it would be.'

'Not easy when somebody dies. I'm sorry,' Medwick said.

'No, not easy,' Jorge agreed.

Before he could say anything more, his head went up like a hound's when it took a scent. He didn't smell anything, but he heard trouble in the air. Gabe Medwick shouted it louder than he did: 'Incoming!' They both dove for the closest hole in the ground.

It wasn't really big enough for both of them, but they made do. And when the U.S. shells started bursting around them, they both tried to make themselves as small as they could, which made the hole seem bigger. That had to be crazy, but Jorge thought it was true.

The damnyankees had shelled Confederate positions in front of Chattanooga before, but this was different. That had just been harassing fire. This time, they meant it. They wanted to blow a big hole in the Confederate line right here, smash on through it, and head straight for the city the soldiers in butternut had defended so long and so hard.

They were liable to get what they wanted, too. Jorge had never been in a bombardment like this, not here and not back in Virginia, either. Beside him, Gabe Medwick was screaming for his mother. He wasn't hurt – he was just scared to death. Jorge couldn't blame him, not when he was scared to death, too.

As suddenly as it had begun, the barrage stopped. 'Up!' Jorge said. 'We've got to get out and fight, or they'll murder all of us.'

He looked around . . . and found he might have been in the mountains of the moon. After a pounding like that, *could* the Confederates fight back?

If you wanted something and the fellow who had it didn't feel like handing it over, one way to get it was to put a big rock in your fist and then slug him. The USA wanted Chattanooga. The Confederates didn't feel like giving it up. Lieutenant Michael Pound knew a certain amount of pride at being on the pointy end of the rock.

As soon as the U.S. bombardment let up, he got on the wireless circuit to the other barrels in his platoon: 'Let's go get 'em! They think they can stop us. I say they're wrong, and I say we'll prove it.'

In war, proving the other guy was wrong often meant proving he had no business breathing. Pound was ready to use that kind of logic against Jake Featherston's men. Why not? Featherston had tried using it against the United States.

As his barrel rumbled forward, Pound wondered if he would spot General Morrell. This was Morrell's operation, and Pound knew how Morrell thought, how he fought, better than anyone else except possibly George Patton. One thing Morrell did was lead from the front. He'd be here somewhere.

'Old home week,' Pound muttered.

'What was that, sir?' Sergeant Scullard asked.

'Nothing. Woolgathering,' Pound said, embarrassed the gunner had overheard him. He still wasn't used to getting called *sir,* either.

The bow machine gun chattered, knocking over a couple of soldiers in butternut unlucky enough to get caught away from cover. Another Confederate dropped his submachine gun and raised his hands over his head. 'What do I do, sir?' The question came back to Pound over the intercom.

'Let him live,' Pound answered. 'We've got infantry along to scoop up prisoners, and he doesn't look like he'll do any more fighting. We'll play fair when we can.' And when they couldn't – and there would be times like that – he would do whatever needed doing, and he wouldn't lose any sleep over it.

He stood up in the turret, riding with head and shoulders out so he could see more. Only a little small-arms fire was coming back at the barrels; the barrage had left the Confederates more discombobulated than usual. Maybe they were finally starting to crack. He could hope so, anyhow.

More soldiers in butternut threw away their weapons and surrendered – or tried to, anyway. A machine gun behind them opened up and cut down several of them. Even the enemy's machine guns packed more firepower than their U.S. equivalents. C.S. machine guns fired too fast to let you hear individual rounds going off; the noise sounded like the Devil tearing a sail in half.

It was enough to make Pound duck down into the turret and slam the cupola lid shut behind him. He didn't mind taking chances, but he didn't like taking dumb ones, and you couldn't get much dumber than to offer that gun a clean shot at you. 'Can you spot the son of a bitch?' he asked Scullard.

'Haven't yet, sir,' the gunner answered. 'Shall I give him a round or two of HE if I do?'

'Damn straight,' Pound said. 'They're starting to shoot their own people now. They might as well be Russians or Japs.'

They rolled past wherever the machine gun was concealed without spotting it. Pound wasn't too worried about that. Another barrel or the infantry would take care of it. He just hoped it wouldn't cause many casualties before that happened. Any which way, the machine gunners were in more trouble than they knew what to do with. Somehow or other, soldiers who served machine guns – especially soldiers who served them right up to the last minute – had a lot of trouble surrendering.

Pound peered through the periscopes set into the cupola. It wasn't as good as riding with his head out, but it would have to do. He wondered where the Confederate barrels were. They couldn't stay very far behind the line, not unless they didn't intend to fight this side of the Chattanooga city limits. So . . . where?

'Front!' The gunner spotted the first enemy machine before Pound did. It squatted hull-down behind the rubble of what had been a roadside diner. And its crew had seen this barrel before anyone spotted it. Even as the gunner yelled for an armor-piercing round, the enemy cannon swung toward the barrel and spat fire.

Clang! Less than a second later, the enemy AP round hit the turret. It was like having your head stuck in God's cymbals when He clashed them together. But the thick, well-sloped armor kept the round from penetrating.

'Thank you, Jesus!' Scullard said.

'Amen!' Michael Pound laughed from sheer relief at being alive. By the shape of its turret, the enemy barrel was an old model, one that carried only a two-inch gun. That cannon was better than good enough when the war started, but not any more. 'Give him some of his own medicine, if you please.'

'Yes, sir!' The gunner's enthusiasm surely also sprang from relief. He fiddled with the gun-laying controls – but not for long, because they'd be reloading with frantic haste in that other barrel, and they might get lucky the second time around.

The U.S. barrel's gun spoke before the enemy got off his second shot. It wasn't an easy target, not with only the Confederate machine's turret showing. Pound wished he were making it himself. Not that Scullard wasn't a damn good gunner – he was. But Pound knew he was better than a damn good gunner himself. He commanded the barrel, though. He couldn't hop into the seat on the other side of the turret. Sometimes you had to trust the men under you, no matter how hard that was. Times like this, he wished he had his stripes back. Being an officer was no fun at all.

And then, suddenly, it was. The 3½-inch AP round punched through that old-fashioned turret as if its steel armor were so much cardboard. It knocked the turret half off the ring, knocked the enemy gun all askew. Then the ammunition stored inside the turret started cooking off. Better not to think about what happened to the Confederate barrelmen when a tungsten-pointed projectile started ricocheting around inside that crowded space. *Much* better not to think about it, because it had almost happened here instead.

'Good shot, Scullard!' Pound said. 'Hell of a shot!' You could talk about the shot as if it were part of a game. You could talk about the enemy barrel as if it fought by itself, as if it had no crew inside. That way, you didn't have to think about what happened to the men in there, what you'd just done to them.

'Thank you, sir.' The gunner laid an affectionate hand on the cannon's breech. 'If our turtle didn't have a thick shell, those fuckers would've done unto us before we could do unto them.'

'First shot is better, but we made – you made – the second one count.' Pound gave credit where it was due.

Scullard sent him a sly grin. 'Bet you wished you were doing the shooting yourself.' He knew Pound had been shifting in his seat.

'Well, maybe a little,' the barrel commander admitted – he couldn't very well deny it. But he went on, 'Probably just as well I wasn't. You know the controls for this weapon better than I do.' That was not only polite but true. He'd fired a few rounds to familiarize himself with the cannon in case something happened to the gunner, but it was Scullard's baby. Pound always thought he could do anything. Maybe getting reminded every once in a while that that might not be true was good for him.

'You're a gent, sir,' Scullard said.

Pound laughed. 'Only shows you don't know me as well as you think you do, Sergeant.' He called the driver on the intercom: 'Let's get moving again. We keep sitting around, we give those bastards too good a shot at us.'

'Yes, sir,' the driver said. The barrel lurched forward.

A couple of minutes later, machine-gun fire started clattering off the machine's armored side and the turret. It sounded like hail on a corrugated-iron roof. Pound traversed the turret to the left. There was the machine gun, sure as hell, muzzle flash winking like a lightning bug. It had a damn fool running it – he couldn't hurt a barrel with all the ammo in the world. 'Front!' Pound sang out.

'Identified, sir,' Scullard replied. He spoke to the loader: 'HE!'

'You got it.' The high-explosive shell went into the breech.

'Fire!' Pound yelled, and the gunner did. The shell casing leaped from the gun and clattered off the turret floor. Dirt and smoke fountained up a few yards in front of the machine-gun nest. 'Short!' Pound said. 'Give 'em another round or two. We'll shut the bugger down, by God.'

'Yes, sir,' Scullard said, and then, 'HE again.' His sensitive fingers raised the cannon a hair. He fired the gun. This time, the sandbags that warded the Confederate machine gun went flying. One of the men from the crew started to run. Scullard cut him down with a burst from the coaxial machine gun. 'That takes care of that.'

Pound didn't answer. He was turning his head this way

and that, trying to look through all the periscopes set into the cupola. Somewhere not far away, a U.S. barrel was burning. It wasn't one from his platoon, but that didn't matter. He watched a rocket with a tail of fire brew up another U.S. barrel.

That made him angry. 'Goddammit, where *is* our infantry?' he said. 'They're supposed to keep those bastards with the stovepipes too far off for them to shoot up our barrels that way.'

Then he forgot about enemy soldiers with rocket launchers. The Confederates weren't saving all their armor inside Chattanooga – no, indeed. Butternut barrels rumbled forward. So did barrelbusters: self-propelled artillery pieces without turrets, so they had only a limited traverse, but with larger-caliber cannon than barrels carried. The United States were starting to use them, too. They could be dangerous, both because of the punch they packed and because their low silhouette made them easy to hide and hard to spot.

They were well armored, too, but not well enough – as Pound rapidly proved – to hold out a 3½-inch AP round. The armored melee was as wild as anything Pound had ever seen . . . till U.S. fighter-bombers appeared overhead and tore into the Confederate machines with rockets of their own. The enemy had no answer to those flaming lances slicing down from the sky. Several barrels and barrelbusters went up in flames. Others pulled back toward better cover.

'Forward!' Pound called to his platoon. One of the barrels couldn't go forward; it had a track shot off, and needed repairs. The other four, including his, pressed on. 'They can't stop us!' he exulted.

Maybe the Confederates couldn't, but nightfall did. He wouldn't have minded storming forward after dark, but he got explicit orders to hold in place. He tried to tell himself it might be just as well. If green-gray infantry did come forward in the night, the enemy wouldn't be able to use their rocket launchers against U.S. armor come morning. And if the infantry didn't come up, Pound wanted to know why not.

He didn't mind the chance to get out of the barrel and stretch his legs – and to empty the bottle into which he and the rest of the turret crew had been pissing all day long. He whistled softly when he got a good look at the groove the enemy AP round scored in the hard steel of the turret before bouncing off. 'That was closer than I really like to think about,' he said to Scullard.

'Bet your ass – uh, yes, sir,' the gunner answered. He greedily sucked in cigarette smoke. Lighting up inside the turret wasn't a good idea.

U.S. artillery came down on the Confederates not far ahead. Pound approved of that. Things seemed to be going . . . well enough, anyhow.

Jorge Rodriguez wasn't just glad to be alive after everything he'd been through the past few days. He was amazed. The damnyankees were throwing everything they had into their drive on Chattanooga. His own side was throwing in everything it had to stop them. If anyone came out of the collision point still breathing, it meant one side or the other was falling down on the job.

If he saw the U.S. soldier who'd traded him ration cans for cigarettes, he knew he would shoot the son of a bitch in a minute – unless the Yankee shot him first. This wasn't trading time, not any more.

He'd hoped the coming of night would slow the U.S. armored advance. It did, but U.S. artillery lashed the Confederates in their trenches and holes. Nobody talked about artillery much, but it was a worse killer than gun-fire. It reached farther back from the line, and it could kill you even if you stayed in your hole. Staying down kept you out of the way of bullets. If a 105 shell came down where you were . . . If that happened, then you weren't, not any more.

During a lull a little before midnight, Gabe Medwick called, 'Hey, Jorge! You still alive?'

'I think so.' That was about the most Jorge could say. 'How about you?'

'Last time I looked.' His friend's laugh was shaky. 'Way that last barrage came in, I wouldn't bet on anything.'

'You guys want to shut the fuck up?' Yes, Sergeant Blackledge was still breathing, too. *He would be,* Jorge thought darkly. Blackledge went on, 'You goddamn well better believe there's damnyankees close enough to hear you runnin' your mouths. Sniper with a scope on his rifle spots you moving around in your hole, you're a Deeply Regrets wire waiting to happen.'

He wasn't wrong. Somehow, that made listening to him more annoying, not less. Voice sly, Gabe Medwick said, 'What about you, Sarge? You just now talked more'n both of us put together.'

'Yeah, but I ain't dumb enough to let those shitheads draw a bead on me, and you dingleberries are,' Blackledge said. Jorge didn't know what a dingleberry was, but he didn't think it was anything good. He wouldn't have sassed the sergeant. He'd been brought up to respect authority, not to harass it. His father's hard hand made sure of that.

His father . . . He still didn't know what to make of his mother's letter. Why would his father kill himself? He'd jumped at the chance to put on the uniform of the Confederate Veterans' Brigades. From his letters, he'd been proud to guard the camp in Texas. What could have made him change his mind? Nothing but *mallates* in the camp, not from what his father had said. It wasn't as if they were real people or anything. So why would his old man have flabbled about them?

The artillery barrage picked up again. Crouching in his hole with clods of earth thudding down on him from near misses, wondering if the next one in wouldn't be a near miss, Jorge felt more comfortable than he did wondering what was going through his father's mind in the last few seconds of his life. He'd learned to master simple terror. Incomprehension was a different story.

In spite of the shelling, he snatched ten minutes of sleep here, twenty there, so that when the sun came up over Missionary Ridge he felt weary but not quite ready to keel over. If the Yankees felt weary, they didn't show it. Their barrels growled forward even before sunrise. Jorge looked in vain for Confederate armor to throw them back.

An antibarrel gun set one enemy machine afire. A mine blew a track off another. The stovepipe rockets some soldiers were getting stopped a couple of more. But most of the green-gray barrels kept coming, with foot soldiers loping along between them. If you didn't have a stovepipe, what could you do? You could fall back, or you could die.

Jorge fell back. He fired at enemy infantrymen. He had no idea if he hit anybody, but he made the damnyankees hit the dirt. Even slowing them down felt like a victory. Once, sprawled behind what was left of a stone fence, he saw Sergeant Blackledge on his belly not far away. Blackledge nodded to him. They were both still fighting, even if they were retreating. Jorge looked around for Gabe and didn't see him. He hoped his buddy hadn't stopped something for his country.

On that battlefield, an upright man was a prodigy. An

upright man in dress uniform seemed like a hallucination. But the officer who came forward wore a chromed parade helmet with a general's three stars in a wreath on the front in gold plate – or, for all Jorge knew, in solid gold. This spotless apparition also had a pearl-handled revolver in a holster on his left hip, and another one in his right hand.

However magnificent he looked, he sounded like Hugo Blackledge. 'Come on, you stinking, cowardly scuts!' he roared. 'Drive these Yankee bastards back! They're not getting into Chattanooga, and that's flat. It's ours, and we're damned well going to keep it. Come on! Do you want to live forever?'

Yes, Jorge thought. *Oh, yes.* But the general fired that revolver and ran forward.

'Get moving, you sorry bastards!' Sergeant Blackledge yelled. 'Anything happens to General Patton, you fuckers'll wish the Yankees blew your asses off! Move, God damn you!'

General Patton, fighting at the front line? General Patton, fighting like a private soldier? Like a crazy-brave private soldier? Jorge supposed it was possible. He'd heard weird things about Patton. A general who actually liked fighting for its own sake was a rare breed. Patton filled the bill.

Jorge did go forward to protect the crazy general. He believed Sergeant Blackledge. If anything happened to Patton, the unit that let it happen would catch hell. With the damnyankees throwing hell around in carload lots, that wouldn't be hard to arrange.

'Incoming!' Gabriel Medwick shouted – he wasn't hurt after all. Then he added, 'Hit the dirt, General!' Jorge hit the dirt. He knew what that rising, hateful scream in the air was, whether George Patton did or not. *My namesake,* he realized. Patton would be one dead namesake if he didn't get down.

He didn't. The shell burst not far away. Smoke and dirt fountained up. Splinters knifed out in all directions. None of them touched Patton. Certain madmen were supposed to be able to walk through the worst danger without getting scratched. As far as Jorge was concerned, Patton qualified. You had to be *loco* to stay on your feet when you heard artillery coming in.

But if you did it, and if by some accident you lived through it, you could pull a lot of soldiers with you. Jorge and the men near him had started forward to try to keep General Patton from getting himself killed. When they saw he didn't, they kept going forward to share his luck – and they drove the startled U.S. soldiers back before them. The men in green-gray hadn't dreamt that the battered, pressured Confederates owned this kind of resilience. Jorge couldn't blame them. He hadn't dreamt any such thing himself.

And then the spell broke. Patton ran up to a soldier crouched behind a rock. 'Come on, son!' he roared. 'We've got Yankees to kill! Up and at 'em!'

The soldier didn't move. Jorge was close enough to see he was gray and shaking. *Shellshock,* he thought, not without sympathy. Sometimes too many horrible things could happen to a man all at once, or a bunch of smaller things could accumulate over time. Then he'd be worthless for a while, or only good for light duty. If you let him take it easy, he usually snapped out of it after a while. If you tried to make him perform while he was at low ebb, chances were you wouldn't have much luck.

Patton didn't. His face darkened with anger. 'Get up and fight, you shirking son of a bitch!' he bellowed.

'I'm sorry, sir,' the private said. 'I'm doing the best I can, but—'

'No buts,' Patton growled. 'I'll boot your butt, that's what!' And he did, with a jackboot almost as shiny as his helmet. 'Now *fight!*'

Tears ran down the young soldier's cheeks. His teeth chattered. 'I'm sorry I'm not at my—'

He got no further. Patton slapped him in the face, forehand and then backhand. When that still didn't get the kid moving, the general raised his fancy six-shooter.

'Hold it right there, General!' The shout came from Sergeant Blackledge. But his wasn't the only automatic weapon pointed somewhere near Patton's midriff. 'Sir, you don't shoot a man with combat fatigue. You do, you'll have yourself a little accident.'

'You wouldn't dare,' Patton said.

'Sir, you pull that trigger, it'd be a pleasure,' Blackledge replied. Jorge listened in astonished admiration. He'd known Blackledge wasn't afraid of the enemy. Knowing he wasn't afraid of his own brass, either . . . That took a rarer brand of courage.

Jorge waited for Patton to demand the sergeant's name. He didn't know whether the general would want to know to arrest Blackledge or to promote him on the spot. But Patton did neither. 'All right, then. If you want to stick with a lousy, stinking coward, you can,' he ground out. 'But you'll see what it gets you.' As if there weren't U.S. soldiers no more than a hundred yards away, he turned on his heel and stalked off. His gait put Jorge in mind of an affronted cat.

Blackledge called, 'Freedom!' after the departing general. Patton's back stiffened. He kept walking.

'Th-Th-Thank you,' the guy with combat fatigue got out.

'Don't worry about it, buddy,' Sergeant Blackledge said. 'That fancy-pants asshole comes up here for half an hour, so he reckons he's hot shit. Let him stay in the line for weeks at a stretch like us and see how he likes it. Being brave is one thing. Staying brave when all kinds of shit comes down on you day after day, that's a fuck of a lot tougher.'

'I – I'll try and go forward,' the shellshocked soldier said.

Blackledge only laughed. 'Don't worry about it,' he repeated. 'We ain't doin' any more advancing, not for a while.' He raised his voice: 'Everybody dig in! Damnyankees are gonna hear we're getting frisky in this sector, so they'll hit us with everything but the kitchen sink.'

'You forget something, Sergeant,' Jorge said.

'Yeah? What's that?' The sergeant bristled at the idea he could have overlooked anything.

'Any second now, our own side, they gonna start shelling us, too,' Jorge answered.

Sergeant Blackledge stared at him, then grudged a chuckle. 'That'd be a good joke if only it was a joke, you know what I mean? Fucking Patton's probably ciphering out how to get us all killed right this minute.'

'Shoulda scragged him when we had the chance,' Gabe Medwick said. Dirt flew from his entrenching tool as he scraped out a foxhole. Jorge was also doing his best to imitate a mole.

'Nah.' Reluctantly, Blackledge shook his head. 'Somebody woulda blabbed, and we'd all be in deep shit then. *Deeper* shit, if there is shit deeper'n this. Besides, who says the next jerk with stars and a wreath'd be any better? Oh, chances are he wouldn't grandstand so much, but he'd still do his best to get us killed. Generals get their reputations for getting guys like us killed. Some're smart assholes and some're dumb assholes, but they're all assholes, pretty much.'

'Good thing the enemy, he's got assholes for generals, too,' Jorge said.

Before Blackledge could answer, U.S. artillery started coming in. The sergeant called that one right on the button. Jorge hoped the Yankees didn't have barrels to follow up the bombardment. If they did, he knew damn well the outfit would have to retreat. He didn't think they could hold the line they'd been in before Patton brought them forward, either. If they'd had armor of their own, maybe, but one general in a chromed helmet didn't make up for what was missing.

Barrels painted green-gray *did* come clanking south. Jorge retreated, machine-gun bullets nipping at his heels. His other choice was dying. Patton would have approved of that for him. For himself, he didn't like it for beans.

Irving Morrell's barrel rattled forward. The Confederates had done everything they could to fortify the ground in front of Chattanooga. He was doing his best to show them that everything they could do wasn't nearly enough.

'Time to make some more of those poor sorry bastards die for their country, Frenchy,' he told the gunner.

Sergeant Bergeron nodded. 'Long as I don't have to die for mine, sir, that sounds real good to me.'

'You've got the right attitude.' Morrell knew there were times when a soldier didn't have much choice about dying for his country. Sometimes you had to lay down your life to keep lots of your buddies from losing theirs. Frenchy Bergeron knew that, too; Morrell had seen him in enough action to be sure of it. Only a man who did know about it could joke about it. But you could also get killed from stupidity or plain bad luck. You not only could, it was much too easy. That was the kind of thing Frenchy was talking about.

The Confederates weren't crumbling, the way Morrell had hoped they would. They were fighting hard even as they fell back. They knew where he was headed, and they had a pretty good notion of how he would try to get there. That made for slow, expensive combat, not what Morrell wanted at all.

John Abell warned me slicing them up might take two campaigning seasons, Morrell remembered. He hadn't wanted to believe it. He still didn't. But there was a pretty fair chance the General Staff officer knew what he was talking about.

'Sir, an infantry counterattack just pushed us back a few hundred yards in Sector Blue-7,' someone said in his earphones.

'Blue-7. Roger that,' Morrell said. 'I'll pass the word on to the people who can do something about it.' Thanks to the fancy wireless gear that crowded the turret of his barrel, he could. The artillerymen at the other end of the connection promised him 105mm fire and brimstone would start dropping on that map sector in a couple of minutes. The Confederates wouldn't enjoy the little gains they'd made. Satisfied, Morrell went back to commanding his barrel.

It was plowing through what had been the last major land defenses in front of the Tennessee River. Crossing the river and getting into Chattanooga itself would be another adventure, but just getting to it would give the war effort a kick in the pants. From the north side of the river line, the 105s now punishing Sector Blue-7 would be able to knock Chattanooga flat and leave it useless to the Confederate States.

A lot of U.S. generals would have been delighted to do that much. Morrell was a different kind of officer, and always had been. Doing what most people expected and no more didn't interest him. He didn't want to wound the Confederates here. He wanted to ruin them. Chattanooga wasn't a goal in itself, not to him. It was a gateway. With it in his hands, with communications over the Tennessee secured, he could plunge his armored sword into the Confederacy's heart.

Unfortunately, somebody on the Confederate General Staff, or maybe Jake Featherston himself, had seen that as plainly as Morrell had. The depth of these trench lines; the barbed wire; the minefields – now marked by signs painted with skull and crossbones – and the concrete pillboxes, some of them sporting antibarrel cannon, told the story very clearly. So did the stench of death. The fancy filters that were supposed to keep the barrel's interior free of poison gas if it was buttoned up tight were powerless against the stink.

The barrel clattered past a dead pillbox. Scorch marks around the slit that let a machine gun traverse in there told what had happened. Morrell was a brave soldier, an aggressive soldier. Not for all the money in the world would he have strapped the fuel and gas cartridges for a flamethrower on his back. The men who did were either a little bit nuts – sometimes more than a little bit – or didn't know the odds against them.

Along with disposing of unexploded bombs, lugging a flamethrower was one of the military specialties where the average soldier lasted a matter of weeks, not months. Using men who didn't know as much seemed unfair. That didn't stop the Army. Maybe ignorance was bliss – for a little while.

A U.S. helmet sat on top of a rifle stock. The rifle's bayonet had been plunged into the ground above a hastily dug grave. Did the flamethrower man lie there? Morrell wouldn't have been surprised. He saw two other pillboxes that covered the burned-out one. Of course the Confederates would have interlocking fields of fire; they weren't amateurs. An armor-piercing round had put paid to one of those pill-boxes. He couldn't make out what happened to the other one, but a U.S. soldier leaned against it eating from a ration can, so it was under new management.

A salvo of rockets screamed in from the south. The soldier dove into a hole. Morrell hoped that would keep him safe. Sometimes blast from the screaming meemies killed even if shrapnel didn't. As the explosives in the rockets' noses burst, Morrell's barrel shook like a ship on a stormy sea. He hoped he would stay safe himself. Those damn things could flip a fifty-ton barrel like a kid's toy.

'Fun,' Frenchy Bergeron said when the salvo ended.

Morrell looked at him. '*How* many times did your mother drop you on your head when you were little?'

The gunner grinned. 'Oh, enough, I expect . . . sir.'

'I guess so,' Morrell said with feeling, and the gunner laughed out loud.

Were Morrell in Patton's shoes, he would have pulled back over the Tennessee and made the U.S. commander figure out how to get at him on the south bank. Patton seemed to want to fight it out as far forward as he could. Some of the things Morrell was hearing from Intelligence suggested Patton had to worry about political pressure from Richmond: or, in plain English, Jake Featherston was screaming his head off.

Fighting the enemy was hard enough. Fighting the enemy and your own leaders had to be ten times worse. Morrell had had his arguments and squabbles with the War Department himself. The suspicion with which he and John Abell had watched each other ever since the middle of the last war proved that – as if it needed proving. But when a president ran the war himself, something was bound to get screwed up somewhere.

Being sure of that made Morrell keep his eyes open in

a special way. If Patton goofed, or even if he didn't but a U.S. attack threw his men north of the river into disarray, Morrell's troops might be able to get over the Tennessee before the Confederates knew they'd done it. And if they could, Chattanooga would fall.

How angry would that make Jake Featherston? Angry enough to sack General Patton? Morrell hoped so. Patton made no bones about having learned armored warfare from him. Morrell could have done without the compliment, because the Confederate officer made much too good a pupil. The drive into Ohio was a small masterpiece. The one into Pennsylvania almost worked, too. And the counterattack through the mountains in eastern Kentucky and Tennessee was well conceived; Patton just didn't have the men and matériel to bring it off.

Through a cupola periscope, Morrell watched a U.S. barrel commander leading a platoon of new-model barrels toward the hottest fighting. The sergeant or lieutenant or whatever he was stood head and shoulders out of his cupola. Morrell knew a stab of jealousy. He wanted to fight the same way. Only a cold calculation of his own value to the advance kept him buttoned up in here. That fellow out ahead of him had the freedom insignificance could bring.

'Son of a bitch,' Morrell muttered.

'What's cookin', sir?' Sergeant Bergeron asked.

'Nothing,' Morrell said. It wasn't quite a lie – it was nothing that would matter to Frenchy. But damned if the broad shoulders on that barrel commander didn't remind Morrell of Michael Pound. He knew they'd finally dragged his old gunner up into officer country, kicking and screaming all the way. Pound was on this front, too. So why wouldn't he be in charge of a platoon of barrels? No reason. No reason at all.

That barrel stopped and fired. Something too far away

for Morrell to make it out very well burst into flames. Morrell slowly nodded. He wouldn't want to be Michael Pound's gunner, not for anything. Pound knew the business too well. Chances were he made an impossibly demanding commander. But the gunner in that machine had scored a hit. Pound couldn't complain there.

'Steer left a little,' Morrell called to his driver. 'Follow that platoon up ahead of us. They look like they're going places.'

'Yes, sir,' the driver said, and he did.

Sweat rivered off Morrell. He wished he were on the cool north German plain, pushing the British back through Holland. You could stand staying buttoned up in a barrel in weather like that. Doing it in late summer in southern Tennessee was a recipe for hell on earth, or possibly a New England boiled dinner. Barrelmen poured down water by the gallon and gulped salt tablets like popcorn. It helped . . . some.

Michael Pound's barrel – if that was Pound in the cupola – fired again. Something else blew up. Morrell mentally apologized to that gunner. He was good enough to meet anybody's standards.

A shell clanged off another barrel in the platoon. The round didn't penetrate; the sparks that flashed as it ricocheted away made a pretty fair lightning bolt. The barrel kept moving forward. That hit would have wrecked one of the early models, and probably would have killed a second-generation machine, too. But these babies didn't just dish it out. They could take it, too.

'I'll be goddamned,' Morrell said: one of the more reverent curses he'd ever used. 'There's the river.'

'The Tennessee, sir?' Bergeron said.

'Damn straight. Maybe half a mile ahead,' Morrell answered.

'Let's go grab the bank.' Yes, Frenchy's promotion was way overdue – he had plenty of aggressive spirit.

And Morrell nodded. 'Yeah. Let's. Then we see what happens next.'

Getting there wasn't easy. An antibarrel round disabled one of the machines from the platoon ahead. The barrel lost a track; the crew, safer than they would have been if they bailed out, stayed inside and fired back. Machine-gun rounds clattered off Morrell's barrel. He had an advantage over junior officers: he could call in air strikes and artillery and get what he wanted when he wanted it. He could also summon reinforcements. He did all those things, and resistance faded.

'Careful, sir,' Frenchy Bergeron said when he opened the hatch and stood up in the cupola. He *was* being careful – or he thought he was, anyhow.

The loop of the Tennessee River protecting Chattanooga was summer-narrow, but still too broad and swift to be easy to cross. Beyond lay the city. Smoke from the pounding it had taken partly veiled Lookout Mountain to the south. Morrell wasn't sorry to see that, not in the least. The Confederates would have observation posts and gun emplacements up there. If they had trouble seeing his men, they would also have trouble hitting them.

He cupped his hands and shouted to the platoon commander whose barrel idled not far away: 'That *is* you, Michael! You did a good job getting here.'

'Thanks, sir. I was hoping to see you again.' Pound patted the top of his turret. 'We've finally got what you could have given us twenty years ago. They should have listened then.'

'Ifs and buts,' Morrell said with a shrug. He wasn't done being angry, but he was done thinking being angry made any difference.

Pound pointed south, toward Chattanooga. 'How do we

get over the river?' Even more than Frenchy, he had a grasp of the essential.

Morrell shrugged again. 'I don't know yet, but I expect we'll think of something.'

'Georgia,' Jerry Dover muttered 'I'm back in fucking Georgia.'

He wasn't very far inside of Georgia, but he was south of the Tennessee line. There was no place in southeastern Tennessee Yankee artillery couldn't reach. Bombers were bad enough. But you couldn't keep a major supply depot in range of the enemy's guns. They would ruin you.

As Dover had farther north, he built another dump, a dummy, not far from the genuine article. Experience made him sneakier. Instead of leaving this one out in the open, he camouflaged it . . . not too well. Instead of leaving it empty, he stored things he could afford to lose there: umbrellas, condoms, a good many cigarettes, cornmeal. He put more noncoms at the dummy depot, too, though he made sure they had the best bomb shelters they could. The more realistic the dummy seemed, the better its chance of fooling spies and reconnaissance aircraft.

It got bombed, but not too heavily. The real depot also got bombed – again, not too heavily. The damnyankees dropped explosives on anything that looked as if it might be dangerous, even a little bit. Dover wished his own side could use bombs – and bombers – with such reckless abandon.

One reason the depots didn't get hit harder was that the United States seemed to have decided the most dangerous things in northwestern Georgia were the highway and railroads up from Atlanta. In their place, Jerry Dover probably would have decided the same thing. If reinforcements and ammunition and rations couldn't get close to Chattanooga, supply dumps didn't matter.

Dover felt sorry for whoever was in charge of keeping the railroad line supplied with rails and crossties and switches and whatever the hell else a railroad line needed. That included everything you needed to fix bridges and reopen tunnels, too. He laughed to himself, imagining that harried officer requisitioning a new tunnel from some-where, waiting till he got it, and then driving it through a mountain.

When he told the joke to Pete, the quartermaster ser-geant laughed fit to bust a gut. Then he said, 'You know, sir, nobody who ain't in the business would reckon that was funny.'

'Yeah, that crossed my mind, too,' Dover answered. 'But what the hell? There are doctor jokes and lawyer jokes. Why not supply jokes?'

'Beats me,' Pete said. 'Just having anything to laugh about feels pretty goddamn good right now, you know?'

'Tell me about it,' Dover said.

The more antibarrel cartridges and rockets he sent to the front, the more trouble he figured Confederate forces were in. Gunboats had almost stopped going up the Tennessee to shell U.S. positions. Fighter-bombers descended on them like hawks on chickens when they tried. The gunboats couldn't steam far enough south by daybreak to get out of danger. Several lay on the bottom of the river. The day of the river warship had come and gone.

A field-post truck brought the mail to Dover's depot. That kicked most people's morale higher than any jokes could. Men who heard from home glowed like lightbulbs. The handful who didn't seemed all the gloomier by con-trast.

Jerry Dover had two letters from his wife. He also had one from Savannah. He put that one aside. His family came first. He read the letters from home in order of postmark. Everything back in Augusta was fine. His son and daughter were flourishing. He wasn't sorry that Jethro, at thirteen, was too young to worry about conscription. No, he wasn't one bit sorry, not the way things were going.

But he read Sally's letters with only half his attention. His eye kept going back to the envelope from Savannah. At last, having gone through the news from home three times, he picked up the other envelope. It looked no different from the ones from Augusta, not on the outside: same cheap, coarse paper on the envelope, same four-cent stamp with a barrel and the word FREEDOM printed across it. No matter how it looked, he picked it up as warily as an Army engineer dug up a land mine.

Yes, it was from Melanie. He'd known that as soon as he saw the handwriting, let alone the postmark. It wasn't so much that he'd once had a lady friend his wife didn't known about. If that were all . . . If that were all, he wouldn't have opened the envelope with so much trepidation.

It wasn't even that she wanted money every now and then. She never asked for more than he could afford – and she seemed to know just how much that was. He'd sent Xerxes down to Savannah with cash one time when he couldn't get away himself.

Sometimes, though, Melanie didn't want money. When he was managing the Huntsman's Lodge, she'd sometimes been interested in knowing who came to eat there and what they had to say. She'd made it much too plain that she would talk to Sally if he didn't tell her. So he did. Why not? If she was blackmailing other people besides him, he wouldn't lose much sleep over it.

But what could she want now that he was back in uniform? If it was only money, he'd pay off. If it was anything besides money . . . In that case, he had a problem. If she wasn't just a homegrown blackmailer, if she was looking for things another government – say, the USA's (yes, say it – say it loud) – might find interesting, then having Sally find out about her was the least of his worries.

She knew where to find him. He hadn't told her. He didn't know anyone who would have told her. She knew, though. He didn't think that was a good omen.

The faintest whiff of perfume came from the stationery she used. Unlike the envelope, the paper was of excellent quality. It had to date back to before the war. He unfolded the letter and apprehensively began to read.

Her script was fine and feminine. *Dearest Jerry,* she wrote, *I hope this finds you well and safe. I know you are doing all you can to keep our beloved country strong. Freedom!*

He muttered under his breath. Did she mean that, or was it window dressing to lull any censors? He didn't think the envelope was opened before he saw it, but he could have been wrong. Only one way to find out: he kept reading.

Things here haven't changed much since the last time I wrote, she went on. *Prices have gone up some, though, and the stores don't have as much as I wish they did. If you could send me a hundred dollars, it would help a lot.*

He breathed a sigh of relief. He had a hundred dollars in his wallet. He'd had good luck and a good partner at the bridge table two nights before. If that was all . . .

But it wasn't. He might have known it wouldn't be. Hell, he had known. *You ought to tell me about your friends,* she wrote. *I never hear about how things really are at the front. Where are you exactly?* Dover snorted. As if she didn't know! *What are you doing? How are you going to lick the damnyankees?*

Jerry Dover didn't snort this time. He sighed. He feared he knew what she was asking for. He'd wondered if she would. He hadn't wanted to believe it, but here it was.

And he was liable to end up in trouble on account of it. He'd end up in worse trouble if he told her the things she wanted to know, though. He sent a soldier after his second-in-command here, a bright, eager captain named Rodney Chesbro. 'Don't let them steal this place while I'm gone,' he said. 'I've got to talk to the Intelligence people.'

'Find out how we're going to kick the damnyankees in the slats?' Chesbro asked – yes, he *was* eager. 'If they tell you, will you tell me, too?'

'If they say I can,' Dover answered, which was less of a promise than it sounded like.

He drove a beat-up Birmingham north toward Chattanooga. The road was in bad shape. He was glad no U.S. fighter-bombers showed up to strafe him or drop explosives on his head. It was only a few miles to Division HQ, but getting there took twice as long as he'd thought it would.

As always, the tent where the G-2 men worked was inconspicuous. Intelligence didn't advertise what it was up to. If you didn't need to talk to those people, they didn't want you around. Dover wished he didn't. But he did. A few words to a scholarly-looking noncom got him sent over to a Major Claude Nevers. 'What can I do for you, Colonel?' Nevers asked.

'I have a problem, Major,' Dover answered. 'I've got a lady friend who's been quietly squeezing me for money for quite a while. I wouldn't waste your time if that were all, but now she's trying to get information out of me, too.' He showed the Intelligence officer the letter.

Nevers read it and nodded. 'I think you're right. She's

smooth, but that's the way it looks to me.' He eyed Dover. 'You realize we're going to have to look at you, too?'

'Yeah,' Dover said without enthusiasm. 'But you'd look a lot harder, and you'd have some nastier tools, if I kept mum and you found out about this anyway. So do whatever you need to do, and I'll worry about that later.'

'All right, Colonel.' Nevers didn't call him *sir*. 'Most of the time, I'd remove you from active duty, too. But we're strapped for men now, and I've heard more than a few people who ought to know talk about what a good job you're doing. So give me the particulars about this, ah, Melanie.'

'Melanie Leigh.' Dover spelled the last name. 'Brunette. Blue eyes. Maybe thirty-five, maybe forty. About five feet four. Nice figure. You've got the address there. I've been sending her cash now and then for years so my wife wouldn't hear about her. She can't live on what I give her, though. I have no idea if she has other guys on the string, or how many. I don't know how she'd get word out, either – but she likely has a way.'

'Uh-huh,' Nevers said. 'Send her this hundred she wants. Write her a chatty letter about the kind of stuff you do. Tell her funny stories, nothing she can really use. With luck, we'll drop on her before she can write back saying that isn't what she wants.'

'Tunnel requisitions,' Dover murmured. Major Nevers looked blank. 'I understand what you're talking about, Major,' Dover told him. 'I'll do it. Maybe I'm seeing shadows where nothing's casting them, but. . . .'

'Yes. But,' Nevers said. 'Go tend to it, Colonel. We'll be in touch.'

'Right,' Dover said unhappily.

When he got back to the dump, he had to explain to Captain Chesbro that he didn't know how the Confederate

States were going to drive the Yankees back to the Ohio by Wednesday next. Writing a cheery, chatty letter to a woman he feared was a spy wasn't easy, but he managed. He let Major Nevers vet it before he sent it out; he didn't want the G-2 man thinking he was warning Melanie. He left it and the money and an envelope with the major to mail. Then he tried to worry about logistics.

He got a call from the major that night – in the middle of the night, in fact. A noncom woke him to go to the telephone. Without preamble, the Intelligence officer said, 'She flew the coop, dammit.'

Dover said the first thing that came into his mind: 'I didn't have anything to do with it.'

'I know that,' the Intelligence officer answered. 'We've had you under surveillance since you came to me earlier today.'

We? You and your pals? You and your tapeworm? You and God? Dover was silly with sleepiness. 'How did she know to disappear, then?' he asked.

'Good question,' Major Nevers said. 'I hope we find out – that's all I've got to tell you. You've exposed a security leak, that's for damn sure. I suppose I ought to thank you.' He didn't sound grateful. Dover, yawning, didn't suppose he could blame him.

Every time Major General Abner Dowling saw a pickup truck these days, he winced. The Confederates' improvised gun platforms had caused him a hell of a lot of grief. Their flanking attacks had stalled his drive on Camp Determination and Snyder. They hadn't made him fall back on Lubbock, let alone driven him over the border into New Mexico, the way the enemy probably hoped. But his men weren't going forward any more, either.

And so he grimaced when a pickup truck approached

Eleventh Army headquarters out there in the middle of nowhere, even though the truck was painted U.S. green-gray and he could see it had no machine gun mounted in the bed. No matter what color it was painted, guards made sure it wasn't carrying a bomb before they let it come up to the tent outside of which Dowling stood.

He started to laugh when the truck door opened and a brisk woman not far from his own age got out. 'What's so damn funny, Buster?' Ophelia Clemens demanded, cigarette smoke streaming from her mouth as she spoke.

'The guards were looking for explosives, but they let you through anyhow,' Dowling answered. 'You cause more trouble than any auto bomb or people bomb ever made.'

She batted her eyes at him, which set him laughing all over again. 'You say the sweetest things, darling,' she told him. 'Do you still keep a pint hidden in your desk?'

'It was only a half pint,' he said, 'and now I'll have to put a lock on that drawer.' That made her laugh. 'Come on in,' he continued. 'I'll see what I can find. It's good to see you, by God.'

'People I talk to aren't supposed to tell me things like that,' the reporter said severely. 'They're supposed to say, "Jesus Christ! Here's that Clemens bitch again!" ' She was kidding, and then again she wasn't.

'I never do things I'm supposed to. Would I be here if I did?' Dowling held the tent flap wide. 'Won't you walk into my parlor, said the fly to the spider?'

'That's more like it.' Ophelia Clemens ducked inside. Dowling followed her. He did produce some whiskey, and even a couple of glasses. As he'd seen her do before, Miss Clemens – she'd never married – knocked hers back like a man. 'And *that's* more like it, too,' she said. 'Thanks.'

'You're welcome,' Dowling said. 'I don't suppose you

came way the hell out here just to drink my booze, so suppose you tell me why you did.'

'I want to do a piece on Camp Determination,' she answered. 'I want to show people in the USA what that murderous son of a bitch in Richmond is doing to his Negroes.'

'That would be good,' Dowling said carefully, 'but a lot of what we know is classified. I don't know how much I'm authorized to show the press. Some of what we have shows how we got it, which isn't so good.'

'This will have to pass the censors before it goes out,' she said. 'As for authorization . . .' She fumbled in her purse, which held only a little less than a private's pack. 'Here.' She thrust a folded piece of paper at him.

He unfolded it. It was a letter from Assistant Secretary of War Franklin D. Roosevelt, allowing and indeed requiring him to tell Miss Clemens what he knew 'since this information, when widely publicized, will prove valuable to the war effort.' He set it down. 'Well, you've persuaded me,' he said. 'I'm putty in your hands.'

'Promises, promises,' Ophelia Clemens said. They both grinned. The game of seduction played for farce, with neither of them intending to conquer, was almost as fun in its own way as it would have been for real. 'What have you got?'

Dowling produced aerial photos. 'Here's the camp. The side north of the train tracks – that's *this* way – holds women and children. The other side, which is older, is for men.'

'Uh-*huh*.' Like him, the reporter wore bifocals. 'How big is this thing?'

'You see these little tiny rectangles here by the men's side?' Dowling waited for her to nod, then went on, 'Those are trucks. They're about the size of our deuce-and-a-halfs.'

Ophelia Clemens blinked. 'The place is *that* big?' Now Dowling nodded. She whistled. 'It's not a camp. It's a god-damn city!'

'No, ma'am,' Dowling said. 'There's one big difference. A city has a permanent population. People go into Camp Determination, they go through it, but they don't come out again – not alive, anyway.'

'And your evidence for that is . . . ?'

He passed her more photos. 'This is – was – a stretch of Texas prairie not far from the camp. Barbed wire keeps people out, not that anybody who doesn't have to is likely to want to go out to the back of beyond. The bulldozers give you some idea of scale here. They also dig trenches. You can see that most of those are covered over. The couple that aren't . . . Those are bodies inside.' He gave her another picture. 'A low-level run by a fighter-bomber got us this one. You can really make out the corpses here.'

'Jesus!' She studied it. 'How many bodies are in here? Have you got any idea?'

'Only a rough one,' Dowling answered. 'Hundreds of thousands of people, that's for sure. The experts who are supposed to be good at figuring this stuff out say it's unlikely there are more than a million . . . so far, anyway.'

'Jesus!' Ophelia Clemens said again, more violently than before. 'Give me that bottle again, will you? I need another drink. Hundreds of thousands, maybe a million – what did they do to deserve it?'

'They were born colored,' Dowling said. 'To the Freedom Party, that's a capital offense.'

'If that's a joke, it's not funny,' she said as he passed her the bottle. Her throat worked when she drank.

'I wasn't kidding,' he told her. 'The other thing you have to remember is, this isn't the only camp the Confederates have. We think it's the biggest, but we've also been able to disrupt operations here better than anywhere else. The ones farther east, in Louisiana and Mississippi, they go right on working all the time, because we can't reach them.'

Ophelia Clemens looked from one photograph to another with the kind of horrified fascination a bad traffic accident might cause. But motorcars hadn't banged together here – whole races had. And one was running over the other. 'If they keep this up, there won't be many Negroes left in the CSA by the time they're done.'

'No, ma'am. That's not quite right.' Dowling shook his head. Ophelia Clemens made a wordless questioning noise. He explained: 'They don't aim to leave *any* colored people alive. Not one. That's what they're aiming for. They don't even bother hiding it. Hell, some of the Freedom Party Guards we've captured brag about what they're doing. Far as they're concerned, it's God's work.'

'God's work.' She spat out the words as if they tasted bad. 'If I believed in God, General, these photos would turn me into an atheist. These photos would turn the Pope into an atheist.'

'I doubt it,' Dowling said. 'The Vatican kept quiet when the Turks slaughtered Armenians. It hasn't said boo about the Russian pogroms against the Jews. So why should Pope Pius give a damn about what happens to a bunch of coons who mostly aren't Catholic on the other side of the ocean?'

'Who mostly aren't Catholic,' Ophelia Clemens repeated. 'Yes, that's about the size of it, I'm afraid. He'd bellow like a bull if they were. But since he doesn't care, what are *you* doing about it?'

'I'm trying to take Camp Determination, that's what,' Dowling answered. 'It's not easy, but I'm trying.'

'Why isn't it easy? This ought to be one of the most important things we're doing,' she said. 'Hundreds of thousands of bodies . . . Attila the Hun didn't kill that many people, I bet.'

'There weren't so many people to kill back then,' Dowling said. 'And why isn't it easy? Because this is a secondary front, that's why. I'm short of men, I'm short of barrels, and I'm short of artillery. I used to be short of airplanes, too, but I'm not any more. Of course, the Confederates are even shorter on everything than I am. That's why I've managed to come as far as I have.'

'It's criminal that you're short.' Ophelia Clemens' pencil raced across the notebook page. 'That smells as bad as all those bodies put together, and I'm going to let the world hear about it.'

'No!' Dowling exclaimed. She stared at him in surprise, anger, and something not far from hatred. 'No,' he repeated. 'Don't raise a fuss about it. Please. Don't.'

His earnestness must have got through to her. Her voice was hard and flat when she said, 'You're going to have to explain that,' but she didn't sound as if she would poison a rattlesnake when she bit it.

Glad she didn't, Dowling said, 'I will. I used to think different, but it's simple, when you get down to it. The best way to put Camp Determination out of business is to lick the CSA. That's what General Morrell is doing over in Tennessee, and more power to him. More power to him, literally. If I had two or three times the men and matériel I do, I'd be taking them away from him, and I don't want to do that. I can annoy the Confederates. I can embarrass them. He can win the war. Do you see the difference?'

She didn't answer for a long time. At last, she said, 'I never thought I'd want to punch a man in the nose for being right.'

'It happens,' Dowling said. 'Look at George Custer, for instance.'

'A point,' she admitted. 'I can't tell you how many times I wanted to punch him, but he won the Great War, didn't he?'

'Oh, not all by himself, but more than anybody else, I think,' Dowling answered. 'He saw what barrels could do, and he made sure they did it no matter what the War Department said. General Morrell was in on that, too, remember, though he wasn't a general then, of course.'

She pointed at him. 'So were you.'

'Maybe a little.' Dowling's main role had been to lie through his teeth to the big wigs in Philadelphia. Had Custer's brutal simplicity failed – as it was known to do – Dowling would have lied away his own career along with his superior's. But for once Custer was right, and success, as usual, excused everything else.

'Modest at your age?' Ophelia Clemens jeered. 'How quaint. How positively Victorian.'

'You say the sweetest things,' Dowling told her. 'Just don't say I want more men, because honest to God I don't. I'm keeping the Confederates busy. They can't send reinforcements east from this front. They've had to reinforce it, in fact, to keep me away from Camp Determination. And every man they send out here to the far end of Texas is a man they don't have in Tennessee.'

' "They also serve who only stand and wait," ' she quoted.

'Is that Shakespeare?' To Dowling, anything that sounded old had to be Shakespeare.

But she shook her head. 'Milton, I think.'

'If you say so. It's true here, though. Except I'm not standing. I'm staying busy with what I've got. I think I can go another forty miles.'

'If you go thirty, you can shell the camp,' she said.

'We haven't bombed it because we don't want to go into

the Negro-killing business ourselves,' Dowling said. 'Same problem with shelling. The people in the camp would be on our side if they got guns. They *are* on our side. They just can't do anything about it.'

'Any way to change that?' Ophelia Clemens asked.

'I don't see one,' Dowling said regretfully. 'I wish I did.'

XVI

Artillery was coming down not far from the supply dump where soldiers unloaded Cincinnatus Driver's truck. The Army had put everything as close to the front as it could. With U.S. soldiers on the north bank of the Tennessee River, with the big brass trying to work out how to get across, nobody wanted to run short of anything.

'You need me to, I take this shit right up to the fellas doin' the fighting,' Cincinnatus called to the quartermaster sergeant checking things off on a clipboard.

'That's awright, buddy,' the noncom said in a big-city accent. 'We'll move it forward – that ain't no skin off your nose. What you gotta do is, you gotta go back, get some more shit, and bring it down to us here.'

'I'll do that, then,' Cincinnatus said. This fellow didn't mock him. He argued from efficiency, which was reasonable enough.

As soon as the big trucks were empty, the convoy did start north to fill up again. Armored cars and half-tracks escorted it. By now, U.S. forces had a pretty good grip on the roads leading down to Chattanooga. But pretty good wasn't perfect. Holdouts or civilians fired at the convoy. They knocked out two windows and gave a truck a flat. Cincinnatus didn't think they hit anybody, though, which made the northbound journey a success.

When the convoy got to the supply dump, soldiers in green-gray surrounded it. *Something's up,* Cincinnatus thought, and wondered what. A full colonel came forward to lead the trucks to tents that hadn't been pitched when they set out a few hours earlier. The troops the colonel commanded spread out; they set up cloth barriers to make sure no one outside the depot could watch what was going on inside.

'What the hell?' Hal Williamson shouted from the cab of his deuce-and-a-half. Cincinnatus was glad to find he wasn't the only driver wondering if somebody'd slipped a cog – or more than one.

'This is a special transport mission,' the colonel shouted. 'You are not to talk to anybody about what you're going to see. Do you understand that? Anyone who doesn't care to go along can withdraw now without prejudice.'

Nobody withdrew. After that buildup, Cincinnatus was too curious to back out. He and the other truckers hauled vital munitions all the time. What could be more special than the stuff soldiers needed to blow Featherston's fuckers to hell and gone?

'All right!' the colonel said. 'The other thing I need to warn you about is, don't panic and don't reach for your weapons when you see what's going on. These men are on our side, the side of the United States of America.'

If he hadn't said so, Cincinnatus wouldn't have believed it. As things were, Cincinnatus had trouble believing it anyway. The soldiers who came out of the tents wore Confederate uniforms. They had on Confederate helmets. They all carried submachine guns or automatic Tredegars.

'The fuck?' Cincinnatus was far from the only driver to say that or something very much like it.

'They're on our side,' the colonel repeated. 'This is the 133rd Special Reconnaissance Company. They're all U.S. citizens who grew up in the CSA or lived there for years. They look like Confederates, they act like Confederates, they talk like Confederates – and they're going to screw the Confederate States to the wall. The enemy did this to us in Pennsylvania last year. Turnabout, by God, is fair play.'

Cincinnatus stared at the pseudo-Confederates. 'Do Jesus,' he said softly. Little by little, a wide, predatory grin spread across his face. If these fellows sounded as good as they looked, they could cause the Confederates a world of grief.

Were they going to cross the Tennessee? If anyone could do it on the sly, this was the outfit. If they got caught, they'd get killed – probably an inch at a time. You had to have balls to try something like this.

Even so, Cincinnatus' hackles rose when some of them got into the back of his truck. Those uniforms, those weapons, that accent . . . They all screamed *Murderers!* to him.

'Don't worry, pal,' one of them said through the little window between the rear and the cab. 'We don't bite, honest.' He sounded like an Alabaman, which didn't help.

After the 133rd Special Reconnaissance Company boarded the trucks, the guards at the depot took down the screens. No one from outside could hope to see into the deuce-and-a-halfs. But then everybody just sat there. The trucks didn't roll south. Cincinnatus wanted to *go*. He wanted to get these men out of his truck. They looked so much like the enemy, they gave him the cold horrors, and he couldn't do anything about it.

He must have been wiggling on his seat, because that counterfeit Confederate spoke up again: 'Don't flabble, man. It's better if we get there after dark. If those fuckers don't see us coming, we can surprise 'em better.'

'I guess,' Cincinnatus said. 'Makes sense.' And it did. No matter how sensible it was, nothing could make him like it.

Sundown seemed to take forever. He knew it didn't, but it sure seemed to. At last, as twilight deepened, the lead truck rumbled to life. Cincinnatus thumbed the starter button with vast relief. The engine caught at once. He wouldn't have been heartbroken had it died. The false Confederates could have found another truck, and he would have stayed here. No such luck.

He turned on his headlights. He might as well not have bothered. The thin strip that masking tape didn't cover gave a little more light than a smoldering cigarette, but not much. The truck convoy wouldn't hurry down toward Chattanooga, not at night it wouldn't.

It did keep its escort. That was good. In case anything went wrong, soldiers in real U.S. uniforms in the half-tracks might protect the impostors from men who didn't know who and what they were. Those soldiers might protect the drivers, too. If ordinary U.S. troops spotted these fellows in butternut, everybody anywhere near them would need a hell of a lot of protecting. Cincinnatus was sure of that.

He rattled along at about fifteen miles an hour. Every once in a while, on a straight stretch of road, he got up to twenty or so. No shots came from the woods. Maybe all the bushwhackers went to bed early. He could hope, anyway. He followed the narrow stripe of tail light the truck ahead of him showed, and hoped that driver didn't get lost. If he did, all the trucks behind him would follow him straight into trouble.

After a while, Cincinnatus went past the depot he'd visited earlier in the day. He thought it was the same one, anyhow. The artillery duel seemed to have flagged with the coming of night. A mosquito bit him on the arm. He swore and slapped and didn't squash it. Next to the bite of a shell fragment, though, it seemed almost friendly.

Those stripes of red got a little brighter: the truck ahead was hitting the brakes. Cincinnatus did the same. The driver in back of him was paying attention, too, because that truck didn't smack his rear bumper.

Somebody by the side of the road gestured with a dimmed flashlight. 'You guys with the special cargo – over this way!' he called.

Like the rest of the convoy, Cincinnatus went over that way. The trucks were crawling along now. That made them quieter, but not what anybody would call quiet. With luck, though, gunfire masked most of their noise. This was about as close to the front as Cincinnatus had ever come. Peering through the windshield, he could see muzzle flashes across the river.

Another soldier with a feeble flashlight said, 'Lights out!' Cincinnatus hit the switch and went from dimness to darkness. His eyes adapted fast, though. He soon spotted strips of white tape somebody – engineers? – had put down to guide the convoy to where it was supposed to go. He nodded to himself. They'd done things like that during the Great War, too.

'Here we are!' A loud, authoritative voice, that one. If it didn't belong to a veteran noncom, Cincinnatus would have been amazed. He hit the brakes.

'Let's go!' *That* voice came from the back of the truck. The U.S. soldiers in butternut piled out. They gathered with their pals from other trucks.

'Good luck.' Cincinnatus almost couldn't force the words out.

Had the ordinary U.S. soldiers here been briefed? If they hadn't, there'd be hell to pay in nothing flat. The thought had hardly crossed his mind before gunfire broke out. Some of the weapons were U.S., others Confederate. Shouts and screams filled the air.

'Do Jesus!' Cincinnatus burst out. He'd feared things might go wrong, but he hadn't imagined they could go as wrong as this. *Only shows what I know,* he thought bitterly. The Army could screw anything up.

And then, little by little, he realized the chaos and the gunfire weren't screwups after all. They were part of a plan. The fake Confederates got into rubber rafts and paddled across the Tennessee toward the southern bank, which real Confederates held. Tracers came close to those rafts, but Cincinnatus didn't think they hit any of them.

He started to laugh. If the shooting fooled him, wouldn't it fool Jake Featherston's troops on the far bank? Wouldn't they think some of their buddies were getting away from the damnyankees? And wouldn't the phonies be likely to have all the passwords and countersigns real Confederates should have?

So what would happen to the genuine Confederates who greeted the troops they thought were their countrymen? They would get a brief, painful, and probably fatal surprise.

And what would happen *then*? Cincinnatus didn't know, not in detail, but he could make some pretty good guesses. When he did, he laughed some more. The only thing he wished was that he were a white man in one of those rafts, carrying a Confederate automatic rifle. He wanted to see the look on the face of the first real Confederate he shot.

The counterfeits in butternut would be getting close. He couldn't hear the shouts across the water, not for real, but he could imagine them in his mind's ear. He sat in the cab of his truck and swatted at more mosquitoes. He wished for a smoke, but didn't light up. He waited and waited and . . .

Sudden gunfire on the south bank of the Tennessee.

As if that was a signal – and no doubt it was – U.S. artillery opened up. Cincinnatus could see where the shells came down by the flashes of bursting shells across the river. It made a tight box around the place where Featherston's phony fuckers had come ashore. The artillerymen would have range tables and maps marked with squares so they could put their bombardment right where they needed it.

And more boats started across the river. These weren't paddle-powered rubber rafts; Cincinnatus could hear their motors growling. They would land real U.S. soldiers in real U.S. uniforms and, no doubt, everything the troops needed to fight on the far side of the Tennessee: mortars and antibarrel guns and ammo and command cars and maybe even barrels. The invaders would secure the bridgehead, punch a hole in the enemy defenses, and then try to break out. And the whole enormous force on the north bank would slam in right behind them.

Cincinnatus waved, there in the deuce-and-a-half. 'So long, Chattanooga!' he said. 'Next stop, fuckin' Atlanta!'

If things worked. Why wouldn't they, though? Somebody'd planned this one to a fare-thee-well. Once the U.S. forces punched through the lines the Confederates had fortified, what could stop them? They'd be fighting in the open, and the enemy would have to fall back or get rolled up.

Small-arms fire on the other side of the river suddenly picked up. Cincinnatus whooped. He knew what that meant, knew what it had to mean. U.S. soldiers in green-gray were across the Tennessee. 'Go, you bastards!' he yelled, as if they were his favorite football team. 'Go!'

Jake Featherston didn't order Clarence Potter court-martialed and shot for his failure in the flanking attack on the damnyankees in Tennessee. There was plenty of failure to go around. Featherston extracted a nastier revenge on the Intelligence officer: he kept him in a combat slot.

Potter protested, saying – accurately – that he was more valuable back in Richmond. No one felt like listening to him. The Confederate States needed combat officers. He wasn't the only retread – far from it. Officers from the Quartermaster Corps, even from the Veterinary Corps, commanded regiments, sometimes brigades. When you ran short of what you needed, you used what you had.

They were using Potter. He hoped they didn't use him up.

He wanted to do in Chattanooga what the United States had done in Pittsburgh. He wanted to tie the enemy down, make him fight house by house, and bleed him white. He thought Jake Featherston wanted the same thing. He hoped that, even if Chattanooga fell, the Confederates could take so much out of the U.S. forces attacking them that the Yankees would be able to go no farther. That would give the CSA a chance to rebuild and regroup.

With C.S. forces holding Lookout Mountain to the south and Missionary Ridge to the east, the defensive position should have been ideal. But Potter couldn't get anybody to listen to him.

George Patton had gone up to talk to the President. Even so, he kept fighting the campaign his own way: hurling troops and – worse – armor into fierce counterattacks, trying to throw the men in green-gray back over the Tennessee. (Potter hated to learn that U.S. soldiers in butternut had confused Confederate defenders long enough to help the main U.S. push get over the river in the first place. That was one more trick the enemy had stolen from his side. As he'd feared from the beginning, any knife that cut the USA would also cut the CSA.)

'Dammit, we can hit them in the flank and smash them!' Patton shouted, again and again. 'It worked in Ohio! It worked in Pennsylvania till they got lucky! It'll work here, too!'

He didn't mention that it hadn't worked in Kentucky and here in Tennessee not long before. And he didn't seem to realize that the Confederates enjoyed the edge in fire-power and doctrine in Ohio and also, for a while, in Pennsylvania. Now the U.S. forces understood what was what as well as their C.S. counterparts.

And the Yankees had the firepower edge, damn them. Whenever the Confederates surged to the attack, they got hit by artillery fire the likes of which they'd never seen in the fondly remembered days of 1941. Fighter-bombers roared across the battlefield, adding muscle to the bom-bardment. They had a much better chance of getting away to do it again than the slow, ungainly Confederate Asskickers did.

Even more revolting, the United States had not only more barrels but also better barrels. The Confederates des-perately needed a new model to match or surpass the latest snorting monsters from Pontiac. They needed one, but where was it? Where were the engineers who could design it? Where were the steelworkers and auto workers who could build it?

Clarence Potter knew where they were. Too damn many of them were in uniform, doing jobs for which they weren't ideally suited, just like him. The Confederacy was running headlong into the same problem that bedeviled it during the Great War: it couldn't walk and chew gum at the same time. One or the other, yes. One *and* the other? Not so well as the United States.

After Patton's third ferocious lunge failed to wipe out or even shrink the Yankee bridgehead on the south bank of the Tennessee, he called an officers' meeting in an elementary-school classroom. Sitting at one of those little desks, smelling chalk dust and oilcloths, took Potter back over half a century.

'What are we supposed to do?' Patton rasped. 'We've got to stop those bastards any way we can. If they get into Chattanooga . . . If they get past Chattanooga . . . We're screwed if that happens. How do we stop 'em?'

Though for all practical purposes only an amateur here, Potter raised his hand. Again, he thought of himself in short pants. He hadn't been shy then, and he wasn't shy now. Patton pointed to him. 'Let's make the enemy come to us for a change,' he said. 'Let's pull back into the city and give him the fun of digging us out. *That* worked up in Pennsylvania. We can make it work for us, too.'

'It means abandoning the river line,' Patton said.

'Are we going to get it back, sir?' Potter asked.

Patton gave him a dirty look. Chances were the general commanding had intended his remark to close off debate, not keep it going. Potter nodded to himself. Yes, Patton had more than a little Jake Featherston in him. Well, too bad. He shouldn't have called this council if he didn't want to hear other people's ideas.

'We will if we can get some more air support,' Patton said.

'From where?' Potter said. 'The damnyankees have had more airplanes than we do ever since the Pennsylvania campaign went sour.'

Patton's expression turned to outright loathing. He'd been in charge of the Pennsylvania campaign, and didn't like getting reminded it hadn't worked. *Too bad*, Potter thought again. He spoke his mind to Jake Featherston. A mere general didn't intimidate him a bit.

'If the airplanes come—' Patton tried again.

'Where will we get them from?' Potter repeated. 'We can't count on things we don't have, or we'll end up in even hotter water than we're in now.'

'You talk like a damnyankee,' Patton said in a deadly voice. 'I bet you think like a damnyankee, too.'

'By God, I hope so,' Potter said, which made Patton's jaw drop. 'About time somebody around here did, don't you think? They've done a better job of thinking like us than we have of thinking like them, and we're paying for it.'

'You haven't got the offensive spirit,' Patton complained.

'Not when we don't have anything but our mouths to be offensive with, no, sir,' Potter said. 'The more we keep charging the U.S. lines, the more they slaughter us, the worse off we are. Let them come to us. Let them pay the butcher's bill. Let them see how well they like that. Maybe we'll be able to get out of this war with our freedom intact.' He used the word with malice aforethought.

'I'll report you to the President,' Patton said.

'Go ahead. It's nothing I haven't told him, too,' Potter said cheerfully. 'Having people who love you is all very well, but you need a few men who are there to tell you the truth, too.' He mocked Featherston's wireless slogan as wickedly as he took the Freedom Party's name in vain.

Several officers moved away from him, as if afraid whatever he had might be contagious. He saw a few men nod, though. Some people still had the brains to see that, if what they were doing now wasn't working, they ought to try something else. He wondered whether Patton would.

No such luck. Potter hadn't really expected anything different. He thought about going over Patton's aggressive head and complaining to Jake Featherston himself – thought about it and dismissed it from his mind. Featherston was as fanatic about the offensive as Patton was, or he would have pulled back sooner in Pennsylvania and lost less.

'We open the new counterattack at 0800 tomorrow,' Patton declared. 'General Potter, you *will* be generous enough to include your brigade in the assault?'

Potter didn't want to. What was the point of throwing it into the meat grinder now that it was rebuilt to the point of becoming useful again? Wasted matériel, wasted lives the Confederacy couldn't afford to throw away . . . But he nodded. 'Yes, sir. Of course, sir. I don't disobey orders.'

'You find other ways to be insubordinate,' Patton jeered.

'I hope so, sir, when insubordination is called for.' Potter was damned if he'd let the other general even seem to put him in the wrong.

He got the brigade as ready as he could. If they were going to attack, he wanted them to do it up brown. He didn't think they could reach the objectives Patton gave him, but he didn't let on. Maybe he was wrong. He hoped so. If they succeeded, they really would hurt the U.S. forces on this side of the Tennessee.

It all turned out to be moot.

At 0700, Confederate guns in Chattanooga, on Lookout Mountain, and on Missionary Ridge were banging away at the Yankee bridgehead. Potter looked at his watch. One more hour, and then they would see what they would see.

But then a rumble that wasn't gunfire filled the sky. Potter peered up with trepidation and then with something approaching awe. What looked like every U.S. transport airplane in the world was overhead. Some flew by themselves, while others towed gliders: they were so low, he could see the lines connecting airplane and glider.

One stream made for Missionary Ridge, while the other flew right over Chattanooga toward Lookout Mountain.

'Oh, my God!' Potter said, afraid he knew what he would see next.

And he did. String after string of paratroopers leaped from the transports. Their chutes filled the sky like toadstool tops. Confederate soldiers on the high ground started shooting at them while they were still in the air. Some of them fired back as they descended. By the sound of their weapons, they carried captured C.S. automatic rifles and submachine guns. The damnyankees had seized plenty, and the ammo to go with them, in their drive through Kentucky and Tennessee. Now they were using them to best advantage.

As the paratroopers landed atop Lookout Mountain and Missionary Ridge, a captain near Potter said, 'They can't do that. They can't get away with it.'

'Why not?' Potter answered. 'What happens if they seize the guns up there? What happens if they turn 'em on us?'

The captain thought about it, but not for long. 'If they do that, we're fucked.'

'I couldn't have put it better myself – or worse, depending on your point of view,' Potter said. The racket of gunfire from the high ground got louder. The USA had dropped a lot of men up there. They weren't likely to carry anything heavier than mortars – though God only knew what all the gliders held – but they had the advantage of surprise, and probably the advantage of numbers.

They caught Patton with his pants down, Potter thought, and then, *Hell, they caught me with my pants down, too. They caught all of us.*

'We're not going to go forward at 0800 now, are we, sir?' the captain asked.

'Sweet Jesus Christ, no!' Potter exclaimed. 'We – our side – we've got to get those Yankees off the high ground. That comes ahead of this counterattack.' If Patton didn't like it, too bad.

But no sooner were the words out of his mouth than a wireless operator rushed up to him. 'Sir, we're ordered to hold in place with two regiments, and to bring the third back, fast as we can, to use against Lookout Mountain.'

'Hold with two, move the third back,' Potter echoed. 'All right. I'll issue the orders.' He wondered if he *could* hold with two-thirds of his brigade. If U.S. forces tried to break out of the bridgehead now, at the same time as they were seizing the high ground and guns in the C.S. flank and rear, couldn't they just barge into Chattanooga and straight on past it? He hoped they wouldn't try. Maybe their right hand and left didn't have even a nodding acquaintance with each other. It had happened before.

Not this time. Twenty minutes later, as his rearmost regiment started south toward Lookout Mountain, U.S. artillery north of the Tennessee awakened with a roar. Green-gray barrels surged forward. It was only August, but winter came to live in Clarence Potter's heart.

Dr. Leonard O'Doull worked like a man possessed. In part, that was because the new senior medic working with him, Sergeant Vince Donofrio, couldn't do as much as Granville McDougald had. Donofrio wasn't bad, and he worked like a draft horse himself. But Granny had been a doctor without the M.D., and Donofrio wasn't. That made O'Doull work harder to pick up the slack.

He would have been madly busy even with McDougald at his side. The United States hadn't quite brought off what they most wanted to do: close off the Confederates' line of retreat from Chattanooga with paratroops, surround their army inside the city, and destroy it. Featherston's men managed to keep a line of retreat open to the south. They got a lot of their soldiers and some of their armor and other vehicles out through it. Down in northern Georgia,

Patton's army remained a force in being. But the Stars and Stripes floated over Chattanooga, over Lookout Mountain, over Missionary Ridge. The aid station was near the center of town.

Up in the USA, newspapers were bound to be singing hosannas. They had the right – this was the biggest victory the United States had won since Pittsburgh. It was much more elegant than that bloody slugging match, too.

Which didn't mean it came without cost. O'Doull knew too well it didn't. He paused in the middle of repairing a wound to a soldier's left buttock to raise his mask and swig from an autoclaved coffee mug. His gloved hands left bloody prints on the china. He set the mug down and went back to work.

'Poor bastard lost enough meat to make a rump roast, didn't he, Doc?' Donofrio said.

'Damn near. He'll sit sideways from now on, that's for sure,' O'Doull replied. 'Like the old lady in *Candide*.'

He knew what he meant. He'd read it in English in college, and in French after he moved up to the Republic of Quebec. But Sergeant Donofrio just said, 'Huh?' O'Doull didn't try to explain. Jokes you explained stopped being funny. But he was willing to bet Granny would have got it.

He finished sewing up the fellow's left cheek. The stitches looked like railroad lines. It was a nasty wound. You made jokes that didn't need explaining when somebody got hit there, but it was no joke to the guy it happened to. This fellow would spend a lot of time on his belly and his right side. O'Doull didn't think he would ever come back to the front line.

After the stretcher-bearers carried the anesthetized soldier away, they brought in a paratrooper who'd got hurt up on Lookout Mountain. He had a splint and a sling on his right arm and a disgusted expression on his face. 'What happened to you?' O'Doull asked him.

'I broke the son of a bitch, sure as hell,' the injured man replied. 'Looked like I was gonna get swept right into a tree, so I stuck out my arm to fend it off, like. Yeah, I know they teach you not to do that. So I was a dumb asshole, and I got hurt without even getting shot.'

'Believe me, Corporal, you didn't miss a thing,' O'Doull said.

'But I let my buddies down,' the paratrooper said. 'Some of them might've bought a plot 'cause I fucked up. I shot myself full of morphine and took a pistol off a dead Confederate, but even so. . . . I wasn't doing everything I should have, dammit.'

'What did you do when the morphine wore off?' Donofrio asked.

'Gave myself more shots. That's wonderful stuff. Killed the pain and kept me going just like coffee would. I've been running on it two days straight,' the corporal said.

Sergeant Donofrio looked at O'Doull. 'There's one you don't see every day, Doc.'

'Yeah,' O'Doull said. Morphine made most people sleepy. A few, though, it energized. 'You've got an unusual metabolism, Corporal.'

'Is that good or bad?'

'Neither, I don't think. It's just different. Why don't you get up on the table? We'll put you under and make sure your arm's set properly and get it in a cast. That'll hold things together better than your arrangement there.'

'How long will I take to heal up?' the soldier asked as he obeyed.

'A couple of months, probably, and you'll need some more time to build up the arm once you can use it again,' O'Doull said. The paratrooper swore resignedly. He wasn't angry at being away from the fighting so much as for letting his friends down.

O'Doull gave him ether. After the soldier went under, the doctor waved for Vince Donofrio to do the honors. Setting a broken bone and putting a cast on it were things the medic could do. He took care of them as well as O'Doull might have.

They fixed several more fractures: arms, ankles, legs. Paratroopers didn't have an easy time of it. Coming down somewhere rugged like the top of Lookout Mountain was dangerous in itself. Add in the casualties the desperate Confederates dealt out and the U.S. parachute troops suffered badly.

But they did what they were supposed to do. They silenced the enemy guns on the high ground. They turned some of those guns against the Confederates in and in front of Chattanooga. And they made Featherston's men fear for their flank and rear as well as their own front. If not for the paratroopers, the Stars and Bars would probably still fly above Chattanooga.

The wounded men seemed sure the price they'd paid was worth it. One of them said, 'My captain got hit when we were rushing a battery. "Make it count," he told us. He didn't make it, but by God we did like he said.' He'd had two fingers shot off his left hand, and couldn't have been prouder.

'Only thing worse than getting hurt when you win is getting hurt when you lose,' Donofrio remarked after they anesthetized the paratrooper. 'Then you know your country got screwed along with you.' Maybe sergeants thought alike; Granny'd said the same thing.

They treated wounded Confederates who went a long way toward proving the point. 'You bastards win, you're gonna screw us to the wall,' said a glum PFC with a bullet through his foot. 'I gave it my best shot, but what the hell can you do when you stop one?' He seemed sunk in gloom.

'You came through alive,' O'Doull said. 'Whatever happens, you're here to see it.'

'Hot damn,' the Confederate answered. Donofrio put him under. O'Doull did what he could to patch up the damage from the bullet. He didn't know if the wounded man would ever walk without a limp, but he was pretty sure he saved the foot.

Away went the wounded PFC. Next up on the table was a much more badly hurt Confederate, with an entry wound in the right side of his chest and a far bigger exit wound in the right side of his back. Bloody foam came from his mouth and nostrils. He wasn't complaining about how the war was going. He was gray and barely breathing.

Sergeant Donofrio got a plasma line into him before O'Doull could even ask for it. O'Doull wished he could transfuse whole blood. They were supposed to be working the bugs out of that, but whatever they were doing hadn't got to the field yet. This guy needed red cells to carry oxygen, but he would have to use his own.

That means I've got to keep him from bleeding to death in there, O'Doull thought unhappily. He opened the Confederate's chest even as Donofrio stuck the ether cone over the man's face. The wounded soldier was too far gone to care.

The bullet had torn hell out of his right lung. O'Doull hadn't expected anything different. He cut away the bottom half of the organ, tying off bleeders as fast as he could.

'Make it snappy, Doc,' Donofrio said. 'His BP's dropping.'

'I'm doing everything I can,' O'Doull answered. 'Keep that plasma coming.'

'I gave him the biggest-gauge needle we have,' the medic answered. 'Only way to get it in there faster is with a fuckin' funnel.'

'All right,' O'Doull said, but it wasn't – not even close. Too much blood loss, too long trying to breathe with that ruined lung . . . He knew exactly when the wounded man died, because he felt his heart stop. He swore and tried open-chest massage. He won a couple of feeble contractions, but then the heart quivered toward eternal silence. O'Doull looked up and shook his head. 'Shit. Close the line, Vince. He's gone.'

'Oh, well. You tried, Doc. Don't feel bad about it.' Every time they lost somebody, O'Doull heard the same thing. There wasn't much else *to* say. Donofrio went on, 'Not like he was one of ours, anyway.'

'I work just as hard on them,' O'Doull said. 'That way, I can stay honest when I hope they work just as hard on our guys.'

'Well, yeah,' Donofrio said. 'But even so . . . You know what I mean.'

O'Doull nodded. He knew exactly what the younger man meant. He worked as hard as he did on enemy wounded not least because he knew. As long as he was honest about that, losing Confederate casualties bothered him as little as possible. If he only went through the motions, if he lost men he might have saved by working harder . . . Well, how could he shave in the morning without wanting to slice the razor blade across his throat?

Corpsmen lifted the dead Confederate off the operating table and carried him away. O'Doull peeled off his gloves. He threw them into a trash can. He had blood on his arms up past the gloves; he'd been deep inside the soldier's chest. He scrubbed with strong soap that smelled of carbolic acid, then went to get a towel with his wrists bent up so the water would run away from his fingers. Hands dried, he took a deep breath. 'Whew!' he said. 'Feels like I'm coming up for air.'

'Enjoy it while you can,' Vince Donofrio said. 'Chances are it won't last long.' He stretched and twisted his back. Something in there crackled. He was grinning as he took off his mask. '*That's* better. Wonder what Chattanooga's like. Haven't hardly had a chance to look around.'

'Chattanooga's a mess,' O'Doull said, which was true in the same sense that Jake Featherston was not a nice person. Chattanooga was bombed and shelled and shot up. But that wasn't all of what Donofrio meant. O'Doull went on, 'Probably not all the women refugeed out.'

'Sure as hell hope not.' Chasing skirt was Donofrio's hobby, the way fishing was for some men and carpentry for others.

'Be careful what you catch. After you've got it for a little while, you'll decide you don't want it any more.' O'Doull knew a lot of skirt-chasers, and didn't understand any of them. He was happy enough with one woman. Oh, he looked at others, but he didn't touch. Plenty of men did.

'Yeah, yeah. I'm a big boy, Doc,' Donofrio told him impatiently. The medic was ready – eager – to comb through the ruins of Chattanooga for anything that didn't take a leak standing up.

'Just remember your initials,' O'Doull warned.

'Funny. Fun-*ny*,' Vince Donofrio said. 'Har-de-har-har. See? I'm busting up.'

'Yeah, well, use a pro station when you're done laughing,' O'Doull said. 'Sulfa's pretty good for the clap, but it doesn't do anything about syphilis.'

'I know, I know. I'll be careful,' Donofrio said. 'Is that other new stuff coming out of the labs – that peni-whatever-the-hell – is that as good as everybody says it is?'

'Haven't got my hands on any, so I don't know for sure,' O'Doull answered. 'The literature sure makes it sound like the Second Coming, though, doesn't it?' He'd seen plenty of literature like that for one patent medicine or another, and that always turned out to be less than met the eye. But people raved about penicillin in professional journals. That was different. He hoped it was, anyway. Drugs that killed germs without poisoning patients gave doctors an edge they'd sorely missed in the Great War.

'I'm gonna slide outa here if I get a chance,' Donofrio said. He didn't; not even a minute later, corpsmen brought in a Confederate groaning with a shattered shoulder. The medic went to work without complaint. If he was thinking about women while he did, well, wasn't that better than brooding about blood and bullets and broken bones?

Armstrong Grimes was new to the rituals of the repple-depple. He'd stayed with the same unit from Ohio to Utah to Canada. Now he didn't belong to anybody or anything. He'd been dissolved away from everything that went before, and was floating free. He was a – what the hell did they call them in chemistry? He muttered to himself, flogging his memory. An ion, that was it. He was an ion.

The replacement depot had been a high school some-where in the middle of Tennessee. He didn't know exactly where, or care very much. All he knew was that it was a hell of a lot hotter and muggier than Manitoba. And he knew the locals here, like the ones up there and the ones in Utah, didn't like U.S. soldiers worth a damn. A barbed-wire perimeter with sandbagged machine-gun nests around the depot rubbed that in.

He lit a cigarette. Confederate tobacco was easy to come by around here, anyway. He sucked in smoke, held it, and blew it out. The kid in the seat next to his said, 'Bum a butt off you, Sergeant?'

'Sure.' Armstrong held out the pack.

'Thanks.' The kid took one, pulled a lighter out of his

pocket, and got the Duke going. He smoked it halfway down, then said, 'You rather go to the front, or do you want occupation duty?'

'Christ! The front!' Armstrong said. 'I've done occupation duty. You can have it. I want to get some licks in at the real enemy for a change. What about you?'

'I got wounded when we were outflanking Nashville,' the kid answered. 'If I could find a nice, quiet spot where nothing much happens . . .'

'You're an honest goldbrick, anyway,' Armstrong said, laughing.

'I'd have to smoke funny cigarettes to really believe it, not nice ones like these,' the young private said. 'The only guys who draw duty like that are Congressmen's kids.'

'Not even them. There was one in my outfit – well, a nephew, but close enough,' Armstrong said. 'He was a regular joe, Yossel was. Did the same shit everybody else did, took the same chances when the shooting started. He had balls, too – sheenies must be tougher'n I figured.'

Up at the front of the repple-depple, where the principal would have given the students what-for, a personnel sergeant sat reading a paperback with a nearly naked girl on the cover. A young officer came up and spoke to him. He nodded, put down the book, and picked up a clipboard. He read off several names and pay numbers. Men grabbed their gear and went out with the shavetail.

A few more soldiers came in and found seats. The personnel sergeant called other names and numbers. Men slung duffel bags or shouldered packs and found themselves part of the war again. A poker game started. Armstrong stayed away. He'd played a lot of poker in the hospital, and had less money than he wished he did because of it.

Another lieutenant talked with the personnel sergeant.

The sergeant looked at his clipboard. Among the names he read was, 'Henderson, Calvin.' The kid next to Armstrong got up and walked to the front of the room. Then the noncom said, 'Grimes, Armstrong,' and rattled off his pay number.

He got up, too. His leg hurt a little, but he got around all right. He went up and said, 'I'm Armstrong Grimes.'

'Hello, Sergeant. I'm Lieutenant Bassler,' the officer said. 'I've got a squad for you. You've led a squad before?'

'I've led a platoon, sir,' Armstrong answered.

Lieutenant Bassler took it in stride. 'Good. You'll know what you're doing, then. Where was that?'

'In Utah, sir, and up in Canada.'

'All right. And you're in the repple-depple because . . . ?'

Did you foul up? Did they take your platoon away from you? Armstrong could read between the lines. 'I got wounded, sir.' He touched his leg. 'I can use it pretty well now.'

'Ah. I caught one about there myself last year,' Bassler said. 'Gives us something in common, even if we don't much want it.'

'Hell of a lot better to shoot the other guy,' Armstrong agreed.

'Well, you'll get your chance. Come on,' Bassler said.

'Hold it.' The personnel sergeant held up a hand. 'I gotta sign these guys out.' Armstrong and Cal Henderson and the other men signed on their lines on the clipboard. Now the military bureaucrat nodded approval. He reminded Armstrong of his own father. He wanted all the i's dotted and the t's crossed, and he didn't think anything was official till they were.

When the soldiers got outside, Armstrong said, 'Sir, you mind if I load my weapon? Never can tell what's waiting out here.'

The question wasn't just practical, though it was that. It would also show him something about how Lieutenant Bassler thought. The officer nodded right away. 'You'd all better do that,' he said, and pulled his own .45 from its holster.

Armstrong put a clip in his Springfield and chambered a round. All but one of the other men also had Springfields. The odd man out – his name, Armstrong remembered, was Kurowski – carried a submachine gun: not a Confederate model, but a big, brutal Thompson, made in the USA.

The lieutenant had a couple of command cars waiting to take his new men down to the front. He said, 'I'll handle the machine gun on one of these. Who wants to take the other one?'

'I'll do it, sir,' Cal Henderson said. 'I've used a .30-caliber gun before. Haven't fired one of these big mothers, but they work the same way, right?'

'Near enough,' Lieutenant Bassler said. 'A .50-caliber gun shoots farther and flatter and harder, that's all.'

'Sounds good to me,' Henderson said. It sounded good to Armstrong, too.

But Lieutenant Bassler didn't put him in with the kid. The officer stuck Armstrong in his own command car, and grilled him as they thumped down the battered road. He got more out of Armstrong about where he'd fought and what he'd done. He probably also learned a bit about how Armstrong thought, but that didn't occur to Armstrong till later.

When they came into Chattanooga – luckily, without needing to use the machine guns on the way – Bassler said, 'Ever see anything this torn up?'

'Sir, this isn't a patch on Ogden and Salt Lake City,' Armstrong answered. 'The Mormons hung on till they couldn't hang on any more. Then they pulled back a block and did it again.'

An old man picking through ruins with a stick glared at the command cars as they went by. If he had a rifle . . . But he didn't – not here, anyway – so he could only hate.

'What do we do with them – what do we do to them – once we lick them?' Bassler said. 'How do we keep from fighting another round twenty, twenty-five, thirty years from now? How do we keep them from putting bombs under their shirts and blowing themselves up when they walk into a crowd of our soldiers?'

Armstrong remembered that woman in Utah, when he was heading for R and R. He shivered despite the humid heat. 'Sir, I wish to hell I knew,' he said. 'I'm just a dumbass sergeant. What do *you* think? How do we do it?'

'Either we make them like us—'

'Good luck!' Armstrong broke in. 'Uh, sir.'

'Yeah. I know.' Bassler wasn't more than a few years older than Armstrong. When he grinned, the difference hardly showed. 'Fat chance. But if we could do that, it would sure save us a lot of trouble down the road. If we can't, maybe we can make them too scared of us to turn terrorist very often.'

'That's what they tried in Utah,' Armstrong said. 'It sort of worked, but only sort of. You start shooting hostages and stuff, you just make people hate you worse.'

'I'm afraid you're right,' Bassler said sourly. 'And the Confederate States are a lot bigger than Utah. We occupy them all, there are bound to be lots of places where we're too thin on the ground to do it right. And those are the places where trouble starts.'

'I know one thing we could do,' Armstrong said. Bassler raised a questioning eyebrow. Armstrong went on, 'We could give what's left of the nigger's guns. If half the shit they say about what Featherston's fuckers are doing to them is true, they'll want payback like you wouldn't believe. They may not love us, but they sure as hell have to hate the bastards who've been screwing 'em over for so long.'

Lieutenant Bassler stayed quiet for so long, Armstrong wondered if he'd said something dumb. Well, too bad if he had. Bassler shouldn't have asked him if he didn't want to know what he thought. Then the young officer said, 'You know, Grimes, I'm going to pass that up the line. We don't think about the Negroes in the CSA as much as we should. I'm sure we're doing some things to help them, same as the Confederates did what they could to help the Mormons in Utah.'

'Mostly the Mormons used our weapons, sir,' Armstrong said. 'That way, they could get ammo from us. Sometimes they took our guns, too. But they already had a lot when we got there, yeah.'

'Uh-huh,' Bassler said. 'But that's not my point. My point is that we ought to be using the Negroes systematically, and we aren't. Somebody with stars on his shoulder straps needs to think about that. Maybe the President does, too.'

Armstrong was convinced they wouldn't think about it on the suggestion of a no-account noncom. Then they drove through the gap between Lookout Mountain and Missionary Ridge, the gap U.S. forces now held. Barechested gun bunnies fed 105s that sent death down into Georgia. Eyeing the high ground to either side, Armstrong said, 'My hat's off to those paratroopers. They saved us a world of grief.'

'You can sing that in church, Sergeant,' Bassler said. 'We got over the Tennessee with a ruse, and we took the mountains with a trick. Makes you wonder what we'll have to do to go forward from here.'

'Well, the country looks easier, anyway,' Armstrong said. 'If we start banging barrels through the gap, can those butternut bastards stop us?'

'Good question. I think we'll find out before too long, once the logistics buildup gets done,' Bassler said. They were close enough to the front to watch incoming artillery burst less than a quarter of a mile away. Bassler tapped the driver on the shoulder. 'This'll do. We'll hoof it from here. They'll start aiming at the command cars if we come much closer.' Looking grateful, the driver hit the brakes.

Armstrong ended up with Cal Henderson in his new squad. He was introduced to Whitey and Woody and Alf and Rocco and Hy and Squidface and Zeb the Hat. When he said, 'Let's try not to get each other killed, all right?' they all nodded.

'You've been through some shit,' Squidface opined. 'That's good.'

'A little bit,' Armstrong allowed. 'You guys look like you have, too.'

'Hell, we're here,' Squidface said. He was a PFC, skinny and dark and needing a shave. He didn't have tentacles or even particularly buggy eyes. One of these days, Armstrong figured he'd find out how the nickname happened. Till then, he didn't need to flabble about it.

The Confederates threw a little more artillery at the U.S. positions. Nobody in Armstrong's new squad even moved. These guys were veterans, all right; they could tell by listening when falling shells were liable to be dangerous. They watched Armstrong as the shells burst, too. They wanted to see if he got all hot and bothered. When he lit up a Duke and went on talking as if nothing were happening, they relaxed a little.

'You guys think we can break out?' he asked. He'd heard what Lieutenant Bassler had to say. These men would have to do the bleeding. *So will I,* Armstrong thought. (So would Bassler – second lieutenants were expendable, too. But Armstrong didn't worry about him.)

They all loudly and profanely insisted they could. Armstrong figured that meant they'd get the chance to try before real long.

Jonathan Moss counted himself lucky to be alive. He didn't think what was left of Spartacus' band would attack another airstrip any time soon. Doing it once had cost the black guerrillas too much.

'They was layin' for us,' Spartacus said. He, Moss, Nick Cantarella, and a dozen or so Negro fighters sat around a couple of small campfires. 'Was they layin' for anybody who come by, or did somebody rat on us?'

That was an ugly thought. A Negro would have to be crazy or desperate to betray his comrades to whites in the CSA, but it could happen. If a man knew his loved ones were in a camp, could he make a bargain with the Devil? Of course he could. Moss could find other reasons that might make a black turn traitor – simple jealousy of Spartacus came to mind – but saving kin stood highest on the list of likely ones.

'Some lyin' nigger might be sittin' right here next to me,' Spartacus said. 'Damn cottonmouth might be gittin' ready to bite again.'

The guerrillas stirred. One of them, a heavyset fellow called Arminius, said, 'We went to the damn airstrip on account o' these ofays. Anybody sell us out, reckon they's the ones. Like calls to like, folks say.'

'It couldn't very well have been us,' Moss said. 'You people have kept an eye on us ever since we joined the band. You think we don't know that? I don't blame you for doing it, but it's no secret.'

He talked like a lawyer: he reasoned from evidence. No surprise – he *was* a lawyer. Sometimes, though, legal tactics weren't what the situation called for. Moving quickly but without any fuss, Nick Cantarella got to his feet. 'Anybody says I kiss Jake Featherston's ass can kiss mine.' He eyed Arminius. 'Shall I drop my drawers for you?'

The black man jumped up with a roar of rage. He charged Cantarella. He was a couple of inches taller than the escaped POW, and much wider through the shoulders. He wasn't afraid of anything – Moss had seen that plenty of times.

He swung an enormous haymaker, intending to knock Cantarella into the middle of next week. No doubt the white officer tried to infuriate him so he would fight foolishly. Cantarella got what he wanted. He grabbed Arminius' arm, jerked, and twisted. The Negro let out a startled squawk as he flew through the air. He landed hard. Cantarella kicked him in the side.

Arminius groaned, but tried to yank Cantarella's foot out from under him. 'Naughty,' the U.S. officer said, and kicked him above his left ear. Arminius groaned and went limp. The brawl couldn't have lasted half a minute. Cantarella looked around. 'Anybody else?'

No one said anything. 'Sit down,' Spartacus told him. 'I don't reckon you done nothin'. I reckon you did, you be dead no matter how fancy you fight. You gots to sleep some o' the time.'

'Throw water on Arminius,' Cantarella said. 'He'll be fine once his headache goes away. I don't think I broke anything – didn't do it on purpose, anyhow.'

A bucket – *no, they call it a pail here,* Moss thought – from a nearby creek revived Arminius. He didn't remember the fight or what led up to it. He did say, 'My head bangin' like a big ol' drum.'

'I bet it is,' Spartacus said. He eyed Cantarella. 'Where you learn dat?'

'Here and there,' Cantarella answered.

'You learn me how to do it?'

'Probably,' the U.S. officer said. 'Most of the time, it's no damn good. Somebody got a gun, he'll punch your ticket for you before you get close enough to throw him through a wall.'

'Learn me anyways,' Spartacus said. 'Mebbe I got to impress some niggers, git 'em to jine up with me. I do dat fancy shit, dey reckon I's tough enough to suit.' He paused. His mouth twisted. 'Hope I find me some niggers to impress. Ain't so many left no more, 'cept for the ones already totin' guns.'

He was right about that. Ten years earlier, the country-side hereabouts would have been full of sharecropper villages, full of blacks. Mechanization and deportation had taken care of that. Not many Negroes remained out here, and fewer all the time. Mexican soldiers and Freedom Party stalwarts and guards from the towns took ever more to train stations. Off they went to one camp or another. And it grew clearer and clearer that the camps didn't house them, or not for long. The camps just killed them, as fast as they could.

'Assembly line for murder,' Jonathan Moss murmured.

'What you say?' Spartacus asked.

'Nothing. Woolgathering, that's all.' Moss was glad the guerrilla chief hadn't understood him.

Nick Cantarella had. 'Army's coming,' he said. 'Won't be too fucking long, either. Chattanooga's fallen. Even the Confederate propaganda mill can't spew lies about that any more. If our guys aren't in Georgia already, they will be pretty damn quick. Territory north of Atlanta's rough, but it's not *that* rough. I don't think Featherston's fuckers can stop 'em once they get rolling again.'

'We still be breathin' when they gits here?' Spartacus asked. 'Can't hardly think about hittin' towns no mo'. Got to stay alive first.'

'What happen to me?' Arminius asked, holding his head as if afraid it might fall off any minute now. Considering what Cantarella did to it, it might, too. Moss wouldn't have wanted a well-aimed shoe clomping into the side of *his* noggin.

'You done did somethin' dumb, dat's what,' Spartacus answered, and then came back to the problem at hand: 'Wanna *hit* the damn ofays. Don't wanna jus' lurk out here like swamp niggers in slavery days.'

'You can get dynamite, right?' Cantarella asked. Spartacus nodded. Cantarella went on, 'And you can get alarm clocks, too, yeah?'

'Reckon so,' Spartacus said. 'What you thinkin' 'bout? People bombs is too risky, even if we finds folks willin' to do it. These days, ofays see a nigger they don't know, they jus' start shootin'. Can't get close enough to blow up a lot of 'em.'

'Auto bombs,' Cantarella said. 'Set the timer for sunup, but drive in during the middle of the night, park the son of a bitch, and then get out if you can. All the shrapnel flying, auto bombs make a mess of things even if they don't have a big crowd around 'em.'

Spartacus sighed. 'Yeah, we do dat. Dey don't patrol as good as dey oughta. But it ain't the same, you hear what I say?'

'We hear,' Moss said. He didn't want to make himself too prominent right now. The guerrillas had attacked the airstrip on his account. He would have enjoyed strafing Confederates in Georgia if he'd stolen an airplane. He would have enjoyed flying off to U.S.-held territory even more. Instead . . . Instead, the band wrecked itself. That was all there was to it. Spartacus and the surviving Negroes – fewer than half those who'd gone to the airport – didn't want to admit that, even to themselves, for which he couldn't blame them. But it was true.

They'd fought the Mexicans on even terms before the debacle. Now they ran from them. They had to. They would get chewed to bits if they didn't.

A buzz in the air overhead made everybody look up nervously. 'Reckon the woods hides our fires good enough?' Spartacus said.

'We'll find out,' Nick Cantarella answered.

That wasn't what Moss wanted to hear. And, a minute or so later, he wanted even less to hear the screech of falling bombs. They wouldn't be big ones – ten-pounders, say, thrown out of the airplane by hand the way bombardiers did it back in the early days of the Great War. But when he had no trench or foxhole to jump into, all he could do was flatten out on the ground and hope for the best.

The Confederate pilot wouldn't be aiming any fancy bombsight, not in an obsolete airplane like the one he was flying. He'd just fling the bombs out and hope for the best. Not much chance of doing damage that way, not unless he got lucky. But when the first bomb knocked down a tree less than a hundred yards from the fires, Moss wasn't the only one who cried out in fear.

More bombs rained down, some bursting farther away, others closer. Fragments snarled past. One man's cries went from fear to pain. Moss got up and bandaged the gash in the Negro's leg. He didn't have needle and thread, but used a couple of safety pins to help close the wound.

'Thank you kindly, suh,' the guerrilla said, and then, 'Hurts like a motherfucker.'

'I'm sorry – I don't have any morphine,' Moss said.

'Didn't reckon you did,' the black man answered.

'Somebody 'round here will, mebbe. When the bombs let up, he get up off his ass an' stick me. You got balls, ofay, movin' while they's comin' down.'

'Thanks.' Moss didn't think the risk was especially large, which was why he'd done it. He didn't say that, though. Being old and white isolated him from Spartacus' band. No one till Arminius had blamed him for the fiasco at the airstrip, but it stuck in his mind – and, no doubt, in the guerrillas' minds, too. Any way he could find to win back respect, he gladly accepted.

After a few minutes, the little puddle-jumper of an airplane buzzed and farted away. The Negro Moss had bandaged was the only man hurt. Spartacus said, 'We gots to git outa here. That pilot, he gonna tell the ofays an' the greasers where we at. They come after us in the mornin'.'

'We ought to pull out, yeah,' Nick Cantarella said. 'But we should set up an ambush, blast the crap out of those bastards when they poke their noses where they don't belong.'

Spartacus thought about it. At last, reluctantly, he shook his head. 'Can't afford to lose nobody now. Can't afford to lose no machine gun, neither.'

Cantarella looked as if he wanted to argue. After a moment, he shrugged instead. 'You're the boss. Me, I'm just a staff officer.'

'Nah. Them fuckers never come up where they kin hear the guns,' Spartacus said. Moss and Cantarella both guffawed. Most of the guerrillas looked blank. Sure as hell, Spartacus had seen staff officers in action – or in inaction – when he wore butternut during the last war. The men he led weren't old enough to have fought for the CSA the last time around.

If they'd had the chance, if they'd been treated decently, they might have done it this time. How many divisions could the Confederates have squeezed from their colored population? Enough to give the USA fits; Moss was sure of that. But the Freedom Party didn't want Negroes on its side. It wanted them gone, and it didn't care what that did to the country.

Moss shook his head. He didn't have it quite right. The Freedom Party thought getting rid of Negroes was more important than using them. That struck Moss as insane, but it made whites in the CSA happy. Jake Featherston wouldn't have got elected if it didn't; it wasn't as if he ever made any secret about what he had in mind.

The guerrillas had to rig a litter of branches and a blanket to take the wounded man along – he couldn't walk. He offered to stay behind and shoot as many soldiers and stalwarts as he could, but Spartacus wouldn't let him. 'Can't do enough with no rifle, and we ain't leavin' no machine gun here,' he said. They got the Negro – his name was Theophrastus – onto the litter and hauled him away.

Moss let out a mournful sigh. If things had worked out the way he wanted, he would be back on the U.S. side of the line now. He might be flying a fighter again. How much had they improved while he sat on the shelf here? He didn't – couldn't – know. But he was still fighting the enemy, which he hadn't been while stuck in Andersonville. It wasn't much, but it would have to do.

'Way to go, Pat!' Sam Carsten held out his hand. 'I knew you'd do it. Now get out there and give 'em hell.'

'Thank you, sir.' The exec shook the proffered hand.

'You don't call me *sir* any more. I call you *sir* now . . . sir,' Sam said. Cooley was getting his own ship, and getting promoted away from the *Josephus Daniels*. He hadn't yet put on his oak leaves or sewn the thin gold stripe that transformed him from lieutenant to lieutenant commander onto each sleeve, but he had the rank even without its trappings.

Rank or no rank, he shook his head. 'Doesn't seem right. It *isn't* right, dammit. You've taught me so much. . . .'

'My ass,' Carsten said like the old CPO he was. 'You knew more than I did when I got here. Now you know a lot more than I do, and the Navy Department's finally figured it out. We both knew this day was coming. You're headed for the top, and I'm doing the best job I know how, and that's the way it ought to be.'

'You ought to have a carrier, not a destroyer escort,' Cooley blurted.

'What the hell would I do with a carrier? Run it on the rocks, that's what.' Sam had to belittle that; he didn't want to – he didn't dare – admit how much he wanted it. He thought he knew what to do. He'd spent enough time aboard the *Remembrance,* first as a rating and then as an officer. But even the baby flattops they were cranking out now had three-stripers in command, and he knew he'd be lucky if he ever made two and a half. He was damn lucky to have made a lieutenant's two.

'You could swing it,' Pat Cooley said. 'You can handle men. You know guns. You know damage control. For everything else' – he winked – 'you could lean on your exec till you got the hang of it.'

Sam laughed. 'You remember to lean on yours,' he said. 'You're the Old Man now. You're the good guy, the mild guy. Let him be the professional son of a bitch. That's his job. It's not yours any more.'

'I won't forget.' Cooley slung his duffel over his shoulder.

As he walked off the deck and onto the gangplank that led to the Boston Navy Yard, the crew called out good luck and good wishes to him. Cooley waved and grinned. He hadn't been an out-and-out Tartar, the way a lot of execs were. The sailors might not love him, but they did respect him.

'Wonder who we'll get now,' one grizzled petty officer said to another.

'Some hotshot who shaves once a week,' the other CPO predicted. 'Well, we'll break him in, by God.'

'Yeah, we'll—' The first chief noticed Sam listening and shut up with a snap.

'I know what you guys will do,' Sam said, holding in a smile. 'Remember, I've done it myself. If you don't ride the guy *too* hard, everything'll be jake.'

'Sometimes we forget you're a mustang, sir,' the first chief said sheepishly. 'You just act like an officer, you know?'

Was that a compliment or an insult? Sam didn't try to parse it. With a snort, he said, 'Yeah, like the oldest god-damn lieutenant in the U.S. Navy. If I'm not a mustang, I'm a screwup. Better for the ship if I came up the hawser.'

Those were the magic words. If something was good for the ship, nobody would say a word about it. The two chiefs didn't hang around, though. They went off some-place where they could slander the outgoing and incoming execs – and probably the skipper, too – without getting overheard.

As for Sam, he walked back to his cramped cabin and wrestled with the ship's accounts. After a spell in combat, you could always write some things off as lost in action, which simplified your life. He thought about keeping accounts for an airplane carrier. That almost made him decide not to touch the job with an eleven-foot bohunk, which was what you used when a ten-foot Pole wouldn't reach. But if he ever got the chance, he knew he would leap at it.

He laughed, but he was angry, too. Pat Cooley had given

him a new itch, even if it was one he didn't think he'd ever be able to scratch.

More shells and small-arms ammunition came aboard. So did all kinds of galley supplies. The ship got refueled, too, and he had to sign off on everything. One of these days, if the *Josephus Daniels* didn't get sunk under him, he'd have to turn her over to somebody else, and he wanted the books to balance, or at least get within shouting distance of balancing, when he did.

The new exec came aboard the next day. Lieutenant Myron Zwilling couldn't have been more different from Pat Cooley had he tried for a week. He was short and squat and dark. He was also fussily precise; if he had a sense of humor, he kept it so well hidden, even he didn't know where it was. He stared at Sam's right hand.

A glance at Zwilling's hand told the skipper what he was looking for: an Annapolis ring. Zwilling's was lovingly displayed, and couldn't have been polished any brighter. 'Reporting as ordered, sir,' he said, trying to hold in his disappointment at not finding Sam a Naval Academy graduate. When he saluted, the ring flashed in the sun.

'Pleased to meet you, Mr. Zwilling,' Sam said, reflecting that the new exec was either an optimist or a jerk, one. How could a two-striper in his mid-fifties possibly be anything but a mustang? 'We'll give 'em hell, won't we?'

'I hope to aid in making this ship an efficient fighting unit, sir,' Zwilling said, and Sam's heart sank. He had nothing against efficiency. But he didn't want to sing hymns to it, and Zwilling plainly did.

'Have you ever served on a D.E. before?' Sam asked.

'No, sir,' Zwilling replied. 'My last tour of duty was aboard a fleet oiler, and before that I was a junior officer on the *Idaho*. I have my personnel records with me for your review.'

Of course you do, Sam thought. That wasn't fair, but he couldn't help it. Trying not to show what he was feeling, he said, 'Well, let's give you the quick tour, then. There'll be places where you want to watch your head – not a lot of room in one of these babies.'

'I'll be careful, sir,' Zwilling said, and Sam believed him. He was unimpressed with the pair of 4.5-inch guns that made up the *Josephus Daniels'* main armament. 'The secondary weapons on a battleship are bigger than these,' he sniffed.

'Tell me about it. I fought a five-incher on the *Dakota,*' Carsten said.

'As battery chief?' Zwilling asked with his first show of interest in his new skipper as a human being.

'Nope.' Sam shook his head. 'I was a loader when the Great War started, and ended up running a gun.'

'A loader. I see.' Zwilling looked as uncomfortable as if Sam had admitted to eating with his fingers when he was a kid. There wouldn't be any talk about professors or courses, not on this ship there wouldn't.

Sam took him through the destroyer escort: galley, bunkrooms, engines, and all. Finally, he said, 'What do you think?'

'Everything seems orderly enough,' the new exec allowed. 'Still, I'm sure there's room for improvement.'

'There always is,' Sam said, not liking the way the commonplace sounded in Zwilling's mouth. 'Do you think you can find your way back to your cabin from here?'

'I do.' Zwilling didn't lack for confidence, anyhow.

'Well, ask a sailor if you get lost.' Sam inserted the needle with a smile. 'I'll let you get settled, and we'll talk some more in the wardroom tonight.'

'Yes, sir.' Zwilling saluted again and strode off.

After Sam went up on deck, he watched a sailor standing on the pier kissing a redheaded woman good-bye. A couple of sniffling little boys in dungarees stood by her, so she was probably the sailor's wife. After a last embrace, he slung his duffel bag and asked the officer of the deck for permission to come aboard.

'Welcome to the *Josephus Daniels*,' Sam said. 'Who are you, and what do you do?'

'I'm George Enos, Junior, sir,' the sailor answered. 'I jerked shells on a 40mm on the *Townsend*. Goddamn Confederate Asskicker sank her in the Gulf of California.'

'Well, we can use you.' Carsten paused. Enos? The name rang a bell. He snapped his fingers. 'Wasn't your mother the one who . . . ?'

'She sure was,' Enos said proudly. 'My father was a fisherman before he went into the Navy, and so was I.'

'Good to have you aboard,' Sam said. 'Good to meet you, too, by God.'

'Thank you, sir.' The sailor cocked his head to one side. 'Have we ever met before? You look kind of familiar.'

With his very blond hair and pink skin, Sam sometimes got mistaken for other fair men. He shook his head. 'Not that I know of, anyway. You live around here?' After Enos nodded, Sam went on, 'I've been through more times than I can count, so you may have seen me somewhere, but I've got to tell you I don't remember.'

'Maybe it'll come to me.' Enos grinned like a kid. 'Or maybe I'm talking through my hat. Who knows? Will I go on a 40mm here, sir?'

'Have to see how everything shakes down, but I'd say your chances are pretty darn good,' Sam answered. 'Go below for now and sling your duffel somewhere. The chiefs will take charge of you.'

'Aye aye, sir.' With a crisp salute, George Enos headed for a hatch.

He could have been a kid when we bumped into each other,

Sam realized. *But if he was, why would he remember me?* He shrugged. He had no way of knowing. Maybe it would come back to Enos. And maybe it wouldn't. The world wouldn't end either way.

Orders came the next day: join up with a task force heading east across the Atlantic to raid Ireland. *This is where I came in,* Carsten thought. He'd run guns to the micks during the Great War, and shelled – and been shelled by – British positions in Ireland afterwards. The difference this time around was an abundance of British land-based air. He wondered how much the Navy Department brass down in Philly had thought about that.

When he showed Myron Zwilling the orders, the new exec just nodded and said, 'That's what we'll do, then.'

'Well, yeah,' Sam said. 'I'd like to have some kind of hope of coming back afterwards, though.'

'If they need to expend us, sir—' Zwilling began.

'Hold your horses.' Sam held up a hand. 'If they need to expend us on something important, then sure. We needed to take Bermuda back if we could – I guess we did, anyhow. I've pulled some raids on the Confederates that I think really hurt those bastards. But this? This looks chickenshit to me.'

'You don't know the big picture, sir,' Zwilling said.

He was right. Sam didn't. 'What I do know, I don't like.'

'You can't refuse the mission,' the exec said.

He was right again. That would mean a court-martial, probably, or else just an ignominious retirement. 'I'm not refusing it,' Carsten said hastily. 'I'm worrying about it. That's a different kettle of fish.'

'Yes, sir.' The way Zwilling said it, it meant, *No, sir.*

You're not helping, Sam thought. An exec was supposed to be a sounding board, someone with whom he could speak his mind. He wasn't going to get that from Myron

Zwilling. He didn't need to be an Annapolis grad to see as much.

'We'll give it our best shot, that's all.' Sam thought about George Enos, Jr. 'And we'll make damn sure all the anti-aircraft guns and ashcan launchers are fully manned.'

'Of course, sir,' Myron Zwilling said.

XVII

Georgia. Chester Martin looked south and east. He was really and truly in Georgia, if only in the northwest-ernmost corner of the state. When he looked across it, though, he knew what he saw on the other side.

The end of the war.

Damned if I don't, he thought. If the U.S. Army could grind across Georgia, it would cut the Confederate States in half. It would take Atlanta, or else make the city worth-less to the CSA. How could the enemy go on fighting after that? Oh, both halves of a worm wiggled for a while if you sliced it in two . . . but not for long.

And the Confederates had to know that as well as he did. Their artillery stayed busy all the time. They staged night raids with everything from big bombers down to little puddle-jumping biplanes that flew along at treetop height and peeked right into your foxhole.

No matter what they did at night, the USA ruled the daytime skies. Two-engine and four-engine bombers pounded Confederate positions. So did U.S. fighter-bombers. After they dropped their bombs, they climbed to go after the outnumbered C.S. Hound Dogs that still rose to challenge the U.S. air armada. And fewer Hound Dogs rose each week than had the week before. Little by little, the Confederate States were getting ground down.

U.S. artillery on Lookout Mountain and Missionary Ridge sent volleys as far into Confederate territory as they would reach, announcing that the high ground had a new owner. Some of the guns up there had belonged to the Confederacy. Unlike small arms, their artillery shared several calibers with its U.S. equivalents. They must have thought they would capture U.S. guns, not the reverse. But those streams of paratroopers floating down from the sky caught them by surprise.

Captain Rhodes came forward and cautiously looked at the fields and pine woods ahead. He didn't use field glasses – they were a dead giveaway that an officer was up there snooping, and an invitation to a sniper to draw a bead on him. He looked from one end of a trench, walked fifty feet with his head down, then popped up for another peek.

Some of the fields out there were minefields. The Confederates had marked some of them with signs that said MINES! or warned people away with skulls and crossbones. Some of the signs were genuine. Others, by what Chester had seen before, were bluffs. And real minefields sometimes went unmarked, too. Advancing U.S. soldiers and barrels would find them the hard way – and probably come under machine-gun fire once slowed down in them.

'We can take those bastards,' Rhodes said.

Chester Martin nodded. 'Yes, sir. I think we can, too. Won't be too easy, won't be too cheap, but we can do it.'

The company commander turned and looked west. 'We ought to be cleaning out the rest of Tennessee, too, so we don't have such a narrow front here. We can sure as hell do that. Even now, the Confederates have a devil of a time getting men and matériel from east to west.'

'Yes, sir,' Chester said again. 'That's how Nashville fell – almost an afterthought, you might say.'

'Sure.' Rhodes grinned. 'Goddamn big afterthought, wasn't it? But you're right, Sergeant. Once we pushed past to the east, once we got over the Cumberland, Nashville stopped mattering so much. The Confederates had bigger worries closer to home. So they pulled out and let us march in, and they tried to hold Chattanooga instead.'

Chester looked back over his shoulder toward the city Captain Rhodes had named. 'And they couldn't do that, either,' he said happily.

'Nope.' Rhodes sounded pretty happy, too. 'They're like a crab – they've got claws that pinch, and a hard shell to go with it. But once you crack 'em, there's nothing but meat inside.'

'Sounds good to me – except the meat in our rations is better than the horrible tinned beef they use,' Martin said. 'Even they call it Dead Donkey. But their smokes are still good.' He took a pack of Dukes out of his pocket and offered it to Rhodes. 'Want some?'

'Thanks. Don't mind if I do.' The company CO took one, lit it, and started to hand the pack back.

'Keep it,' Chester said. 'I've got plenty. Lots of dead Confederates these days, and lots of POWs who don't need cigarettes any more.'

'Thanks,' Rhodes repeated, and stuck the pack in his shirt pocket. He took a drag, blew it out, and then shook his head. 'Hate to pay you back for your kindness this way, Chester, but I don't know what I can do about it.'

'What's going on?' Chester grew alert. It wasn't the same sort of alertness he used around the enemy, but your own side could screw you, too.

'Well, I hear repple-depple's coughed up a shiny new second looey for us, so I'm afraid you're going to lose your platoon,' Rhodes said.

'Oh.' Martin weighed that. It stung, but not too much. 'I'll live. When they made me a first sergeant after I reupped, I figured they'd have me breaking in shavetails. I've had some practice by now. I think I'm halfway decent at it.'

'Fine.' Rhodes set a hand on his shoulder. 'You've got a good attitude. I'm glad you're not getting pissy about it.'

'Life is too short.' On the battlefield, Chester had seen how literally true that was.

Second Lieutenant Boris Lavochkin turned out not to be what he expected. Oh, he was young. The only second lieutenants who weren't young were men up from the ranks, and they didn't need a graying first sergeant to ramrod them. Lavochkin was squat and fair and tough-looking, with the meanest, palest eyes Chester Martin had ever seen.

'You're going to show me the ropes, are you?' the youngster asked.

'That's the idea, sir.' Martin sounded more cautious than he'd thought he would.

'And you've done what to earn the right?' Lieutenant Lavochkin seemed serious.

'I lived through the Great War. I ran a company for a while. I've seen a good bit of action this time around, too . . . sir.'

Those icy eyes measured Chester like calipers. 'Maybe.' Lavochkin took off his helmet to scratch his head. When he did, he showed Chester a long, straight scar above his left ear.

'You got hit, sir?' Chester said. That had to be why Lavochkin was coming out of the replacement depot.

He shrugged broad shoulders. 'Only a crease. You've been wounded, too?'

'Once in the arm, once in the leg. You were lucky, getting away with that one.'

'If I was lucky, the shithead would have missed me.' Lavochkin peered south. 'Give me the situation in front of us. I want to lead a raid, let the men see I'll go where they go. They need to know I'm in charge now.'

A lot of shavetails wouldn't have been, even with the

rank to give orders. Lavochkin . . . Lavochkin was a leader, a fighter, a dangerous man. He'd go places – unless he stopped a bullet. But they all took that chance.

'Sir, maybe you'd better check with Captain Rhodes before we go raiding,' Chester said.

Lavochkin scowled. That made him look like an even rougher customer than he had before. In the end, though, he nodded. 'I'll do that,' he said.

Rhodes came up to Chester a couple of hours later, a small, bemused smile on his face. He glanced around to make sure the new lieutenant wasn't anywhere close by before remarking, 'Looks like we've got a tiger by the tail.'

'Yes, sir. I thought so, too,' Martin said. 'You going to turn him loose?'

'I sure am,' the company commander answered. 'He needs to find out what he can do, and so do we. And if things go wrong, well, you've got your platoon again, that's all.'

'If I come back,' Chester said. 'I'm not gonna let him take my guys out by himself. I'm going, too.'

Lieutenant Lavochkin didn't like that. 'I don't need you to hold my hand, Sergeant.'

'I'm not doing it to hold your hand, sir,' Chester said evenly. 'I'm doing it for my men.'

'In case I don't cut it?'

'Yes, sir.' Martin didn't beat around the bush.

Lavochkin gave him one of those singularly malignant stares. Chester just looked back. The young officer tossed his head. 'Well, come on, then. We'll see who learns something.'

The raid went in a little before midnight. Lavochkin knew enough to smear mud on his face to darken it. He carried a captured Confederate submachine gun along with the usual officer's .45. He also had a Great War trench knife on his belt. Was he showing off, or had he been in some really nasty places before he got hurt? *We'll find out,* Chester thought.

Lavochkin moved quietly. The Confederate machine-gun nest ahead sat on a small rise, but brush screened one approach most of the way up. Chester would have gone at it from that direction, too. Lavochkin slid forward as if he could see in the dark.

Suddenly, he stopped moving. 'They've got wire, the bastards,' he said. He didn't ask for a wire-cutter – he had one. A couple of soft twangs followed. 'This way – stay low.' Chester flattened out like a toad under the wheels of a deuce-and-a-half. He got through.

Before long, he could hear the Confederates at the machine gun talking. He could smell their tobacco smoke, and see the glow of a cigarette coal. They had no idea U.S. soldiers were in the neighborhood.

'Everybody ready?' Lavochkin whispered. No one denied it. Chester was close enough to the lieutenant to see him nod. 'All right, then,' he said. 'At my signal, we take 'em. Remember, we want prisoners, but shoot first if you're in trouble. Runnels, scoot over to the left like we planned.'

'Yes, sir,' the soldier said softly. He was little and skinny; Lavochkin had picked the right guy for quiet scooting. *He's a prick, but I think he knows what he's doing,* Chester thought.

Lavochkin's signal was nothing if not dramatic. He pulled the pin from a grenade and tossed it about halfway between Runnels and the Confederate position. As soon as it burst, Runnels, who carried a captured automatic rifle, fired several quick rounds.

Naturally, the Confederates in the machine-gun nest started shooting at the noise and muzzle flashes. Chester saw the flame spurting from their weapons. He hoped

Runnels was all right. He hoped he would be all right himself, too, because he was up and running for the enemy entrenchment as fast as he could go.

Runnels squeezed off another burst to keep Featherston's men thinking about him and nobody else. He yelled like a wild man, too. The deception worked just the way Lieutenant Lavochkin hoped it would. The Confederates didn't notice the footfalls of the onrushing U.S. soldiers till the men in green-gray were right on top of them. Martin heard a startled, 'What the fuck?' as one of the machine gunners tried to swing his piece around.

Too late. Lavochkin cut him down with three accurate rounds from his submachine gun. Then he leaped down into the entrenchment. The rest of the U.S. soldiers followed. Chester hadn't used a bayonet for anything but opening cans and holding a candle since trench raids a generation earlier. He discovered he still knew how. He stuck a machine gunner who was grabbing for a submachine gun of his own. The sharpened steel grated on a rib, then went deep. The Confederate let out a gurgling shriek as he crumpled.

Seeing one of their buddies spitted like a pig made the rest of the Confederates quit trying to fight and surrender. 'Let's get 'em out of here,' Lavochkin said. 'Get the guns off the tripods and take them, too.'

'Let's get *us* out of here,' Chester said. 'We woke up the rest of the butternut bustards.'

Sure as hell, shouts and running feet said the Confederates were rallying. Runnels alertly fired at them. That made them hit the dirt. They didn't know if he was there by himself or had buddies close by. The raiders scrambled out of the nest with captives and booty and hurried back toward the U.S. line. A few wild shots sped them on their way, but they made it with nothing worse than a sprained ankle and a fat lip from one of the Confederates before three men jumped on him.

Intelligence officers took the prisoners away for grilling. In the trench from which they'd started out, Lavochkin eyed Chester Martin. 'Well, Sergeant?' he said. 'Do I pass?'

'So far, so good, sir,' Chester answered. 'The other half of the test is, not doing that kind of shit real often. You know what I mean?' Lavochkin scowled at him, but slowly nodded.

George Enos thought the *Josephus Daniels* was a step down from the *Townsend* as a ship. She was smaller and older and slower and more crowded. But she seemed a tight ship, and a happy one, too. From what he'd seen and heard, those two went together almost as often as the cliché claimed.

He'd slept in a hammock on the *Townsend*. Having to sling one on the *Josephus Daniels* was no surprise, and no great disappointment. He started to make himself at home, learning, for instance, that her sailors hardly ever called her by her last name alone. He also found out that Josephus Daniels had been Secretary of the Navy during the Great War. After all the time he'd spent on the *Townsend*, he still didn't know who Townsend was. With the ship at the bottom of the Gulf of California, he wasn't likely to find out now.

Everyone liked the skipper. Sam Carsten's craggy face and pale, pale hair kept trying to ring a bell in George's mind. He'd seen Carsten somewhere before, and not in the Navy. He kept picturing an oak tree. . . .

Nobody had a good word to say about the exec. That was also normal to the point of boredom. But people did speak well of the just-departed Pat Cooley. 'This Zwilling item ain't fit to carry Cooley's jock,' said Petty Officer Second Class Clem Thurman, who was in charge of the

40mm gun near the bow whose crew George joined.

'No?' George said. Somebody was plainly meant to.

'Fuck, no.' Thurman spat a stream of tobacco juice into the Atlantic. 'Cooley was the kind of guy who'd find out what you needed and pull strings to get it for you. This new one, he looks in the book for reasons to tell you no.' He spat again.

'That's no good,' George said.

'Tell me about it,' Thurman said. 'You ask me, this mission we're on is no damn good, either. Ireland? I got nothin' against micks – don't get me wrong. We give them guns so they can yank on Churchill's nuts, that's great. We get our ass shot off tryin' to give 'em guns – that's a whole different story, Charlie.'

George looked east. Nothing but ocean ahead there. Nothing but ocean all around, ocean and the rest of the ships in the flotilla. None of those ships was a carrier. They didn't have even a baby flattop along. The cruisers carried scout aircraft, but how much good would those do when enemy bombers appeared overhead? *Not enough* was the answer that occurred to George.

'Yeah, well, maybe we're better off without an escort carrier,' Thurman said when he grumbled about it. 'Eighteen knots? Hell, they can't get out of their own way – and if we get jumped, thirty airplanes probably won't be enough to stop the limeys, especially since most of 'em won't be fighters.'

'No wonder the skipper has us at gunnery practice all the time,' George said.

'No wonder at all,' the gun chief agreed. ' 'Course, the other thing is, he served a gun himself when he was a rating. He knows what's going on.'

'He seems like a pretty good guy,' George said.

'Bet your ass,' Thurman said. 'He's on our side – and

I'm not just saying that on account of the new exec is a dipshit. Carsten knows what makes sailors tick. He works us pretty hard, but that's his job. I was in this ship when he took over, and the difference is night and day.'

George had been part of a good gun team on the *Townsend*. This one could beat it. They went through more live ammo than the *Townsend*'s skipper would have wanted to use. Sam Carsten's attitude seemed to be that everything was fine as long as they had enough to fight with when action came.

They went on watch-and-watch a little more than halfway across the Atlantic: at the point where, if they were unlucky enough, a British patrol aircraft flying out of Limerick or Cork might spot them. The Irish rebels were supposed to be trying to sabotage those patrol flights, but who could guess how much luck they'd have?

'Now hear this.' Lieutenant Zwilling's cold, unpleasant voice came on the PA system. 'We have a wireless report that one of our submersibles just torpedoed a British destroyer about 300 miles east of here. No reports of other British warships afloat in that area. That is all.'

'Sounds good to me,' Petty Officer Thurman said. 'The gatekeeper's gone. We hope like hell he is, anyway.'

They made the closest approach at night. At midnight, they lowered a speedboat into the ocean. It replaced two lifeboats; its skeleton crew consisted of men either from Ireland or of Irish blood. They were making a one-way trip to the Emerald Isle. George passed crates of weapons and ammunition to the crane handlers, who lowered them into the speedboat. Each ship in the flotilla was doing the same thing. The irregulars battling the British occupation of their homeland would get a lift . . . if the munitions and men arrived.

Big, powerful gasoline engines rumbling and growling,

the speedboats roared off to the east. The *Josephus Daniels* turned around and hightailed it back toward the USA. The black gang pulled every rev they could out of her engines. They wanted to get as far away from the Irish coast as they could by the time the sun came up.

She *was* slower than the *Townsend*. Thurman had mocked an escort carrier's eighteen knots. George wasn't happy with the destroyer escort's twenty-four or twenty-five. The *Townsend* broke thirty easy as you please. The flotilla stuck together to help with antiaircraft protection. With really fast ships, it could have got thirty or forty miles closer to home by dawn.

And if it had, maybe the British flying boat wouldn't have spotted it. The cruisers' scout airplanes went after the big, ungainly machine. They even shot it down, but the damage was done. George was sure of that. Somewhere in the direction of the rising sun, armorers were loading explosives onto bombers. Maybe fighters would come along as escorts, if they could fly so far. George shuddered, remembering the carrier-launched fighter that shot up his fishing boat.

Waiting was hard, hard. Time stretched like taffy. Maybe nothing would happen. Maybe . . .

'This is the captain.' Sam Carsten sounded much more sure of himself on the PA than Zwilling did. 'The Y-ranging officer says we'll have visitors in a bit. Give them the kind of friendly American welcome they expect. Do your damnedest, boys. If we ride out this wave, chances are we get past the range where their low-level bombers can hit us. They may send high-altitude heavies after us, but those babies have to be lucky to hit a moving target from three miles up. That's all.'

George looked back toward Ireland again. He felt silly as soon as he did. Of course the Y-ranging set reached farther than the Mark One eyeball. It wouldn't be worth much if it didn't. But those airplanes with the blue-white-red roundels were on the way.

'At least I can shoot back now,' George muttered.

'What's that, Enos?' Petty Officer Thurman asked.

'When I was a fisherman, a limey fighter shot up my boat. I was lucky – everything missed me. But the son of a bitch killed a couple of my buddies.' George set a hand on the 40mm's breech. 'This time, by God, I've got a gun, too.'

Thurman nodded. 'There you go. Pay those fuckers back.'

'Hope so,' George said. 'Don't much like the idea of air attack again, though, not when my last ship got bombed out from under me.' The Gulf of California had been warm and calm. The North Atlantic in the latitudes of Ireland was rarely calm and never warm. If the *Josephus Daniels* went down, how long could he stay afloat? Long enough to get picked up? He had to hope so.

'We'll get 'em.' Thurman sounded confident. Like a captain, a gun chief was supposed to. Underlings could flabble. The guys in charge stayed above all that.

The *Josephus Daniels* built up speed. As far as George could judge, pretty soon she was going flat out. Even so, the cruisers in the flotilla could have walked away from her and the other destroyer escorts. They could have, but they didn't. George was glad to see them stick around. They put a lot of shells in the air – and, he told himself in what was half cold-blooded pragmatism and half shameful hope, they made bigger targets than destroyer escorts did.

'Bandits within ten miles,' Lieutenant Zwilling said over the PA system. 'Bearing 090. Won't be long now.'

Everybody stared back the way they'd come. George pointed and yelled, 'There!' as soon as anybody else. And if he could see the enemy airplanes, they could see his ship, too.

One of them flew in low and slow, straight for the *Josephus Daniels*. 'Fuck me if that ain't a torpedo bomber!' Thurman yelled. He swung the twin 40mm mount around to bear on it. 'We've got to blast the bastard!'

'Fuck me if it's not a two-decker!' George exclaimed as he passed shells and the gun began to roar. 'Which war are we in, anyway?' Next to Japanese airplanes, it seemed downright primitive.

Tracers shot red, fiery streaks toward the biplane. 'It's what they call a Swordfish,' Thurman said. 'Looks like a goddamn stringbag, don't it? But it can do for us if we don't knock it down first.'

They did. The Swordfish's right wing tilted down and touched a wavetop. Then the airplane cartwheeled and broke up. It never got the chance to launch the torpedo.

'One down!' Thurman shouted exultantly. He couldn't be sure his gun had nailed the British torpedo bomber. Several others were also shooting at it. Another Swordfish, this one trailing smoke, went into the Atlantic. But white wakes in the water said some of the slow, ugly two-deckers managed to launch their torpedoes.

The *Josephus Daniels* zigzagged as hard as she could. George automatically adjusted as the ship heeled first one way, then the other. He kept passing shells. The gun never ran dry. After this, if there was an after this, he would really be part of its crew – this was baptism by total immersion.

British fighters buzzed overhead like wasps. Every so often, they would swoop down and sting, machine guns blazing on their wings. George had never got a good look at the one that shot up the *Sweet Sue*. Now he did. The fighters seemed much more up-to-date than the torpedo bombers. He wished they didn't.

One of them raked the *Josephus Daniels* from end to end, bullets clanging and whining as they ricocheted off steel and striking home with soft wet thwacks when they met flesh. Wounded men's shrieks rang through the gunfire.

Petty Officer Thurman caught two bullets in the chest. Looking absurdly surprised, he flailed his arms a couple of times to try to keep his balance. Then, crumpling, he tumbled off the gun mount and splashed into the sea. Only a puddle of blood said he'd ever stood there.

'Jesus!' George said.

One of the aimers, a guy named Jorgenson, stepped up to take over the twin 40mm. The loader took his place. And George stepped into the loader's slot. Jorgenson screamed at a sailor running by to jerk shells. The man started to squawk, but then settled down and started doing it.

The British fighter got away anyhow.

George had practiced as loader, both here and on the *Townsend*. He knew what to do, and he did it. It kept him too busy to see what was going on, which might have been a blessing in disguise. After a while, Jorgenson said, 'Hold up.' George did. That gave him his first chance in several minutes to raise his head.

No more airplanes. He looked around in dull wonder. Where did they go? Back toward Ireland, he supposed. He didn't think they'd come off a British carrier. A couple of U.S. ships had fires, but they were all still moving. With luck, they'd get out of range before the next limey strike – if there was one – could come this far. With more luck, the speedboats had landed their weapons without getting spotted. To the brass in the Navy Department, that was the only thing that mattered.

*

In a way, getting out of Richmond was a relief for Jake Featherston. He felt stifled in the concrete bunker under the Gray House, and in the Confederate capital as a whole. The damnyankees were clobbering the city with everything they had, and they had more than Jake ever dreamt they would. He'd done his best to flatten Philadelphia, and his best was pretty good, but the United States were doing worse in and to Richmond.

In another way, though, leaving the bunker, leaving the capital, made him sweat bullets. As long as he stayed in the bunker, he was safe. All the reinforced concrete above his head laughed off even direct hits. It had taken several, without any damage to speak of. Once he got down to Georgia, he felt secure enough. But getting there . . .

The trouble was, you never could tell who was reading your signals, even the ones in the codes your cryptographers swore were unbreakable. Those codes might not be such an ultra enigma to the USA. Maybe traitors had delivered cipher machines to the enemy. Maybe the Yankees were just better codebreakers than anybody in the CSA figured.

And if they were, and if their fighters bounced Jake's transport airplane or their bombers hit his train . . . Well, in that case Don Partridge became President, and the Confederate States went straight down the crapper.

But it hadn't happened, not this time. He was down here talking things over with General Patton. And the Yankees were in Georgia. Not much of Georgia, but they were over the state line. Not Kentucky. Not Virginia. Not Tennessee. Georgia. They'd never got into Georgia in the last war. He hated their being here now.

'You want my head, sir? You can have it. I won't say boo,' Patton told him, as he had up in Richmond. 'I promised I'd hold Chattanooga, and I didn't do it. It's my fault, no one else's. If you need a head to roll, here's mine.'

Not without a certain reluctance, Featherston shook his own head. 'Nah. Who would I get that was better? Besides, could they have run you out unless the paratroopers dropped on Lookout Mountain and Missionary Ridge?'

'No way in hell – uh, Mr. President,' Patton said.

'Well, I didn't reckon so myself,' Jake said. 'All right – they fooled us once, damn them. Can they do it again?'

'Not that way, anyhow,' the general answered.

'I didn't think so, either,' Jake said. *If they can, we're in even worse shape than I figured.* 'So your job now is to hold 'em where they're at, not let 'em break loose into Georgia.'

'I understand the need, sir,' Patton said. 'I know how important Atlanta's industry and rail junctions are. I'll do everything I know how to do with the men I've got. I wish I had more.'

'You've got everything we can give you. Tell you the truth, you've got more than I can afford to give you,' Featherston said. 'Manpower . . . Well, we're moving more women into factories and onto farms. That frees up some new soldiers, anyhow. And we've got some new weapons we'll be trying out here.'

'New barrels?' Patton asked eagerly. 'You have no idea how galling it is to see the Yankees outgunning and out-armoring us. Barrels are supposed to be our strength, not theirs.'

'The new ones are on the drawing boards,' Jake said. 'They'll go into production as soon as we iron out the kinks. It would've happened sooner, but U.S. bombers pounded the crap out of the factories in Birmingham, and that set us back.' If the United States weren't able to base bombers in Kentucky and Tennessee, they would have had a much harder time bombing a town in Alabama. Featherston couldn't growl too loud about that, not when Patton had offered his head and he'd declined to take it.

'Well, all right, Mr. President.' By the way Patton said it, it wasn't. It didn't come close. Gathering himself, the general asked, 'What have you got for us, then?'

'New rockets. These babies can reach way the hell up into Tennessee from here, maybe even into Kentucky,' Jake said. 'They aren't *real* accurate yet, but they'll let us shoot at things we haven't been able to touch for a while. They're better than bombers, that's for sure – we don't lose a whole crew of trained men whenever one fails.'

'I hope they help.' Patton sounded less delighted than Featherston hoped he would. Most generals – most officers, come to that – were stick-in-the-muds. Jake had seen as much during the Great War. After he took over, he'd tried to get rid of as much dead wood as he could. But he couldn't retire or shoot the whole Confederate officer corps, no matter how tempting the idea was.

He could put Patton in his place, though. 'What's this I hear about you slapping an enlisted man around?'

'Yes, sir, I did that, and I'd damn well do it again.' Patton had the courage of his convictions, anyhow. 'The yellow coward wouldn't go forward after a direct order. He blathered about combat fatigue. What nonsense!' He spat with magnificent contempt. 'I would have got him moving, too – hell with me if I wouldn't – if not for some near-mutineers. I hope the Yankees killed the lot of them when they overran Chattanooga. Some good would come from the loss in that case.'

'General, I don't like slackers. Nobody does. But I've seen shell-shock. Some men do break,' Jake said. 'When I took the oath in 1934, I promised that soldiers would get a square deal from their officers. Christ knows I didn't last time around. I'll give you the benefit of the doubt – once. But if I hear about anything like this again, you'll have dug yourself one goddamn deep hole. You got that?'

'You always make yourself very plain, Mr. President.' Patton plainly didn't like it.

Too bad, Jake thought. Had they promoted him to lieutenant for scenting the Negro uprising of 1915, he probably never would have become President of the CSA. The boiling resentment he still felt at being passed over fueled his rise to power.

A young officer came up to the President and the general. Saluting nervously, the kid said, 'Sir – uh, sirs – Y-ranging reports Yankee airplanes on the way. You might want to think about getting under cover, in case they decide to unload on us up here near the front.'

'Y-ranging,' Jake muttered. That was one more place where the USA had the jump on the CSA. If not for some quiet help from Britain, the Confederacy might still be without it. But he nodded to the kid and to Patton. 'Come on, General. No phony heroics today. The country needs us, and we'd better stay alive.'

'What do you mean, "phony heroics"?' Patton asked as the junior officer led them to a well-reinforced bombproof. 'Some men even of high rank are fond of fighting at the front. In my opinion, that is as it should be.'

'Not if they throw their lives away to do it,' Jake said. 'We can't afford gestures like that, not in the spot we're in. You don't see me going right up to the front any more, do you? You reckon I don't want to?'

Patton might have wanted to make a comment or two along those lines. Whatever he wanted, he didn't do it. Featherston's record for fighting up near the front all through the Great War spoke for itself. And, when things were going better, he'd already served the guns this time around. You could say a lot of things about him – he knew the things his enemies did say. But the only way you could call him yellow was to lie through your teeth.

Bombs started thudding home a few minutes after Jake and Patton went to the shelter. Dirt pattered down between the planks that shored up the ceiling. Kerosene lamps lit the bombproof. Their flames wavered and jerked when bombs hit close. Once, the junior officer moved one of them back from the edge of the table on which it sat. Jake didn't get the feeling he was in any great danger, not down here.

'How long you think this'll go on?' he asked the kid.

'Twenty minutes to a half hour, sir, if it's the usual kind of raid.'

'They're trying to wear us down,' Patton said.

They were doing a pretty damn good job of it, too. Jake held that thought to himself. If Patton couldn't see it for himself, he didn't need to hear it. 'What will the Yankees be doing up top?' Featherston asked the youngster.

'Maybe some raids to grab prisoners and squeeze them.' The officer looked unhappy. 'We lost a machine-gun nest like that last week. But they may just sit tight and let the airplanes pound on us.'

'How many do we usually shoot down when they come over like this?'

'A few. Not enough. The antiaircraft guns do what they can, but we really need fighters to make the enemy pay.'

'We need more fighter pilots, too,' Patton said. 'Some of the kids who get into Hound Dogs these days . . . don't have enough practice before they do. Let's put it that way. If they live through their first few missions, they learn enough to do all right. But a lot of them don't, and that costs a man and a machine.'

'I know. Ciphering out what to do about it's not so easy, though,' Jake said. 'If we slow down the training program, the pilots pick up more experience, but we don't get 'em soon enough to do us much good. If we rush 'em, they're still green when they come out. Like you say, General, the ones who live do learn.'

'Sometimes they get killed anyway, uh, sir,' the junior officer said. 'The damnyankees just have too many airplanes.'

Featherston glared at him. He didn't like being reminded of that. And, since the front had moved south, Confederate bombers weren't hitting U.S. factories so hard. The ones out in California and the Pacific Northwest, which the CSA could hardly hit at all, were also making their weight felt. In a war of production, the United States had the edge – and they were using it.

After a little more than half an hour, the bombs stopped falling. 'Let's get up there and see what the hell they did to us this time,' Jake said.

They'd turned the area into one of the less pleasant suburbs of hell, that was what. Craters pocked the red earth. Smoke rose here and there from fires the bombs had set. Several motorcars lay flipped over onto one side or on their roofs. Stretcher bearers and ambulances took casualties back to aid stations. The wounded men groaned or screamed, depending on how badly hurt they were. Nobody shouted, 'Freedom!'

Biting his lip, Featherston said, 'It's a bastard, isn't it?'

'Can't fight a war without casualties, sir,' Patton said.

'I know that,' Jake said impatiently – he couldn't let the general think he'd found a weak spot. 'But I didn't reckon they could do so much damage so quick. What if they did push through after an air raid like that? Could we stop 'em?'

He watched Patton pick his response with care. Patton, after all, was the general whose flank attack through the mountains hadn't driven the USA out of Tennessee and Kentucky, and the general who hadn't held Chattanooga when it desperately needed holding. 'Sir, we'd make it mighty warm for them,' Patton said at last.

That meant he didn't know. Jake had no trouble reading between the lines. 'If they break out again, we're in a lot of trouble. A *lot* of trouble, you hear me?'

'We're doing everything we can with what we've got,' Patton said. 'That's the Lord's truth. If you can pull any more rabbits out of your hat, I'd love to have 'em. Maybe those rockets you talked about will do some good. I hope so. But if there's anything bigger, I sure want to get my hands on it as quick as I can.'

Jake thought of Professor FitzBelmont and his team at Washington University. He could still win – the CSA could still win – if they got their uranium bomb built faster than the damnyankees did. If the USA beat them to that punch . . . Well, if that happened, a breakout in Georgia wouldn't matter any more.

'I may have something for you, General, but I don't know when yet,' Featherston said. 'When you get it, though, it'll be a humdinger.'

Patton looked northwest. 'Sir, it had better be,' he said.

Flora Blackford smiled whenever she got a letter from Joshua. That wasn't often enough to suit her – two a day wouldn't have been enough to suit her – but he did write two or three times a week, when he found the chance and wasn't too tired. Camp Pershing was in upstate New York, between Rochester and Syracuse. To Flora, that was the back of beyond. Joshua liked the weather. How he'd like it when September turned to November and then to January was liable to be another story.

He even liked the food in the mess halls, which was a truly alarming thought. By what Flora gathered from his letters, they fried everything and let him eat as much as he wanted. To an eighteen-year-old, that made a pretty good start on heaven.

He wrote about how they were whipping him into shape, and how he was stronger and faster than he'd ever been. They were turning him into the best kind of killer they knew how to manufacture. Part of Flora hated that – she didn't want him conscripted at all. But if he had to wear the green-gray uniform, shouldn't he be a fit, well-trained soldier? Wouldn't that give him the best chance of coming home in one piece?

She wished she hadn't thought of it that way. She wished she didn't have to think of it that way. As a Congresswoman, as a President's widow, her wishes usually came true. Not the ones that had to do with Joshua, not any more. He had wishes of his own, and the will to thwart her. He had them, and he used them, and she had to pray his enthusiastic patriotism didn't get him killed.

The next morning, someone blew himself up while Flora was on her way in to the battered hall where Congress met in Philadelphia. The blast was only a couple of blocks away, and made the taxi's window rattle. '*Gottenyu!*' she exclaimed. 'Was that what I'm afraid it was?'

'I think so, ma'am.' The driver was close to sixty, and one of the hands he put on the wheel was a two-pronged hook. 'Those crazy bastards don't know when to quit.'

'You don't even know who it was,' Flora said.

'Do I need to?' he returned. 'Whoever'd strap on explosives and push the button's gotta be nuts, right?'

'You'd hope so.' But Flora wasn't so sure. Apparently rational, cold-blooded groups were starting to use people bombs for a very basic reason: they worked. Nothing else disrupted life the way they did. Every time you got on a bus, you looked at all the other passengers, wondering if you could spot the one about to martyr himself – or herself – for the sake of a Cause. And those other people were looking at you, wondering if you were that one.

A Mormon unhappy with the truce terms? A Confederate agent who'd got close to somebody Jake Featherston wanted dead before pushing the button? Somebody with a personal grievance and access to explosives? A genuine nut? She wouldn't know till she heard over the wireless or read the answer in the paper.

She tipped the driver heavily when he dropped her off. 'Thank you, ma'am, but you don't have to do that,' he said.

'I didn't do it because I had to. I did it because I wanted to,' she told him.

He touched the hook to the patent-leather brim of his cap. 'Mighty kind of you,' he said, and drove off.

Kind? Flora doubted it. She'd given him extra money not least because cabs like his saved her from worrying about the other passengers on a bus. That was less egalitarian than it should have been, but she couldn't make herself feel very guilty about it. She didn't want to get blown up, and that was that.

She had to show her ID to get into the building. Before she could get past the entrance hall, a burly guard checked her purse and briefcase and a policewoman patted her down. By the woman's smirk, she enjoyed it the way a man might have. Flora didn't know what could be done about that, either. Nothing, probably.

She hurried to the room where the Joint Committee on the Conduct of the War was meeting. Several Senators and Congressmen were already there. 'Morning, Flora,' one of them said. 'We pounded the, uh, crud out of Atlanta last night, if half of what they say on the wireless is true.'

'Good,' Flora replied. About half of what they said on the wireless usually was true.

'You all right?' the Congressman asked. 'You look a little

poorly.' Foster Stearns was a granite-ribbed Democrat from New Hampshire: a reactionary, a class enemy, and a good fellow. One of the things Flora had found in Congress was that the people on the other side of the aisle didn't have horns and a tail. They were just people, no worse and no better than Socialists, and as sincere about what they believed.

'I've been better,' Flora said. 'I heard a people bomb – I'm pretty sure that's what it was – go off when I was coming in.'

'Oh!' everybody exclaimed. Foster Stearns pulled out a chair and made her sit down. Somebody – she didn't see who – gave her a paper cup. She took a big swig, thinking it was water. It turned out to be straight gin, and almost went down the wrong pipe. She managed to swallow before she had to cough. She wasn't used to straight gin right after breakfast – or any other time. But the swig seemed to help. She was less upset afterwards than she had been before.

More committee members came in. They knew about the bomb, too. 'Took out quite a few folks, the miserable son of a bitch,' one of them said, and then, 'Excuse me, Flora.'

'It's all right,' Flora answered. 'That's not half what I think of him.'

'Are we all here? Shall we get started?' A Senator and a Congressman asked the same thing at the same time.

Along with everybody else, Flora looked around the conference room. Robert Taft wasn't there. And that meant something was wrong. They should have convened five minutes earlier, at nine on the dot. He was always on time, as reliable as the sunrise. 'Somebody call his apartment,' Flora said.

Somebody went outside to do that, and came back a couple of minutes later. 'His wife says he left forty-five

minutes ago. He was walking in – trying to lose ten pounds.'
More than one committee member chuckled, remembering
his rotund father.

Flora knew where Taft lived – much closer to
Congressional Hall than she did. And she could make a
pretty good guess about how he would have come here.
When she did, she gasped in dismay. 'I hope I'm wrong,'
she said, 'but . . .'

'What is it?' Congressman Stearns asked. Then he must
have drawn his own mental map, for he went pale as milk.
'Sweet Jesus Christ, you don't think the people bomber got
him?'

'I don't know,' she answered, 'but he would have been
in about the right place at about the wrong time. And the
Mormons and the Confederates both hate him like rat
poison. The Canadians, too, come to that.'

'We'd better find out.' Foster Stearns and three other
committee members said that or something very much like
it. Stearns added, 'We don't even have to adjourn, because
we never convened. Come on!' They all hurried toward the
entrance.

'Has Senator Taft come in?' Flora asked the butch policewoman.

'Not by this way,' she answered, and he would have.

Flora and the rest of the committee members looked at
one another, their consternation growing. Somebody said,
'Maybe we'd better start calling hospitals. Philadelphia
Methodist is closest to where the bomb went off, isn't it?'

'That's right,' Foster Stearns said while Flora was still
forming the picture in her mind. He nodded to the policewoman. 'Where's the nearest telephone we can use?'

'Down that hallway, sir, on the left-hand side.' She
pointed. She was more polite to him than she had been to
Flora. With a wave of thanks, Stearns trotted off.

Along with the other committee members, Flora followed him. Maybe there would be more than one telephone, so they could call several hospitals at once. And even if there weren't, they would hear the news as soon as he got it.

He was already talking when Flora came up. 'You do have casualties there?' he asked. 'How many? Have any gone to other hospitals, too?' To the other Representatives and Senators, he said, 'At least a couple of dozen. It's a bad one.' He spoke into the handset again: 'Is Senator Taft there? . . . He is? How is he? This is Congressman Stearns. I'm on a committee with him.' He waited. Someone spoke into his ear. Flora knew the answer right away – he looked as if the person on the other end of the line had punched him in the stomach. 'Thank you, Miss.' He hung up the telephone like a man moving in the grip of a bad dream.

'He's gone, isn't he?' Flora said.

'He is.' Stearns nodded dazedly. 'Massive internal injuries, she said. They did everything they could, but. . . .' He spread his hands.

'Do they know who the bomber was?' Two or three people asked the same question.

Now Stearns shook his head. 'Only pieces left. The woman at the hospital said it was a man. Maybe what he's got in his pockets will tell them more – or maybe it won't.'

Something flashed through Flora's mind. A story she'd read to Joshua, back when he cared about stories and not Springfields. 'Pocketses,' she muttered, but the memory wouldn't take any more shape than that. 'Whoever did it, he hurt us when he did. Robert was a good friend to his friends, and a bad enemy to his enemies.'

'He was a stiff-necked old grouch,' she heard one of her fellow Socialists whisper to another.

That was also true; no one who'd ever had much to do

with Robert Taft would or could deny it. Taft had no patience for people who didn't measure up to his own stern notions of rectitude. Despite wide political differences, he and Flora had got on well for years. Beyond any doubt, that said something about her. They made odd friends, the austere Ohio aristocrat and the New York garment worker's daughter, odd but good.

And now they didn't. *I'll have to go to the funeral,* she thought. She had a black dress that was getting too much wear these days. Part of that was the war's fault, part her own for reaching her fifties. No matter how often you told them not to, people kept dying on you.

'I think,' Congressman Stearns said, 'we'd better go back and let some unhappy Army officers know we're adjourning.'

Going on the way Taft wanted would have meant convening the committee and raking those bungling officers over the coals. Flora was sure of that. She was just as sure she had no more heart for it than her colleagues did.

Two of the officers – a brigadier general and a colonel – were in the conference room when the committee members returned. 'Good God!' the colonel exclaimed when he heard the news. 'He was a son of a bitch – everybody knew that – but he was *our* son of a bitch, and everybody knew that, too.'

His words more pungently echoed Flora's. She kept feeling at the hole losing Robert Taft left in her spirit. It seemed as real, and as painful, as the hole from a lost tooth in her mouth. The dentist gave her codeine after doing his worst to her. There was no codeine for a hole in the spirit. It would have to hurt till time turned it from an open, bleeding wound to a scar.

Before she even knew she was doing it, she started to cry. So much already lost in this war. And she thought about Joshua's latest letter. She'd lost so much – and she still had so much to lose.

Jefferson Pinkard thought Humble, Texas, was mighty well named. It lay twenty miles north of Houston, and was about the size of Snyder – three or four thousand people. For a while after the turn of the century, Humble might have been Proud: they struck oil there, and a lot of people got rich. Then the mad inflation after the Great War wiped out everybody's money, rich and poor alike, and after that the wells started running dry. Some of them still pumped, but they weren't making anybody rich these days. Lumber from the pine woods around the town helped business keep going.

Humble would just about do, Jeff decided. He'd looked at a lot of small towns in southeastern Texas, and this one seemed best suited to his purposes. A railroad ran through it; building a spur off the main line would be easy. Local sheriffs and Mexican soldiers had already cleaned most of the Negroes out of the area. If he had to build a new camp here, he could do that.

He'd rather have stayed in Snyder, but that wouldn't fly much longer. Who would have thought the United States cared enough about Negroes to try to keep the Confederates from getting rid of them? What business of the damnyankees was it? If they wanted to let their blacks live, they could do that. But they didn't like them well enough to let more from the CSA come over their border.

Jeff could see advantages to starting over. He could do things the right way from the beginning. The bathhouses that weren't would go up as an organic part of the camp, not as add-ons. He could build a proper crematorium here, get rid of the bodies once and for all, instead of dumping them into trenches. Yes, it could work.

It would disrupt routine, though. To a camp commandant, routine was a precious thing. Routine meant the camp was operating the way it was supposed to. When routine broke down, that was when you had trouble.

Of course, if you looked at it another way, routine at Camp Determination had already broken down. Damnyankee bombing raids and the U.S. Eleventh Army's drive toward Snyder had ruined it. How could you run a proper camp when you weren't sure how much population you needed to reduce from one day to the next? How could you when you didn't know whether soldiers in green-gray would start shelling you soon? That hadn't happened yet, but Jeff knew it could.

When he talked to the mayor of Humble about running up a camp outside of town, that worthy said, 'You'll use local lumber, won't you? You'll use local labor?'

'Well, sure,' Jeff answered. 'As much as I can, anyways.'

'Sounds good, General,' the mayor said, eyeing the wreathed stars on either side of the collar on Jeff's uniform. Pinkard didn't explain about Freedom Party ranks – life was too short. The mayor went on, 'Once you get this place built, reckon you'll want to keep some local boys on as guards? And some of the older fellas who maybe got hurt the last time around or maybe aren't up to marching twenty-five miles a day?' The mayor himself, with a big belly, a bald head, and a bushy white mustache, fell into that last group.

'I'll do what I can,' Jeff said. 'If they've got what it takes, I'll use 'em.'

The mayor beamed. He thought Pinkard had made a promise. Jeff beamed, too. He knew damn well he hadn't. The mayor stuck out his pudgy hand. 'Sounds like we got ourselves a deal,' he said.

'I hope so,' Jeff said, shaking on it. 'Still have to clear

things with Richmond, too, you understand.' *If you don't understand that, you don't understand anything.*

But the mayor did. 'Well, sure, General. That's how things work nowadays, isn't it?' he said. 'You want to use my telephone?' He seemed proud to have one on his desk.

'I sure as hell do,' Pinkard answered. He slid the telephone over to his side of the desk, but didn't pick up the handset or dial the long-distance operator till the mayor ate humble pie and scurried out of his own office. Then Jeff listened to the inevitable clicks and pops on the line as his call went through. And *then* he listened to the voice of Ferdinand Koenig's secretary, which was sultry enough to fit into any man's wet dream.

'Oh, yes, sir,' she purred. 'I'm sure he'll speak to you. Hold on, please.'

'I thank you kindly.' It wasn't even that Jeff was a week and several hundred miles away from his wife. Edith could have been standing beside him and he would have been extra polite to a woman with a voice like that.

'Koenig here.' The Attorney General of the CSA, by contrast, sounded like a raspy old bullfrog. But he had Jake Featherston's ear, so he didn't need to be sexy. 'You find what you were looking for, Pinkard?'

'Reckon I did, sir. I'm in a little town called Humble, up north of Houston. Got a railroad line, and a spur to a new camp'd be easy to build. Mayor's damn near wetting his pants, he wants it in his back yard so bad.'

'Humble, you say? Hang on. Let me look at a map.' There was a pause while Koenig rustled papers; Jeff listened to him do it. He came back on the line. 'All right – I found it. Yeah, that looks pretty good. Yankee bombers'd have a devil of a time getting there from anywhere, wouldn't they?'

'If they wouldn't, sir, we are really and truly fucked,' Pinkard replied.

A cold silence followed. Then the Attorney General said, 'You want to watch your mouth. I've said that before, haven't I?'

'Yeah, I reckon you have.' Jeff wasn't eager to kowtow to a voice on the line from Richmond, no matter how important that voice's owner was. 'But wasn't I telling you the truth?' He used Jake Featherston's catchphrase with sour relish. 'Things don't look so good right now, do they?'

'Maybe not, but we'll lick the damnyankees yet. You just see if we don't.' Ferd Koenig sounded absolutely confident.

'Hope like hell you're right, sir.' Jeff meant that. 'Can we talk about this Humble place some more?' The biggest advantage he saw to closing down Camp Determination was purely personal: it would let him get his family the hell out of Snyder without looking as if they were running away. They'd come through every Yankee bombing raid so far, but how long could they stay lucky? Long enough, he hoped.

He wondered if Koenig felt like raking him over the coals some more, but the Attorney General backed off. 'Yeah, let's do that,' he said. 'Reckon it'll suit.'

'All right, then. Next question is, how do we get it built? I used niggers to run up Camp Determination, but I don't figure that'd work this time around. Can I get me a team of Army engineers, or are they all busy over in Tennessee and Georgia?' That Jeff could mention the Army's being busy in Georgia said how badly things were going.

Ferd Koenig didn't hesitate. 'You'll have 'em,' he promised. 'Population reduction is a priority, by God. We'll take care of this, and in jig time, too. You get ready to finish what you've got going on at Camp Determination, and we'll run up the camp by Humble. Plans'll be about the same as the ones you used before, right?'

'Yes, sir, except we'll want the bathhouses built in instead of tacked on, if you know what I mean,' Pinkard said. 'And I'd like a crematorium alongside, too. More ground in use around here – not so much room for dozers to scrape out the big old trenches we'd need.'

'Don't worry about that,' Ferd Koenig said. 'We've got 'em in place at a couple of other camps. Design's already taken care of, so all we've got to do is run up another one.'

'That sounds good. I thought so, but I wasn't sure,' Jeff said.

'Let me write it down so I make sure I have it straight.' Koenig did, then read it back. 'That about cover things?'

Jeff thought before he answered. If he'd forgotten something, getting it fixed after the engineers left wouldn't be so easy. But he couldn't think of anything – and then he did. 'Mayor here wants to make sure you hire locals for some of the work.'

'Oh, sure – we always take care of shit like that. Gotta keep those boys happy, too,' the Attorney General said indulgently. 'You get ready to move, 'cause this one'll go up faster'n hell. We don't want to pull the engineers off the line any longer than we have to.'

'I'll handle that, sir,' Jeff said. 'You can count on it.'

'If I couldn't, somebody else'd be there. Freedom!' Koenig hung up.

The mayor was plainly worrying about his telephone bill when Jeff called him back in. Jeff wondered if the man had ever called anywhere as far away as Virginia. He would have bet against it. But the mayor's face lit up when Jeff said, 'Well, Ferd Koenig reckons Humble will suit us as well as I do. Some Army engineers'll come in to run up the camp, and then, by God, then we'll get down to business.'

'That's mighty fine news – mighty fine,' the mayor said.

'Uh – you do recall I'd like some of our people from around these parts to help do the work?'

'Ferd says the engineers'll take care of that,' Pinkard told him. His repeated use of the Attorney General's nick-name seemed to impress the mayor even more than the near-promise.

'Good news. Damn good news.' The mayor reached into his desk and pulled out a bottle and a couple of glasses. 'We ought to have us a drink to celebrate.'

'I sure don't mind,' Jeff said. The mayor's whiskey turned out to be rotgut, but Jeff didn't flabble. It wasn't as if he hadn't drunk rotgut before. One drink led to several, and to his staying over in Humble a night longer than he'd intended. The mayor offered to get him a girl for the evening, but he turned that down. He was more practical than virtuous. Any woman the mayor got him would be a pro, and with a pro you never could tell what you were bringing home to your wife. That wouldn't be so good, especially not with a baby on the way pretty soon.

He set out across Texas for Snyder the next morning. As usual, the sheer size of the state flabbergasted him. The drive in the old Birmingham felt more like crossing a country. Even real cities like Dallas and Fort Worth seemed dwarfed by the immensity all around them. Bomb damage seemed diminished and spread out, too. He knew the USA had hit both towns hard the year before, but he saw only a few battered, fire-scarred buildings.

West of Fort Worth, woods grew scarcer and the prairie stretched as far as the eye could see. Every so often, Jefferson Pinkard began to spot shot-up motorcars by the side of the road. Some were merely pocked with bullet holes. A couple had bloodstains marring the paint of one door or another; a hasty grave was dug beside one of those. And some were charred wrecks: autos where a bullet had gone through the engine or the gasoline vapors in a mostly empty fuel tank.

Pinkard kept a wary eye on the sky. The Birmingham had nowhere to run and nowhere to hide if U.S. fighters or fighter-bombers swooped down. Maybe he could get out and hide in a ditch while they shot up the auto. That was his best hope, anyhow.

When he stopped for gas in a little town called Cisco, the woman who pumped it said, 'Reckon you're either mighty brave or mighty damn dumb, comin' so far in broad daylight.'

'I can go faster,' Jeff said.

'Yeah, but you can end up dead faster, too,' she replied. 'Your funeral – if you get one.'

Jeff remembered the grave next to the motorcar. He remembered the bloodstains he'd seen, too. And he stayed in Cisco for a roast-beef sandwich and a couple of bottles of beer, and waited till twilight deepened to get going again. Maybe he wasted a few hours. Maybe he saved his own life. He never knew one way or the other.

Crawling along with headlights masked down to slits, he didn't get into Snyder till not long before dawn. He drove with special care in town, because craters scarred so many streets. You could crash down into one before you saw it. But he made it home, and found he still had a home to come back to. 'Sorry to bother you, hon,' he told Edith. 'We'll be able to clear out, go somewhere safer, before real long.'

'Thank you, Jesus!' she said, and squeezed him tight despite her swollen belly.

Cassius was proud of his new boots. They fit him perfectly, and the Mexican soldier who'd worn them before didn't need them any more. Somebody – Napoleon? – said an army marched on its stomach. Food mattered, all right, but so did your feet. The shoes in which Cassius got out of Augusta were falling apart, so he was glad to get such fine replacements.

'Lucky bastard,' Gracchus said. His feet were very large and very wide. Cassius' were of ordinary size, like the rest of him. He'd never thought of that as luck before, but maybe it was.

'We'll get you some, boss,' he said – as much of a title as the guerrilla leader would take.

'Have to slit 'em,' Gracchus said morosely. The shoes he wore now were slit on either side, to make room for his uncooperative feet. What that lacked in style, it more than made up for in comfort. Gracchus eyed Cassius thoughtfully. 'You know how to drive?'

'Wish I did.' Cassius shook his head. 'Folks never had an auto or nothin', though. How come?'

'Want to steal me a pickup truck from somewheres, mount a machine gun in the back,' Gracchus said. 'Some of the other bands been doin' it, I hear tell. Raise all kinds of hell that way. Ain't as good as havin' our own barrel, but it's about as good as a bunch o' niggers can hope for.'

About as good as a bunch o' niggers can hope for: eleven words that spoke volumes about how things were in the Confederate States of America. Crouched in pine woods, hoping the whites and Mexicans wouldn't put airplanes overhead to hunt for the band and hoping the trees would screen the fires and guerrillas if they did, Cassius had his own worm's-eye view of what those words meant.

He also had his own reasons for wanting to hit back at the Freedom Party and everyone who stood with it: everyone in the CSA who wasn't black, or as close as made no difference. 'Don't know how to drive,' he said, 'but you bet I do me some fancy shootin' if you put me in the back o' that truck.'

Gracchus chuckled. 'Every nigger in the band I talk about this with say the same thing. A couple o' the gals, they say they give me what you ain't even got if only I put 'em back dere.'

Cassius hadn't dared approach the handful of women who marched and fought along with Gracchus' men. They were tougher than he was, and he knew it. The word *intimidated* probably would have sprung to his father's mind. It didn't occur to Cassius; he just knew that those gals scared hell out of him.

'Where you gonna get a pickup?' If he thought about the truck, he didn't have to think about the women.

'Off a farm, I reckon,' Gracchus answered. 'Damn ofays mostly keepin' 'em locked up tight nowadays, though. They know what we kin do if we git our hands on one.'

Locks didn't usually stop Gracchus when he set his mind on whatever lay behind them. His scouts didn't need long to find a farm with a pickup truck that would do. The farm had a telephone line so the whites there could call for help if guerrillas attacked them. Gracchus only smiled when he noted that. Among the tools his irregulars carried were several wire cutters.

'Dey kin call all dey please,' he said. 'It don't go through, ain't that a shame?'

The guerrillas grinned, white teeth shining from dark faces. Despite those grins, they spent a couple of days sizing up the farm before they made their move. If the whites brought in riflemen or a machine gun of their own under cover of night, they could give raiders a wicked surprise. Gracchus couldn't afford to get surprised that way.

After the telephone line was cut, he pitched a rock through a farmhouse window to get the attention of the people inside. When curses said somebody was awake in there, he shouted, 'Throw out the keys to your truck an' we goes away. We don't hurt nobody. We jus' takes the truck an' goes.'

'Over my dead body!' the man inside yelled. In a lower voice, he went on, 'Sal, call the militia!'

'Can't get the operator!' Sal said in despairing tones.

'Las' chance, ofay!' Gracchus shouted. 'We kin hot-wire the truck if we gotta, but we gonna have to shoot you to make sure you don't start shootin' your ownself when we takes it away.'

A rifle shot split the night. The bullet didn't miss Gracchus by much, but it missed. The guerrillas knew what to do. Some of them started banging away to make the people inside keep their heads down. Others, Cassius among them, ran toward the farmhouse. He wished he had a helmet to go with his boots. But a helmet wouldn't stop a rifle round, either.

The defenders had several firearms. If they raised enough of a ruckus, someone at a nearby farm might telephone the authorities or go out to get help. The guerrillas had to win quickly, take the truck, with luck kill the whites, and disappear before superior force arrived.

'I'll shift them fuckers,' a Negro called. 'Break me a window an' see if I don't.'

Cassius was close enough to a window to smash it with the butt of his Tredegar. Had one of the farm family waited on the other side of the glass, he would have caught a bullet or a shotgun blast with his teeth. That crossed his mind only later. He did know enough to get away fast once the stock hit the window.

A few seconds later, a Featherston Fizz sailed in through the opening he'd made. He heard it shatter on the floor inside. That would spread blazing gasoline in a nice, big puddle. 'Burn, you goddamn ofays!' he yelled. 'Burn in your house, an' burn in hell!'

Flames lit that room from the inside. They showed a white man standing in the doorway to see if he could do anything about the fire. Cassius snapped a shot at him. He wasn't the only guerrilla who fired at the white man, either. The fellow went down, either hit or smart enough not to offer a target like that again.

Another Featherston Fizz flew into the farmhouse. Cassius liked the idea of roasting whites with a weapon named for the founder of the Freedom Party. He'd run into a phrase in a book one time – *hoist with your own petard*. He didn't know what a petard was (though his father likely would have), but he got the sense of it anyhow. Those Fizzes were petarding the devil out of the family in there.

They stayed in the burning building as long as they could. They stayed a lot longer than Cassius would have wanted to. Then they all charged out the back door at once, shooting as they came. Had they made it to the woods, they might have escaped. But they didn't. In the light of the fire behind them, they made easy targets. An old man in a nightshirt killed a woman with him before he went down. Another woman, hardly more than a girl, blew off her own head with a shotgun.

They had to fear what the Negroes would have done with them – to them – had they taken them alive. And they had reason to fear that. Revenge came in all kinds of flavors. If you could get some with your dungarees around your ankles . . . well, why not? It was nothing whites hadn't done to blacks through the centuries of slavery. Cassius' own mother couldn't have been above half Negro by blood. He himself was lighter than a lot of guerrillas in Gracchus' band. He wasn't light enough to pass for white, though – not even close. In the CSA, that was as black as you had to be to get reckoned a Negro, as black as you had to be these days to get shipped off to a camp and have your population reduced.

'Let's get outa here!' Gracchus shouted. 'The ofays, they see the fire fo' sure.'

'We oughta stay, shoot the bastards when they come,' somebody said.

'You dumb fuckin' nigger, you reckon dey think a fire in the middle o' the night go an' happen all by itself?' Gracchus said scornfully. 'They don' jus' bring the fire engines. They bring the armored cars an' the machine guns, too – bet your ass they do. I say get movin', I mean get movin'!'

No one argued any more. Cassius did ask, 'We got us the pickup?'

'Oh, hell, yes,' Gracchus answered. 'Leonidas done drove it off five minutes ago.'

'All right by me,' Cassius said. 'I was busy five minutes ago.'

'Lots of us was,' the guerrilla leader allowed. 'Ain't busy now, though, so git.'

Cassius got. Part of him regretted missing the chance to ambush the whites who'd come to the farm family's rescue. But he knew Gracchus was right: who would ambush whom wasn't obvious. Best not to tempt fate.

Somewhere up in the northwestern part of Georgia, the Stars and Stripes already flew in place of the Stars and Bars. Sooner or later, the Yankees would break out into the rest of the state. Cassius could see that coming. All the black guerrillas could. If they could stay alive and keep harrying the Confederates till the U.S. Army arrived . . .

If we can do that, we win the war, Cassius thought.

Then he wondered whether winning the war would be worth it. What did he have to go back to in Augusta?

Nothing. His family was gone, his apartment not worth living in. The rest of the guerrillas were no better off. They'd already lost, no matter how the war went.

'Boss?' he said as the guerrillas loped away.

'What you want?' Gracchus asked.

'Suppose the United States lick Jake motherfuckin' Featherston. Suppose we're still breathin' when that happens. What the hell we do then?'

'Don't know about you, but I got me a big old bunch of ofays I wants to pay back,' the guerrilla leader answered. 'Reckon that'll keep me busy a while.'

Cassius nodded. 'Sure enough, we can do that for a while. But what kind of *life* we gonna have? What kind of country this gonna be? Can't kill *all* the damn whites – wouldn't be nobody left then. Gotta live with 'em some kinda way. But *how*? How we go on, knowin' what they done to us?'

'Fuck, I dunno. I ain't never worried about it. Ain't had time to worry about it – been too worried about stayin' alive,' Gracchus said. 'Lookin' down the road . . . You don't want to think too goddamn much, you hear what I'm sayin'? Spend all your time thinkin' 'bout tomorrow, you ain't gonna live to git there.'

That made some sense. But Cassius said, 'We ain't old or nothin'. We make it through this goddamn war, we got a lot o' time ahead of us. Maybe we go on up to the USA. They ain't so hard on niggers there.'

'That's a fact – they ain't,' Gracchus said. 'But here's another fact – they don't like niggers much, neither. If they did, they woulda let more of us git away when the Freedom Party first took over. But they didn't. They closed their border so we had to stay in the CSA an' take whatever Featherston's fuckers done dished out. Yankees like us better'n they like Confederate sojers, but it don't go no further'n that.'

He didn't just make some sense there – he made much too much. 'What're we supposed to do, then?' Cassius wanted to wail the question. Instead, it came out as more of a panting grunt. It was the sort of thing he would have asked his father when he and Scipio weren't quarreling.

His father would have had a good, thoughtful answer for it. Gracchus just shrugged and said, 'We gots to stay alive. We gots to hit the ofays till the war's done, an' go on hittin' 'em afterwards. Past that . . . Hell, I don't know nothin' past that. Find out when I gits there, if I gits that far.'

The way things were, maybe that *was* a good, thoughtful answer. If you were someplace where you couldn't make plans, didn't trying only waste your time? For now, what was there besides fighting and taking whatever vengeance you could? Cassius trotted on. He couldn't see anything besides that now himself.

XVIII

Every time an officer Lieutenant-Colonel Jerry Dover didn't know came to the supply dump, his stomach started knotting up. He kept wondering if someone from Intelligence would take him off and do horrible things to him because of Melanie Leigh. Every time it didn't happen, Dover relaxed . . . a little.

He saw plenty of unfamiliar officers, too, enough to keep his stomach sour, enough to keep him gulping bicarbonate of soda. Lots of that came to the front; given what soldiers ate, they needed it.

Some of the new officers he dealt with came from outfits just arrived in northwestern Georgia to try to stem the Yankee tide. Others were men in new slots, the officers they replaced now being wounded or dead.

One day, a brigadier general showed up and asked, 'You fought in the line in the last war, didn't you?'

'Yes, sir,' Dover answered. 'I was only a noncom then, though.'

'I was a first lieutenant myself,' said the officer with the wreathed stars. 'We've both got more mileage on us than we used to. I have a regimental command slot open – Colonel McCandless just stopped some shrapnel with his face, and he'll be on the shelf for weeks. If you want it, it's yours.'

'Sir, I'll take it if you order me to,' Dover answered. 'But I don't think I'd be better than ordinary in that slot. As a supply officer, I'm pretty goddamn good. If somebody ordinary replaces me here, that might hurt the war effort worse than if you have some different ordinary officer take charge of your regiment.'

The brigadier general studied him. *Wondering if I'm yellow,* Dover thought. The officer's eyes found the ribbon for the Purple Heart above Dover's left breast pocket. 'How'd you get that?' he asked.

'A scratch on my arm. Not worth talking about,' Dover answered.

Maybe the general would have decided he was a liar and a blowhard if he came up with some fancy story of a wound suffered in heroic circumstances. His offhand dismissal seemed to satisfy the man. 'Stay where you are, then, Dover,' the brigadier general said. 'You're doing well here – I know that, and it's one of the reasons I thought about you for a combat post. But you have a point: this work is important to the war effort, too, and it needs to be done right. I'll find somebody else for the regiment.'

After the general left, Dover lit a cigarette. He had to stir the butts in the glass ashtray on his cheap desk to make room for it. One of the sergeants who helped keep the depot going stuck his head into the tent and asked, 'What was that all about, sir?' Like any sergeant worth his stripes, he assumed he had the right to know.

Dover saw no reason not to tell him. 'About what you'd figure, Pete – he thought about moving me up to the front, but he decided I can do more here.'

'Christ, I hope so!' Pete said. 'You're really good at this shit. I don't even want to think about how much trouble I'd have breaking in some new asshole, and some of those clowns just never do get what's going on.'

'Nice to know I'm a comfortable old asshole,' Dover said, and Pete laughed. Dover tossed the sergeant the pack of Raleighs.

'Thanks,' Pete said. 'Even smokes are getting hard to come by, the way the damnyankees keep tearing things up between here and Atlanta. That never happened the last time around, did it?'

'I don't think so,' Dover answered. 'I don't remember running short, anyway.' He looked north and west. His personal worries weren't the only ones he had. 'You think we can stop the Yankees if they try to break out again?'

'Reckon we'd better,' Pete said dryly. 'They start heading for Atlanta, we better start trying to see how much they'll let us keep if we quit.'

That was about how Dover saw it, too. 'Careful how you talk,' he told Pete, not for the first time. 'Lots of people flabbling about defeatism these days.'

'Yeah, well, nobody'd be defeatist if we weren't getting fucking defeated,' the sergeant said, which was nothing but the truth. 'I'd almost like to see Atlanta fall, to tell you the truth, just so I could laugh while some of the Quartermaster Corps fat cats there got it in the neck. Those cocksuckers have done more to lose us the war than any three Yankee generals you can think of.'

'You expect me to argue? You're preaching to the choir,' Dover said. 'Now they use the bad roads and the torn-up train tracks for excuses not to send us what we need.'

'Did I hear right that you told one of the shitheads down there you were gonna send Jake Featherston a wire about how lousy they were?' Pete asked.

'I said it, yeah,' Dover admitted. 'Don't know that I'd do it. Don't know that it would do any good if I did.'

'You ought to, by God. They've been getting fat and living soft off Army goods since the war started,' Pete said. 'If Featherston can't rein 'em in, nobody on God's green earth can, I reckon.'

Maybe nobody could. Jerry Dover was inclined to believe

that, which was another reason he hadn't sent the telegram. Before he could say so, air-raid sirens started howling. Somebody clanged on a shell casing with a hammer, too, which was the emergency substitute for the sirens.

'Head for shelter!' Dover said. He heard U.S. airplane engines overhead even before he got out of the tent. The dugout into which he and Pete scrambled was as fancy as any he'd known in the Great War. It had all the comforts of home – if your home happened to be getting bombed.

'Maybe they aren't after us,' Pete said.

'Here's hoping,' Dover agreed. Northwestern Georgia had plenty of targets. Then explosions started shaking the ground much too close. The supply dump was one of those targets.

Something on the ground blew up – a roar different from the ones bombs made. Jerry Dover swore. He hoped the secondary explosion didn't take too much with it. He was as careful with ordnance as he knew how to be. He didn't store much of it in any one place, and he did build earth revetments around each lot. That minimized damage, but couldn't stop it.

Another secondary explosion proved as much, as if proof were needed. Dover swore some more. A couple of other soldiers in the bombproof laughed, as much from nerves as for any other reason. A lucky hit and the bombproof might not be; it might turn into a tomb.

'Sometimes the bastards get lucky, that's all,' Pete said.

'I don't want them to get lucky, goddammit,' Dover said. 'What if they're starting the big push now? The guys at the front will need everything we can send 'em.'

'And if the damnyankees break through, *we'll* be the guys at the front,' Pete said.

That made Dover wish he hadn't already used up so much good profanity. Then, instead of cussing, he started to laugh himself, which made Pete send him a fishy stare. He still thought it was funny. Here he'd gone and turned down a combat command, but he was liable to get one whether he wanted it or not.

A *big* explosion sent dirt trickling down between the planks on the shelter's roof. 'I hope to God that was one of their bombers crashing,' Pete said.

'Me, too,' Dover said. 'Why don't they go away and bother somebody else?' He knew why perfectly well. That didn't keep him from wishing anyway.

The bombers stayed overhead for more than two hours. That had to mean several waves of them were pounding Confederate positions. Now that the United States had airstrips down in southern Tennessee, they were only a short hop away. And they were making the most of it, too.

After no bombs had fallen for fifteen minutes or so, Dover said, 'Well, let's see what's left upstairs.' He hoped something would be. He also hoped he wouldn't come out when a new wave of enemy bombers appeared overhead. *That'd be just my luck, wouldn't it?* he thought sourly.

The passage out from the bombproof's outer door had a dogleg to keep blast from getting in. It also had several shovels stashed near that outer door, in case the men inside needed to dig their way out. But Jerry Dover could see daylight when he got the door open.

He could see daylight, yes. He could also see smoke, and smell it: smoke from burning rubber and explosives and wood and paint and several other things. His eyes stung. He coughed again and again.

Behind him, Pete said, 'How bad is it?' He was coughing, too. Dover wished he were wearing a gas mask. He hoped the Yankees hadn't blown up any gas shells, or he might really need one.

'I don't think it's good,' he answered. Getting out of the

trench was easy. A near miss had built a nice, convenient ramp. If that one had burst a hundred feet to the left . . . No, you didn't have to fight at the front to see combat these days.

He and Pete and the other soldiers hurried up to ground level and looked around. 'Fuck,' Pete said softly, which summed things up pretty well.

Enemy air strikes had pounded Jerry Dover's supply dumps before. That was part of the cost of doing business in a war. He didn't think one of his depots had ever taken a beating like this before, though. Eight or ten fires raged. Yes, one of them was an enemy bomber's pyre – he could see the airplane's tail sticking up. But the damnyankees had done a lot more damage here than they'd taken doing it.

Hoses were already playing on some of the worst blazes. Dover felt proud of his men. They knew what they had to do, and they did it. And in doing it, they took chances front-line soldiers never had to worry about.

Of course, the men at the front had worries of their own. Pete cocked his head to one side, listening. 'Firing's picked up – fuck me if it hasn't.'

Dover listened, too. He said the worst thing he could think of: 'Yeah, I think you're right.'

'They're trying to break out.' Pete found something bad to say, too.

'Sure sounds that way,' Dover allowed.

'Think they can do it, sir?' Any time Pete used an officer's title, he needed reassurance.

Right now, Dover longed for reassurance, too. 'Hope to hell they can't.'

A telephone rang. He would have bet the bombardment had blown up the instrument or broken the lines that made it work, but no. He ran over to it and admitted he was there and alive.

'Dover, you've got to send me everything, fast as you can!' He recognized the voice of the brigadier general who'd offered him a regiment. 'They're coming at me with everything they've got. If you have a division's worth of dehydrated infantry, pour water on 'em quick and get 'em up here.'

In spite of everything, Dover smiled. But he had to say, 'Sir, I don't know what the hell we've got right this second. They just bombed hell out of the dump, too.'

The general's opinion of that violated all the Commandments with the possible exception of the one against graven images. 'We're doing all we can, dammit, but how can we hang on if we don't have enough bullets and shells?' he said.

'I'll get you what I have, sir.' Dover slammed down the handset and yelled orders. He had to interrupt himself when the telephone rang again. 'Dover here,' he said.

'Rockets! Antibarrel rockets!' another harried officer screamed in his ear. 'Damnyankee armor's tearing holes in my lines! They've got these goddamn flail barrels to clear mines, and they're going through us like a dose of salts. If we don't stop 'em quick, we are dead meat, you hear me? Fucking dead meat!'

Dover didn't know what a flail barrel was. He didn't know how many antibarrel rockets had escaped the Yankee bombs. He didn't even know who was yelling at him. He managed to find that out. He rapidly figured out one other thing, too: the United States were pushing hard here. If they did break through . . . *If they break through, we've lost the damn war for sure,* Dover thought. He dashed off to do what he could to stop them.

Signs with skulls and crossbones on them warned the world a minefield lay ahead. Lieutenant Michael Pound was pretty sure the signs and the field were genuine. When the Confederates bluffed, they usually slanted the bones and the word MINES. These stood straight.

He was a hard charger, but he didn't want to tear across that field and blow a track or maybe get the bottom blasted out of his barrel. And he didn't have to. 'Here comes a flail,' he said happily, ducking down into the turret to relay the news to his gunner and loader and to get on the wireless to the other machines in his platoon. He'd had to make himself remember to do that when he first became an officer. Now he did it automatically.

Sergeant Mel Scullard grinned. 'Those bastards sure are funny-looking,' he said.

'Well, I won't argue with you,' Pound told the gunner. 'But who gives a damn? They do the job, and that's what counts.'

Some engineer must have been smoking funny cigarettes when he came up with the flail barrel. He mounted a rotor drum on a couple of horizontal steel bars out in front of the barrel's chassis. The barrel's engine powered the contraption. Lengths of heavy chain came off the drum. As it rotated, the chains spanked the ground ahead of the oncoming machine. They hit hard enough to touch off mines before the barrel itself got to them. And other barrels could follow the path the flail cleared.

Naturally, the Confederates did everything they could to blow up flail barrels before they got very far. But, after the pounding U.S. artillery and aircraft had given the defenders here, they couldn't do as much as they wanted to. The Confederate Army remained brave, resourceful, and resilient. It wasn't so responsive as it had been earlier in the war, though. You could knock it back on its heels and stun it if you hit it hard enough, and the USA had done that here.

'Follow the flail!' Pound commanded, and his driver did. They all wanted to get past the minefield as fast as they could. The pine woods ahead weren't cleared yet. That meant they were bound to have Confederate soldiers – and, all too likely, Confederate barrels – lurking in them.

The other machines in Pound's platoon followed him, as he followed the flail barrel. Every commander rode with his head and shoulders out of the cupola, the better to see trouble. He was proud of them. He hadn't ordered them to do it. He wouldn't have given an order like that. They got out there on their own.

Fires in the woods sent up smudges of smoke. There weren't enough of them to drive out the lurkers, however much Pound wished there were. If they had an antibarrel cannon waiting . . .

They did. Sensibly, they fired at the flail barrel first. If they knocked it out, all the machines behind it would expose themselves to danger among the mines. Their AP round scored a direct hit . . . on the flail. The gadget fell to ruins, but the barrel kept going. Now it was as vulnerable as any of the others.

'Front!' Pound sang out – he'd seen the muzzle flash.

To his relief, Mel Scullard sang out, 'Identified,' which meant he'd seen it, too. To the loader, he added, 'HE!'

With a thrum of hydraulics, the turret traversed to the left. As it steadied, Pound ordered the barrel to stop to give the gunner a better shot. If the gun in the woods was drawing a bead on him at the same time . . . Well, that was the chance you took.

Several cannon spoke at once: the antibarrel gun and at least four barrels' main armaments. An AP round dug a furrow in the dirt a few feet to the right of Pound's machine. He was surprised it didn't touch off a mine or two. The other shells all burst close to the same place in the woods.

'Gun it!' Pound yelled to the driver. If they hadn't knocked out the gun or wounded the crew, more murderous projectiles would come flying out of there. 'Stay behind the flail barrel,' he added a split second later.

'How come?' the driver asked. 'He's not gonna do any more flailing.'

'Well, no,' Pound said, and let it go at that. Some people weren't very bright, and you couldn't do anything about it. The lead barrel's flail might have taken a knockout, but it could still show where at least one mine lay – the hard way.

Pound wished he hadn't thought that – it might have been a jinx. A few seconds later, the flail barrel did hit a mine. It slewed sideways and stopped, its right track blown off. It didn't catch fire, but it was hideously vulnerable out there. The commander traversed his turret till it faced the woods, putting as much armor as he could between himself and the enemy. Past that, he had to wait for a recovery vehicle and hope.

Losing the flail barrel left Pound in the lead. He could have done without the honor, but he had it like it or not. He got on the wireless to the other barrels in his platoon: 'Stay behind me. If I make it through, you will, too. And even if I don't, you won't have far to go, so you may make it anyhow.'

He could see the signs at the far edge of the minefield. Only a couple of hundred yards to go . . . Maybe a hundred yards . . . Maybe fifty . . . It would be a shame to run over one now, with the end of the field so close. . . .

'Made it!' he said, a great whoop of relief, as if all his troubles were over.

No matter how much he savored the moment, he knew better. The Confederates had a strongpoint up ahead on some high ground called Snodgrass Hill. They'd put a lot of guns up there, most of which could fire AP ammo. Hitting a moving barrel with an artillery piece wasn't easy, but horrible things happened when gunners did. Not even the latest U.S. barrel had a prayer of surviving a tungsten-tipped 105mm round. Pound drove past a couple of burnt-out hulks that showed as much. One of them had the turret blown off and was lying upside down ten feet away from the chassis. That wasn't the kind of thing a barrel commander wanted to see.

Much more welcome were the fighter-bombers working over Snodgrass Hill. They hit the Confederates again and again, bombing and strafing. Two or three of them went down, but the fire coming from the hill decreased dramatically.

'Couldn't have done that in the last war,' Pound said.

'No, sir,' Sergeant Scullard agreed. 'But their goddamn foot soldiers wouldn't have been carrying stovepipes then, either.' He sprayed some bushes up ahead with a long burst from the coaxial machine gun. If any Confederates with antibarrel rockets crouched there, they didn't get the chance to fire them.

Machine guns at the base of Snodgrass Hill held up U.S. infantry. Barrels painted green-gray knocked out the machine-gun nests one by one. Antibarrel cannon farther up the hill knocked out some U.S. barrels. Michael Pound got on the wireless and screamed for artillery support. Being only a lowly platoon commander, he didn't have a set that let him talk directly with the gun bunnies. He yelled loud enough to make the soldier he did talk to say, 'Keep your hair on, pal. I'll get the word through, honest to Pete.'

'You'd better,' Pound said. 'Otherwise, if they find you mysteriously strangled with telephone wire, they'll know just who to suspect.' On that encouraging note, he switched off.

He couldn't have been the only barrelman yelling for HE. The barrage didn't land on Snodgrass Hill fast enough to suit him, but it would have had to go in yesterday to do that. Land it did. The lower slopes of the hill went up in smoke and shrapnel and poison gas. Watching all that come down on the Confederates, anybody would have thought nothing could stay alive under it.

Pound knew better. Featherston's fuckers had trenches, and they had gas masks, and they had balls. As soon as things eased off even a little bit, they'd pop up and start serving all the guns that weren't knocked off their wheels. He didn't want that to happen – it was the last thing he did want.

He had no idea if he was the highest-ranking barrel officer down near the bottom of Snodgrass Hill. He didn't care, either. He sent his platoon an order barrels didn't hear every day: 'Charge!' A moment later, he added, 'And bring everybody else with you if you can. Let's get them before they get us!'

He stood up in the cupola to wave all the U.S. barrels forward. The commanders in his other machines were doing the same thing. A short round from his own side burst much too close to his barrel. Shell fragments whined past his head. He turned the wave into an obscene gesture aimed at the artillery he'd wanted so badly only a few minutes before. You were just as dead if your buddies got you as you were if the bad guys put one between your eyes.

With a few more barrels of their own, the Confederates probably could have broken up the charge before it got rolling. But they didn't have enough, and one of the U.S. barrels killed the first C.S. machine that showed itself. The infantrymen in butternut with stovepipes mostly stayed down in their holes; they wanted to live just like anybody else. And the charge pounded on.

Before long, Pound ducked down and closed the cupola hatch. By then, rounds didn't have to fall short to be dangerous. He was brave enough, but not suicidal. He thought of himself as a coldly practical man. Whether that kind of man would have led a charge up the heavily defended hill was a question he never worried about.

Both his barrel's bow machine gun and the one beside the main armament chattered. Brass casings clanked down onto the floor of the fighting compartment. 'This is kind of fun, you know? – like a pinball arcade,' Sergeant Scullard said. 'They pop up here, you shoot 'em, then they come up somewhere else, so you gotta knock those guys down, too.'

'I can tell you one difference,' Pound said dryly.

'Yeah? What's that, sir?' Scullard didn't even need to look at what he was doing to feed a new belt of cartridges into the coaxial machine gun.

'In the arcade, they don't shoot back,' Pound answered. Machine-gun bullets and shell fragments clattered off the barrel's thick steel skin.

'God knows we've been through worse.'

'You aren't wrong,' Pound agreed. They were almost to the top of Snodgrass Hill now, and resistance was thinning out. Too much had landed on the Confederates too fast. They were groggy, like a boxer who'd taken too many rights. In the ring, the ref would have stopped the fight before the loser got badly hurt. Hurting the other side was the point of the exercise here.

Pound's barrel rolled over the tube of an overturned 105. Even if the Confederates drove the USA off this hill, they'd never use that gun again – or if they tried, the first round would blow up inside it. *Wouldn't that be a shame?* Pound thought.

He looked around for more enemy soldiers to shoot or

guns to wreck, and he didn't see any. He wasn't quite at the crest of the hill – why give somebody on the far side a clean shot?

More airplanes appeared. He needed a moment to realize they were Confederates: Asskickers with rockets slung under their wings. When the dive bombers salvoed them, they looked like lances of fire slashing across the sky. They tore into the U.S. forces on Snodgrass Hill like lances of fire, too. And Pound couldn't do a thing about it. He'd seen a few barrels with a .50-caliber machine gun mounted in front of the commander's cupola to serve as an antiaircraft weapon. He didn't have one, but he was thinking he'd get one as soon as he could.

The Asskickers sped off to the south. They couldn't linger, or U.S. fighters would hack them down. They'd done damage, no doubt about it. But they hadn't driven U.S. forces off of Snodgrass Hill. They didn't have a chance of doing that, not by themselves, and no Confederate ground counterattack materialized. The strongpoint seemed to be the center of the C.S. position here, and it had just fallen.

Clarence Potter knew the wintry pleasure of being right. The Confederates had hit the United States as hard as they could, and the USA didn't quite fall over. Now the United Sates were hitting back, and they had the CSA on the ropes. The Confederates' problem was that they'd kept trying to land haymakers when they should have been doing their damnedest not to get hit. He thought of everything his country had squandered on aggressive counterattacks that it should have kept under cover or in reserve. If that wasn't enough to drive a man to drink, he didn't know what would be.

If Chattanooga had held, they still might have had a chance. Chattanooga was the cork in the bottle. U.S. paratroopers had yanked the cork. Now the damnyankees could spill out into the heart of the Confederacy, into country that hadn't seen Yankee invaders even in the War of Secession.

And the enemy knew it, too. It didn't do any more to expect U.S. generals to stay half a step behind their opposite numbers in butternut. The United States banged through the improvised C.S. lines in northwestern Georgia . . . oh, not with the greatest of ease, but not with the kind of effort that ruined them, either. They could bang some more whenever and wherever they chose to.

Meanwhile, General Patton was trying to piece together another line. This one, of necessity, was longer than the one centered on Snodgrass Hill. It was also weaker. Fewer men and barrels were doing their damnedest to cover more ground. Their damnedest, Potter feared, wouldn't be good enough.

His own brigade was stationed near Calhoun, Georgia, defending the line of the Oostanaula and Coosawattee Rivers. He wished the rivers were as wide as their names were long. But even if they were, how much difference would it make? The Yankees had crossed the Ohio and the Cumberland. They would be able to deal with obstacles like these.

Right now, they weren't trying very hard. Their artillery and his fired at each other across the rivers. Not a half hour went by when his brigade didn't take at least one casualty. Replacements trickled in more slowly. He would have bet the commander of the U.S. outfit to the north didn't have that worry.

His stomach started to knot up when General Patton paid him a call. He feared he knew what Patton would want, and he was right. 'How soon do you think your brigade can be ready to strike a blow for—'

'Freedom?' Potter interrupted, turning the Party slogan into a jeer.

Patton turned red. 'You still don't have the proper attitude, Potter.'

'That's a matter of opinion, sir,' Potter replied. 'I don't think we can win the war any more, not on the battlefield.' He thought about U-235 and Professor FitzBelmont. If the Confederacy still had hope, it lay there. Did Patton know about uranium bombs? Potter hoped not. He went on, 'Seems to me what we ought to do now is try not to lose it on the battlefield.'

'You're a defeatist. I'll report you to the President,' Patton snarled.

Such a threat would have chilled the blood of ninety-nine percent of the officers in the Confederate Army. Potter yawned in Patton's face. 'Go ahead. He knows how I feel.'

Patton stared at him. 'Then why doesn't he throw you in irons, the way you deserve?'

'Because he knows I think with my head, not with my heart or my balls,' Potter answered. 'It's really a useful technique. You ought to try it one of these days . . . sir.'

'You can go too far, General,' Patton warned. 'Watch yourself.'

'Sir, you can do whatever you please to me, and I really don't care. I'm Clarence Potter, and I'm here to tell you the truth.' Potter appropriated President Featherston's phrase with malicious glee. Patton gaped at him. Smiling a chilly smile, Potter went on, 'We can't afford the head-knocking style you've been using. What will it take to make you see that? The damnyankees in Atlanta? In Savannah, on the ocean? In Mobile, on the Gulf of Mexico? From where I sit, you're greasing the skids to get them there.'

'How dare you say such a thing to me?' Patton thundered. 'How *dare* you? I'll have you court-martialed and drummed out of the Army, so help me God I will!'

'Good luck,' Potter said. 'I've got a Stonewall in my pocket that says you can't do it.' He took out the goldpiece and tossed it up and down. 'Worse thing that'll happen is that the President'll overrule the court and order me back to Richmond. My bet is, he'll overrule the court and keep me right here.'

His calm voice must have held conviction. Patton stood there breathing hard, his cheeks a mottled and furious red. Then, suddenly, he lashed out and slapped Potter in the face. While Potter was grabbing – successfully – for his glasses, Patton ground out, 'All right, you son of a bitch! Will you meet me on the field of honor tomorrow morning? *Have* you honor? One of us will go down in history as a casualty of war, and the other will be able to continue the campaign as he thinks best.'

He was dead serious. He was also deadly serious, his hands hovering near the fancy pistols he wore on each hip. He looked ready – more than ready – to plug Potter on the spot. Replacing his spectacles on his nose, Potter said, 'As challenged party, I believe I have the choice of weapons, sir?'

Patton actually bowed. Did he imagine himself a knight in shining armor? Hadn't he got that idiocy knocked out of him during the Great War? Evidently not, for he was courtesy itself as he replied, 'That is correct, sir. Pistols, swords, rifles at long range if you prefer a contest of skill . . . I am entirely at your disposal in that regard.'

'I'd like to choose horse turds at five paces to show you what a fool you are,' Potter said.

'Do not make a mockery of this, General. I will not abide it,' Patton warned. 'I have challenged; you have accepted. The weapons must be lethal.'

'I just said I'd like to. I didn't say I would,' Potter answered. 'Lethal, is it? All right, sir. I'll give you lethal weapons, and see how you like it.' By the carnivorous smile on Patton's face, he expected to like it very much. Then Potter said, 'I choose flamethrowers at ten paces.'

General Patton's jaw dropped. Some of the high color left his face. 'You are joking,' he got out with some effort.

'Not me,' Potter said. 'Isn't that lethal enough to suit you? We'll both be burnt meat in nothing flat. Well, sir? You wanted a duel. I goddamn well gave you one. Do you still want it?'

For a horrible moment, he thought Patton would say yes. His superior might be furious enough to immolate himself if he could take the man he hated with him. But Patton, though his lips drew back from his teeth in a furious grimace, shook his head. Nobody who'd ever seen what a flamethrower could do wanted one to do it to him. Back in gaslight days, a moth would sometimes fly into the flame of a lamp. That was about what jellied gasoline did to a man.

Then, to Potter's amazement, George Patton started to laugh. 'By God, General, you have more spunk than I gave you credit for!'

He admires *me*, Potter thought, more bemused yet. *I made myself into a bigger jackass than he did, and he* admires *me for it.* Some of the Austro-Hungarian alienists who were probing the shape of man's psyche would probably have had some interesting things to say about that. Wearily, Potter said, 'The United States are the enemy, sir. You're not, and I'm not, either. They're the ones we've got to lick – and the ones we've got to keep from licking us.'

'Well said! Very well said!' In a final surreal touch, Patton bowed again. 'Please accept my apologies for the slap and the insult. While I was provoked, I see now that I was hasty.'

'I'll let it go.' But Potter had enough of the old code in him – and enough pride – to go on resenting what Patton had done. Aiming a flamethrower at him would have been a treat. It would, unfortunately, have been a last treat.

Patton, perhaps still unnerved, made what was for him an astonishing choice: he condescended to ask, 'Since you seem unhappy with my plans for engaging the Yankees, General, what would you do instead?'

'Fight for time,' Potter answered at once, thinking again of Professor FitzBelmont and U-235. How far were he and his crew from building a bomb that could give the CSA a fighting chance again? And how far were their U.S. counterparts from building a bomb that would end all the Confederacy's chances?

'You will perhaps understand a campaign needs more detailed goals and objectives than that.' Patton could have sounded snotty. In fact, he did; that was part of his nature. But he didn't sound anywhere near as snotty as he might have, and Potter gave him reluctant credit for it.

'Yes, sir,' Potter said. 'If you ask me, our goal is to keep the Yankees out of Atlanta. We can't afford to lose it, partly because of all the factories and partly because it's such an important rail junction. Transit between the East Coast and everything from Alabama on west goes to hell if Atlanta falls, and that goes a long way toward losing the war for us. Objectives would have to do with containing the U.S. advance as close to the Georgia-Tennessee border as we can.'

'And driving it back,' Patton said.

Potter shrugged. 'If we can, at this stage of things. But mostly I want to make the U.S. forces come at us. I want to use the defender's advantage for everything it's worth. I want the United States to have casualty lists three, four, five times as long as ours. They're bigger than we are, but they can't afford that kind of thing forever. If they bleed enough, maybe they'll get sick of banging their heads against a brick wall and give us a peace we can live with.'

And if we drop uranium bombs on them a year after that, it'd damn well serve them right, he thought. *Would they hit us first? I don't know. I didn't used to think so. Now, though, we may have given them too many reasons not to let us have another chance.*

'In your opinion, then, we cannot hope to win the war on the ground.' Patton spoke like a judge passing sentence.

Potter didn't care. 'Sir, they're in Georgia. Doesn't that speak for itself? They're cleaning up the pockets of resistance west of their thrust through Kentucky and Tennessee, too, and we haven't been able to keep them from doing that. Between Richmond and Philadelphia, we've stayed even with them in the air. Everywhere else? Here, for instance? You know the answer as well as I do. We haven't matched their latest barrel yet, either.'

'We're ahead of them in rockets,' Patton said.

'Yes, sir,' Potter said. 'Those will hurt them. Those *have* hurt them. They'll make us lose slower. Do you really think they can make us win?' *Maybe if we put a U-235 bomb in the nose of one. But how much does one of those damn things weigh? When will we have a rocket that can get it off the ground? In time for this war?* You'd have to be a wild-eyed optimist to believe anything like that.

'Yours is a counsel of despair,' Patton said.

'I don't want to throw my brigade away charging their guns,' Potter said. 'I want to make them throw their brigades away charging my guns. I don't think that's despair. Where we are now, I think it's common sense.'

'When I give you orders, I expect you to obey them.'

'When I get orders, I expect them to be ones I'm better off obeying.'

They glared at each other. Neither had convinced the other – Potter knew that. Swearing under his breath, Patton stormed out of Potter's tent. Potter wondered what he would do if Patton commanded him to go over the river line and attack the enemy. *I'll refuse,* he decided. *Let him do what he wants after that. It'll keep the brigade in being a while longer, anyhow.*

The orders arrived two hours later. Potter's men were to hold in place. Patton laid on a counterattack farther west. Potter sighed. Patton had grasped the letter, not the spirit. He didn't know what he could do about that. Well, actually, he did know: he couldn't do a damn thing.

Guns blazing, the counterattack went in. It drove U.S. forces back a couple of miles, then ran out of steam. Potter wished he'd expected anything different.

The *Josephus Daniels* rode the waves in the North Atlantic – rode them like a roller-coaster car going up and down ever taller, ever steeper bumps. George Enos took the motion in stride: literally, as he had no trouble making his way around the destroyer escort despite the roughening seas. Though not a big warship, the *Josephus Daniels* made a platform ever so much more stable than the fishing boats that bobbed on the ocean like little corks in a bathtub . . . and sometimes sank as if going down the drain.

He wasn't worried the *Josephus Daniels* would sink – not on her own, anyhow. She might have help from British, French, or Confederate submersibles, though.

At least she was out of range of British land-based airplanes. George had gone through too many attacks from the air, both here and in the tropical Pacific, ever to want to help try to fight off another one.

'We're still floating,' the sailors boasted. Most of them were kids. They'd helped rescue men whose ships had gone to the bottom, but they'd never been sunk themselves. They were cocky because of it. It hadn't happened to them, so they were sure it couldn't.

With the *Townsend* at the bottom of the Gulf of California, George knew better. The water there was shallow. Maybe one day somebody would salvage her for scrap metal. Unless someone did, she'd never see the surface again. Neither would the men who'd died aboard her or who hadn't been able to get off before she went down.

Sam Carsten knew better, too. The captain sometimes talked about how he'd been on the *Remembrance* when the Japanese sank her. That made George wonder if he'd seen the skipper in the Sandwich Islands.

It seemed logical, but he didn't think so. The memory, if it was a memory, felt older than his stint there. When he thought of the skipper, he thought of Boston, and not of Boston the way it was now, either: not the Boston he'd occasionally come back to since joining the Navy. When he thought of Sam Carsten, he thought of his home town a long time ago, back in the days when he was a kid.

Sunshine flashing off the gilded dome of the State House, seen from across Boston Common . . .

When that came back to him, his mouth fell open in amazement. He felt like a man who'd just scratched an itch he'd thought he would never be able to reach. 'Son of a bitch!' he said softly. '*Son* of a bitch!'

Then he wanted to tell the skipper about it. That would have been next to impossible on a battlewagon or an airplane carrier. For an able seaman to get an audience with the captain of a ship like that was like getting an audience with God. It shouldn't have been that hard on the *Josephus Daniels*. Sam Carsten was only a two-striper, and a mustang to boot. He should have had – he probably did have – a soft spot for the men from whose ranks he'd risen.

He wasn't the problem. His exec was. Lieutenant Myron Zwilling seemed convinced God Himself needed to stand in line to see the skipper. As for a mere rating . . . Well, in Zwilling's mind the question hardly arose.

But there were ways around the executive officer. The skipper was a gunnery fanatic. He lavished most of his attention on the two four-inch guns that gave the *Josephus Daniels* what little long-range bite she had, but he didn't forget the 40mm mounts, either.

Picking a time when Carsten seemed a bit less rushed than usual, George said, 'Ask you something, sir?'

'What's on your mind, Enos?' The captain of a bigger ship wouldn't have known all his men by name, but Sam Carsten did.

'You've been in Boston a good many times, I expect,' George said.

'That's a fact – I told you so once. Anybody who's been in the Navy as long as I have, he says he hasn't been in Boston a lot, he's a damn liar,' Carsten replied.

'Yes, sir. Do you remember one time when you were out on the Boston Common and you went under a tree to get out of the sun?' George said. 'There was a family having a picnic under there – a woman, and a boy, and a girl. This would have been – oh, some time around the start of the Twenties. I was ten, eleven, maybe twelve. Does that ring any kind of bell, sir?'

Sam Carsten's face went far away as he thought back. 'No,' he said, but then, 'Wait a minute. Maybe. Damned if it doesn't. Somebody said something about the *Ericsson*.' Because of what had happened to the destroyer at the end of the Great War, any Navy man who heard about it was likely to remember.

And, when the skipper remembered that, it brought everything flooding back to George. 'I did!' he said. 'I told you my father was on her.'

'There was a girl along with you, yeah,' Carsten said slowly. 'She was younger than you, I think.'

'My sister Mary Jane,' George said.

Carsten shook his head in slow wonder. 'Well, if that doesn't prove it's a small world, I'll be damned if I know what would. I wanted to get under that tree so I wouldn't burn, and your mother was nice enough to let me share it.'

He was almost as fair as a ghost; George had seen him blotched with zinc-oxide ointment several times, and it wasn't much paler than his skin. No, he wouldn't have liked summer sun in Boston, not one bit. And . . . 'My mother *was* a nice person,' George said.

'Nice-looking, too. I remember that,' the skipper said. Would he have tried to pick her up if he'd met her without her children? Had he tried anyhow, in some way that went over the kids' heads? If so, he'd had no luck. He eyed George. 'You say *was*? I'm sorry if she's not living any more.'

'She's not.' That brought memories back, too, ones George would sooner have left submerged. 'She took up with the writer who did the book about how she went and shot the Confederate submersible skipper. Bastard drank. They would fight and make up, you know? Except the last time, they didn't. He shot her and then he shot himself.'

'Jesus!' the skipper said. 'I'm sorry. That must have been hell.'

'It was . . . pretty bad, sir,' George said. 'If he wanted to blow his own brains out, fine, but why did he have to go and do that to her, too?'

Carsten set a hand on his shoulder. 'You look for answers to stuff like that, you go crazy. He did it because he went around the bend. What else can you say? If he didn't go around the bend, he wouldn't have done anything like that.'

'I guess so.' That wasn't much different from the conclusion George had reached himself. It made for cold comfort. No – it made for no comfort at all. What he wanted was revenge, and he couldn't have it. Ernie robbed him of it when he turned the gun on himself.

'Sure as hell, you were right about one thing – I did look familiar.' Sam Carsten tried to steer him away from his gloom. 'I wouldn't have known you in a million years, but you were just a kid then. Damned if I don't recall that day on the Common, though. How about that?' He walked down the deck shaking his head.

'So you weren't just blowing stack gas when you said you ran into the Old Man once upon a time,' Petty Officer Third Class Jorgenson said. He still had charge of the 40mm mount. 'How about that?'

'Yeah, how about that?' George agreed. 'I thought so, but I couldn't pin it down till now.'

The crew for the gun spent as much time working together as they could. Because of casualties, just about everyone was in a new slot. Till they figured out how to do what they had little practice doing, they would be less efficient than the other gun crews. That could endanger the ship.

Because the skipper was a fiend for good gunnery, he encouraged them and kept their usual bosses from loading extra duty on them. Carsten wanted them to spend as much time at the gun as they could. They steadily got better. Fremont Dalby would have had some pungent things to say about their performance. Jorgenson *did* have pungent things to say about it. But they improved.

The *Josephus Daniels* went back to patrolling east of Newfoundland. The men who'd been in her for a while told stories of earlier adventures on that duty. If a quarter of what they said was true, she'd had some lively times. The limeys worked harder at smuggling arms into Canada than the USA did at smuggling them into Ireland. Canada and Newfoundland had a much longer coast than the smaller British isle, which gave the enemy more chances to slip through.

Navy Department doctrine was that stopping the arms smuggling would snuff out the Canadian rebellion. The sailors didn't believe it. 'What? The fucking Canucks can't find any guns of their own? My ass!' Jorgenson said when the talk got around to the patrol.

Klaxons hooted. That killed a bull session. George and Jorgenson raced toward the bow. They got to their gun in a dead heat. The rest of the crew wasn't more than a couple of steps behind them. 'What's going on?' asked the new shell-jerker, a big blond kid named Ekberg.

'Beats me,' Jorgenson answered. 'Maybe it's a drill.' He was even bigger than Ekberg, and almost as fair, though neither of them matched the skipper.

'Now hear this!' The PA system crackled to life. Lieutenant Zwilling's harsh voice got no sweeter blaring from the speakers: 'Y-ranging gear has picked up an unidentified aircraft approaching from the south. Exercise caution before opening fire, as it may be friendly. Repeat, exercise caution before opening fire, as it may be friendly. But do not endanger the ship.'

George swore, and he wasn't the only one. The exec wanted to have his cake and eat it, too. Don't shoot the airplane down, but don't let it make an attack run, either? How was that supposed to work?

A minute or so later, the PA came on again. 'This is the captain,' Sam Carsten said. 'The ship comes first. If we have to fish some flyboys out of the drink afterwards, we'll do that. We're trying to find out who's in the airplane, but no luck so far. If we open up on the wireless, we tell everybody in the North Atlantic where we're at, and we don't want to do that.'

'See, the skipper tells us what's what,' Jorgenson said. 'The exec just bullshits.'

'Lieutenant Cooley, he was all right,' Ekberg said. 'This guy, though – you can keep him.'

'Damn airplane *ought* to be one of ours,' Jorgenson said. 'Don't see how the limeys could've snuck a carrier this far west without us knowing.' He paused. ' 'Course, sometimes they fly fighters off their merchantmen. One of those assholes carrying a bomb could be real bad news.'

'Confederate seaplane?' George suggested.

Jorgenson frowned. 'Right at the end of their range. They couldn't get home again unless they refuel somewhere.' The frown turned into a scowl. 'They might do that, though. Maybe the limeys have a station or two on the Newfoundland coast. We can't keep an eye on everything. So yeah, maybe. Whatever it is, we'll find out pretty damn quick.' He swept the southern sky with a gun commander's binoculars.

Somebody farther astern spotted the airplane first and let out a yell. George had a shell in the breech of each gun in the mount. He was ready to open up as soon as Jorgenson gave the word. The gun chief swung the twin 40mms to bear on the target.

'It *is* a seaplane,' he said, still peering through the field glasses. George felt smart for about fifteen seconds. Then Jorgenson went on, 'It's one of ours. That's a Curtiss-37, sure as shit. Stand easy, boys – we're all right.'

'Don't shoot! Repeat – do not shoot!' Lieutenant Zwilling blared a few seconds later. 'The airplane has been positively identified as nonhostile.'

George needed a moment to translate that into English. Then he realized the exec said the same thing as Jorgenson, though not so clearly.

The seaplane buzzed past, the eagle and crossed swords plainly visible on its sides. It waggled its wings at the *Josephus Daniels* and flew on toward the north. 'Nice *not* to need to fight for a change,' George said, and none of the other sailors at the mount told him he was wrong.

When a bath meant a quick dip in a creek, Jonathan Moss did what anybody else would: he mostly did without. Sometimes, he got too smelly and buggy to stand himself, and went in for a little while. He came out with his teeth chattering – fall was in the air, even in Georgia.

'Jesus, I miss hot water!' he said.

'Yeah, no kidding.' Nick Cantarella had just taken a brief bath, too. 'We're both skinny bastards these days, you know?'

Moss ran a hand along his ribs. 'You mean this isn't a xylophone?'

'Funny. Funny like a crutch. And you've got more meat on your bones than I do,' Cantarella said.

'Not much,' Moss said. 'You started out built like a soda straw, and I didn't. That's the only difference.'

They both got back into the ragged dungarees and collarless work shirts that would have been the uniform of black guerrillas in the CSA had the guerrillas enjoyed anything so fancy as a uniform. In one way, the only difference between them and the rest of Spartacus' band was their lighter skin. In another . . .

'You ofays!' Spartacus called. He used the word as casually as a white Confederate would have used *niggers*. Most of the time, it meant the Confederate whites the guerrillas were fighting. But it could mean any white at all, too.

'What is it, boss?' Jonathan Moss asked. The band didn't

run on anything like military discipline, but Spartacus fancied his title of respect.

'How come the United States done lost the War of Secession? You lick them damn Confederates then, nobody have to worry 'bout 'em since.'

Moss and Cantarella looked at each other. Any school-child in either country knew the answer to that, or at least the short version. But Spartacus and the rest of the blacks with him were never schoolchildren. The Confederate States always did everything they could to discourage Negroes from getting any kind of education. They didn't want them to be anything more than beasts of burden with thumbs.

'Shall I do the honors, or would you rather?' Cantarella asked.

'I can, unless you're hot to trot,' Moss said.

Cantarella waved him forward. 'Be my guest.'

'Well, the first thing that happened was, the Confederates had a good general in Virginia and we had a lousy one,' Moss said. 'McClellan was never a match for Robert E. Lee – not even close. And Abe Lincoln didn't get rid of McClellan and put in somebody who knew what he was doing. We blame Lincoln for a lot, and it starts right there.'

'He wanted to be good to niggers, though,' Spartacus said. 'Ofays down here don't reckon so, they don't secede in the first place.'

That was probably true. From the U.S. viewpoint, it was one more thing for which to blame Lincoln. If someone sensible like Douglas had won the election . . . In that case, there wouldn't have been a War of Secession in the first place.

'It gets worse,' Moss said. 'Lincoln couldn't do anything when England and France recognized the CSA after Lee beat McClellan up in Pennsylvania. Neither could anybody else in the United States.'

'What difference recognizing the Confederate States make?' Spartacus said. 'They there whether they recognized or not.'

'After the limeys and frogs recognized them, they broke our blockade,' Moss said. 'They had better navies than ours. Then they shipped the Confederates whatever they needed, and got cotton back. And they could blockade U.S. ports if we didn't make peace with the CSA.'

'They could, and they did,' Nick Cantarella put in.

'They ganged up on us again twenty years later, after the Confederates bought Chihuahua and Sonora from Mexico,' Moss said. 'When we lost the Second Mexican War, that's what made us decide to line up with Germany. That way, we had a . . . what would you call it, Nick?'

'A counterweight,' Cantarella said.

'There you go.' Moss nodded. 'With Germany on our side, we had a counterweight to England and France. And that's how things have been for the last sixty years.'

'How come y'all don't let niggers in the USA when things is tough fo' us down here?' Spartacus might not know much about what had happened a long time ago, but he had that piece of recent history straight. Chances were every Negro in the CSA did.

Moss and Cantarella eyed each other again. They both knew the reason. They both feared it would be unpalatable to the Negroes around them. And they both feared the guerrillas would recognize a lie.

Sighing, Moss told the truth: 'A lot of whites in the USA don't like Negroes much better than whites here do.'

A low hum ran through the guerrillas. It was, Moss judged with more than a little surprise, a hum of approval. 'Leastways you don't put no sugar on a spoonful o' shit,' was how Spartacus put it.

'I don't care if them Yankee ofays likes us or not,' another guerrilla said. 'Ain't never had no ofays like us. Don't hardly know what I'd do if'n they did. Long as they ain't tryin' to murder us, that'll do fine.'

Several other Negroes nodded. One of them said, 'Wish them damnyankees'd come farther down into Georgia.'

'Amen!' Two or three Negroes spoke together, as if responding to a preacher. One of them added, 'That'd be about the onliest thing that could save the niggers down here. That or the Second Coming, one.'

'Don't hold your breath,' Spartacus said dryly.

'Well, hell, I know Jesus ain't comin',' the guerrilla said. 'But the damnyankees, they might.'

'They're moving again. *We're* moving again,' Nick Cantarella said. 'I don't think the Confederates can stop us from breaking out of our bridgehead south of Chattanooga. And once we're loose in north Georgia ... '

'Yeah!' Again, the response might almost have come in church.

'They gonna get here soon enough to do us any good?' Spartacus answered his own question with a shrug. 'We gots to las' long enough to find out, dat's all.'

One way the guerrillas survived was by never staying in one place very long. Mexican soldiers and white militiamen hunted the Negroes – not all the time, but too often. Not staying around to be found was simple common sense.

Of course, moving had dangers of its own. You could walk into trouble as well as away from it. But Spartacus' point man, Apuleius, was as good as anybody Jonathan Moss ever saw. He was as good as anybody Cantarella ever saw, too. 'Put that little so-and-so in our uniform and he could sneak a division of barrels right on into Richmond,' Cantarella said.

'Wouldn't be surprised,' Moss agreed. 'Or he could, anyway, if we let Negroes join the Army.'

'Yeah, well, that's horseshit, too,' Cantarella said. 'You know smokes can fight, and I know smokes can fight, and if Philly's too goddamn dumb to know smokes can fight, then fuck Philly, you know what I'm sayin'?'

Apuleius held up the band outside an abandoned sharecropper village. He didn't think it *was* abandoned. 'Somebody in dere,' he told Spartacus after crawling back through the forgotten, overgrown vegetable plots around the place.

'How you know?' Spartacus asked. 'Looks quiet enough. Ain't no smoke or nothin'.'

'Not now,' the point man said. 'But sure enough was some not long ago. An' when I git close, I smell me some people ain't had no baths in a hell of a long time.'

He kept himself cleaner than most of the other guerrillas. Moss had thought that was because he was unusually fastidious, and had even wondered if he was a fairy. Now he saw good sense lay behind it. If Apuleius didn't smell himself, he had a better chance of sniffing out other people.

'You reckon they ofays or Mexicans?' Spartacus asked.

'Likely ofays,' Apuleius answered. 'They stink worse. The Mexicans, they washes when they gits the chance.'

'How we gonna smoke 'em out?' Spartacus suddenly grinned a predatory grin. 'Reckon you kin wiggle back close enough to chuck a grenade into the middle o' things?'

'I kin try.' The point man didn't sound thrilled, but he didn't say no.

'Well, why don't you wait a bit?' Spartacus said. 'Let us set up the machine gun at the edge o' the brush. Then we be ready to give them ofays a proper how-do-you-do.'

The two-man machine-gun crew positioned their precious weapon. The rest of the guerrillas, riflemen all, took cover where they could. Moss hoped the bush he crouched behind wasn't poison oak.

Apuleius worked his way forward again. Moss presumed he did, anyhow; were the point man visible to him, he would have been visible to whoever was inside the village, too. Moss didn't see the grenade fly, either.

He sure heard it when it went off. And all of a sudden that village didn't seem abandoned any more. Militiamen, some in gray uniforms, others with clothes no fancier than the guerrillas wore, boiled out of the tumbledown shacks that hadn't been anything much when they were in good repair and looked even more sorrowful now. The white men were cussing and clutching their weapons and pointing every which way. Some of those flying fingers aimed at Apuleius, but others flew in the opposite direction.

'Now!' Spartacus said.

Along with the rest of the riflemen in the band, Moss started shooting at the youths, mutilated men, and old-timers who made up the local militia. The machine gun spat death at the village. Death had visited it before – where were the sharecroppers who once lived there? Where were their wives and children? Gone to camps, most of them, if they were like most of the Negroes in Georgia.

As soon as the gunfire gave him cover, Apuleius tossed another grenade into the village. This one made the militiamen yell and scream even more than they were already doing. The kids, the ones who'd never seen real fighting before, suffered worse than the veterans. Men who'd come under fire knew they needed to get down and get behind something when bullets started flying. The youngsters stayed upright much too long – and paid for it.

'Fish in a barrel,' Nick Cantarella said happily, sprawled behind a bush not far from the one that hid Moss.

A bullet snapped past between them. 'Fish don't shoot back,' Moss said.

One of the militiamen had got his hands on a fancy

C.S. automatic rifle. He sprayed bullets back at the guerrillas almost as fiercely as the machine gun fired at his side. A couple of Negroes howled when they were hit, but the noise they made was as nothing beside that from the militiamen caught in the ambush.

When Spartacus ordered a withdrawal, the machine gun gave covering fire. The militiamen didn't seem to have any stomach for coming after them, anyhow. Were Moss one of them, he wouldn't have, either, not after the way they got shot up.

'Keep movin'!' Spartacus called. 'They be all over the place round these parts now.' He was sure to be right, though Moss wasn't sure how many militiamen and Mexican soldiers the local authorities could scrape together.

Litter bearers carried one of the wounded men. The other, shot through the right arm, was able to walk – and to swear with remarkable fluency. Moss looked around for Apuleius. He didn't see the point man, but that proved nothing. Apuleius might need to wait till dark before making his getaway, and he'd caught up with the band before. Odds were he could do it again.

Would any of it matter? Could they hang on till the U.S. Army came down here or put the Confederates out of business? Moss had no idea. With his scheme for stealing an airplane as dead as too many of the men who'd helped him try, he could only hope.

'Bad one, Doc!' Eddie called as he brought the casualty into the aid station.

Leonard O'Doull knew the medic was right even before he saw the casualty. When you smelled something that reminded you of a pork roast left too long in the oven . . . then it was a bad one, all right.

Vince Donofrio wrinkled his nose. 'Christ, I hate burns!' he said.

'Me, too,' O'Doull said. 'But I sure don't hate 'em near as much as the poor bastard who's got one.'

The wounded man came out of a barrel. That much was plain from what was left of his coverall. One leg was charred, and he was howling like a wolf. 'Has he had morphine?' O'Doull asked.

'Three shots, Doc,' Eddie answered. O'Doull bit his lip. Sometimes even the best painkiller was fighting out of its weight. Eddie went on, 'Ether'll put him out.'

'Yeah.' O'Doull turned to Sergeant Donofrio. 'Get him under, Vince.'

'Right,' Donofrio said tightly. The man's hands were burned, too, and so was his face, though not so badly. He tried to fight when Donofrio put the ether cone over his mouth and nose. As gently as Eddie could, he held the wounded man's arms till they went limp. His screams faded then, too.

'How much can you do for him, Doc?' Eddie asked.

'Me? Not much. I just want to get rid of the tissue that'd go gangrenous if I left it. Then the specialists take over.'

'That tannic-acid treatment they give 'em?' Donofrio asked.

'That's right,' O'Doull said. 'Tans their hide, scars it fast so they don't weep fluid out through the burns. They get better results with it than with anything they used to do.'

'Tans their hide . . .' Donofrio shuddered. 'Must hurt like hell while the poor guy's going through it.'

'I bet it does, yeah,' O'Doull said. 'But if you've got burns like that, you already hurt like hell. You heard this guy before you knocked him out. How many syrettes of morphine did you say he had in him, Eddie?'

'Three,' the medic answered. 'I hear these guys with the

burns, a lot of 'em turn into junkies 'cause they need so much dope to get 'em through it while it's bad.'

'I've heard the same thing,' Donofrio said.

'Yeah, so have I,' O'Doull said. 'You can't blame 'em, though. If they didn't have the drugs, a lot of them would kill themselves. There just isn't pain much worse than a bad burn.'

He methodically went on debriding flesh that would never heal. The smell made him hungry and nauseous at the same time. That was one more reason to hate burns. 'What happened to the rest of the barrel crew?' he asked.

'Don't know for sure,' Eddie said. 'All I know is, he's the only one we brought back. Maybe the other guys all got out and didn't get hurt. Here's hoping.'

'Here's hoping,' O'Doull agreed. His eyes met Sergeant Donofrio's over their masks. They both shook their heads. Much more likely that the other four men in the crew never made it out at all. Much more likely that they burned to death. What kind of memories were now dimmed inside this fellow's head? Would he hear his buddies' shrieks for the rest of his life? *Too bad there's no morphine for the soul,* O'Doull thought.

The burned soldier was still mercifully unconscious when the corpsmen took him off for more treatment farther back of the line. O'Doull shed his mask. So did Vince Donofrio. 'That was a tough one,' Donofrio said.

'Burns are about as bad as it gets,' O'Doull agreed. 'I'm going outside for a cigarette. You want one?'

'After a case like that? What I want is a good, stiff drink. I guess a butt'll have to do.' Donofrio was another one who didn't drink when he might have to deal with patients soon. O'Doull approved, though he wouldn't have said anything as long as the medic didn't show up smashed.

He pulled out a pack of Raleighs, gave one to Donofrio,

and lit another for himself. After the first drag, he said, 'Getting away from the smell in there is good, too.'

'Bet your ass,' Donofrio said. 'That's another thing smoke is good for.' He inhaled, held it, and then blew out a blue-gray cloud. Even after that, he made a face. 'You know what it reminded me of? Like there's spare ribs in the oven and the telephone rings, you know, and it's the gal's sister, and she gets to yakking and doesn't look at the clock till she smells stuff burning – and then it's too damn late.'

'That sounds about right,' O'Doull said. 'I wonder why they call them spare ribs. I bet the pig didn't think so.'

Donofrio laughed. 'Good one, Doc! I bet I steal it.'

'You better not,' O'Doull said, so seriously that the medic looked surprised. He went on, 'You'll cut into my royalties if you do.'

'Royalties?' Donofrio snorted. 'You want royalties, go to Mexico or France or England.'

'Sure, tell an Irishman to go to England for the king,' O'Doull said. 'You know how to win friends, don't you?'

'In a poker game, right?' Donofrio could be even loopier than Granny McDougald.

'Poker game.' O'Doull shook his head. He couldn't get the wounded barrelman out of his thoughts. 'That poor son of a bitch sure had the cards stacked against him.'

'Yeah.' The medic scowled, too. 'One good thing – his face came through pretty good. He won't have to go through life like that guy in the book – *The Phantom of the Catacombs,* that's what the name of it was. You ever see the movie they made from it? Scared the crap outa me when I was a kid.'

'I was grown up by then, but I know what you mean,' O'Doull said. 'They ought to do a talking version now. They have for a lot of the old silents, but not that one – not yet, anyway.'

'Who do you suppose they'd get to play the Phantom?' Donofrio asked. 'You could put anybody in one of the other parts, but the Phantom? Everybody who saw the movie would be comparing him to Lon Chaney.'

'Not everybody,' O'Doull said. 'The silent version's more than twenty years old now. Most people younger than you never saw it. They would have stopped showing it as soon as talking came along. When was the last time you saw a silent movie?'

'Been a while,' Donofrio admitted after a little thought. 'You don't even worry or wonder about crap like that, but it disappears when you aren't looking. Like Kaiser Bill mustaches, you know? Now it's just a few stubborn old farts who wear 'em, but my old man sure had one in the last war. Everybody did. Hell, I think even my mother did.'

O'Doull laughed. 'You said it – I didn't.'

'My mother's a nice lady,' Donofrio said. 'She heard me going on about her like that, she wouldn't beat me up . . . much.'

A green-gray truck pulled up. 'You guys get ready to take your aid station forward,' the driver said. 'Front's moving up again. You're too far behind the line.'

He sounded as if he came from Kansas or Nebraska. All the same, O'Doull said, 'I don't know you from a hole in the ground. Give me the password.' Confederates in Yankee clothing remained a nuisance. O'Doull hoped U.S. soldiers with drawls were also making the enemy sweat.

'Oh – Sequoyah!' The truck driver couldn't sing worth a damn, but that was the opening for a hot new Broadway show, and the day's password. He pointed at O'Doull. 'Now give me the countersign, or I'll figure you're one of Featherston's fuckers in disguise.'

Fair was fair. 'Away we go!' O'Doull said dutifully. The

driver nodded. O'Doull turned to Donofrio. 'Time to pack up and leave our home sweet home.'

'Leave, my ass – we take it with us,' Donofrio said, and then, with a shrug, 'What the hell? It's not like we never did it before.'

'I'd rather go forward than back,' O'Doull said, and the medic nodded.

As Donofrio said, they'd had practice knocking down the aid station. And it was designed to fit inside the rear compartment of a deuce-and-a-half. Military engineering extended to things besides rifles and barrels. Making aid stations go into the trucks that had to move them fit the bill, and the people who'd put things together knew what they were doing. Even the operating table folded up for a smooth fit.

'Let's roll,' the driver said.

Roll they did, down past Dalton, Georgia, toward Resaca. O'Doull and Donofrio rode in the cab with the driver; Eddie and the other corpsmen who gathered casualties stayed in the back of the truck. Several bodies hung in the Dalton town square. HE SHOT AT SOLDIERS, said the placard tied around the neck of one of them. The others bore similarly cheery messages.

'They love us down here,' Donofrio said, eyeing the bodies.

'Who gives a damn if they love us?' the driver said. 'Long as they know they better not screw with us, that's all that counts.'

Oderint dum metuant. An ancient Roman playwright had put that into three words. *Let them hate as long as they fear.* English was a less compact language than Latin. O'Doull didn't suppose he could expect a truck driver to match a poet's concision.

War's wreckage littered the landscape: burnt-out barrels from both sides, crashed airplanes, smashed houses and barns, hastily dug graves with helmet-topped rifles taking the place of headstones. O'Doull nodded to himself. The aid station had got too far behind the front. Smelling death again reminded him what war was like.

Brakes squealed when the driver stopped. Small-arms fire came from up ahead. 'This about right?' the man asked.

'Should do,' O'Doull answered. Vince Donofrio's head bobbed up and down.

They got out and started setting up what they'd taken down not long before. The corpsmen wrestled with canvas and ropes and tent pegs. As soon as they had the tent up, O'Doull and Donofrio put in the operating table and medical supplies. Before long, the doctor and senior medic were ready for business again. Eddie and his pals headed up toward the front to see what kind of business they could bring back.

'Hope we don't see them for a while,' O'Doull said.

'That'd be nice, wouldn't it?' Donofrio cocked his head to one side, listening to the gunfire up ahead. 'You really think all that shit's flying around and nobody's getting hurt?'

'No,' O'Doull admitted. 'But you're right. It would be nice.'

They had a respite of most of an hour. That was about how long the corpsmen would have needed to walk up to the fighting, find someone wounded and give him emergency first aid, and then lug him back to the relocated aid station.

The first wounded man came back cussing a blue streak. A bandage swathed his left hand. Another one soaked up blood from his left buttock. 'Same fucking bullet clipped off a finger and a half and got me in the ass,' he growled.

'Could've been worse,' Donofrio said. 'Could've been your other hand.'

'Up yours, Jack,' the wounded man told him. 'I'm a lefty.'

'Oh.' For a moment, the medic looked as foolish as he sounded. 'Sorry. How was I supposed to know?'

'You coulda kept your goddamn mouth shut.'

'Let's get you on the table,' O'Doull said. 'I'll do what I can for your hand, and I'll see if I can dig out the bullet.'

'Hot damn! So I get to turn the other cheek, huh?' the soldier said.

O'Doull winced. Donofrio reached for the mask attached to the ether cylinder with nothing but relief. Putting this guy under would shut him up, anyway.

XIX

Rain poured down from a leaden sky. Off in the distance, lightning flashed. Irving Morrell counted hippopotamuses – or was it hippopotami? Whichever, he counted twelve of them before the dull boom shook his barrel. The stroke was more than two miles away. But the rain, dammit, was here, there, and everywhere.

The barrel squelched forward through mud that was starting to look like tomato soup. U.S. armor all over northern Georgia was squelching – except in the places where it was flat-out stuck. The low ceiling grounded fighter-bombers. Even regular artillery was less accurate in godawful weather like this, and shell bursts spent themselves in the mud instead of spreading as they did most of the time.

'Dammit, we need to keep rolling,' Morrell muttered. But how? He'd broken out of the bridgehead south of Chattanooga. No way in hell the Confederates could drive U.S. forces back into the bottle and pound down the cork.

But Morrell didn't think small. He wanted Atlanta. He wanted it so bad he could taste it. He wanted to see Jake Featherston try to fight a war with the Stars and Stripes flying over the chief Confederate junction between east and west. And he thought he could take Atlanta – as long as his men kept moving, kept pushing, didn't let up on the bastards in butternut, didn't give them a chance to regroup, reorganize, catch their breath.

October wasn't listening to him. The summer had been drier than usual. Fall seemed to be making up for it all at once. 'Unfair,' Morrell said. The enemy couldn't stop him. The enemy had a devil of a time even slowing him down. Why was the weather doing the Confederacy's dirty work for it?

Dirty work it was. Plowing through this gunk, the command barrel kicked up a bow wave like a destroyer at flank speed. But seawater was clean, not mixed with mud. Anyone this bow wave splashed would turn the color of rust – if he hadn't already from trying to make his own way through the muck.

More lightning flashed. After a dozen or so hippos, thunder boomed. The rain came down harder than ever. Swearing under his breath, Morrell ducked down into the turret and closed the hatch behind him.

'Thank you, sir,' the new gunner said. Clark Ashton had an infectious grin. 'Wondered if I'd have to start bailing there.'

'Not that wet,' Morrell said, though it didn't miss by much. Frenchy Bergeron had shoulder straps with gold bars on them now, and a platoon somewhere around here. So did Michael Pound, if he hadn't got hurt since Morrell saw him last. *My gunners – a substitute for OCS?* Morrell thought with a wry grin.

'No forty days and forty nights?' Ashton said. 'Sure coming down like it. If you see a big boat with giraffes and elephants and a guy with a beard, you better watch out.'

'The Ark came down on Mount Ararat,' Morrell said. 'That's in Armenia, not Georgia. The Turks and the Russians have to worry about it. Not us, thank God.'

'Isn't there a Georgia right next to Armenia?' Ashton asked. 'Maybe we've floated over from this one to that one.'

'Maybe you've floated clean out of your skull,' Morrell

said. The gunner took a seated bow, which wasn't easy in the crowded turret. Morrell rolled his eyes. That only made Ashton bow again.

Word coming in on the command circuits made Morrell do worse than roll his eyes. Unit after unit reported that it couldn't go forward. Artillery was bogging down too far behind the line to give any kind of worthwhile support. Armored cars couldn't leave the roads to scout; their tires made them more prone to getting stuck in the mud than barrels or armored personnel carriers. Even infantry units were having heavy going . . . and soldiers hated nothing worse than flooded trenches and foxholes.

At last, Morrell decided struggling to go forward would cost more than it was worth. He ordered all front-line units to hold in place to give the artillery and logistics train a chance to catch up. He wanted to be ready to reopen the attack when the rains let up – if they ever did.

'You don't think we'll sink in the mud if we stop here, sir?' Ashton asked.

Morrell muttered under his breath. That didn't just strike him as possible; it struck him as likely. He ordered the driver forward till they came to a paved road. That also had its drawbacks. The barrel was too exposed to make him happy. But the curtain of rain drumming down hid the machine almost as well as a smoke screen. And he didn't want to have to summon an armored recovery vehicle to rescue him if he did bog down. His reputation would be a long time recovering from something like that.

'Here we are,' Ashton said. 'The middle of nowhere. Isn't it lovely this time of year?'

'This isn't the middle of nowhere,' Morrell said. The gunner raised an eyebrow, as if to say he was too well-bred to argue but it sure looked that way to him. 'It isn't,' Morrell insisted. 'Where we are right now, this has to be the southern end of nowhere. Down a little farther, you've got Atlanta, and Atlanta's definitely somewhere.'

Clark Ashton thought for a bit, then nodded. 'Somewhere we can't get to right now,' he said.

'Well, no. Thanks for reminding me,' Morrell said. 'When this barrel rolls into Atlanta, the war's just a long spit from being over.'

Ashton listened to the rain pounding on the barrel's metal skin. 'Seems to me God's got the long spit right now.'

Morrell grunted. 'Seems that way to me, too, and I wish to hell it didn't.' He patted the front pocket of his coveralls. 'And I wish I could have a cigarette.'

'Good luck, sir,' the gunner said. Morrell's chuckle was distinctly halfhearted. He wasn't about to light up inside the turret. Barrelmen did that every once in a while, but you had to be really desperate for a butt to take the chance. He would have growled like an angry bear if Ashton or the loader smoked in here, which meant he couldn't do it himself. Normally, he would have just stood up in the cupola if he wanted a nicotine buzz. With water coming down in buckets, that wouldn't work, either.

'Won't kill me to go without,' he said mournfully, and patted that front pocket again.

'How long do you think it'll be before we can start advancing again?' Ashton asked.

Laughing, Morrell said, 'What is it about gunners? You guys can't stand not to know about anything, can you?'

'I don't know about anybody else, but I sure can't,' Ashton said.

'Tell you what,' Morrell said. 'Talk to God. If you can make the sun come out and dry up the mud, we'll roll. Till somebody does . . . we won't.'

'If God listened to me, sir, I wouldn't be in a turret with you – no offense. I'd be in bed with a blonde – or a brunette, or a redhead. I'm not a fussy guy. Any kind of girl would do.'

'Blonde,' the loader said. 'If you're gonna ask, don't be shy, for Chrissake. With big jugs, too.' He gestured.

'There you go,' Ashton said. 'That'd work for me.' He glanced over at Morrell. 'What about you, sir?'

'One of these days, I wouldn't mind leave to go back to Kansas,' Morrell said. 'That's where my wife and daughter are.'

'Yes, sir,' the gunner said. 'But you're here now, and there's plenty of broads around, and some of 'em'll put out even if you're a damnyankee.'

'I don't need it that bad,' Morrell said. 'Agnes isn't fooling around on me back there, and I don't feel right about cheating on her.'

Ashton and the loader looked at each other. He could read their minds, though they said not a word. *Poor old guy,* they had to be thinking. *If he had more get up and go in him, he'd nail some of these Confederate bitches any which way.* Maybe they were right. Morrell hoped not, but he recognized the possibility. A man in his twenties was a hard-on with legs. A man in his fifties damn well wasn't, and never looked or acted more idiotic than when he pretended he was.

His earphones crackled with a new report: 'Sir, our forward scouts say there's a Confederate buildup centered on map square Red-14.'

'Have you called artillery in on it?' Morrell asked, maneuvering the map so he could see where the devil Red-14 was. Folding and unfolding the damn thing inside the turret reminded him of a crowded flat with laundry drying on lines strung across the front room. The square lay south and east of Resaca, not too far from where he was himself.

'Yes, sir,' said the voice on the wireless. 'Doesn't seem to be enough to break 'em up. Sure could use a spoiling attack.'

'Well, I believe you,' Morrell said. 'Haven't got a whole lot to spoil with, though. And this damn rain . . .'

'How much trouble can they cause if they break through there?' the voice asked.

Morrell looked at the map again. He did some more muttering. If everything went precisely wrong, the Confederates could retake Resaca. That would complicate his life. It would mean Atlanta wouldn't fall any time soon. And it would put him in hot water with the War Department, where you were only as good as what you did yesterday.

'How big a buildup is it?' he asked. If it was brigade strength, maybe even division strength, he *would* put in a spoiling attack. He wouldn't just put it in, either – he'd lead it himself. He knew he couldn't put his hands on anywhere near a division's worth of men and matériel, but he didn't care. The Confederates wouldn't be so sure of that. When barrels came at them out of a curtain of rain, wouldn't they think twice before they tried attacking? He thought so – they couldn't afford to get too intrepid. On the other hand, they couldn't afford *not* to get too intrepid, either. How did you judge?

He knew how he judged. If they were there in corps strength, he'd have to receive an attack instead of delivering one. That was where he drew the line between aggressiveness and stupidity.

'Sir, best estimate is division strength,' said the man at the other end of the wireless connection.

'Heigh-ho,' Morrell said. 'Let's go.' He thumbed the TRANSMIT button. 'Well, we'll see if we can knock 'em back on their heels. Out.' Then he started calling the armored and infantry in the neighborhood. He wondered if their COs would groan and fuss and flabble and say they couldn't possibly move in this downpour. Nobody did. They wanted to hit the Confederates. 'We've been thumping 'em like a big bass drum from Pittsburgh down to here,' an infantry colonel said. 'Let's do it some more.'

Clark Ashton beamed at him when the command barrel squelched forward. 'Frenchy told me to expect action when I rode with you,' he said. 'He wasn't blowing smoke, was he?'

'We aren't here to give those butternut bastards a big kiss,' Morrell answered. 'We're here to blow 'em to hell and gone. And I aim to.'

His scratch force pushed in the Confederate pickets with the greatest of ease. Featherston's men didn't seem to dream that anybody could bring off an attack in weather like this. Some of them panicked when they found they were wrong.

Barrels loomed up out through the rain. Morrell called out targets. Clark Ashton hit one after another. Maybe Frenchy Bergeron had told him he'd better be a good gunner if he was going to get along with his new commander. Or maybe even the powers that be feared what Irving Morrell would say and do if they saddled him with a gunner who didn't know his trade.

The Confederates fell back. Morrell started laughing fit to bust. The rain that had helped the CSA was helping him instead now. The enemy couldn't tell how small his force really was. The way the U.S. barrels and soldiers pushed forward, they had plenty of weight behind them. They'd have to be nuts to push like that if they didn't. Featherston's men, sure they were sane, fell back. Irving Morrell, just as sure he wasn't, laughed and laughed.

★

Carefully conned by a pilot who knew his way through the minefields, the *Josephus Daniels* came into New York harbor. Sailors stood at the rail admiring the tall buildings and boasting of the havoc they would wreak when they got liberty. Sam Carsten remembered leaves of his own when he was a rating, from Boston all the way to Honolulu.

He fondly recalled the lady – well, woman – he'd visited just before he first met George Enos, Jr. And wasn't that a kick in the head? Funny the kid remembered it after all these years. Actually, Enos was no kid any more – he had to be past thirty. *And how many miles have you got?* Sam asked himself. Some questions were better left unanswered.

As usual, the pilot knew his business. A good thing, too, since in his line of work your first mistake was much too likely to be your last. Blowing a ship halfway to the moon would get you talked about, and not kindly, even if you lived through it.

'We have the first liberty party ready?' Sam asked Myron Zwilling as the ship approached its assigned quay.

'Yes, sir,' the executive officer answered. 'All men with good disciplinary records.'

'That's fine for the first party,' Sam said. 'But I want everybody to be able to go ashore unless we get called back to sea sooner than I expect right now.'

'Yes, sir,' Zwilling repeated, but he didn't sound happy about it. 'Some of them don't deserve the privilege, though.'

'Oh, come on,' Sam said. 'Nobody's knifed anybody, nobody's slugged anybody, nobody's got caught cooking hooch.' There was some illicit alcohol aboard the *Josephus Daniels*. There'd been some aboard every ship in which Carsten ever served. As long as the chiefs kept things within reasonable bounds, as long as nobody showed up at his battle station too toasted to do his job, the skipper was inclined to look the other way.

'No one's been caught, no.' By the way the exec pursed his lips, he was inclined to act like a revenuer in the hills of West Virginia. Only Sam's manifest unwillingness to let him held him back. 'But I'm morally convinced there's a still on this ship, and I'd like to get rid of it as soon as possible.'

'We'll see,' Sam said. 'Meanwhile, though, we'll do it the way I said.'

'Aye aye, sir.' Zwilling couldn't disobey an obviously legal order, no matter how much he wanted to.

Happy sailors poured ashore after the destroyer escort tied up. Sam went ashore, too, not to roister but to consult with his superiors. 'We keep getting good reports about you, Carsten,' said a captain not much younger than he was.

'Sir, I deny everything,' Sam said, straight-faced.

The officers in the conference room chuckled. One of them sent up smoke signals on his pipe. The captain who'd spoken before said, 'How's the new executive officer shaping?'

'He's brave and he's diligent, sir.' Sam believed in getting the good out ahead of anything else. But there was more to say, and he said it: 'He's . . . kind of a stickler for rules and regulations, isn't he?'

'Does that interfere with how well he does his job?' the captain asked.

'No, sir, but I had a happier ship with Pat Cooley in that slot,' Sam answered.

'Would you say he's disqualified from command?'

'No, sir.' Sam left it right there.

He tried to, anyhow. The captain asked, 'Would you be happy serving under him?'

Sam had to answer that one truthfully, no matter how little he wanted to. 'No, sir,' he repeated.

One of the officers who hadn't said anything wrote a note in a little book whose pages were held together by a spiral wire. Sam hoped he hadn't just murdered Lieutenant Zwilling's career. 'Why not?' the captain asked.

'He'll do everything by the book,' Sam replied. 'We need the book. It's a good thing we've got it. But you need to know when to throw it out, too.' He waited to see if they would contradict him. When they didn't, he went on, 'I'm afraid he doesn't.'

The officer with the notebook wrote in it again. 'Thanks for being frank with us,' he said.

'Sir, I'm not happy about it,' Sam said. 'Within his limits, he's a solid officer. He's plenty brave – I already said that. He's conscientious. He works hard – nobody on the ship works harder.'

'That's what the exec is for,' said the captain who did most of the talking.

'Well, yes, sir, but over and above that,' Sam said. 'He sticks his nose in everywhere – sometimes, probably, when people wish he wouldn't. Even when somebody who does that is right all the time, ratings resent it. When he isn't, that only makes things worse.'

'You're saying Lieutenant Zwilling sometimes intervenes mistakenly?' the captain asked.

He wasn't twisting Sam's words, but he was interpreting them harshly. 'It's not too bad, sir,' Carsten said.

'It's not too good, either, or you wouldn't be talking about it,' the captain returned. 'Will you tell me I'm wrong?'

'No, sir,' Sam said once more. Lieutenant Zwilling wouldn't love him – he knew that. But he didn't love his new exec, either. Pat Cooley had spoiled him.

'Anything else about your ship that we ought to know?' the captain asked.

'Nothing you don't already know about the class, sir,'

Sam answered. 'She's not fast enough to run from a fight, and she doesn't have the guns to win one.'

That made the officer taking notes smile. 'Didn't you outfight one of the limeys' merchant cruisers?' he said.

'Yes, sir, but only 'cause they couldn't shoot straight,' Sam said. 'If they'd hit us a couple of times, it would have been all over – the wrong way.'

'Destroyer escorts do a fine job in the roles for which they're designed,' the captain who did most of the talking said primly.

'Yes, sir,' Carsten agreed. 'For escorting convoys, for going after submarines – no problems there. But the *Josephus Daniels* has done a lot of things she's not designed for, too. If she keeps doing them, her luck'll run out one day. I know it's a busy war. I'm not complaining – but you asked.'

'Most people would say everything was fine and let it go,' the captain remarked. 'They'd be afraid of messing up their careers if they popped off.'

Sam laughed. 'What have I got to worry about, sir? I'm never going to command a cruiser, let alone anything bigger. Either I stay on my ship till the war's over or I get a real destroyer. The difference isn't worth flabbling about. So I guess I can tell the truth if I feel like it.'

'Yond Carsten has a hard and mustang look,' the note-taking officer said. 'Such men are dangerous.'

That rang a bell in Sam's mind. He had to reach way back to figure out why. '*Julius Caesar!*' he exclaimed. 'We did that in English the semester before I chucked school and chucked my father's farm and joined the Navy.'

'If you still remember, you either had a really good teacher or a really bad one,' the officer said. 'Which was it?'

'Miss Brewster was good,' Sam answered. 'I can still

quote the start of *The Canterbury Tales,* too. . . . But this isn't a literature class.'

'No,' the other officer said – wistfully? 'But you've told us what we need to know. Why don't you go enjoy New York City? If you can't have a good time here, chances are you've got no pulse.'

'Thank you, sir. I'll do that.' Carsten got to his feet and saluted. The captain who'd done most of the talking returned the gesture. Sam left before the assembled officers changed their minds. A young lieutenant commander was waiting to go before them next. Saluting him as he went, Sam hurried out.

He flagged a cab. 'Where to, Skipper?' the driver asked. He almost dropped his teeth – she was a woman, a brassy blonde somewhere around forty-five.

But why not? If she was pushing a hack, a man could do something more closely connected to the war. 'Why don't you take me to a show?' he said. 'Something with singing and dancing and pretty girls in it?' He didn't want to go to a burlesque house and watch strippers. Well, actually, he did, but he didn't want to run into sailors from his ship when he did it. Being the skipper had a few drawbacks.

So he let the lady cab driver take him to Broadway instead. That was a longer ride and a classier destination than he'd had in mind, but what the hell. The Winter Garden was a big, fancy theater. JOSÉ S HAYRIDE, the marquee said. 'This'll do it?' Sam asked as he paid the driver.

'Pal, if this doesn't do it, you're dead,' she answered, unconsciously echoing the officer with the notebook.

Quite a few Army and Navy men were buying tickets, which seemed encouraging. They cost a five-spot, which was either encouraging or appalling, depending on how you looked at things. A pretty usherette guided Sam to his seat.

He liked the music – Woody Butler was one of his favorites. The comic had his trademark greasepaint glasses marked on his face. He spent most of his time leering at the female lead. So did Sam. The cab driver hadn't been kidding. Daisy June Lee had a beautiful face, legs to die for, and a balcony that outdid anything in *Romeo and Juliet*. By the howls and whistles from the audience, she was wreaking havoc on every man there. Sam gave forth with his share and then some.

She didn't show as much of herself as a stripper would have, but what she did show was more worth watching. It wasn't one of Woody Butler's best scores, but it was better than most of what the competition put out. Besides, when Daisy June Lee was on stage the orchestra could have been playing kazoos and bazookas for all Sam cared. And even when she wasn't, the comic with the painted-on spectacles kept him laughing.

He joined the standing ovation when the show ended. When Daisy June Lee took her bows, he hoped she would explode out of her tight top. She bowed extra low, too, as if challenging the laws of gravity. That made the applause even louder and more frantic. The top, of course, stayed in place. She grinned out at the servicemen; she knew what they wanted.

Then the comic came out and made as if to unbutton his shirt. He looked wounded unto death when the crowd laughed instead of cheering. That only made people laugh louder, which made him look more wounded yet.

Sam hated to leave, even if he knew perfectly well that Daisy June Lee was bound to have a boyfriend – and even if she didn't, she wouldn't give a damn about an overage two-striper. *A man's reach should exceed his grasp/ Or what's a heaven for?* – another fragment from his lit class ran through his head.

He waved down another cab in front of the Winter
Garden. This driver was a man: a man with a hook doing
duty for his left hand, the one that stayed on the wheel.
He drove well enough. Sam tipped him better than he had
the woman who'd taken him to the theater.

'Everything all right?' he asked Lieutenant Zwilling
when he came aboard the *Josephus Daniels*.

'Yes, sir,' the exec said. 'You're back sooner than I
expected.'

Sam shrugged. 'I had a good time.' *Except when I was
talking about you, I'm afraid.* 'You want to see a gal you'll
never forget, go watch *José's Hayride* at the Winter Garden.'

'Maybe I will, sir.' By the way Zwilling spoke, he didn't
mean it. What did he do for fun? Anything? *Poor bastard,*
Sam thought. Zwilling probably got his kicks telling other
people what to do. If that wasn't a dead-end street, Sam
had never seen one.

Flora Blackford turned on the wireless in the kitchen and
waited for it to warm up as the coffee started to perk and
she used a spatula to turn the eggs frying in a pan. The
eggs got done about the time the wireless came on. A few
seconds later, two slices of toast popped up. The coffee,
running behind schedule, didn't get dark enough to suit
her till she'd almost finished breakfast.

She almost didn't recognize the patriotic song coming
out of the wireless. The singer and her band didn't seem
well matched. She was more than good enough, in a con-
ventional way. The band, by contrast, did things with syn-
copation and harmonies nobody else in the USA would
have imagined. Flora paused with a bite of fried egg halfway
to her mouth. *Is that . . . ?* she wondered.

The song ended. 'That was Kate Smith, with "God Bless
the Stars and Stripes," ' the announcer said. 'Backing her

is the famous colored combo, Satchmo and the Rhythm Aces.'

'Thought so!' Flora said, and got up to pour herself a cup of coffee.

'Satchmo and his musicians *do* bless the Stars and Stripes,' the announcer continued, laying on the propaganda with a trowel. 'They know too well the bars in the Stars and Bars stand for the imprisonment of their people. We'll be back with the news on the hour following these important messages. Please stay tuned.'

Those messages were important only to the advertisers who paid for them: a soap company, a cosmetics company, a prominent brand of fountain pens, and a cigarette maker that said its products came from 'the finest tobacco available.' She didn't know how many letters she'd had from constituents in the armed forces complaining about the cigarettes that came with their rations. She couldn't do anything about those complaints, however much she wanted to; U.S. tobacco simply didn't measure up to what the Confederates grew.

'And now the news,' the announcer said once his station finally ran out of commercials.

'U.S. forces report significant advances in northern Georgia and western Tennessee despite the rainy weather that has slowed operations in recent days,' the newscaster said. 'Our bombers punished Atlanta and Birmingham in heavy raids on industrial areas. Damage to both cities is reported to be extensive.'

'Good,' Flora murmured, though she wondered how true the reports were. If clouds covered the targets, the bombers would drop their loads anywhere they could. If the bombs came down on houses instead of factories . . . well, who lived in the houses? People who worked in the factories. Any which way, bombardment hurt the C.S. war effort.

'Farther north, our bombers also pounded Richmond,' the newscaster said. 'Our losses were light. Little by little, we continue to beat down the enemy's air defenses. Confederate strikes against Washington and its environs produced only slight damage. No enemy bombers appeared over Philadelphia last night.'

As far as Flora knew, that was true. She hadn't heard any sirens. They were loud and insistent enough to make sleeping through them almost impossible. She'd done it once or twice, but no more than once or twice.

'Significant advances have also taken place in northern Arkansas, in Sequoyah, and in western Texas, where Confederate resistance seems to be crumbling,' the newsman said.

Flora hoped that wasn't intended only to keep listeners happy with good news from a front far enough away that they couldn't easily check up on it. The U.S. Eleventh Army was driving on Camp Determination now. If it fell, U.S. propagandists really would have something to crow about. And, if it fell, wouldn't that also mean the Freedom Party would have a harder time killing off Negroes in the CSA?

'In an amphibious assault, U.S. Marines recaptured Wake Island, west of the Sandwich Islands,' the newsman said. 'There was no fighting, the Empire of Japan having withdrawn its forces before the Marines landed. Japan no longer holds any U.S. possessions.'

And about time, too, Flora thought. That conflict would probably peter out now, the way it had a generation earlier. One of these days, there would have to be a reckoning with Japan – but not yet. Fighting through the fortified islands of the western Pacific to reach the enemy's homeland was a distinctly unappetizing prospect.

Had Japan been able to seize the Sandwich Islands, the USA would have had a devil of a time getting them back.

The U.S. West Coast would have become vulnerable to Japanese air raids. Flora remembered the Japanese strike on Los Angeles during the Pacific War, the strike that nailed the lid down on the coffin of her husband's reelection hopes. Japan and the CSA could have worked together to cause more trouble in the eastern Pacific these days. But that wouldn't happen now.

'In foreign news,' the broadcaster continued, 'the Kaiser's forces have inflicted a heavy defeat on the Russian Army east of Kiev, and it now appears certain that the capital of Ukraine will remain in German hands. The Tsar's wireless broadcasts speak of renewing the offensive as the Russians find the chance – as close to an admission of failure as we are likely to hear from them.'

Flora's smile was wry. One rule held true in this war: everybody lied. Some countries lied more than others – the Confederate States, France, and Austria-Hungary came to mind. But everyone was guilty of what Churchill called terminological inexactitude now and again. You couldn't stretch things too far. Otherwise they'd break, and the truth would bite you. But you could let your own people down easy and persuade the other side you still had plenty of fight left . . . whether you did or not.

'Heavy German bombing raids on Petrograd, Minsk, and Smolensk damaged Russian factories and railroad yards in those cities,' the newsman said. 'And the Germans have promised to aid the nationalist uprising in Finland, and say they will recognize the Finnish provisional government.

'As if to counter that German move, the Tsar is appealing to the Russians' "little brothers in the Balkans" – his term – to rebel against Austria-Hungary, whose government he terms "unnatural and detested by God." In Vienna, the King-Emperor Charles was quoted as saying that if God ever hated any regime, it was surely Russia's.'

Takes one to know one, Flora thought. *Yeah, and you know 'em all.* The schoolyard taunts carried more weight when backed up by millions of men and all the munitions two industrialized countries could turn out.

'In western Europe, Germany claims to have begun the liberation of Belgium from British occupation. Prime Minister Churchill says this is utter rubbish, and claims the British Army is merely readjusting its lines. Time will tell.

'German wireless has warned that, if the war continues much longer, England, France, and Russia face what the broadcaster termed "unprecedented destruction." The French government's response is too crude to repeat over the air.'

Flora wondered whether the French knew as much as they thought they did. Germany had split the uranium atom before the United States did. The Kaiser could call on an impressive array of nuclear physicists. The United States were getting close to a uranium bomb. Wasn't it likely the Germans were closer yet?

How close were the Confederate States? That was Flora's biggest worry. All she knew was what she heard from Franklin Roosevelt, and the Assistant Secretary of War knew less than he wished he did. Flora shook her head. Roosevelt admitted to knowing less than he wished he did. It wasn't the same thing.

When the newsman started talking about the weather and the football scores, Flora turned off the set. She drank another cup of coffee, did the dishes, called a cab, and went downstairs to wait for it. It showed up in about ten minutes, which was par for the course. The driver held the door open for her.

'Congressional Hall, please,' Flora said as she got in.

'Yes, ma'am.' The man had gray hair and walked with

a limp. Flora couldn't remember the last time she'd seen a healthy young man who wasn't in uniform. Her own son was a healthy young man . . . and now he was in uniform, too. Maybe the CSA's uranium bomb wasn't her biggest worry after all.

The cabby knew the shortest way through the maze of bomb damage that still tied up Philadelphia in the third autumn of the war. Flora gave him a big tip for making good time.

'Thanks a bunch, ma'am.' He tipped his cap.

'Thank *you*,' she said, and got out her ID to show to the guards at the entrance.

'Go on in, Congresswoman,' one of them said – but only after he carefully examined it. When would these painstaking inspections relax? At the end of the war? Ever? The soldier went on, 'One of the ladies will finish checking you.'

In front of a blast barricade, a uniformed woman went through Flora's handbag and briefcase and patted her down. Then she said, 'Go ahead.'

'Thank you,' Flora said resignedly. She doubted the new security measures would end with the war. Too many splinter groups would still have causes and people ready to die for them.

She navigated the maze of drab corridors to her office. A good thing no birds flew these hallways; she was often tempted to leave a trail of bread crumbs, and she couldn't be the only person who was. Her secretary looked up from the typewriter. 'Good morning, Congresswoman.'

'Good morning, Bertha.' Flora let herself into her inner office and closed the door behind her. She telephoned Franklin Roosevelt.

'He's in a meeting, Congresswoman,' Roosevelt's secretary said. 'He should be back in about an hour.'

'Have him call me when he can, please.' Flora had plenty to do while she waited. The paperwork never went away, and the elves never took care of it when she went home at night. And the telephone rang four or five times before it was the Assistant Secretary of War.

'Hello, Flora,' Roosevelt said. 'What's up today?'

'I wondered if you noticed the news item where the Germans warned England and France and Russia about unprecedented destruction,' Flora said. 'Does that mean they're getting close?'

'I missed it,' Roosevelt answered after a thoughtful pause. 'I hope someone close to the project heard it. I hope so, but I don't know, so I'll pass it along. In case you're wondering, we haven't heard a word from the Germans about this yet.'

'I didn't think we had,' Flora said. If uranium bombs worked the way the people with slide rules thought they would, the postwar world would have two kinds of country in it: the ones with those bombs, which would be powers, and the rest, which . . . wouldn't. 'That reminds me – any new word about how the Confederates are doing?'

'Nope. I wish there were, but there isn't,' Franklin Roosevelt said. 'Their number one man in this area hasn't gone anywhere. He's still right where he was before the war.'

'But they're still working on it?'

'Well, we sure think so. They know we are – we found that out. They wouldn't just ignore it themselves.'

'No, they wouldn't. I wish they would, but no,' Flora said unhappily. 'Are they working on it there, then?'

The Assistant Secretary of War paused again. 'Don't know,' he said at last. 'We haven't been able to prove it, not even close, but. . . . Maybe some people ought to pay a call on them there if they really are. It's a backwater place, not a lot of targets, so nobody's gone after it much. Not a lot of obvious targets, I should say. We can probably spare some personnel to find out. Even if the answer is no, we remind more Confederates that they never should have started this war in the first place.'

'Yes.' Flora wondered what her question would end up doing to a backwater place somewhere in the CSA. Some people who'd passed a quiet war would suddenly discover that hell had decided to picnic on their front lawn. She shrugged. If that helped keep Joshua safe, she didn't care.

Cincinnatus Driver liked the idea of being in Georgia. Georgia was, without a doubt, the deep South. In Kentucky, he'd been right across the border from the USA. Foreign ideas easily wafted south; people said Louisville and Covington were the least Confederate cities in the CSA. Tennessee reminded him of Kentucky, though it seemed . . . more steeped in the Stars and Bars, perhaps.

But Georgia – Georgia was something else. It was a sign that the United States were really getting somewhere in this war. And it was a scary place for a Negro in the service of the USA to be.

'Ofays here ain't gonna catch me,' he told a couple of the other truck drivers as they ate supper in a half-wrecked house on the outskirts of Jasper, Georgia, in the hill country north of Atlanta. 'I got one bullet I save for me if I'm ever in that kind o' trouble. Quick and clean is better'n the other way.'

'I guess I can see that,' Hal Williamson said. 'White folks around here don't like you one whole hell of a lot, do they?'

'White folks around here don't like anything that's got anything to do with the USA,' Bruce Donovan said. Before Cincinnatus could get mad, he added, 'But they especially don't like colored folks – that's plain enough.'

'Yeah – ours or their own,' Williamson said.

That made Cincinnatus want to start clobbering white Georgians with his cane . . . or else to put a clip in his gun and start shooting them. He didn't think U.S. authorities would arrest him if he did. Odds were they'd just take the gun away from him and send him home. That had temptations of its own, but he thought he did more to hurt the CSA by hauling supplies than he would by murdering a few Confederate civilians.

Williamson lit a Duke, then held out the pack to Cincinnatus and Donovan. After he lit up, he said, 'Stories the Negroes tell – man, they'll curl your hair.'

'Do Jesus!' Cincinnatus said. His hair was already as curly as it could be. He'd seen the same thing in Kentucky and Tennessee and now Georgia: U.S. soldiers were a magnet for the surviving Negroes in the Confederate States. They mostly came in by night; they hid during the day so white Confederates couldn't finish the job of capturing them and sending them to camps or killing them on the spot.

They were ragged and filthy and skinny, some of them starvation-skinny. They couldn't tell stories about the camps farther south and west, except to say that people who went in didn't come out. But they could talk about years on the dodge, scrounging and stealing and hiding. A few talked about whites who protected them for a while. Those stories relieved Cincinnatus; he'd known some decent whites in Covington, and didn't want to think the Freedom Party had turned all white men in the Confederate States into devils.

Donovan tossed his ration can into a dark corner of the room. The clank it made alarmed all the drivers. You never could tell who was lurking in the dark. Maybe it was a Negro, looking for a new lease on life from the U.S. invaders. Or maybe it was a sniper, a bypassed soldier in butternut or a civilian with a hunting rifle and a grudge against damnyankees.

'What the hell?' To Cincinnatus' relief, that half challenge came in unmistakable U.S. accents.

'It's just us. Sorry,' Donovan said, also in tones that could only have been forged north of the Mason-Dixon line.

'Well, watch it. Get your dumb ass shot off if you do shit like that very much.' For all the soldier knew, he was cussing out a general. He didn't care.

Donovan sighed. He knew he'd been careless, too. He needed a couple of minutes to get back to the subject at hand. When he did speak again, it was much more quietly: 'Some of the colored gals who come in, they're damn good-looking.'

'How come you're so surprised?' Cincinnatus asked, a certain edge in his voice.

'He musta figured they'd look like you,' Hal Williamson said dryly, which deflated him and set them all laughing.

How many Negro women had Bruce Donovan seen in person before he started driving a truck through the Confederate States? Any? Cincinnatus had no way of knowing. Maybe not. If he came from a small town in the Midwest or the mountains, he might have gone his whole life without running into anybody who wasn't the same color he was.

Then Donovan and Williamson shared a glance that excluded Cincinnatus. He didn't call them on it, but he knew what it meant. Some of the colored women coming to the U.S. lines were pathetically anxious to make sure the soldiers in green-gray didn't turn them back. They had ways to persuade that black men didn't. Several thunderous bulletins about fraternization and VD had already come down from on high.

When you had to order something more than once, it was a sign people weren't listening to you. Soldiers *would* screw if they got the chance. Who wouldn't? And Confederate blacks *were* more likely to carry the clap and syphilis than whites. Who would have bothered treating them, back in the days before the war? Even up in Covington, Cincinnatus knew he might easily have got himself a dose if he hadn't married young. Plenty of guys he knew had.

'What the hell are we going to do with this country once we get done stomping it flat?' Williamson asked, as if his fellow drivers had an answer that eluded the President of the United States and the Congress in Philadelphia. 'Everybody white who stays alive'll hate our guts. All that means is another war as soon as these assholes get back on their feet.'

'Sure worked that way last time around,' Cincinnatus said.

'Anybody sticks his head up and causes trouble, we got to kill him. Simple as that.' Donovan made it sound simple, anyhow.

'How does that make us any better than Jake Featherston?' Williamson asked.

'I'll tell you how.' Cincinnatus did have an answer for that. 'If you're black here, you don't gotta stick your head up. Freedom Party don't care. They want to kill you any which way. Long as we leave folks who don't cause trouble alone, we're miles ahead of them bastards, miles and miles.'

Williamson grunted. 'Well, you're right about that.' He pulled out the pack of cigarettes again, looked at it, and shook his head. 'Nah. This'll keep. I want to grab some shuteye, is what I really want to do.'

'Yeah!' Cincinnatus and Donovan both sounded eager. Cincinnatus always sounded eager for sleep these days. He was working harder than he would have in civilian life, and he wasn't as young as he had been once upon a time.

His back wouldn't like sleeping on the floor wrapped in a blanket, with a rolled-up jacket doing duty for a pillow. The rest of him didn't care at all. He sank into slumber like a submersible slipping below the surface of the sea, and he dove deep.

It was still dark when he woke. For a muzzy moment, he thought another thunderstorm was pummeling northern Georgia. Then he realized this was manmade thunder. Muzzle flashes flickered on the walls of the battered house where he slept. The artillery roared and roared and roared again.

'Gun bunnies are working overtime.' Hal Williamson sounded as drunk with sleep as Cincinnatus felt.

'Hope they blast the shit outa whatever they're aimin' at.' Cincinnatus waited for some comment from Donovan. All he heard was a snore. He would have thought this barrage loud enough to wake the dead. Evidently not. A few minutes later, he was asleep again himself. You could get used to damn near anything.

Were the fellow who shook him awake at sunup in the Army, he would have been a top sergeant. The man had a leg gone below the knee and was a couple of years older than Cincinnatus, so he was a civilian, too. But he sure as hell acted like a top kick. 'Come on, you lazy bums!' he yelled. 'You think the goddamn war's gonna wait for you to get your beauty rest?'

'Have a heart, Ray,' Cincinnatus groaned – a forlorn hope if ever there was one. But hot coffee and real fried eggs resigned him to being conscious. What the ration cans called scrambled eggs weren't worth eating, even if the ham that came with them wasn't too bad.

'Where we going?' Williamson asked as he refilled his tin coffee mug.

'Southeast.' Also like a good top sergeant, Ray had all the answers. 'Soon as we break out of these fucking chick-enshit mountains, get out into the flat country, the Confederates can kiss their sorry ass good-bye. They can't stop us now. Weather can sometimes, but they can't. We get down into the flat country, they won't even slow us down.'

Maybe he was right. Maybe he was wrong. It sounded good to Cincinnatus any which way. The latest depot was only a few hundred yards off. He drove his truck over to it. Soldiers filled the back with heavy wooden crates of artillery ammunition. He liked that. If they needed more shells farther forward, things were going the way they were supposed to.

He didn't know exactly where the truck convoy was heading. All he had to know was that he was going the same way as the truck in front of him. He shook his head. No, one more thing: if they got bushwhacked, he knew he had to fight back. He had plenty of ammo for the piece on the seat beside him.

But the convoy got through. There'd been more bush-whacking farther north. Here, the Confederates still seemed startled to see Yankee invaders. Cincinnatus feared that wouldn't last long. If the Confederates could raise hell behind U.S. lines in Kentucky and Tennessee, they could do it here, too.

The gun bunnies were happy to see them. Even though summer was gone and the day was cool, a lot of artillerymen stayed stripped to the waist. 'Keep this shit coming, buddy!' said a blond kid with a skull-and-crossbones on his left upper arm. 'We'll blow the whole damn CSA to hell and gone.'

'Sounds good to me,' Cincinnatus answered.

'Yeah, I bet,' the youngster said. 'If you could push a

button and smash up the country, you'd do it like *that*, I bet.' He snapped his fingers.

'You was in my shoes, wouldn't you?' Finding a white man who understood what a Negro might be feeling always surprised Cincinnatus.

Then the gun bunny winked at him. 'Bet you can keep a secret,' he said. Cincinnatus made a noncommittal noise. The artilleryman went on, 'One of my great-great-grandfathers was about the color you are. Maybe we're cousins, way the hell down the line.'

'Maybe we are.' Cincinnatus kept his voice neutral as he asked, 'So you're passin', then?' The fellow with the tattoo couldn't have more than one-sixteenth Negro blood in him: less, probably, since Cincinnatus had some white blood in him. If the gun bunny hadn't said he was part colored, Cincinnatus never would have guessed.

'Yeah, I'm passing. It's easier. You've got to know that. None of my girlfriends ever knew – that's for damn sure. And besides, if the government thought I was a nigger, they never would have let me join the Army. And you know what? I want to kick Jake Featherston's ass just as much as you do.'

'More power to you, then,' Cincinnatus told him. Would the artilleryman's kids, when he had them, ever find out they were part Negro? And would it be good or bad if they didn't? Some of each, probably – most things worked out like that. After a moment, Cincinnatus added, 'I got me a couple of half-Chinese grandbabies in Des Moines.'

'How about that? Country's turning into a regular zoo.' The kid grinned. Cincinnatus grinned back. They reached out at the same time and shook hands.

Driving away from the front, Cincinnatus wondered how many people with a thin streak of Negro blood were passing for white in the CSA. As many as could get away with it;

he was sure of that. Acting white instead of black made things easier and more convenient in the United States. Down here, it was a matter of life and death.

He rolled past a burnt-out Confederate barrel in a field. U.S. technicians were salvaging what they could from the machine. Four hastily dug graves lay nearby. Cincinnatus nodded to himself. Death wasn't coming just to Negroes in the CSA. Whites were getting their share, too. 'Good,' he muttered, and drove on.

Jake Featherston stared at the situation maps pinned to the wall of his underground office. He swore under his breath. Despite everything George Patton could do, the abscess in northwestern Georgia was bursting, and damnyankees were spreading all over the landscape. How the hell was the country supposed to hang on to Atlanta? How the hell was it supposed to go on with the war if it couldn't?

He swore again. He knew the answer to that: uranium bombs. Somehow, the Confederacy had to stand the gaff till they were ready, and to hope like anything the USA didn't get them first. 'Got to hang in,' Featherston said softly. 'Got to hang on. Got to.'

A moment later, Lulu poked her head into the office. 'Professor FitzBelmont is here to see you, Mr. President,' she said, and sniffed slightly. She didn't know why the tweedy physics professor was so important to the Confederate States. Jake didn't think she did, anyhow. Whenever he put something about the uranium-bomb project in writing, he took care of it himself, bypassing her. Security for this couldn't be too tight. He wouldn't have let his own shadow know about U-235 if he could have helped it.

All he said now was, 'Thanks. Send him in.'

Henderson V. FitzBelmont closed the door behind him.

He nodded to Jake. 'Mr. President,' he said, and then, belatedly, 'Uh – freedom!'

'Freedom!' Jake didn't get angry at the forced way the professor brought out the slogan, as he would have with most people. He waved him to a chair and asked, 'How are you?'

'Sir, I'm alive,' FitzBelmont said wearily as he sat down. 'I'm alive, and I'm not hurt. I've always tried to be a rational man. I don't have much use for the idea of miracles. Things are what they are, that's all. But if anyone wants to say it's a miracle that I'm here now, I won't argue with him.'

'I heard Lexington got hit hard,' Featherston said sympathetically. From all the reports he had, Lexington had got one night's worth of what Richmond took several times a week. 'You see what it's like when you come here. Now you've been through it yourself.'

'Seeing it's one thing. Going through it . . .' The professor shook his head in stunned disbelief. 'How does anybody go through *that* and stay sane?'

'It's like anything else, Professor – the first time it happens, it's the worst thing in the world, but when it happens twenty, fifty, a hundred times, it's just something you've got to deal with and go on,' Jake said.

'If they bomb Lexington fifty times, there won't be anything left,' Henderson FitzBelmont said, horror in his eyes. 'There's not a whole lot left now.'

'Town's been lucky up till now,' Jake remarked. Off in the Blue Ridge Mountains, without much industry to draw enemy bombers, Lexington had largely escaped the war. The President of the CSA leaned forward. He could think of only one reason bombers would visit Lexington. 'How much damage did they do to the project?'

'Well, sir, the works weren't badly hurt. A lot of bombs

hit around them, but not very many on them,' FitzBelmont answered.

'That's good news!' Jake meant it from the bottom of his heart. The sooner the CSA got uranium bombs, the better – it couldn't be too soon.

FitzBelmont raised a warning hand. 'It's not so simple, Mr. President. I wish it were. We lost several men who specialized in enriching the uranium we have and extracting element ninety-four from it – jovium, we're calling that.'

'Wait a minute. Ninety-four? Uranium's ninety-two, right? What happened to ninety-three?' Jake Featherston could no more become a nuclear physicist than a clam could fly. But he had a devil of a memory for details.

'Element ninety-three – saturnium, we're calling it right now – doesn't have an isotope that yields a useful fission product,' FitzBelmont answered.

'It won't go boom?' Jake Featherston translated academese into English.

'It won't go boom.' The professor looked pained, but he nodded. 'And Martin, Collins, Delancey, and Dean knew more about isolating jovium than anybody else, and the raid killed three of them and left Delancey . . . well, maimed.' He grimaced. 'I saw him afterwards. It's not pretty.'

Jake had seen a great many horrors in his life. Henderson FitzBelmont probably hadn't. He looked a little too young to have fought in the Great War. Chances were he didn't go in for street fighting, either. 'How long will he be out?' Featherston asked.

'I don't know yet, sir. He's lost a leg and a hand,' FitzBelmont answered. 'He won't be back soon – I can tell you that.'

'Damn!' Jake said. FitzBelmont wasn't kidding when he said Delancey'd got maimed. 'All right, then. Who are your next best people in Lexington? Who can you bring in from somewhere else? The work has to go on, even if you take casualties. That's part of what war's all about.'

'I understand that, but physicists are harder to replace than riflemen,' Professor FitzBelmont said stiffly. *So there,* Featherston thought. The professor went on, 'Just about everyone in the Confederacy who could help is already in Lexington. There weren't very many nuclear physicists here to begin with. We might be able to bring in a few men from Tulane. They won't begin to fill the shoes of the people we lost, though. The ones I mentioned were only the most important.'

'Damn!' Featherston said again. 'So that means the Yankees sure as hell know where we're working on the bomb.' Henderson V. FitzBelmont blinked behind his spectacles. Jake spelled it out for him: 'Why the fuck else would they plaster Lexington? Your uranium works is the only thing going on there that matters to the war.'

'How . . . unfortunate,' FitzBelmont muttered.

'Tell me about it!' Featherston pointed to the situation map. 'The country's in trouble, Professor. If anybody's got a chance to save it, you're the man. Whatever you need, we'll give you.'

'What I need most is time. If you hadn't sent me packing when I first came to you . . .'

FitzBelmont had nerve, to remind Jake of his mistakes. The President of the CSA sighed heavily. 'Ask me for something I've got, dammit. Yeah, I was wrong. There. You happy? Not many people ever heard me say that, and you better believe it. But I thought you were selling me snake oil. Can you blame me? It sounded too fantastic to be true. Still does, but I reckon it is.'

'Yes, sir, it is. The United States think so, too,' FitzBelmont said, which made Jake wince. The physicist went on, 'If the Yankees hit us once in Lexington, aren't they likely to do it again? We may take more damage the next time around.'

'I've already pulled four antiaircraft batteries away from Richmond and sent 'em west,' Jake said. 'I've pulled two wings of night fighters, too. We'll get hit harder here, but we can live with that. We can't live without you. I didn't want to do anything special about Lexington before. If we had all kinds of defenses around a no-account little college town, the United States'd be bound to wonder why. Well, now the damnyankees know why, so we'll do everything we can to hold 'em back.'

'Thank you, Mr. President.' FitzBelmont hesitated, then asked his question: 'What do you think the odds are?'

'Not as good as I wish they were.' Featherston wanted to lie, but feared the USA would show he was lying in short order. 'We can make hitting Lexington expensive for them. I know that for a fact. I can't promise we'll keep everything off you. How much time would you lose if you packed up and went somewhere else?'

'A good deal. Several weeks, anyhow – maybe months.' Henderson V. FitzBelmont eyed the map to which Jake had pointed. 'Besides, where would we go?'

That was a much better question than the President wished it were. With airstrips in southern Tennessee, the United States could strike most of the Confederate heartland. 'Miami? Houston? Habana? Those look like about your three best choices.'

By the expression on FitzBelmont's face, he liked none of them. Neither did Jake Featherston. But he didn't like leaving the facility where it was, either. *The devil and the deep blue sea,* he thought. Yet the devil lurked *in* the deep blue sea. U.S. submersibles prowled the Confederate coast. If they sank a ship with the uranium project aboard, they sank the CSA, too.

'How much of your work can you move underground?' he asked. 'That'll give the damnyankees a harder time, anyhow.'

'It will also involve delay.' But Professor FitzBelmont looked thoughtful. 'With reinforced concrete above it, perhaps . . .'

'You need concrete? I'll give you concrete till it's coming out your ass,' Jake said. 'And we'll give the Yankees something new to think about pretty soon, too.'

'May I ask what?' The professor was starting to get the hang of security.

Normally, Jake wouldn't have said boo, but he needed something to buck up FitzBelmont's spirits – and his own. He made the rules. He could break them. 'Yeah,' he said. 'We've got us a project down in Huntsville, too. Pretty soon – any day now, matter of fact – we'll be able to fire rockets with a ton of TNT in the nose a couple of hundred miles into Yankeeland. Let's see 'em try and stop those, by God!'

'That would help. I can see as much. How accurate are they?'

'They can hit a city. They can't hit a city block.' Jake stabbed a finger out at Professor FitzBelmont. 'How heavy will your uranium bomb be? Put one of those in a rocket and it'd be the perfect weapon, near enough.'

'Calculations are still theoretical. The best estimate is on the close order of ten tons,' FitzBelmont answered.

'Shit!' Jake said feelingly. 'Need bigger rockets or smaller bombs. Which do you reckon I could get first?'

'Since we don't have any bomb at all yet, getting larger rockets would seem easier,' the professor said.

'Makes sense,' the President of the CSA agreed. 'I'll tell the boys in Huntsville to get on it, and pronto. Damnyankees haven't sniffed them out yet, so they can work without having the sky fall on 'em.' He muttered under his breath.

'Only a matter of time, probably. Spies everywhere. Everywhere, I tell you.' He made himself brighten. It wasn't easy. 'Wouldn't that be something, though? A rocket big enough to throw a uranium bomb all the way to San Francisco and Seattle?'

'That would be . . . remarkable,' FitzBelmont said. 'Of course, a just peace would be even better.'

'I offered the United States a just peace two years ago,' Featherston said angrily. His definition of *just* boiled down to *just what I want*. 'They wouldn't take it, the bastards. I figured we'd better grind it out of 'em, then, on account of they sure aimed to grind it out of us.'

Henderson V. FitzBelmont started to say something. It probably would have been something like, *Look how things are now. Would they be worse if you'd made a softer proposal?* Had he said any such thing, Jake would have blown up in his face. The physicist wasn't so good with people, but he saw that, all right.

'We are going to win this sucker. *Win* it, you hear?' Jake growled. 'We are going to lick the Yankees right out of their boots. Lick 'em, by God. Lick 'em so they stay licked, so we never have to worry about 'em again. It *will* happen, and you'll help make it happen. That's how it's gonna be. Got it?'

FitzBelmont said the only thing anybody with an ounce of sense would have said: 'Yes, Mr. President.'

Maybe he meant it. Maybe he didn't. But he said it, and he *would* produce for Jake Featherston and for the Confederate States of America. He *would* produce, and the Confederate states *would* win. Jake looked at the unfortunate situation map, then deliberately turned away from the unfortunate situation it portrayed. No matter what was going on in northern Georgia, the Confederate States *would* win.

*

The house Jefferson Pinkard rented in Humble, Texas, was one of the finest two or three in town. Edith and Willie and Frank liked it fine. Of course, they would have liked a tent in the woods outside of Humble almost as well. Anything that got them away from the Yankee air raids on Snyder would have looked like paradise on earth to them. Getting away from Snyder looked pretty damn good to Jeff, too.

And Camp Humble looked even better. Ferd Koenig had wanted to call it something fancy: Camp Devastation, or maybe Camp Destruction. Jeff talked him out of it. 'Look,' he said in a long, angry telephone call, 'any nigger who hears he's goin' to Camp Destruction, he'll know he's got nothin' to lose. He'll be more dangerous than a god-damn rattlesnake. There's such a thing as asking for trouble, and giving a camp a name like that – well, it's the picture in the book.'

He got his way. The Attorney General grumbled and harumphed, but the Attorney General was way the hell off in Richmond. He wouldn't have to live with the consequences of a name like that. No – he'd just blame Jeff for the riots and dead guards that sprang from it.

Camp Humble, now . . . What could sound more harmless? And what could be more deadly? This camp was done *right*. Everything Jeff had learned the hard way at Camp Determination went into Camp Humble from the start. The bathhouses had a bigger capacity than his old ones. He had more trucks to help them along. And he had a big, fancy crematorium set up right at the edge of the camp. No more mass graves, no, sir. When Camp Humble reduced its Negro population, it would reduce the coons right down to nothing.

Leaves no evidence behind, he thought. He couldn't do anything about the mass graves outside of Snyder. Now that Camp Determination was empty and blown to hell and gone, he doubted that the Confederates would bother trying to hold on to Snyder and the territory nearby. They needed soldiers even more farther east. Those graves handed the United States a propaganda victory on a silver platter.

Well, too bad. They could yell all they wanted. It wouldn't make a dime's worth of difference in who won the war.

He sighed. Back when he ran up Camp Determination, he'd figured it was in a damn good spot. So had everybody set above him in the CSA. That only went to show people weren't always as smart as they thought they were. Yes, Snyder, Texas, was out at the ass end of the Confederacy. The damnyankees could reach it anyhow. The older, smaller camps farther east were still going great guns.

And now Camp Humble was, too. Negroes who came in here got dealt with in jig time. All the improvements Jeff had designed into the new camp paid off. Camp Humble also had a Y-ranging station, massive antiaircraft batteries all around it, and a fighter wing assigned to help protect it. U.S. bombers could get here, even if they had to come a long way to do it. They wouldn't meet a friendly reception if they tried.

So far, they hadn't tried. Maybe they didn't know where the new camp was. If they didn't, they would soon enough; you couldn't keep a place this size secret very long. But making air raids expensive might be enough to keep them away.

Jeff muttered under his breath. Over by Spencer, the CSA hadn't been able to make Yankee air raids expensive enough. The USA battered down C.S. air defenses, and went right on battering till U.S. warplanes dominated the skies. That couldn't happen here – not so far inside C.S. territory. Pinkard hoped like hell it couldn't, anyhow. If

U.S. airplanes started owning the sky over Houston and Humble, the Confederate States were in deep.

He muttered again. By the news filtering out of Georgia, the Confederate States were in deep anyhow. That there *was* news out of Georgia – no matter how the Party and the government tried to keep it quiet – told how very deep his country was in.

A train whistle blew, off in the distance. Jeff kept the window to his office open a little way so he could hear those three blasts whenever they came. He intended to go on doing that unless it was snowing outside or something. As usual, he wanted to know what would happen before it did. He still prowled through Camp Humble with a sub-machine gun, looking for trouble spots before they showed up. And when he heard those three toots from the train whistle, he still erupted from the office and headed for the unloading point like a jackbooted force of nature.

Guards in gray uniforms hustled to take their places where the spur from the line through Humble stopped at the camp. Some of them led big, mean, snarling dogs – coon hounds, they laughingly called them, though the German shepherds were nothing like the beasts that went after four-legged coons.

'Come on!' Jeff shouted. 'Move your lazy asses!' Anybody who got in position after he did was in trouble, and everybody knew it. Some of the guards, the men from the Confederate Veterans' Brigades, moved slower than their younger counterparts. He could put the old farts in the stockade or ship them home, but that was about it. He could send younger guards straight to the front if they fucked off. He'd done it, too, though only twice.

The train whistled again. Jeff Pinkard was anything but an imaginative man, but he couldn't help thinking how mournful that sound was. And yet . . . Who would mourn the Negroes who went into the bathhouses and the trucks and the crematorium? Nobody white in the CSA, that was for damn sure.

Here it came, smoke puffing from the stack. Sparks flew as steel wheels ground against steel rails. The engineer knew just what he was doing. He stopped the locomotive along-side the flagpole that was his mark and waved to Jeff. As Pinkard waved back, the fellow in the tall cap inside the engine took a pint of whiskey out of his coat and swigged from it. Then he gave a throat-cutting gesture, and then a thumbs-up.

If he hadn't added the thumbs-up, Jeff would have reported him for drinking on duty and for political unre-liability. As things were, the camp commandant just grinned.

'Out! Out! Out!' the guards screamed as they unlocked the crowded cars. 'Get moving, you stinking, rasty niggers! Form two lines! Men on the left! Women and brats on the right!' When the Negroes stumbled out of the cars, the guards reinforced the orders with cuffs and kicks. A dog leaped forward and bit a woman. Her shrill scream made the blacks move faster to keep the same thing from hap-pening to them.

Into the camp they went, those who could move. Other Negroes – trusties – carried and dragged those who couldn't move straight to the trucks. The story was that they were going to a clinic some distance from the camp. In fact, the trucks would go far enough to make sure they were dead, then bring them back to the crematorium. More trusties, these always under the watchful eyes of guards, would load the corpses into the fire, and that would be that.

Before long, the trusties would get it in the neck – in the nape of the neck, to be precise – and go up in smoke themselves. They didn't know that yet; they thought they were saving their worthless black hides by going along with the guards. But Jeff and the others in gray uniforms had plenty of Negroes to choose from. Blacks were flooding into Camp Humble faster than even this magnificent facility could get rid of them.

Guards and trusties went through the train together, pulling out corpses and the live Negroes who were either too far gone to come out on their own or were playing dead. The bodies went straight to the crematorium. The shammers went straight to the trucks.

One of them saw the wreathed stars on Jeff's collar and stretched out his hands in appeal. 'I didn't do nothin', suh!' he said, plainly sensing that nothing good was likely to happen to him. Trusties holding him tight and guards aiming automatic weapons at him gave pretty fair hints.

'You broke a rule,' Jeff said stonily. 'They said come out, and you damn well didn't. There's a punishment barracks next to the clinic.' By now, he brought out the soothing lies with the greatest of ease. 'You spend some time in there, you'll learn to behave yourself when you get back here.'

The Negro went on squawking, but these weren't the bad kind of squawks. As long as he thought he would be coming back, he was willing to go where the trusties were taking him – not eager, maybe, but willing. He would have kicked up all kinds of trouble had he thought he was heading for his last truck ride.

Before long, the crematorium went to work. The trusties took jewelry and dental gold from the corpses and gave them to the guards. Keeping any of that stuff sent a trusty into the flames alive. So far, the guards hadn't caught any of them sticking rings up their ass or anything. Sooner or later, it was bound to happen. Some people *would* try to steal no matter what.

Smoke belched from the stacks. Jeff swore softly. The smoke smelled like greasy burnt meat. The outfit that ran up the crematorium had sworn on a stack of Bibles that the smoke would be clean, that you'd never know in a million years they were burning bodies. 'Lying bastards,' Pinkard muttered. Yeah, some people tried to steal, all right, no matter what. They weren't all black, either.

He wrinkled his nose against the stink. Sometimes half-charred bits of flesh came flying out of the stacks, sucked up along with the hot gases. There was a lot more soot than the manufacturers promised, too.

Pulling out a notebook, Jeff scribbled in it. Before long, he'd send Richmond a nasty letter. With luck, he could put the company's ass in a sling. He did some more muttering. He hoped the people back in Richmond weren't too busy with the war to come down on some not so petty grifters who'd grabbed a fat contract by promising more than they could deliver.

He wondered if he ought to see where he could put mass graves in case the crematorium just didn't work out. That would be harder around here than it was around Snyder; this country was more thickly settled. And the ground here was a lot swampier than it was farther west. The stink from graves might be even worse than what the crematorium turned out. All those bodies might pollute the ground water and start epidemics, too. He supposed he'd have to talk to a doc about that.

So goddamn many things to worry about.

But Camp Humble was up and running, even if it had a few rough spots. Camp Determination was nothing but a memory. Jeff could go home to Edith and his stepsons every night proud of what he'd accomplished. And pretty soon he would have a baby of his own. Wouldn't that be something?

One of the guards came up to him. 'Sir?'

'What's up, Cromartie?' Jeff tried to know everybody's name.

Cromartie looked shamefaced. 'Sir, I've got the clap,' he blurted. 'Troop Leader Mauch said I had to tell you, or he'd tear off my dick and stuff it up my. . . . Well, he said I had to let you know.'

'You fucking idiot,' Jeff said, which was exactly Cromartie's trouble. 'Did you catch it here?'

'Reckon so, sir. I sure didn't have it before.'

'All right. Get your sorry ass over to the doc. He'll have some pills for you. I'm gonna gig you three days' pay, and word of this will go on your record.'

Miserably, Cromartie nodded. Even more miserably, he shuffled away. Jeff laughed, but only quietly – no fool worse than a horny fool. The laughter didn't last. No matter how well Camp Humble ran, he wished he were still several hundred miles farther west. That would have meant the Confederacy was winning the war.

XX

Abner Dowling walked the mayor of Snyder, Texas, through what was left of Camp Determination. The mayor was a plump, middle-aged fellow named Jethro Gwynn. He walked with a limp and a stick; he'd fought for the CSA in the Great War. 'You say you didn't know what was going on here?' Dowling growled.

'That's a fact, sir,' Gwynn answered. 'All the barbed wire and everything . . . They kept people out, you know.' He sounded earnest and persuasive. Dowling didn't believe him for a minute.

Neither did Major Angelo Toricelli. 'Well, what did you think was going on when all those trains stopped here? People got off those trains. Thousands and thousands and thousands of them got off. Nobody ever got on. Didn't that kind of make you wonder?'

'No, sir,' Gwynn said blandly. 'All them trains went through Snyder sealed up tight. Couldn't prove by me they had people in 'em.'

'What are we going to do with this lying son of a bitch, sir?' Dowling's adjutant demanded.

'Here, now. You got no cause to talk about me like that,' Jethro Gwynn said. 'Whatever went on here, it was none of my damn business, and I didn't ask no questions.'

Major Toricelli's hand dropped to his pistol. 'For three cents cash I'd blow your lying brains out. It's more than you're worth, too.'

'Nobody who lives in town paid much attention to this place,' the mayor of Snyder insisted. 'It was just here, that's all.'

That was too much for General Dowling. 'All right, Mr. Gwynn,' he said. 'You're going to come for a little ride with me.'

'Where are we going?' Gwynn asked, sudden apprehension in his voice.

'Don't worry – it's not far,' Dowling answered. 'And even if it were, you'd be smart to come along. I bet if I looked in my pocket I could find three cents for Major Toricelli.' His hands folded into fists. He wanted to beat the snot out of this Texan, the kind of urge he hadn't had since his West Point days. 'Get moving. You think you're unhappy now that the United States are here, you give me any trouble and you'll find out you don't know jack shit about unhappy – not yet you don't, anyway. But you will.'

He must have been persuasive. Without another word, Jethro Gwynn walked back to the command car that had brought him out from Snyder. The driver and the other two soldiers waiting in the vehicle glared at him. Dowling didn't think he'd need to give them three cents. If the mayor got even a little out of line, he could have an unfortunate accident for free.

'Take us to that field, Clancy,' Dowling told the driver. 'You know the one I'm talking about?'

'Oh, yes, sir. I sure do,' Clancy said. The motor was still running. The driver put the command car in gear. It rolled along a well-paved highway – a remarkably well-paved highway, seeing that it ended in the middle of nowhere.

The wind was blowing from the field. Dowling's nose wrinkled. So did Jethro Gwynn's. 'Maybe we don't need to go any further,' the mayor of Snyder said.

'Shut up,' Major Toricelli said, his voice hard and flat.

'I think we'll keep going,' Dowling said. 'We're almost there anyhow, eh, Clancy?' He gave Gwynn a sour stare. 'Clancy and I have been here before. Have you, Mr. Mayor?'

'No!' Gwynn said. 'Christ, no!'

'I wonder why not,' Dowling said. Jethro Gwynn didn't answer. Nothing was the best thing he could have said, but it wasn't nearly good enough. The command car passed through a barbed-wire gate a barrel might have flattened. To the driver, Dowling added, 'Stop by the closest trench – the open one.'

'Yes, sir,' Clancy said, and he did.

'Well, let's get out of here and have a look around, shall we?' Dowling descended from the command car. He waited for the mayor to join him. Plainly, the mayor didn't want to. Just as plainly, the savage expressions the U.S. soldiers wore told him he had no choice. Looking as glum as a man possibly could, he got down, too. Major Toricelli followed him.

'Come over here, God damn you.' Toricelli shoved him toward that trench, which hadn't been covered over like the rest. 'Take a good look. Then tell me you didn't know what the hell Camp Determination was up to.'

'Please . . .' Jethro Gwynn said, but nobody wanted to listen to him. Feet dragging in the dirt, he scuffled his way forward.

Even in October, curtains of flies buzzed above the trench. Crows and ravens and vultures flew away as the men approached, but they didn't go far. The rations were too good for them to want to leave. The stench was overpowering, unbelievable; it seemed thick enough to make the air resistive to motion. Dowling knew it would cling to his uniform, his skin, his hair. He also knew he would have to bathe several times to get rid of it.

'Go on,' he said harshly. 'Take a good look.'

Gwynn gulped. How many Negroes – men, women, children – lay in this trench, all bloated and stinking and flyblown and pecked by scavenger birds? Thousands, surely. The trench was long and deep and about two-thirds full. Had the Confederates not pulled out of Camp Determination and blown the place up, they would have filled the trench with corpses and then scraped out another trench, closer to the entrance, and started in on that one, too. They'd set this up very efficiently.

'Well?' Dowling said. 'What do you think, Mr. Gwynn? How do you like it?'

'I had no idea,' the mayor of Snyder gasped, and then he leaned forward and threw up. He was neat about it; he missed his shoes. Wheezing, coughing, spitting, he went on, 'Honest to God, I didn't.'

'You lying sack of shit.' Dowling pointed to the closed trench beyond this open one, and then to the next closed trench, and then to the next and the next. 'What did you think they were doing here? Running a hospital?'

'I didn't ask any questions,' Gwynn said. 'I didn't want to know.'

'That sounds a little more like the truth, anyway – not much, but a little,' Major Toricelli said.

'Not enough,' Dowling said. 'Nowhere close to enough. Come on. Let's go back to the command car.'

'Can we head back to town?' the mayor asked eagerly.

'Not yet, Charlie,' Dowling said. After they got in, he told Clancy, 'Go on all the way up to the first trench.'

'Yes, sir,' the driver said.

Again, Jethro Gwynn didn't want to get out. This time, Major Toricelli gave him a shove. 'We had to look at this, asshole,' he said. 'You damn well can, too.'

Bulldozers had scraped off the dirt from part of the

first trench. The bodies in there were a couple of years old. They were mostly bones, with rotting clothes and bits of skin and hair here and there. Halloween in hell might have looked like this.

'They've been doing it ever since this camp opened up, for the last two years or so. How many bodies are here all told, do you think?' Dowling said. 'And you have the brass to try and tell me you didn't know what was going on? God, what a shitty excuse for a liar you are.'

'What a shitty excuse for a human being,' Toricelli said.

Gwynn puked again. He didn't try denying things any more, though. Maybe that was progress.

'And do you know what the best part is?' Major Toricelli said. 'Once your smokes here were dead, the guards had people who went into their mouths with pliers or whatever the hell and yanked out all their gold fillings. Waste not, want not, I guess.'

Gwynn looked revolted in a new and different way. 'You're making that up. Nobody would do such a thing.'

'It's the God's truth, Mr. Gwynn.' Abner Dowling held up his right hand as if taking an oath. 'So help me. We had Graves Registration people put on gas masks and look at the bodies up close. They didn't find any dental gold. None – not a crown, not a filling, not a bridge. Nothing. What they did find was lots of dead colored people with teeth yanked out or teeth broken to get the gold from them. And how do you like *that*?'

Had Gwynn looked any greener, Dowling would have been tempted to mow him. The mayor of Snyder said, 'I swear on my mother's name, General, and by our Lord Jesus Christ, I never knew nothin' about that. Nothin'. Pulling teeth? That's . . . just sick.' He bent over and retched some more. This time, he had nothing in his stomach to bring up.

The dry heaves were nasty. Dowling watched without

sympathy till Gwynn's spasm finally ended. 'So you really did know they were killing off Negroes at the camp, then?' he said.

'Well, I had a pretty good notion they were,' Jethro Gwynn admitted in a ragged whisper. 'I didn't ask any questions, though. None of my business, I reckoned.'

'You passed by on the other side of the road, like the priest in the Good Book,' Dowling said in a voice like iron.

By then, Gwynn was in no shape to quarrel. 'I guess maybe I did.'

'I've got one more question for you. Then I'll take you back to town,' Dowling said. 'Why don't you like grubbing gold out of Negroes' mouths once they're dead? They don't need it any more then. Isn't killing 'em what's really wrong?'

'You know, I never looked at it that way,' the mayor of Snyder said seriously. 'I mean, they're just a pack of rebels and troublemakers. But this . . .' He gulped. 'It's different when you see it with your own eyes.'

'You liked the idea. You didn't want to know what it meant, that's all. Or have you got the nerve to tell me I'm wrong?' Dowling asked.

'No, that's a fact, a true fact,' Gwynn said. 'You think about gettin' rid of niggers and you think, *Hell, country'd be better off without 'em.* You don't reckon they're – people, or anything.'

'Well, what the hell are they, then?' Dowling demanded. When Jethro Gwynn didn't answer the question, he did it himself: 'They're dead, that's what. And I bet the worst of 'em has a better hope of heaven than you do, Mr. Gwynn. Come on, damn you.' He shoved the mayor of Snyder toward the command car.

Gwynn didn't say anything as Clancy drove him back to town. The U.S. soldier let him off in front of his real-estate agency. The mayor fled inside and slammed the door behind him, as if that would keep Dowling and his men from coming back.

Having shown Jethro Gwynn what Camp Determination was all about, Dowling grabbed Snyder's leading (and only) banker, two attorneys, an accountant, and a doctor. With a happy – for him, anyhow – afterthought, he also grabbed their wives. He took them out to the camp together in a deuce-and-a-half. They all denied they'd had any idea what it was doing.

'I thought you might say that,' he told them.

The truck driver drove them to the mass graves. They turned pale even before the stink started filling the back of the truck. All but one of them vomited at the first trench. Two women fainted. So did one of the lawyers. The doctor passed out when he heard about taking dental gold from the corpses.

'We ought to bring the whole town through here, sir,' Major Toricelli said on the way back to Snyder.

'By God, I'm tempted,' Dowling said. 'Maybe I will.'

His own headquarters were well upwind from the mass grave. He bathed and bathed that night, and still smelled, or thought he smelled, the stench of death clinging to him.

His telephone rang early the next morning. The accountant in Snyder had shot his wife and three children, then turned the pistol on himself. Another call came in a few minutes later: the banker's wife had swallowed rat poison. Then the telephone rang again: Mayor Gwynn had hanged himself from the chandelier in his real-estate office.

'Maybe they've got consciences after all, if you kick 'em hard enough,' Dowling said, not altogether without satisfaction. 'Who would have imagined that?'

Sergeant Armstrong Grimes hadn't been in the big fight since the Confederates came north into Ohio. He liked fighting on enemy turf much better. He liked facing the real enemy much better, too. Utah, Canada . . . It wasn't that they weren't dangerous places. His leg still pained him in wet weather like they were having now. No, the point was that he'd got shot in a fight that didn't matter, a fight that said nothing about who would win the war.

Lieutenant Bassler pointed to a wooded hill in front of Hollysprings, Georgia: a nowhere town that never would have mattered to anyone more than five miles away if it didn't lie on a road leading south toward Atlanta. 'The Confederates are dug in there,' he said. 'We're going to be part of the force that takes the high ground away from them.'

'Yes, sir,' Armstrong said. Cautiously – Confederate snipers were loose in front of the hill – he peered forward. After ducking down again, he added, 'Don't hardly see 'em. They're probably just waiting for us there under the trees.'

'Afraid you're right,' the company commander said. 'Nothing we can do about it, though.'

'I hope they pound the crap out of the place before they send us in,' Armstrong said. 'Will we have a lot of armor support?' He assumed they'd have some, which wouldn't have been a sure bet in the sideshows where he'd fought before.

'They say we will,' Bassler told him. 'Maybe they're blowing smoke up my ass, but I don't think so. Softening-up is supposed to start tomorrow at 0500. We go in two hours later.'

'Yes, sir,' Armstrong repeated. He probably wouldn't have slept late tomorrow anyhow, but now he knew damn well he wouldn't.

He took the news back to his squad. The men greeted it with the enthusiasm he'd expected. 'Hot shit,' Squidface said. 'Featherston's fuckers get another chance to blow my dick off. Just what I've been waiting for – yeah, you bet.'

'I wish one of these Confederate broads *would* blow my dick off,' Woody said. The other soldiers laughed. Then they went back to studying the hill. They might not be strategists, but they'd learned tactics the hard way.

Cal Henderson summed it up: 'Taking that place out is liable to be expensive as shit if they're laying for us under those pines.'

'Air bursts. Lots of air bursts,' Squidface said. Armstrong found himself nodding. You could fuse a shell so it went off as soon as it touched anything at all – a branch, for instance. Air bursts like that slashed the ground below with fragments. Unless you were in a bunker dug into a trench wall, you'd catch hell.

'Grab as many Z's as you can now,' Armstrong said. 'Artillery opens the show at five tomorrow morning. We go in a couple of hours later.'

No, he didn't get much sleep himself. Having nerves was silly – he couldn't do anything about whatever would happen soon – but he did all the same. Because he was awake at least as much as he was asleep through the night, he heard barrels rattling up to the start line under cover of darkness. Lieutenant Bassler had got that right, anyhow.

The bombardment started at five on the dot. Star shells lit up the hill bright as day. High-altitude bombers droned overhead, dropped loads of death, and kept on going. They'd blast Atlanta or some other C.S. town, then fly north and land, after dawn let them see what they were doing.

Confederate artillery woke up in a hurry. Quite a few shells fell on the U.S. front line, but none dangerously close to Armstrong's squad. The men huddled in their foxholes and waited for the brass whistles and the shouts that would send them forward.

It was getting light when U.S. fighter-bombers zoomed in to put the finishing touches on the preliminaries. Armstrong was glad to see them. They could hit targets the high-altitude airplanes were too likely to miss.

'Boy!' Whitey yelled. 'They're beating the holy bejesus out of that place, aren't they?'

'Here's hoping,' Armstrong said.

Several soldiers nodded at that. They were like the guys he'd fought beside in Utah: they'd been through the mill, they knew it was no damn good and wouldn't get any better, and they kept going anyway. He didn't have anybody just out of the repple-depple in his squad, though the company carried several replacements. He took another look at that hill. By the time they got to the top of it, he feared the squad would need some new men. He hoped to hell it wouldn't need a new sergeant.

Engines roaring, U.S. barrels clattered forward. Lieutenant Bassler's whistle shrilled. 'Let's go!' the company commander shouted. 'Keep your heads down, don't bunch up, and I'll see you when we get there!'

He made a good leader for a front-line outfit. He always sounded confident, and he didn't send his men anywhere he wouldn't go himself. Armstrong feared they were going into a meat grinder now. Sometimes that came with the job. He didn't like it, but he couldn't help it.

Mortar bombs started falling as soon as the U.S. barrels and soldiers began to advance. Screams followed some of the bursts. Medics scooped up the wounded and carried them back to the rear. Other bursts sounded curiously subdued. They didn't throw many fragments. Armstrong knew what that meant. Swearing, he shouted, 'They're heaving gas at us!' and put on his mask. One more annoyance, one more inconvenience, in a war that seemed full of nothing else but.

A bullet cracked past him, about belly-button high. He was flat on his belly in the muddy grass before he knew how he'd got there – reflexes really did take over in time of danger. A moment later, he got up and started running again, dodging like a star halfback in a professional league.

Another bullet missed him by not nearly enough. He hit the dirt again. This time, he spotted the muzzle flash. 'There!' he yelled, pointing toward a foxhole just in front of the edge of the trees.

With several U.S. soldiers shooting in his direction, the Confederate took his life in his hands whenever he popped up to fire. The men in green-gray worked their way closer to the foxhole. One of them shouted for him to give up. He answered with a burst from his automatic rifle. A shriek said he wounded someone. But two grenades flew into the hole. After that, he didn't fire any more.

Other Confederates farther back did. Armstrong was glad when he got in among the trees himself. He had plenty of cover then, from upright trunks and from those the U.S. bombardment had knocked over. Not least because of all the havoc the shells and bombs had wreaked, the woods smelled powerfully of pine. The fresh, clean, spicy scent made an odd backdrop for the brutal firefight that went on under the trees.

Armstrong ran past a young Confederate he thought was surely dead – the man had stopped a couple of fragments with his belly and another with his chest. But the soldier in butternut groaned and moved, and almost scared Armstrong out of a year's growth.

Crouching beside him, Armstrong asked, 'How bad is it?'

'I'm done, Yankee,' the enemy soldier answered, gasping against the pain. Blood ran from his mouth and nose.

'You want morphine?' Armstrong said. 'I'll give you some.'

'Already got it.' The kid had to be younger than Armstrong himself, and Armstrong was only twenty. After another gasp, the Confederate said, 'Don't help much.' Armstrong believed him; nothing would help much, not with those wounds.

That led to another question: 'Shall I finish you or yell for the medics?'

'I'm done. Told you that.' The soldier took as deep a breath as he could. 'Get it over with. No blame on you. I'll thank you for it.'

'All right, then.' One quick round did the trick. Armstrong hoped somebody on either side would do the job for him if he ever needed it as bad as this kid did. He hurried on, leaving the corpse where it lay.

The Confederates had several machine-gun nests with interlocking fields of fire on the forward slope. You couldn't approach one without exposing yourself to fire from another. The shelling and bombing hadn't hurt them; they were made of cement, not sandbags. A soldier with a flamethrower tried to deal with one of them, but a bullet to the fuel tank drenched him in the fire he hoped to shoot. That was a bad way to go; the stench of burnt meat made Armstrong's stomach heave.

Then two barrels ground close enough to shell a Confederate bunker. After three or four hits, the guns inside stopped shooting back. 'Careful!' Armstrong yelled when U.S. soldiers started moving forward again. 'They might be playing possum.' They weren't, but Lieutenant Bassler thumped him on the back for worrying about it.

The barrels methodically smashed three more machine-gun nests. Then one of them hit a mine and threw a track, while a Confederate with a stovepipe rocket set the other one on fire. One last concrete emplacement went on hurling death at the men in green-gray. Two U.S. soldiers with captured Confederate automatic rifles sprayed bullets back. The machine guns focused on them, which was what the men with the automatic rifles had in mind. While they kept the Confederates inside the emplacement busy, another soldier with a flamethrower crept toward it.

A jet of golden fire spat from the nozzle of his infernal device. It shot through the narrow concrete slit that let the machine guns traverse. Armstrong heard screams from inside. They didn't last long. He got another whiff of that charred-pork smell as he loped past the machine-gun nest. It was dead now, and so were the men inside it.

Up till then, the Confederates resisted fiercely. After the last bunker fell, the spirit seemed to go out of the soldiers in butternut. Instead of dying in place or falling back to fight again from another position, more and more of them tried to surrender. Some succeeded, and went to the rear with hands high and with broad grins of relief on their faces. Others ran into U.S. soldiers in a vengeful mood or just without the time or manpower to bother with prisoners.

Armstrong trotted past a Confederate soldier out in the open who looked to have got shot while trying to give up. That was too bad. If he ever found himself in a mess like this, he hoped the men on the other side would let him yield. But not a damn thing in war came with a money-back guarantee.

He made it to the top of the hill before he quite realized he was there. A couple of mortar teams were launching bombs at Hollysprings to announce that the hill had changed hands. A lieutenant from another company in the regiment was yelling for men to go on and take the town. After the fight on the hill, nobody looked thrilled about rushing into another big one right away.

'You made it, Sarge.' There was Squidface, smoking a

Duke some Confederate wouldn't need any more. He held out the pack to Armstrong without being asked.

'Thanks.' Armstrong took one and leaned close to get it started. He sucked in smoke, then blew it out. It eased the worst of his nerves, anyhow. 'Yeah, I'm still here. Looked like they started to lose it a little bit once we took out their machine guns.'

'Uh-huh. I thought so, too,' Squidface said. 'Don't hardly see that with these butternut bastards. Say what you want about 'em, they fight hard.'

'Maybe they see the writing on the wall,' Armstrong said. 'Wouldn't that be something?' He tried to imagine Jake Featherston giving up. The picture didn't want to form. Neither did one of the United States' accepting anything less than unconditional surrender and full occupation of the Confederacy.

Artillery shells screamed in from the south. Armstrong hit the dirt and started digging. Sure as hell, the Confederates hadn't quit yet.

Cassius relaxed in a hut that had once belonged to a share-cropper. The roof leaked. The mattress was ancient and musty. He didn't much care. Right this minute, nobody seemed to be hunting Gracchus' guerrilla band. With the damnyankees pounding toward Atlanta, central Georgia had more urgent things to worry about than a few blacks with stolen guns.

Not being dogged wherever he went felt wonderful to Cassius. Gracchus, by contrast, was insulted. 'They reckons we don't count fo' nothin',' the guerrilla leader grumbled. 'Gots to show 'em we does.'

'Ought to lay up for a while first.' That wasn't Cassius; it was a scarred veteran named Pyrrhus. 'Rest and relax while we can.'

Gracchus shook his head. 'They shippin' all kinds o' shit up toward the no'th. We hit some o' dat, make it harder fo' Featherston to fight the Yankees.'

'We get hit, make it harder for us to fight anybody,' Pyrrhus said.

'You don't got the nerve, you kin stay where you's at,' Gracchus told him.

The older Negro refused to rise to the bait. 'Got me plenty o' nerve, an' everybody knows it. Got me some sense, too, an' you sure ain't showin' none.'

'Only way we live through this is if the Yankees come,' Cassius said. 'Yankees stay away, sooner or later the militia an' the Mexicans hunt us down an' kill us. If we can help the USA, we oughta do it.'

'Hear dat?' Gracchus said. 'This is one smart nigger. You don't want to listen to me, listen to him.'

'You reckon he smart on account of he say the same thing you do. That ain't reason enough,' Pyrrhus answered. 'United States're comin' whether we do anything or not. You reckon they get down into Georgia on account o' what niggers done? Wish it was so, but it ain't likely.'

Gracchus scowled at him. So did Cassius. It wasn't likely at all. Another Negro said, 'Sure enough wouldn't mind a little rest-up, anyways.'

At that, Gracchus looked almost ready to explode. Cassius caught the guerrilla leader's eye and shook his head, ever so slightly. If Gracchus blew up now, he could split the band. Where would they come by new recruits to make either half big enough to be dangerous if that happened? Negroes were thin on the ground in rural Georgia these days.

To Cassius' relief, Gracchus got the message, or enough of it to keep from losing his temper. He went on glowering at the men who'd thwarted him, but at least he had the sense to see he *was* thwarted for the time being. 'We lay up,' he said reluctantly. 'We lay up fo' now, anyways. But if we sees a chance, we takes it.'

'Fair enough,' Pyrrhus said. Some of the other black guerrillas nodded, all seeming relieved the quarrel wouldn't explode in their faces.

They didn't live off the fat of the land. The land had little fat to live off. White farmers had armed guards. Some had squads of Mexican soldiers garrisoned on their land. The henhouses and barns might have been bank vaults. Before too long, the guerrillas would have to raid to eat.

Birdlime and nets brought in songbirds. Cassius had never imagined eating robins and doves, but they weren't bad at all. 'My granddaddy, he used to talk about all the passenger pigeons when he was a pickaninny,' Gracchus said. 'Way he told it, you could eat them birds fo' weeks at a time.'

'Where they at now?' Pyrrhus asked. 'Sure don't see 'em around none.'

'Po' birds got their fuckin' population reduced,' Gracchus answered. 'Might as well be niggers.'

Two nights later, a Negro sneaked out of Madison, Georgia, the town closest to the tumbledown sharecropping village, with word that a truck convoy had stopped there for the night and would go on to the northwest in the morning. 'You ain't goin' back,' Gracchus said. 'You comin' wid us. You lyin', you dyin'.'

'Give me a gun. I want a shot at the ofays my ownself,' the Negro replied.

'I gives you a gun,' Gracchus said. 'I gives you one after we gits away. You kin shoot the ofays then.'

'You don't trust me none,' said the town Negro, whose name was Jeroboam.

'Bet your ass I don't,' Gracchus said. 'I don't know you

from a cowflop. Ain't got no reason to trust you – yet. But you give me one, we git on fine.'

Jeroboam knew the road that led to the front. Like a lot of rural roads, it was badly potholed; money'd gone into guns and barrels and murder camps and main highways, not the roads that meandered between them. One of those potholes let the guerrillas plant explosives without digging under the roadbed from the side, which would have taken longer and been much too conspicuous once done.

Gracchus placed his men in the high grass and bushes to either side of the road southeast of the bomb. The CSA had too much to do to bother clearing weeds, either. With any luck at all, the white Confederates would pay for their neglect.

Jeroboam lay in the bushes only a couple of strides from Gracchus. He was bound and gagged; nothing he did or said would warn the men in the approaching truck convoy – if there was an approaching truck convoy. He hadn't squawked when Gracchus told him what they were going to do. Cassius hoped that argued he was truthful. If it didn't, it argued that he was a good actor.

With autumn here, fewer bugs bothered Cassius than would have a few months earlier. He scratched anyway. He knew he was lousy. The only thing he had to kill lice was kerosene, a cure almost worse than the problem. He'd always been clean; his mother was neat, his father downright fastidious. Now they were almost surely dead, and he had nasty little bugs crawling over his scalp.

'Heads up!' somebody called. Cassius flattened himself into the grass. Why did people say that when they meant *duck down*? He supposed it came from football or some other game.

Then, catching the low rumble of approaching trucks,

he stopped worrying about things that didn't matter. How much protection did they have with them? If four or five armored cars and half-tracks were in the convoy, the plan was to blow up the lead vehicle and then just slip away. Getting into an expensive skirmish was the last thing Gracchus wanted.

Closer . . . Closer . . . The machine in front was a truck. It was, in fact, a captured U.S. truck – blockier than C.S. models – with a coat of butternut paint slapped on over the original green-gray.

Gracchus had the plunger whose wires led to the explosives in the roadway. He jerked down on it at just the right moment. The truck went up in a fireball that engulfed the one behind it, which was following too close. The other trucks in the convoy slammed on the brakes. As soon as they did, Cassius and the rest of the black guerrillas started shooting.

He'd never fired a rifle till he joined Gracchus' band. He sure knew what to do with one now. He fired again and again, working the bolt on the Tredegar and slapping in a fresh clip when the one he was using ran dry. The rifle butt slammed against his shoulder again and again. He'd be sore tomorrow . . . assuming he was still alive.

The drivers had rifles and submachine guns of their own, and started shooting back. And then Cassius heard an unmistakable machine gun banging away, and ice walked through him. That sure sounded as if it came from a weapon most likely to be mounted on an armored vehicle. He hoped the guerrillas had some Featherston Fizzes, but getting close enough to throw one could prove more dangerous to the man with it than to his intended target.

And then he heard something else: a deep rumble from the northwest, rising swiftly to multiple screams in the air. Yankee fighter-bombers had spotted the convoy with the burning trucks corking its way forward. The airplanes glee-fully swooped down for the kill.

Cassius had imagined hell on earth, with the Confederate military playing a star role in the roaster. Now he saw it: truck after truck smashed by bombs or by machine-gun and cannon fire. Gouts of flame erupted from the road. The trucks couldn't run, couldn't hide, couldn't even shoot back. The men inside them died where they sat – or, if they tried to run for cover, the black guerrillas shot them.

Only one thing was wrong with the fire and brimstone visited upon the convoy – some of it slopped over onto Gracchus' band. Not all the bombs hit right on the road. Neither did all the shells and bullets. Chances were the U.S. pilots didn't even know the Negroes were there. If they knew, they didn't give a damn. Their mission was to smash up enemy transport. They did that up brown. Everything else was just a detail.

To them, it was a detail. It was liable to get Cassius killed. He hugged the ground while bullets smashed down much too close and blast tried to pick him up and throw him away. Somebody close by screamed, 'No! No! No!' After a little while, he realized he was making those noises.

The U.S. warplanes couldn't have lingered more than ten minutes. They came, they saw, they destroyed. And the truck convoy was much more thoroughly wrecked than either Gracchus or Jeroboam could have imagined.

'Shitfire!' Gracchus cried in a mix of awe and outrage. 'Ain't even nothin' left fo' us to steal!'

'Hell you say,' Pyrrhus answered, and paused to shoot a dazed and bloodied Confederate truck driver who stag-gered toward him. As the white man fell, the guerrilla went on, 'Almost got myself squashed by a big old crate of rations – landed in these bushes here.'

'Well, that's somethin'.' Gracchus sounded as if he didn't know how much it was. Cassius didn't, either. You could eat Confederate rations and you wouldn't be hungry afterwards. Past that, he had nothing good to say for them. He'd heard even Confederate soldiers traded cigarettes or coffee with the enemy to get food better than their own.

'Mother!' a dreadfully wounded Confederate screamed. *'Motherrr!'* Cassius drew a bead on him and shot him through the head.

'Why you go an' do dat?' a Negro asked. 'Shoulda let the damn ofay suffer.'

'I'd shoot a dog,' Cassius said.

'Yeah, but a dog, he wouldn't shoot you,' the other rebel said.

After a moment, Cassius decided he had a point. Instead of admitting it, he changed the subject, calling out to Gracchus, 'You gonna let that Jeroboam loose?'

'Reckon I better,' the guerrilla leader said. 'He wasn't lyin', that's fo' damn sure. An' we ought to write a nice thank-you to them Yankees. They done a lot of work fo' us.' He laughed. 'Reckon they done mo' work than we coulda did our ownselves.'

He wasn't wrong. 'Wonder how many of us those U.S. pilots hit,' Cassius said, and laughed at himself. He was sure he was the only rebel in the band – maybe in the state – who would have said *those pilots*. To the other Negroes, it would have been *them pilots*. Like it or not, Cassius was his father's son.

The guerrillas had lost one man dead and two more wounded, neither seriously. 'Watch what happen to them trucks, an' do Jesus! I don't hardly mind gettin' shot,' one of the injured men said. The dead guerrilla had stopped a 20mm cannon shell with his chest. Chances were he wouldn't have agreed.

Carrying the rations and other small bits of loot, the black rebels made their getaway. Behind them, the shattered convoy sent up great dark plumes of smoke. Before long, whites would come out from Madison to see what had happened – not that they could be in much doubt – and do what they could for anyone left alive.

Cassius smiled as he trotted away. God hadn't come down from the heavens to give the guerrillas a hand, but the next best thing had.

Jorge Rodriguez wondered how long he could go on. He wondered how long the Confederate States could go on, too. If the damnyankees kept pounding on them the way they had been, it wouldn't be much longer. Autumn or no autumn, rain or no rain, the United States were driving on Atlanta, and Jorge didn't see how the Confederacy could stop them.

He didn't worry about it all that much, either. He worried about staying alive. With everything the damnyankees were throwing at his regiment, that was plenty all by itself.

Kennesaw Mountain was heavily wooded country. U.S. artillery was firing shells fused for air bursts. If you didn't have a good foxhole, the fragments knifing down from above would cut you to ribbons. Jorge did. He was proud of the hole, which he'd dug himself. He could fire from it when enemy soldiers drew near. But it also had a small shelter strengthened with boards – what they would have called a bombproof in the Great War – scraped out under the forward lip. When the shelling got bad, he'd duck under there and stay fairly safe.

Right this minute, there was a lull. He could get out of his hole, ease himself behind a tree, smoke a cigarette. He could, yes, as long as he stayed wary as a cat at a coonhound convention. Things had a way of picking up with no warning. If you didn't dive back into your hole in a hurry, you'd be a casualty.

'Stay alert, men!' Captain Malcolm Boyd called. 'They're liable to throw paratroops at us like they did in Tennessee.'

If the United States tried an air drop here, they had to be crazy. It looked that way to Jorge, anyhow. Too many paratroops would get stuck in trees and die before they could start fighting.

'We've got to hang on to Marietta no matter what, too,' the company commander added. 'We don't hang on to Marietta, how the hell can we hold Atlanta?'

There he made more sense to Jorge. Marietta was the cork in the bottle – probably the last cork in the bottle in front of Atlanta. If it fell, Atlanta almost had to. And if Atlanta fell, the Confederate States were in a hell of a lot of trouble. So everybody said, anyhow. Jorge knew things everybody said weren't always right, but this one felt too likely to laugh off.

He wished he wouldn't have heard so many things like, *We've got to hang on to Chattanooga no matter what.* The Confederates couldn't hang on to Chattanooga. Now they were paying for losing it.

An automatic rifle rattled up ahead. When Jorge first went into the Army, that would have meant the man with the rifle wore butternut. No more, not necessarily. The Yankees had captured a lot of C.S. automatic weapons on their long drive south. They'd captured the ammo the rifles used, too – or maybe they were making their own. Jorge didn't know about that. He did know he had to wait and hear more before he could be sure who was out there.

Sure as hell, the bangs that followed came from U.S. Springfields. In the CSA, nobody but home guards and Mexican soldiers used bolt-action rifles these days. The damnyankees were still a long step behind when it came to small arms. Some Confederate soldiers wondered what the enemy was doing in Georgia if that was so.

To Jorge, the answer looked clear enough. Yes, Yankee soldiers carried Springfields. But whole great swarms of Yankee soldiers carried them. U.S. artillery matched anything the Confederacy turned out. So did U.S. airplanes, and the United States had more of them than the Confederate States did. As for barrels ... Jorge didn't want to think about barrels. The USA's new monsters outclassed everything the CSA made.

He peered down the forward slope of Kennesaw Mountain. He couldn't see the enemy troops, but he had a pretty good idea where the gunfire was coming from. The damnyankees were probing in front of his regiment, trying to find a way through. He could have done without the compliment, if that was what it was.

The automatic rifle chattered again. *Right about ... there,* Jorge judged. If the fellow who carried it kept coming forward, he'd probably show himself somewhere near those two pines.

And, a couple of minutes later, he did – not for very long, but long enough. Jorge fired a short burst from his own automatic rifle. The U.S. soldier threw up his hands and toppled. Jorge didn't think he'd get up again. He looked around for a new target.

Easier to think of what he'd just done as hitting a target. If he thought of that figure in green-gray as a soldier, as a man, then he had to think about everything shooting his fellow soldier, his fellow man, might mean. But a target was only a target. You could shoot at a target for fun, if you felt like it.

Almost as much to the point, targets didn't shoot back.

Jorge wondered if another U.S. soldier would try to retrieve the automatic rifle. If a man in green-gray did, it would be his last mistake. But the rifle lay where it fell. The damnyankees seemed confident they could drive the Confederates back and then retrieve it. Jorge had to hope they were wrong.

He waited for the next artillery barrage or armored assault or gas attack or air raid or whatever the enemy had in mind. Instead, a U.S. officer waved a white flag from behind a tree and shouted, 'Can I come forward?'

Firing on both sides died away. Sergeant Blackledge shouted back: 'Yeah, come ahead. What do you want?'

The Yankee emerged, still holding the flag of truce. As he approached the Confederate lines, he answered, 'Want to try to talk you people into surrendering, that's what. You keep fighting, we'll squash you flat.'

'Yeah, now tell me another one,' Blackledge jeered. 'You want to win one on the cheap, that's all.'

'Not this time,' said the man in green-gray. 'We'll take some of your guys behind our lines, show you what we've got. I don't believe you can stop us, or even slow us down very much.'

'You'll do what?' The sergeant sounded as if he couldn't believe his ears. Jorge didn't blame him. The damnyankees had never said anything like *that*, not where he could hear it. He'd never heard of anything like it, either.

Calmly, the U.S. officer repeated himself. He went on, 'Will you take me back? This is what they'd call a limited-time offer on the wireless. If you don't take me up on it pretty damn quick, you'll find out whether I'm lying or not. Oh, yeah – better believe you will.'

If he was acting, he could go out on the road. The confidence that filled his voice seemed frighteningly convincing. Maybe Sergeant Blackledge thought the same thing, because he said, 'Come on up, damn you. I'm gonna put a blindfold on you before you go back of the line, though. You won't do any spying under flag of truce.'

'Have it your way,' the Yankee said. 'Like I told you, you can look at what we've got.' He walked forward. The sergeant put a rag over his eyes and led him back toward C.S. officers. Nobody on either side fired. A few U.S. soldiers came out and swapped rations for smokes and coffee. Jorge just sat tight and waited.

After about twenty minutes, the blindfolded U.S. officer returned, three worried-looking Confederates in his wake. He took off the rag and nodded to Sergeant Blackledge. 'Cease-fire will last till these gentlemen come back,' he said. 'After that, it's up to them.'

'We won't open up unless your guys do,' the noncom replied.

Away they went, the one man in green-gray and the three in butternut. Jorge was sure the Confederates would see only what their enemies wanted to show them. That was liable to be plenty. He waited. He smoked. He climbed out of his hole to take a leak. He didn't want to be a POW; one of his brothers already languished in a camp. He didn't want to get killed, either.

An hour and a half later, the C.S. officers returned. Their U.S. guide stopped between the lines. 'You can still change your minds,' he said. 'This is your last chance, but you can. You'll spare your men a lot of grief.'

'We're obliged to defend this position, Major,' a Confederate colonel said. 'We will do so to the best of our ability.'

'You'll be sorry,' the Yankee said. 'Your men will be sorrier. I can't answer for what will happen to them when we cut loose.'

'We have to take the chance, sir,' the Confederate replied. 'We have our duty, as you have yours. With our country in danger, our personal safety is of small concern.'

'That sounds very pretty. You'll find out what it means. You're sure?' The U.S. officer waited. No one said anything more. The major shrugged and returned to his own lines. One of the Confederates used a field telephone to tell their headquarters what they'd done. All three of them stayed on the front line. Jorge admired that. They could have retreated to safety. Instead, they were sticking it out.

Somewhere between five and ten minutes went by. Then the United States opened up with everything they'd shown the Confederate officers and more besides. Jorge didn't think he'd ever gone through a bombardment like this. Fighter-bombers stooped on the C.S. line and added their weight of hellfire to the mix. He heard shrieks through the thunder of exploding ordnance. Jorge carried a rosary in his pocket, and fingered the beads to thank God and the Virgin that his own shrieks weren't among them.

Wise in the Yankees' ways, he popped up from his hole the instant the barrage lifted. Sure as the devil, soldiers in green-gray scrambled forward. He shot one of them. Another alert Confederate nailed a different one. The rest hit the dirt or ducked behind trees. But they weren't giving up. That would have been too much to ask for. They kept on coming. They just didn't think it would be a walkover any more.

More shells and some mortar bombs started dropping on the Confederates. Shouts and curses off to the left warned that enemy troops had reached and were probably piercing the line there. A moment later, enfilading fire made the probability a sure thing.

'Back!' Sergeant Blackledge yelled. Jorge might have known nothing the USA fired at the Confederates could hurt him. 'They'll cut us off if we stay!'

'The sergeant's right!' Captain Boyd added, perhaps

relieved Blackledge spoke up before he had to. 'We need to save ourselves!'

Jorge didn't want to get out of his hole, any more than a mouse wanted to come out into the middle of the floor. Bullets and flying fragments did dreadful things to soft, tender flesh. But he'd get captured or killed if he stayed here. Out he came, and ran up the north slope of Kennesaw Mountain toward one of the two crests.

A bullet slammed into a tree trunk just to his left. A big shell burst behind him – at least a six-incher. None of the fragments tore into him, but blast – a St. Bernard puppy the size of a building – picked him up and shook him and dropped him on his face. He scrambled up again, knowing he was lucky to be able to. Blast could kill all by itself. Had that shell come down a little closer . . .

Best not to think of such things. He ducked behind another tree to see how close the damnyankees were. Two or three were too damn close for comfort. He fired at them. They went down, though he didn't think he'd hit them. But he would have done the same thing in their boots. Why take chances when you were winning?

'Way to go, Rodriguez,' Sergeant Blackledge said from behind another tree. He seemed to be everywhere at once. 'Make 'em earn it, by God. They won't come on like their pants are on fire now, the bastards.'

'Sure, Sarge.' Jorge hadn't thought of anything more than saving his own skin. He still wasn't sure he could do that. The U.S. major hadn't been kidding. The United States put a rock in their fist before they hit Kennesaw Mountain. More shells came down. He huddled in what wasn't enough shelter. *'¡Madre de Dios!'* When he got scared into Spanish, things were pretty bad. 'What can we do?'

'Try and stay alive.' As usual, Blackledge was relentlessly pragmatic. 'Try and find some place where we can make a stand, slow the shitheels down. Try and hit back when they give us the chance. Sooner or later, they will – I hope.' He swore, plainly wishing he hadn't tacked on the last two words.

'Marietta's gonna fall, isn't it?' Jorge asked. The sergeant didn't answer. For a second, Jorge thought he didn't hear. Then he realized the noncom didn't want to say yes. If Marietta fell, Atlanta was in deep trouble. If Atlanta fell, the Confederate States were in deep trouble. And Marietta *would* fall, which meant. . . .

Purple martins perched in the shattered trees in the park square at the center of Marietta. The birds were flying south for the winter; they didn't care that the trees had taken a beating. There were still plenty of bugs in the air. All the artillery in the world couldn't kill bugs.

Chester Martin, in green-gray, didn't care that the trees were burned and scarred, either. As far as he was concerned, the Confederate States were getting what was coming to them. And he hoped he was going south for the winter. Atlanta wasn't that far away. How much did the enemy have between here and there? Enough? He didn't think so.

A man with a white mustache hung from a lamppost. A sign around his neck said, I SHOT AT U.S. SOLDIERS. He'd been there a couple of days, and was starting to swell and stink. Chester hardly looked at him. Maybe he'd do a little good; maybe he wouldn't. Confederate bushwhackers and diehards and holdouts and red-ass civilians kept on harrying the occupiers all the way back to the Ohio River. Hostages kept dying because of it. Which side would run out of will first remained unclear.

The trees in the park weren't all that had been shattered in Marietta. The Confederates fought hard to hold it. Not many houses were whole. Glassless windows might have been the eye sockets of skulls. Scorch marks scored clapboard. Chunks of walls and chunks of roofs bitten by shellfire gave the skyline jagged edges.

And Marietta's people seemed as ravaged as the town. They were skinny and dirty, many of them with bandages or simply rags wrapped around wounds. They stared at the U.S. troops trudging south through their rubble-strewn streets with eyes that smoldered. Nobody said anything much, though. As Chester had seen in other Confederate towns, his buddies were quick to resent insults. A man with a rifle in enemy country could make his resentment felt.

A scrawny woman whose hair flew every which way cocked a hip in a pose meant to be alluring. 'Sleep with me?' she called.

'Jesus!' said one of the soldiers in Chester's squad. 'I've been hard up before, but not *that* hard up.'

'Yeah.' Chester nodded. 'I think she's a little bit cracked. Maybe more than a little bit.'

An old man whose left sleeve hung empty scowled at him. Chester nodded back, more politely than not. He understood honest hate, and could respect it. He wondered if the respect he showed might change the Confederate's mind. It didn't, not by the look on the man's face. Chester didn't suppose he should have been surprised.

A burnt-out C.S. barrel sat inside the ruins of a brick house. The last few feet of the barrel's gun poked out through a window. The gun tube sagged visibly. Eyeing it, Chester said, 'Must've been a hell of a fire.'

'Yeah, well, it couldn't happen to a nicer bunch of guys,' said the soldier who didn't want the scrawny woman.

Chester grunted. He didn't love Confederate barrelmen. What U.S. soldier did? Those enemies were too good at killing his pals. But he didn't like to think of them cooking like beef roasts in a fire so hot it warped solid steel. That was a bad way to go, for anybody on either side. He wanted the enemy barrel crew dead, sure. Charred to black hideousness? Maybe not.

'Come on, step it up!' Lieutenant Lavochkin yelled. 'We aren't camping here. We're just passing through, heading for Atlanta.'

Chester looked forward to fighting for Atlanta the way he looked forward to a filling without novocaine. Atlanta was a big city, bigger than Chattanooga. The United States couldn't take it by surprise, the way they had with the Tennessee town. If U.S. forces tried smashing straight into it, wouldn't the Confederates do unto them as the USA had done to the Confederacy in Pittsburgh? Fighting one house at a time was the easiest way Chester knew to become a casualty.

Maybe the brass had a better plan. He hoped like hell they did. But if so, nobody'd bothered passing the word down to an overage retread first sergeant.

A kid wearing what looked like his big brother's dungarees said, 'Get out of my country, you damnyankee.'

'Shut up, you lousy brat, or I'll paddle your ass.' Chester gestured with his rifle. 'Scram. First, last, and only warning.'

To his relief, the kid beat it. You didn't want to think a nine-year-old could be a people bomb, but he'd heard some ugly stories. Boys and girls didn't fully understand what flicking that switch meant, which made them more likely to do it. And soldiers sometimes didn't suspect children till too late.

'Hell of a war,' Chester muttered.

Some of his men liberated three chickens to go with their rations. They didn't have time to do anything but roast poorly plucked chicken pieces over a fire. The smell of singeing feathers took Chester back half a lifetime. He'd done the same thing in the Great War. Then as now, a drumstick went a long way toward making your belly stop growling.

He was smoking a cigarette afterwards when a grenade burst not far away. Somebody screamed. A burst of fire from a submachine gun was followed by another shriek.

'Fuck,' said a soldier named Leroy, who was more often called the Duke.

'Never a dull moment,' Chester agreed. 'We're licking these bastards, but they sure haven't quit.'

As if to prove it, the Confederates threw in a counter-attack the next day. Armor spearheaded it: not barrels, but what seemed more like self-propelled guns on tracked chassis. They weren't mounted in turrets, but pointed straight ahead. That meant the enemy driver had to line up his machine on a target instead of just traversing the turret. The attack bogged down south of Marietta. A regiment of U.S. barrels made the C.S. barrelbusters say uncle.

Chester examined a wrecked machine with a professional's curiosity. 'What's the point of these, sir?' he asked Captain Rhodes. A U.S. antibarrel round had smashed through the side armor. He didn't want to think about what the crew looked like. You could probably bury them in a jam tin.

'These things have to be cheaper to build than barrels, and quicker to build, too,' the company commander answered. 'If you've got to have as much firepower as you can get, and if you need it yesterday, they're a lot better than nothing.'

'I guess,' Chester said. 'Ugly damn thing, isn't it?'

'Now that you mention it, yes – especially if you're on the wrong end of it,' Rhodes said. 'Get used to it, Sergeant. You can bet your ass you'll see more of them.'

He was bound to be right. And if they were cheap and

easy to make . . . 'What do you want to bet we start cranking 'em out, too?'

Captain Rhodes looked startled, but then he nodded. 'Wouldn't be surprised. Anything they can do, we can do, too. We're lucky we've kept our lead in barrels as long as we have. Maybe the Confederates were too busy with these things to pay as much attention to those as they should have.'

'Breaks my heart,' Martin said dryly.

The company commander laughed – but not for long. 'Be ready for a push of our own, soon as we can move more shit forward. When the Confederates hit us, they use stuff up faster than they can resupply. Might as well kick 'em while they're down.'

'Mm?' Chester weighed that, then nodded. 'Yeah, I bet you're right, sir. I'll get the men ready. You think we're going into Atlanta?'

'Christ, I hope not!' Rhodes blurted, which was about what Chester was thinking himself. Rhodes went on, 'We do try to go straight in there, a lot of us'll come out in a box.'

'Looks like that to me, too. So what do we do instead?' Chester asked. 'Just bomb it flat? Or maybe try and flank 'em out?'

'My guess is, we go that way.' Captain Rhodes pointed east. 'We do that, we cut the direct train and truck routes between Richmond and Atlanta. Yeah, the Confederates can get around it, but we put ourselves in a good position for hitting the lines and the roads coming up from the south. I'd sure rather do that than charge in with my head down.'

'Me, too,' Chester said fervently. 'Amen, in fact. You think the brass has the smarts to see it like you do?'

'Well, we'll find out,' Rhodes replied with a dry chuckle. But he didn't seem too downcast. 'Start of this campaigning

season, we were chucking the Confederates out of Ohio.
Now they're trying to get us out of Georgia. I think maybe
General Morrell knows what he's doing.'

'Here's hoping,' Chester said, which made the company
commander laugh out loud.

The U.S. push went in three days later. The Confederates
had done what they could to build a line south of Marietta,
and it held for most of a day, but once U.S. armor cracked
it the enemy didn't have much behind it. Then Confederates
fired what had to be half the rockets in the world at the
advancing men in green-gray. They were scary – hell, they
were terrifying. They caused casualties, not a few of them.
But, without enough men in butternut on the ground to
hold it, the rockets couldn't stop the U.S. forces.

And the main axis of the U.S. attack aimed not at
Atlanta but at Lawrenceville, almost due east of Marietta.
Captain Rhodes looked uncommonly smug. Chester
Martin didn't say boo. How could he? The captain had
earned the right.

Heavy bombers and fighter-bombers stayed overhead
all the time, tearing up the countryside south of the U.S.
advance and keeping the Confederates in and around
Atlanta from striking at the U.S. flank. Lots and lots of
artillery fire came down on the enemy, too. Chester
approved of every single shell and wished there were more.

Every time U.S. forces crossed a railroad line, demoli-
tion teams tore hell out of it. Every time U.S. forces crossed
a paved road that ran north and south, engineers dynamited bridges and blew craters in the roadway. Even if the
Confederates rallied and drove back the men in green-gray,
they wouldn't move much into or out of Atlanta any time
soon.

For the first time, Confederate prisoners seemed to lose
heart. 'Thanks for not shootin' me,' one of them said as

he went to the rear with his hands high. 'Reckon we're whipped any which way.'

'See what Featherston's freedom got you?' Chester said.

'Well, we're rid of most of our niggers, anyways, so *that's* good,' the POW said. 'But hell, Yank, you're right – we coulda done that without gettin' in another war with y'all.'

'You started it,' Chester said. 'We'll finish it.'

Freedom Party Guards, by contrast, still believed they'd win. 'Wait till the secret weapons get you,' said a man in camouflage overalls. 'You'll be sorry then.'

'Yeah, the bogeyman'll get you if you don't watch out,' Chester jeered. The captured Confederate glared at him. Under the guns of half a dozen soldiers in green-gray, he couldn't do more, not if he wanted to keep breathing. 'Take him away,' Chester said. 'Let him try his line of bullshit on the Intelligence boys.'

'It ain't bullshit!' the Freedom Party Guardsman said. 'You'll find out! And you'll be sorry when you do, too.'

'Yeah, sure, buddy,' Chester said. Two men took the POW off to the rear.

'The crap they come up with,' another U.S. soldier said, lighting up a Habana he'd taken from a prisoner. 'He sounded like he believed it, too.'

'People used to believe the world was flat,' Chester said. The soldier laughed and nodded. But the Guardsman *had* sounded mighty sure of himself. And Chester remembered all the rockets the Confederates seemed to have pulled from nowhere. He was a little more worried than he let on – not a lot, but a little.

Flora Blackford hurried into the House chamber. She'd got the summons to the joint session of Congress only a little while before. Other Representatives and Senators were grumbling at having to change plans to get here on time.

She understood why. The President wouldn't ask for a joint session much in advance. That would give the Confederates – and maybe other enemies – more time to come up with something unpleasant.

The Speaker of the House rapped loudly for order. When he got something close to quiet, he said, 'Ladies and gentlemen, I have the distinct honor and high privilege of introducing the President of the United States, Charles W. La Follette!'

Applause rang through the hall. Charlie La Follette took his place behind the lectern. He was tall and ruddy and handsome, with a splendid shock of white hair the cartoonists loved. He'd been President for almost a year and a half now, but still didn't seem to have stepped out from under Al Smith's shadow. Maybe today was the day.

'Ladies and gentlemen of the Congress, my fellow Americans, 1943 has blessed our arms with victory,' he said. 'When the year began, we were driving invaders from western Pennsylvania. Now Pennsylvania and Ohio have been liberated, and our armies stand not far from Atlanta, the hub of the Confederate States of America.'

More applause washed over him, loud and fierce. He grinned and held up a hand. 'We have also driven deep into Texas, and seen with our own eyes the horror the Confederates have visited on their Negro population. The murder factory called Camp Determination, at least, will perpetrate those horrors no more.'

This time, the applause was more tentative, though Flora clapped till her palms hurt. Pictures of those enormous mass graves – the words hardly did them justice – had been in all the weeklies for a while. Even so, the furor was less than she'd hoped for. People either didn't care or didn't want to believe what they were seeing was true.

'Everywhere, Confederate forces are in retreat,' the

President said. 'Even Jake Featherston must see that he cannot hope to win the war he started two and a half years ago. This being so, I call on him to surrender unconditionally and spare his country the bloodshed further resistance would cause.

'Though they do not deserve them, I promise him and his leading henchmen their lives. We will take them into exile on a small island, and will guard them there so they can no longer trouble North America and blight its hopes. Confederate soldiers will be disarmed and sent home. All Confederates, white and colored, will be guaranteed life, liberty, and property.

'Think well, President Featherston. If you reject this call, both you and your country will regret it. We will leave wireless frequency 640 kilocycles unjammed for your reply for the next forty-eight hours. You *will* be sorry if you say no.' He stepped away from the microphones on the lectern, putting notes back into an inside pocket of his jacket as he did.

Flora applauded again. So did most of the other members of Congress. If the war ended now . . . *If it ends now, Joshua won't get hurt,* she thought. That alone gave her plenty of reason to hope. Hope or not, though, she feared Featherston would ignore the call.

The hall emptied as fast as it had filled. Now no one had a great big target to aim at. Flora hurried to her office. She tuned the wireless set there to 640. She didn't know how long the President of the CSA would take to answer, but she wanted to hear him when he did.

He needed less than two hours. 'Here is a statement by President Featherston of the Confederate States of America,' an announcer said.

'I'm Jake Featherston, and I'm here to tell you the truth.' That familiar, rasping, hate-filled voice snarled out of the wireless set. 'And the truth is, people of the USA and President La Follette, we aren't about to surrender. We've got no reason to. We're going to win this war, and you'll be laughing out of the other side of your mouth pretty damn quick.

'Philadelphia will get the message in just a few minutes. Philadelphia will get it twice, matter of fact. You wait, you watch, and you listen. Then you figure out who ought to be doing the surrendering. So long for now. You'll hear more from me soon.'

Terrorists inside the city? People bombers waiting to press their buttons? Flora's mouth tightened. She knew those were both possibilities. Could Featherston be so sure they'd do their job on short notice? Maybe that was why he hadn't answered right after President La Follette's speech. Or . . .

A loud explosion rattled Flora's teeth and put ripples in the coffee in her half-full cup. Long experience told her that was a one-ton bomb going off not nearly far enough away. No air-raid sirens howled. It hadn't fallen from an enemy bomber. Flora was sure of that.

Maybe three minutes later, another blast echoed through Philadelphia, this one a little farther from her office. *'Vey iz mir!'* she exclaimed. She didn't know what Featherston and his minions had done, but no denying he'd kept his promise.

After about a quarter of an hour, he came back on the wireless. 'I'm Jake Featherston, and I'm here to say I told you the truth,' he crowed. He must have waited till he got word his plan, whatever it was, had worked. 'See how you like it, Philadelphia. Plenty more where those came from, and we'll spread 'em around, too. Surrender? Nuts! We just started fighting.'

If anyone in Philadelphia knew what the Confederates

had done, Franklin Roosevelt was likely to be the man. What point to having connections if you didn't use them? Flora dialed his number, hoping she'd get through.

She did. 'Hello, Flora!' Roosevelt still sounded chipper. As far as she could tell, he always did. But he went on, 'Can't talk long. Busy as the Devil after a fire at an atheists' convention right now.'

'Heh,' Flora said uneasily. 'You must know why I'm calling, though. What did the Confederates just do to us?'

'Well, it looks like a rocket,' the Assistant Secretary of War answered. 'Two rockets, I should say.'

'Rockets? You mean they had them set up somewhere outside of town and fired them off when Featherston told them to?'

'No, I don't think that's what happened, not from the first look we've had at what's left of them.' Franklin Roosevelt kept that jaunty air, but he sounded serious, too. And he wasted no time explaining why: 'Our best guess is, they shot them up here from Virginia.'

'From Virginia? *Gevalt!*' Flora said. 'That's got to be – what? A couple of hundred miles? I didn't know you could make rockets fly that far.'

'Unfortunately, *I* can't. But Jake Featherston can, damn his black heart,' Roosevelt said.

'What can we do to stop them?' Flora asked.

'At this end, nothing. They get here too fast,' he said. 'If they've got bases or launchers or whatever you call them, maybe we can bomb those. I hope so, anyway. But I don't know that for a fact, you understand.'

'How much damage did they do?' Flora found one bad question after another.

'One blew a big hole in a vacant lot. The other one hit in front of an apartment building.' Now Roosevelt was thoroughly grim. 'Quite a few casualties. But it would have been worse at night, with more people at home and fewer out working.'

'Do they aim them at Philadelphia? Or do they aim them, say, at the corner of Chestnut and Broad?' Yes, all kinds of nasty questions to ask.

'Right now, your guess is as good as mine. If I had to bet, I'd say they just aim them at Philadelphia. A rocket can't be *that* accurate . . . can it? But that's only a wild-ass guess – excuse the technical term.'

In spite of everything, Flora smiled. 'Thanks, Franklin. I needed that. What are we going to do? If we can't stop these rockets and we can't even warn against them, how do we go on?'

'As best we can,' Roosevelt answered. 'Stick a rabbit's foot in your purse if you don't already have one. Remember that every time the Confederates build one of these, they don't build something else. And some will be duds, and some will go boom without doing much damage. As much as anything else, they're trying to scare us.'

'They're pretty good at it, aren't they?' Flora said. Roosevelt laughed merrily, as if she were joking. What he hadn't said was that some of the rockets would blow houses and apartments and factories to kingdom come. Then something even worse than that occurred to her. 'Can they load anything besides ordinary explosives onto these . . . things?'

'You mean like gas? I think explosives would hurt us more,' Roosevelt said.

Flora had no doubt he was being dense on purpose. 'Gas, maybe,' she said. 'Or other things.' She didn't want to say too much on the telephone.

Obviously, neither did he. 'Not right away,' he answered. 'I've already talked with some people. They need a bigger rocket or a smaller thing. So that's all right for a while, anyhow.'

'For a while. How long is a while?'

'I have no idea. If it's not till we finish licking them, it doesn't matter. And now I've got to go. Other people to talk to. Stay safe.'

'How?' Flora asked, but she was talking to a dead line. Sighing, she hung up, too. She heard no more bangs out of the blue. That was something. Maybe Featherston had only two ready, and more would have to wait a while. Again, though, how long was a while? Not nearly so long as the Confederates would need to load a uranium bomb on a rocket – Flora was all too sure of that.

Her secretary looked into the inner office. 'Were those booms the Confederates or the Mormons, Congresswoman?'

'Mr. Roosevelt says they were the Confederates, Bertha,' Flora answered.

Bertha nodded. 'Figured you'd be talking to him. How did they sneak the bombs in? Can't we stop stuff like that?'

Were the rockets secret? The War Department would probably like to keep them that way, but it would be like trying to classify the sunrise. Like it or not, everybody would know about them before long. Flora told Bertha what she'd heard.

'All the way up from Virginia? How do they do that?' Bertha said.

'If we knew, we'd do it, too,' Flora said dryly. 'I bet like anything we're trying to figure it out, though.'

'Oh, boy.' Bertha didn't sound impressed, for which Flora could hardly blame her. 'What's to keep us all from getting murdered in our beds without even any warning?'

Nothing, Flora thought. 'We're going to take Atlanta pretty soon. If we smash the Confederate States to pieces, they won't be able to go on with the war.'

'Oh, boy,' her secretary repeated. 'How long will that take?'

'I don't know. Not too long, I hope.' *Please, God, let it be before they send Joshua into action. I haven't asked You for much, but give me that.*

'They'll be shooting off these skyrocket things all the time till then?' Bertha asked.

'Not if we can bomb the places where they shoot them from,' Flora said.

'Hmp.' Bertha made a noise redolent of skepticism. 'Did anybody know what a nasty war this would be before they went and started it?'

'Does anybody ever?'

'What are we going to do?' Bertha asked.

'What can we do? We're stuck in it. We've got to win,' Flora said. Bertha didn't say no, but she didn't say yes, either.